The Kell Stone Prophecy Complete Trilogy

Book One
CHILDREN OF PATH

Book Two
THE WRETCHED

Book Three
MARK OF THE FAIRE

BOOK ONE

Children of Path

Chapter One

In the time of the beast...

Kiergan smelled the rotting flesh a hundred yards before he reached the stream. When he stepped into the glade abutting the water he put his hand to his face to stop the vulgar stench reaching his nose. Fat flies buzzed and hummed over two bodies, an angel and what looked to be a small, frail, though now bloated, folk—a felid.

The swollen felid's body was darkened with rot and lay against the thick trunk of a pine, while the angel lay curled as a fetus at the other end of the glade, enlarged, bloodied, half eaten by roster fiends and hundrats.

Kiergan stumbled through the clearing to the stream and vomited several times into the cold waters, falling to his knees on the shore. This was not the adventure he was looking for in running away from an inopportune marriage in Ruhm. He sat on the knotty earth of Kell, wet a kerchief and wiped his face with an icy chill, considering his next move.

A felid—akin to the large cats found only on the southern continents—in folk form, and an angel. Dead and rotting in the northern forests of the Great West, far beyond the rocky hills of Galdred. The Hass of Emorah would give quite a reward for the report of an oddity such as this. The stories they could weave around it would bolster their beliefs, no doubt. But to gain a reward would mean a return home—and a marriage he did not want.

Perhaps he could ignore it, pretend he did not see it. But there was something perplexing about the scene. Clambering to his feet he wrapped his damp kerchief about his face, tying it in a knot behind his head, and returned to examine the puzzle.

Beside the felid folk sat a plate of roasted fawn and dew-berries. He was felled quickly, without struggle. The angel's left wing had been hacked off, leaving a black and bloodied stump. She was leaving the felid, reaching for something, when she was attacked, probably by the fiends. But why had the fiends, or hundrats, or any other scavenger left the fawn untouched? Why had they left the felid whole and only attempted to devour the angel?

With the foul odor seeping through his kerchief and sting-ing at his eyes, Kiergan took himself back to the stream where he could breathe and think. The angel had poisoned the felid and tried to leave. But why? He returned to the angel, holding his breath, and walked away from her, in the direction her body suggested, into the woods and to a gathering of smooth white boulders. There, in a crevice, he saw it.

Suddenly Kiergan could breathe freely. His future was now his own. He could return to Ruhm and marry whom he pleased—any fair folk lass he chose would be his. Lifting the heavy green stone from its safekeeping, he held it up and watched as the sunlight streamed from the sky and lit it up like a beacon.

Kiergan had solved his people's beast problem. He had found the kell stone.

1280 Autumn

"Twaddle and nonsense, Fenn Foster. Grubs are no more demonic than gnomes."

"You lied to me?" Fenn's voice cracked.

He stared at the gaping, dirt hole in the wall. In Father Treacher's lantern light, only a few feet inside were visible, like a mouth that would swallow him down a dark, monstrous throat. The dankness of the earth and the smell of mud sent a shiver of fear through Fenn. He was not allowed in the tunnel.

"It's not as if I'm the only adult in the Ruud who told children about grub demons. Besides, if I had not told you about them, would you have stayed out of the tunnel?"

Before Fenn could answer, Father said, "Of course not."

"But you never lie. If you said there were grub demons, there must be grub demons. Maybe you're lying now just to get me to go into the tunnel? But you don't lie."

"Stop babbling, boy." Father shoved his knapsack at him. "Listen to me. This is important."

Fenn held his breath and stared at Father's weathered, lined face and mossy green eyes aglow in the yellow lamp light. His wild gray hair dangled carelessly across his mouth and poofed out with each breath as he spoke.

"Keep your birthmark secret—show no one. Never return to Path.

Never, do you hear me?"

Fenn nodded, dumbstruck. Yanked unceremoniously out of bed before dawn, his short boots barely laced, dragged into the musty storage room below the cellar of the wissenry, told to get into the forbidden tunnel and never return home—Fenn could only hope he was dreaming.

"The tunnel will take you to the high crossing at the river. Get into Aaronland and make your way south through the divide wood to the Cold Sea wissenry and Father Britt. He will know what to do."

"But what about the grub demons?"

Father grabbed Fenn's shoulders and gave him a bit of a shake.

"There are no such things, I tell you. Everything you will need is in your knapsack. And most of all, remember the night curse and be cautious of it. Remember that it isn't real; the visions are not real."

Father's face softened and Fenn let out a breath.

"Can you remember all of that?"

"Yes, sir." His voice was small, like the squeak of a mouse—Fenn hardly recognized it as his own.

Father smiled. "Good boy. Now, find your way to Father Britt. Use your head. Keep hidden."

Handing him the small lantern, Father motioned for him to enter the monster's throat.

"Luck be with you, boy."

Fenn paused, worrying about the grub demons, before obeying and climbing in.

"Fenn," Father said and Fenn turned back to him.

Father looked worn and defeated, but he smiled.

"You would have made a fine wissende."

"But, Father..."

"I will miss you, Fenn Foster."

"I'll see you again, Father," Fenn said. "You can come visit me at Cold Sea Port."

Father looked at him sadly for a moment too long.

"One last thing," he sucked in a breath as if for courage. "The kell stone. Promise me you won't go near it."

"The what?"

"Whatever you hear, whatever you learn, Fenn, don't go out looking for it."

Noises erupted upstairs, muted and distorted through the earthen walls.

"Keep your head." Father said.

The door swung shut over the entrance to the forbidden tunnel and

Fenn was left alone in the dark, cold earth, listening to Father stack potato bins against his retreat.

Chapter Two

Prince Welk of Michelruud paced the floor of the king's library, his black eyes scanning the seventy musty volumes settled amid the cobwebs and dust. He was no great reader, that was true. But he'd at least skimmed the most important parts of the books on his father's shelves. There was nothing in them about the new bairn, or the mark, or the prophecy and the plot to have the king killed. And yet the story was common knowledge—except for the mark...that was new.

Years ago, in their colonizing of the eastern continent, the folk of the Ruud battled the beasts into the forest and the outlands. And the felid sage, Dag Anfang, threatened them with the prophecy of a bairn who would come to destroy them all. The folk waited and feared and waited years more, but it never came to pass. Now stuff of legend, the prophecy tale is told on stormy nights by firelight to scare wee ones. It was done, over—nothing came of it—if it ever happened.

And yet, hundreds of years later, rumors of the bairn of prophecy, born into the wasteland, are circulating; and the folk grow fearful again.

Why was the story not in the history? Was it not true? Even the folk of the kingdoms of the Ruud, though unso-phisticated no doubt, couldn't believe such nonsense without evidence. Weren't they all descendants of the wissendes of the Great West and the Kingdom of Ruhm? Weren't they blessed by the virtues of wisdom and logic?

Even as he muttered these words to himself he chuckled. How far they'd come since their ancestors brought them out of tyranny in the west to freedom in their little section of the eastern continent. How many of the folk could even read these days?

But to think that a child could kill a king and destroy the Ruud? He reached a hand to a thick volume on the bookshelf and wiped dust from the title, *The History of the Ruud*. No, he'd read that one. There was nothing in the history about the prophecy, nothing about a war with the beasts. It *could* be no more than a fairy tale.

"Your Highness."

Welk jumped a bit, turned, and wiped the dust from his hand onto his vestment. Dunham, his father's steward, had entered the room and cleared his throat.

"I'm sorry to disturb you, Highness."

"Quite all right. Just looking for some reading."

"There's nothing there. I've read them as well."

Welk smiled. Ever the vigilant servant. Was there anything he could think that Dunham had not already considered?

"I bring you news of the king." Dunham's gaze fell to the floor and Welk knew the man had information he shouldn't share. But they had an agreement, the two of them. Welk, the son of an errant king, and Dunham the son of a disgraced steward. They knew the importance of allies.

"What has he done?"

Dunham shook his head as if it weighed the world and sighed. He clicked his tongue against his front teeth a few times and said. "The prophecy, you know. He's allowed Sorgood to take the folk's fear into action."

"Action? Of what sort?"

"He plans to round up the children, Highness. Mostly of the village of Path, as they believe the new bairn is there."

"And do what with them?"

"Imprison them, I would imagine."

"Imprison the children of Path?"

"Aye, it is madness."

"The folk won't stand for that...will they?"

Dunham sighed again and pressed the tip of his tongue against his teeth rapidly. "The folk are unlikely to resist Sorgood's troops...or the king's orders; and they're frightened, Highness. They believe there is a plot afoot to destroy the Ruud."

Welk put his rough hands to his face and rubbed his eyes. "I don't understand, Dunham. What's become of the folk of the Ruud?"

"Highness?"

"We have always been told that wissendes are of a special breed, of the highest of intellectual prowess. And we are the ancestors of the great sage Michelruud who brought us out of persecution in the west. What happened? I confess, I myself have not taken to academic pursuits. Was I not born to it? Have the wissendes lost their status?"

"Not all folk of the Ruud are descended from the wissende class," Dunham said. "You forget the servants, the farmers and laborers—they also sought freedom from the Hass of Emorah in Ruhm. And there has been a small but steady stream of freedom seekers who have managed to escape since that time."

"And the criminals," Welk said with a short laugh. "Ruhm has no qualms about releasing undesirables to seek their fortunes here. I hear they send them off with a map to the Straits of Winkin and fare for the boat."

Dunham smiled at the prince. "Yes, Highness. So, you see..."

"No, I still don't see. Where are the great thinkers who descended from the wissendes?"

Dunham sighed. "They're still here, Highness, no doubt. But, the truth of the matter is that even skills that are ours by inheritance can become dull from misuse. And to put it quite simply, thinking is hard."

Here Welk let out a loud laugh and Dunham joined him.

"If I am to become King, Dunham, I will set up wissende schools. And the wissende class will champion reason once again."

"*If,* your Highness?"

"There's always the chance that I will take the route of my brother, Elrundt."

Dunham's eyes flew open and Welk offered him a wink. "Not to fear, Dunham. I've no plans to disappear today. After all, someone must protect the Ruud from the bairn of prophecy. Send Pierston to the stationer's to see if he has any volumes of history that might help us."

"Stationer Pratt is in Damon Wall. But we can see if his apprentice knows of any."

Welk laughed. "I've met Jeopard Link. He's not got a wit about anything other than the books on flowers and trees. There's something not right with that one."

"He'd make a fine horticulturist, if his heart wasn't set on books and printing."

"We don't need a horticulturist. We need a child of proph-ecy."

"You mean to find him yourself?"

"I do. If we are to see the children of Path safe at home, we must end this nonsense one way or another."

"Very well, Highness." Dunham seemed to expand with a renewed energy. "As soon as the stationer returns home, I will send Pierston to him." He bowed low and at the door, turned back to Welk.

"I should like to say, Highness, if it is not presumptuous; I am glad you have no plans to disappear."

Welk winked at him and smiled. When the door closed behind Dunham, he turned once again to the dusty books on the shelf. "No worries," he muttered. "I have a much better plan in mind."

6

Chapter Three

L eah Hallowsing breathed in the damp air of the early morning hours, lifted her dress hem slightly above her slippers, and scuttled through the empty cobbled streets of Ruhm in the dark. She'd done it at last! All her years of studying at the Hass school, all the hours she'd given up, the parties, and the festivals, all for this one grand honor: Aide to the High Priest of Hass. A little more diligence, a few more years, and the coveted post of Historian of Ruhm would be hers.

She ran up the stone steps of the stationers' and pushed open the door.

"Hello Marigold," she called out to the second apprentice. "Where is father?"

Marigold smiled, gave a tired little curtsey, her short curls bobbing about her head, and said, "Congratulations, mistress. Aide to the High Priest of Hass. We're so very proud."

"Is he here?"

Marigold nodded, motioning to the back of the shop, and Leah made her way through the shelves of maps, books, stock papers, and printing supplies into the back room where the presses stood motionless with expectation. The smell of ink and paper and burning candles surrounded her. She knew she'd been abrupt with Mari, but the girl was always phoney. Her first job as aide to the High Priest would be to study the blasphemy laws; there ought to be something a folk could do to keep snotty girls like Marigold in check.

"Father?" Her voice was dampened by the walls stacked with books and paper. As organized as her father was, there was always too much at the shop than the shop had room for. But her father was not there. She wandered the large room, looking under desks—for she had indeed once found him crouched on the floor with a magnifying glass doing goodness knows what—and behind crates of ink and supplies. "Father?"

A slight shuffling echoed from behind her. She turned and wove her way through the maze of tables, presses, and desks to the far corner where a door stood ajar. Her hair stood on end and a chill swept through her chest. The forbidden closet. Her father's private office, where no one was allowed.

She approached the door and peered into the darkness behind it. "Father?"

"Yes, Leah," he said. "Come in."

"Come in?"

7

"Yes, yes."

"Are you certain Father?"

"I am."

She pushed the door open and stepped in. Her father sat behind a small desk. The room was much larger than she'd imagined—about the size of the family kitchen. Her parents' bedchamber lay behind it and so, having never entered there either, she'd never had much occasion to calculate the size of her father's office, though she admitted to often contem-plating it—he spent so much time there.

The walls were lined with shelves crammed with books in every available space. Candles, poised atop the cases and on his desk, gave off a dim, spooky glow, casting odd flickering shadows on the walls. One tiny, yellowed, glass window on the outer wall was home to a dusty web.

"You read in here, Father?"

"Only when I must," he said. "Come, sit."

He motioned to a small wooden bench in front of his desk. Leah danced her way through the cluttered office and pulled her long bound tresses out of the way to take the seat.

"So you are off to the eastern continent," he said. "The land of the betrayer, Michelruud."

A smile touched her father's lips and though she knew he was not speaking of Michelruud with the required vehemence, she forgave him. Many of the older citizens of Ruhm had trouble of late, feeling hatred where hatred was due.

"We leave in two days' time." She paused for a moment while her father watched her. "Are you not proud of me, Father?"

Surprisingly, he did not answer right away. He tapped a finger on the desk and frowned. "Being the aide to the High Priest is a great honor indeed."

Leah lowered her head. "I know you don't approve. But I'd hoped..."

He leaned forward and folded his hands together. "We are proud of you, my dear. You have studied hard and earned your honor well. It's just that..."

Leah also leaned in with anticipation. But when her father hesitated she said, "I know it's a long trip and I'll be away for some time, but it's perfectly safe."

Her father shook his head. "Leah, my dear child. Do you know who you are?"

Stunned, she sat straight and cocked her head to one side. "I'm Leah Hallowsing, of course. Daughter of Edwin, Stationer to the King of Rhum." She did not shrink from the pride in her own voice.

"Ah," he said and pointed a finger at her. "Your concise-ness gives you away."

"Conciseness? I am who I am, am I not?"

"You are the daughter of wissendes, Leah. Logic, precision, learning."

"Wissendes?" She shuddered just a bit at the word and that her father had said it so loudly. But she would not let him cow her. "There are no more wissendes in Ruhm, Father. There is only the Hass."

"But there were once wissendes. Folk of great knowledge and understanding—of great compassion and love of freedom."

"Father." She trembled. "You come close to blasphemy."

"And here you've just been promoted to the Circle of the High Priest. It is a quandry for you, indeed."

Her head shook nervously. "What are you on about? Is this a test? Shall I tell my superiors?"

He stared hard at her face with a look of sad resignation. "If you must. But only after you hear what I have to say."

Now a bit perturbed at her father's game, she said, "Well, go on then."

"As I said. You are descended of Dakenruud, a grand premier of Hass long ago. Oh, don't look so impressed. He was nothing more than a wissende. But as you say, the Hass had no time for truth or logic and so turned them all into premiers and whatnot."

"Father—"

"Do let me finish before you make your accusations of blasphemy. You may not know the history, as it's not allowed—your blasphemy prevents this sort of information—but it was your great, great grandfather —I'm not sure how many greats there are, seven or eight, I would think. Brother to the aforementioned Michelruud, the wissende who fled persecution to the east and set up his own little kingdom, to which you will travel tomorrow. Yes. You are kin to the apostates! What do you think of that?"

Leah grimaced. Kin to Michelruud the Betrayer. This was unsettling, indeed. "Do others know? Wouldn't the Hass know this?"

"Pfft. The Hass cares nothing for history or genealogy or reading in general."

"But, Father." Leah rolled her eyes. "I'm going to be the Historian of Ruhm one day. And here you sit telling me the Hass cares not for history."

"I think you may find, daughter, that words and titles are often stripped of their meaning by despots."

"Despots?"

"Now, now. I mean to say that your Hass's idea of historian and yours may differ remarkably."

"I studied history in school and quite liked it." She almost rolled her eyes again. This was always how conversations with her father went. They neither seemed to understand the other at all.

"Nonetheless, your connection to the Ruud has its origins in long, long ago. Not the sort of thing the Hass would be interested in. No. Your secret is safe with your mother and me. But it's what Dakenruud did that is of import to us. Michelruud and his little settlement is nothing. Dakenruud held the kell stone himself—"

Leah gasped. "What do you know of the kell stone?"

"Ah, they have told you."

Ashamed that she'd given away the very thing she'd been told to keep to herself, her cheeks reddened. "A little. Only a very little."

"I see it in your eyes." Her father winked at her. "You want to know more. And I will oblige. Yes, the kell stone is real. Or so say the stories. So it could just as well be only legend."

"Well, is it real or not?"

"It seems to me," he said, "that as Dakenruud was very real and his name is listed in our family's ancestry, the stories about him are likely to be truthful. And the story is this. Michelruud had a beast problem. The felidae and centaurs and angels, especially the accursed angels, would not get off his land. Hah! *His* land, what to do you make of that? Anyway," he waved his hand about in front of his face.

Leah had never seen her father so animated. She couldn't tell which was more engrossing, his excitement or the story he told.

"In exchange for help from Ruhm and her weapons, Michelruud gave the kell stone to Dakenruud."

"Where did Michelruud get it from?"

"Why from here, from the mines of Galdred, where it was hidden, of course. Oh, it's a long and silly story. There is legend and there is fact and what we know may lie somewhere in between. The beasts got it from Krone Mountain, and we stole it—"

"Stole it?"

"Yes, we stole it from them. Certainly the Hass isn't trying to whitewash that event. The point is that Michelruud stole it from the Hass and planned to return it to the beasts. But instead, he gave it to Daken."

"So, the stone is not in the east, after all?" Leah was filled with energy. She had information that the Hass would want. This could elevate her even higher in the Circle and hasten her to her coveted appointment as historian. Perhaps this was why her father told her this. He truly was proud of her.

"They don't know where it is. When the Hass was unable to destroy it, Daken was charged with traveling the entire world and finding a place deep within the earth to hide the stone. He was to tell no one of its whereabouts. He returned home two years later."

"And?"

"And what?"

"That's it? That's the story? Of what use is that to me?"

"Use? My dear, did you think I meant to offer you useful information?"

"Well...yes, I suppose I did."

"But do you not simply enjoy a good story?"

Leah couldn't help but laugh. "A going away story? Very well done, Father."

"Yes, a going away story. And it has a moral as well." Now her father seemed to grow hardened and serious. "As a descend-ant of the wissendes, you are a thinking creature. You cannot help yourself. I have watched you struggle in your endeavors with the Hass."

"I don't know what you mean."

"Yes, you do. You question too much. They told you this early on when you first wanted to go to the Hass school instead of the common school your friends attended."

"I wanted a proper education."

"Twaddle. You wanted to wear the uniform and play on their grand grounds with their contraptions."

"I did not."

"You were six years old, Leah. Of course that's what you wanted. How long before you realized that they brought the students out to the play yards only in the mornings and afternoons when the common school children passed by?"

He stared at her and she raised her chin in defiance.

"How long?"

Leah's shoulders fell. "About three days."

"Yes, you see. You were not meant for the Hass."

"I am meant for the Hass. I love the Hass. The Hass keeps the peace. It is because of the Hass that we live in an ordered society as we do. If it were not for the Hass—"

"Poppycock, don't feed me your memorized propaganda."

"Father, you play too much at blasphemy."

"And will you turn me in? Would you really turn anyone in, to have them stocked or whipped...or worse?"

They stared at each other, neither willing to yield.

"Then why did you let me go to the Hass school?" she asked. "If you

11

don't approve. Why not keep me out as the other parents?"

Here her father's face softened and he smiled a bit. "It is not in a parent's heart to deny his child the best education possible. Even if it is with the Hass. Your scores were far above your friends', and the Hass did its best to recruit you. And so you went. I feared you would become too much like them, but I saw that you learned to keep your questions to yourself. They're still there." He pressed a finger to his fore-head. "And one day they'll pester you until you let them out."

"More dancing with blasphemy, Father?"

Truly she was confused. Had her father always been this irreverent? How could she have missed it? Yes, she could admit to herself that she was a small girl and wanted to wear the silky blue dress of the Hass school and play on the equip-ment and walk up the tall steps to the impressive marble building. She was a child. What child wouldn't want it?

But she had grown into a sensible woman, had she not? She'd worked hard for her position with the Inner Circle. And she deserved it. What was there to question, anyway? The Hass interpreted the laws of Emorah—sacred morality —given to them by the savior Rett eons ago, when he sacrificed himself for the purity of the folk of Ruhm.

Certainly, she didn't accept all the legend as absolute truth, nor did she participate in the rituals of Rett as some of the more excitable members of Hass did. But that didn't mean she wasn't completely in support of the Hass and its government.

"Are you not curious about Dakenruud's fate?"

Her father's voice startled her from her thoughts. She stared at him. "I assumed he...no. I mean, yes. What happened to him?"

"He returned home after his journey, instead of to the palace and the Hass. He wanted to see his family. And he gave to his brother Abueruud a journal of his travels. Two days later, the Hass burst into the family home and dragged Daken away. He was never seen again."

A silence hung between them. Tiny bits of dust floated about and the ticking of her father's pocket watch was suddenly very loud.

Chapter Four

After Father's steps, muffled on the cold earth of the cellar, scuttled away, Fenn sat still for some time at the tunnel entrance, grasping at the hemp rope he wore around his neck, wanting desperately to pound on the old wooden door. He could cry convincingly and beg Father not to make him go. Somewhere in the darkness there must be a trigger for the bell, for he'd heard it sound a few times and followed Father to the cellar to let in some poor refugee or the occasional lost gnome who must have fallen into the tunnel, unable to find his way out.

He dangled the lantern about him in the dark, casting ominous shadows on the root-knotted, dirt walls. Where was the bell? He would ring the bell. Would Father come for him? Would he let him back into the wissenry?

He'd certainly been able to change the old wissende's mind about many things with a few tears in the past. But he knew, somehow, that he *must* go. He must make his way out into the Ruud to Cold Sea Port. Father's face was sincere with fear and alertness. Something horrible was happening and he was trying to save Fenn. But Fenn didn't feel saved. Instead, he was paralyzed with indecision.

Slowly, he calmed his breathing and told himself sternly, "Stop being a baby. You can't go crying back and you can't sit here in the dirt forever. So you must crawl."

And crawl he did—slowly at first, finding his rhythm with one arm holding the lantern out in front of him. His hand, grasping its handle, seemed to warm from it—he felt an odd connection between the lantern and Father. Visions of Father carrying it about the cellar and dark storage came to him, comforting him. Father shuffling with a rat beneath his feet; Father dropping the lantern and nearly falling himself; Father swinging it about casting shadows in an attempt to entertain; and then Father holding it while denying the existence of grub demons. At that thought, Fenn crawled faster and faster, stopping for the briefest second to switch the lantern to his other hand.

He had time now, in the dark tunnel, to ponder the grub demon situation. When had Father lied? Was it years ago, when he'd told Fenn that if he entered the tunnel, the grubs would wriggle into his socks and pants and lay eggs under his skin? Was it a lie that the eggs would hatch and as the demons grew inside him, they'd slowly take over his body? They'd make their way to his brain and soon control him; he'd be a grub zombie—the living dead. Fenn shuddered and moved faster, shaking off his legs in case any grubs might be trying to get hold of his pants.

Or, on the other hand, had Father lied just now, when he said that there were no such things as grub demons? Had he wanted him in the tunnel so desperately that he'd risk his becoming a grub zombie? Could anything possibly be that horrific to run away from?

No. The simplest explanation had to be that grub demons didn't exist and Father just scared him away from the tunnel with that story long ago. It had certainly worked. He never set foot in the tunnel for fear of grubzombiism. He'd never even dared move the potato bins to have a look at the door, as his foster brother Lucas had done many times. Still, hadn't other kids talked about the grub demons? Did everyone have tunnels? Were all the other kids in the village of Path right now crawling through tunnels fearing grub demons and realizing their parents were liars?

Fenn stopped and stared into the blackness in front of him.

"Lucas didn't come," he said aloud.

Lucas was still at the wissenry, as far as he knew. Why hadn't Father sent Lucas away? He started to turn back, but thought better of it. He ought to do what he was told—after all, he didn't do as told very often.

After a few minutes, the tunnel opened out around him and he could stand and walk. He was much less worried about grub demons while walking. They were just grubs anyway, weren't they? They'd be fat and sticky—he could feel them, maybe, before they laid any eggs. He stopped his thoughts with a chuckle. There aren't any grub demons, he reminded himself. But in the hollow of his stomach, and in the tiny skip of his heartbeat, he knew that he still feared what likely didn't exist.

Lucas' teasing laugh echoed through his mind. Of course, Lucas would know the truth about grub demons; Lucas always seemed to know everything. A pang of grief hit Fenn's chest. He didn't want to leave Lucas behind. He didn't want to live at the wissenry at Cold Sea Port. Granted, the port held many excitements. Maybe he'd be allowed to actually enter the city.

Still, he wondered if there were any orphans living there who could possibly be as annoying, as bothersome, or as funny and endearing as Lucas Foster? Fenn doubted it. He didn't want to leave. Though his feet kept taking him farther and farther from his home, his heart was being left behind.

Michelruud had to be the best kingdom of the realm. It had the best apple orchard, there was no doubt. And the pond in the woods to the north, where Gettel and Drew—though they didn't care much for wissenry orphans—let Fenn and Lucas swim and fish had to be the most serene body of water in the entire Ruud, if not the continent.

And the village of Path was surely the best village in all of Michelruud, and all the Ruud. Timber may abut the beast forest with its mysteries and chills. But who needed scary stories, anyway? What Fenn wanted—what he'd always longed for—was a simple life in Path, living at the wissenry, visiting the stationer's, noshing apples, reading, and learning. He thought he'd live with Father Treacher always.

When his eyes brimmed with tears, he wiped them on the back of his sleeve and decided he should think about the grub demons some more.

14

No sense getting all blubbery about leav-ing. Maybe this trip to Cold Sea was temporary. Or better yet, maybe it was all part of a secret wissende training. He just had to show he could make it to Father Britt and then he could go home—in a carriage, he hoped.

He felt he'd walked for an hour when the tunnel began to shrink again and soon he was back onto his hands and knees and crawling upward. The opening must be near. He came to a pile of large rocks and felt cool night air on his face. After putting out the lantern and setting it aside, he climbed to the opening of the tunnel—nothing more than a crevice between boulders, covered with brush. He stopped and listened. At first, he heard nothing. Then he realized the river rushed in the distance, and wind whispered through the pines. He moved his hand to push aside the bushy covering, but heard something new. Voices.

Hunkering down in the crevice, Fenn listened hard.

"What are you doing here?" a girl said.

"Quiet," said a boy, but awfully loud for wanting silence.

"There's nobody else out here."

"You don't know that," he said.

"I know as much as you, waiter boy."

When Fenn realized it was Sadie Pratt's voice, he pushed the brush away from the tunnel opening and crawled out. Rounding a rock as tall as he was, to where they stood, he said, "I agree. We should stay quiet."

They jumped when they heard him and he chuckled. Sadie was standing with Grayson Steppe, a boy from the inn—an odd pair, he thought.

"Who is that?" Sadie said, peering through the darkness.

Fenn walked out of the shadow of a tree so they could see him in the moonlight.

"It's me. Fenn Foster of the wissenry," he said, tossing his pack against a rock where Sadie's and Grayson's knapsacks lay.

"One of the orphans," Grayson said. "Well, come on over."

Fenn had never actually talked to the innkeeper's son before. Grayson kept to himself, same as Fenn. He was a quiet kid, tall and scrawny—the opposite of his brothers. All the Steppes were sturdy, red-haired, and fair-skinned like their father, except for Grayson who favored his dark-eyed mother. Not a woman in the Ruud could mention Grayson without noting it. "Has the look of his dear departed ma, that boy does." And then they'd shake their heads mournfully and wipe nonexistent tears from their eyes.

On more than one visit to the stationer's, Fenn would jump when he realized Grayson Steppe was curled up in a corner of the shop engrossed in a book, still wearing his dirty apron from the inn.

Though he knew Sadie Pratt fairly well, he now realized he'd barely spoken a dozen words to her, either. Her house, or at least the stationer's office on the first floor, was full of books and papers and Fenn was always sure to accompany Father Treacher on his errands there. Stationer Pratt was very generous in lending books, but only to Fenn, he'd say often, with a wink. Sadie wasn't usually at home. If Fenn saw her at all, she was bouncing loudly down the stairs and out the door shouting to her ma she'd be back for supper.

Sadie was one of those who sometimes found themselves at the wissenry with their mothers at their wits end because of their mischief. Not that Fenn hadn't let Lucas drag him into some mischief on occasion, for which he was almost always blamed. But Sadie never paid them any attention. They were wissenry orphans, well past the age for adoption. Everybody in the village knew he and Lucas would be wissendes. They weren't for playing with—one day Lucas and Fenn would be helping them with their neighbor troubles, reading their letters for them, or sorting out their transgressions against one throne or another in the Ruud—you don't play with kids like that.

"Are we the only ones who made it out?" Grayson asked.

Sadie laughed. "Don't be stupid."

"It's not stupid," Fenn said.

Only now did Fenn realize there was little hope of his being on a secret wissenry training mission. As he imagined in the tunnel, all the kids of Path must have been sent away from home. What kind of threat had befallen them?

"There are lots of others, all over," Sadie confirmed. "They'll have been told, same as us. Get out and hide for a while."

"You mean you're to go back?" Fenn asked.

"Sure. I was told to sneak back to the cellar after dark today." She plopped herself down, pouting, on a rock. "It's going to be a long wait."

"I'm to wait until my father or my brother comes for me," Grayson said. "It shouldn't be more than a day."

Fenn took a seat on the big rock beside Sadie and thought that maybe Father Treacher had overreacted. Maybe he should do as they were doing and go back after a while. Their parents seemed to think the trouble, whatever it was, would be over soon.

"So, you're to go back then."

Even in the dim moonlight, Fenn could tell Sadie rolled her eyes. "That's what we said. Why? Aren't you going back?"

"Sure I am."

"This is stupid," she said. "I'm going to give it an hour and then go

16

back home."

"You can't just march back into the village," Grayson said. "You'd have to sneak in and make sure the guard are gone."

"The guard?" Fenn asked.

"The king's guard." Sadie looked exasperated. "You know, the ones we're hiding from."

Fenn wanted to ask them what the guard wanted, but he felt stupid now for not knowing. Sadie and Grayson seemed to know exactly what was going on and acted as if this sort of thing happened all the time. And while Fenn didn't care for the feeling of not knowing, he cared even less to let on that he didn't know. What was it Father Treacher always said? It's preferable to keep our mouths closed and let others think we know nothing, rather than open our mouths and give them proof of it.

"If we're going to have to sneak anyway, why don't we go back now and have a look?" Sadie said.

"A look at what?" Grayson said.

"At what the guard actually does."

"My da said the guard is looking for kids our age. Why would we go to the village where they can find us?"

Sadie let out something of a laugh. "What are you? Scared?"

"I'm not scared; I'm cautious. And I obey my parents."

"Now that's a laugh. How many times have you been whipped back home from my dad's shop when you were late for chores? Anyway, even my ma isn't sure what's happening. All she heard was a rumor about the guard coming into the village to check the kids. For all I know she heard the rumor from your da."

"What's that supposed to mean?" Grayson said.

"It means—" Sadie shook her head at him—"That there might not be anything going on at all."

"But there must be or Father Treacher wouldn't have sent me into the tunnel, believe me."

"What tunnel?" Grayson said.

"There's a tunnel? Can we see?"

"You're easily distracted, aren't you?" Grayson said to Sadie and laughed.

Sadie stood and grabbed her back pack. "I am not easily distracted. Come on. Let's stow our packs in this tunnel of Fenn's and sneak into town."

Fenn waited to see what Grayson would do. He knew it was a bad idea. If it was just Sadie pushing it, he'd rather not. Sadie wasn't the best judge of safety. She'd fallen out of trees, got caught swiping one of the

Kessler's pups, and fell off a lamb trying to ride it up a hill. Not the sort of folk you follow into danger. But Grayson stood and nodded and grabbed his knapsack.

So, against his better judgment, but admittedly very willingly, Fenn led Grayson Steppe and Sadie Pratt to the tunnel opening and they tossed their sacks in.

"You have to swear to secrecy," he told them. "This tunnel's for refugees and secret messages and all that. Don't go blab-bing or all the kids in Path will be using it for hides and chases."

"Yeah, okay, okay," Sadie said. "We swear. Now—" she put her fists on her hips and glared at them both in the morn-ing darkness—"I don't suppose the two of you have ever played nab a gnome."

Grayson sputtered. "That cruel game?"

"I've heard of it." Fenn said, feeling rather proud of himself. "You sneak around and grab gnomes."

"First team back to base with one wins," Sadie said. "Have you played?" She looked from Grayson to Fenn and back again. "I should have known. Okay, look, the goal is to move quickly without running. Watch your step. No twigs or cones. Keep to the soft needles or dirt. The guard will be coming from Michelruud castle on the other side of Path, so we should be okay. We'll go through the woods to the bramble knot, you know the bramble knot, I hope?"

They both nodded. Fenn realized that not having played nab a gnome had put him and Grayson on Sadie's dumb list. Who wouldn't know where the bramble knot was?

"There's a dirt path I know through the brambles."

"Through the brambles?" Grayson said.

"Are you afraid of a few scratches? It'll take us right to the stationer's on the square."

"And your mom put up those lattices for vines on either side of your place," Grayson said. "We can hide behind those and see what's going on."

"Nice thinking, waiter boy."

"I'm not a waiter—"

"Shh," Sadie said. "Single file, don't lose sight of me. And quiet."

And so it was that Fenn followed Grayson Steppe and Sadie Pratt back to Path, once more in his short life, disobeying Father Treacher. He could see the old wissende's red, splutter-ing face in his head as he loped toward the village.

Sadie avoided the houses nestled in the woods, and their paths that would lead them straight to the village square, and instead led Fenn and

18

Grayson in a maze of a trek through the trees and shrubs.

His heart pounded in his chest at every sound, from the twigs Grayson couldn't seem to miss to the early morning chatter of an awakening bird. He was not made for hides and chases.

They came upon the back of Sadie's house and she led them quietly across the yard to the corner where she peered around to the front.

"All clear," she said. "We can hide behind the lattice and wait to see what happens."

Fenn and Grayson made their way past her toward the front of the house. From behind him, Fenn heard Sadie gasp and shout.

Chapter Five

Ow, ow, ow, ow!"

Fenn turned to see Ma'am Stationer glaring at him and Grayson. She had Sadie by the ear. Fenn sucked in a breath and held it. He'd seen Sadie's ma take her by the ear plenty of times over some mischief, but he'd never seen her truly angry as she was now.

"Mutterede's law, Sadie Pratt, what are you doing back in the village? This way."

She dragged Sadie by the ear toward the back of the house.

"You too. Dratted willful..." Her voice trailed off.

"Ow. Ma."

"Hush."

She pulled Sadie up the back steps, pushed open the back door and shoved her in. "You too," she said to Fenn and Grayson and they dutifully followed Sadie into the back room of the stationer's. It was dark, the heavy drapes closed against the early morning light.

Jeopard Link pulled aside the curtain from the front doorway and looked into the room, his eyes as wide and round as his spectacles and his blond mustache twitching. "I heard carriages ma'am. I think the guard have arrived."

"Into the basement with you."

Ma'am Stationer pulled open a door and handed Sadie a lit candle. Sadie took it, rubbed at her ear with her other hand and descended wooden steps to the cellar. Fenn and Grayson followed.

"I'll be down directly," Sadie's ma whispered loudly down the stairs and they were left in the darkness, the candle casting their warped shadows onto the shelves. Sadie bumped her way across the small room and used her candle to light a lantern hanging from a hook on one wall.

"One folk you can never get past is my ma," she said, pouting.

Fenn eyed the room. The shelves were lined with canned goods and fresh produce, much like the cellar at the wissenry. He took a seat on a crate and squirmed. All three of them jumped when they heard a thump from above. The door opened and a large, dark figure, breathing heavily, followed a lantern down the wood stairs.

Ma'am Stationer had a round, kind face, but it was full of concern and flecked with ire, as she stood in the middle of the small cellar looking at them.

"What's happening Ma?" Sadie asked.

Ma'am shook her head. "Just what I told you might happen. They'll be bringing up a criminal cage at any moment —they're looking for the bairn. What in Mutterede's name are you doing here?"

"We just wanted to see for sure," Sadie whined. "We thought it was all just a rumor."

"So did I," Ma'am said. "And if I could catch the nosy busybody who started it, I'd tan his hide, I would. Now, Sadie, I'm not going to tell you again—no need to come back tonight for news—make your way to Damon Wall; and you ought to take these two with you. Your uncle may be able to hide you until the guard leaves. But they don't look likely to leave for some time."

"Why not?" Fenn asked.

She shook her head sadly and tears welled up in her eyes. "They said...they said they know he's here. The bairn is here in Path. And they aren't leaving until he's dead."

"Dead?" Grayson said with a hollow voice.

The hair on the back of Fenn's neck stood on end and his breathing quickened.

"Who said that, Ma?"

"I heard it from the baker."

Sadie sighed loudly. "So it could just be another rumor."

"We're not taking any chances," Ma'am said.

She grabbed hold of Sadie and pressed her hard into her soft belly, weeping quietly.

"It's okay, Ma," Sadie tried to soothe her, her faced smashed against the laces of her mother's bodice. "We'll get away. I promise."

Letting Sadie go, she wiped her face with the back of her hands. "And here," she said, taking a slim leather book off a shelf. "Your da put these together for you. It's maps of the Ruud...and parts beyond—just in case."

Sadie looked up at her mother with her mouth open, a horrified look on her face. But she only mumbled. "Thanks Ma. Thanks."

20

"You understand, Sadie, don't you?" her mother said. "You have a mark, small as it is. You must flee and stay away until the guard leaves us be. You understand that?"

"Yes, Ma'am."

"I don't know what your situation is, sons. But as you're of the age, you best stay out of Path as well. If you don't find safety in Damon Wall, don't bother with Aaronland—I know no one there to help you. Go straight out to the hill country and stay as long as needs be."

Her brow creased with worry.

"We'll be all right," Grayson said, standing up. "We'll stick together and we'll be fine."

Sadie's mother grabbed them all into her huge arms and gave them a squeeze. Fenn thought she smelled like ink and cider. Waves of emotions rattled through his head at her touch: love, fear, anger, frustration, pity, pride—Fenn could barely contain them all and felt the urge to pull away from the woman. When she finally let him go, through the rush of relief as the feelings fled, he realized he'd never been hugged by a woman before and stared at her for a few seconds longer than was proper, his cheeks hot with flush.

"All right then. Stay to the woods. Avoid anyone on horseback, I'd say, or in carriages, for that matter. Avoid everyone, to be sure. And may the spirit of Elrundt be with you."

Sadie rolled her eyes. "Ma. You don't really believe in Elrundt, do you?"

Ma'am Stationer rose to her full height and slapped her fists onto her hips. "He was a real prince; I saw him myself with my own two eyes. He disappeared before you were born and well, you never know. Maybe he really is out there protecting the lost and weary, like they say."

"Ma."

She threw up her hands. "I know, I know. And your father would be laughing at me, too. But give me this one little hope. Reach out for his help if you find yourselves in trouble."

Sadie started to protest but paused and nodded. "Okay, Ma. May Elrundt be our guide."

Fenn and Grayson nodded as well, mumbling the mantra of many a traveler setting off into the unknown parts. "May Elurndt be our guide."

"Now hurry, before they start searching houses."

They climbed out of the cellar and quietly left the station-er's by the back door; Fenn heard the lock click after them. He started for the yard, but watched as Sadie made her way again to the corner of the house. She turned and waved for Fenn and Grayson to follow her.

"What are you doing?" Grayson whispered.

"I want to see for myself."

They all made their way to the lattice work jutting out from the side of the house and peered through at the town square. A carriage pulling a caged cart behind it rolled up the lane.

Chapter Six

Lucas walked with Father Treacher down the lane toward the village square from the wissenry at the southern edge of Path. He opened his mouth wide and yawned, rubbing his eyes and shaking off sleep.

"Are you certain about this," Father said halting, and turning to him, worry in his voice.

"The only way to be of use is to be in the thick of things, Father. Nothing will happen at the wissenry. Nothing ever happens there."

"You joke," Father said, giving his shoulder a smack with the palm of his hand. "Anyway, I'm sure it will not be as dangerous as all that."

Lucas looked up at the old man and smiled. "Of course not. They'll take the children to Steingefan for questioning, realize what fools they've been and let them go." He smiled broadly, charmed at how easily the lie rolled off his tongue.

Father Treacher nodded several times. "Yes, yes, of course."

They took up their walk again and the air around them lightened just a bit. Day was dawning.

As they came to the village square the sounds of horses —thudding hoofs, whinnies—rushed at them from the north. Shouts rang out as members of the king's guard pounded on doors.

"Into the square," they shouted. "Everyone into the square."

Father Treacher sighed. "So it is true."

"You expected it was not?"

He nodded. "Some large part of me wished they would not come and that Britt would send Fenn back to us and all would be as it was."

A large guardsman plodded toward them on foot, shaking off sleep.

Lucas smiled at Father Treacher. "Is that the objective reasoning of the wissenry, Father?"

"The bittersweet desires of an old man, I'm afraid. When this has ended, I fear our little Ruud will never be the same."

The guard grabbed Lucas by the arm and shoved him.

"Stand in the center," he demanded. "By the well."

"Please," Father Treacher said rather haltingly. "He's just a boy of

22

twelve."

Lucas smiled and winked at Father before walking to the stone well. Treacher was not the liar Lucas was. But the guard bought it and that was all that mattered.

Lucas watched as children were dragged from their mother's arms and forced to stand with him in the middle of the square near the well. When the carriage rolled in, pulling a criminal cage, and stopped in front of the stationer's, he turned to give Father a hard stare.

Parents huddled in groups watching their children as Sorgood, the head of King Evan's guard, pranced his horse about shouting at them to stand back. Sorgood sneered, taking in their fearful gazes like a vile spider tracking prey.

"All children will bare their shoulders," he said.

Lucas waited for a guardsman to approach him. He could feel Father Treacher's eyes searching for him through the crowd. When Tildon Weeks stepped in front of him, he nodded and pulled at his tunic, baring his left shoulder.

Tildon looked at it and said, "Other arm, please."

Lucas smiled and bared his right.

"What's that?" Tildon asked him.

"I don't know what you mean."

"Come on, now, Lucas, it looks like you drew on your arm."

"Really?" Lucas turned his head in the dim morning light to look at the three squiggly lines he'd drawn on himself with his ink pen. "No," he said. "I didn't draw that."

Tildon looked confused.

"I think you're to send me to the cage now," Lucas told him. "Even if I didn't have a mark, I'm of the age."

"Are you now, Lucas?"

"Sorgood will think so, Til. You better do it."

Tildon nodded slightly. "All right then, onto the cart with you. It's a bad omen, sending a wissenry orphan into the cage."

"No more so than sending Lara Cole. What is she, five?"

"But she has a real mark, Lucas."

Lucas climbed onto the metal-enclosed cart behind the carriage and helped the smaller children in. The damp morning air was filled with sobs, some mild protests, and shouts from the guard. Sorgood caught him glaring at him, and so he turned from the scene to the other side of the cage.

His attention was drawn to the lattice work beside the stationer's. Ma'am Stationer had never been successful at growing a full lattice of vines and so the fingers sticking out from behind it were easy to see. The face and eyes belonging to the fingers, only a felid would be able to find.

"Mutterede's laugh, Fenn," Lucas whispered. "Pull your fingers in before you're seen."

Chapter Seven

Fenn let go his grasp of the lattice and pulled his hands in, thinking he must have imagined he heard Lucas' voice. He made to move around the lattice but Sadie grabbed him.

"What?" she said. "What is it?"

"It's Lucas," Grayson told her. "He's in the cage."

"Well, you can't do anything about it now."

Fenn looked at the scene through the lattice once more. Most was blocked by the carriage and the cage behind it. But he could see a few guardsmen on horseback and hear Sorgood's sneering voice telling mothers to let go of their children.

"What is this?" he muttered. Then he heard Lucas again.

"What are you about, Fenn Foster? Why are you here?"

"What's going on?" Fenn whispered.

"I think it's pretty clear," Sadie said.

"Shh." Fenn nudged her.

"Hey." she pushed back.

"Don't worry about me," Lucas told him. "I'll be fine. But you should have been halfway to Damon Wall and the port by now. Cross the river and get into Aaronland as soon as you can, and then make your way to the Cold Sea. Hurry."

Before Fenn could react, he heard Sorgood's voice shout, "Search the village."

"Run," Lucas said. "Now."

"We have to get out of here," Fenn said. "Meet me at the tunnel."

Fenn didn't think about the nab-a-gnome strategy. He just ran—as fast as he could. He went around the bramble knot, even while he saw Sadie head straight into it on her path. But he could hear Grayson's padding feet behind him and so led him around the brambles, through the wood, some two miles, until they stopped, panting and bent over, at the tunnel entrance.

"It's about time," Sadie said, tossing them their sacks. "Let's get out of here."

"But I'm to wait," Grayson said between breaths.

24

"Wait for what?" Sadie said. "To be captured and put in a cage? They're searching. They'll find us."

"Out here?" Fenn said.

"Like my ma said, I'm taking no chances. I'm going to do as she told me."

"Where will we go?" Grayson said.

"Were you not paying attention at all? To my uncle's in Damon Wall," she said. "Ma said maybe he can help us."

"What *was* that?" Fenn blurted out. "What happened back there?"

They both looked at him briefly, confused.

"They're looking for the new bairn," Grayson said. "From the rumors."

"What rumors?" Fenn said. "Somebody tell me what just happened."

"It's stupid," Sadie said.

"The king's guard doesn't think it's so stupid, do they?" Grayson turned to Fenn. "You've never heard the story of the new bairn and the prophecy?"

He shook his head.

"I told you it's stupid," Sadie said. "The elder villagers used to tell about a prophecy that said a new bairn would be born to the folk who would one day kill the king and destroy the Ruud."

"That is a little silly," Fenn said, and Sadie nodded.

"Not everyone thinks so," Grayson said. "The beast lord made the prophecy a long time ago."

"Still, if it's just a story..." Fenn said. He felt his steady breath returning.

"But lately there are rumors going around that the new bairn was born some time ago and that he has a mark on his right shoulder so everyone will know him."

Fenn shuddered. Father Treacher's trembling voice echoed in his head, telling him to keep his mark secret—show no one. But his fears were nonsensical. How could Fenn be in a prophecy? If he had plans to lay waste to a kingdom, he'd know about it, wouldn't he? Why would anybody want to do such a thing, anyway?

"Just wild rumors," Sadie said.

"Everybody's afraid," Grayson said. "So they're looking for the bairn—to try to stop him."

Sadie said, "How is a bairn going to destroy the Ruud?"

"Well, he's not a bairn anymore; they think he's about twelve now."

"Then why do they keep calling him that?"

"Anyway," Grayson continued, ignoring her, "they say he's come now, to destroy the Ruud."

"But why?"

"To avenge the beast folk."

"Avenge them for what?" Sadie said.

"We pushed them out of the Ruud, stole their land." Grayson said.

Sadie's brow furrowed. "Really?"

"Sure. You think they just gave us this land when our ancestors came over from Ruhm?"

"Well, I never thought about it."

"Thinking isn't your strong point, is it?" Grayson said.

But Sadie wasn't listening. "If we forced them all into the outlands and the beast forest... They got the felidae and the centaurs and the chimera...harpies, doppelgangers, duergar and the like. All of 'em mad as a caged troll at us for all these years just waiting for this new bairn to come along and make mincemeat of the Ruud."

"I thought you didn't believe any of it," Grayson said.

"I think it's a stupid rumor," she said. "But I can see where the beast folk wouldn't be too happy with us if what you say is true."

"Well, I've never heard any of that," Fenn said. "How do you know about it?"

Grayson said, "It's all part of our history."

Fenn knew that it wasn't part of the history of the Ruud he'd read. "So, they're looking for kids with marks?"

"The rumors say the bairn was born with a mark." Grayson said. "I've got one."

"Me too," Sadie said.

They both pulled at their tunics, exposing their right shoulders.

"But, that's just a mole," Fenn told Sadie. "And yours is a little scar," he said to Grayson.

"Doesn't matter," Grayson said. "Nobody knows what the mark is. Do you have one?"

Fenn hesitated. "No."

"It wouldn't matter," Sadie said. "My ma said they'd be taking all the kids around eleven, anyway. And you're about... what, ten?"

Fenn blushed. "I'll be twelve soon."

He thought briefly of Lucas who was fourteen, but not much taller than Grayson. He might be mistaken for twelve on some days. Was that why they put him in the cage? And why was he so calm?

There were always two parts of Lucas. One was a mischie-vous kid snickering and playing tricks. And the other was quiet, contemplative, and wise with advice. Which one was it who had told Fenn about the secret history of the Ruud?

"If the main folk pushed the beast folk out of the Ruud and into the forest and the outlands, why isn't it in the *History of the Ruud*?" Fenn said.

"Isn't it?" Sadie asked. "I wouldn't know."

Grayson shrugged.

"Haven't you read the history?" Sadie asked him, laughing. "All the bragging you do about how smart you are and how much you read books, and you haven't even read the history of the Ruud?"

"Have you read it?" Fenn asked Sadie.

"Of course not. But I don't claim to be a great reader."

"Of course I've read the history," Grayson said. "It was one of the first books I read."

Sadie smiled. "I know you've read it. I've seen you. I don't know why you have to come to my da's shop to read it, when you've got your own copy at the inn."

"Exactly," Grayson said. "You've got a copy. Why haven't you ever read it?"

"What, boring old history?"

"It's not boring."

There were four copies of the *History of the Ruud* that Fenn knew about. One was at the inn, on a stand in a corner, gathering dust. Father told him it used to be brought out of doors every morning and retrieved every evening; but it was left out to be rained on too many times and so it sits in the corner at the inn, ignored. The second copy was at the stationer's, on a table piled high with other books and papers. Nobody ever looked at it there, except for Grayson, apparently. The third copy was in the front room at the wissenry, on a special table by the window, where folk could sit and read it in comfort—though no one but wissendes and orphans ever did. This was the copy Fenn had read many times. It was the first real book Father Treacher had assigned to him in school.

"Read this several times," he'd said, opening the thick padded cover and flipping the gold-lined pages. "But do not become too attached to it. Once you begin your training as a wissende, you will find that many things are not as you once thought."

It was Lucas who told him about the fourth copy of the history. Some time last year, when Father Treacher was out, and Fenn stood in the front room leafing through the huge gold-trimmed book on the table. Lucas showed up behind him, startling him. He'd slammed the book shut and gasped. Lucas laughed at him.

"You should be ashamed, reading that nonsense," he'd said. "If it's history you're after, wait until you're twelve and you can read the real history of the Ruud."

"Real history?"

"Yep. That thing's just made up for anyone bored enough to learn to read it. The real history is in *The Book of Katze*, and it's kept under lock and key in the secret rooms downstairs."

"Why under lock and key?"

Lucas smiled that devilish smile and his eyes glistened with daring. "It's forbidden," he'd said. "A secret history. Only wissendes know of it."

Fenn stared at him, wide-eyed and trance-like, until Lucas shouted, "Boo!"

That was Lucas. But he was telling the truth. Fenn had seen the book for himself. He followed Father Treacher into the secret rooms dozens of times to help him carry books back and forth. And after Lucas told him about it, he saw *The Book of Katze* there in the locked book cabinet.

"Why do we keep some books in the locked cabinet, Father?" he'd asked, several months ago.

"Some knowledge is dangerous to the unlearned mind."

"But what is that book, there, that looks so much like the *History of the Ruud?*"

Father Treacher smiled his dreamy smile and said some-thing like, "Many things look the same outside, but can be quite different inside."

Father was always saying things like that—things that seemed to mean a great deal and nothing at all, both at the same time.

"I don't understand."

"All in good time, Fenn."

"May I read that one?" he said. "*The Book of Katze*. What is it about?"

Father Treacher looked at him carefully and said, "You may read it when you are twelve and begin your training."

"It's a training book, then."

"Yes."

"Can't I start early?"

"What has Lucas told you?" Father took the stack of books from him and sat him down on a crate in the dank, dim cellar.

"Nothing. He didn't tell me anything."

Father sighed knowingly. "I will tell you a bit. But first you must understand what it is to be a wissende."

"I know what it is to be—"

Father held his hand up to stop him. "To be a wissende is to be a keeper of secrets. It was not always that way. The wissenry of the Ruud is quite changed from its glory days in the Kingdom of Ruhm."

"Glory days?"

"Fenn Foster, if you cannot keep your mouth closed, how will you

28

stop all the wissenry secrets from spilling out?"

"Yes, Father."

"I am going to tell you a small portion of a secret, in hopes that you will not repeat the suspicions running through your head just now. But you must understand that you are to repeat none of this. Not one word. To anyone. When you are a wissende, you will be able to discuss it cautiously with other wissendes. But no one else. Do you understand me?"

Fenn nodded.

"Very well. It was Roarn of Michelruud who commissioned the rewriting of the history of the Ruud in the year 1072. Before that time, the official history of the Ruud told the truth and was kept by the wissendes and printed and bound by the Stationer to the King. But, things happened in our little Ruud, things that the kings of the Ruud wished to forget; and things they wished to keep hidden. So a new history was written by the stationer, with some help from the wissenry and Roarn, the king. This new history was to be displayed at all wissenry buildings, at all inns in the Ruud, and at the stationers. The folk of the Ruud were free to read it. But, of course, few could read and fewer still wished to."

"You can rewrite history?"

"Indeed."

"To make it any way you like?"

"I'm afraid so."

"So, the *History of the Ruud*...isn't?"

"Well, it is, partially."

"And *The Book of Katze*?"

"Katze was a wissende. He was not happy with Roarn's commission. And so, he secreted away a copy of the original history. He added his own thoughts, not very pleasant ones, I'm afraid. And he published that book—only one or two copies were made as far as we know."

"And you were allowed to have one?" Fenn whispered, amazed.

Father held up a warning finger. "No, my dear boy. Not at all. It is forbidden. And that is why you must never speak of it."

"Until I'm a wissende, you mean."

"And then only to other wissendes. And even then, you will be taught to be wary."

Fenn's eyes widened as he walked toward the cabinet, its door standing open. There, the secret history of the Ruud beckoned him. "Aren't you afraid someone will find it there?"

Father Treacher chuckled. "Some things are best hidden in plain sight."

"I can't wait to read it, Father."

"But wait, you will."

Fenn shook his head, frustrated. Father Treacher had told him nothing helpful—just to get out of Path and off to Cold Sea. And now Lucas was in a cage. Why didn't Father send Lucas away with Fenn? It didn't make any sense. He knew that all he could do now was as Father said and leave.

A crunch of twigs echoed behind them and they all crouched down by the tunnel, startled and alert.

Chapter Eight

Morning had dawned and the cobbled streets of Ruhm were coming alive as Leah made her way to the Hall of Hass. The aromas of the bakers filled the air and Leah breathed in: fruit pastries, twisted dough, fresh breads. All the smells of wonder mixed with the horse dung and carriage axle oil into a pleasing welcome to the day.

She came upon Kettering's flower cart, and stopped to sniff a deep red rose. When she looked up to Kettering she felt herself freeze somewhat. The old woman's face was deeply lined and sad; and she was looking, Leah was sure, at the crest of the Circle of Hass on her vest lapel.

"Just smelling it," Leah said.

A shy smile touched Kettering's mouth.

Leah moved on. It was true, she had to admit to herself, that members of the Circle often took from the merchants without paying. It was their right by law. She could have had the rose and enjoyed it all day. But she didn't take it. A tiny trickle of fear ran up her back. Was her father right?

She'd always known she was a descendant of wissendes. This was why she was always quick to stay her objections when her father said something nearly blasphemous against the Hass. He couldn't help himself, she surmised. But now she knew that she was also descended from Dakenruud, and through him, related to Michelruud the Betrayer. Was this why she knew, somehow, deep in her heart, she would never mention her father's indiscretions to the Hass? Did she not really have it in her to be a member of the Circle?

Though the three towers of the young king's palace loomed over the city, there was no building so beautiful as the Hall. Forty-seven stone steps led up to the ornately carved main arch of the entrance, and two smaller arches on either side, all two stories tall. The venerable priests of

30

Hass, long dead, were carved into the stone, and watched Leah as she climbed the steps, their delicately chiseled faces stern and sad.

She pulled open the heavy main door and entered the nave where Lord Kirche's secretary, Prenalin, was waiting for her.

"Prompt, as usual, Hallowsing. This way."

He led her through the main hall down the center aisle and to the crossing where he turned and brought her into the chambers of the High Priest. Leah shivered with delight and pride.

"Will I meet Lord Kirche today?" She trembled at the thought. She'd only seen him from a distance a few times, but he reminded her of the carved faces over the archway outside.

"I'm afraid Kirche is busy preparing for the journey. But you will meet him soon enough. You can't take the boat all the way to the Ruud without it, I'm sure."

Prenalin pushed open a door and gestured for Leah to make her way inside to a large, plushly decorated round room with a heavily carved desk by a row of windows. Before Prenalin could say, "Sit," Leah was at a window gazing out at the city. "Is this Lord Kirche's office?"

Prenalin chuckled. "It's mine."

She turned to him. "Lord Kirche's is nicer than this?"

"Indeed. Sit please."

Prenalin walked around the large desk and took a seat in the velvet-covered, high-backed chair and smiled at her. She crossed the soft, thick maroon rugs and sat in the padded chair in front of his desk. She realized, taking quick stock of the office, that there were ornate chairs and small tables, but no shelves, and no books.

Though it was Prenalin who had chosen Leah, out of her class of fifty-seven, to be Aide to the High Priest, she often thought he didn't like her.

"Very well, Leah Hallowsing. Today you begin your profession with the Inner Circle of Hass. Do you have any concerns?"

"No sir."

He raised an eyebrow. "Not a one?"

"I imagine I will be told what is expected of me. Is there a book to read?"

"Ah, a book. You were studious, weren't you? No. There is no book. You will simply do whatever I tell you to do."

"And what of Lord Kirche? I am his aide, am I not? Will he tell me what to do as well?"

"Of course."

Leah decided to say nothing of the silly questions in her head. Was she also Prenalin's aide? Would she be required to call Lord Kirche, Lord Kirche every time? Or could she call him Kirche as Prenalin did? Would she get an office? All of these questions were certainly stupid, so she kept them to herself. But one burned at her and she had to ask.

"Will I have any clerical duties, or am I to be only a ser-vant?"

While she realized this question came off as quite arrogant, she could think of no better way to say it.

"Everyone in the Circle has a purpose," Prenalin said.

"I see." He hadn't answered her question at all. She tried on a battered smile but she was quickly losing excitement for her new position. And so soon.

"Your parents are pleased for your success," Prenalin said.

Leah stared at him wondering how to respond. He hadn't actually asked a question after all.

"Of course," she said.

"They are not members of the Hass, are they?"

Ah, here was the rub, she thought. "No sir."

"And why is that?"

Leah smiled gently. "My father has always said that as stationer to the king, it would be inappropriate to be a member. He should like to stay neutral."

"And yet—" Prenalin raised his brows at her—"The king answers to the Hass, does he not?"

"Yes, of course. I'm just telling you my father's opinion."

"What is yours?"

"My opinion? Well, it..." Leah's brain filled with thoughts and fears. Was this a test? She somehow knew her opinion would fail her, but she couldn't seem to stop it from leaving her mouth. "It's my understanding that membership in the Hass is not obligatory."

"True, of course. But there are so many benefits to member-ship. Your father has never found those benefits appealing?"

"I would have to say that he does not, else he'd have joined."

"And your mother?"

Leah couldn't help but let out a sigh. "My mother thinks for herself as well."

"Are you saying that members of the Hass do not have free will?"

"Of course not, Prenalin. Only that my mother has chosen not to join the Hass and I can find no fault with that choice."

"Really? You find no fault with those who don't join?"

"It's their choice, is it not? By law. Why would I find fault?"

Prenalin seemed to digest this while Leah screamed awful words at herself in her head, even words she'd heard the butch-er say. She shook her head briskly as if to rid herself of these horrid slurs and looked at Prenalin. He was studying her, his dark eyes closed up somewhat. If he didn't have that hint of a smile at his lips, Leah would have thought him angry. But he was...amused.

"Very well," he said. "You must ready for your journey. I have made you a list of things you must purchase for Kirche and yourself, if you do not have them already. And here is a general packing list you might use. The trunks you must get from Habersher's; you shouldn't need more than two for yourself, if that many. Have Kirche's things sent to the Hall."

"What do I purchase these with?"

Prenalin waved his hand in the air. "Charge it to the Hass of course."

"Even my own things?"

"Of course. You are a member of the Inner Circle now. We take very good care of our own."

No doubt. As soon as the thought entered her mind, she winced.

"What is it?"

"Nothing, sir. I'll be at the dock first thing in the morning in two days' time, ready to sail."

On her way out, Leah clenched her fists until her nails dug deep-pink half moons into her palms. This was all her father's fault. She'd have done perfectly well if he hadn't put it in her head she was too much a thinking creature to find a place with the Inner Circle. And now she was off to a rather bad start with Prenalin. Still, he didn't fire her.

She looked at the papers he'd given her. Kirche needed a case of sacramental wine, three pewter mugs, and a journal. A journal? Leah couldn't help thinking Prenalin had put that on the list on purpose. How could she choose a journal for the High Priest? She walked into Zygot's general shop; the little bell on the door tinkled above her and Hannah looked up from behind the counter.

"Leah, dear. What can I do for you?"

She made her way through the tables of cloth and cook-ware to the counter.

"Journals, Hannah. I need two."

Hannah pulled a selection from a shelf behind her and placed them on the counter in a row. Leah pointed to a dark brown leather book with a burgundy ribbon peeking out the bottom.

"This one will do for me, but I need something much nicer for Lord Kirche."

"Ah." Hannah's voice fell.

She doesn't think she'll get paid, Leah thought. "I'm to charge it to the Circle."

Hannah forced a smile and nodded. "Of course." She pulled a grand, plum-dyed leather book from the shelf and set it before Leah. "This is our finest journal. Fit for the king, if you ask me."

"Lord Kirche isn't the king," Leah said, smiling. "It's much too expensive."

Hannah raised her brows. "Too much, you say? For the High Priest of Hass?"

Leah knew she must sound like she'd lost her mind; but she couldn't help wondering if charging merchandise to the Inner Circle meant the same as the license members of the Circle had to take small items without pay, like Kettering's roses, or the butcher's lamb chops, or the cracker boxes in the rack at Zygot's door. She'd seen members of the Circle take these things with nary an attempt to pay.

"Let me pay in doars for mine," she said and pulled her pouch from under her tunic. "And I suppose you'll have to charge this one to the Circle." She picked up the black leather with gold trimmed pages. "It's not so expensive is it?"

"No ma'am," Hannah said, sounding relieved. "I'll wrap them."

When she left Zygot's, Leah realized she might never become Historian of Ruhm.

Chapter Nine

We have to get going," Grayson said, his voice hollow. He crossed his arms at his waist and tried to rub the chill out of his bones.

"Let's do it, then," Sadie said. "It could be fun. An adventure."

"Fun?" he said.

"Sure. Maybe we'll see an angel or one of the eis—"

"Angels in the Ruud?"

"—or maybe even something out of the beast forest. Wouldn't you like that?"

Grayson glared at her. "You must be the most addle-brained girl in Path. Do you know how dangerous angels are? And the beast forest? I told you they were all mad at us."

"I'm just trying to get you to see the fun side of it, that's all."

Grayson shook his head and looked at Fenn. "This is what comes of all play and no study. Do you think it will be fun?"

He raised his shoulders and tilted his head. "It's just to Damon Wall to see her uncle."

"But what if he can't help us? You heard my mum. She gave me these maps..." Sadie yanked her knapsack off her
back, dug through it and pulled out the leather notebook. "She expects I will have to leave the Ruud."

"So, maybe we *will* see an angel," Grayson said. "Does that make you happy?"

"I'm just saying a little adventure never hurt anyone."

"Let's just get to your uncle's and see what he has to say. And then we'll go from there. One step at a time." Fenn said.

"Good idea," Sadie said. "No need to panic now. We can panic later."

"I'm not panicked," Grayson sputtered. "Do I look panicked? Just because I don't want an angel encounter does not mean I'm panicked."

Sadie rolled her eyes and sighed. Shaking her head, she shoved the book back into her pack. "It's obvious you're panicking, waiter boy."

"We'll take the bridge to Aaronland," Fenn said, leading them east, through the wood to the high crossing. Father Treacher had wanted him to take the bridge anyway. It was important to him that Fenn get out of Michelruud as soon as possible. Better late than never, as Father Treacher often said.

As they approached the opening of the trees where the rickety wood bridge crossed over the fast-paced river into Aaronland, Grayson, up front, stopped short and put his hands out to his sides to stop them. He stepped backward several feet before turning to them and putting his finger across his lips. They all quietly made their way back into the woods several feet and huddled together.

"Troll," Grayson whispered. "Sitting on the bridge."

They nodded and quietly crept back to the tree line, keeping very low. They watched as the round, hairy beast, barely as tall as Sadie, shifted positions on the bridge, snorting with effort as he settled back down. Something moved near the foot of the bridge on the opposite shore, hidden in the shade of pines. Fenn suddenly realized there were horses tied to a tree on the far side.

He nudged the others and pointed. They nodded and snuck back into the woods.

"They'll be watching all the bridges," Grayson said. "They're probably patrolling the river. I can't believe they were at the bridge the whole time we were here—and you with your loud mouth running," he poked Sadie's shoulder. "It's a wonder we weren't captured."

"No need to scold me now," she said. "We didn't get caught, did we?"

"No thanks to you and your booming voice. And you're still not whispering quietly enough."

"We'll have to make our way to South Bridge," Fenn said.

"But there must be a guard there, too," Sadie said.

"Still too loud," Grayson whispered, glaring at her. He put his forefinger to his lips.

Sadie mouthed the words "all right" and rolled her eyes.

Fenn said, "If there's a guard, we keep going until we find a safe crossing."

As they began their trek along the river, keeping to the woods, Grayson whispered, "I can't believe they'd be using a troll."

"I suppose they'd use whatever means they can," Fenn said.

"But a troll? After the way they treat them, always push-ing them around, tricking them into falling into holes and such; and now they have the nerve to sleep and let a troll do their jobs for them."

Sadie let out a loud sigh.

"You aren't bothered by it at all?" he said.

"It's the troll's business. He's probably making a gold coin for his trouble."

"He's probably desperate for something to feed his family."

Sadie laughed. "Trolls eat roots. Roots are free."

Grayson harrumphed and kept walking in silence for a few moments before he turned around to face Sadie.

"Trolls don't just eat roots. They're omnivores."

"Quiet down," Fenn warned.

"Omni-what?" Sadie said.

"Omnivores you ignoramus. Just like you."

"Trolls are ignoramooses?"

Fenn thought Grayson looked as if he might explode, so he did his best not to laugh, but as soon as Grayson turned back to the path, he nudged Sadie with a smile.

As they walked in silence, Fenn's thoughts returned to Lucas in the criminal cage.

"So...your brother who was to come for you..." he said, catching up to Grayson. "He stayed behind because he's older?"

"Both of my brothers are well over the age. And my sister is way too young. And none of them have a mark. How come you haven't heard about all this? It's all over the village."

Fenn shrugged. "I don't get out much. Stick to the wissen-ry, mostly."

Fenn expected Grayson to make a joke, but instead he said, "I thought they knew everything at the wissenry. It's got that funny name and all. The Wissenry of Sacred Knowledge and Understanding."

Fenn smiled slightly, uncomfortable. He didn't know any of the folk knew the full name. The truth of the wissenry had been forgotten in the last two hundred years and now the folk thought they were just counselors and lawyers. "Our job," Father Treacher had told him long ago, "is to find out the truth, and decide how best to keep from upsetting the folk with it." The wissendes would dismiss a story about a bairn of prophecy with barely a nod.

But weren't there times when he was led out of the room when certain of the village folk came to see Father for advice? He now thought he recalled whispers when he entered a room, or looks exchanged between Lucas and Father. Had they been discussing the prophecy and didn't want him to know about it?

"Where are they taking the kids?" he asked.

"Who knows?" Sadie said.

"We had a traveler at the inn yesterday who said they took a couple of boys from Aaronland already. Said they just put them on horses and led them right out of town, through the woods and across the border; and nobody did anything to stop them. The folk are scared."

"But you're not?" Sadie asked him.

"I'm not afraid of a prophecy," Grayson said. "But it would be wise to be cautious of what the guard might do."

"It's just a story some old gossips started," Sadie said. "You'll see. The grown-ups will all calm down when they don't find anything more than moles and scars. How dangerous can kids be, anyway?"

Fenn nodded in agreement, but his heart wasn't in it. Grayson had it right. For years now, Father Treacher had been teaching him the ways of the folk and the beast. Fearful, superstitious creatures, the lot of them. If they'd got as far as rounding up village kids looking for some evil bairn, it wasn't likely they'd be easily stopped.

Chapter Ten

The rickety cart wobbled to and fro across the broad field of high grass north of Path. Lucas stood, holding fast to the bars of the criminal cage; it was old, rusted, and useless. The door was tied only with a rope. It had been many years since the king's guard had hauled prisoners this way. But the guardsmen worked their way through the grass beside and behind them on horseback; no one would escape.

The old stones of Steingefan loomed in the distance. The decrepit castle had been turned to a prison when Castle Michelruud was built a hundred years before. He couldn't imagine a worse place for a prison: cold, drafty, moldy. No place for children. Morning was in full swing and the sun had dried the dew. Lucas could smell the grass, the pipes and rolled smokers of the guards, the horse sweat, and...felidae.

He turned to face the west, the logical point of attack, weaving his gaze between the taller boys hoping to catch a glimpse. What could they want? Why would they risk leaving the forest?

There! Figures shifted the long blades, parting them, but remained close to the ground and hidden as they neared the slow, rambling cart.

One of the guardsmen, oblivious, blurted out in song, "So long goes the road, so low sinks my weary heart." The cart driver and other guards joined in, "Take my tired bones home to my love."

"Everybody down," Lucas whispered as the felidae came within striking distance. "Down." He pushed the taller kids down one by one; they looked at him annoyed. "If the door opens," he said quietly, "make a break for it."

"We're squished in here like pickles in a barrel, Lucas. What are you doing?"

At that moment, enormous dark figures leapt from the grass. Lucas ducked, but watched as the felidae climbed the carriage ahead of the cage and pulled it over. Several cats roared and grabbed at the cage, it tipped onto its side, the door swung open and hit the ground with a thud. While Lucas made his way toward it, the others pressed to the front, fearful of the felidae. Only then did Lucas remember that most of the kids in town believed felidae ate folk for sport.

"It's okay," he called over the din of shouting guards, whinnying horses, and roars. "Let's get out of here."

Before any of them moved, he felt a hard thud on his back. It was Lara Cole's screams he heard as the giant cat bit him on the back of the neck and dragged him through the grass. Lucas frantically tried to pummel the cat's head.

"Stop it! Stop it now!" But the more he squirmed the harder the cat bit. He was helpless in its powerful jaws and could only watch the landscape pass as he was carried away.

Finally, when the screams and cursing of the guards and kids was far in the distance, the cat dropped him and panted, drooling above him. Lucas turned onto his back, looked up and saw the pines; he was at the edge of the western woods. He looked to the felid and growled.

"Why now?"

Chapter Eleven

Prince Welk paced his quarters on the third floor of Michelruud castle. His back was feverish and his hair damp at the nape of his neck, but he was cold through to his bones. His thoughts had not settled since hearing about the capture of children from the village of Path. While at first, he'd wanted to bolt into his father's chambers and strangle the old man until he repented, he knew his father was near death, and not the true instigator of the attack. And he knew, too, that the imprisonment was certain to quiet the angry protests of the folk who demanded protection from the bairn. It was, he hated to admit, a good idea.

"Send Sorgood to me," he barked at his servant.

Pierston, Welk's mousy, lean steward bowed and made his way to the door to escort the king's master of the guard, who had been waiting outside for the invitation, to the prince's hearth.

Welk motioned Sorgood to sit on the wood bench by the fire and forced himself to take the large, comfortable chair opposite. He knew his restless nerves would make him appear weak to Sorgood; he did his best to quell them. The king's master of the guard clearly felt himself above the rank of a mere prince. Welk had surmised long ago that Sorgood controlled his father. He had to be wary of how the man was handled. He watched as Sorgood sat, scrawny and twisted, like a gnarled twig of the poisonous hex vine.

Welk had learned that after clearing Steingefan of adult prisoners, banishing them all to the wasteland, the children of Path were rounded up and would be held there.

"Tell me of the children of Path," he said. "Did any have the mark? Do you suspect any of being the bairn?"

Sorgood sneered only slightly, he did not answer to the prince, after all. But Welk was sure he would not be able to keep himself from bragging of his exploits.

"Thus far, we have found nothing truly out of the ordinary, Highness. But we rounded up all the children of the age and a few who had moles or scars or other suspicious markings. We continue to police the village, picking up those not found in the first raid."

"You did not catch them all?"

"Some were simply not there."

"Where could they be? They're children."

"We will continue to search, Highness."

Welk could see Sorgood squirming and enjoyed it.

"The mark ought to be telling," he mused. "It must be recognized to

39

have meaning...one would think. I understand you received information from a nurse in the wasteland."

Sorgood lowered his face, casting his eyes to the floor at Welk's feet. The prince could almost read the man's struggle between showing off his skills and treating the prince as inferior. His ego won.

"Our spies heard talk of a butcher in Aaronland, some-what befuddled, bragging of being the ward to a bairn with a foreboding mark. He gave up much information—including the name of the child's nurse in the wasteland. She has residence in a tiny hut far from the main village, along a creek."

"What did the old nurse say?"

"She said, as you might suspect, Highness, that the child is to be found in Path. He was first taken to the wissenry at Waverly and then to the Cold Sea and finally to Path where she believes he remains."

"But how does she know?"

Sorgood let his eyes briefly rise to the prince's chin before casting them down again. "She was his nurse, Highness."

Welk gnashed his teeth together in annoyance, but tried to stay calm. "Yes, I know she was his nurse. As you just said, the old butcher said as much. But how does she know where the child was taken after he left her?"

Sorgood had the audacity to shrug his shoulders in the presence of the prince. "She claimed that she received news from the butcher regularly."

"From the butcher?"

"Yes. It turns out he was once a wissende, banished to the wastelands himself."

"Yes, of course," Welk mumbled. Another piece of the puzzle. A wissende would attend such a birth. He would have this sort of knowledge.

"And how old was the bairn when he arrived in Path? Was he adopted out to a family in the Ruud? Is he one of the orphans of the wissenry?"

"She didn't know, Highness, and the butcher could not say. But she confirmed that he had a mark of some kind on his arm."

"Did she describe it, then? Do we know what we look for?"

"She has lost much of her mind and is fragile. I could not exert much pressure on her without fear of losing her. She may be needed in the future."

"And the butcher?"

Sorgood shook his head. "Neither could describe it, Highness. They're neither quite right."

Welk tried not to let the frustration show on his face. An elderly nurse and an addled butcher were their only sources of information. The prophecy could still be nothing more than wild tales and rumors.

Sorgood had already taken two boys from Aaronland, suspiciously linked to the old butcher. They were his strong-est suspects, but they had no marks. King Arnot had sent emissaries to Welk's father demanding an explanation for the abduction of the boys. But of course, King Evan, on his deathbed, was unable to answer for it.

What could Arnot do, anyway? What could Ricker of Damon Wall do? Nothing. The main folk of the Ruud feared the return of the bairn who would destroy their lives and their kings. No. Arnot and Ricker would not risk the folk's loyalty to stop Sorgood.

Sorgood could imprison the children at Steingefan—or banish them all. But would that be the end of it? Was the new bairn truly in Path? Or was he far from the Ruud and not to return until it was time for him to fulfill the prophecy? Was the prophecy even real? Or was all this just the result of nervous old women and hungry wastelanders spreading ru-mors?

Welk shrugged. No matter. If he decided to produce an heir and save the throne of Michelruud, if he was determined to unite all three kingdoms of the Ruud under that throne, he must take the story seriously and rid himself of the threat of the new bairn, real or imagined. And to do that, he must let Sorgood continue with his plans. He must deal cruelly with the children of Path.

"You have folk to care for the children in the prison?"

"Of course, Highness. They will be well tended until we find the bairn."

"Very well." Welk did not hesitate. "Do not bother with permission to enter the other realms of the Ruud. But only take the most suspicious of Aaronland and Damon Wall. I feel certain we are correct and we will find the bairn in Path."

Sorgood nodded.

And with that, Welk began to assert his control over Sorgood and the kingdom of Michelruud.

Chapter Twelve

As they neared the south bridge about an hour later, Sadie, Grayson, and Fenn approached with caution and spied a guardsman posted there, pacing the bridge with a firearm. The wide river rushed beneath him and he seemed mesmerized by it, even while continuing his strides.

"Where'd he get that?" Fenn asked as they headed farther south.

"Lots of the guard have them now," Grayson said. "Power-ful deadly aren't they?"

"So I've heard."

"You don't think they mean to shoot the children do you?" Sadie asked.

"It might be a quicker death than hanging," Grayson said. "But as for pain, I'd say it looks like it hurts more."

"Have you seen one fired, then?" Fenn asked.

"No, but I've heard stories."

Fenn wished he'd been raised at the inn instead of the wissenry. Nobody interesting ever showed up there—just wissendes and orphans. Either the wissendes had no stories to tell, or they did so in secret. The village folk came daily, of course, and Fenn assisted Father in helping them with their complaints. But they weren't as special as travelers from all over the Ruud. All they wanted to talk about was whose chickens were in their house and whether or not they were dreaming when they thought they saw a dancing gnome.

"We have to get out of Michelruud soon," Fenn said. He could still hear the urgency in Lucas' voice at the village square. He didn't know how he could have heard him when no one else did, but he was sure Lucas was speaking.

"We can cross at the Timber bridge into Damon Wall," Sadie said. "Then we go to my uncle's as planned."

"It's too far. Michelruud is too dangerous. Let's head south to the shallow bend in the river and cross there."

"In the river?" Grayson said.

"Afraid of water are you?" Sadie said.

"It's the fastest way out of Michelruud." Fenn didn't like the idea any more than Grayson did. He could swim well enough in the lake; but crossing the river was serious business —something he doubted wissendes ever trained for.

As if sensing his thoughts, Sadie said, "Why do they keep you wissenry orphans locked up the way they do?"

"That's rude," Grayson said.

"We're not locked up."

"But you're never out by the well in the morning; you never find us over in the grazing field for a game. My da says they keep you under lock and key."

"That doesn't mean they're locked up," Grayson said. "It's a meta-phor."

"A what?"

"Never mind."

"So, you're not locked up in there?"

"No," Fenn said, almost disappointed. At least being locked up would sound exciting. "I know you've seen me in the village. You nodded at me once."

"True enough. Then why don't you play?"

"They're going to be wissendes," Grayson said. "They have to study the law and philosophy and such."

"Is that true?"

Fenn nodded. "We do study. We practice mathematics, writing, spelling, and reading."

"What for?"

"To be wissendes, silly," Grayson scolded. "They're the smartest folk around."

"My da's as smart as a wissende and he doesn't do any of that."

"He must read," Fenn said. "He's the stationer. And he's got to know mathematics to keep the accounts."

Sadie seemed to puzzle over that for a moment. Then she let out a groan. "You mean I'm going to have to learn mathematics?"

Grayson laughed. "Don't you know how to add already?"

"Well, sure, everybody knows how to add."

"Wissendes know a lot more than just adding and sub-tracting," Fenn said. "So be thankful you won't have to learn as much."

"I still say my da's as smart as any wissende."

Fenn thought he should change the subject; he knew that nobody could possibly be as smart as Father Treacher. Except, smart as he was, Father Treacher was also a bit addlepated on occasion. But when a folk's brain is as stuffed with knowledge as Father's was, it must rattle him now and then.

"There's also a lot of work to be done at the wissenry," he said. "There's just not much time for playing."

"You have to work at the inn, too, Grayson," Sadie said.

"And you at the stationer's but you still have time to play."

"I suppose," she said. "Do you never want to play?" She asked Fenn.

Fenn thought about the question for several seconds. After morning chores there were lessons. After afternoon chores, he often had a fine, long walk into the village with Father or Lucas. They always brought their history or philosophy books with them and found time to sit and read after visiting and shopping. On days he was on his own, he'd walk Castle Road to the castle village and prop himself against an apple tree in the king's orchard, have an apple or two and read a novel. There were games at times, with Lucas, in the front room at the wissenry: word switch, number pattern, or chess. And in the warmer months he and Lucas often walked north to Gettel's pond and fished or lazed in the sun...and they always had their books. But the best pastime of all was sitting on the back porch of the wissenry with Father Treacher, Lucas, and visiting wissendes, listening to them haggle over philosophy and truth.

Did he never feel the urge to play with the other kids?

"I guess, if there had been more time to play..."

"My da says you're not allowed to play with us," Sadie said.

"Is that true?" Grayson asked.

"No one ever told me I couldn't. And Lucas is friends with some of the older kids in the village, isn't he?"

"That's true, I guess," Sadie conceded. "But he never came to ball games or tug matches."

"I guess Lucas and I are more of the reading and board sorts."

"Like chess? The men play some of those games in the inn and let me join in. But they gamble. Are you allowed to gamble?"

"Honestly, Grayson," Sadie said. "You ask some of the strangest questions. Of course wissendes don't gamble."

"That's probably true," Fenn said.

"Maybe they chose you to be a wissende because you don't like to play."

"I wouldn't say I don't like it."

"But if you liked it, you wouldn't spend your free time under the oak with a book. You'd have been in the field kicking the tether ball or something."

Fenn laughed. "All right then. We'll say I don't care much for field games. But neither does Grayson."

"Isn't that the truth," Sadie said. "Why don't you go in for the wissenry, waiter boy?"

"Stop calling me that."

"At least you weren't locked up in chains," Sadie said.

"You really thought we were kept locked up?"

"Nah, not really. But you're sure?"

"I think I'd know if I'd been locked up."

"You have to believe him," Grayson said. "He's in training to be a wissende. It's probably rule number one. 'A wissende never lies.'"

"I'm not in training yet," Fenn said with a laugh. "Not until I'm twelve. And I'm sure I could tell a lie if I wanted to." After all, he thought, Father Treacher certainly lied about the grub demons.

"Twelve?" Sadie said. "I've been training to take over as stationer

44

since I was eight."

Grayson chortled and shook his head.

"What are you laughing about? Because I'm a girl? I'll be the first woman stationer in the Ruud. My da says it's about time." She beamed.

"It's not that," Grayson said. "I've yet to see you pick up a book or a pen. Can you even write?"

"Of course I can write. At least I spend time at my studies. You spend too much time at my da's shop instead of the inn."

"Are you training to be innkeeper?" Fenn asked him.

"Well, my da has it in mind that I'll take over one of his inns at the port."

"That would be exciting," Sadie said. "I'd love to be an innkeeper at the port."

Grayson shrugged and shoved his hands deep into his pants pockets. "Maybe. I'd rather be a stationer."

"Well, we already have a stationer. And he has an appren-tice and a daughter. So you'll just have to run an inn some-where," Sadie said.

"I'd like to open a school," Grayson said.

"A school? What for?" Sadie said.

"For the kids in the village. To read and write."

"What do they need to read and write for?"

Grayson fell silent.

"A school is a nice idea," Fenn said, hoping to make him feel better.

"If you're not going to get training until you're twelve," Sadie said. "Maybe you need a wissende school. If your da was a wissende, I'd bet you'd have started already."

"It wouldn't matter if my da was a wissende. I'd still have to wait 'til twelve. It's the rules."

"Maybe your da *was* a wissende," Sadie said.

Grayson gave Sadie a stern look.

"Sorry," Sadie mumbled. "I guess I shouldn't have..."

"I don't mind," Fenn said.

"Sure," Sadie said, smiling now. "You're not the first or-phan in town, anyway."

"Sadie," Grayson scolded.

"Well, I am an orphan," Fenn said. "No sense pretending I'm not."

Grayson looked at Fenn, his face filled with concern. "You don't mind folk talking about it?"

Fenn shrugged. "Why should it bother me?"

"Well..." He hesitated. "Not to know who they are, your parents, I mean. It just sounds awful."

"Maybe that's because you've always known yours. Not knowing them now seems bad. But I never had parents to know. It's just the way things are." Fenn's chest tightened and his breath shortened.

"But don't you want to know who they are?" Sadie asked.

Fenn shrugged again, now wishing he hadn't allowed the subject. "Sometimes. But I'm told they're dead and nobody knows who they were."

"Seems a bit odd, don't you think?" Sadie said. "I mean, there can't be that many folk in the Ruud. How can nobody know who your parents were?"

"There are thousands of folk in the Ruud," Grayson said, rolling his eyes.

"Still," Sadie said. "Somebody's got to know."

Fenn didn't respond, hoping now the conversation would stop. His parents were a part of him somehow, even though he didn't know who they were. But he didn't think Sadie or Grayson would truly understand that; and it sounded too silly to say out loud, anyway.

"So, you haven't learned all the secrets of the wissenry, yet?" Grayson said.

"Huh?"

Sadie laughed. "There aren't any secrets of the wissenry. You'd make a really bad wissende, waiter boy. It's not some secret club, you know. They just deal with boring old facts. You go and complain about the ghosties or the demons steal-ing your pies and they tell you there's no such thing and it's probably the neighbor kid or some rogue gnome. They aren't very cheerful, them wissendes—spoiling everybody's fun."

"There are secrets," Grayson said, looking seriously at Fenn. "You know there are secrets, right?"

Fenn shrugged. "I know some things."

They looked at each other for a brief second as they walked and Fenn got the feeling Grayson knew things he shouldn't. Was he talking about the secret history in the locked cabinet? But Grayson couldn't know about that, could he? And even if he did, he couldn't know any more than Fenn did: two histories. That's it. What made them different was still unknown to Fenn.

Eying Grayson curiously, Fenn had a new feeling that made his chest tingle. Even learning that Father Treacher had lied about the grub demons hadn't felt quite like this. Fenn's heart was unaccustomed to distrust and suspicion.

Chapter Thirteen

After his degrading capture, Lucas followed the felidae through the western woods southward to the beast forest. None of the felidae would speak to him or answer his questions. "That is for the lord to explain," they said, over and over again. Four remained in their feline state, patrolling the edges of the group while four others took their folk form, clad in smooth fur cloaks and hoods, hiding their pale faces from him.

"I am Walden," the felid who'd dragged him from the tall grass told him when they surrounded him and he stood to greet them. He introduced the others in folk form: Matthew, Arberdeen, and Shelton. The cats he called Lister, Cratchen, Nerol, and Quarn. "We have watched you, waiting. And now you are called," he said. And that was all he would say.

The forest was darker and colder than the woods. Quiet fell all around them, but for the occasional breeze whistling through the pines above them.

"Even the roster fiends sense your presence, young Lucas," Walden said.

Lucas turned to him, hoping he would continue, but he lapsed back into his brooding silence. Deeper they traveled into the dense forest until finally a clearing opened around them and a dozen centaurs emerged from the trees on the opposite end.

"Hallo, young Lucas," the lead centaur said coming for-ward. His orange red coat and mane were paler than his dark hair and beard, and his eyes were hazel brown. Compared with the svelte, wiry felidae folk, the centaurs were rugged and hearty.

"Red Lichen—" Lucas bowed—"It is good to see you again."

"You remember me? After all these years?"

Lucas smiled. "A centaur makes quite an impression on a child, my friend. Why have they brought me here, Lichen? The felidae won't speak to me."

Lichen laughed. "They rarely speak to anyone."

"Don't be absurd," Matthew said. "Of course we speak."

"Not the least willfully or joyfully," Lichen said. "Come Lucas, meet my fellows and we will take you to Dag Voorspeld."

"But why? I was on important business."

"He was in a cage," Walden growled.

Lichen looked down at Lucas with concern. "Is this true?"

"Yes, but it was necessary."

"Necessary to put a beast in a cage?"

"They don't know what I am."

"Nonetheless," Walden said. "We would not allow it. It was unbecoming."

"And being dragged off by the neck was, of course, honorable, I presume."

"You were called to the lord."

"But you don't just abduct a folk and drag them away. And in front of children no less."

"Is this true?" Lichen now turned on the felid.

"We have our orders. What did you expect us to do, ask for his release?"

Lichen shook his large head violently, sending shivers down his mane and to his tail. "I will never understand felidae...or folk for that matter. Come Lucas. You'll have answers soon enough."

As they neared the lair of the beast lord, beast of the forest joined them in their trek, all taking time to introduce themselves and their tribes to Lucas. He knew he'd never be able to remember them all, and yet knew he must somehow, at some point. But this was not the time, he protested to Lichen and Walden. There were children in danger in Path. He did not have the leisure to meet with the lord just now. Of course, even Lucas knew one didn't simply shrug off the orders of Dag Voorspeld. And so on he walked with the beasts of the forest.

Finally, he found himself in the misty green lair, surrounded by representatives of the beasts, Lichen of the centaurs, and the felidae, some cat and some folk. Dag Voorspeld sat purring in his rock throne beside the stone with the trickle of clean water running down its edge. Lucas remembered being there as a child, but it all still seemed hazy and new.

When Dag rose and shimmered and changed his form, all bowed, except Lucas who stood and stared. Once in folk form, Dag pulled his cloak hood from his white face and glared at Lucas with deep blue eyes.

"What have the folk lost their minds with now?" he purred, his smooth voice nearly penetrating Lucas' chest like a vibrating drum.

"Lord." Lucas bowed his head slightly, but only for a second, in acknowledgment. "They have rumors that the bairn of prophecy has been born and now will attempt to level the Ruud."

Voorspeld smiled.

"They are looking for one with a mark. They are taking children near the age and holding them prisoner until they find him."

"And you wish to help him?"

"It is imperative he is safe. He doesn't know who he is. The wissendes won't tell him."

"Why not?"

48

"They can't tell him what they themselves don't under-stand. They fear he will attempt to fulfill the prophecy."

Voorspeld was quiet for a moment, then said, "Nonsense."

"They are merely folk. They fear him."

"They believe he will find the kell stone."

"Perhaps, but how could he?"

"I think you know."

"It is time," Lichen said stomping his front hooves into the needle-covered ground. "The kell stone will soon be returned to us and the council of the Rad will convene. A new era of the beast will commence."

"Yes, yes, it may be so. Walden," Voorspeld said. "Find the hunter and bring him to me." He turned back to Lucas. "Very well, you may keep an eye on the situation. But it is unseemly to be held captive."

"I only intended to see where they would take the children."

"And now you have seen. We will assure their safety. Mingle with the folk and keep us informed."

"But what of the boy?"

"Leave the folk eis to me."

Chapter Fourteen

Supper with her parents was hushed and uncomfortable. Leah opened her mouth to speak several times only to realize she could think of nothing to say. Her mother dabbed at her eyes with her napkin as often as at her lips and her father shoveled food into his mouth continuously; Leah surmised it was to keep himself from saying something that would start an argument.

Finally, her mother said, "You've all you need for your packing up tomorrow?"

Leah nodded. "Laundry is done, chests are aired, lists are made."

"And you're excited?"

"Yes ma'am."

"You don't sound excited."

"I'm not happy to be leaving; but I am glad to be on an adventure."

Her mother made a small noise and put the napkin to her lips again.

Finally the meal was done and Leah made her way to her room upstairs, over her father's little office. She walked a bit, in tiny circles, on the rug, imagining she were down there now, listening to him tell her of Dakenruud and the kell stone once again. Though they were so often at odds, she liked being in his office with him; it brought them closer somehow.

Pulling her new leather journal from her desk drawer, she sat there by her window where the last of the evening light shone through the yellowed glass panes. She opened the journal and on the first page, wrote: *The Adventures of Leah Hallowsing.* And on the next, she wrote the date.

I set off morning after next for my first great adventure. Prenalin has instructed me to use this journal for my trip and for my position as Aide to the High Priest. He says it will be useful. As a devotee of journaling in particular, I could assure him he is correct. Nothing clears the mind so much as regurgitating it onto paper.

I look so forward to finally meeting Lord Kirche. He has been High Priest of Hass since I was a young girl of thirteen. I will always remember the first time our eyes met as he rode by in a grand parade. Our class was escorted to every Hass parade during school and while the other children saw an opportunity for play, I was always on the lookout for our dear leader. This brings to my mind my former teacher Madam Always, who often stood beside me, her face aglow with pride as we watched the spectacles. I do often think of Ma'am Always and what's become of her.

Ah, well, I am now employed with our beloved Hass and will soon meet him! Not only that, I will work for him directly. I can only imagine how proud of me Ma'am Always would be if she knew.

Closing the journal, Leah pressed her palms to her hot cheeks to cool them. It was surprising, she thought, that she could still feel the energy of her teenaged years and the fervor with which she wanted to be a part of the Hass. And yet, in her more lucid moments, she could not get her father's admonition out of her head: You think too much, Leah Hallowsing. You've too many questions.

"So much for clearing the mind," she muttered and tossed the journal into her travel pack. Either way, she knew her trip to the eastern continent, to the kingdoms of Michelruud the Betrayer, would be enlightening. How could it not be?

She only wished she would be able sleep the two nights remaining before her adventure.

Chapter Fifteen

After another hour, Sadie paused and sat to rest on a fallen tree. Fenn sat in front of her on the pine needles covering the forest floor in a spot where the sun shone through an opening in the trees; Grayson laid down and put his arms over his eyes.

"Why'd the guard have to come to the village so early," Sadie said.

Grayson yawned in response. "How far is it to your uncle's? I don't think I've ever walked so much in my life."

"It's a fair trip. We could try to cross the river here," Sadie said.

A permanent worry wrinkle had etched itself in Sadie's forehead; Fenn wished he could wipe it away. She was smaller somehow, than when he first came upon her by the boulders at the tunnel. Ever since her ma handed her that book of maps, she hadn't smiled once.

"Or make our way almost to Timber," she continued. "There's a better crossing there and it's closer to the divide wood. What do you think?"

Grayson rubbed his eyes with his fingertips and said, "Don't ask me. I've never been out of Path."

"Never?" Sadie said.

"I'm not sure where the divide wood is, but I've seen it on the maps in your da's shop. It runs between Damon Wall and Aaronland."

"How can you have never been to Aaronland, at least? It's right over the bridge," Sadie said.

"I know where Aaronland is," Grayson said. "I've studied the maps of the entire Ruud, and the wasteland and hill country to the north. I'm just not the folk to ask about getting anywhere, that's all."

"Didn't you ever cross one of the bridges?" Sadie asked.

Grayson shook his head.

"Never? Not even hunting rabbits?"

Grayson looked horrified. "You aren't allowed to hunt in Aaronland. You'll be arrested."

Sadie laughed. "They don't arrest kids for hunting rabbits."

"It's the law," Grayson said.

Fenn smiled. "Once Ma'am butcher brought Jack into the wissenry. He'd been brought home by the Aaronland guard; he was across the bridge shooting arrows at lizards." He laughed. "Jack couldn't sleep for days he was so scared and Ma'am wanted Father Treacher to tell him he'd done nothing wrong."

"See," Sadie said. "They didn't arrest him."

"Lizards," Grayson said. "Aaronland doesn't care about lizards. But you can't hunt their rabbits or squirrels or even gnomes."

"Gnomes? Why would anyone hunt a gnome?"

"That's not the point. And besides, you hunt gnomes."

"I just nab gnomes. It's completely different."

"I say we cross here," Fenn said. "We should get on the other side of the river as soon as possible."

"What difference does it make?" Sadie said.

"We'll be out of Michelruud," Grayson said.

"So what?"

"The guard took kids from Aaronland," Fenn said. "Maybe King Arnot set up a post to keep King Evan's guard out of his villages."

"On the other hand, Arnot could be on King Evan's side and looking for kids from Michelruud to hand over to him," Sadie said. "That guard at South Bridge was on the Aaronland side, you know."

"But there's a chance we'll be protected there," Fenn said.

"You heard my mum," Sadie protested. "We're not to go to Aaronland."

"Still, better on their side of the river than ours, I'd think."

"We're crossing here," Grayson said, standing up and making his way to the river shore.

Fenn beamed at Sadie and held out his arm directing her to go after Grayson. She rolled her eyes and grimaced; but she followed Grayson to the river. They would have to wade through the icy deep water, with nothing to hold on to but the rocks. They put their knapsacks on their heads to keep them out of the water, tying the straps around their chests, should they fall off.

"Me first," Fenn said. "Sadie to follow and Grayson, you head up the rear."

"The rear." Sadie snorted with laughter. "Aye sir. Grayson is the rear end."

Fenn was glad to hear her laugh. And while she made a lot of fun of Grayson, Fenn got the feeling Sadie was glad to have him around. He was taller and stronger than the two of them, after all, slender as he was.

As they began their careful trek through the rapid river, Fenn too, was grateful for Grayson's presence behind them, urging them on. From stone to stone they carefully inched their way across, at one point up to their waists in water. One hand on their heads, holding their sacks, the other fumbling in the waters for a grip on a large stone. The river rushed around them, forcing its way between the huge white boulders, pulling them off their balance and tossing them against the rocks. Halfway in, Fenn stumbled and fell, taking in a big gulp of the icy water and trying to stay quiet.

"Fenn," Sadie whispered loudly over the surging water.

"I'm okay." He grabbed at his sack and held it up as high as he could to keep it out of the water and struggled for his footing.

Finally, Fenn climbed onto the opposite bank and turned to pull Sadie along; together they helped Grayson out of the freezing water and up the slope. They lay there panting, cold and numb.

Sadie, her teeth clattering, said, "My mum would kill me if she knew we did that."

"Do you think she really believes Prince Elrundt's ghost is out here to help us?" Grayson said.

Sadie shook her head. "Sometimes she's a bit superstitious."

"Well, it's too bad he's dead," Grayson said. "But I'm glad if the thought of his spirit gives your ma hope. She'd be awfully worried otherwise."

"You don't believe in spirits?" Sadie asked him.

Grayson sat up and looked north up the river. "Nah," he said.

"But what about your ma?"

Fenn thumped Sadie lightly on the shoulder and frowned at her.

"It's okay," Grayson said, standing. "I don't believe in spirits—even my ma's. What about you, Fenn? What do you believe?"

Fenn stood up as well and wiped the seat of his pants with his hands. He thought of his visions and how real they felt. Father called them his night curse. Dreams that were not dreams, they felt solid and true, and yet, not connected to any memory he had—they left him confused and questioning.

"I don't want to believe anything I can't know," he said.

He remembered Lucas, suddenly, and his teasing about the history— the history he knew and Fenn didn't—and the *Book of Katze* that he could read and Fenn couldn't. And he remembered lying awake in the darkness of early morning, thinking of stealing the key to the book cabinet in the cellar from Lucas' top drawer; he'd read the book and Lucas would have to stop teasing him. That was just before Father had pulled him from bed and pushed him into the tunnel—it seemed so long ago already, and it was just last night.

"All right then," he said, trying to focus on the present moment. "Let's get into the divide wood before evening and get a little sleep."

They hid from one another behind the trees to change their clothes, and carried their wet tunics and pants over their arms to hang out to dry, once they found a place to stop.

Following along the river's path, keeping to the pine woods, they reached the large divide wood between Aaronland and Damon Wall hours later. They went in as deep as they could before they needed to sleep. It was early evening when Fenn's head was heavy on his arm and he felt himself falling into a deep slumber. His body melted into the ground; his ears filled with a rush of static. Suddenly he was standing at the well in the center of Path, watching the children being forced into caged carts pulled by carriages. They were led out of the village calling out for help as Fenn stood at the well, his hands tight over his ears to block out their voices. Then he heard himself say, "You did not find them all."

He startled awake in the foggy morning light, his eyes blinking, trying to adjust. Was that a vision or a dream? He couldn't tell; it seemed to be both. It shouldn't matter. Father Treacher told him again and again his visions weren't real—they meant nothing. It was just the curse of an orphan, he said, that he'd think he saw things or heard things like a dream—visions that seemed very real, but were just out of his imagina-tion.

From behind him, Fenn heard a low-pitched mumbling, the rustling of cloth and a tinkling of metal. Frightened, he turned slowly and sat straight up, now terrified, at the sight of an enormous brown bear nuzzling in Sadie's knapsack.

Chapter Sixteen

Fenn could feel a scream forming in the back of his throat, even as his thoughts warned him not to make a sound or he might alert a nearby guard.

"Darnit!" a booming voice called out and a large, bearded man stumbled out of the woods toward the bear. "Get out of that. That don't belong to you." He swatted the bear's back with his hand—*thwap*; the bear shook its massive head back and forth, mumbling a low growl, before lumbering over to a tree and sitting down.

The dark-haired man smiled at Fenn. "Sorry about that. He's not trained very well."

"Who...who are you?"

Sadie and Grayson now sat up as well, their eyes wide with surprise.

"I'll be Rogget," he said. "Just a wayonder. Sorry I hap-pened upon your camp—it was Darnit there; somebody must have jerky."

"What's a wayonder?"

"Oh, you know...I'm away yonder there one week, and away yonder somewheres else the next. I'm always yonder and about. But are you all by yourselves? Children ought not be in the divide wood all alone."

"That's not your concern," Fenn said.

They stood and stretched, keeping wary eyes on the bear—and the bear man—and began to pack their sacks. The large man looked as if he carried his entire life with him in the bulging pack on his back. Perhaps he told the truth and he was nothing more than a traveler who accidently happened upon them. Hung over his shoulder, Rogget carried a quiver of arrows and a bow; and though Fenn didn't see any evidence of a musket,

54

he was sure he must have several knives tucked here and there, and could see the straps of what was most likely the leather sheath for a dagger, peeking out just above the lip of his right high-boot.

"Heading out then?" Rogget said. "Where to?"

Fenn looked at him with suspicion. "That's not your concern," he said again.

Rogget's eyebrows lifted. "Oh, well, I've been told now, haven't I, Darnit?" He looked to the bear, who seemed to shrug in response. "I s'pect you're headed to the port. I hear tell King Evan's guard crossed over into Damon Wall and took off with some children. I even hear they went so far as the castle village and Ricker didn't do nothin' to stop 'em. The Ruud isn't a safe place for children of your age, these days."

"Why would the kings of Aaronland and Damon Wall let King Evan's guard just ride in and carry off kids?" Sadie asked no one in particular. "And why aren't the parents doing anything about it?"

"Ard," Rogget shrugged. "There you'd need to be knowin' all the history of the Ruud. The three kingdoms have had their share of warrin' and Michelruud has always come out best. They got the fiercest and most loyal soldiers, trained up from their eighth year to fight for the king. I'd say—" he lowered his voice—"if I didn't think I might be overheard, that Arnot and Ricker are plain scared."

Sadie frowned. "That doesn't explain parents letting the guard just walk away with their kids."

Grayson nudged Sadie with a warning look.

Again Rogget shrugged. "They're scared, too...of the evil bairn. And if they didn't let their kids go, well, they'd be called traitors, wouldn't they?"

"Well," Sadie said as she pulled her sack onto her back, "thank you for the warning. We'll be going now."

"Mind you be careful and stay hidden. There's lots of bad going on about now."

"Yes, thanks," Grayson said, pushing Sadie and Fenn forward and away from Rogget.

Sadie and Fenn followed Grayson through the wood and as soon as they were out of Rogget's hearing, Sadie said, "I've been to Damon Wall lots of times. We can't follow the south road, because the last few miles it's out in the open. But if we keep south here, I think we'll run into Woodside village. Then we can make our way straight from there to Damon Village and my uncle's. There are patches of wood across the range; and I'm guessing the guards will stick to the roads."

"Maybe," Fenn said. "But we have to wait until dark again."

"Agreed," Grayson said. "We need a place to camp away from bear man."

They made their way to the edge of the wood where they could see the outskirt cottages of Woodside dim in the fog of the cold autumn morning, and sat down to cold biscuits and apples.

Grayson asked Sadie for her map book.

"You like maps, waiter boy?" Sadie said.

"What's not to like?"

"It's just the Ruud."

"It's more than that. It's a piece of history."

"There's not much history in our Ruud. Nothing exciting ever happens here."

"All sorts of things have happened here," Grayson said. "The Ruud wasn't always like this." He poked at the map. "It was all one realm at first. But King Michelruud divided it up and gave a piece to each one of his sons. Legend says they were identical, but they weren't. Michelruud, his first son who was named after him, got the biggest part in the north here, where we live." He pointed to the map. "Damonruud, the second oldest, but some say his father's favorite, got the southern section with the port. And Erinruud got this north-east part."

"If Damonruud was his father's favorite, why didn't he get the bigger part?" Sadie asked.

"Exaclty, see?" Grayson said. "Damonruud thought the same thing. And his grandson Obervan set out to avenge him this slight and murdered his cousin King Alfred of Michelruud. But the Michelruud guard rallied behind Alfred's widow Eleen and they retook the kingdom for her son, coincidentally, named Fenn."

"Fenn?" Fenn said, surprised. "There was a King Fenn of Michelruud."

"There sure was."

"That's not in the *History of the Ruud*," Fenn said.

Sadie nodded, impressed. "That is exciting. Were there any other murders like that?"

Grayson laughed. "Plenty."

"But they aren't in the history," Fenn said, irritated now. "You're just making this up."

"I'm not making it up."

"But it's not in the history."

"You just have to know the right books to read to find out the real history," Grayson said with a sly wink at Fenn.

"Why do you like maps so much if you don't go any-where?" Sadie said.

"How can you travel the Ruud and not like maps?"

Sadie dug through her knapsack and pulled out two pieces of fried chicken wrapped in a cloth. "There's just one thing I don't understand. How could they have known that the bairn was born and that he has a mark?"

"Someone must have seen him—someone who knows the whole story," Grayson said.

"But they're taking kids with any ole' mark, so they must not know what the mark looks like. How stupid is that?"

"There must be some basis for the rumor," Grayson said.

"What basis could there be?" Fenn said. "Why would everyone start thinking some evil little bairn has been born somewhere with a mark on his arm. It just doesn't make any sense."

"Just because we don't know the source, doesn't mean it isn't true," Grayson said.

"Yeah, and just because you've been told a story is true, doesn't make it true. It's just like the grub demons."

"What do grub demons have to do with anything?" Sadie said.

"I don't think there are any such things as grub demons. I was in that tunnel for maybe an hour and I never felt anything like a grub on me."

"That doesn't mean anything," Sadie said. "They're not just sitting there waiting for you to happen by. They live under-ground; they've got things to do. They'd only come up if they felt your body shaking up their home. And they're slow, anyway."

"I was in there forever. They had plenty of time to come up and climb on me. What could a grub demon have to do with his time, anyway?"

Sadie smirked. "Maybe they were sleeping."

"*That's* your explanation?" Fenn said with a chuckle. "Do grubs even sleep? Do demons sleep?"

"You don't know, do you? And just because you didn't see any, or feel any, doesn't mean they didn't get on you."

Grayson looked at him nervously.

"I'm not going to be a grub zombie," he told him. But he didn't look entirely convinced.

"I don't know about grub demons," Sadie said. "But, the prophecy is just a silly story."

Grayson's voice rose. "If it was just a kid's story, they wouldn't be taking us away in cages, now would they?"

Sadie nodded and admitted, "That's true."

"No. That doesn't make the story true," Fenn persisted. "Grown-ups get scared of things, just like kids. They might be scared about the story, but that doesn't mean it's real."

"It doesn't matter for us, either way, though, does it?" Grayson said.

They all sat quietly for a moment and then Sadie mumbled, "You can't prove they weren't there and just sleeping."

Once night fell over them again, they crossed the range amid patches of trees toward Damon Village. Sadie walked fast and stayed up front, Fenn thought to prove she could outwalk Grayson, who lagged behind often whining about his disrupted sleep habits. Fenn stayed behind with him.

"In the history," he said, "it doesn't say anything about Obervan murdering Alfred. All it's got is a chart of the geneal-ogy of the kings."

"Yeah, so," he said breathlessly. "Why didn't you know there was a King Fenn."

"I don't remember seeing one."

"Maybe your history is missing some pages."

"I don't think so."

"Maybe you just didn't read it well enough."

"Well, I admit I never really looked at the genealogy. But I've read the history a few times—okay, I also admit there were parts I skipped over, but only the really boring stuff. I wouldn't skim past a murder. And what you said about Alfred isn't in there."

"So?"

"So, you're wrong."

Grayson said nothing, but kept trudging along in the darkness. Fenn suspected he knew the secret history of the Ruud. But how could he?

Finally it occurred to him. "Does Sadie's father have a copy of *The Book of Katze* at the stationer's?"

After a pause, he whispered, "Yes."

"You've read the secret history of the Ruud?"

"Yes," he said.

"But, that's forbidden to everyone but the wissenry."

"Why?"

"It just is."

Fenn wasn't sure he was telling the truth; but that's what Lucas told him and as playful as Lucas was, he'd never lied to Fenn before. And that's what Father Treacher told him, though he now knew that Father was indeed capable of lying.

"Well, Sadie's father is stationer to the king. He has a copy."

"He isn't supposed to have a copy of the old history."

"How do you know?"

"I just know, that's all."

"Well, he has one."

"And you weren't supposed to read it."

"Well, I did."

"It's forbidden to anyone but wissendes. You could be hanged for reading it."

"What are you two talking about?" Sadie whispered from up ahead. She'd stopped and turned and was standing with her fists on her hips, pouting in the moonlight.

"What did you hear?" Grayson said as they approached her.

"Nothing but you loud-mouths. You complain about my yapping, but apparently it's okay for you."

"You're right," Grayson said and looked at Fenn. "We'll be quieter, won't we?"

"Can we rest?" Sadie whined.

"No," Grayson said and walked past her.

Fenn chased him through the trees and checked to make sure Sadie was well behind them.

"There's only supposed to be one copy—a secret copy."

"Maybe Roarn of Michelruud distrusted the wissenry. Maybe he didn't know the wissenry had a copy. And maybe he left a copy in the hands of his stationer?"

"But Roarn of Michelruud is the one who commissioned the rewriting of the history."

"Is that what your wissende told you?"

"What's that supposed to mean?"

Grayson shushed him and looked behind them at Sadie. "I'm not sure I should say any more about it. Apparently, it's forbidden and I'll get into trouble."

"I agree."

"Okay then, let's not talk about it."

"Well, maybe you should be more careful what you say in front of Sadie."

"She doesn't know enough to know what I'm talking about."

Midway, the south road curved toward them and they heard horse-drawn carriages rolling along it. Fenn imagined the carriages were pulling cages, like the one he saw in Path. Children might be struggling against the metal bars, reaching out to him in the dark. He shuddered, and kept walking.

After the carriages passed and there was only the wind in his ears, they entered a small wood. Fenn heard a thud behind them, as if something hit the ground.

"What was that?" he whispered, and peered back into the dark trees.

He saw nothing, but thought he heard the grunt of a bear, or a bear man.

Chapter Seventeen

Sorgood approached the prince where he sat at the king's table and Prince Welk's stomach tightened. There went any hope of enjoying his evening meal. He must remem-ber to dine alone in his own quarters more often. There in the keep, in the drafty great hall, where his father's servants always set a place for the king at his throne, even while knowing he was busy dying in his bed a few feet away, Welk was generally uneasy. Too many tittering ladies and greedy men eating his food, drinking his wine, and looking at him with expectation. But Sorgood's presence always put an extra knot in his stomach. The man was positively frightening—akin to a swarthy, six-foot tall praying mantis; and his simpering reports to Welk left him distrustful.

He waved his hand as an invitation to Sorgood to sit before him and nodded to his wine steward to offer the vile man a drink. Sorgood chose to stand, but took the drink and primly sipped from the goblet, his little finger, with its dirty nail, lifted daintily in the air. Licking his lips, and keeping his eyes to the ground in front of the prince's table, he said, "Highness, we have imprisoned all the children we could find of Path and Timber. We've taken some from Damon Wall villages as well."

Welk smiled. "So now we have another enemy within the family, eh? Does Ricker know we've stolen some of his child-ren?"

Sorgood shook his head. "I don't think so, Highness. Not yet. But no doubt he'll meet with King Arnot when his sub-jects complain of the assault."

"Yes," Welk snickered. "They will meet to talk out their feelings, but they will not have the courage to move against me. You say, all that you could find of Path and Timber. Do we know how many we still lack?"

"No. We believe from Path, one of the wissenry boys is missing, as well as the innkeeper's son and the stationer's daughter. But we are told they are on visits of business. And from Timber, quite a large group is missing. We fear they've taken to the beast forest."

Welk stopped his chewing and frowned at Sorgood. The man looked rightfully fearful.

"You've lost them to the forest?"

Sorgood trembled as he nodded. Suddenly a lady across the room burst out in laughter, and several ladies stood to run across the hall with a few gentlemen tossing flowers at their backs. Sorgood bristled, but kept his face toward Welk. But Welk watched the gaiety of the game until it settled down.

"The ladies appear to need distraction," Welk said to his servant.

"But you have not finished your meal, Highness."

Welk waved him away. "Music for the ladies." He paused to recapture his line of thought. Then he smiled. "No bother, Sorgood."

The relief on the man's face was clear.

"Your lost children will come out of the forest soon enough. The beast lord won't tolerate their presence. And they're from Timber, as you say. It is the children of Path who matter most. Do what you must to find them."

Sorgood nodded with a slight smile at his lips. "Yes, Highness."

Welk felt a great urge to shudder. "Will you not stay and dance? I'm sure we can find a lady to tolerate you."

Sorgood looked to the ground. "I do not dance, Highness," he seethed.

"No, I don't suppose you do. Too dedicated to your duties."

He waved his hand in dismissal and Sorgood slithered away.

Over the low hum of conversation, the fiddlers tuning their instruments, dishes being cleared away, and the vibrating echo in the hall, Welk pondered the situation. The young orphan of the wissenry was missing. The wissendes, of all folk, would know much about the prophecy. Could they be hiding him? And the innkeeper's son, that gangly boy, along with the stationer's daughter—still not found. Certainly they were children of those most likely to know about such things. There is always much talk with travelers at the inn. And the stationer has a library to rival the wissenry. Sorgood must find these three children.

Over the din, the east-tower bell tolled its mournful count-down of the king's illness. Twenty-one days now King Evan had lain dying in his bed. Twenty-one hollow rings. Welk thought of the day when all the bells in Michelruud would peal out his ascension to the throne.

Chapter Eighteen

In cold and darkness, Fenn and Grayson followed Sadie around the southern outskirts of Damon Village to a cottage in the clearing of a wood. They paused behind a large pine, watching the house for any hint of danger. Though it was the dead of night, long past when folk would be abed, the canvas-covered windows glowed dimly with lantern light. Her uncle was at home, and awake.

"I'll go alone," Sadie whispered to them. "I'll see if it's safe."

She stepped out from behind the tree into the moonlit night and approached the tiny home of stone. Gingerly, she crept up the wooden steps and tapped lightly on the door. She waited, nervously shifting her weight from one foot to the other, but no one came. She tapped a bit harder and suddenly the door opened, casting lantern light on her face, and a tall man with white hair glared at her.

"What is it, Ralph," a woman's voice called sleepily from inside the cottage.

"Raccoons," he bellowed back at her. "Or gnomes."

Then he turned to Sadie and whispered to her before darting back inside and reappearing shortly with a leather, drawstring bag. Putting it in Sadie's hand, he kissed her on the top of her head, whispered something more, and closed the door again.

Sadie stood on the top step, very still, for several seconds. Then she looked all around and suddenly dashed into the wood to where they stood watching her from behind the trees.

"Run," she said as she passed them. They followed her westward deeper into the woods darting among the trees. Fenn struggled to listen for horses, or voices behind them, but over their footsteps and panting, he heard nothing but their knapsacks jolting against their backs. When he thought his lungs would burst, and his nose and ears were numb with cold, they finally stopped, all three of them gasping for breath. They sat against pines on the needle-covered dirt drinking in the air in large gulps. If anyone was following them, Fenn thought, they would just have to be caught; he couldn't run anymore.

"Uncle said the guard is hiding out in the village looking for children who are missing from Michelruud. He told me to run as fast as I could into the wood and then go back home and hide in Ma's cellar. There's no place for us here."

"You're saying nobody's chasing us?" Grayson's face was lit with surprise and anger. "I nearly ran my lungs out."

"My uncle said to run. So I ran."

"What did he give you?" Fenn asked her.

She held out her hand, still grasping the bag and opened it. "It's money," she said. "A few pents and a doar."

Fenn nodded. Not much, but it could be useful. There was nothing left now, but to go to Father Britt, as he was told to do in the first place. Guilt for disobeying Father Treacher stabbed at his conscience. Suppose Father was waiting for word from the Cold Sea wissenry—some coded message of a sort, letting him know Fenn had arrived safely. He could be beside himself with worry. And all along, Fenn had been running around the Ruud just daring the guard to catch him. Then a taste of resentment hit him. Why hadn't Father Treacher told him what was going on? Why had he sent him through the tunnel with no mention of the guard?

"What do we do now?" Grayson asked. "Hill country?"

"Do you know anyone who's been there, Fenn?" Sadie asked.

He shook his head. "Visitors talk. But I've heard no details, other than it's dangerous. How about you?"

"There are stories at the inn," Grayson said. "Folk dis-appear some-times, criminals and misfits; usually they're in big trouble. And it's said they take to the wasteland or the hill country—"

"Or to the port and out to sea," Fenn added.

"So, none of them are places we want to be," Sadie frowned. "If they're filled with rotten folk."

"Well," Fenn began, and then winced at having to admit the truth, "I have to go to the Cold Sea wissenry."

"At the port?" Sadie asked, wide-eyed.

Fenn nodded. "I'm to see Father Britt."

"Were you supposed to go to Cold Sea from the begin-ning?" Sadie asked and Fenn nodded again. "Why didn't you say so? Why did you come home with me, and to my uncle's?"

He shrugged his shoulders. "I didn't know if maybe Father was overreacting. But he told me to go to Father Britt. I think Britt can help us."

"What, put us on a boat to somewhere?" Grayson's voice rose with panic.

"Well," Sadie said, "I suppose if the wissenry has ways ....we could be pirates."

"I don't want to be a pirate."

Sadie shook her head. "No sense of adventure what-soever."

Fenn laughed. "I'm sure we'll have protection, Grayson. The wissenry wouldn't make you become a pirate."

Sadie shivered. "Well, let's go while there's still dark. It's another good hike."

"How far do you suppose we've been already?" Fenn asked.

"I dunno. Twenty-five miles?" Sadie said.

Grayson whistled. "No wonder my feet are sore."

After crossing South Road, which ran from Damon Wall back to Michelruud, they marched southwestward toward the sea and the air grew colder; the wind picked up and brought pine needles twirling down onto their heads.

"Ow," Sadie complained regularly.

In the midst of the great wood, a strong wind whipped at the trees overhead and Sadie said it again—"Ow."

"Shh." Fenn stopped and turned to them. "Did you hear that?" he whispered.

"It was just me—"

"Shh." Fenn glared at Sadie. "Listen."

They stood silently in the breezy wood, surrounded by darkness, until they heard it. A grunt. The grunt of a bear...or a bear man. Fenn pulled them close and whispered his plan.

Sadie moved forward, talking aloud as if she were having a conversation with the boys, while Grayson and Fenn spread out on either side of her path and waited. As soon as she was just barely out of hearing, along came Rogget and his bear. As they passed, Fenn waved a bit of jerky in the air and then tossed it back the way they'd come. Darnit sniffed, turned, and caught sight of Grayson in the trees. Fenn could tell Grayson was looking across the path at him, frightened, though he couldn't see his face in the dark shadows of the trees. Finally, Darnit lumbered off to search out the jerky.

Grayson still looked panicked when they met in the path-way and Fenn smiled at him and motioned him to remain quiet as they followed Rogget along the path. When they caught up to Rogget, at Fenn's signal, they jumped onto his back, expect-ing to knock him to the ground, but instead clung to his over-stuffed knapsack and hung there as the huge man turned this way and that, flinging their legs around him.

"Argh," Rogget yelled, falling to his knees, his voice echoing in the forest all around them. He turned, flung the boys off him, lost his balance, and fell over onto his back. "Darnit," he called, but Grayson climbed on his chest and wrapped his knapsack strap around Rogget's head filling his mouth.

"Whf duyu thnk yuf doon?"

"Why are you following us?" Fenn demanded.

Rogget sat up, pushed Grayson off him and removed the strap from his mouth. "What do you think you're doing? Eh?"

"Why are you following us?"

Sadie appeared from the trees, pale and frightened.

"It's all right," Rogget said. "I'm protecting you, that's all."

"We don't need protecting. And we didn't ask for it, either." Grayson said with a trembling voice.

"No matter. I'm to protect you."

"Well, stop."

"I can't stop. But I'll...I'll protect you from farther away."

Grayson rolled his eyes. "What good will that do?"

"I'll be farther back, see? So you won't be thinking I'm going to pounce on you or something."

"Why can't you just go a different way and leave us alone?" Sadie asked quietly.

"I just can't."

"Well, fine then," Fenn said trying to sound much older than he was. "But when we get where we're going, you'll be dealt with."

He hoped he sounded mean enough to scare Rogget. After all, Rogget couldn't know who they were, or where they were going. They were headed seaward, where all sorts of pirates and gangs came to port. What did he know but that they would set their gang of thugs on him as soon as they got there?

"Come on," he said and they left Rogget sitting in the wood with Darnit chewing on jerky.

They made the rest of the journey quietly, always listening out for Rogget or Darnit. Once Fenn's heart stopped racing with excitement, he considered the odd feeling he'd had when he jumped on Rogget. Swinging this way and that on the large man's back, Fenn could only think of him as kind and gentle. He didn't feel as if he should fear him at all. It seemed odd to him that he would think so just at that moment, and then go back to distrusting the woodsman soon after.

They settled down to sleep at the edge of the wood and Fenn nestled snugly under his blanket against the cold night wind. As he felt the sinking of sleep settle over him, the hemp rope around his neck grew warm and the heat spread through his body. He found himself in a dark, cold, stone room with a blazing fire at the hearth. As he approached the fire, the flames bathed him in warmth. There was a place for him by the fire and a mug of hot cider on a table. He sat and sipped until his cheeks burned with heat and a calm fell over him. Slowly, he became aware of a presence in the room. It was his father, standing just behind him. A large, warm hand rested on his shoulder and nudged him. Suddenly he was shaken awake.

Chapter Nineteen

Leah tipped the handler who lugged her trunks onto the ship, but, despite a welcome by the captain, remained on the dock waiting for Prenalin and Lord Kirche. It would be presumptuous of her to board before them. She breathed deeply of the misty sea air and smiled up at the gulls squawking for their early morning meal of fish guts.

The port was busier even than the city, she thought and it was not yet dawn. Men loaded and unloaded cargo, sailors sang as they disembarked from faraway lands hurrying to see their families again. And they sang as they prepared ships to sail for months at sea. The fishmongers sold right off their boats where servants, chefs, matrons, and innkeepers all vied for a good price.

A group of urchins darted through the throng of folk, snickering, barefoot and thin. They should be readying for school, Leah thought. She turned this way and that looking for their mothers—but no caring woman came after them.

As she peered through the crowd, she saw him. Tall and slender, his shimmering blond hair falling down his shoulders. His robe was pure, clean white, lined in purple. He nearly glowed among the filthy dregs of the port. Atop his head was the conical mitre trimmed in purple and gold. And on his chest, in the center of his vestment, hanging from his neck, was the gold medallion with the flame tree carved into it.

Leah had stopped breathing and caught herself mesmer-ized by Lork Kirche's piercing blue eyes before she realized she was staring right at him. Quickly she cast her gaze to the ground as did the others as they passed him on the dock.

"Lord," every man and woman muttered, bowed slightly and hastened away.

"Lord Kirche," she said and curtseyed when he stopped in front of her.

Her heart fell when he ignored her, turned to Prenalin and ordered his trunks taken aboard ship. At least Prenalin smiled at her before walking up the ramp, leaving her on the dock to board behind Kirche's trunks.

She heard her father's voice calling her name and turned to see him running down the dock; her mother struggled to catch up.

She shouted from the plank, "You come to see me off."

"Indeed, of course," he said, panting. "Good sailing, child."

"Mutterede's blessings with you," her mother said.

Leah flinched, turned to look up the ramp and there, to her dismay, stood Lord Kirche, one eyebrow raised and a sour look on his face. She turned back to her parents with a weak grin.

"Blessings of Hass be with you while I'm away," she said half-heartedly. As she waved and blew a kiss, tears formed in her eyes, but she dared not wipe them away and let her father see. She turned from them and made her way up the plank to where Lord Kirche stood glaring at her.

66

"Mutterede's blessings, indeed," he said.

Leah marveled at his steely smooth voice and chastised herself for thinking it a wonder. But she couldn't help it. She wanted to hear it again.

Chapter Twenty

"Fenn, wake up."

Fenn darted up, throwing off his blanket. "Wha?"

"Wake up," Sadie said. "I want to go to the port now."

"Is it morning, yet?" Fenn said groggily.

"No," Grayson moaned. "She's woken us in the dark."

"Come on," she urged them, stuffing their blankets into their sacks. "Come on, let's go."

"But why?"

"You'll see."

Fenn felt like a grub zombie, stumbling through the wood. He couldn't have had more than two hours of sleep. What could be so important?

Like walking into another room, the pine forest gave way to a brief grassy plain, and the land sloped southwestward toward the sea, caught in the darkness of pre-dawn. Salty wind whipped against their faces.

"Hurry," Sadie called and ran ahead of them through the knee-high grasses.

They followed until they were at the edge of the slope and stood staring at the ebbing darkness spread below them. As the eastern sky began to lighten with a pale glow on their left, images in gray emerged—a wooden pier, spotted with boats and ships, stretched out like the arms of an octopus across the deep bay. Atop a jutting ridge on the western end of the city sat a beacon, a stone tower containing a great light made by candle and mirrored glass. To their left, a hundred yards away, sitting atop the highland ridge on which they stood, was the wissenry building, overlooking Cold Sea Port.

"Wow," Grayson whispered as they stood and stared down at the great city emerging into morning. "I've never seen the like of that before."

"Me either," Sadie said. "My da's told me stories of the sunrise, but it's even better than he described."

"Is this what you woke us for?" Grayson said.

Sadie nodded.

"Thanks," he said.

A large curving path, for horses and carriages, and sets of rocky steps, led down the long grassy slope into town. As they stood and continued to stare at the sea, small sounds of the waking port carried over the wind; ships approached, a bell rang out. Suddenly, they heard hoof beats and carriage wheels behind them.

"Drop," Fenn said and they fell to the ground. "Flat," he said.

Fenn carefully lifted his head to peer out through the grass. Across the plain he saw a carriage emerge from the wood, heading west.

"It's the road," Grayson said. "From Damon Wall, the road runs west through the wood and down the slope into town on the west side."

They waited for the carriage to pass and make its way down a curvy path toward the port city below. Grayson stood. "I wish we could go into the port."

"It looks scary big," Sadie said.

"When you and your da come to the wissenry here to deliver copies and books," Fenn said, sitting up. "You never go into town?"

"I haven't come to Cold Sea with my da since I was seven. And he never took me to the city then. Too dangerous," Sadie said, her voice hollow.

"But you're in training to be stationer. Don't you make trips here all the time?"

"Why do you think my da has Jeopard Link?"

Sadie tugged at a tall blade of grass. Looking up, she caught each of them in a brief gaze before turning her face away. "It's because I haven't taken to it. I'm never wanting to read or write, just like you said. I hate copying books. Don't like the print press. And I don't want to ride the carriage to Cold Sea or Aaronland wissenries or the other stationer's. It's boring."

Grayson and Fenn exchanged glances.

"Sure it is," Fenn told her.

Sadie looked up at him with a smirk; she stood and wiped bits of grass off her tunic and pants.

"No, really, it is. I only go because I'm made to go," Fenn admitted.

"I have to be made to do my training, too," Grayson said with a laugh.

"Have you been into the city, then?" Sadie asked Fenn.

"No, Father would never let me go. Too much carousing and gambling."

"At least you've been here before," Grayson said. "And you've led us all this way from memory."

"I still go to my uncle's often. And getting here from there was pretty easy."

"Still, it's rather brave of you to lead the way like this."

"You haven't ever been out of Path," she said. "You seem awfully brave, too, considering."

Grayson lit up slightly and smiled.

"Really, you should have seen him stuff that knapsack strap in Roggett's mouth last night," Fenn said and Grayson's smile grew wider.

"That sounds very fitting for an innkeeper," Sadie said.

"And you'll make a fine stationer, too, I'm sure," Grayson told her.

They kept their attention downward on the fascinating town as they made their way across the ridge toward the wissenry. They could see folk, like tiny creatures, and children their age running about. Though the distance was great, they saw nothing that resembled the king's guard in the little port city.

"I don't think the guard's been here," Grayson said. "Nobody down there's acting scared or anything."

"Let's just get to the wissenry quickly," Fenn said and led them along the ridge to the building overlooking the ocean and the port city. They approached from the back, hiding behind a shed and watching the wissenry for suspicious activity—of what sort exactly, they weren't sure.

"All right," Fenn said, feeling a little silly. "Let's just go."

They crossed the yard to the back of the building, climbed the stone steps, and Fenn knocked on the door. It opened almost immediately and a young man of about seventeen smiled down at them. "Orphans?"

"Fugitives," Fenn said.

"Well, come in then."

They entered into a roomy kitchen on the left, with a large table to the right and beyond that, a corner desk at a window.

"I'm to see Father Britt. Has King Evan's guard been here?"

The boy snickered. "They'd be a might bold to come to the port, eh?"

"Fenn." Father Britt bounded into the room. "Finally."

Father Britt was the opposite of Father Treacher. Not much taller than Grayson, he was very round. His brown hair matched his woolen robe, and was cropped short all around his head as if wore a bowl for a hat. He smiled at them all showing off dimples in his ruddy cheeks.

"I'm sorry Father. I was to come straight away but I..."

"I see you found some mates. But you're here now. And don't you look half asleep! Come, come, we best get you settled into the hidden rooms."

Father Britt lit a lantern and led them out of the kitchen and down a long, dim hallway, through a maze of passage-ways and rooms, and down a set of creaky wooden stairs into a dank cellar. He pulled storage trunks away from one wall and guided them through a short tunnel and down earthen steps, taking them under the cellar floor.

"These are secret chambers," he said, guiding them through the small set of rooms. "You can stay here for a while."

"Do all the wissenries have secret rooms and tunnels?" Fenn asked.

Father Britt cast a glance at Grayson and Sadie before looking back at Fenn with a wary smile. "Perhaps. Here at the Cold Sea we often harbor fugitives from the kings; folk who wish to take to the sea."

"Are we going to sea?" Grayson asked.

"Oh, no, son. It's not safe."

"Can we stay here?" Sadie asked.

Father Britt shook his head. "Not for long."

"You think the guard will come soon?"

"Eventually," he said. "I think..."

Fenn found Father Britt's behavior odd and unsettling. Did he know anything at all or was he just making up answers?

"Why haven't they come already?" he asked.

The wissende lit more lanterns in one of the rooms and they dropped their knapsacks on the beds lining the walls, and sat down. "I'll get you some food and let you rest."

"We'd really like to know what's going on, Father. If you don't mind," Fenn said, though he was suddenly very heavy and his eyelids felt puffy and tight.

"The kings of the Ruud don't have much control here, Fenn. They must barter with the captains and tradesmen for goods and transport. If they could ever get along well enough, they might manage some authority. But they always bicker amongst themselves—and we pay the price. This is a lawless port, for the most part. King Evan's guard will not come here unless he feels it is absolutely necessary. And then they will need many men."

"But you think they will come?"

"Rest now. Then eat. We'll talk more later."

Father Britt left them and they all lay down on the beds along the walls. Fenn woke later, wondering how he'd managed to fall asleep with all the questions running through his mind, but he had, and it was a dead sleep, dreamless, without visions. He felt more rested than he had since he was pushed into the tunnel by Father Treacher. There was food on the table in the front of the room and when he sat down to eat, he found himself stuffing it into his mouth quickly.

Sadie and Grayson woke as well and joined him.

"This is really good," Sadie said smiling. "I was starving on apples and jerky."

70

When they'd eaten their fill of thick soup and crusty bread, Grayson said, "I think Father Britt is right. I think the king's guard will get here eventually. Unless they find their bairn."

"But if they don't know who the bairn is or what his mark looks like..." Sadie said.

"Exactly," said Grayson. "They won't find the bairn because they don't know who they're looking for. So, they'll be here eventually."

"Maybe Father Britt has a plan for us," Fenn said.

"Alas," Father Britt said, entering the room and startling them. "We did have a plan for you once, Fenn. But now it seems...well, it seems we're at a loss."

Chapter Twenty-one

The three-masted *Treasure of the Seas* was Lord Kirche's ship, owned by the Hass and maintained for the Lord's personal use. His cabin was aft, with Prenalin's next to it, portside, while Leah's cot was down below in a closet next to the galley. At least she didn't have to share like the washer woman and kitchen staff did.

Their party were nine, not including the sailors and crew. Kirche, Prenalin, and Leah were aided by three of Kirche's body guards and three porters who would carry luggage and handle any other duties of that nature. While body guards Kipling, Redd, and Alphonse, were prone to standing silent and muscular at doors or in corners, glaring, Leah found the porters friendly enough. Gretchen would babble in a whisper about most anything going on in her head at the moment if you sat with her at table or on deck. Zelda, large and strong, had an infectious loud stuttering laugh. And Xavier, though thin and very young—Leah thought no more than fourteen —was always quick with a kind word and worked the luggage like a man three times his size.

Leah's duties were simple. She would rise before dawn and make her way to the galley to oversee preparations for Lord Kirche's breakfast and bitter kaff. She was to clear his dishes, send his laundry to the washer woman, keep his desk and belongings neat, sharpen his pencils, keep his ink filled, maintain a constant supply of kaff in his mug, see to his meals, and all his demands for apples, oranges, crackers, pickles, and tiny pastries. Prenalin saw to Kirche's more personal needs of bath, dress, and toilette and appeared to otherwise be his confidant.

Leah couldn't help thinking how silly it all seemed. There was no reason she could fathom why Lord Kirche couldn't pour his own kaff when he needed it. But she supposed that was why Kirche was the High Priest and she was merely an aide.

Kirche said barely four words to her that first morning and she curtseyed so often he told Prenalin to make her stop.

"Our Lord Kirche," Prenalin said, as he would always begin when relaying Kirche's messages to others while Kirche stood mute beside him, "tells me you look like a bobbing buoy and would wish that you cease the adolescent obsequious bowing."

"Yes, sir," she said and curtseyed again which brought a snort from Prenalin and a smirk from Kirche. Leah knew she should be ashamed, but instead felt a rush of pride: she had made the Lord smile.

"Don't be too excited to visit the Ruud," Prenalin told her as she set up the small table in Kirche's cabin for his lunch.

"Do I seem excited?"

"Indeed, you do. But the Ruud is a crude, uncivilized realm. They haven't any streets to speak of, beyond the port city. The folk live in tiny huts and wear muslin tunics still—the women all wear pants. I dare say they rarely bathe."

"It's still a new place," Leah said. "And I'm told there is more green there than anywhere in Ruhm."

"Forests, yes. Where you can be lost forever and eaten by felidae. Do not be so fond of green, my dear. Green is untamed and therefore holds much immorality."

Leah felt a laugh in her belly and stifled it. Immoral forests? Prenalin clearly took himself too seriously.

"And what does Lord Kirche think of the Ruud?"

"Why, he can barely stand his visits. If they weren't demanded of him, I dare say he would not go."

"Why could he not send you in his place, then?"

"That would be undignified. Tribute is always collected by the Lord himself. To show his dominance, and his power. Every realm ought to see its king regularly."

"But Kirche is not king of the Ruud."

"Semantics, my dear. Semantics. The Ruud pays tribute to Ruhm. Their kings are our vassals. That makes the Hass their allegiance, and Kirche their king."

Leah had to wonder what the kings of the Ruud thought about that sort of logic. She went below to the galley to collect Lord Kirche's meal.

The rules of the *Treasure of the Seas* stated explicitly, according to Prenalin, that the galley crew, and only the galley crew, may carry plates to the cabins. However, no galley crew member is allowed to set a plate before the Lord or his secretary. And so, Leah followed the midshipman up the ladder and back to the stateroom. She took the plate from the sailor and placed it on the table just as Kirche entered the room.

He said nothing as he sat and lifted the lid of his lunch plate. He sat down, sniffed, picked up a fork and poked at the half chicken, then looked up at Prenalin.

"I would wish you to lunch with me."

Leah curtseyed half way and remembered herself, nodded at Prenalin and scurried below for another plate. She was out of breath when she took the second plate from another midshipman and placed it opposite Kirche at his little table.

As she turned to leave, Kirche said, "And you, Leah. I would have you join us."

She smiled as best she could and left the room for another plate. This one she carried herself and placed on the table.

"Lord Kirche's plate is now cold," Prenalin said. "Give him yours."

"You would have me eat Lord Kirche's meal?" Leah was astonished.

"Of course not," Kirche said. "Prenalin will take mine and you will take Prenalin's."

"But then," Prenalin said, "I will have the coldest meal and Leah will have a warm meal."

"Very well, then," Kirche said. "After you take my meal and I take Leah's, you may then give your meal, which was earlier my meal, to Leah, and she will give hers, which was earlier yours, to you. And that way, Leah will not have my meal at all, but yours."

"Yes, quite right," Prenalin said and they began passing plates.

Leah caught Prenalin's eye as she took Lord Kirche's plate from him and she resisted smiling. She was sure he was laughing inside.

Chapter Twenty-two

Fenn and the others looked at Father Britt with questions on their faces and he sat down at the table with them and rested his arms across it, patting Sadie's hand.

"You must understand, Fenn. The original plan was for you to travel the unknown southern continents, to explore for the wissenry. But, not until you were of age. Treacher must be barking mad to expect me to put you on a ship south now, what with the pirates and beast folk and the lawless, and..."

"An explorer? Really?" Fenn said. Father Treacher had never said anything about him leaving the Ruud.

Britt nodded and raised his brows. "As I was saying, you're better off running alone in the woods with the guard at your heels." He paused, shaking his head. "No. I'm sorry to say it. But soon enough they will discover your whereabouts and come after you here."

"Me?" Fenn said. "Why me?"

Father Britt waved his hand in the air and continued, flustered. "Well, all of you, of course. They'll figure out where you've run to and find you out. It appears to be the children of Path they want...so my sources tell me. And I imagine they know which they have and which are missing."

"We could hide here," Grayson said hopefully.

"Oh, I think the wissenry is one of the first places they'd look for Fenn, don't you?"

Grayson and Sadie nodded and looked at him.

"No, I think what's best is that you rest here for a short time, eat your fill, bathe if you like, and then take the divide wood between Aaronland and Damon Wall and on to the hill country in the north. There you may find some safety if you keep moving. I'll provide protection, of course."

"Rogget," Fenn said.

"Did you come upon my man, then? He was supposed to be discreet."

"He was following us with a bear."

"Yes," Father Britt nodded with a smile. "I suppose he's not as slippery as I'd like; but he knows the guard well enough to keep them from you, and volunteers for jobs such as this are hard to come by."

"He did say he was supposed to protect us. We thought he wanted to rob us," Grayson said.

"How long do we have to hide?" Sadie asked.

Father Britt sighed. "When the prophecy is forgotten you may return."

"But what if it's never forgotten?"

"Well, then, you must wait until you are older, fifteen at least, before returning to the Cold Sea wissenry. And then you may both follow Fenn into the southlands, if you wish."

Fenn shook his head in frustration. "You mean you are sending us into the hill country for years with no real hope of ever returning home?"

"Ever?" Grayson echoed.

Father Britt was silent.

"Why am I to..." Fenn looked at the rotund wissende carefully. "Why am I supposed to hide...things? What would I have to do with this prophecy story?"

Father Britt seemed to think carefully for a moment before he answered. "You have nothing more to do with it than any other boy of your age." But he grimaced slightly as the words came from his lips. "The prophecy was made by the beast lord too long ago to remember. It had almost been forgotten until about ten years ago."

"Do you believe it, Father? Do you believe there is a child who will grow up to destroy the Ruud?"

"I cannot say."

Fenn stared at him, angry. He either believed it, or he didn't—why could he not say which? Father Britt left them, telling them to rest, but as his footsteps sounded on the stairs to the cellar above them, Fenn stood and paced the room.

"We can't just go into the hill country," he said.

"But why not?" Sadie asked. "My ma would want us to be safe from the guard."

"If the prophecy is true, we could be waiting in the hill country for years for it to come to pass and be over with. The bairn may not be found until it's too late and we're practically grown."

"What choice do we have?" Grayson said.

"And if the prophecy is not true, we would never be allowed to return home."

"Never?" Sadie said with a whine.

"Don't you see? If the prophecy isn't true, they'll never find the bairn. They'll be looking for him forever. We'll have to hide forever."

They sat and stared at him as he paced back and forth between the small beds.

"What should we do?" Grayson asked.

Fenn sat down on his bed and looked carefully at both of them. "I think we should go into the beast forest."

Sadie laughed. "Are you out of your mind? Are you crazy?"

"Keep your voice down," Grayson said to Sadie and then turned to Fenn. "You want to see the beast lord?"

Sadie's face contorted, and she whisper-screamed, "The beast lord? You *are* out of your mind. We can't go into the forest. Do you know what's in there?" She paused as if think-ing hard and said, "Well, beasts of all sorts."

"You don't think seeing one of the larger beasts up close would be an adventure?" Grayson said.

"There's a big difference between spotting a centaur and actually having the nerve to walk straight into the forest. The beast folk hate us, you said so yourself."

"That's history. We don't know how they feel now," Grayson said. "The beast folk and the main folk lived together peace-fully for many years before..."

"Before we stole their land and banished them to the forest. Who cares what happened before that? You think they're going to be happy to see us now?"

"I should never have told you about that," Grayson said.

"You'd rather go to the hill country and hide out for the rest of your life?" Fenn said.

Sadie shook her head. "Well, let's see...starve to death in the hill country ...or be eaten by roster fiends."

Grayson laughed. "Roster fiends? What are they going to do? Peck at your toes?"

"You don't have to come with us," Fenn told Sadie. "We can send you off with Rogget."

"Oh, thanks. That's much better. Eaten by a bear." But she smiled just a bit. "No. I'll go with you. Besides, you need me; someone has to be the cautious one. I guess I'm the brains of this outfit, after all."

Grayson laughed. "The brain isn't made of mush, Sadie."

"Oh, like you know all about brains."

"Your father's library is the best in the Ruud," he protested. "Maybe on all of Kell. You should try reading some of the books there."

"Fine then," Sadie said. "You be the brains. I'll be the muscle."

"We need brains *and* muscle," Fenn said.

"She doesn't have muscle, either," Grayson said.

"More than you, waiter boy."

"Enough already," Fenn said and they both looked at him, pouting.

They found the bath room down the hall. Father Britt had lit the lanterns, filled delicately carved ceramic bowls with clean water, and laid out freshly washed towels for them. They cleaned up, ate a little more, and searched their way out from the hidden rooms and upstairs. Once on the main floor, they were unsure of the path to the kitchen and began wandering around the wissenry, past offices with writing tables, papers and crates, past doorless bedrooms, and past non-furnished rooms with mats on the floors.

Fenn led them down a long, dark hall, heavy with quiet. A dim light shone from one tiny room and he realized the hall-way was a dead end. Knowing the room must be occupied and not wanting to disturb someone possibly in meditation, they turned to go back. But Fenn stopped when he heard Rogget's voice echo from the room.

"But his abilities could be very useful to us."

Father Britt replied, "No, Rogget, no. He must discover this connection on his own. I warn you; the possibility of bad consequences demands that he *not* be told."

"But Father—"

Their voices went suddenly quiet, and Fenn thought he heard Father Britt whisper. He pushed for Sadie and Grayson to hurry away. Once back in the main hall with more light, Fenn realized they'd been turned around coming up the stairs and wandered into the front rooms of the wissenry by mistake. Finally, heading toward the back, they found the kitchen.

Standing at the large table in the middle of the room chopping vegetables, the boy who'd let them in earlier startled at their approach.

"Hello again," he smiled broadly.

"Are you well rested already?" Britt asked, surprising them by coming up behind them and clapping his hands together. "Want a bit of tea? Sit down, sit down."

He guided them fully into the room and bade them all sit at the table, glancing suspiciously at Fenn, who did his best to pretend he hadn't overheard Father's conversation with Rogget.

"This is Tom, Lesser Wissende."

Tom nodded with a smile. "I hear you're to head into the hill country with Rogget. We'll get you well set with provisions."

They nodded solemnly. What abilities might come in handy in the hill country, Fenn wondered. And whose abilities were they?

"Aw, don't be scared," Tom said. "Rogget will protect you. And it's beautiful in the hill country."

"You've been there?" Grayson asked.

"Well, no. Nobody has, have they? But it sounds quite nice, doesn't it?"

Sadie turned to Fenn and put on a stern face, nodding, as if to say that had settled it—she'd definitely take the beast forest over the unknown hills.

"You will stay with us for a time," Father Britt said. "We will take stock of the guard situation, make a plan for you, procure provisions, and locate our man Rogget."

"And we can rest," Sadie said.

Fenn smiled at Grayson and Sadie and wondered if the same dark, half moons deepened the skin under his eyes as he saw on theirs.

"Very well," Father Britt said. "Fenn, if you'll follow me. I have something for you."

Fenn glanced at Sadie and Grayson before following Britt out of the kitchen, through the main lobby, and into the maze of halls they'd been lost in. Down the dark hallway, Father turned into the small, doorless room where Fenn heard him talking to Rogget earlier.

Surprisingly cluttered, the room contained a table with a chair behind it and another in front. Papers and books littered both the table and several spots on the floor. Tall chests of drawers and bookcases lined every wall. The room was lit by dozens of candles under glass, sitting atop tables, the desk, and in corners of bookcases, much too close to books for Fenn's liking.

"Have a seat there," Britt told him, waving toward a hard-backed chair in the corner nestled between two towering piles of books—too many to fit in the cases against which they were stacked.

Fenn waited for the scolding he thought he deserved—wandering about and listening in on private conversations were certainly not the behaviors of a wissende. At least, he suspected they weren't.

But Father Britt turned from him, walked to a tall, stand-ing chest at the far end of the room and pulled opened the top drawer. He took out a small box and carried it over to Fenn, removing the lid as he walked. And out of the box, he drew what looked like an oblong gold coin with a hole at one end.

"This is yours." He placed it in Fenn's hand. "It belonged to your mother."

"My mother," Fenn echoed. "What is it?" He turned it over and over in his palm. It was warm, when he expected it to be cold, and it sent waves of comfort through him.

"A charm. She wore it around her neck on that braided hemp rope of yours."

Fenn reached to his chest and touched the thin rope. "This was my mother's?"

Britt nodded. "We wanted you to keep something of hers. But the charm...well, it's very valuable. It would draw attention. I think you should have it now, as I may not ever see you again. But keep it hidden. If you must wear it, keep it under your tunic."

Fenn nodded and continued examining the charm. On the front, lightly carved into the gold, was a dragonfly. And on the back, deeply engraved, were the letters RoE. He rubbed it with his thumb. That was his mother: RoE.

"What was her name?"

Britt shook his head. "No one knows, I'm afraid. I'm sorry son."

But if no one knows, he wondered, how do they know this charm was hers? Father Britt was not being truthful with him; he was sure of it.

"Where was I born?"

"In the wasteland, I think. That is what I was told."

"And the mark on my shoulder?"

"Scar. Animal scratch, I think." Father Britt shrugged. "I don't know much. I wasn't there at the time."

"It doesn't look like a scar," Fenn said.

"It *is* unusual; that is why you must keep it secret. I'm afraid you could be killed for it."

"For having a strange mark?"

"I know it makes little sense to a boy your age, but, yes. Fearful folk are capable of vile acts."

"But what are they afraid of and what does it have to do with my mark?"

Father Britt sat on the edge of the chair at the desk and looked kindly across the room at Fenn. Candlelight cast odd shadows on his face.

"Oh, folk are afraid of many things. But mostly, they're afraid of what they don't understand. Stories and rumors fill their imaginations with terrible ideas and they'll do anything to make themselves feel safer."

"But the mark..."

"Yes, I'm afraid very few folk in the Ruud would know the true meaning of it."

"It has meaning?"

Father waved his hand. "Never you mind any of that, now. It's best you get to a safe spot and wait out this nasty business with the prophecy."

"The hill country is connected to the wasteland in the north, isn't it?" Fenn said. "What if one day I were to travel there and search for my mother."

Father Britt stood and turned away to replace the empty box in its drawer. "Oh, I wouldn't dare do that if I were you, son. The wasteland is more dangerous than the beast forest."

For a moment Fenn worried Father Britt had overheard their plan. But when he turned back to him, his face was pleasant, a concerned frown at his lips.

"But, if I did, do you have any idea who I might talk to about my parents? Someone there must have heard of them."

"Fenn, my boy." Father Britt shook his head and smiled down at him. "Orphans are born in the wasteland and sent into the Ruud all the time. You must consign yourself to the truth: your parents are dead and you have no history to be recovered."

Fenn looked to the ground at Father's sandled feet. His heart pounded heavy and mournfully in his chest and he strug-gled to keep his breathing steady. Something was not right; he was certain. Father Britt had answers, but they were at the same time not answers at all. Britt did not know his mother, and yet, he knew the charm was hers. Fenn had a distinctive mark, and yet, he had no history of importance to search for.

There were pieces missing and Fenn was determined to find them.

"Do stay safe," Father Britt said, laying a chubby hand on Fenn's shoulder. "And come back to us when you're of age to handle the pirates. Eh?"

Fenn smiled up at him. "I'll do my best, sir."

Pulling his hemp rope from around his head, he untied it and threaded it through the hole in his mother's charm. When he retied it and put it back around his neck, Father Britt watched as he lifted it, and dropped it behind his tunic.

Chapter Twenty-three

Welk was summoned to the king's bedside but delayed as long as he could. With his father's advisor, Dunham, hovering around him making that nervous click-clicking noise with his teeth, however, he began to believe that facing his dying father might be less bothersome than trying to avoid it.

He took a deep, staggering breath and left his quarters, marching with feigned confidence across the third-floor landing to the stairs. Dunham followed him down to the king's floor, where they were joined by Sorgood, looking strangely merry.

At the huge double doors leading to the king's chambers, Welk stopped and paused just long enough to start Dunham's teeth chattering again before pushing open the doors and entering the dimly lit room.

His father's large bed was surrounded by the usual syco-phants, trying to look loyal in the hopes of a deathbed bequest of what small land or fortune could be had from the Ruud. Welk wondered if they also didn't hope to look dutiful and kind for his own favor. For as soon as his father drew his last breath, he would be King of Michelruud.

Approaching the bed, he scornfully waved off the fawn-ing weasels, and looked down on the pale, drawn face of his dying father. The stuffiness of the room suddenly closed in on him. How hot it was, and musty-smelling. For a brief second he wondered if it wasn't sickness in the air that threatened to choke him, and was it contagious. He wanted to bolt, to never return, but that would be foolish. This frail, skeletal man was nothing. Once a great king, Evan the Fearsome was revered and loathed by the entire Ruud and many lands beyond. Welk himself had hated him for more than ten years. He tried to remember the man he knew as a child; but he could not forget what his father had done to him.

The dying king sucked in a breath as if he'd been gone and come back to life. He reached up a bony hand and let if fall back to the bed.

"Forgive me," the king said.

"Forgive you? You took me by force from my betrothed. You caused her death, if you didn't do the bloody deed your-self."

The power with which Welk still felt the pain of the event, now more than ten years past, startled him.

"I didn't intend for her to die."

"And what of Elrundt? You cast him out, banished him from the Ruud, only because he married against your wishes."

"Her family was against it as well."

"As always you blame the eis. How would you know what they felt about it?"

"I promise you I did not intend for anyone to die."

"It was not but a few years after the attack on our party in the hills that stories of the new bairn began. It was your evil act that brought the prophecy to bear. The fates will not deal kindly with a king who tears apart the sacred vow of marriage."

"You could not marry her. She was...not...like us." The dying king closed his eyes, waiting for another breath.

"Forgive me..." he whispered finally, and let out a choppy sigh.

Welk watched him, waiting for him to breathe again, but his face relaxed; he had passed on into the ether. It was done. His nurse's wail seemed far away, through the thick and heavy damp air. Welk stared, blinking, for several seconds, trying to fathom his own feelings. His father was dead. Was there not, somewhere deep within him, some sorrow? All he felt, he admitted, was anger, and he unconsciously gnashed his teeth together with disgust on his face.

The weasels fluttered back to the bed, fretting and weeping for a few moments, whispering prayers for the dead. Mutterede's blessings for safe passage. The nurse wailed again, clutching her apron to her face. Then Dunham's voice shattered the suffo-cating atmosphere as he roared, "The king is dead! Long live the king!"

In the room, there was a shout of, "Long live the king!" They all bowed and wallowed before him, murmuring words of solace. Scum. He pushed through them and back through the double doors. As he raced up the stairs to his quarters, he heard the bells in the towers already ringing out the news. Evan the Fearsome was dead. Welk was King of Michelruud.

He threw open the door to his chambers and, breathing hard, collapsed into his best chair by the hearth and put his head in his hands. There he sat, calming himself, forcing his hands and legs to cease their trembling, defying tears that never came.

He startled when he became aware of Dunham's presence in the room. "Orders, Sire?" Dunham said.

"You serve me now?" Welk asked him, turning his face away from the man and wondering if it was wise to take on his father's advisor. Dunham, he knew, was already faithful to him. But how would it look? Nonetheless, the king was dead, was he not? Welk could do as he pleased. And as vile as Evan had been, Dunham had served them both faithfully and rationally.

"I am the king's loyal servant, Sire."

"Very well then." He turned to him, finally feeling control over his emotions. "My father and I have said little to each another these last ten years."

Dunham nodded.

"Am I prepared to take his throne?"

"I have done my best, over the years, to keep you up to date, Sire."

"Where do I stand then? What knowledge do I lack?"

"Not that much. You are aware that emissaries from the eis in the ice realm have thrice approached the king demand-ing he rid the hill country of land pirates. The last group was turned away on your father's order... through Sorgood, of course."

Welk frowned. "Turned away with reason?"

"No, Sire. They were shown to the edge of the Ruud and summarily dismissed. We may be on the brink of war with the eis."

Welk winced and rubbed his forehead. He knew well the troubled truce between the main folk of the hills and the natives of the ice realm, the faire eis. Tall, swarthy creatures, appearing frail but with great strength, the eis had lived a settled peace with the Ruud, until the hill country started filling with folk.

From the beginning, the eis demanded the hill country remain uninhabited, as a neutral expanse of land; but as much as the realms tried to contain them, folk managed to make their way across all the warmer parts of the continent. And it was known that refugees from the Kingdom of Ruhm in the Great West had made their way to the hills as well.

The eis were intolerant of all other creatures, except, lately, the angels. They wished to remain in their ice mountains, left alone. But they had made it clear that they would venture out into the warmer climes to rid themselves of what they considered pests.

King Evan, along with the other kings, determined it was not the concern of the Ruud. But the faire eis saw little difference between the squatters in the hill country and citizens of the Ruud. There would be war, a war like the main folk had never seen before, if the matter wasn't handled with care. For on the side of the eis now stood the angels. Fearsome, magical beasts whose numbers were unknown and most certainly under reported.

"What of the rumors about the usurper queen?"

Dunham nodded. "Yes, Sire. There is a rift in the ice realm. The usurper eisen sits on the eis throne pretending to be queen, while her niece acts as princess. She is defended by a majority of their guard. The emissaries often appear split in loyalty between them."

"Anything else?"

"The Hass of Emorah, Sire. They are due for their annual visit."

"Tribute, yes. Send out the usual warnings to the folk, remind them of the proper attitude and behavior. We must tolerate the Hass once again."

"They have grown more daring of late, Sire. Last year the High Priest attempted to claim lordship over Michelruud."

Welk looked at him, stunned. "The Hass? In control here?"

"Yes, Sire. Your father suspected they have bided their time over the years, demanding their tribute, waiting for a vulnerable moment to strike at us. They tried to force your father to turn over his power, but I would not allow him to sign, Sire."

"Good man. Interesting, isn't it, that each autumn when the Hass approached, my father took violently ill?"

"Yes, Sire. Do you suspect anyone?"

"I have my suspicions. Anything else?" As if the threat of war from the north and from the west were not enough.

"As might have been expected, Sire, there is now an outcry over the children. They've been held in the old prison for a week now. A constant stream of visitors flows through Steingefan to see them. Fears are now of illness and exposure to the harsh weather."

"We won't keep them much longer. I feel sure that we will find the bairn before long."

"And if you do not?"

Welk shrugged. "I suppose we'll have to send them all back home. But at least the folk will then admit we did what we could. What do you make of the missing children of Path?"

"Sire?"

"The innkeeper's son and the stationer's daughter, along with a wissenry orphan. All three missing and claimed to be on business."

"The stationer has returned to his post, Sire. I will send Pierston, to inquire after them."

"Yes, do that. But you go. It is of high import. And see what the stationer found on the history."

Dunham bowed slightly at the request.

"Sorgood tells me they've searched all the wissenries for the children."

"Except Cold Sea. He says he needs more men to force his way there."

Welk shook his head. "It will be unseemly and quite out of the ordinary to use military force against a wissenry. But, I suppose it must be done. If the missing ones are not to be found there, they must be off to the hills already."

"If they have escaped us, the folk will remain fearful of the prophecy for some time. They may demand further action."

"Yes." Welk pondered that thought briefly. "How do you gauge the movement for uniting the realms of Ruud into one kingdom?"

"The folk seem not to care as they come and go freely. But your cousins are adamantly against it."

"Naturally. And what has been the folk's feeling of late, regarding me?"

Dunham paused as if he regretted the question. "They have named you, Sire."

"Already? But I haven't done anything noteworthy, yet. Well, let's have it; what have they come up with?"

Dunham paused again, bringing a frown to Welk's face.

"They call you the Dead King, Sire." He winced.

Welk chuckled, both at the epithet and Dunham's fear. "The Dead King, eh? That would be because of my famous oath, I take it?"

"Yes, Sire, I believe so. There is hope among the gentry, as well as the peasantry, that you will change your mind and wed."

Welk nodded. Would he break his oath never to marry, never to produce an heir? He'd only sworn against it to rile his father, to threaten him with no legacy. Without an heir, Michelruud would fall into the hands of Aaronland or Damon Wall. And believing Elrundt to be long dead, his father was caused years of suffering and anxiety at the thought of such a loss. Welk had done all he wanted—he'd let his father die believing Michelruud would pass away, into the hands of his cousins.

Welk laughed again. "The Dead King. It has a nice ring to it."

"Yes, Sire." He paused. "I feel I should tell you something, though I do not understand it myself."

"Very well."

"The Hass, over the years, especially in the last decade, seem preoccupied with searching for something."

"Searching?"

"Indeed, Sire. Your father, at first, forbade searches of the Ruud, but as his health faded, the Hass had more power to do as they would. I believe they searched the castle, as well as several shops in Michelruud, at least. And they read the history on each visit. Pored over it, as if it contained some hidden information."

Welk peered at him. "That's odd. What are they searching for?"

Dunham lowered his eyes to the floor. "I hesitate to say, Sire. It sounds silly. But I thought I heard them refer to a stone."

"A stone?" Welk chuckled; but in the back of his mind there tickled a small recollection. "Perhaps a gem stone they believe they deserve from our historical treasures."

"Perhaps, Sire. But it has grown in importance to them over the years."

"Very well, then, Dunham. I will keep all in mind."

Dunham left the room and Welk chuckled again. Such pettiness could be expected from the Hass.

Chapter Twenty-four

Rogget and Darnit followed them closely, along the ridge overlooking Cold Sea Port. The brisk, salty wind whipped through the darkness, battering their bodies and dampening their voices.

They'd spent a restful five days at the wissenry. Wanting to leave after the first day, Fenn was disappointed when Father Britt declared the king's guard was in the port and they must stay hidden until the threat passed. They were kept in the secret rooms underground for so long, Fenn was glad they left by moonlight, for even it was harsh on his eyes.

"It's the other way to the divide wood," Rogget said from behind them.

They pretended not to hear him, continuing on through the tall grasses of the plain, wrapping their arms around them-selves against the chilly sea breeze. Though it was nearly mid-night, the port city below was abuzz with action, the center at the water's edge lit with lanterns.

"I wish we could go down the hill into town," Grayson said.

"What about all the gambling and carousing?" Fenn said.

"I've seen it before at the inn."

"And you still want to go?" Sadie asked.

Grayson laughed. As they continued on, Sadie held back, watching the port as long as she could. Grayson walked beside Fenn for some time without speaking. Then he whispered, "Did you tell Father Britt?"

"Tell him what?"

"About the history?"

Fenn smiled to himself. "No."

"Why not?"

Why not? He had no idea why not. He almost told. When Father Britt burst into the kitchen at their arrival, his first thought was to blurt it out. The stationer to the king has a copy of *The Book of Katze* and Grayson has read it. But he didn't really want to tell. The only reason he felt like telling was because he was jealous of Grayson for getting to read it before he could. But there was more to it, he knew.

"I don't know," he said.

"Yes you do."

Fenn shrugged. "Maybe I don't trust the wissenry so much as I did before." His gut ached for the past, before Father Treacher forced him into the tunnel, when there was nothing to do but learn and read; the days were quiet and uneventful. Now his head was constantly filled with questions and worries and fears.

"Father Treacher never said anything about me becoming an explorer for the wissenry. I didn't even know they had ex-plorers."

"It sounds exciting."

"I suppose."

"It's not what you want to do?"

"I thought I was going to be wissende in Path. If anyone was made for exploring it would be Lucas."

"It's that-a-way, I tell you." Rogget called out, stopping and pointing behind them.

Reluctantly, they halted their trek and turned to him.

"We're taking a different route," Sadie said.

"The long way," Grayson added.

"And why would you be going the long way?"

"It's safer," Fenn said, and smiled.

They turned from Rogget again and walked on across the plain, until they heard him wheezing and coughing.

"You're not," he gasped. "You're not."

"We're not what?" asked Grayson with a devilish smile at his lips.

"You're not headed to the beast forest. I'll go back and tell Father Britt."

"Go on and do it," Fenn said. "What's he going to do about it?"

Rogget spluttered and stomped his foot in the grass. "You can't," he said. "You can't enter the beast forest. It's forbid-den."

"Who's going to stop us?" Grayson said.

"The beast folk will."

Grayson looked at Fenn, his eyes nervous and question-ing. Fenn turned to Rogget.

"We're going to see the beast lord. The beast folk can try to stop us; but that's what we're doing."

"What in Mutterede's name for?"

"We want to know about the prophecy."

"The beast lord is the leader of all the beast folk; the keeper of their lore. He won't take kindly to folk children pestering him about things that happened so long ago."

"But we can try."

Fenn and Sadie turned and continued the hike. Grayson paused for a second, but turned to join them. They all walked on, with Rogget following, heaving sighs and moaning moans and making puffing noises.

The enormous trees of the beast forest rose up slowly before them as a dark wall on the horizon. The closer they got, the more Rogget complained. "Beast lord'll have 'em for dinner," he said again and again. "They'll never make it past the river." And once he shouted out, "Arachnids!"

But they ignored him.

They knew they'd reached the boundary of Damon Wall when the tall grasses of the ridge plain were abutted by a dense timberland of evergreens reaching so high they couldn't see their tops without falling over backward; and nailed to each tree, down the line in front of them, was a signboard.

"What's it say?" Rogget demanded.

The salty wind whipped across the plain as a violent warning, muffling Grayson's reply.

"Beware," he read. "All who enter here. Kings of men are paupers and fools."

"The beast lord," Rogget whined, dancing on his feet. "I can't enter the beast forest. Now come away all of you and we'll get out to the hill country."

"It's after midnight," Sadie said. "And I'm still tired. Let's sleep and make our way through in daylight."

"I agree," Grayson said. "Traveling the beast forest in the dark is not a good idea."

"Yes, that's right," Rogget said. "Let's stop here a while and think this through."

"Not yet," Fenn said. "I don't want to camp until we're out of the Ruud."

Grayson and Sadie nodded and they all walked toward the wall of trees.

"I can't enter there," Rogget said. "If you go on, I can't help you."

"But why?" Grayson said.

"It's Darnit...for the most part."

"But he's an animal. Won't he get along fine in the beast forest?"

Rogget stared at him in outrage. "Do you think that's where you're going, then? Into an animal forest with the deer and porkypines?"

"Well, not exactly."

"Right not exactly. What about the cat folk, and the harpies? You could catch a doppelganger." He gasped and turned pale. "What if you meet up with an *angel*? You'll be killed on sight."

"Don't be silly, Rogget," Grayson said with a smile. "Angels are only found in the northeast, near the ice realm."

"And how would you be knowing that?"

"I read it in an encyclopedia."

"An encyclo-what?"

"An encyclopedia. It's a big book filled with information. Back home, the stationer has one just on beast folk of the eastern lands."

"Sounds handy," Rogget said. "But clumsy for lugging around the Ruud. Does it have pictures?"

"Of course," Grayson said.

"Look, Rogget, can't Darnit just wait out here for us?" Fenn asked.

"I can't go in, I tell you." He paced back and forth and rubbed his hands in his hair. "I can't go in and I can't protect you."

They looked at one another and shrugged.

"Sorry, Rogget," Fenn said. "You'll have to stay here with Darnit, then."

Visibly shaken, Rogget took in a deep breath and looked to the ground. He paused and twisted his lips this way and that as if deep in agitated thought. Then he nodded and said, "All right-y then. Two days, you hear? You walk in. You camp until daylight. You get to the lord, and you walk back out without stopping. I'll be waiting..." He looked side to side. "Round here somewheres safe."

"That's only one day," Grayson said holding up his finger as if counting.

"Eh?"

"It's one day. We go in, we camp for a bit. Then it will be morning still, and we'll go see this beast lord and come back tonight or early morning tomorrow. That's one day."

"It's two days," Rogget said holding up a finger. "One, you walk in tonight and sleep." He held up a second finger. "Two, you see the lord and come back. Today, and tomorrow. That's two days."

"But it's just after midnight, we're already in today. And twenty-four hours is a day. We'll be back in about twenty-four—"

"You'll be back tomorrow," Rogget persisted. "That's two days."

"Is this really important?" Sadie asked, trying not to smile.

Rogget and Grayson looked at her.

"It's as if he's expecting to get back in one day." Rogget said.

"All right then," Fenn said. "Two days."

"But—" Grayson protested, but Fenn held up his hand to quiet him.

Fenn found it hard to move his legs. He had trouble be-lieving Rogget was actually going to let them walk into the beast forest alone. And he couldn't tell if Rogget was just scared, or had some other very good reason for not being able to enter the forest. What if Rogget knew more than they did? Would Rogget let them go in if he knew something so terrible was in there that they'd be eaten...or worse?

Finally Fenn nodded and stepped forward, shaking Rogget's big hand with both of his. "Two days," he said. He could see Grayson rolling his eyes.

Rogget stared at Fenn, their hands clasped tightly togeth-er as if he feared to let go. Fenn imagined Rogget with a fire-arm, suddenly, tears in his eyes, shouting, "I didn't mean to do it. I swear I didn't mean to." Fenn pulled his hand from Rogget's grasp and turned away.

Sadie hugged the wayonder and Grayson shook his hand. Fenn watched, trying to get the picture of a sobbing Rogget out of his mind. Father Treacher was right; these visions, now enter-ing his head both day and night, no doubt due to his disrupted sleep habits of late, were just the wild imaginings of an orphan.

Leaving Rogget and Darnit behind, they walked hesitatingly across the border into the beast forest. Immediately the air was fresh and clean and floated lightly around them without wind. Everywhere, darting between the trees, were tiny, dancing bits of illuminated gold.

"Lightning bugs," Grayson said. "Da told me about them. They used to be all over Path. Every night kids would chase them, lock them up into lanterns and let them glow through the glass." He let out a melancholy chuckle. "I didn't believe him, of course."

Sadie reached out her hand and grabbed one as it lit up. Laughing, she watched her hand glow on...off...and on again.

Fenn thought of Rogget and looked back, but they'd already lost him to the darkness. "How far in?"

"Little farther," Sadie said.

They walked on until they came to a clearing in the trees where the moonlight bathed the ground.

"Here," Grayson said.

They took their blankets from their knapsacks and spread them on the cold pine needles.

"I have to admit," Sadie said, lying down, "I'm a little disappointed."

"You thought the roster fiends would eat us straight away?" Grayson said smiling.

"Something like that."

"It does seem a bit ordinary," Fenn said, closing his eyes, and wondering if he could sleep. He still pictured Rogget standing at the wall of trees peering after them and Darnit sitting at his side shaking off the cold. It seemed weeks ago now, since he'd left Path—weeks since he'd met Sadie and Grayson. His eyelids became heavy and he felt himself drifting.

Though Fenn could see the slender-fingered hand clutching at a robed arm from a distance, he could feel it, too. His was not the arm of the wissende, but he felt the hand grasping and pulling at his thick woolen sleeve. His was not the woman's hand, but he could feel himself grasping with it. As he floated upward, toward consciousness, he heard his own shallow gasping. Just as he darted awake, a woman's voice whispered desperately, "Keep him safe."

He opened his eyes, paralyzed, lying flat on his back with sweat at his brow, despite the cold. His mother's gold charm burned on his chest. He tried to lift his hand to touch it, but he couldn't. He tried to turn his head to look for Sadie or Grayson, but he could not. He could only lie there listening to his own breathing, feel the cold air chilling the sweat on his forehead, and watch the lightning bugs frolic among the trees above him. He closed his eyes and went back to sleep.

The sun warmed them, nudging them awake the next morn-ing and they rubbed their faces and stretched. Father Britt and Tom had provided them with fresh fruit and biscuits, sausages, and roasted chicken legs.

"It's nice here," Sadie said.

"Like a faire patch," Grayson agreed.

"I suppose it does seem greener than the Ruud; but maybe that's the business with the guard."

"No, I think it really is greener here," Grayson said. "There's something I'm wondering, Fenn. I know I'm not this new bairn folk, because I'm just the son of the innkeeper in Path and my family's been doing that for generations. And Sadie's not likely an evil bairn either, now is she?"

Fenn nodded.

"But you," he continued and Fenn stopped chewing. "We don't really know much about you, do we? *You* don't even know much about you, right?"

"You think I'm the bairn?" Fenn laughed. "I'm an orphan."

90

"I know. And normally I would think your mum and da were poor dead folk or something. But..."

"But what?"

"Well, I see you're wearing some gold there around your neck."

Fenn was startled and reached for the charm, tucking it down behind his tunic. Grayson and Sadie looked at him and he looked back. "So?" he said.

"Well. Let's just say that my mum never had a gold charm."

"How do you know it's my ma's?"

"Tom told us," Sadie said, looking guilty. "When you went off with Father Britt. He said he was likely going to give you the charm. He told us about how he found it one day and Father Britt nearly whipped him for snooping. Anyway...he told us."

"I don't think he was supposed to," Fenn said.

"And see there's that, too," Grayson said. "There's secrets all around you."

"Are not."

"Well, there sort of are," Sadie said, and Grayson pointed at her.

"See, even Sadie thinks so."

"What secrets?"

"Well..." Grayson took a bite of sausage and seemed to ponder the question for a moment. "It's just odd that you came out of that tunnel not really knowing why you were in it."

Fenn's cheeks warmed up. That much was true, he had to admit.

"And, when we showed you our marks...you didn't show us your arm."

"I told you I don't have one."

"I know. But I just guess if it were me...I'd have shown you my arm."

"Are you saying I'm lying?"

"He didn't say that," Sadie said. "You didn't say that, right Grayson?"

"I don't think you're lying. I just think you're... secretive."

"You think I'm the evil bairn. That's what you think."

"Nah." Grayson shook his head. "Not really."

"Good, because it's a stupid idea. I'm not any kind of a bairn. I'm just an orphan. I'm out here for the same reason you two are."

"Okay, okay," Grayson said. "Forget about the evil bairn. I'm just saying that you're different from us. Your mother was somebody important."

Fenn put his hand to his tunic where the charm was now cold against his chest. "No, she wasn't," he said.

"How do you know?"

"I just know that's all."

"Well, okay," Grayson said. "But..." He paused as if to think better of it, but then went on, "But you could be some-thing more than what you appear to be, and even you wouldn't know it."

They sat quietly avoiding one another's eyes until Fenn stood up and packed his sack. An awkward distance had formed between them and he wasn't sure how to get through it. He knew that Grayson was right...about everything. He hadn't shown them his arm, and he'd lied about not having a mark. He didn't tell them about Father Britt, when they'd told him what they were supposed to do after being sent away from home. And he didn't show them the charm Britt had given him. They had every right to be suspicious of him. But still, he couldn't bring himself to say so.

"We should get going now, if we're going to get back to Rogget in time."

Grayson chuckled. "Within the day, you mean."

"That's two days, now, Grayson." Fenn smiled at him. "Don't you forget it."

"Don't make fun of Rogget," Sadie said as she pushed past them farther into the forest. "He's nice."

"Oh, sure, of course...he's nice," Grayson said. Nudging Fenn, he whispered, "Nice and crazy."

The beast forest was not at all what Fenn had expected. It was supposed to be dark and dismal. Danger was said to lurk behind every tree. And while he knew there must be scary beast folk everywhere, it was mostly a pleasant timberland with soft yellow sunlight streaming through the enormous pines, spruce, and hemlock. There were occasional dark patches where the branches above were so thick they blocked out the sun, but even there, Fenn found the deep greens and blacks of the shrubs and cold dampness of the air a wonder.

Gold dust seemed to float through the air all around them. Flowers filled their noses with perfume and tiny tinkling noises sounded off every now and then.

"Fairies," Grayson said when they first heard them. "Did you know fairies used to live in the divide wood? My da says there's an abandoned faire glade there. But he never traveled through it. It's not exactly on the way to anywhere."

"I never heard of it," Sadie said. "Listen, I'm thinking something's following us."

Fenn looked all around, but the trees were so fat and thick that as they moved between them, anything could follow them, from tree to tree, unseen.

"We'll keep a lookout," he told the others and they walked on in silence for some time.

Fenn sensed something was walking along with them, to their right, keeping their pace, but at a distance. He thought he heard padded feet, like the peddler's dog's, only slower and heavier, crunching the pine-needle covered forest floor; and once he heard something like a heavy hum...a purr. His breathing picked up. He felt his heart leap. He caught a glimpse of sleek black fur, huge yellow eyes, and long white fangs. But in an instant it disappeared behind a tree. Pushing forward a bit, past Sadie, he strained to see what would come out on the other side of that particular tree. He stopped and gasped.

"What?" Sadie turned and stopped as well.

Chapter Twenty-five

Lucas took a needed break from the rough and tumble with the young wolverines and sprawled out in the clear-ing with Red Lichen and the others. He noshed an apple and breathed in the heady forest air, glad he had agreed to stay for a time with his kin. The morning was passing quickly, how-ever, and he knew he must be on his way soon.

"You could stay," Lichen told him.

He shook his head. "Nope."

"But you know you ought."

"I do not know I ought."

"Well, you ought."

Lucas laughed. It was true he had much to learn. He'd spent most of his time in the forest meeting with representa-tives of the beast tribes. They brought him impromptu gifts, hurriedly made when they learned he was with them for a short time.

Leorin of the fairies brought him a handful of star dust which she combed through his hair. Lichen laughed, but the tiny amount she could hold brought a sparkle to his blond locks and the fairies oohed and aahed with pleasure and didn't say anything about his feet, which pleased the centaurs.

Bruce of the trolls brought him a fork with one bent tine; and Lichen didn't have to poke him to be sure to be appreciative. Lucas could only imagine it was one of the trolls' treasured possessions.

"I thank you much," he said to Bruce. "I fear I take from you something too valuable. May I offer a coin in return?"

Bruce jumped several times and squealed with delight and Lichen nodded with great respect.

The brownies were represented by Woolrich of the displaced and Eeberdeen of the woodland—the only brownies known to the forest who kept their names for life. They brought Lucas a basket of biscuits, still warm and buttery from their stone ovens. They were shared all around as was customary.

Glenndary of the sluagh, those spirits of the dead folk who still wandered the kell and had come to be accepted in the forest, brought Lucas the dearest gift of a silent song, which Lucas was pleased to embrace. It wasn't often the sluagh could bestow the song, as they were rarely allowed in the presence of folk.

Even the duergar Streetch brought a gift—a string of infant skunk skulls tied with a ribbon.

"I thank you very much, Streetch, for your kindness."

She huffed and flew off, her tiny fairy sisters twittering after her.

"You did well with the representatives last night," Lichen now told him. "I was much impressed."

"So, you are all good with my leaving."

"I would like to know how you learned so much in the village."

"Father has *The Book of Katze*."

Lichen startled. "I didn't know it was still in existence."

"It is. He let me study the early parts of the beast history and culture. And the felidae visited often for lessons."

Lichen's large head bobbed up and down. "Good. Good. I am glad you were not neglected."

Walden leapt into the clearing, startling the centaurs into pounding their hooves and sending the fairies skittering back up to the trees.

"We have found the hunter," he said to the felidae guard. "Quarn and Nerol, you are with me. Woolrich—" he turned to the leader of the displaced brownies—"A word. And Lucas, there is news of your Michelruud."

Lucas stood to hear it.

"The king is dead."

"Thank you for telling me, Walden." He bowed slightly to him.

Woolrich and the other brownies followed the felid out of the glen and Lucas turned to Lichen.

"What do they want with the hunter?" Lucas asked him.

"He will pay his debt to us now."

"His debt? But he didn't do anything wrong. You still live, Lichen."

"But he does not know that."

"It is immoral to punish a folk for something he did not do."

94

"He is being punished for his attempt. That he did not succeed is evident. If he had, he would be dead himself."

Lucas sighed. "But you let him believe he killed you. It's not right."

"You have lived among them too long. You forget what they did to us—what they still do."

"I do not forget. But, the folk of the Ruud are not the same as those of Hass." Lucas stood and brushed the greenery off his pants and began to pack his things. "I choose to forgive and work toward a peace."

Bruce's son Carver handed Lucas a wrapped piece of ox meat, cooked on the open flame. "For travel," he said.

Lucas nodded his appreciation and pressed a small coin into Carver's palm.

"You may work for peace," Lichen said as he followed Lucas north. "But you will remember who you are, yes?"

Turning back to him, Lucas bowed. "That I will always do, Red Lichen. I will see you again. Hopefully not too soon."

Lichen pounded a hoof into the ground and snorted. "This ancient way is highly out of the ordinary."

"Indeed it is. But it was once revered...to offer freedom of choice."

"Freedom? Freedom to remain an infant for so long?"

Lucas laughed. "I am not an infant, Lichen."

The centaur snorted again with displeasure. "You should have been turned long ago."

"Would you wish to do the deed?"

"I would, if I were given permission."

"Ah, but you don't have it. Only Dag Voorspeld can give it. You wouldn't go against the wishes of the lord, would you?"

The irritation on his friend's face brought out another laugh from Lucas.

"Don't worry, Lichen. It is for the best. There is work to be done. I will turn. I promise. All in good time."

Chapter Twenty-six

Staring at Fenn with large, glowing, yellow eyes was a ghostly white woman. She stood not ten feet from them, wrapped in a black, velvety cloak that seemed to billow around her body. Reaching up with a slender, deathly-pale hand, she stroked the velvet on her arm and purred. When she grinned at them, sharp white fangs appeared at either side of her mouth. Looking away from them, she glided into the forest, disappearing. Fenn heard the low hum of purring again and then it was gone.

"Was that—?"

"A felid," Grayson said.

"Was it? Have you read about them?"

He looked back at both of them with wide, frightened eyes and nodded.

"It didn't eat us," was all Sadie said before beginning to walk again.

"I don't think they eat folk at all."

"But they've dragged a few away," Sadie said. "What else would they do with them?"

"There have only been two recorded instances of folk being dragged away by felidae. And both times they were young orphans."

"Orphans?" Fenn said.

"That's right. Coincidence? Maybe."

"You don't think so?"

"I have my theories..." Grayson said.

Fenn waited for Grayson to say more but he remained quiet as they continued the hike, cautiously aware that there were indeed beast folk about. After only a few moments, a centaur appeared suddenly, several feet ahead, glaring at them with a creased forehead. His wild, brown hair stood out all around his head like a lion's mane and his beard fell scraggly and knotted to his chest. He stood tall and proud, his horse tail twitching and flicking across the lustrous chestnut coat of hair on his back.

They were so frightened by him that they said nothing. Trying to keep an eye on him without looking directly at him, they continued walking, hoping he wouldn't attack. He didn't; but after they passed, they heard his hooves hit the ground rapidly, thump-thump, thump-thump. The bushes rattled as he vanished.

Several wolf-like creatures, black and gray, their hair stand-ing on end across their spines, passed by ahead of them but didn't stop to stare. A rugged brown unicorn twitched and sped away at their approach. They heard whispers, echoing in the air around them and they each looked this way and that with wide, spooked eyes.

"Ghosts?" Sadie murmured.

Fenn shook his head. No. It was something else—some-thing small, but alive and well, and speaking their language. The beauty of the forest was disappearing as their anxiety grew.

Grayson claimed there were fairies following them in the trees above their heads, but every time Sadie and Fenn looked, they disappeared.

"I tell you they're there."

Grayson became so aggravated he shouted at them all to scuttle off already. And at that, there was audible fairy giggling and Sadie and Fenn laughed.

"We knew you were telling the truth," Sadie told him.

"Darn fairies." Grayson pouted.

"Don't be insulted," Fenn said. "They were just teasing."

Grayson raised his eyebrows at Fenn. "Eh?"

"The fairies—I'm sure they didn't mean it."

Grayson chuckled. "I think you've been too far from the wissenry, there, Fenn. I don't know what you're talking about."

Sadie stopped and turned to Fenn. "Are you saying you heard the fairies saying something to Grayson?" She was smiling broadly at him.

"Didn't you hear them?"

"We heard fairy song," Grayson said. "But folk don't understand fairy song. Even when they heard it all the time, ages ago, they couldn't make it out."

"Well..." He felt self-conscious now. "I thought I heard them making fun of your big feet."

Sadie put her hands on her hips and tilted her head to one side. "Very funny, Fenn. Very funny."

Suddenly loud screeching and the flapping of wings sounded overhead. Something dark brown darted at them from the air.

"Roster fiend," Sadie screamed and pushed the others to the ground. "Cover your faces."

They huddled together as fiends gathered around them flapping wildly, shrieking, pecking and nipping at their clothing, hair, and skin.

"Ouch!" Sadie screamed as they bit her hands.

Fenn tried to push them away but one of them grabbed at his arm with a sharp talon and wouldn't let go. He waved it wildly, the wind from its flapping wings hitting his face, finally sending it sailing off against a tree.

Sadie screamed again and curled tighter into a ball and Grayson put his body over hers to protect her while fighting the fiends out of his hair.

Suddenly they heard a booming little voice call out, "Kwitcher! Kwitcher!" And a loud pop, pop, pop sent the roster fiends flying toward the sky, leaving the three of them still huddling in fear with brown and white feathers floating to the ground around them.

"Gone," the strange voice said and Fenn looked up to find a very small folk-like creature, no higher than his own kneecap, beaming at him proudly, with a smoking firearm in one hand and a stick in the other. "Don't like the pop, pop," he said.

They sat, brushing pine needles, dirt, and feathers off their clothes and examining their wounds. The little man peered intently at them through round, lashless eyes, his head tilting one way and then the other. His leathery face was deep brown and lined with age. He wore a dark brown leather cap and a matching tunic with a belt of braided grass.

"Thank you," Fenn said.

"Are you a brownie?" Grayson asked.

"*Displaced* brownie," he said, raising his chin and looking along his stub nose at Grayson, insulted.

"Displaced brownies once lived in the village...in our homes and barns," Grayson said.

"Are there any other kind?" Sadie said sarcastically.

"Course there are," the brownie said. "Woodland brownies." He squinched up his face distastefully. "Dirty, backward sorts."

"Well, thank you for the help...what was your name?" Fenn said.

"Name?" He laughed. "No names, Nearly Orphaned."

"You're nearly orphaned?"

"Not me." The brownie pointed at Fenn. "You." He sniffed the air around Fenn and said, "Are you a fairy?"

"Do I look like a fairy?" Fenn crinkled his face in confusion while Grayson laughed.

"What do folk call you, if you haven't got a name?" Sadie asked.

"Whatever they want to call me."

"Well, I'm Sadie," she said.

"You are Scared and Bitten. And he is Tall. And that one is Nearly Orphaned."

Fenn smiled. "Those sound a lot like names to me."

The brownie shook his head. "Not names at all. I'll call you something different when I feel like it."

"Fine then, what will we call him?" Fenn asked the others.

"Kwitcher," Grayson said.

The brownie beamed at him. "Am liking that. Too bad you must change it tomorrow."

"Were brownies this annoying when they lived with us?" Sadie asked.

Kwitcher peered darkly at her, but Grayson said, "Folk rarely saw them. I think...if I recall...once they'd been seen, they disappeared. Moved into another cottage. Is that right, Kwitcher?"

He shrugged. "Many generations since the displaced lived in the villages. The rules—" he waved his hand regally—"Like names, change when we want them to."

"Can you help us?" Fenn asked. "We're looking for the beast lord."

Kwitcher laughed. "Thought you were lost. The beast folk told me to take you back home. You want the lord?"

"Yes, please."

"Villagers don't see the lord unless they're dead."

"Dead?" Sadie's eyes widened. "Then there *are* ghosts in here?"

Kwitcher ignored her.

"We need to see him. We need information," Fenn said.

"I can give you information. I know everything he knows."

"We want to know about the prophecy."

"What is the prophecy?"

"That's what we want to know," Sadie said.

"You must know," Kwitcher said. "How can you know to ask if you know nothing."

"We know there's a prophecy."

"What is a prophecy?"

Sadie rolled her eyes. "The beast lord will know."

Kwitcher frowned. "If you tell me what a prophecy is, I will know all about it."

"A prophecy is like a prediction," Fenn told him. "One of the beast lords said something bad was going to happen to the Ruud and we want to know exactly what he said."

"I think you need to see the beast lord for that."

Grayson put his hands together as if he were choking Kwitcher and Sadie slapped at him.

"Good idea," Fenn said. "Will you take us to see the beast lord?"

Kwitcher shrugged. "Guess so. I'm not sure I'm allowed to."

"We'd appreciate your help," Sadie said.

Kwitcher smiled at her. "All right Scared and Bitten. This way."

They followed Kwitcher through the forest as he sang about everything he was doing.

"I walk, I walk, I walk the forest. I lead the young folk to the lord." Or more dully, "trod, trod, trod, left, right, left, look a tree, I see three..." On and on, unless he was talking. "I think Scared and Bitten will be frightened of the beast lord and will want to stay far back from the lair, with Kwitcher. Tall will be slapped I'm sure; he is not very nice." On and on, and on, until Grayson put his hands over his ears as he walked.

"Listen," Fenn said, pulling at Grayson's left hand. "The river."

They could hear the rushing water in the distance and the air began to fill with mist.

"Not *the* river," Sadie said. "The one we crossed?"

"That's the one."

"What's it doing way over here?"

"Meandering," Grayson said with a smile.

"It curves west, runs up against Timber and then disap-pears into the forest," Fenn said.

"You mean we have to cross it again? I didn't much care for it the first time."

"Folk say it runs through the beast lands, falling over an enchanted cliff face into the sea," Grayson said. "There's a permanent rainbow there...they say. And folk used to travel through the forest for days and days until they were starved and disoriented, and then flung themselves over the falls."

"What for?" Sadie said.

"Love, mostly."

Sadie rolled her eyes. "What a stupid thing to do...go and kill yourself for something as silly as love."

"But they didn't die," Grayson said, intriguing her again. "They fell, sure, but they floated slowly into the water. They say the fairies hold them up as best they can until they drop into the sea and then the mermaids guide them through the rocks and crags to safety on the beach."

Fenn shook his head. "Just more old fairy tales."

"Yes, fairies have many tales told of them," Kwitcher said.

They came to a clearing at the river where a wooden bridge arched over it and Kwitcher stopped them.

"Must pay the troll," he said and dug into his tiny pockets. "I have nothing. We maybe have to cross the river in the wet."

"I've got a coin," Sadie said and turned away from him while she dug one out of the pouch her uncle had given her. Kwitcher was too curious for Fenn's liking so he tried to distract him.

"Where is the troll, Kwitcher? I don't see one."

"Under the bridge of course," he said. "Don't you ever read stories?"

Fenn smiled. "Not really."

"Ah, forgot. You are nearly orphaned. You probably grew up in the wissenry or as a stable hand of a benevolent master. No silly story books for you."

"Why do you keep saying I'm nearly orphaned?"

Kwitcher looked at him as if he were insane. "Smell like it, of course."

"He's all the way orphaned, you—"

"Found one," Sadie interrupted, holding up one of the pents.

"To the bridge," Kwitcher said. "Walk fast, drop coin."

They walked quickly over the sturdy wooden bridge, the icy waters rushing beneath them. Just as Fenn was thinking there was no troll after all, the bridge shook. They stopped.

"Keep walking," Kwitcher ordered.

Again, the bridge shook and over the side in front of them swung a fat, brown troll. Only slightly shorter than Fenn, he was hairy and greasy...and angry. His bulging eyes glared at each of them in turn while his thick tongue licked his pudgy oversized lips.

"Who woke troll?" he demanded.

"Just give the coin," Kwitcher sang as he continued across the bridge past the beast.

Sadie held out the coin between the tips of her fingers as if she hoped to drop it in the troll's wide hand without touching him.

"Sorry for disturbance, Ugly Brown," Kwitcher said.

Fenn winced at the insulting name and hoped the troll wouldn't take it out on Sadie. It held out its plump, dirty hand and Sadie dropped the coin into it and kept walking. As Fenn and Grayson passed, the troll bit the coin and marched its feet into the air one by one singing, 'wee' in a high-pitched voice.

Fenn wanted to stop and have a word. It seemed likely that information about passing trolls might be helpful in the future. After all, Father Britt told him that the wissenry planned to send him out to the southern lands to explore. He ought to ask questions of everyone he met, now that he thought about it.

He'd want to know, for instance, what else might the troll have taken as payment. That could be very useful information to other travelers. He tried to make himself turn around and go back to ask, but his legs were weak and shaking. While he told himself, "go back, go back," his body would not obey. The troll's as tall as I am and twice as wide, he told himself. Curious shouldn't be stupid. Now there was something a traveler might find useful, he thought.

Deeper and deeper into the forest, they followed Kwitcher; and as it grew darker Kwitcher grew more and more quiet until he was not speaking or singing at all. The three of them ex-changed fearful, questioning looks and Fenn knew they must wonder the same thing. Should they have trusted Kwitcher? He seemed so silly and kind. But...what if he worked for an arachnid, for instance, and was actually leading them to its web for dinner? Fenn shuddered and decided to keep a wary eye on their path. Sadie would never let him hear the end of it if he'd led them into the forest just to be eaten by an arachnid; she might have much preferred the hill country and the bear.

They rested for lunch in a clearing where the air was again lighter and brighter and Kwitcher told them they were very close. They should eat first, though, he said. The beast lord would have nothing to feed them.

"Who is the beast lord?" Sadie asked.

"Dag Voorspeld," he said. "Day Foretold. He is felidae."

"The cat folk?"

Kwitcher nodded. "Will be in the folk form I am sure, or he would not be able to understand you."

"Don't felidae eat folk?" she asked warily.

Kwitcher laughed and snorted through his nose. "Once, maybe. When cats. Now they are undead. Silly."

Sadie nodded as if she understood, but the look on her face told Fenn she didn't. The beast folk of the forest were a little more confusing than they all had expected.

After lunch, Sadie walked to the edge of the clearing and pulled at a short shrub with large leaves—as wide around as wash tubs.

"Kwitcher, what's this?"

He shook his head. "It's a bush," he said.

"Yes, I know, but what kind? I've never seen it before. These leaves are huge."

"We call it oliphant," he said.

"The leaves look like oliphant ears," Grayson said. "Would it be all right if we took some?"

"What do you want to do that for?" Sadie said.

"To show Jeopard; he studies plants."

"But when are you going to see him again?" Sadie said, her voice softened.

"Take some," Kwitcher said. "The bush doesn't mind."

Grayson's face had fallen in sadness, but nonetheless, he pulled at several of the large leaves, rolled them up and put them in his knapsack.

They began their journey again and as Kwitcher led them closer to the lord's lair, others joined in their trek, though keeping their distance. The centaur returned and followed them several yards behind. Brownies often appeared, running along beside their group hissing at Kwitcher and, on occasion, pelted him with rocks.

"Kwitchet," he screamed.

Duergers, fairy-like but malformed and vicious, fought with the fairies for a better look at the travelers, flitting from tree to tree above them. And circling just above the treetops, roster fiends shrieked, sending echoes down all around them.

Finally Kwitcher stopped and pointed. "There."

Ahead of them was an entrance into a thick stand of trees. Two large pines overrun with vines, created an archway under which they were to pass. Fenn, Grayson, and Sadie waited for Kwitcher to lead them, but he stood staring at them.

"Well, go on," he said.

"You first," Grayson said.

Kwitcher laughed. "Brownies don't go first."

Fenn looked at him suspiciously, and then looked around at the gathering of beast folk watching them—the centaur, with his arms folded across his furry chest; the fairies and duergers, flittering nervously; wolves; brownies; and various others more heard than seen. There was nothing to do but enter, he thought. He nodded at Sadie and Grayson, and walked under the arch into the beast lord's lair.

Chapter Twenty-seven

As soon as they entered the lair, the moist, cold air turned their breath to fog and a deep pulsing hum filled Fenn's ears. Lightning bugs danced around them, guiding them through the dimness. They fumbled about for several yards, the droning growing louder and louder, until they came upon a glade where the late afternoon sunlight shone through the opening in the trees above and the hum echoed all about.

A large boulder, three times taller than Fenn, stood across the clearing opposite them. Water trickled noisily down its face and dripped over a natural ledge into a pool at its bottom. Stuck in a hole in the stone to the right of the pool was a tall staff topped with what looked like the claw of a giant roster fiend, slightly open, grasping at nothing. And to the left of the rock was a stone throne, and in that throne sat an immense black cat, staring at them with stern green eyes, purring loudly.

Sadie startled when she saw it and turned to run but Grayson stopped her.

"It's all right," Fenn whispered. "It's him."

She turned back and trembled as the cat lifted a wide paw to its mouth, licked the back of it several times with its large salmon-colored tongue, then drew it over the side of its head and licked it again. After settling its paw back on the throne, the feline began to shiver and shake until it seemed it was breaking into a million tiny pieces of itself. It stood and grew larger, as its bits rearranged themselves. Slowly it morphed into a ghostly form with a folk face, retaining its fangs and green eyes; its skin was pale, and a black, velvety cloak hung on its shoulders.

While Sadie's breathing had calmed, her eyes darted around them, and Fenn realized more felidae had appeared. Some remained as cats, sitting or lying down, encircling them. Others took their folk shape and paced back and forth, watching them warily with glowing eyes.

"Dag Voorspeld?" Fenn said, his voice shaking.

The felid on the throne nodded but said nothing.

"We have come about a prophecy."

For a long moment, Fenn feared the felid did not under-stand him, or would refuse to speak to them. The air seemed to grow colder as they stood there waiting; he could see the breath floating out of the lord's nose and from his own mouth.

Finally, Voorspeld removed his pale hands from his cloak and reached behind his neck to pull the hood over his head.

"There is no prophecy," he said, his deep voice silky smooth with the hint of a throaty purr behind it.

Fenn started to correct him, to tell him he was wrong, but thought better of it.

"Can you tell me why the main folk think there is one, and that it was made by one of the beast lords?"

"Main folk?" Voorspeld hissed. "As if you are the norm and we are marred? There are two kinds of folk in the land: sentient beast and mortal."

"What about the immortals?" Grayson murmured and Sadie looked at him in surprise.

Voorspeld turned his head away slightly. "They are of the beast, so far as the mortal are concerned, are they not?"

"Can you tell me why the folk of the Ruud think there is a prophecy?"

"Yes," Voorspeld said and took his seat on the throne.

When the beast lord sat, the standing felidae around them sat as well and began hissing; Fenn quickly sank to his knees, and pulled the others to the ground with him.

"Many years ago, the beast and the folk of the Ruud shared the land and the forest. But Michelruud demanded all the domain for his progeny. He divided it up and built them castles of stone. The beast were forced to retreat into the forest. Eventually, all the beast left you to your own devices. I hear you have done poorly—always at war."

"We see a troll or a harpie now and then," Sadie said with a nervous giggle.

The felid nodded. "You might see more if you paid more attention."

"And the prophecy?"

"Dag Anfang said it. To frighten the Ruud and to make the folk kings reconsider what they had done. But the future cannot be foretold. The mortals' fate is unwritten."

"Can you tell me what he said?"

Voorspeld nodded and lifted his hand to the boulder. "Drop your beloved into the pool."

Fenn looked at the slick rock and the water dripping into the stone basin below it. He slid his knapsack off his back, got up, walked toward the rock and looked into the clean, clear liquid.

"What do you want me to do?"

"Drop your beloved into the pool." The cat was growing impatient with him.

"My beloved?"

"What is it that you cherish?"

Fenn felt the gold charm at his neck grow warm.

"Will I get it back?"

Slowly turning away, Voorspeld ignored him, clearly tired of his questions. Pulling the hemp rope from around his neck, Fenn looked at it one last time. He felt the rough braid between his fingers, and memorized the look of the dragonfly carved into the charm. Then he held the rope above the pool and dropped it in.

Voorspeld arose and walked to the pool to stand beside him.

"Anfang. *Risen ant memren.* Rise and remember."

Suddenly, out of the pool rose dark, velvety vapors that danced and swirled on the face of the rock. They slowly took shape and Dag Anfang stood before them as a ghostly wisp of his former self.

"Prophecy to the kings of mortals," Voorspeld said to the memory of Anfang, and the shadow laughed.

"Michelruud, the dirty king, who laid waste the lands of the beast, forcing us into the ancient forests," Anfang sneered. "A selfish and simpering folk. The felidae, drawn to the kell, stalked him and laid siege to his castle walls, cast spells to make fire and snow, bringing him, fearful and caterwauling, out to beg us to leave."

"The prophecy," Voorspeld muttered impatiently. And turning to Fenn said, "The ancients are often long-winded."

"A new bairn," Anfang echoed. "Born of the kings, cast into the wasteland, raised an orphan. He will rise up against you, King of Michelruud. Dead you are. Dead you will be." Anfang chuckled, pleased with himself.

Hairs on the back of Fenn's neck rose up and tickled his skin. The wasteland...an orphan.

Anfang roared and said, "The kell stone will be his to wield and all folk will harken to his command. The dragon flies above him! All laid waste below!" A chill of silence wafted across the glen as Anfang shrank and grew dim.

"It did nothing," Voorspeld said and Anfang frowned.

"It did not work," the shadow admitted. "The folk of the Ruud continued to deny the beast folk their right to the land and we were forced to retreat into the ancient forest where we will remain until the mortals decide their own fate."

"When will the prophecy come to pass?" Fenn asked.

Anfang's memory looked at Fenn, as if seeing him for the first time, and hissed, "Have you not been listening?"

Voorspeld nodded to the memory, and Anfang gradually disappeared saying, "Is that it? Is that all you wanted?"

The beast lord waved a pale hand in dismissal. "I am too old for this foolishness. I wish to return now to my form. You must leave quickly," he said and walked slowly back to his throne.

Fenn, sensing the lord's restlessness and eagerness for them to be gone, began to shiver before asking what he knew he must.

"My beloved," he said.

"Oh, yes, yes. Take it out."

Fenn reached into the icy water and pulled out the braid and charm. When he put it back around his neck the charm was hot against his skin. Turning to Grayson and Sadie, who still stared at the large, wet rock in surprise, he ushered them back through the circle of hissing and growling felidae and out through the vine-covered archway.

Chapter Twenty-eight

As they appeared outside the lair of the beast lord, the beast folk who had followed them to the archway dis-persed frantically. Kwitcher peeked at them from behind a tree.

"Have survived," he said somewhat surprised. "This way now. Quickly." And he led them back the way they had come.

Darkness was drifting into the forest as the sun had fallen well below the trees.

"Can you take us to where you found us?" Fenn asked Kwitcher.

He nodded. "Will need another coin for the troll."

"A bairn," Sadie said quietly as they walked. "Just like the rumors."

Grayson and Fenn nodded.

"The son of a king," she said.

"Born of the kings," Grayson corrected. "Whatever that means."

"So you agree now that it's not me?" Fenn said.

Grayson looked at him, but said nothing.

"What's a kell stone?" Sadie said.

Fenn could feel Grayson's eyes on him. Was this another secret?

"Anyway, you heard Dag Voorspeld," he said. "It was just a story Anfang told to scare the folk."

"A prophecy is different from a story," Grayson protested. "Folk might be afraid of a story, but a prophecy has power, whether or not the folk who makes it believes in it or not."

"You're saying that a folk can make a prophecy without meaning to?" Fenn turned to him, stopping in the wood. "That's crazy."

"Is not," Grayson said. "Anfang spoke a prophecy, whether he knows it or not."

Fenn rolled his eyes. "And what was all that nonsense about dragons? There aren't any dragons, Grayson. Dragons don't exist."

"You don't know. You haven't been everywhere."

"Not that again. Look, dragons are huge and fly and breathe fire, right?"

"Well, we don't know for sure, do we?"

"And you think something like that could exist and we'd never see one?"

"I never saw a cat turn into a folk until today."

Fenn sighed, frustrated. "But you knew of the felidae."

"And I know of dragons."

"Aargh!" Fenn clenched his fists and walked faster.

"It doesn't matter either way," Sadie said. "Prophecy or not, we still can't go home."

On their way out of the beast forest, instead of gathering around and following them, beasts seemed to scatter as they went. They could hear them darting through the bushes and trees; and fairy whispers echoed through the wood but no fairies could be seen. Even the roster fiends left them alone.

"Why aren't you afraid of us, Kwitcher?" Sadie asked him.

"Known you longer, I suppose." He shrugged. "Besides. I think it's grand he didn't kill you. Makes you something special, not cursed."

"The others think we're cursed now?"

"Probably are. But I don't think curses rub off, do you?"

Sadie laughed a little. "No, I don't think so."

They walked a few hours until Fenn felt woozy and disoriented.

"I'm confused," he said. "Do we sleep in the day or in the night?"

Sadie laughed. "I can't remember either."

"Our rest at the wissenry turned us all around. We're traveling at night and sleeping during the day," Grayson said.

"But we walked all day yesterday to see the beast lord."

"That was today."

"Let's sleep," Sadie whined. "Please."

Grayson laughed and Fenn couldn't help himself—he bent over holding his belly and laughed until tears formed in his eyes. Sadie sat down and laughed and cried.

"This is punch drunk," Kwitcher said. He shook his head. "Not to worry. I do fire."

They sat around Kwitcher's small fire, huddled under their blankets, and listened to him weave stories of the beast folk. They shared their biscuits and chicken with him and he gave them small hard nuggets that tasted of honey. And as they nodded off to sleep, Fenn thought he heard Kwitcher tell them about the kell stone.

Fenn dreamed of the fire and the strong hand on his should-er. His face was warm and he was smiling. A soft, earthy voice sang of the kell and Mutterede and magic. Fenn was sure it was an eisen—her song echoed in his body as if he were empty. He could feel himself sink deeper and deeper into sleep's spell and he did not fight it.

They awoke at dawn the next day and followed Kwitcher toward the bridge.

"This is bad," Grayson said. "We're all turned around again."

"Turned around?" Sadie said.

"Now we'll have to stay up all night to get turned back."

Fenn started laughing again. "And I hate to tell you this, Grayson, but Rogget was right. It's two days."

"He was not right."

"But it will be another half day or more before we get to the bridge. It'll end up being almost two days."

"I agree, it will have been a day and a half, but that's not what Rogget meant. He said—oh, never mind."

"Don't talk about it; it's too funny," Fenn said, wiping tears from his eyes.

"How can it be funny," Sadie said. "I want to go home."

"I know, I know," Fenn said. "I'm sorry."

They reached the bridge well after lunch and Sadie fished for another coin out of her pouch, while Fenn again dis-tracted the curious Kwitcher. When the troll pounced onto the bridge before them, Fenn stopped and breathlessly asked him, "What other payment would you take?"

"No coin?" he said.

"We have a coin. But what else would you take?"

"I want coin."

"You'll get the coin. But supposing we didn't have a coin?"

"Do you have coin or not?" The troll frowned.

"We have a coin, see?" Sadie said and dropped it in his hand as she and Grayson passed him by and ran to the other side of the bridge.

"But what else might you take?"

The troll looked at him and tilted its head. "You want to give me something else?"

"Next time," he said. "What can we bring next time? We have no more coins."

The troll scratched its head and looked into the air. "Mini-ature squirrel," he said.

"A squirrel?"

"Yes, Mm. Squirrel."

"Do you want us to kill it for you?"

The troll looked horrified and stepped back. "Dead squir-rel? What do I do with a dead squirrel?"

"Eat it?"

"Eat it," the troll roared. "Why would I eat my squirrel?"

"You want a pet squirrel?" Fenn asked, incredulous.

"Or paste."

"Paste? You mean, like stationer's binding glue?"

"Paste," he said.

"You want to paste some things together?"

The troll looked at Fenn as if he was stupid. "To eat," he said.

"You eat paste?"

Stomping his feet and shaking his head, the troll said, "Never mind. Don't come back again without coin." And he swung himself over the side of the bridge.

Fenn watched the troll disappear without a sound and leaned far over the rail looking for him. He turned to see Kwitcher standing at the foot of the bridge with his hands on his hips and shaking his head, his tiny left foot tapping madly.

"No splash," he said. "How'd he do that?"

"Talk to a troll?" Kwitcher scolded.

Fenn shrugged. "I just wanted to know."

"Don't ask," Kwitcher said. "Just give something."

"How is it all the beast folk get along so well when none of you make sense when you talk? And the folk of the Ruud are always at one another's throats when we understand perfectly what we're saying to each other."

"Ah," Kwitcher said and smiled. "You answer your own question."

Chapter Twenty-nine

It was late afternoon when Lucas made his way into the center of Path. He'd spent his time hiding in the tall grasses outside Steingefan listening and watching the windows in the west tower for any signs of distress. He waited at the road to Michelruud Castle, the old stone prison in the distance, for Hutt. When he appeared on the road, noshing an apple, the juices flowing down his chin and dripping onto his tunic, Lucas stepped out from the trees and startled him.

"Lucas Foster," he nearly shouted and spit fleshy yellow bits at him. "You scared the livin' Mutterede out of me."

Lucas laughed and slapped at his shoulder. "You off to work this evening?"

"Aye, I'm on for a three day shift. They've got the kids up there in the west tower, did you hear? It's much better than having real prisoners, not to say the kids ain't prisoners, mind you. Hey, hold on. Weren't you taken?"

"There's not a cage in the Ruud can hold me."

Hutt let out a beefy roar and gave Lucas' thin arm a punch. "That's no doubt true."

"You're taking good care of the kids, aren't you, Hutt?"

"Course. My ma, too. We'll not let out a peep if you stage a rescue."

"No, that won't do any good. They'd just round them back up again."

"It don't make much sense to keep them," Hutt finally dragged a sleeve across his mouth. "The folk are happy to think maybe they got the evil one up there with the innocent; but they all thought Welk, er, that's King Welk, would set them all free when he ascended the throne."

"Is there anything going on in the village I ought to know about?"

"Aye, you've no idea. There's some kids still missing and the folk are not happy, not at all. They figure if their own child-ren are stuck up in the stone prison, might well as all of them should be. And they're thinking if none of their children are the bairn, maybe it's one of the missing kids and they ought to let the others go free. They're not treatin' the innkeeper, nor the stationer with much respect these days. You'd best get back to the wissenry, as I've heard one or two awful propositions about your Father Treacher, too. Namely to put him behind bars."

"What for?"

"For that kid you had over there. Fenn. He's been missing with Sadie and Grayson for a week now, and all kinds of speculations are running about the village. They're in cahoots, they are, so they're saying at the general store. Too much time on their hands if you ask me. And don't you go traipsin' through town neither. They like to wonder why you're not locked up like you should be."

And yet, there Lucas was, walking through Path as the stationer and the apothecary were closing up shop. The market stands were already deserted, but as Hutt had said, several folk had gathered on the front porch of the general store watching the goings on around them. He could hear them talking about him—they recognized him.

"Oh, that's just Lucas Foster of the wissenry," Ludvolk said.

"But he was taken, I'm sure of it. What's he doing out?" Ma'am Hardy said.

"They like to find out he's fourteen or so and tossed him out."

"It's true Maddy, he's well over the age."

"You know what I think," Ludvolk said. "I think it's one of them missing kids."

"It is," Ma'am Hardy agreed. "I know it is. And there Pratt and Steppe just walk free as you please around the village like nothing's bothering them. They ought to be forced to hand over their children or face punishment."

"Aye, Karner and Bolt have already petitioned the new king. You'll see. And that wissende, too. They'll all be turned in, you'll see."

"Quiet, Ludvolk," Karner said. "Lucas might hear you."

"He's over to the stationer's you dolt. What do you think, he's got eis ears or something?"

Lucas smiled and walked on down the path toward the wissenry. When he was sure to be out of sight of the folk, he broke into a run.

Chapter Thirty

The sun was setting in the western sky behind them as they approached Cold Sea Port. Leah stood at the gunwale, port side, and watched as the forested land, dim and mysterious, drew near. Cold sea wind whipped at her long locks and she pulled at her velvet ribbon until it was free. Shoving the ribbon in her pocket, she ran her fingers through her hair, shook it out, and gathered it once again. Just as she reached for her pocket, she glanced up to find Kirche standing beside her on deck, looking rather startled at her appearance.

"Lord." She curtseyed. "So s-sorry," she said and couldn't help herself but giggle. "Honestly, Lord Kirche, you must allow me to curtsey, as I can't seem to stop."

He smiled a bit, though his eyes remained, as always, cold, and she dug deep in her pocket for the ribbon. With trembling hands, under his steady gaze, she tied up her hair and pressed her palms smooth against it to be sure it was contained.

"Look there," she said, spotting a centaur standing at the tree line on a cliff.

"And there," Kirche pointed to the sea, dotted white with foam below a waterfall.

"Mermaids?"

"They would swim to the ship," Kirche said. "But they know our flag."

Leah turned to look up toward the stern where the flag of Ruhm, gold and purple, fluttered in the wind and above it, the flag of Hass, white with the flame tree ablaze in its center.

"Which one?" she asked Kirche.

"Does it matter?"

I wouldn't have asked, she thought, if it didn't. She looked back to the centaur who reared and stomped its hooves on the ground before turning back into the trees. Leah gasped, amazed at the proud creature.

"Filthy beasts," Kirche said.

She turned to him, her eyes wide, realizing too late she was behaving like an excited child—her cheeks burned. She'd only seen beasts in the zoo in Ruhm. To see them in the wild, living free, was frightening, and joyful. But, she knew she must contain herself.

"Leah Hallowsing." He said her name in the same manner as he'd said 'filthy beasts' and yet she enjoyed hearing it.

"Yes, Lord."

"We will go ashore this night and stay at the Snapping Turtle Inn. I would prepare you for the journey."

"Prenalin has told me much of what to expect."

"Crudeness, yes. Their manners are awful. And you will no doubt find yourself seeing trolls and gnomes as often as rats and curs. You mustn't be alarmed."

"No sir."

Leah couldn't help but continue to be spellbound by Kirche's deep, soothing voice. Even when giving orders, he spoke smooth-ly and calmly. While the captain of the *Treasure of the Seas* often barked orders until he was hoarse, Kirche, quiet and arrogant, commanded much more respect, in Leah's view...and fear.

"We seek the kell stone, as you probably know."

"Prenalin says we've been looking for it for years."

"Indeed." He looked down his nose at her and smirked.

Leah cringed. It seemed she couldn't help insulting Lord Kirche every time they spoke.

"Every trip we make here, we attempt to search new places for information."

"What makes you think there is information in the Ruud?"

"Our source told us it was left here."

"Source?"

"The thieving betrayer, Michelruud, stole the stone from us and cowardly ran with it here. He foolishly believed the beasts were good and would live in peace with his folk. It was not long before he was begging Ruhm for help in defending them from the creatures."

"And so you bargained for the stone?"

"We simply impressed upon him the necessity of keeping it from the beasts. So we sent an emissary to retrieve it. Our ancestors tried to destroy it, but it contained powerful magic. So, they sent the emissary to hide it deep in the earth some-where. He was told to reveal the spot to no one. But upon returning home, he refused to tell even the Hass. Under torture, he finally revealed that he felt the best place to hide it, was the last place anyone would expect to find it."

"Torture?" Leah murmured.

"I beg your pardon?"

"The emissary was tortured?"

"Torture, when used toward the righteous ends of Hass, is always acceptable."

"Yes, of course," Leah said, her voice hollow and distant. "And the Ruud would be the last place anyone would expect him to hide the stone."

"Exactly."

"And so it must be here." She turned again and watched as the green forest opened up to the port city, sloping its way up an enormous hill as if trying to climb out of the sea. She remembered her last morning with her father in his cramped office and his story of Dakenruud. Her heart sank; she would have to tell him that Dakenruud gave way under torture and revealed the stone's whereabouts.

"But you do not know exactly where..."

"Sadly, our history says the emissary died before divulging that most important detail."

"Oh, that's...that's so sad."

"Not to worry. We will find the stone."

"May I ask, Lord. Our ancestors wanted it hidden...and yet they wanted to know where...and I assume they never made a move to find it again."

"Naturally one wants to know the whereabouts of one's enemy, even while he wants him underground."

"Then why do we search for it now?"

"Ah, the rumors. Prenalin did not tell you."

Leah shook her head.

"Some years ago we heard stories of a prophecy being on the verge of fulfillment. A child was born with a mark in the wastelands of the east, and he will one day find the kell stone and use its magic to destroy the Ruud."

"And we do not want this to happen?"

Kirche tilted his head to one side and then another in thought, but his face did not change. Leah marveled at his composure, for she knew her mouth would be twisted and her brow furrowed. Her father called it her thinking face; a sudden pang of homesickness twinged at her heart.

"The Hass would not mind if the Ruud were destroyed and this family of wissendes humbled," he said finally, turning to watch the port city as they neared the piers. "But we do not want the kell stone in the hands of the beasts again. They would use its power against us as they did long ago in Ruhm. If we can get the kell stone and use it to defeat the beasts once and for all...without destroying the Ruud...that would be best."

Leah, to her dismay, let out a chuckle and Kirche turned to give her a hard stare.

"Forgive me, Lord Kirche. It just seems like such a monumental task. I fear I giggle when I am afraid." Or hear a plan for the impossible, she thought.

"Something to remember about you in the future, no doubt."

She curtseyed and laughed again, but this time Kirche's gaze was softened. Her father's voice echoed in her head, "You think too much, my dear." Did not Lord Kirche realize that simply by finding and exposing the kell stone and attempting to use it, according to legend, the beasts would regain their former power and become a greater challenge to the folk?

"If I may, Lord," she said. "If you want to rid the country of the beasts, why not just use our firearms and go to war?"

"You speak the mind of the folk in Ruhm," he said, as if it was an insult. He turned toward her and rested his right elbow on the railing. "We have reason to believe that he who wields the stone controls its power."

"I know of no legends that would give us that idea."

"The prophecy itself tells us that a folk child will destroy the Ruud with it. We hypothesize that the beasts kept the stone from us because they have known all along it would make us more powerful than they."

He was nodding as if he'd laid out a great and wondrous new vision. But Leah could only think the Hass had no idea what the kell stone could do, or would do. They only equated it with power, and they wanted it.

"You have your journal, do you not?" he said.

"I do."

"Good. You must write in it often. Make note of what you see and hear. While we are in the realms of the Ruud, you will listen, and pay attention, for any clue of the stone's whereabouts. Your journal may help you by putting pieces of information together, as a puzzle; and when you come upon something that may be of import, you will let me know."

"Yes, Lord." Leah's mind was feverishly repeating his last words, "Let me know." He wanted her to report directly to him and not through Prenalin. She could speak to him on her own!

"And you will also pay close attention to any talk of politics: kings, unification, war, infighting. Anything of the sort."

"Is Ruhm interested in the politics of the Ruud, Lord?"

"Did Prenalin not tell you? We are planning a grand eastern reunification."

"Reunification?"

"Yes. Yes."

Kirche was excited now and his eyes gleamed in the evening light. "You spoke of war earlier. You may have the pleasure of one. For we will take back the descendants of our wissendes, banish the beasts from these lands, and rule here. And the kell stone is going to help us do it."

Chapter Thirty-one

The sky was growing dark when they came to the border of the beast forest and Kwitcher stopped and turned to them.

"I leave you here."

Sadie reached down to shake his hand. "I'll miss you, Kwitcher," she said.

He nodded. "Be careful, Pretty."

She blushed.

"And you, Protector," he said turning to Grayson. "Do so."

"Do so?"

"Protect her."

"Right, I'm Protector now, I get it."

Kwitcher rolled his eyes and Fenn laughed. "Protect her," Kwitcher said again, this time pointing to Sadie.

"Oh, okay, yeah, sure," Grayson said and shook Kwitcher's hand.

"And you, Nearly Orphaned. You must fulfill."

"Fulfill what?"

"Your destiny."

"Don't we all have to do that?"

Kwitcher shook his head. "Not all folk have true destiny. Most are lucky to live out their lives in the land or in the wood in peace and contentment. But you—you have a destiny and you must fulfill it."

"Okay then," he said, thinking it was best to change the subject. "But tell me, Kwitcher...what else can you give to a troll for payment?"

"Almost anything. I usually give buttons. Buttons are amazing things. Trolls love buttons. And paste."

Fenn slapped himself on the forehead and groaned. "We could have given him anything?"

Kwitcher looked puzzled. "We passed. No worries, now."

Fenn shook Kwitcher's hand. "Thank you for all your help, Kwitcher. Would you like a button?"

"Oh, no. Only trolls require payment. And water quacks, you know. Oh, and merfolk."

Fenn laughed. He really did have a lot to learn before he could explore the southern continents.

They waved once more and left the beast forest.

It was dark now and they carefully headed toward a distant smell of campfire, but backed away into the trees when they spotted horses.

"The king's guard," Grayson whispered.

"I'm surprised they're all the way over here," Sadie said.

"Rogget would have spotted them too, I hope," Fenn said and led them south in hopes of finding him.

They came upon him about ten minutes later, asleep and snoring loudly out in the open. Darnit roared upon their arrival, startling him awake.

"Ard, you scared Darnit, now didn't you?"

They laughed. "It's a good thing you have him," Grayson said. "There's a guard not ten minutes out and you were snor-ing loud enough for them to hear in a quiet moment."

"Really Rogget," Sadie said. "What were you thinking? Sleep under a bush at least."

"Then how would you find me?"

"He has a point," Fenn said.

Together they set up kindling against a boulder for a small fire and sat watching in the darkness as Rogget tried to use flint sticks to ignite the

116

brush; he struck them against a rock but they burnt out before he could get them to the dried leaves and weeds. Fenn found this behavior curious. He knew Rogget, who lived in the wild for the most part, ought to be better at lighting fires. On Rogget's third attempt with a new flint, Fenn felt the urge to put his hands over the wood and call the fire to light itself; and thought it might make a fine joke if the fire would actually come to life. He glanced up at Rogget just then and caught him peering at him with a hopeful look in his eyes. Odder behavior still. Rogget shrugged and scratched the third flint against the rock, bringing it to flame and lit his clump of brush. The flame gradually took to the sticks making a glowing fire. They stood around it with their hands outstretched as if they could soak up its warmth through them.

"Well, now, tell me the story. You survived the forest, I see," Rogget said.

"We did.'"

"But you're wounded."

They looked at their hands in the campfire light.

Sadie smiled. "Roster fiends."

"Hmph," Rogget snorted, looking satisfied.

"About that," Grayson murmured. "I'm sorry I made fun. I didn't realize roster fiends could be so vicious."

"Yeah, well now maybe you'll listen to me," Sadie said, but she smiled.

They told Roggett of their adventure, each interrupting the other with excitement. The roster fiends, Kwitcher, the troll, the various beasts of the forest. Sadie and Grayson forgot about Fenn hearing the fairies speak and he decided he'd prefer to let them forget. He was sure he heard the fairies using folk language, but he'd had enough of feeling different.

"And the lord," Roggett said, rubbing his hands near the flames. "Was he kind to you?"

"He acted impatient," Fenn said. "Like he didn't really want us there. But he did what we asked."

"What did you ask?"

"We wanted to hear the prophecy," Grayson said. "For ourselves."

"And he recited it for you?"

"Even better," Sadie said. "He called up the spirit of the lord who said it."

"And the prophecy then, what was it?"

"I have to say," Sadie said digging a biscuit from her pack. "I'm surprised King Evan didn't send in the guard to hear the prophecy, before gathering up kids and putting them in the stone prison. You'd think he'd at least want to know the truth, first."

"Ard, now, that wouldn't be allowed. Fenn—er, kids may-be," Roggett said. "But no adult is allowed into the forest without express permission, or a summons."

"Is that why you couldn't go in?" Grayson asked him.

Roggett looked startled. "Yes. That's right. That's why I couldn't follow you in."

Fenn eyed Roggett carefully. It made perfect sense, and yet, he was sure that was not the reason Roggett couldn't enter the beast forest. Why is everyone so full of mystery? And why only now, after Father forced him from home in Path? Fenn was sure he never knew such deception in folk before.

As if realizing Roggett must know much more about everything than he pretended, Fenn found himself blurting out, "What do you know about a kell stone?"

Rogget stared into the fire, twisting his face into a knot. "I, uh, I don't rightly know. I ain't sure I ever heard of a stone. But the kell...it's the core of the planet—it's why we call her Kell, ain't it?"

"That's the kern," Grayson said. When they all looked at him he said, "Isn't it?"

"Yeah," Fenn said. "That's the kern."

"Na, Na," Rogget said rubbing his beard. The kern is made of kell—pure kell. There, see. They're not exactly the same."

"I do seem to remember something like that," Grayson said with a distant voice.

Fenn looked at him curiously. Again, he sensed deception all around. A dull headache prodded his forehead.

"Do you have to know everything?" Sadie said to Grayson.

"I'm just saying it sounds familiar is all."

There was a slight smile at his lips and he glanced at Fenn before darting his eyes away. Fenn pushed past his suspicions and rubbed his eyes.

"Well, how would you wield a stone of kell?" he said, to no one in particular. "It doesn't make sense."

"Well if there's no such thing as dragons," Sadie said, "maybe there's no such thing as a kell stone either."

Fenn glared at her; why did she have to decide to follow logic now?

Rogget shrugged. "I've no idea. No idea. Let's move on now. Let's get as far from the beast forest as we can." He began packing his gear.

"We just made a fire," Sadie protested, stepping closer to the warmth.

"Well, I don't mean this second. But have a rest and let's move on."

Sadie suddenly collapsed into her knees, covered her head with her hands and began to sob. Rogget stopped his packing and looked frantically about.

"What is it? What'd I say? We can stay by the fire longer if you want. I didn't mean to..."

Fenn turned to Grayson. Sadie was crying, of all things. What should they do?

Sadie lifted her head and rubbed the tears from her eyes. "It's nothing," she said. "It's just that...we have to go now. To the hill country."

Rogget squatted and frowned. "You knew you'd end up doing that in the end...didn't you?"

"I just wish my mum and dad knew I was safe."

Grayson sat beside Sadie. "I can't see my da either. But they'll know. Somehow, they'll know we're okay."

"Father Britt would have sent word about our visit," Fenn said. He realized then how much hope Sadie must have had that they'd find a solution and not have to leave home. No wonder she'd followed him to the port and into the forest.

Rogget made a growling noise and stood again, pacing back and forth a few times. "I could go to Path and give them a message," he said, rubbing his chin. "I could only tell them you're all right. Father Britt said not to tell anyone where we're off to."

"That would be okay," Sadie said, cheering up a bit. "Just so she knows I'm okay. And...and I'll know she's okay."

Grayson looked at Fenn. "Can we do that?"

"I'm sure Father Britt would have sent word."

"But we don't know that," Sadie said, tears welling up in her eyes. "And I just want to make sure everything is all right at home, before ...before we leave the Ruud."

"Okay, okay," Fenn said. He couldn't argue with home-sickness. He almost wished he felt more of it himself. "And you could see Father Treacher, too, in case he didn't get any word. But you'll have to be careful. You don't want to make the guard suspicious."

"It would seem very odd that you're visiting them, if they know we three are missing," Grayson said.

"I can just visit one, then, and that one can get the news to the others. Besides, the wissenry will get word to Treacher eventually."

They agreed that Rogget would visit Sadie's mother at the stationer's; he could pretend to be looking for an encyclopedia, though Grayson was sure he'd forget how to pronounce it before he got there.

"I'll only do it on one condition," Rogget said. "You prom-ise me you'll wait for me at the faire glade in the divide wood. Promise me you'll wait for me there and we'll go to the hill country together."

"We promise," Fenn said.

"I don't know about these two," Sadie said, "but I don't want to go into the hill country without you."

"All right then," Rogget said rubbing his hands together. "It's a plan. You head south, bordering on Cold Sea Port where the guard is less likely to be."

"How do we find the faire glade?" Sadie asked.

"Oh, it's not hard. It's just about in the middle."

Fenn thought that sounded easier than it must be. He had no idea how big the divide wood was, so he doubted he could find the middle.

"It might be on my map of the Ruud," Sadie said, digging out the leather atlas her mother had given her. "But once we're in the wood, I'm not sure a map will do much good."

"So how will we know it when we get there?" Grayson asked.

"Have none of you ever seen the faire glade?" He looked at each of them in surprise as they shook their heads at him. "Well, you'll know it. Trust me."

After packing up Rogget's camp and putting out the fire, they said good bye to him and Darnit, and made their way back to Cold Sea Port in the dark. As they approached the high ridge, they heard music and shouts carried over the wind. They walked to the edge and looked down into the town, lit with lanterns. Sadie breathed in deeply, the wind picking up her hair and lifting it straight back behind her.

"Roast chicken," she said dreamily.

"With gravy," Grayson said rubbing his belly.

They watched the streets below as a group of children ran from one building, down the cobbled road to another, scream-ing and laughing as they went.

Sadie drew in a gasp. "It's the night of the dead."

Chapter Thirty-two

Grayson looked at her and frowned. "We're missing trolling night."

"I never got to participate, anyway," Fenn said, watching the small cottages below, waiting for the children to reemerge and move on to the next.

"The Path kids never stayed up this late for it," Sadie said. "It must be after ten."

"I think Path is darker," Grayson mumbled. "Quieter."

Sadie looked back and forth at them and Fenn looked at Grayson.

"They don't appear to be dressed up special," Fenn said and raised his eyebrows. "Shall we?"

Grayson shook his head. "We really shouldn't. We might get caught."

"By who?" Sadie said. "You heard Tom and Father Britt. The guard stay out of the port for the most part. And they've already come searching for kids with marks and now they've gone. We'll be fine."

"What about Father Britt himself?" Grayson said.

Fenn looked back to the town below, abuzz and alive with celebration. As much as he wanted a chance to participate, he wanted it more for Sadie. Her spirits needed lifting.

"We'll be careful," he said.

"But we don't have masks," Grayson said. "We can't troll without masks."

Sadie dropped her knapsack and grabbed at Grayson's pulling it off his back. "Your oliphant leaves," she said. "Get a knife, we'll cut holes for our eyes."

"I was saving those for Jeopard."

"Oh, never mind Jeopard. You can draw him a picture. How'll we keep them on. Fenn, you got any string?"

"Just my boot laces."

They each took a lace from one of their boots and used it to tie an oliphant leaf to their faces. They stood for a moment looking at one another in the darkness and laughed.

"We look ridiculous," Grayson said.

"Perfect," Fenn said. "Come on." And he headed down the steep slope toward the rambling port city with Grayson and Sadie behind him.

The first cottage on the outskirts of town, built into the sloping hill, was adorned with a cauldron, bubbling with steaming stew, the twig symbol of the crone—a woman flying on a stick—and a jack-o-lantern on the step. Fenn knocked on the door and they heard brittle, high-pitched laughter from within. He smiled at Grayson and Sadie through his mask and could only assume they did the same.

When the door opened, they were bathed in soft candle light as a woman held up a lantern to see them.

"Impish spirits of the dead," she said with a giggle. "Go off with you, be dead again come the sun." She held out a wooden pail filled with apples and they each took one and bellowed, "A treat!"

"Now be off with your bribe and do me no harm," the old woman cackled and they ran down the street to the next home and the next, stuffing their knapsacks with food treasures. As they got closer to the bay, the air hung heavier with salt and the cottages were replaced with inns, shops, and ware-houses. Still, the proprietors stood at their doors, laughter and shouting erupting from within, with treats for the children.

At the wharf, they found an open door and inside travelers were eating and drinking. Just inside the door was a table at which sat a large bearded man with a patch over one eye.

"Ard, there be village dead. Quick, Passel, something to throw at them to make them leave us be."

"Here, Duit, some nuts from the gathering," a man called from the bar where he sat with a pint of cold brew. He tossed a bag across the room and the bearded man dug through it.

"Aye, this'll keep 'em at bay." And he tossed nuts at them, pelting their chests as they giggled and picked them up off the floor. "Now off, and be dead no more come the sun."

They ran out into the street again.

Sadie gasped for air under her leaf and said, "This is ten times better than at home."

"Where next?" Grayson said, breathless, but lifting his mask to take another bite of apple.

"This way," Sadie said and Fenn followed them closer to the harbor, as they looked for more open doors and willing givers. Fenn noticed that there were no other children this close to the water just as a woman burst out of an open door to screech at them.

"You're too far in, gets back up to the cottages. You've no business this deep."

They stopped, startled, and Sadie murmured, "Yes, ma'am."

They turned and took off their masks.

"Where are we exactly?" Sadie asked, looking around. Her hair was wild and damp on her head.

Fenn pointed. "The ridge is up there. We've come all the way to the wharf. I guess kids aren't allowed down here."

"If we went on just a bit more," Grayson said, "we'd be able to see the ships."

"And be taken aboard one as captive," the old woman said, still staring at them.

"Yes, ma'am," Grayson said, losing his enthusiasm.

"We have to go this way to get back up," Fenn said, lead-ing them back along the block looking for the road they'd taken south toward the sea.

At once they came upon a short cobbled road leading southward to the pier where a group of folk nearly ran them off the path.

"Out of the way," one of them scolded and they backed up against a stone wall as the folk filed past them, heading up the road to where the old woman stood. Most were dressed in fine linen, unlike anyone wore in the Ruud. Two of the men were adorned in velvet cloaks of purple. One wore a velvet tam, but the other wore a hat like Fenn had never seen before, shaped like a huge arch on his head, and he wore a chain of large gold links with a medallion hanging from it against his velvet cloak. On the medallion was a tree in flames.

Grayson and Sadie gasped and Fenn turned to them.

"The Hass of Emorah," Grayson whsipered and looked wide-eyed and frightened at Fenn.

The group passed, then their luggage bearers, and finally, a young woman, dressed in a fine tunic and long skirt, her green silk slippers peering from beneath it with each step. As she passed, Fenn was awestruck at the sight of her chestnut brown hair, tied at the nape of her neck with a black ribbon, and falling down her back to well below her waist. As the group continued on, forcing their way through the night crowds, she turned back to them and cast a worried look at Fenn.

Once they reached the cottages, all was quiet. The night of the dead had ended for the children of the port and they climbed back up the slope, weary and tired, but full in the stomach and satisfied.

Fenn caught up with Grayson, who marched quickly across the ridge, and grabbed at his arm, but he silenced him with a glance at Sadie and a finger to his lips.

They camped in the wood just south of Damon Village in the early morning, building a small fire and lying near it with their blankets. Sadie began to snore almost as soon as her head hit the ground. Fenn turned to look Grayson in the firelight. He was still awake.

"What was it? Back at the port. You said something about those men."

"Did they not tell you about the Hass of Emorah at the wissenry?"

He shook his head. "No. But I've seen them before."

"They come to the Ruud every year."

"Then why were you scared?"

"You'd be scared too, if they let you out more. And if you'd been allowed to read *The Book of Katze*."

"Tell me."

"They come to the village every year and find some fault every time. Last year they put Ma'am Hardy in the stocks. Ma'am Hardy!"

"In the stocks?"

"Quiet, don't wake Sadie. She's scared to death of the Hass. All the kids are. They'll whip you just as soon as look at you."

"What? Just up and start whipping?"

"If you walk in front of their horse or bump them, yes. Mean folk. The meanest you'd ever meet."

Grayson said no more and Fenn watched the small blaze of fire, fuming. Maybe Sadie was right. Even if only figuratively, he was beginning to see that he'd been kept locked up at the wissenry. But the girl with the long tresses—she didn't look mean at all. Was it possible?

Fenn dreamed of the tall blond man with the gold medal-lion striding purposefully toward him. The strange hat on his head opened and out flew a roster fiend. It darted at him, pecking at his eyes and he woke with his own screams in his ears, his mother's charm and hemp rope burning on his skin.

Chapter Thirty-three

Leah woke the next morning woozy from dreams of sail-ing and rocking back and forth and to and fro. She near-ly toppled when she stood from the bed too quickly and staggered to the window. Throwing open the sash, she peered out onto the glorious port city of Damon Wall, the sun rising over the ridge in the distance, and gulped in the sea air.

Crude indeed. The Snapping Turtle Inn was just as nice as her own home, with clean wood floors and soft feathery beds. Perhaps Kirche and Prenalin slept in marble castles on silk, but few in Ruhm would scoff at the pleasures of the Ruud, so far as what she'd seen.

After a knock at the door, a plump girl entered with a tray.

"Ard, mum, you're up already," she said and curtseyed. Leah laughed at the gesture and gave a little dip herself before crossing the room, hand outstretched to greet her.

"I'm Leah, of Ruhm," she said.

The girl put the tray on the tiny table by the wall, wiped her trembling hands on her clean apron, and took Leah's hand gratefully.

"I'll be Wanda Kay. I'm to make the beds and fetch your meals, if you want to eat in. And I'll draw water for the bath if you like. I'll even comb out your hair. Such lovely hair 'tis."

"Oh, no," Leah gasped, reaching behind her head to pull her hair off her shoulders and shake it out onto her back. "Only those of my tier may touch my hair—or a member of my immediate family."

It was barely dawn and already Wanda's deep auburn locks were escaping her head scarf in frizzy twirls, as if she'd been hard at work scrubbing floors. She cocked her head to one side and said, "Is that so?"

Leah plopped herself back on the bed and smiled at the girl. "Is your tier system different?"

"I don't rightly know what you mean, ma'am. What is a tier...exactly?" Wanda gave another nervous curtsey.

Leah began to understand Kirche's distaste for the gesture.

"It's a level of society. Do your kings and queens wear their hair differently from shop keepers or servants?"

Wanda put a wide face on and opened her mouth to speak but no sound found its way out.

"In Ruhm," Leah said. "Only those in the higher tiers may wear their hair long. When I entered the Hass school at age six, my locks were shorn right up to my head, to symbolize my status as a servant to Hass. And thereafter I was not to cut my hair until I graduated and was given my status."

"Ah, I see, mum. So you've grown your hair for some time."

"Eleven years. And as a member of the Inner Circle of Hass, I am to keep my hair at just this length." Instinctively, Leah tugged at her hair, pulling it from under her, and laid it out on the bed in a deep brown fan.

"And no one may touch it, you say?"

"No one below me." She winced as she said it, only then realizing how it must sound to someone unused to tiers and status. "You must have servants here in the Ruud who don't enjoy the same privileges as the kings...of course."

"Well, yes, of course, mum. I apologize if I worried you. I won't touch your hair. But I can do all the other things you might require of a... servant."

"I can do most for myself," she said. "But don't let me do anything that would get you into trouble. I wouldn't have you put in the stocks or whipped on my account."

Wanda frowned. "No 'm. I won't. Tis my father's inn—he wouldn't whip me for naught. I've brought some biscuits and hog-sausage gravy and an autumn apple salad for your breakfast. The men of your'n are downstairs but they told me to tell you to eat and take your time."

"Did they now?" Leah laughed. "Have you traveled much Wanda?"

"Oh, no 'm. Not at all. Why, I've never left the city."

"Honestly?"

"I swear by Mutterede's daughter."

"Well, I feel wonderfully free and...and I dare say, mischie-vous."

"Do you now?"

"I do. And I wondered if it was the travel. I've never traveled before either, you see."

"Ah, well ain't we a pair? I'd say to ask your gent'men friends, but I'll be telling you straight now that they do not appear free or mischievous this morning ma'am."

"Well, that's the Hass for you."

"Yes 'm."

"You know of the Hass?"

"Everyone in the Ruud knows the Hass. Our king folk pay tribute every year in thanks for the Hass' help in settling our little Ruud. It was kind of Ruhm to see us off so graciously."

Indeed, Leah thought.

"Is Ruhm as they say ma'am?" Wanda said. With a curtsey she shooed Leah off the bed and to the table for her meal, before pulling the sheets back into place. "Is it grand and made of marble?"

"Much of it is. Our main village is as busy and crowded as your port city, but ten times bigger."

"That much?"

"But our shops and homes are not unlike yours. It's just the halls and palaces and libraries and such that are sleek and ornate."

"Sounds lovely. I hear you have no beasts in Ruhm."

"We have some. In zoos, of course. And in the mountains of the north there are still some loose. I hear I might see a gnome or some such on my visit."

"Surely, you might, as you travel through the woods and forests. Don't be fearing them; they're harmless."

"So, is it only the larger beasts that are violent?"

"Violent?" She stopped plumping the pillows and turned to Leah. "Why I wouldn't rightly call them violent. We hear a centaur often pulls rowdy children into the beast forest, but he only does it as a lesson. No one gets hurt. And secretly I think the children like it. Else why would they continue to play so near the edge?"

"The folk of the Ruud aren't afraid of the beasts?"

"Well, now, they might be afraid, especially with the new bairn on the loose and all. But they fear war, more than violence ...if you take my meaning, mum."

"Yes, I think I do. Who is this new bairn then?"

"Oh, he was born some ten or twelve years ago. I have it on good authority that he's here somewhere in the Ruud, plotting and planning. You'd best be on your way soon as your tribute business is done with. You don't want to be caught up that frightful magic."

"You mean the kell stone?"

Wanda tucked the bed cover under the pillows and again looked at her.

126

"I don't know anything about a stone. I just know the bairn has some magic power. And he's got the mark of evil on his arm, so they say. And I heard it on good authority. The king of Michelruud—Evan it is, though he's dead now—he took to rounding up possibles and hauling them off to Steingefan."

"Where's that?"

"It's the first castle of the Ruud. Quite old and falling apart, now. But it does nicely as a prison."

"Your king is putting children in prison?"

"Well, not *my* king, that I'll tell you. No, no. The king of Michelruud. This here's Damon Wall. Our good King Ricker wouldn't do such a thing. Though, I hear it on good authority that he ought. We're torn, I tell you. Somes of us think all the children of age should be harnessed and kept an eye on. And others think it's just old wives tales. And it's true, old wives do tell quite the tales. I'm keeping you from eating. Eat, eat."

"I'll eat; I promise. But tell me more about the bairn." Leah pulled apart a biscuit and poured creamy gravy on it.

"Well, there's not much to tell, exceptin' we all thought he was going to destroy our Ruud and kill King Evan. Not that King Evan didn't deserve it. Don't go tellin' I said that." Here she let out a chortle and a cough. "But King Evan up and died, so now it'll be his son King Welk the bairn will be after. After all, it was his father who did the deed and brought on the prophecy."

"What deed?"

"Well, as I hear it, he had a party of eis murdered all be-cause one of them was engaged to marry his son. That's the story as it's being told. And this is his punishment—the time of the bairn has come. Of course, the bairn was predicted long ago and I s'pose the murders was just the tipping point—yes'm, Evan's evil deed brought the prophecy to pass. I have it on good authority."

"I see. And you know nothing about a stone?"

"There are lots of lovely stones in the mines up north there, if that's what you're after. I hear tell your Hass likes the stones for tribute. I'd take the apples were I Hass. I hear tell there aren't so good apples on any continent on Kell."

"They are wonderful," Leah said munching the apple salad. It was mixed with walnuts, dried grapes, and berries. "We get them over in Ruhm."

"Not near so good, I'm sure."

"No, I mean, we get them sent to us from the Ruud. We call them Ruud apples."

"Oh, well, then I guess if you already have 'em...I suppose rocks are nice, too."

Leah laughed. When Wanda finally bustled herself out of the room, Leah dressed and took her journal from the top drawer in the chest by the window. Her room had a small desk with an inkwell and quills and a row of sharpened lead writers, her favorite.

Skimming past her previous entries, she relived the memories of her days and nights on the *Treasure of the Seas*, of the gentle soothing rock of the ship that made all three porters and even Redd, the largest of the body guards, sick for much of the journey. She read of her brief encounters with Kirche and the last evening on deck when he spoke to her for nearly five minutes. She read of the shifting of plates and her stifling of laughter. And she read with renewed sadness about learning of the torture of her ancestor, Dakenruud.

So much adventure had already happened. She picked up a lead writer and dated a new page.

I wanted desperately to tell Lord Kirche, last evening on the ship, the story Father told me on my last morning visit with him in his tiny office. Something about Kirche's voice...well, it makes a folk melt a bit and want to tell him everything. But I kept my wits about me. And when Kirche mentioned my journal, the very one I write in now, I was instantly taken back there to Father's office, to his loud ticking pocket watch on the desk and the dim light of the room. Dakenruud gave a journal of his travels to his brother Abueruud. Could he have disclosed the very place he hid the kell stone? Does Father have that journal? I can hardly wait to return home to find out.

A loud knock at the door startled her and she snapped the book shut. Her heart raced as she returned it to the top drawer of the dresser, covering it with her delicates. Certainly not even Prenalin would touch those.

"Leah," Prenalin called through the door. "We are ready for our day in the port. Do hurry."

She smiled and sang out, "On my way," as she tied her hair behind her back. It would not hurt, she thought, to keep some information from Lord Kirche and reveal it at the appropriate time. After all, she couldn't mention a journal that might not exist; that would only lead to trouble for her father. But if she could find the location of the kell stone, she would be rewarded greatly, and it would certainly please Lord Kirche.

They spent a tiring day wandering the port city inspecting the shops and warehouses. Prenalin ran a constant lecture of the proceedings, while Kirche walked ahead with his guard, scarcely aware of Leah's presence.

The folk of the Ruud could trade only with Ruhm. Even goods that came from other continents must go through Ruhm. At the docks, foreign ships and boats were inspected to be sure they weren't carrying these illicit goods.

Leah carried the leather book in which Kirche kept his notes. Interspersed with Prenalin's constant lectures, he'd nod at a number or notation Kirche would tell him and then tap the leather book of papers in Leah's hands and bark the information at her. She noted which ships were in port and what Kirche found on the manifests.

The folk were allowed only a small number of firearms and certain types of weapons, the numbers of which were also regulated. Leah wrote down how many short knives, daggers, and swords the blacksmith had on hand. All firearms were counted and entered. Folk were stopped on the street and questioned about how many firearms they saw in the course of a day and when was the last time they shot one.

Kirche would then put on a satisfied smile, turn to Prenalin and nearly whisper, "none." After which Prenalin would cease his yapping and call out "none from stout woman carrying basket." And Leah dutifully jotted it down on the "Street Answers on Firearms" page. It was all very senseless and silly. But Leah reminded herself, every few minutes or so, that it must be deadly important to Ruhm.

The folk all seemed friendly enough; they smiled and bobbed their heads in deference. Lord Kirche and Prenalin basked in their affection. But Leah sensed tension in their manners. Fear, perhaps. While Prenalin and Kirche let them bow, listened to their answers to routine questions and moved on with nary a second thought, Leah often turned back to watch the folk sigh in relief, wipe a brow, or shake off nervous hands.

This was more than tribute, she began to understand. The Hass exerts much control here, she thought. She nearly shivered herself at the idea. By the end of the day, Leah felt she'd walked a thousand miles on the cobbled streets, though often they rode in a carriage—she was forced to sit on the perch beside the driver.

That evening she fell onto her soft bed and closed her eyes as Wanda set up tea at the little dining table.

"Your'n gentlemen folk will sup downstairs. Would you be joining them?"

"No, I think not," she said.

"I'll bring up your supper then. Can I get you anything else?

"Yes, you can." Leah sat up on the bed. "Don't sigh in relief when you leave the room."

Wanda stared hard at her, her face frozen with a small smile. Leah thought she must think her mad, but finally the girl dipped her head just a bit and said, "I'll do my best, mum."

Chapter Thirty-four

Welk stood in the great hall watching as a gathering of folk from the village of Path moved his father's belongings from his chambers upstairs into storage and his own down into the king's quarters.

"Keep it up, folk, good work," he said occasionally, reminding them that pork pies and steins of ale were their reward as soon as the work was complete.

Welk allowed the customary three day mourning whereby his father's body was displayed in the great hall and the folk covered it with flowers. But he forbade the wearing of full black. He feared that so few would show any grief it would make a mockery of his father's legacy, such as it was.

Dunham approached and bowed. "Sire, I have been to the stationer's three times now and each time he has evaded my questions."

"Explain."

"I told him the king asks about our history; he wishes books. At first, Stationer Pratt told me he would search for some and bade me return the morrow, and so I did. Then he regaled me with a story about the transfer of books from one stationer's office to another, seeming to say he'd lost them."

"Seeming to say?"

"Yes, Sire. I felt certain he was not being forthright. And so I returned once more today and inquired again, upon which he said he'd never had any books on the history of the Ruud. I pointed to the very obvious *History of the Ruud* on one of his tables and he said, 'oh, yes, well that one of course.' He nearly sputtered, Sire. He's hiding something."

Welk grinned at Dunham. "You're quite the detective, my man. I think you are right. Certainly his answers regarding his daughter and the innkeeper's son were vague at best."

"Indeed, Sire. To think we would accept that they were on some sort of sight seeing tour in the wasteland. Of all the silly notions."

"I have a plan." Welk led Dunham to the king's library and closed the door. "Hear me out, Dunham, before you balk. I would have Sorgood arrest the stationer—"

"—arrest the Stationer to the King?"

"And the innkeeper and Father Treacher of the wissenry."

"Sire...but...but."

"Hear me, Dunham. This is a tangled mess. We must find the child who was born in the wasteland, whether he be a child of prophecy or not. Or at the very least, we must let the folk of the Ruud believe we are doing all we can, to allay their fears. I for one would like nothing more than to find this child and keep him under watch. But none of the children in Steingefan appear to be our target. I fear to say so, but, these children are simply average."

"You would expect this prophecy child to be special."

"Wouldn't you? And who more special than the stationer's daughter?"

"But she wasn't born in the wasteland, Sire."

"How do we know? The stationer and his wife travel often."

"I'm sure we can find out, Sire."

"You miss my point, Dunham. I'm not saying I believe the stationer's daughter is the child of prophecy. But the folk of Path and Michelruud want something done. We must find the missing children. And perhaps they will return from hiding if we put some pressure on their parents."

"But arrest a wissende?"

Welk sighed. "I know it's highly out of the ordinary. But of the three missing children of Path, you must admit the one most likely to have been born in the wasteland is the wissenry orphan."

"But arrest the stationer? And Father Treacher?"

"What about the innkeeper?"

"And the innkeeper—Sire, you mock me."

Welk smiled. "I told you to hear me out. They will not wait long in the prison. And what we really seek, our history, might also be had with a little pressure."

Dunham opened his mouth and started to speak, but hesitated and closed it again. "Now there you have a point."

Welk laughed and slapped the old man on the back.

"And it is a comfortable jail," Dunham said.

"Of course it is. There are many things to gain from this. The folk will be further calmed at our progress—we've had petitions to arrest these folk already. We may lure the missing children out of hiding. And we may have our history."

"Indeed, Sire. But it is a nasty business."

Welk balked. "All your time serving Evan the Fearsome and you quiver at this minor thing?"

"'Tis too true, Sire."

Dunham was doubtful, Welk could see. The old man had, perhaps, served too long under King Evan and was jaded. Welk would do more to reassure him that he intended no harm to anyone. But he admitted, at least to himself, that he wasn't sure how far he would go. What if he found proof that there was a child of prophecy who meant to destroy the Ruud? Would he not do whatever a king must do to save his folk?

Chapter Thirty-five

In darkness the next evening, they crossed the Damon Wall range, and hiked into the divide wood to camp again. They woke at mid-day and made their way eastward in the wood. Fenn hadn't any chance to question Grayson further about the history, or the men in the port and his mind raced feverishly whenever they were all quiet, trying to sort out this puzzle that had become his life.

"So, I'm guessing there will be fairies there," Sadie said. "That's how we'll know it."

"I told you before," Grayson said. "The fairies have aban-doned it."

"You don't know. You've never been there, either."

Grayson looked insulted. "If it says so in the encyclopedia, then it's so."

"Well your encylo-pede didn't help you much with the roster fiends, did it?" Sadie looked triumphant.

"Maybe I didn't read up on roster fiends? Don't blame the book."

"Well, if there aren't any fairies in it, how will we know when we get there?"

Fenn heard a rustling up ahead of them and stopped. "Shh."

They moved forward carefully. As they neared a clearing, Sadie gasped. Huddled against a pine stump was a small child, whimpering and shivering, wearing only an under tunic. Her thin lips were slightly blue from the cold and her eyes were wide and red from crying. She covered her face with her hands when she saw them.

Sadie approached and knelt beside her.

"Are you all right?"

The child stared at her from between her fingers, too frightened to speak.

"How long have you been lost?"

Still, she said nothing.

Grayson looked around at the trees surrounding them. "She must have wandered from home earlier this morning. She'd have never lasted a night out here without a blanket. We need to get her to the nearest village. Where do you suppose we are?"

"It would have to be Woodside," Fenn said. "That's the only village near here."

"Do you live in Woodside?" Sadie asked.

"She's not yet three years old," Grayson said. "She probably doesn't even know."

"Well, come on. We have time to get her to the outskirts."

Sadie took the child's hand and she got up and walked with them taking tiny steps and stopping to be lifted over a branch.

"This will take forever," Grayson said. "Let me carry her." He lifted her up and she buried her face in his neck and wrapped her arms around him.

Sadie smiled. "She likes you."

"I have a little sister," he said. "They like to be carried."

They hiked south again and before they reached the end of the wood voices rang out from far and near, calling, "Illeya!"

"They're looking for her," Sadie said.

When they reached the edge of the wood, they peered out from behind the trees.

"Illeya!" a woman called from several yards away, coming toward the wood, startling them back into hiding.

Grayson put the girl down and Sadie pushed her forward. "Go on," she said. The tot walked a few steps out from the wood, looked back, and then ran away from them screaming, "Mama!"

Darting back behind the trees when they saw the woman approach, they heard her scream and begin sobbing. Sadie smiled and turned back into the forest. Grayson followed, but Fenn lagged behind. The woman's crying echoed in his head, his mother's charm throbbed on his chest, and his hemp braid twisted back and forth, irritating his skin.

They turned east again, and headed toward the middle of the wood where the faire glade was said to be. The farther toward the glade they got, the hotter Fenn's charm grew against his chest, until it burned his skin and he was overcome with the feeling of being lost and abandoned.

He stopped. "Wait."

They turned back to him with puzzled looks on their faces.

Pulling at the charm under his tunic to get it off his skin, he said, "We have to save the children of Path."

They stared at him.

"We can't go to the hill country. We have to go to Steingefan and somehow set them free."

Sadie and Grayson looked at each other. Then Grayson said, "But even if we could save them, where would they go? They'd just be rounded up again, wouldn't they?"

"Maybe," he said "But we have to do it."

Sadie said, "Maybe they could go to the hill country."

"A gang of children living alone?"

"Maybe everyone can go. The kids and their families?" she said.

"What, the families of Path just up and leave? Who would farm? Who would trade?"

"Just the kids, then," Sadie said.

"I agree it's the right thing to do," Grayson said, looking sad. "But I just don't see that it would do any good...in the end."

"It is the right thing," Fenn said.

Grayson nodded.

"But you don't want to do it?"

"Not really, no. What good will it do? The kids can't survive alone."

"We're surviving," Sadie said.

"But grown-ups gave us food. And we've had Rogget."

"We can all figure out how to get food. And we'll still have Rogget."

"But what about the beast folk in the hill country? Not to mention the main folk."

Sadie shrugged. "I don't know. Together we could do it."

"Rogget would never let us go."

"He couldn't stop us going to the beast lord," Fenn said.

"This is different. We're in the middle of the Ruud now. There's no way he'd let us go to Steingefan."

"Then we go without him."

"We can't just leave him. Imagine how worried he'd be."

"We'll leave him a message. We'll tell him we'll meet him a little later than planned."

Grayson shrugged. "It doesn't seem at all crazy to you?"

Sadie laughed but said nothing, looking defeated and bewildered.

Grayson seemed to think about it for a while before he said, "So we'd leave Rogget a message at the faire glade...if we decided to do it."

"All right then," Fenn said. "We continue on to faire glade and decide there. And if we go to Steingefan, we leave a message for Rogget."

This was agreeable to all three of them and they hiked to the faire glade in silence. The charm, too, seemed satisfied and cooled slightly to gently warm Fenn's skin. He pulled at the hemp rope and brought the charm out to look at it. He was hollow in the pit of his stomach as he held it in his fingers; and though his legs kept moving him forward, it was as if they were made of lead. Suddenly, he felt a hand cover his and squeeze it slightly. Startled, he stopped moving and dropped the gold to his chest, looking around frantically.

"Ghosts," he said and the others turned to him.

"There aren't any ghosts in the divide wood," Grayson said.

"Are you sure?" Sadie asked, now looking around with Fenn.

"I'm sure."

"You can't be positive, though," Fenn said.

Grayson shrugged. "Well I suppose there could be some, but no one's seen any for generations; they all gather in the beast forest now."

"What did you see?" Sadie asked him.

"I felt it. It touched me."

"You'd have seen something. We would have seen it too, if it got that close," Grayson said.

"No, I didn't see anything, but I felt a hand; it touched me."

Grayson shrugged. "We're all tired, Fenn. You probably imagined it."

They continued on and Fenn struggled with what had happened. Had it been one of the sluagh, or was it a vision? If he'd only imagined it, why did his hand still feel the warmth of it?

Chapter Thirty-six

As soon as they stepped into the faire glade, they knew they had arrived. The afternoon sunlight, streaming through the trees, danced with the colors of the rainbow. Specks of gold and silver dust floated in the air. The wind in the trees seemed to recite poetry in an unfamiliar language. And the grass at their feet was warm, soft, and giving.

Filled with peace and contentment, they sat and rested, pulling food from their sacks. They ate in silence and explored the glade for several hours. Grayson pocketed rocks of all colors that glistened as if they were wet. Sadie pulled clovers and daisies from grassy patches and pulled off their leaves and petals, chanting ancient rhymes. Fenn lay on the ground with his eyes closed concentrating on the slight wind in the pines. As the day wore on, he thought more about Grayson's decision. He didn't want to push the issue of the children of Path on him until he was ready to talk about it. But he wanted to leave soon—the fate of the children was uncertain and he felt an urgency that he barely understood.

"I've thought about it," Grayson finally said as the sky was growing dark. "I'll go with you, if you're determined to save them, but the only thing it might do is encourage the parents to fight the guard—if they see we're brave enough to try. And then, in the end, whole families would be in Steingefan. We can't get thirty or so kids our own age to group together and make for the hill country. They'd all be caught again and maybe us with them. And if too many families just up and left Path, the village might be devastated. The folk left behind might spread out around the Ruud and the Michelruud guard would likely use that as an excuse to make a move on Aaronland and Damon Wall. So then there would be war."

"All that," Fenn said, "just because we rescue the children of Path?"

Sadie chimed in, "I agree with Fenn. If Path falls, it will be the king's doing. How long will our parents let us be hunted and imprisoned? And once they've decided they can't find this bairn they're stupidly looking for, the guard will move on the other kingdoms of the Ruud for more children and we'll have war, anyway."

"So, you think our interfering won't matter," Grayson said.

"That's right."

"It won't do any good, it won't matter, but you still think we should do it," he said.

Sadie and Fenn nodded.

He shrugged. "All right then. How do we leave a message for Rogget?"

Sadie looked around. "We'll carve it in a tree. The largest one there."

She pulled a knife from her sack and scraped the bark off the large pine tree at the north end of the glade and said to Grayson, "How do you spell Steingefan?"

As he spelled for her, she carved the words 'to steingefan' in the tree.

"There," she said, smiling proudly at the other two.

Fenn started to turn away, satisfied, but the sound of creaking and rubbing, wood against wood, made him stop; his eyes widened and his mouth fell open as the three of them watched the tree's bark spread out to cover the message. The pine looked just as it had before, as if nothing had been done to harm it.

Sadie was dumbstruck at first, but then twisted her face in determination and scraped the bark off once more. "Spell it again," she told Grayson. This time she repeated aloud each letter as she carved, 'to steingefan.' And, just to be sure, she carved over her message a second time.

"Cover that up, stupid tree."

Obliging, the tree stretched and screeched as the bark regrew covering the message. An audible, frustrated sigh escaped from it when it had finished.

Sadie kicked the tree, scraped the bark off again and shouted, "Spell it again."

Grayson turned a frightened face to Fenn, but dutifully spelled; and Sadie carved once more, this time in very large letters: 'TO STEINGEFAN!' She held her hands against it, in a pitiful attempt to keep the bark from spreading over her message. But the bark regrew seemingly with as much enthusi-asm as Sadie had put into carving.

"Argh!" she screamed and kicked the tree again. A branch shot down from above and smacked her across the backside, knocking Grayson and Fenn to the ground.

"I'm sorry, I'm sorry," Sadie whimpered.

"Forget it," Fenn said. "We'll have to think of something else."

They looked around the glade for a while. Sadie suggested digging up grass to say Steingefan, but Grayson balked at the difficult work. "And it'll probably just grow right back."

"Rocks," Fenn said. "We could arrange rocks to spell it out."

"Where can we find that many rocks?" Sadie whined. "We'll be looking all night."

"It's getting dark, already," Grayson said. "We won't have any light."

"Does anyone have a lead writer?" Fenn said digging into his sack. "Grayson, you must have one."

"I do, but we only have Sadie's maps to write on. We shouldn't leave one of those behind."

"I have a biscuit wrapper," Sadie said.

Grayson did his best to write a message on the slick, waxy, biscuit wrapper with his piece of lead and they stuck it through the tip of a twig hanging from one of the trees.

"He'll never see that," Sadie said.

"It'll blow off in the wind," Grayson said.

"It's all we've got," Fenn said. And they gathered up their supplies and headed back toward Path and on to Steingefan. "Maybe we'll pass him on the way and we won't have to worry about it."

Grayson shrugged his shoulders. "Keep your ears open for grunts."

They hiked west again until they heard the rushing of the river and turned to follow it north, keeping on the Aaronland side. About two miles up, they heard voices and splashing and snuck up on a group of three boys trying to fish in the river from the bank opposite them. Fenn sidled cautiously from tree to tree, until he came to the shoreline and called out, trying to whisper, but knowing he wouldn't be heard without some volume.

"Quiet down."

The boys were startled, dropped their fishing sticks, and started to run; but they stopped when they saw him.

"Who is that? What are you doing here?" the larger boy asked.

"Same as you, probably."

"Hiding?"

He nodded. "There are guards posted at the bridges and the high crossing just north of here. You're making too much noise." Fenn realized that as loud as they were talking over the rush of the water, they might be heard by the guard. He looked nervously up the river.

"Where are you from then, Path?"

Fenn nodded. "And you?"

"Timber."

"How many have they taken from Timber?"

"Don't know. We all ran when the guard arrived. Where are you camped? How many of you are there?"

"We're not camped anywhere," Fenn said. "We're headed to Steingefan."

The larger boy said, "What for?"

"We're going to help the others escape."

The three on the other side looked at one another and whispered among themselves. The larger one then called out, "You're lying. You just said you came from Path."

Fenn sighed with frustration. "We went to the port for help and now we're on our way back."

"You can come over to our camp and get warm for a while if you want," One of the smaller boys said.

The larger boy punched him. "We don't even know who he is and you're asking him over?"

Fenn shook his head. "The crossing will soak us. We don't want to freeze crossing twice in one night."

"You wouldn't need to cross back over," the large boy said, sounding suspicious. "If you're headed up north to Steingefan."

"We want to stay on this side as long as possible. But go back and ask your mates if anyone wants to come with us and help us rescue the children of Path. Maybe you'll find some from Timber as well."

They paused staring at him, but finally the large one nodded. "We'll be back in a few minutes."

Fenn turned back into the trees to find Sadie and Grayson.

"What if they're spies and are going to set the guard on us?" Sadie whispered.

"I don't think so. I scared them pretty good when I called out. I think they're hiding, same as us."

"I hope you're right," Grayson said.

They waited fifteen minutes before the large boy returned alone.

"Hey," he called out in a loud whisper and Fenn returned to the shore. "We took a poll and everybody thinks you're crazy."

Fenn smiled. "So nobody wants to come with us?"

138

"Nobody can get into Steingefan. And nobody can get out."

"I guess that means no."

"You'll end up in the prison yourselves."

"Maybe," Fenn said. "If so, we'll see you there soon enough."

Leaving the Timber boy to the darkness, they continued on, making their way to the point they crossed days before when they'd first left Path. Sadie stopped and watched the rushing waters of the river glistening in the moonlight. Path was just on the other side, through the woods, not more than five miles. Fenn could almost see it pulling at Sadie.

"We may not see Rogget again," she said.

"I'm sure he'll be okay," Grayson said.

"But we'll never know if he saw our parents."

"No," Fenn said. "He'll get our message and follow us to the prison. We'll see him soon."

Sadie shook her head. "We can't be sure."

She turned to look at Fenn and he knew what she was thinking.

"You could get caught," he said.

"I have to go."

"What," Grayson said. "You're going to cross? You're going home?"

"Just for a few minutes. I need to find out if my mum and dad are all right."

"We may as well, while we're so close," Grayson said.

"But why wouldn't they be okay?" Fenn said.

Sadie and Grayson looked at him like lost calves, their eyes round with concern. He could almost hear them say it: that connection they had with their parents drew them. They needed comfort, even if only temporary, before they left for good.

"Don't you want to see Father Treacher? What if he has news of Lucas?" Sadie said.

But it wasn't the same. Of course it wasn't the same for a wissenry orphan.

"I want to see him," he said. "But I won't risk getting caught to do it. I know Father Treacher wouldn't want me to."

Tears welled up in Sadie's eyes and she looked to the ground.

"I'm going anyway," she said.

Fenn knew that her heart was pulling at her stronger than her head. He was willing to bet her mother would be angry at what she was risking, but he admired her for her daring anyway.

"I have to go with her then," Grayson said weakly. "We can't let her go alone."

"What's that supposed to mean?" Sadie grumbled. "You think I can't handle the woods on my own?"

"I didn't mean that. I—"

"Oh, admit it, waiter boy, you think girls are not as brave as boys."

"I do not. You're clearly brave."

"Ah, but not smart, is that where you're going with it?"

"You said that, not me."

"Enough," Fenn said. "Did it never occur to you that Grayson just wants an excuse to go home too?"

They both looked at him wide-eyed.

"I do not need an excuse," Grayson said. "And just because I think Sadie shouldn't go to Path alone doesn't mean I think less of her, or girls, or—why does everything have to be so complicated with you?"

"All right, all right," Sadie said. "You can come, I guess."

"What do you mean, you guess? I can go if I want."

"You can't follow me if I don't want you around."

"Will you two stop it," Fenn yelled. "Why can't you get along?"

Grayson turned his face and glared into the woods while Sadie pouted at the river.

"Okay," Grayson said turning to Sadie. "Truce. For the trip at least."

"Truce," she said and shook his hand.

Fenn nodded. "Good. I'll wait here. If there's trouble, I'll make my way south one mile to wait."

"Okay," Grayson said and slapped him on the shoulder. "Get some sleep. We'll be back in a couple of hours."

Two hours later the sun began to dispel the darkness and the smell of pine and jasmine rose up out of the ground to hit Fenn in the nose. He paced along the river bank to keep him-self awake and wondered if Sadie and Grayson had decided not to return. Maybe Sadie's mum thought she should hide in the cellar, after all. And Grayson's father was to come for him the day after they'd run off; maybe he had a place for him to hide as well. It would be too dangerous for them to try to come back to get Fenn. He'd give them more time, he decided, before heading off alone; he needed sleep, anyway. But could he break into Steingefan and rescue the others all by himself?

He felt so near to Father Treacher, but he couldn't get him a message. Had Rogget succeeded? He should have gone too, to make sure everyone at the wissenry was okay and to let them know what had become of him. But Father made him promise never to return to Path. He'd already broken that promise once. Fenn knew Ma'am Stationer had likely told Father Treacher about that visit; and he had to admit part of the reason he didn't want to see Father again, now, was his guilt over disobeying him.

Father would be very angry, he was sure. And if he found out Fenn had been into the beast forest, and that he was now planning a trip to Steingefan—well, Fenn couldn't imagine what Father would do. The last time Father had been truly mad, at Lucas, his face had puffed up and turned red and he'd rolled his eyes to the heavens and squeaked out the numbers one through ten before turning on his heels and leaving the wissenry for three hours. He might explode this time, with Fenn's disobedience.

Tired of waiting at the river, he walked a short distance into the wood and started a small fire with his flint sticks, hoping they would arrive soon. Though the sun was rising fast, they'd be wet and need warmth. Impatiently, he returned to the bank of the river to find them finally making their way quietly through the icy waters toward him. He wrapped them in their blankets and led them to the fire. Their faces were worn and pale.

"What is it? What happened?"

Chapter Thirty-seven

At the sound of Wanda's timid knock, Leah rolled over and pulled the pillow atop her head. She moaned with exhaustion as Wanda cooed, "Breakfast, mum?"

Stretching, and tossing the pillow aside, she sat up, disheveled, and gave Wanda a weak smile.

"It's early, mum," Wanda said as she placed the tray on the small table at the wall. "You're off to Aaronland today, I hear. Your'n men are downstairs a'ready. You had an eventful trip yesterday at the wissenry, as they tell it."

Leah reached her arms over head and yawned noisily. "I did. Your Father Britt reminded me very much of my father, though rounder and shorter. But just as jovial and with just as many books."

"Ah, yes, our Britt is very kind and wise. I hear tell Tom is very nice as well."

Suddenly Leah was wide awake. Had Kirche and Prenalin been telling stories of their day to the folk at breakfast?

"I thank you very much for your hospitality, Wanda. I hope we can stay here for at least a night before we make our way back to Ruhm."

"Ard, it's my pleasure, mum."

Climbing out of bed, Leah drew her robe around her and sat at the table to eat. Wanda curtseyed and turned to the door.

"Wanda," Leah said and she turned back to her. "Might I ask you a question?"

"Of course, mum. Anything you like."

"Why do the folk here fear Lord Kirche?"

Wanda stared at her for a moment, as if she'd said some-thing in a foreign language.

"Fear, mum?"

"Mm hm," Leah said, her mouth full of biscuit. "Sit," she tried to say, and motioned to the chair opposite her.

"Well, I wouldn't say we fear him." Wanda moved slowly to sit. "We respect him, o' course. Our kings pay tribute to Hass, after all. Hass helped us settle way back when."

"No, I'm sure there's fear there."

Wanda's eyes darted nervously about the small table as she appeared to try to form words.

"You think I'll tell Kirche what you say to me, don't you?"

The girl's eyes met Leah's, her face pale against the red twirls peeking out from her scarf; she shuddered a bit.

"You see what I mean? What would happen if you told me something bad about the Hass, or Kirche, and he found out about it? He doesn't rule here. What could he do?"

Suddenly Wanda's face lit up as if she'd found an escape. "Lord Kirche, or any representative of the Hass, don't rule here, that's true enough. But he advises our king about punish-ments and whatnot. And our king, what with his duty to tribute and all, he generally follows with what the Hass says."

"I see. So, Kirche metes out punishments to folk here, does he?"

"Aye, mum, as is his right by the treaty. But only on occasion."

"What sort of punishment?"

"Well..."

Wanda pulled her hands under the table and Leah was sure she was wringing them together in her lap.

"There was one time a few years back. I heard tell that a young man was carrying a yoke balancing two jugs of milk from the dairy to his stall in the market and he swatted your Lord Kirche with one, knocking him to the ground. Forgive me—" She looked down and shook her head. "As it was, the man purposefully hit your Lord Kirche, who was most definitely watching where he stepped, with a bucket of milk. And it was apparently soured."

Leah grinned broadly. "Did he now?"

But Wanda's face, when she looked up, was pale and drawn. "Aye. And though the young man was remorseful, your Lord Kirche would have him publicly flogged."

"Oh." Leah frowned. "Was it awful?"

"Aye," the girl whispered and her eyes filled with tears. "He was but sixteen. Whipped so long and hard, he never fully did recover, mum. Works the stall still, though."

"Well, that explains quite a lot."

There was a silence between them, and Leah was glad that Wanda no longer seemed afraid but wished desperately to cheer her.

"So, I imagine once we've moved along to torment Aaronland and Michelruud, the entire city of Cold Sea will breathe a sigh of relief."

"Oh, no'm, not until you're all back on the boat to Ruhm." And at that she nearly shrieked and put her hand to her mouth, her eyes wide with horror.

Leah laughed and nearly spit biscuit at her. After a second or two, Wanda was able to lower her stiffened shoulders and smile.

"You're not like the others, mum," she said and rose to leave.

"So my father tells me."

After her breakfast, Leah dug her journal from her delicates drawer and situated herself in the chair by the window. She opened the book, sighed, thinking over the events of yesterday. She'd already written about the morning spent visiting the important folk of Cold Sea Port so they could show deference to Lord Kirche and the manner in which Kirche and Prenalin seemed to puff up at each meeting.

And she wrote about her trip to the wissenry up on the ridge, it's quaint building filled with books and wise men who clearly fought to contain themselves in speaking to Kirche, who, she'd noted, asked rather inane questions that flustered Father Britt.

"Why are there no gallows at the wissenry?" was one such inquiry.

The question made sense to anyone from Ruhm, as there are gallows, a head cutter, and stocks in front of the House of Premiers and various Hass buildings there. The premiers and the Hass were in charge of the moral fiber of the citizens of Ruhm, after all.

"As you know, Lord Kirche," Father Britt had said, "the role of our wissenry here in the Ruud is one of advising and conflict resolution. Punishment is only given by the king."

Leah found it odd that Kirche could not understand this, and strange that he asked the question again, but only rephrased, as if he thought Father Britt was an imbecile. And she was left wondering why he would not know the answer from his previous visits. When the conversation ended, however, she realized that Kirche was not asking—he was criticizing. Strange, it was difficult to tell with Kirche which was which, as his voice was always smooth and pleasant.

And she wrote the night before about meeting Tom in the yard out back as he was chopping wood for the kitchen fire; he stopped his work and wiped his hands on his apron to greet her with a wide smile. As they got acquainted, Leah thought she saw a large black cat, something like the legendary wolf panther, in the woods behind the wissenry shed. Tom had laughed heartily, telling her such cats could only be found on the southern continents. He'd been so kind as to lead her inside and show her his books on beasts of the world.

Today, dear journal, she wrote. *I have decided to confide in you what I did not last evening. I wish I could say it was exhaustion at fault, but alas, I simply couldn't bear to put it down in words.*

It worries me that Wanda mentioned Tom, the lesser wissende, at breakfast. It seems my behavior yesterday may have brought gossip to Prenalin and Kirche. And I must admit before yesterday, I wouldn't have thought them capable. But watching them whisper and snicker these last days after meeting such plain and simple folk, I now see that I have put them on too high of pedestals.

Perhaps father was right. The Hass is no different from the folk, they merely think themselves above the rest. I shudder writing that. I fear it borders on blasphemous, if it's not outright so. But I can't help what I think.

Oh, perhaps it is my own failings that make me say it. I admit I am embarrassed and hurt at the thought those two were telling tales on me downstairs at breakfast—or worse, what if they did so last night while enjoying ale with the folk? My behavior will be the talk of the town. An aide to the High Priest of Hass flirting with a wissende? Could there be anything more degrading?

I wish I could lay the blame on Kirche, but he can't help that my heart flutters every time he looks my way. I'm a foolish twit. But one moment he's eying me softly with the hint of a smile at his lips and the next he acts as if I'm a servant to be ignored. So, what girl would not take the opportunity to enjoy the company of such a gallant young wissende as Tom? So what if I let him take my hand off the carriage perch? So what if I took a walk with him to the cliffs and let him teasingly push me toward the edge? So what if I screamed just a bit with delight at the joke?

Oh, all right. It was improper behavior. But it did certainly capture Kirche's notice. He was angry. Very angry. And it made my heart sing.

She closed her journal, smiling with satisfaction. What a silly girl I've grown to be, she told herself as she dressed. Father would not approve.

144

Chapter Thirty-eight

Grayson looked deeply into the crackling, spitting fire while Sadie frowned at him.

"Well, go on," Fenn said. "You two look like you've seen ghosts. What happened?"

"The king is dead," Grayson said, his teeth chattering. "Welk, the Dead King, is on the throne."

"The Dead King?"

He shrugged. "Years ago, he swore he'd never marry."

"I don't get it," Sadie said with a hollow voice. "He's not dead."

"But his line will end. No heir. No one to carry on the succession. No more King of Michelruud."

Sadie stared for a moment and then shook her head, "But he's not dead."

Grayson growled at her through his closed mouth and turned to Fenn.

"The village is under siege," he said. "Sorgood of the king's guard is in charge there, with King Welk's approval. They are certain the bairn is in Path. They're questioning everyone, trying to make them expose their neighbors, tell who they think the child might be."

"And they're searching for us; they know we're missing," Sadie said, looking at Fenn across the glow of the fire. "Our parents have been arrested and are being held at the village jailhouse."

"What? Why? And who's looking after your brothers and your sister?"

Grayson shook his head. "Henry is old enough; so's Jonathan, I guess. And anyway, my gram is there."

"But what good can it do to arrest them?"

"It's a trap," Grayson said. "They're waiting for us to try to see them."

"Who told you all of this?"

"Jeopard Link, my dad's apprentice," Sadie said. "He's at our house, keeping the shop running for the king."

"Will he tell the guard you were there?"

"I don't think so, but he begged me to go away."

"What took you so long to get back?"

"The guard is everywhere," Grayson said. "We had to move slowly around the village and the nearby woods. We almost got caught."

"I guess you didn't have a chance to ask about Father Treacher."

"Of course we did," Sadie said softly. "Father Treacher has disappeared."

Fenn felt a rush of guilt again. "It's my fault Lucas was taken," he said.

"I knew I should have gone back for him. And now Father is missing."

"Why didn't Father Treacher send Lucas through the tunnel with you?" Sadie said.

"He's fourteen...Father probably thought they wouldn't take him."

"He doesn't look fourteen."

"Fenn," Grayson said. "Does the wissenry think you might be the bairn of prophecy?"

Fenn glared at him. "There isn't an evil bairn."

"I know that and I'm not saying I think you are. We all heard Anfang's prophecy about the son of kings and the wasteland. But the grown-ups think there is an evil bairn."

Fenn nodded. "I think..." He wondered if he should trust them. They'd stood by him this long. They'd followed him to Cold Sea, into the beast forest. They were, he realized, his only friends. He felt calmer and more confident, but still cautious. "I think, yes. They probably believe I'm the one told of in the prophecy."

"Why?" Sadie asked.

He shrugged. That was a good question. He should tell them about the mark on his shoulder and that he was born in the wasteland. But he couldn't do it. He'd disobeyed Father Treacher enough already.

"I don't know," he said. His face burned red in the warmth of the fire, and to change the subject quickly he said, "After we rescue the children of Path, we'll return to the village and rescue your parents, as well."

"How?" Sadie said.

Fenn laughed defeatedly. "If we can get kids out of Steingefan, we can do anything."

Grayson said, "We're crazy, aren't we?"

"Yeah, we are," Sadie said.

They couldn't hold their heavy heads up any longer and all laid down by the fire to sleep. Fenn woke suddenly in the early afternoon light filtering lazily through the wood.

"Rogget," he whispered.

"Huh?" Grayson said, rubbing his face and sitting up.

"Did you hear anything about Rogget last night in the village?"

Sadie yawned. "Jeopard said a woodsman came by the shop looking for a 'cycoptic.' He asked after my mum and Jeopard told him my parents were in jail."

"Do you think he tried to see them? Do you think he was arrested?"

"I hope not," Sadie said. "What would happen to Darnit?"

"You think we should look for them?" Grayson said, digging jerky out of his sack.

146

Fenn shook his head. "No. We keep to the plan. Let's get through the wood today and tonight we'll try to get into the prison."

It was not yet dark when they'd hiked the wood far north of the high crossing, climbed across the river on an old log bridge, and made their way to the northern edge of Michelruud, to the road that led from Michelruud Castle to Steingefan. In the distance, across a grassy plain, they could see the two prison towers rising into the evening sky. They climbed atop a group of enormous boulders to have a better look. The castle still stood, but most of the outer wall around the bailey had been dismantled, and the rest crumbled, over the years. They could barely make out the stone barbican in front, still watching over the entrance, though its wooden gate had long since rotted away.

"The grass is taller than we are," Fenn said climbing down from the rocks. "We could probably make our way across the plain without being seen."

Grayson landed with a thud beside him. "It won't work. They'll have guards at the tops of the towers. We'll be seen, if not in the grass, then in the clearing around the castle. And there's the moat."

"Moat?" Sadie looked panicked. "Nobody said anything about a moat."

Suddenly a large figure burst through the wood toward them, panting and wheezing.

Chapter Thirty-nine

"Rogget!"

Rogget, out of breath, bent over to put his hands on his knees and looked up at them. "Out of your minds?" he said and panted. "Ran all the way to catch you."

Sadie rushed to him and hugged him around the neck. He stood, lifting her up and wrapped his arms around her.

"It's okay. I'm here now. Come on, let's get away from the road. Foolish children."

They crossed the dirt road and entered the wood on the other side where they sat on the trunk of a fallen tree.

"I tried to get messages to your folk, but I couldn't."

"We know," Sadie said. "But you got our message in the glade?"

"I went there and you weren't anywhere to be seen. I tell ya I was beside myself; I thought for sure the guard had you."

They all frowned and looked at the ground.

"You didn't find the message then?" Grayson said.

"I got the message, all right," Rogget snorted. "I asked the trees and one of 'em started shouting at me and wouldn't shut up. How many times did you carve it? Once will do, and make for the sweetest voice. But you turned the poor tree into a screaming lunatic. She was might relieved to be done with your message, I have to say."

"The tree talks?"

Rogget shrugged. "Ard, I shouldn't ha' left you be. And now what in beasts' names do you think you're doing here at Steingefan?"

"We're rescuing the others," Fenn said and stared defiantly at him.

Rogget shook his head and rubbed his hands over his face. "Father Britt is never going to trust me again after all of this."

"It won't matter," Sadie said. "After this, none of us will be able to set foot back in the Ruud."

"Well, that much is true," Rogget said. "So how do you propose to get yourselves into Steingefan?"

"It was the first castle of Michelruud," Grayson said.

"Does the stationer have one of those cycopted things for castles of the Ruud?" Rogget asked.

Grayson laughed. "No. But it's in the history of the Ruud. Steingefan isn't as fancy or big as the castles are now. It's basically a square stone box with staircases running up the middle from the main lobby. Two towers at the back were used to spy anything approaching from the wasteland. There are several entrances all around the outside, but from what I've read, they've filled the moat with boobrie and water harpies; the only way over is the bridge in front. But at least it's not a drawbridge anymore. The outer stone walls were dismantled long ago so it's really just a matter of getting across the moat."

"I don't think they're going to just let us walk over the bridge," Sadie said.

"We could," Fenn said. "We could let ourselves be caught and then try to escape."

"No," Rogget said. "There's a way out, but only if you break in."

"Huh?" Grayson said.

"I heard it in the port. Folk talk. Escaped prisoners and whatnot. They say that if you're taken in, you can't get out again. But if you break in, you know the way."

"But if they're escaped prisoners...they must have found a way out from inside," Grayson said.

"Well, maybe they weren't escaped. I never talked to 'em, myself."

"Did you ever hear what this way out was, exactly?" Fenn asked.

He shook his head. "It sounded too silly to ask about. Why would anyone sneak in just to sneak back out?"

"That's exactly what we're planning to do," Sadie said.

"I don't know any other way," Fenn said, "but to cross the bridge. Wait—"

A clattering of carriage wheels in the distance caught Fenn's attention. Voices, talking and laughing, carried over the wind. They looked at one another and all seemed to light up at once.

"We need to stop the carriage," Fenn said.

"Leave it to me," Rogget said and motioned for them all to get up from the huge pine log.

"After we leave," Fenn said, "head west, to the edge of the forest. We'll meet you there."

Rogget nodded. "And if you don't show in two days, I'm going to find a rabble of land pirates from the hill country and force my way in to get you all out myself."

"Really?" Sadie said. "You could do that?"

"Ard, you don't come out, and you'll just see, won't you?"

Rogget grabbed hold of the fallen pine and heaving, dragged it out of the wood and laid it across the road. Grayson, Sadie, and Fenn waited in the wood for the carriages to stop. When they did so, the guard at the front dismounted and called out for help. There was a canvas-covered supply cart being pulled by the first carriage and a cage with children in it pulled by the second.

Fenn recognized the boys he'd spoken to across the river. Looking around him, he picked up several brown pebbles and one by one, tossed them at the larger boy. Finally, with a tiny thump, he hit him on the head and watched him grimace and reach up to rub his hair, looking around for the culprit. Fenn waved his arms to catch his attention. The boy peered at him curiously in the early evening darkness as Fenn pointed toward the driver of the carriage.

The large boy smiled, nodded, and called out, "Hey."

The driver turned around. "What now?"

"This one's sick," the boy said. "Do you got a cloth or something and some water?"

The driver climbed down in a huff and went around to the back of the cage and Fenn led Sadie and Grayson across in front of the carriage where they climbed onto the supply cart, covering themselves with the canvas. There was a sudden rustling of feathers and the clucking of hens.

"Be still," Fenn whispered. "Don't scare the chickens."

"Heave!"

They heard the call of the guard as the soldiers dragged the heavy tree off the road. Finally, the carriages began moving and Fenn peered out beneath the bottom of the canvas, watching the tall grasses pass in the darkness. When they were over the bridge and into the torch-lit prison grounds, he saw the carriage behind them head the opposite direction as they were taken around to the west side of the castle. The cart stopped and the carriage driver jumped to the ground.

"Delivery," he shouted and rounded the side of the cart.

Fenn began to panic; if the driver lifted the canvas now, they'd be caught. But footsteps padded off toward the castle front until they were silent. He sighed with quick relief and lifted the canvas to take a look around. From the front of the castle he heard the boys from the cage talking and the guards yelling for control of them. But there on the west side, it was quiet.

They climbed off the cart and stared up at the gray stone walls rising three stories. A pile of rubbish sat to their right and, to their left, stone steps led up the side of the castle to a wooden door—the supplies would be taken in there. Fenn felt panic rushing at him again. They couldn't go through that door. Any second now someone would come out of it to unload the cart. What had he been thinking? This was impos-sible. They couldn't just walk into Steingefan and let the children go.

Sadie nudged him and pointed. Farther along the castle wall to their left was another stone staircase, but it didn't reach the ground. His eyes followed it up and saw that it led to a small wood door, painted gray to look like the stone of the castle. Grayson, seeing the same thing, went to the rubbish pile, pulled out old wood crates, and stacked them under the last step of the staircase, about six feet off the ground. They climbed the unsteady crates and reached the bottom step just as the kitchen door opened below them.

"Ard, Hutt, come unload the supplies," an old woman shouted into the castle behind her. "Full load." And then she disappeared inside and closed the door again.

Quickly they climbed the staircase to the higher door and pulled it open. Fenn peered inside.

"It's just a passageway," he whispered and climbed in.

"There are tunnels and passageways everywhere," Grayson said. "There always are in the castles."

"You are such a know it all," Sadie said.

They walked down cold stone steps until they came to a large brick in the wall, behind which faint light shone through. The stone didn't fit well in its spot—much too small—and they could peer into the kitchen through the spaces on either side of it. Hutt was now carrying in the supplies from the cart.

"They brought seven more," Hutt said to the large cook.

"Tsk, tsk," she said, shaking her head. "The poor children. They'll have to start putting them in the east tower, too, if they bring in any more."

"No ma'am," Hutt said. "Snell said they'd all go into the west tower. They mean to keep their quarters in the east, no matter how crowded the kids are."

"Least they brought me some decent food this time."

"Yes ma'am. Chickens, too. I'll feed 'em for you."

"Ah, Hutt, you're a good boy." The large cook smiled and patted his cheek as he headed out for another load.

Fenn led them farther along the passage, feeling his way in the dark, until it ended. The exit was covered by a thick piece of cloth, rough like the back of a tapestry, hanging from the wall. Fenn poked at it—it puffed out and fell back again. They listened and heard no sound from the other side. Cautiously pushing the tapestry aside, Fenn slowly peered out, finding they'd come to a room lit only by the moonlight shining through two open windows. It was barely furnished with a stack of wood planks against one wall.

"An abandoned room," he said and they all filed out of the tunnel.

"The passage will continue," Grayson said. "But from another point in the room. We just have to find it."

"But how do we know the passage will take us anywhere?" Sadie said.

"They always end up at one of the staircase landings."

Sadie rolled her eyes. "Like you know all about castles."

"I read," he said.

"That's all you ever do."

"And what's wrong with that?"

"It's not good for a boy to always have his nose in a book. And why can't you have it in a book at your own house?"

"No, he's right," Fenn said, trying to avoid another quarrel. "But the landing passage is usually trickier to find and causes noise when those who don't know how to open it try to do it. That brings out the guards."

"How come you know all about it, too?" Sadie said, glaring at him.

"Father Treacher told me a story once about a great prince who was in love with a princess and..." When he saw the horrified look on Grayson's face, he said, "Never mind."

"Here," Sadie whispered from across the room. "It's be-hind this one."

This tapestry was larger than the other and covered the entire wall.

"They hid the passages better in the newer castles," Sadie said. "You know all about that, don't you, waiter boy?"

"No," he said crawling behind the tapestry. "There aren't any books on the newer designs and I doubt they'd reveal such secrets."

Sadie followed and Fenn heard her voice muffled by the rug. "Ah, but if you'd played in Michelruud castle on Founder's Day with the rest of us, instead of spending your time in my da's shop, you might have discovered a thing or two."

Reluctantly, Fenn joined them, and they entered the pas-sage, following it upward where it came out behind a large chest. It would have to be moved for them to get out. Hearing guards, coming and going on the landing, they retreated to the empty room.

"We'll have to wait until later when everyone's asleep," Fenn said. "We need to cross the landing and climb the left stairs. They should lead us up to the west tower."

They waited in the abandoned room for several hours and when the prison was deathly quiet, made their way out to the third floor landing. It took the three of them to push the wood chest far enough from the tunnel to get out and it scraped loudly across the wood floor as it went. Every inch, they stopped and listened for an awakened guard. Finally, it was away from the hole and they crawled out onto the landing, crossed it, and climbed the creaking wood staircase; it curved upward toward the west tower and opened into a large lobby. Lanterns hung from the walls around the room and several guards lay sleeping at the foot of a smaller staircase. Sadie motioned them away from the guards, to the opposite walls and they looked for another passageway.

They found it behind an enormous animal skin, hanging by its hind legs from the ceiling; pushing it aside, they climbed through. This passage was tighter forcing them to walk single file until it ended at an open window that looked out over the moat and grassy plain and beyond that, to the forest west of the prison.

"What kind of animal was that?" Sadie whispered.

"Shh," Grayson scolded.

"It's a dead end," Fenn whispered after a moment, surprised.

"It can't be," Sadie said. "There's no use for a dead end."

"Who says the passage has to have a use?" Grayson said. "Maybe it's just for looking out the window."

Sadie rolled her eyes in the dim light of the night sky. "There has to be a reason it's here."

"The tower room is just above us, that way," Fenn said, pointing upward and to their right. He leaned out the window to look. Rectangular bricks jutted out all over the tower; and from the window where Fenn stood, they formed steps that led upwards and around. He drew back in, smiling at them.

"Stairs," he said. "They must lead into the tower room. Wait here."

Grayson grabbed his arm and whispered in the darkness. "Are you out of your mind? Look down."

"I did look down. There's a bit of ledge below. If someone fell, they'd land there...probably."

"Then look up. There must be a guard at the top of the tower."

"I don't think so," Fenn said. "And anyway, I'll be up against the wall; he won't be looking for me."

"This is crazy," Grayson said. "How do you even know there's a window in the tower?"

"There's always a window in the tower," Sadie said. "Don't you know that?"

"Oh, really?" Grayson sputtered. "So the princess can see her true love coming to her rescue?"

"Maybe," she said.

"Just wait here," Fenn said. "And stop arguing, you'll wake the guard."

He climbed out onto the window ledge, turning to face the wall, and found there were holes in the stone above the win-dow where he could grab hold. He did so, and then stepped over to the first jutting brick with his left foot. Once safely on the step, he found holes along the stone and he used them to steady himself as he climbed. As he rounded the turn however, the jutting bricks grew thinner and thinner, until he saw ahead that they were barely existent just at the window to the tower room. He turned to face the wall again, keeping his body pressed against it as he continued to climb. Finally, there was no step left, but he reached out with his left hand and found a grasping hole above the tower room window; and he reached out with his left foot and found the window ledge. Frantically searching the stone for more holes for his hands, he pulled himself over, until he was finally able to lower himself into the room.

It was dark and silent. He paused to let his eyes adjust, and moved slightly to let the dim light of the night sky shine into the window behind him.

"Hello?" he whispered.

"Where'd you come from?"

"I came through the window. I'm here to rescue you."

There was a chuckle in the darkness and movement as two boys came to the window where he could see the outline of their faces against the moonlight.

"You came through here?" one of the boys asked incredu-lously.

"He did; I saw him," said the other.

"Does the guard sleep in here with you?"

"No. They're down the stairs. They leave us alone mostly."

Fenn was relieved. "I'm Fenn, from the wissenry in Path."

"Fenn, it's me, Gettel, and Drew. From the north lake, remember?"

"I do remember," Fenn smiled. He'd spent his days two summers before at the north lake fishing with them. "Is Lucas here?"

"Lucas? Don't folks know?" Gettel said.

Other bodies stirred, some sitting up and listening.

"Know what?"

Drew said, "That first day..."

"We were in the cage, on our way to the prison," Gettel said. "We were attacked...by the felidae."

"Felidae? Are you sure? Were they attacking the guard?"

"We thought so at first. They did get the cages open."

"They took him," Gettel said.

"Lucas?"

"They carried him off," Drew said.

Stunned, Fenn took a step back from the boys.

"We tried to get out of the cages and run. But the guard caught us all. All but Lucas."

"So you don't know for sure he was carried off."

"Some of the kids saw it," Gettel said. "He's been eaten for sure."

Fenn remembered Kwitcher's reaction when he found out they believed felidae ate folk. "Only when cats," he'd said. "Now they're undead." But why would the felidae set the kids free to carry off only one of them? And why Lucas? No...they must be mistaken. Lucas was the only one who escaped, that's all. He desperately wanted to believe that.

Drew interrupted his thoughts, saying, "So how are we getting out?"

"Tomorrow night. We all climb out this window and follow hidden passageways through the castle. We end up around there—" Fenn pointed out the window to the left—"On the west side of the castle, just outside the kitchen door. We make it to the forest. From there we decide what to do next."

"I want to go home," Gettel said.

"You can try to sneak home. But you may be sent to the hill country."

"How do we cross the moat?" Drew asked.

"The only way is across the bridge out front."

"There'll be guards," Drew said.

"They don't post guards in the towers," Gettel said. "They're all sleeping indoors."

"But they're bound to post some outside the front door," Drew said.

Fenn shrugged. "We'll either make a run for it, or we'll find a way to sneak across."

Drew shook his head. "I don't like it."

"Well, if you can come up with a better plan, we'll listen."

"How many of you are there?"

"Three. I'll be back for you tomorrow night. Be ready."

He left the boys to watch him climb back out of the window and disappear around the outside of the tower.

"This just isn't going to work," Grayson said later, pacing back and forth in the safety of the abandoned room on the second floor.

"It can work. All the kids are about our age. They can climb out the window if I can. We each take a group and lead them through the passageway."

"And what about the moat?"

Fenn looked to the ground. "I haven't figured that out yet. But I'm thinking maybe we can use stuff from the rubbish pile."

"And all this time, the guards don't notice anything?"

"They didn't notice us before," Fenn said.

"There are three of us. But up there are thirty or more kids."

"What choice do we have? You want to just sneak out and leave them here?"

"No. No, of course not," Grayson said. "I'm just...I'm just yammering that's all. But what kind of moron puts a stone staircase on the outside of a tower?"

"A brilliant one," Sadie smiled.

Chapter Forty

Did you see Lucas?" Sadie asked.

Fenn was startled. "No," he said.

"Wasn't he there?"

He shook his head. "Some of the kids told me he was...they were... The carriages were beset by the felidae and Lucas disap-peared."

Sadie gasped. "I told you they eat folk."

"No," Fenn said. "I'm sure he just escaped when he had the chance."

"But why would the felidae attack the carriages if not for food?"

"Sadie," Grayson hissed. "I don't think we should talk about this anymore. We're all tired."

"Oh, right," Sadie said. She laid a gentle hand on Fenn's arm and he felt warmed by it. "I'm sure he's okay."

They hid in the passageway to sleep, fearing a night watch-man would check the room. Fenn dozed off to the rhythm of Sadie's snoring and dreamed of Lucas, standing ashen and thin, in front of the potato bins in the cellar of the Path wissenry. Lucas was laughing at him, daring him to pull back the woolen curtain hiding the tunnel. He could hear his own frantic breathing as he reached out to draw the woolen cloth away, but it wasn't his own hand that he saw; instead, the delicate, pale hand of the woman in his visions removed the drape as she crooned, "Look carefully; there is nothing to fear." Out of the gaping, dark tunnel rushed a growling felid. Pouncing ferociously on Lucas, it ripped into his flesh and ate away at his face. Fenn screamed, sitting up in the dark passage-way, panting.

"What is it?" Sadie asked.

"Nightmare."

She touched his arm and instinctively he placed his hand over hers; immediately, he felt soothed and calm.

"Did I scream out loud?"

"No, but you made a funny noise...like a squeak."

"Maybe that's what a dream scream sounds like."

"What made you scream?"

"Lucas...and the felidae."

She patted his arm softly. "I'm sure he escaped."

Nodding in the darkness, he lay back down and tried to sleep with Lucas' half-eaten, bloodied face in his mind.

The next day, they explored the room. Grayson found a bevy of spiders and their webs and spent a great deal of time searching out bugs to feed them.

"It's too cold," he said. "We need cold weather bugs."

Fenn was taken with the various drawings and writings on the walls that seemed to be a crude attempt at a history of the castle. They tried to keep as quiet as possible and away from the windows, but Sadie was drawn to them. She sat on a stool next to one and peered out from the bottom corner. When she got tired of sitting, she stood and peered out just the tiniest bit from the side. She saw no guards, she told the boys, but occasionally heard a loud voice in the distance.

"I guess Rogget's over there waiting for us," she whis-pered, looking dreamily toward the western woods. "Fenn," she whispered louder, "come here." She motioned for him to come quickly to the window. Kneeling down, she moved away and pushed him to the spot where she had been standing.

"What?"

"Look that way, into the moat, across from the kitchen door."

He looked down and winced at the glare of the sunlight off the waters in the moat. But then he saw what Sadie wanted him to see. Just below the surface of the water, there appeared to be a bridge.

He laughed quietly. "What's it for? Don't they know it's there?"

Grayson joined them and Fenn moved aside so he could peer out and see the bridge.

"It's probably for the kitchen," Sadie said. "Look there—" she pointed toward a bare spot in the tall grasses about thirty feet from the moat.

"It's a dumping spot," Grayson said. "Like the one behind the inn. For dead stuff, like chicken leftovers. Keeps the wild animals at a distance."

"And the smell, too," Sadie said.

"But prisoners could use it to escape," Fenn said.

Sadie shrugged. "Maybe that's why it's under water. Maybe it's hard to see from the ground."

"And from the tower," Fenn said. "The tower window faces north."

"So, they'd never see it." Grayson smiled. "It's just like Rogget said."

Suddenly the mood in the room was light and carefree; now Fenn believed their plan was possible. They would secret the kids out of the tower, through the passages, across the moat and into the tall grass. They'd all be across into the western forest before anyone knew they were missing. It could actually work.

Long after darkness had fallen and the prison guards finally finished their cards and their ale and had fallen asleep, Sadie, Grayson, and Fenn made their way quietly through the secret passageways, past the guard at the stairs to the tower room, and to the secret steps on the outside of the tower.

Fenn climbed the tapering stairs again and entered the tower room where he could barely make out the figures of the children awake and ready for him.

"We've looked out the window," Drew said. "It's not pos-sible."

"I just did it. You can't see them, but there are holes above for your hands and the steps get wider and wider as you go down."

They were skeptical, and quiet.

"And what about the moat," an unfamiliar boy whispered. "I don't want to break for it just to be caught and punished."

"Just outside the kitchen door, on the west side, there's a bridge. It's a bit underwater, but we could see it yesterday from a window."

Still, they looked doubtful; but Drew stepped forward and said, "Okay, I'll go."

"When you get to the next window, climb in and wait in the passage until about ten are there and Sadie will lead you out."

"Sadie, from the stationer's?"

Fenn nodded.

Drew climbed onto the window ledge and they watched his legs disappear to the left. There was a slight sigh from the group of kids.

"See?" Fenn said. "We can all do it. Just stay calm, go slow, and be careful."

One by one, Fenn sent the children out the window. When the boys from Timber approached, they shook Fenn's hand.

"We thought you were crazy," the large one said.

Fenn laughed. "Maybe we all are."

The children looked at him with awe and fascination. He recognized most of them from Path and hoped they would find a way to be safe after the escape. But what if Grayson was right? What if this was all for nothing? He shook his head. No, they had to try.

Finally, Lara of Path was left—the smallest and youngest. "I have a scar on my shoulder, see?" she told him while waiting her turn. "But I'm not a baron."

She was wide-eyed and shaking as Fenn helped her climb out the window.

"I'll be right behind you," he told her, and she nodded before reaching her hands up to find the clutches. She was so small, Fenn feared she'd not be able to reach, but she stretched well up and had the stones by her fingertips. Before she could begin the climb, the prison walls thundered with shouting and clanging bells.

"Escape! Escape!" Guards yelled from the floors below. The soldiers at the foot of the stairs awakened with startled, drunken shouts and clumsily made their way up the steps to the tower room.

"Hurry," he told Lara as he looked behind him and heard heavy footsteps on the stairs. "They're coming."

Lara stood frozen on the ledge.

"Reach out to the right with your hand, quickly."

She did as he told her.

"Now your leg."

Fenn climbed out the window beside her and helped her find her balance. "Keep going that way, hands and feet."

She nodded, wide-eyed and shaking. Before Fenn could get himself off the window ledge he heard the guard enter the tower room yelling, "Light the lantern." But they couldn't have seen him; they didn't approach the window.

As they rounded the outside of the tower, they met one of the other kids making his way back to the tower room.

"Go back," Fenn whispered loudly. "We keep going."

The boy nodded in the darkness and the three of them made their way down to the other window. Long arms reached out for Lara and pulled her in. It was the boy from Timber. Fenn smiled his gratitude as he lowered himself through the window. The last group, still waiting for him, looked nervous and frightened.

"This way," he said pushing past them to the front of the line.

From the passageway they heard the guard shouting. "They're gone!" More boots trampled into the lobby.

"They snuck right past you," someone scolded. "They're all over the grounds out front. Come on."

The commotion of the guards scrambling out of the lobby, cursing, reminded Fenn of the spooked wild horses Farmer Richard had once accidentally herded into the middle of Path. But the horses were off to the river in seconds, while the guardsmen seemed to stumble down the steps forever.

Finally they were out into the lower levels, and turning to the kids in his charge, Fenn said, "Just follow me as best you can. If you get lost, run for it. Look for the bridge just under the water outside the kitchen door on the west side."

They nodded, but reminded Fenn of startled deer. As he ran across the room and into the secret passage opening, he tried to pretend none of them would be caught, and he would see them all in the west wood. When they came out at the third floor landing, several guards and servants were hurrying down the stairs. The kids waited for them to disappear and then dashed across and slid behind the wood chest still ajar from the hole. Whistles and shouts rang through the castle; then a shot from a firearm startled them all and Lara stood paralyzed, beginning to cry.

"We have to keep going," Fenn said, grabbing her hand and pulling her along. He pushed her into the passageway and they raced through the abandoned room, into the next passage and past the kitchen. Fenn pushed open the little wood door and raced down the stone steps, calling quietly, "This way, this way."

He stood on the bottom step as they filed past him, one by one, and climbed down the wood crate pile. Guards in the front of the castle were ringing bells and tooting whistles and shouting orders, but none came around to the west side.

"Look for the underwater bridge," Fenn called to the kids, but they stood in a clump, dazed in the early-morning dark-ness, waiting for him.

Lara was the last one to the crates and as soon as she was down, Fenn jumped and fell into them, crash-ing to the ground.

"This way," he said, scrambling to his feet, wincing at pain in his right leg. As he neared the moat, he could see large stones just under the water's surface—remnants of the outer wall.

"It's here!" he shouted.

"Fenn," Sadie called as she appeared in the tall grasses on the other side.

"Help me get them across," he said, and began pushing the kids toward the moat. They waded noisily through the water and most had crossed when two guards, one carrying a lantern, came running from the front of the castle. Fenn was in the cold water after Lara, the last of the kids with him. As Sadie reached down for Lara's hand, one of the guards raised a firearm and pointed it at her.

"Hold it!" he shouted.

Fenn stopped and turned in the water to see a young guard with long brown hair pointing a gun at him. The other guard, older with gray hair and whiskers, stood behind him holding the lantern up high and glaring at them.

"All of you," the guard said, "back to this side of the moat."

Shaking, Fenn took Lara's hand and led her back across the stone bridge. The second guard grabbed them and pulled them up out of the water, pushing them to the ground.

"Tie them," said the guard with the gun.

"I don't have any rope."

"Well get some."

"Let's take them around to the front," he said. "Someone will have rope there."

"Not into that mess. You go find rope and round up all the other captured. We'll hold them here away from the chaos."

The other nodded, handed his lantern to the guard with the gun, and scurried off to the front of the prison.

"Up against the building," the guard said.

They scrambled upright and walked, half-soaking and scared, to the prison, and stood with their backs to it near the kitchen door.

The guard hung the lantern from a hook on the stone wall above them and raised his weapon, aiming at Fenn.

Chapter Forty-one

Fenn could feel Sadie trembling on his right side, while Lara's warm, moist hand slipped into his left. He glared at the guard who was pointing his gun, first at one of them, then another, and back again. Fenn realized the young man was shaking and nervous. He was not so much older than Fenn, maybe sixteen.

Glancing toward the moat, Fenn wondered how many got away. He heard screaming from the front and a guard called out, "There are more!" He knew some of the kids had been captured and would be sent to stand with them on the west side, to be held at gunpoint.

Suddenly, out of the grass, he caught sight of three shadowy figures— Grayson, with Drew and Gettel. His mood brightened at the thought of a rescue.

"How did you do it?" the guard said and Fenn's attention was drawn back to his uneasy face. "Did a guard help you? Was it the cook? Or the maid?"

Sadie and Fenn stared at him, silent, but Lara raised her hand and pointed to Fenn.

"He rescued us."

Fenn let out a sigh of disappointment. He knew she didn't realize what she was saying. He knew she was scared. But how stupid could she be? When he turned to look at her, she was staring like a wild animal at the guard with the gun. He could only hope she didn't catch sight of Grayson and the other boys quietly wading across the stone bridge in the moat and start blabbing about that.

"You?" the guard said. "You're just a kid."

He peered at Fenn curiously for a second or two before his eyes widened and he lowered his gun. Stepping forward, he roughly pulled Fenn's tunic off his shoulder. The shock of Fenn's mark, visible in the dim lantern light, sent the guard stammering backward and Sadie gasped.

"It's you!" the guard said and raised his musket again.

Suddenly, they were all pelted with stones, and as the guard turned, Gettel whacked him on the head with a huge rock, knocking him to the ground, causing his weapon to fire into the air. Fenn grabbed Lara and chased Sadie across the moat, with Grayson and the other boys after them.

Sprinting across the plain without a word, Fenn could hear their breathing, their footsteps thudding all around him, and the dry, brown grass rustling as they darted through it. They ran toward the visible treetops of the western forest. Fenn hoped they could run long enough and far enough to avoid the guard.

Once they hit the timberland, they kept running, panting loudly; they could see one another now, disappearing and reappearing as dark shadows from behind trees in the dense wood. Fenn saw Grayson, Drew and Gettel far ahead. Lara was in front of him, sprinting like a deer through the maze of pines and spruce, and Sadie was beside him.

Was that it? Six of them? He kept running. Grayson, Drew and Gettel disappeared into a thicket and Lara followed. Finally, he and Sadie joined them, still running, in the dark wood, where shrubs and bushes grew twice Fenn's size and the trees were almost as thick as in the beast forest. They con-tinued on until they found themselves in a clearing, where there were more than a dozen kids waiting.

Fenn slowed and finally stopped, grasping a tree at the far side of the glade, gasping for breath. He paced for several seconds before plopping down to the ground beside Sadie. The boys from Timber sat against a pine; he nodded a hello.

Grayson came to him, panting. "It was my fault," he said. "All my fault."

"No it wasn't," said a boy with blond hair. "It was Skap. He spilled marbles all over the landing."

"Marbles?" Fenn said.

"Had his pocket full of them."

Grayson rolled his eyes. "There was a guard just down a back room and he called out and came toward us. I didn't want to try for the passageway; then Sadie'd be caught. So we just ran down the front stairs and across the hall out the front door. We had guards after us all the way across the bridge into the grass."

"I followed Grayson," the blond boy said, smiling proudly.

"I couldn't call out to the others," Grayson looked horrified. "That would let the guards know we were heading west."

"It's all right," Sadie said.

"But they've recaptured most of them," Grayson said.

"We have to wait here until things calm down. The guard will be all over the Ruud looking for us," Fenn said.

"It doesn't matter," Sadie said.

Grayson looked at her. "Are you okay?"

"They won't be looking for us," she said. "All the children will be set free soon enough."

Grayson shook his head, ready to argue, but she continued, "They'll just be looking for Fenn."

Grayson turned to Fenn. "What's she talking about?"

"Nothing. It doesn't matter, Sadie. We still need to settle in somewhere until things calm down."

She nodded and Grayson continued to look at her curiously.

"Drew," Fenn called. "And Gettel. We need scouts. Can you sneak back through the grasses and see if the guard suspects anyone is over this way?"

They nodded with adventurous smiles and headed out. Fenn and Sadie gathered the remaining kids together and told them to rest a while. They shared with them what food they had in their sacks.

"It's not enough," Sadie said. "We have to find Rogget and get the kids home."

"But what about the guard?" Grayson asked. "And the other kids?"

"All the kids will be released soon enough," Sadie said.

"Why?"

"It's Fenn."

"I'm not the one," he said and pulled them aside away from the other kids.

"It doesn't matter if you are the one or not, Fenn. You have the mark. They'll be after you."

Grayson looked at Fenn now. "What's she talking about?"

"Show him," Sadie said.

Fenn scowled; but he lowered his tunic over his shoulder. Grayson peered at the mark on his arm and his eyes widened.

"You had the mark all along."

Sadie turned away and lay on the ground with the other kids to sleep. She was angry, Fenn knew; and he supposed she had a right to be.

Grayson shrugged. "You should have told us."

"I couldn't. Father Treacher made me swear."

Grayson nodded and said, "Still, you should have told us."

They settled down to sleep with the others but Fenn kept himself awake until just before dawn when Drew and Gettel returned. The few kids with him in the glade tossed and turned, whispered together, and sat up occasionally to look around. Only Sadie and Grayson were still and quiet.

"There's naught but a few guards walking the outside of the castle," Drew whispered when he and Gettel returned. "None over this way at all. Looks like your plan worked."

Fenn finally allowed himself to relax. Maybe his plan *had* worked, he told himself. Maybe the kids would not be recap-tured. Maybe King Welk was smarter than his father, King Evan, and he'd see what nonsense the bairn story was and stop all this madness.

He felt as if he'd just put his head to the ground when he was startled awake in the bright morning light by Darnit's cold nose against his neck, nudging his head off his sack so he could root for jerky.

"Darnit, no," Rogget whispered loudly.

"Are you out of your mind, letting that bear into camp? One of the kids could have screamed and set the guard after us."

"Sorry, there, Fenn. Darnit's always ahead of me. He's got the four legs, you know. And don't be worrying about the guard. They rode all the way to the southern rim of Michelruud before calling off the search."

"They did?"

"Sure. Where else are the kids going to go, anyway? They'll just come round the villages today and round them back up."

"Maybe not all of them. Some of them will head out to the hill country with us...and maybe their parents, too."

Rogget sniffed. "If you say so."

The others slowly woke, surprised to find themselves camped in the woods north of Michelruud before remembering their daring escape the night before. Rogget and Grayson built a fire and they all gathered around the warm glow.

"Can we go home now?" Lara said.

"Maybe," Fenn told her. "The guard will be coming around the villages looking for you. Do you all have places to hide at home?"

Some nodded.

"Rogget and I can take you to the hill country with us."

"Aren't you going home?" Gettel asked.

Fenn shrugged. "You all need to decide what you want to do."

"We'll take the Path kids home," Grayson said.

After much discussion, the kids from Path decided to make their way home with Grayson and Sadie. Fenn and Rogget were to take the seven children from Damon Wall to the edge of the divide wood where they could easily see their way home.

"We don't need any help finding our way," the large boy from Timber said. "We'll head out now. Thanks."

"Take care you stick to the woods west of the Ruud, and south of home as well," Rogget warned. "Don't come out 'til you're at Timber."

"But that would mean entering the beast forest," the taller boy said.

"Aye," Rogget said. "No need to go too far in, but stay out of sight of the open fields of the Ruud."

They shrugged with acceptance and each shook Fenn's hand and disappeared into the forest before Fenn realized he never learned their names.

"Rogget and I will wait for you in the faire glade three days," Fenn said to Grayson and Sadie. "'Til the full moon."

"I'll be there," Sadie said.

Fenn eyed her curiously. "But if you're right and they only want me, your parents will be free and you can stay home."

"Still, I'll be there. You'll need news of Path before you go."

"I'll be there, too," Grayson said. "No matter what."

"I'll expect you, then," Fenn said with a hint of a smile. "And if you're wrong, Sadie, we can make plans to rescue your parents."

Drew and Gettel shook his hand and thanked them for the help. "Maybe we'll see you in the hill country," they said.

Lara hugged him. "I'm sorry if I got you in trouble," she said.

"It's okay. You were scared. We all were."

Chapter Forty-two

Welk's pacing before the great hearth in the king's chambers was interrupted by a light tapping at the door. Dunham appeared. "He has arrived, Sire."

Sorgood. Finally. Sorgood's lieutenant had brought word of the escape at Steingefan in the early morning hours, disrupting Welk's already restless sleep. Sorgood, he'd said, would give a full report when they'd succeeded in rounding up the children. It must be finished, he surmised. How long could it take to recapture a few children, after all?

He heard voices as he entered the great hall, and saw Sorgood and several of his guards standing at the back end of the room by the hearth, near his throne. They cleared away in front of him and he took his seat, waving away the pleasantries, as Sorgood bowed and attempted to apologize for awakening him.

"Tell me," he demanded.

Sorgood's long face was pale and frightened in the dim, fire-lit hall. "We have reason to believe, Sire, that it was the bairn who entered the castle and released most of the children."

Welk stood up quickly, stunned. "The bairn?"

"Yes, Sire, yes." Sorgood actually met Welk's eyes momen-tarily and proceeded. "Footman Wolf—" he pointed at one of the men with him— "saw the mark."

Welk motioned for the young guardsman to approach the throne and he did so, bowing and keeping his eyes to the floor. A large bruise surrounded a red gash across his cheek; his left eye was swollen shut.

"Look at me," Welk barked and the young man jumped slightly and with difficulty raised his good eye to the king.

"Tell me what happened."

"I found three of them, Sire, crossing the stones in the moat on the west side. I put them against the wall. One of them, very small and scared, told me the boy had rescued them. I was suspicious, Sire, so I pulled at his tunic and...and he had the mark."

Welk watched him speak and believed he was telling the truth.

"What did the mark look like?"

"It was dark, Sire, very dark. But I saw three lines...they ...they were larger on top, smaller on bottom...and...and closer together on the bottom."

The hair on Welk's neck bristled and stood on end. "Draw them," he said. "Find this man a stick."

Dunham snapped his fingers at the chamberlain standing against the wall where the banquet tables had been lined up; the man ran to the corner and pulled a stick from a tall urn and scampered back with it, bowing before the king. Dunham took the stick from him and handed it to the young guard.

Welk led them from the stone floor to one of the hearths, surrounded by hard dirt. His hands shaking, the guard knelt before the roaring fire, and drew the mark in the dirt in front of the king.

"The children say it was Fenn Foster of the wissenry," Sorgood whispered as the guard drew his lines. "He was aided by the innkeeper's son and the stationer's daughter."

Ah, it was all clear now and as he'd suspected. The innkeeper would certainly have known the truth; he received information from the outside regularly. And the stationer, with his books and letters from all over the world. Yes, it made sense. But to sacrifice their children to it? To send them out alone to confront the guard? No; perhaps the children simply knew one another because of their parents' association and found themselves in a position to act.

"Oh," the guard said, pulling Welk's attention back to the ground. "And there were three dots, one at the bottom of each line." He poked holes in the dirt.

Welk could feel the blood draining from his face as the young guard made the mark of the faire at his feet.

Chapter Forty-three

They camped only once, and Rogget let them sleep a mere four hours, arriving at the edge of Woodside Village just after midnight on the second day, where they said goodbye to the children of Damon Wall. Rogget and Fenn made their way from there to the Cold Sea wissenry, arriving mid-morning, where Father Britt, shocked to see them, ushered them quickly out of the yard and into the kitchen.

"Why have you returned? Eat, eat," he said, bustling about pouring tea and handing them biscuits, sausage, and hunks of cheese.

Tom stumbled into the room from the front of the wissenry, wide-eyed and smiling. "I never thought I'd see you again. Didn't you make it to the hills?"

"I know you're going to be mad as a harpie, Father," Rogget began. "But I followed this boy into error all over the Ruud."

Father turned to Fenn with his fists on his hips, shaking his head with a frown. "Having just met with Father Treacher, I can't say I'm—"

"Father Treacher was here? When?" Fenn broke in.

"I was saying, Rogget, I'm not surprised. The stories he told me. A dear boy to be sure, but much too adventurous for his own good."

"Is he okay, then?"

"Yes, yes. He's fine. Hiding out in the port as a drunkard, actually."

The picture that entered Fenn's head brought out a laugh; Father Britt gave him a scolding glare.

"Father, he went into Steingefan and released the children of Path."

Tom dropped the biscuit out of his mouth and Father Britt fell into the chair next to him. "Dear ghostly heavens. And you're still living?"

"He managed it, for the most part," Rogget said. "But the guard was alerted and some of the children were rounded up again. I'm fearing they'll pay a penalty for the attempt."

"But it wasn't their fault," Fenn said.

"They likely knew the risks," Father told him reassuringly. "And from what I hear, most of the guard aren't so beholden to Sorgood's methods. I don't think they'll be too hard on them."

Fenn believed Father Britt was only trying to make him feel better—but he held out hope that he was right.

"But I thought...I thought maybe the new king would stop all this. I thought maybe he'd see how determined we are to be free."

"Did you now?" Britt smiled at him, and shook his head, clucking his tongue against the roof of his mouth. "King Evan was ill for many months before his death. Sorgood, his master of the guard, acted for him in matters military. It's doubtful Welk would not grant him the same powers. He's quite vile, of course, but vile men are useful to kings."

"Oh." Fenn was dejected. Perhaps he was just a stupid kid, after all. He supposed he should have done what he was told from the beginning.

"Come now. You look drained of all life. Get some sleep in the secret rooms and we'll get you out of here into the hill country for good this time. You do plan to go?"

Fenn nodded. He followed Father Britt below to the secret rooms without protest, wanting nothing more than to sleep—to forget that he'd failed—to pretend that he hadn't done the stupidest thing anyone had ever attempted. Grayson was right all along. Maybe a few would make it out to the hill country, or to the port and off to sea. But the children of Path were still in danger. He'd really solved nothing.

He dreamed again of the woman's slender hand grasping the wissende's robes; he was sure now it was a wissende. And he knew the woman must be his mother. She was dying—telling the wissende to take Fenn and protect him—dying in the wasteland with no one to care for her child. He woke with the burning charm against his skin but didn't move to touch it. He let it sear punishment into his chest.

Finally, he climbed out of the comfortable bed and went upstairs. Father Britt was cooking again and Tom was practicing his copying of a book in the corner at his desk.

"Good evening," Father told him. "It's supper time, if you're hungry."

Fenn felt like he would never not be hungry again and sat down to more bread while he waited for Father's roasted chicken and sweet potatoes. The smell wafted through the kitchen reminding him of the days he lived with Father Treacher at the Path wissenry. It seemed so long ago that he was well-fed and happy and learning from books, like Tom. What would he do in the hill country? Would he and Rogget camp every night and struggle to catch rabbits for stew? There'd be nothing for it but turnips, and he hated turnips.

"Where's Rogget?" Fenn asked.

Suddenly the back door flew open and Father Treacher burst in, wearing a worn sailing uniform and smelling of whiskey, uncombed and unshaven.

"Fenn," he said with a startled and curious look at him. "You should be long gone to the hills." He turned to Father Britt. "Has he told you what he's done—what's happened? All our plans were for naught."

"Ah." Father Britt was calm and composed in great contrast to Treacher's messy appearance and breathless entry. "Yes. It seems that Fenn is not the obedient, yet adventurous, boy you described. He's much more on the adventurous side than the obedient."

"It's all over the Ruud by now." Treacher sank weakly into a chair at the table. "They say they've found him—the evil bairn of prophecy. Fenn, why did you come back here?"

"Tell us all the news over supper," Britt said, carving the chicken. "We hear the boy made a daring rescue at the prison."

"Yes," Treacher said. "A guard claims that the bairn snuck in and helped the children to escape. He caught him outside the castle with one of the prisoners and his accomplice. He saw the mark."

Father Britt looked at Fenn. "Is this true?"

Fenn nodded.

Father Treacher put his head in his hands. "It is true, then. Oh, no," he cried. "After all our work. All these years of keeping the secret."

Britt rolled his eyes and nodded toward Father Treacher giving Tom a knowing look and Tom smiled. "No bother," he said. "It will all come to pass as it must."

"Fenn, don't you understand they will kill you?"

Fenn shrugged. It was hard to imagine a great king and his guard killing a little kid. He'd never heard of such a thing before.

"Imprison him or banish him is more like it," Britt said. "And he's going to banish himself later this evening."

"There is no evil bairn," Fenn said. "There was no prophecy."

They all stared at him—Tom and Father Britt with smiling, but vacant, expressions; and Father Treacher wild-eyed and aghast.

"We went to the beast forest and saw the beast lord. The prophecy wasn't really a prophecy at all. It was just meant to scare the king but it didn't work. It didn't say anything about a mark. And the new bairn is supposed to be the son of a king."

Fenn was breathless and frustrated. The more he'd gone on, the more they all smiled, until he thought they were going to laugh at him. Instead, they stared at him in silence and then looked back and forth among themselves until finally Father Treacher said, "We know."

"What do you mean you know? What do you know?"

"We know all of it."

"You know?" Fenn could feel the anger rising in his throat. "You know about the new bairn and about there not being a mark and the son of a king? Do you know about the wasteland? That he was born in the wasteland?"

They nodded.

"Why didn't anyone tell me?"

Father Britt laughed. "But, you're only a boy."

Fenn stood up suddenly, shoving his plate of food away. "A boy with a mark on his arm that makes folk think he's going to kill the king. A little more information might have been helpful to me a long time ago."

"Fenn," Father Treacher shook his head and spoke lightly. "What difference would it have made, really?"

"I'd have been out of the Ruud long ago, for one thing," he said, his voice rising. "I'd never have dragged my friends into the beast forest and all over the Ruud and into a prison. I wouldn't have risked their safety, not to mention the lives of all the kids, especially those who didn't make it out."

"Wouldn't you?" Father Treacher said.

In the tense pause, Tom looked at Treacher and nodded. Father Britt smiled innocently. Morons, Fenn thought. Grown-ups are morons. He turned to leave, planning to get his supplies from the secret rooms. He wanted to get away as quickly as possible, and alone. He didn't want to meet Sadie and Grayson, and maybe their families, at the glade and have to suffer a lifetime of guilt in the hill country with them, knowing it was all his fault. And he didn't want Rogget and Darnit banished to the hills just because he had a funny mark on his arm. But before he could move to the door-way, Father Treacher stopped him.

"There's more," he said. "You need to know all of it. They've released all the children of the Ruud who were recaptured. And they won't be taking any back again. The children of Path are safe."

Fenn looked at Treacher understanding him too clearly. They were now after him and only him. He would *have* to go alone. Suddenly his courage in abandoning his friends and his protection faded; but he nodded.

"That's for the best."

Father Treacher looked pained. "They're now only after you and your accomplices."

"Accomplices?" Fenn said, alarmed. His thoughts raced. "Wait. You did say that the guard saw Sadie. But he never saw anyone else but Lara. They don't think..."

"No. They're after you and Sadie and Grayson."

"Grayson, but why?"

Father Treacher sighed, his thin face defeated. "They forced the children who didn't make it out of the prison to tell them. Most of them were from Path, of course. They knew all of you."

"But if it's just me they want..."

Father Treacher sighed again. "They will use them to get to you."

"Sadie and Grayson can explain that they didn't know who I was,"

Fenn stammered, but all three of them shook their heads.

"Your friends are now tied to you. You must leave at once. Rogget will be your guardian," Father Britt said. "Make your way to the ice kingdom and find the maiden. She may be able to help you. She has powerful magic."

"But she is wicked," Father Treacher sputtered, looking horrified at Britt. "I thought we were to send him to sea."

"I will not debate this with you again," Britt said. "He will make for the ice realm. We don't know the maiden's true nature; we have conflicting stories. So, be wary. Give her your mother's charm and she will know you."

Father Treacher stammered another protest. "A mere story, Britt. We have no reason to believe she knows his mother."

"I admit that is true. But it is said she has the power of touch."

"What's that?" Fenn asked.

"She can sense images from objects. She can hold your mother's charm and learn about her through it."

Fenn's face froze and his mind raced wildly, but he tried to not to let them know he was shocked and frightened. The charm had been burning spots on his skin and sending him visions both in his sleep and while he was awake. And before the charm, the rope on which it hung warmed him and sent him images. Father Treacher called it a curse, exaggerated nightmares and visions, meaningless. But Fenn didn't know that folk could sense things from objects. Was *that* his night curse?

He casually nodded his head. "What is it you expect me to learn from her?"

"We are hopeful she will let you hide there with the eis."

"And what about my friends' parents?"

"They will probably remain imprisoned until Sadie and Grayson are found."

Father Treacher said, "I will return to Path immediately. They must not go to their parents. They must escape."

"It's too late; they would have been there two days ago."

"Still, I will return to Path and do what I can."

"It's suicide, Treacher," Father Britt said. "Your connection with Fenn..."

"The entire wissenry is connected to Fenn. If they don't find me in Path, they will soon be at *your* door."

"Father, I need to tell you about Lucas."

Treacher smiled slightly. "Oh, I wouldn't worry about Lucas; he has skills."

"Skills?"

Britt smiled his now annoyingly pleasant smile and agreed with Treacher. "Yes, special skills. Same as you. No need to worry about Lucas."

"But the Path cart was attacked by felidae on its way into the prison."

At this they all frowned at him.

"Yes. And some of the kids say he was carried off and eaten."

"Eaten?" Father Britt spluttered with laughter.

Treacher shook his head with a smile. "No, no. They wouldn't have eaten him."

"Are you sure? I did hear that felidae don't eat folk... anymore. But are you sure?"

"We're certain, Fenn. And that's so much better than sure."

Better for those who feel the certainty, he thought; but not so much for those who doubt. He could only hope their confidence in Lucas' fate was an indicator that he was safe. Little made sense in Fenn's head anymore. Exhausted, he felt as if he were swimming in mud.

"What if you went to King Welk," he made his last protest. "And explained about Sadie and Grayson?"

"Fenn." Father Britt lost his patronizing smile now. "We have no sway with the king."

"But you're the wissenry."

"Your friends are now allied to the bairn of prophecy."

"There is no bairn."

"We know. The king might even know—and Sorgood certainly doesn't care."

"Then why are they after me?"

"You're the new bairn."

Fenn put his hands over his ears and yelled, "None of this makes any sense. Have all the grown-ups lost their minds?"

Britt smiled. "Folk believe what they will."

"But if the king knows, he can tell the folk that it's not true, that there's no such thing as prophecy."

"The only truth that matters, Fenn, is what folk believe and how those beliefs affect their behavior—how they use them to justify their ends. The folk of late are turned against the evil bairn as soon as they learn to talk. The king's hands are tied in that matter; he must be seen to be of help. And there are benefits to a common enemy of the folk."

"You mean, if it suits folk to think I'm the bairn of prophecy, then I'm the bairn of prophecy."

Chapter Forty-four

Aaronland was not so grand as Damon Wall with its bustling port city. While there were no salty moist winds pulling at her hair, Leah decidedly preferred the smell of fresh pine to fish and seaweed. And while the port was indeed beautiful, especially while looking down on it from its grassy ridge, there was an abundance of sporadic woods and greenery inland.

At Damon Wall, their party had visited King Ricker at his castle and supped with him at a grand feast. But in Aaronland, they were beckoned to take quarters in Aaronland castle.

"This is most unusual," Kirche said to Prenalin. "Most unusual indeed."

Leah found it stifling. She'd been banished to a drafty room on the fourth floor to be overseen by ladies in waiting who would not speak a word to her beyond, yes'm, and no, and I would speak to the queen if you like. Of course Leah begged off. Why would she want the queen of Aaronland bothered about what flower was just outside the northeast window of the great hall? Or who made the tapestries? You don't speak to queens about such things.

She was left to her own devices as Kirche and Prenalin took the opportunity of King Arnot's constant ear. They wined and dined and went on a brief hunt. The feast boars they'd shot were impressive and roasted to tender perfection. After they gorged themselves, the three men retired to the king's library and Leah was summoned to bring in Kirche's journal and papers from his room.

The very idea that she should enter Kirche's private room alone sent shivers through her body and her heart raced. Her legs felt like aspic as she climbed the carpeted wood stair to the second floor, crossed the hall and pushed open his door. Kirche's room smelled of lilac and pipe tobacco and reminded her of the Snapping Turtle Inn, without the salt. His room was impeccably neat, as if a servant cleaned it every time he left it.

She found the desk, at the window, where Kirche said his books and papers would be and there they sat, in a neat pile, the papers clasped in their leather binder. She picked them up, put them to her face and breathed in, then gave them a gentle hug to her chest.

Leah stood for several seconds begging herself not to do it, but in the end, she put the books down, pulled the journal from the bottom and carefully opened it. Her eyes fluttered at the sight of Kirche's strong tight hand, tilted almost too far right; she quivered and quickly closed the book again. What was she thinking?

As she turned to leave, she caught sight of a sheet of parchment peeking out from under Kirche's *Book of Rett*. On it she saw the letters e-a-h. Curious, she stared at it for a moment before putting the tip of her finger on it and sliding it out just far enough to be sure. Indeed, her name was written there in the same tight cursive of Kirche's journal. Not able to help herself, she pulled the paper from under the holy book and read:

While she is working out quite nicely, and will no doubt serve her purpose, I must wonder daily, dear brother Haberson, why Prenalin would choose for me an aide so pretty as Leah.

She sucked in a quick breath and frantically fumbled to get the paper back under the *Book of Rett* just as it had been, before grabbing at Kirche's journal and leather book and darting from his room.

He'd called her Leah. So casual. So intimate. And he thought she was pretty. Her face grew hot and she knew she would look ablush when she took the papers to him. Luckily, she was brought directly before King Arnot once in his den, where she bowed and curtseyed low, and could only hope being in such proximity to the king would be her excuse.

She turned to Kirche and held out his books for him. He took them without looking at her, without a break in his smooth dialogue to the king; he was going on about something to do with the Ruud and its tiny, insignificant kingdoms. Back to ignoring her, she thought. Now her face blushed with anger and she turned to leave the room.

Just at the door, she heard King Arnot say, "I tell you, this child of prophecy lives and has been identified. Welk will not hesitate to use him to force his rule upon the entire Ruud, and once united, I dare say, you and Hass will have a tough time of it."

"I assure you that will not happen. And we will help you find your bairn of prophecy."

Leah turned to look back at the men and caught the king's eye.

Prenalin stood and said sharply, "This is none of your affair."

Dutifully, Leah curtseyed once more to the king and left the room. She made her way to the great hall and left through the eastern door, walking the open corridor to the kitchens.

"Allo miss," one of the cooks called to her as she pulled open the door. "Helps you?"

"I hate to be a bother; but have you anything sweet?"

"Aye, we've got tart cakes. Have a seat there by the window."

Leah sat and watched the cook as she bustled around while others

174

came and went seeing to the needs of the other guests at Aaronland castle. Finally Cook came back to Leah with a small plate on which she'd placed an assortment of tarts.

"I imagine your Lord of Hass is most intrigued at the news," Cook said waiting while Leah took a taste.

"About the child of prophecy? Yes, I imagine. How do they know they've found him?"

"He's got a strange mark on his arm. Very perplexing. An evil omen, no doubt."

"No doubt. And what sort of child is it?"

"It's a young lad of the wissenry, ma'am."

"Not Tom of Cold Sea?"

The woman chortled. "No, no. Young boy, only 'leven or so. Fenn Foster, they call him. Hard to believe such evil can lurk in such an innocent heart, eh?"

Leah's chest seemed to form a hole at Cook's words and swirl away from her. It was unnatural, she thought, to hear a plump and kind-faced woman refer to a child so young as evil.

"Is it Tom of Cold Sea who's broken your heart, miss?" Cook said.

"What?"

"You look forlorn of love."

Leah pulled her brows together and glared at the woman. "I do not."

"If you say so, miss."

Leah vengefully shoved an entire tart in her mouth and turned to look out the window. She startled as she saw Kirche stride across the lawn outside the kitchen and disappear from view. She jumped up and darted out the door with barely a wave of thanks to Cook and sidled the wall, watching him walk straight into the woods.

Looking this way and that for Prenalin, surprised that he was nowhere to be seen, she followed Kirche's path. Once in the woods she crept quietly to a spot where she heard Kirche talking. A strange male voice answered him—squeaky and rather rat like, in Leah's view.

Desperate to catch sight of the owner of such a weasel voice, she tiptoed to a tree and slid across its enormous trunk until she could peer every so slightly around it. He was tall and lanky with long, greasy black hair, in the style of the Hass, but not as clean as it ought to be. He did look very much like a rodent.

"Arnot is willing to help in finding the boy," Kirche said. "He fears Welk will use him to garner support for uniting the Ruud under the Michelruud throne."

"Yes," the weasel sneered. "Welk is ambitious, but weak-hearted. He would not do what is necessary, especially as it involves a child."

"Then you must catch him first," Kirche said. "And don't forget the hunt, my good man."

"Ah, yes. I have found a most abundant spot of forest for you, my lord. Brownies behind every tree."

Brownies? Leah cringed. Did this man mean to imply that Lord Kirche would hunt them? Or are they merely an indica-tor of good game? She must have heard incorrectly.

"Good man," Kirche said, much more relaxed than Leah had ever heard him. "We will be in touch."

Leah stepped back behind the trunk and waited quietly, listening as both men's footsteps left the spot. Somewhere to the west she heard horse hooves trot off into the distance. When she thought she was alone, she allowed herself to breathe. Her heart pounded in her chest and she formed a fist with her right hand and pounded it into the tree.

What had become of her? Looking into his journal; reading his letters; and now following him into the forest to listen in on his private conversations? This was not becoming of an aide of Hass.

Remaining in the woods for at least an hour until it grew dark enough that she thought she wouldn't be seen, Leah raced to the castle, through the great hall without a word to anyone, and up the stairs to her quarters where she would pour out her confessions to her journal.

Not only would she never make Historian of Ruhm on this path, she'd be flogged and stocked in front of the Hall of Hass. But as she opened the door to her room, she could only think of the horror of Lord Kirche hunting brownies—such funny, harmless creatures. She must have been mistaken.

Chapter Forty-five

Lucas packed his knapsack in the hidden rooms at the wissenry at Cold Sea. He'd managed to drag Father Treacher, unwillingly, from the wissenry in Path to Cold Sea Port and set him up there as a vagabond. It was a wonderful disguise and Treacher seemed to enjoy it rather too much. But he heard news of the goings on with the bairn and gleefully reported it regularly to Father Britt while preten-ding to beg a few pents from the old wissende.

He'd then followed Fenn, watched as he and his friends made a daring rescue, saw that Fenn was discovered, and ran all the way back to Cold Sea, knowing Rogget would have the boy there within days. Lucas knew what he must do now.

"Will you follow him? Keep him safe?" Father Treacher asked, entering the candle-lit room.

"Rogget can do that, Father."

Treacher nodded. "He is the best tracker in the land; he's evaded the guard since he deserted. He's our man, yes."

"But?"

Father sighed woefully. "I would have the boy with someone he knows. Family."

Lucas shoved a blanket into his sack and smiled. "I must be with those who chase him. And will you go to Path as you insisted to Britt?"

"Britt forbids it for now. But I would like to be of use."

"I will get you news when I can."

Father Treacher watched him as he checked his wealth and tossed his pack over his shoulder. He followed as Lucas wended his way through the hidden rooms, up into the cellar, into the wissenry and through its maze of rooms to the kitchen where he bid his goodbyes to Father Britt and Tom.

They all stood on the back steps and waved a final parting as Lucas entered the woods behind the building. He would make his way to Path where there was a call for help with search parties.

He'd hiked only a hundred yards through the woods, when he caught the distinct scent of felidae...one, he calculated. But there was something else—an unfamiliar smell. A branch broke behind him and he turned to see the felid as it transformed to its folk form.

"Do I know you?"

"I am Quarn, of the felid guard."

All of Lucas' senses were on edge as he gave the felid a wary glare.

"Is the guard so far from the forest?"

"I come alone."

Lucas waited for an explanation, still sensing another creature lurking nearby.

"Your father Belfen was my brother," Quarn said. "Had he lived, I would have had the honor of turning you as an infant."

"You are kin to me?"

"I am."

"Why did you not say so before?"

"It was not the time."

"What happened to my parents?"

Lucas did not trust Quarn; he wasn't sure he would believe the story he would tell. But he had to ask.

"They attended a party of eis and the young princes of Michelruud in the hill country when they were slaughtered by King Evan's guard. Few survived, Prince Welk being one. Your father saved his life in giving up his own."

Lucas stared at him. "How do you know this?"

"I was in attendance, with two others who escaped. We were in our felid form, while your parents were vulnerable. We thought you dead with the others."

"Why was I not told this?"

"The wissenry found you and so became guardian. Dag Voorspeld, against our wishes, allowed them to raise you in the ways of the ancients, living out your full life as folk before turning. And so, they kept some things from you—with Voorspeld's blessing."

"And why are you here, then, telling me what was to be kept from me?"

"As I said. It would have been my honor to turn you as an infant."

"Did Dag Voorspeld send you?"

"No."

"Then you cannot turn me now."

"I cannot, without losing my place and my honor. But you can be turned."

At this, one of the eis stepped out from behind a large pine. A foot taller than Quarn, the slim figure wore the tunic of an eis hunter, his muscular arms and legs bare to the elements as an open invitation to his enemies—their chances of harming him were remote. An easy smile broke out on his long, sharp face and his green-eyed gaze held steady on Lucas.

"You would have me murdered by an eis?"

"I would have you take your rightful place among your kin. Voorspeld grows old and weary, while you gad about the Ruud like a folk."

"I am a folk."

"Not for long."

The eis stepped forward, flipped a bow from his shoulder and reached behind his back to draw an arrow from his quiver.

"I consider it an honor to be a part of this felid ritual, barbaric as it is," the eis said with a smirk.

"It would be a ritual if you were felid," Lucas said, letting his knapsack fall from his back. "Being an eis, it only makes you a murderer."

"Be that as it may."

As soon as the eis lifted his bow to begin to arm it, Lucas turned and

178

dashed through the wood. He skipped over small boulders and wildly skittered around trees. His heart thumped hard in his chest; it was not his time to die. From the corner of his eye he saw the enormous dark figure before it hit him and rolled to the ground with his neck in its jaws.

Quarn had pounced and now held him. The eis approached, but lowered his weapon and stood, his breathing calm, a smirk still on his lips.

"Let him go, Quarn," he said. "It is undignified to shoot a folk in this manner."

Quarn roared and growled before stepping off Lucas. The eis motioned with his head for Lucas to run.

"If I stand my ground?" Lucas said.

"Then I will shoot you here. I won't have you held, but I needn't chase you."

Lucas turned and fled again; the eis laughed. Arrows twanged against thick pines as he passed them and Lucas knew the eis was toying with him. Part of him wanted to stop fleeing and stand still so as not to give the vile eis pleasure; but his instinct forced his feet farther on. His only hope was the wissenry and he turned wide round and headed back to the building.

Leaping over a boulder, he lost his footing on a second, hidden rock and tumbled to the ground. He turned onto his back and saw the eis coming forward in the wood. Before he could scramble to his feet he heard someone shout, "No," and a body fell on him.

"Stop there," Tom called out.

Lucas heard the click of a firearm. Father Treacher was lying across his chest, struggling to get up, an arrow bounced in the air as his shoulder gave way beneath him.

"Father," Lucas cried.

"I'm all right," Father muttered. "Wounded."

The eis turned and fled and Lucas could hear the solid padded feet of a felid pummel off into the wood.

"It's all right, Tom," Lucas said. "They've gone. Help me with Father."

"Are you certain?" Tom was breathless, turning this way and that with the firearm unfamiliar in his hands.

"I can smell them," he said. "With a good wind."

"Very well," Tom said and lowered the firearm.

Together they lifted Father and helped him through the woods to the wissenry.

"You need a guard, Lucas. It's clear now."

"I don't need a guard, Father. But I'll take that firearm."

Chapter Forty-six

Fenn and Rogget arrived at the faire glade in the divide wood at dawn the next morning to find Sadie and Grayson, alone, waiting for them. "You're a bit late," Sadie said hugging Rogget.

"There was a lot to learn at the wissenry." Fenn paused and looked at both of them. "I didn't know if you would be here."

"Of course they'd come," Rogget said, reaching out a hand and mussing Grayson's hair.

Sadie reached into her knapsack and pulled out a small parcel wrapped in biscuit paper. "The children of Path made this for you."

Fenn unwrapped it to find a stone charm, flat and round, that fit into the small of his palm; it was painted all over with tiny stick-figure children.

"You're a hero now," Grayson said.

"What about you two?"

Sadie shook her head. "We don't have the mark."

Fenn turned the stone over and over in his hand and then removed his hemp rope and added the stone to it. His mother's gold charm tinkled lightly against it with welcome.

"What news?" Fenn said finally, as he and Rogget joined them in sitting around the small fire they'd made.

"They've released all the children."

Fenn nodded. "That much we'd heard. What of your parents? Did you see them?"

They both shook their heads.

"We were hid out in Drew's home by the lake," Sadie said. "The guard searched, but didn't find us. But that was just after we'd arrived...when, I think they were still just looking for all the escaped children. It was later in the day that the proclamation came from the king."

"Proclamation?" Rogget shuddered.

"We three were named enemies of the king—and our parents as well. And there are rumors spreading that Welk plans to take all the realms under his control, to unite them to find and kill you. He's already spread the proclamation through-out the Ruud."

"But they will fight, won't they? Aaronland and Damon Wall will fight for their independence."

Rogget sighed. "They'll be seen as helping you to defeat the Ruud if they don't succumb to Welk."

"Yes," Grayson said. "Welk said that they are either with him...or they are with you."

They all stared into the fire. Fenn was stunned. Sadie and Grayson seemed shocked as well, though they'd had more time to digest this terrible turn of events.

Grayson said, "We left Drew's house right away and headed out here. We didn't want to put his family in any more danger."

"We don't know where to begin in rescuing our parents."

Fenn nodded gravely. "I'm sorry. I should have told you about my mark. Maybe you wouldn't be here in this mess with me if I'd been honest."

Sadie sighed. "No, I guess I understand. I'd be scared to show anyone, too."

"Can I see it again," Grayson asked. "In the daylight?"

Fenn shrugged and pulled his shoulder out of his tunic. They oohed and aahed over it: three lines, like claw marks, two inches long, tapering to points down his arm.

"It's the faire mark," Grayson said.

"Oh, come on," Sadie said. "Do you really have to know everything?"

"I can't help it if I read a lot of books."

"Don't start at each other again," Fenn said.

"I can't believe it," Grayson said. "I saw it in the dark that night and I told myself over and over I was mistaken. It can't be. It just can't be."

"Well, what's the faire mark?" Sadie said.

"The sign of the fairies. I only read about it once in a big book on mythology. The fairies know, somehow, if you're meant for something... some important duty. I can't remember it all. But they mark you. Nobody believes it's real, though."

"You're saying I'm a fairy?"

"Don't be insulted." Grayson smiled.

"Really, we're sitting here in their glade," Sadie said. "Be polite."

"It's said to mean you are somehow related to the beast folk. Maybe it explains how you could understand fairy talk in the forest."

"Oh, well, now everything is clear," Fenn shook his head. Did nothing in his world follow the rules of logic, or at the very least, common sense, anymore?

Grayson shrugged. "It could just be talk."

"Of course it's just talk." After a brief silence he continued, "So, in the end, we didn't really accomplish much."

"How's that?" Grayson said. "We freed all the kids of the Ruud."

"But all we really needed to do was walk up to the guard and show them my mark. We went through quite a bit of trouble for nothing."

"You're looking at it all wrong," Sadie said. "You didn't know your mark would free the children. You did what you thought was right and in the process it all worked out."

"You sound like Father Britt."

"Father Britt is a great man," Rogget broke in. "Don't take him lightly."

It was hard not to, with him smiling all the time. No matter; it wasn't likely Fenn would ever see him again.

"What do we do now?" he asked them.

But no one said a thing. No one looked up from the fire. Not even Fenn, whose mind was so captivated and haunted by all he'd learned that only the focus of the flame seemed to calm him.

Finally, as if awakening from a trance, Fenn said half-heartedly, "I'm told to travel to the ice kingdom to see a maiden."

Sadie nodded slightly. "Sounds like fun."

"Cold," Grayson said.

Fenn nodded.

"I'm so tired. My feet and legs hurt. I feel like I could sleep for days," Sadie said, yawning. "Do you think we've walked a hundred miles?"

"Maybe," Grayson said. "I could try to figure it out with your maps if you want."

Sadie shook her head. "I think I'd rather not know."

After another long pause in which they continued to watch the fire, Grayson said, "So, it's to the ice realm. I feel like one of the travelers at the inn."

"I did always want to travel to the places I'd read about in my dad's books."

"You haven't read any of your dad's books," Grayson said.

"Well, I've looked at the pictures."

"You don't have to come with me," Fenn said. "You could go with Rogget into the hill country and stay safe."

"We stick together," Rogget said.

"Definitely," Grayson said. "Let's agree on that, at least."

"We'll make a pact," Sadie said, holding out her hand, palm down. "We stick together; through thick and thin, with beast or folk, we stay true to each other. No more secrets. We're a team—no matter what. Agreed?"

Grayson put his hand over Sadie's and smiled. "Agreed."

Rogget laid his hand over Grayson's. "Aye. Agreed."

Fenn put his hand on the top of the pile. "Agreed."

They each in turn smacked the pile with their other hand. It was settled.

They spent the day talking over the plan, and though it was well-

182

thought and doable, Fenn still had the sense that they were left open and vulnerable.

What can we do? he kept wondering to himself. How might they rescue Sadie's parents and Grayson's da? How would they stay safe crossing the hill country? How could he avoid Welk's guard? How could they end this nonsensical madness?

They went to sleep in late afternoon, expecting to rise before midnight to start their trek across the border of the Ruud. But the faire glade acted as a tonic, bringing them deep and satisfying slumber difficult to rouse from. Sadie snored; Rogget snored louder; and Darnit louder still.

That morning, in the wee early hours, Fenn alone lay awake in the dark, restless, staring up into the gold and silver dust floating among a few lightning bugs. He'd thought of waking the others so they could see them glow, but appreciated the solitude and the quiet for his nerves. The treetops swayed far above him in the cold night air and the stars twinkled down upon him.

"What can we do?" he whispered, agonizing over his fate.

A wind seemed to pick up and shake the trees; but as he looked carefully, Fenn saw it wasn't the wind that rustled the leaves and needles. Thousands of fairies, no bigger than the leaves behind which they'd been hiding, their fluttering wings shimmering in the moonlight, hovered all around him in the crisp air of the glade. They whispered, at first a cacophony of airy nonsense, but finally merging their lyrical voices into one unified message.

Fenn smiled. "Yes, of course," he said. "That's exactly what we'll do."

BOOK TWO

The Wretched

Chapter One

1268 Autumn

Piercing screams echoed around him as Prince Welk of Michelruud startled awake in the darkness. He clambered up, for a moment unable to remember where he was. His tent had collapsed around him and he battled with it. *The tent.* Yes, the encampment on the grassy plain of Nergens between the Ruud and the ice realm—northeast of the lilac clover fields. He was in his nuptial tent, the morrow his wedding day when he would finally marry his beloved Rue, whose screams now terrified him into action.

Horse hooves pounded the ground around him, whinnies, shouts, and grunts filled the air as he struggled to free himself from the heavy tarp. It was still night, but as he found his opening, the campsite was lit in flames as the other tents burned.

"Rue-Anna," he screamed, and the reality of his terror shook him. His legs trembled violently as he climbed to his feet and darted toward the women's tent. Their screams had ceased. Only shouts of dark figures on foot and horseback thundered in the air—and the shrill cries of the felid folk child Frieden, who stood a few yards away, just outside his father's flaming tent.

"Rue-Anna," Welk cried out.

A rugged folk ran toward him, his hand raised above his head, a wooden mace locked in his fist. When he realized the man's prey was Frieden, Welk dove for the child, scooped him up and tumbled to the ground, shielding him from the swing of the club. A sharp, stabbing pain shot through his head; dazed, a blackness fell over him, even as he fought to hide the felid child from death, even as he realized his attacker was a soldier in his father's guard.

His own name on his brother's lips floated somewhere in Welk's pain-filled fog of sleep. Elrundt lived, and gently shook him into

184

consciousness.

"Wake, brother," he was saying. "Hurry. Wake."

Welk reached for his throbbing head and forced himself to sit, fighting the waves of nausea rippling through his stomach. Fire raged somewhere near—the odor of burning flesh found him and brought him nearly to heaving. Morning had dawned. He squinted against the harsh summer sun.

"Rue," he whispered and winced.

There beside him was young Frieden, whimpering in his sleep.

"Who else lives, brother?" Welk closed his eyes against the sickening pain racking his body.

"None." There was a cold edge of rage to his brother's voice.

Elrundt helped him to his feet and led him through their burned encampment. Fifty yards east, against the backdrop of the snow-capped peaks of the ice realm, flames rose off a pyre and flumes of swirling black and gray smoke billowed into the clear blue morning sky. The eis had come to cremate their dead.

"No," Welk muttered and made toward them, but Elrundt pulled him back.

"They will not allow us. I have tried."

"They cannot be dead." He turned to Elrundt and let out a choked cry. "They are not gone."

He reeled and looked back at the burned nuptial tents, heaps of ashes now. Belfen, the felid folk child's father, lay just outside the tent he shared with his brothers Quarn and Yew, bloodied and deathly still. Staggering, Welk made his way past him to where his betrothed's tent lay in a blackened clump. The tarp had burned away, exposing Vreni's charred remains, her arms stretched forward as if she'd tried to cover and protect another.

"All dead," Elrundt said following him. "Except the felidae Quarn and Yew. They watched as Belfen fought for his life and fled when he was killed. The eis arrived before I regained consciousness."

Welk remembered Frieden and turned back to see him still sleeping on the ground in the middle of the remains of their lives.

"Why didn't Belfen take his felid form?" Elrundt said.

"He and Vreni were bound by the old ways."

"He died for principle?"

"No, brother. Once they took the oath, they could not transform until Frieden was of a certain age. They were physically unable." Welk found his knees loosening and he let himself sit. "Quarn and Yew," he said. "They did nothing?"

"They might have fought valiantly and torn many of the guard apart," Elrundt said. "Before being shot… probably killed. But, they did nothing to stop this."

"It would be better to die fighting than live as cowards. The felidae would agree."

Elrundt shook his head, his eyes empty, his countenance dispirited.

"They cannot be dead," Welk muttered.

He remained on the ground for some time, his brother letting him have his silence; tears streamed down his face until he wiped them away and scowled.

"What happened? What did you see?" he asked Elrundt.

"I was just on the edge of sleep. They buckled the tents first and set the others on fire. I fought, but there were many. I watched Belfen carry Frieden out of his tent and try to get him to run while he fought off the guard. And I watched Quarn and Yew do nothing."

"Not our tents?"

"They knew our colors."

"And you were not harmed?"

"They cudgeled me. Same as you."

"It was Father's guard."

"And that is why we live." Elrundt nearly spat the words.

Welk stood and forced fresh air into his lungs, but it was tinged with the smoke of the bodies of their beloved eisen.

"Then we know what we must do now. We will go home. And kill him."

Elrundt stared at him, and Welk realized, sadness falling over him, that his brother had succumbed finally, to their father's ill will. He'd had his fill of abuse and it had hardened him. His dark eyes, instead of burning with rage, were dulled with pain.

"I will never return to the Ruud," Elrundt said. "I will never look upon our father again. Not even to murder him."

Tiny, muted cries startled them and they turned to see pale Frieden, sitting up and peering around him. Welk hurried to the child and lifted him into his arms.

He whimpered. "Mama."

"We have visitors," Elrundt said and turned to the west.

"From the south as well."

From the west came the felidae, dozens of them, padding through the tall plains grass into the camp in their svelte, black, feline forms—large, formidable beasts, who could kill a folk with a swipe of a paw. Without greeting, they sniffed out the bodies of Belfen and Vreni and several shifted into folk form to lift them.

"Quarn, you coward," Elrundt shouted and made for the group.

"No," Welk warned. "Now is not the time to break the troubled truce between us."

They watched as the party of felidae escorted their folk away with the bodies. But Quarn and Yew remained behind, turned to them, and transformed into frail, wan folk. Elrundt took a few steps toward them as they approached and Welk considered allowing him to take his vengeance on the felidae. But they would only have to shift back into their feline forms to rip him apart.

"Give us the child," Quarn said.

Welk's heart sank into his chest. Turn Belfen's son over to the felidae? "No."

Quarn let out a guttural growl and the pack of felidae stopped their march and turned, waiting.

"Give us the felid child. He does not belong with you."

"You will murder him," Elrundt said.

"That is none of your concern."

"It is," Welk said. "Belfen was my friend. He and Vreni pledged themselves to the old ways of your kind. You must honor them."

"He is mine now." Quarn stepped forward.

"Stop." One of the felidae in the pack had shifted into his folk form and his voice echoed in a loud penetrating hum all around them. "The prince speaks the truth. Our brothers left the forest to live among the folk. It was their wish."

Quarn turned to the felid. "But Frieden is my nephew. Now orphaned. He is my responsibility."

"Not if this folk will take him."

Looking back to Welk, Quarn's face twisted in fury. "I will not leave him in the hands of these vile creatures."

"You will do as I command," the felid folk behind him said.

Quarn's body shook with rage. He took two steps back, shifted to his cat form, turned, and stalked away. He and Elrundt watched the felidae trod across the plain toward the snug villages of the Ruud miles distant, and their beast forest beyond.

Elrundt turned to him. "What do you intend to do with a young felid folk?"

Welk turned south where the old wissende's party made its way into the burned camp. There were five, all in their humble brown wissenry robes, tied at the waist with rope belts. It was unusual to find wissendes so far from the Ruud.

"What has happened here?" Father Britt said. He was a head shorter than Welk and twice as round. His straight brown hair sat about his head like a dirty bowl.

"Our party was attacked in the night," Welk said. "Eis and felidae were killed."

Father Britt stared at them, astonished. "But you live?"

"Yes, Father. And I have a charge for you." He handed the boy into the arms of the wissende.

"Orphaned?"

Welk nodded. "He is Frieden, named so because his parents wanted the freedom to live the felidae ways of old, when their young lived out their folk years as Mutterede intended."

"You wish the wissenry to raise a felid?"

"Indeed. You will find them not so much different from us."

Father Britt handed the child to one of his party and stepped into the camp. "But who did this?"

"What brings you here so far from the Cold Sea, Father?" Elrundt said.

"We look for Father Wold. Have you seen him? He is errant. Banished, but returned uninvited. We wish to see him settled for good in one of the wasteland villages. He was last seen heading north toward the ice realm. We fear for his sanity."

"You banished a wissende?"

"Indeed. Did you see him?"

They shook their heads, perplexed, then turned once more to the camp. Welk felt a great urge to let himself collapse to the ground, to stay there until he starved or died from thirst, to never leave his beloved Rue. But the eis had already claimed her—and they would not let him join her in their afterworld.

"May I offer you words of comfort, my young princes of the Ruud?" Father Britt said.

They shook their heads again.

"There is nothing to say," Elrundt said. "This is what is wrought by kings. My life as a prince of the Ruud is done."

1280 Autumn

King Welk paced the floor of the great hall an hour before dawn. Soon, the nobles of Michelruud Castle would gather for their breakfast, there would be noise and merriment, feasting and stories, before they'd all be off for horse races, hunting, or apple picking. Welk would allow them to go; the folk should not be alarmed as yet.

The threat from the ice realm in the northeast was merely percolating —a territorial dispute only. Why the eis were so adamant that no folk be allowed to settle in the hills abutting their realm was beyond him. If they weren't content to use the land, why keep it from others? Did they despise mortal folk so much?

The threat from the Hass of Emorah in the Great West was only brooding, as well. Their desire to retake the folk of the Ruud and abolish their self-rule was only rumor at this point. And as for the trouble with the bairn of prophecy, the guard alone could handle that. Although, Welk wondered at their prowess. They'd already let Fenn Foster run amok in the Ruud without one sighting. The devilish child broke into the great stone prison Steingefan and helped all the other children escape.

Welk thought the rumors of a bairn born in the wasteland, following an old prophecy of the felidae, was nonsense. And yet the king's guard found the boy with a distinct mark. Could it be true? Was Fenn Foster, a wissenry orphan, fated to destroy the Ruud and kill him? A boy, kill a king? Destroy his homeland? No. It was ludicrous.

Back and forth before the large hearth on the western wall, Welk paced, stopping occasionally to look at the dirt in front of the smouldering fire, shuddering. He could still picture the mark, drawn by the young guard days ago after he'd seen it on young Fenn of the wissenry. He could still hear the oily Sorgood's curious voice, quivering with questions.

"What is it, Sire? What does it mean?"

But he'd refused to tell him anything. The mark of the faire was unknown to the folk. Welk himself had only learned of the design when he saw it for the first and only time on the upper arm of his beloved, Rue of the eis. She'd laughed at him playfully when he asked about it.

"I am special." She smiled and her eyes danced. He'd replied, "Of course you are," and the matter was settled.

Why would Fenn Foster bear that mark? Perhaps it was a mark typical of the eis. Welk had never found himself in a position to examine the arms of any other of the eis. His experience of them was limited to Rue and her sister Aliara—and he couldn't recall any such mark on *her*. If it *were* a mark distinctive of the eis, Welk was certain no one in the Ruud resembled the tall, pale folk of the frozen realm—certainly not Fenn Foster, though he couldn't place the boy's face in his memory.

Welk had turned to the guards who'd discovered Fenn and the stationer's daughter at the old prison, where they'd led the daring escape.

"What did he look like, this Fenn of the wissenry?"

They stared blankly at him.

"Was he tall? What were his features?"

"Tall?" Footman Wolf said. "No, Sire. Very small, for a boy they say be twelve. Rather small for any sort of threat."

"Was he blond?"

"No, Sire, quite the opposite. Very dark of hair and eye. Like yourself, if you don't mind my saying. But very pale, very pale. Unlike you in that respect."

If he was not an eis, why did he have the mark? Now more than ever, Welk needed access to the stationer's library of tomes. He knew him to possess books on the beasts of the realm. There must be an explanation. And the stationer's daughter, raised surrounded by those books would have known, surely. And the innkeeper's son, who spent a lifetime listening to stories of the Ruud and beyond, who had teamed up with Fenn Foster, sporting his faire mark—perhaps he too had learned of its importance.

If this mark signified some connection to the beast, it would all make sense. His beast blood would give the boy the power and daring to rescue the imprisoned children from Steingefan. It would be no wonder, then, that the king's guard was unable to track him. He would be instinctively more cunning than other children.

Welk dragged his tired bones to his throne next to the fire. Though it was little more than a large chair covered in pelts of eleshag and rabbit atop a dais, he found it imposing and ridiculous; but he liked the height and watching the room as if a large bird. Here now, in the dim candle-lit silence of the great hall, he recalled his fear and awe as a small child in watching his father's great ceremony in taking the seat, and grimaced.

He could still see it. He could still smell the burnt hides and tents. He could not wipe from memory the bloodied body of his friend Belfen. The pyre on which his beloved burned. And Father Britt, gaping, horrified at the massacre, the felid boy clinging to him.

Turning on this throne to look again at the hearth where the mark of the faire had been made in the dirt, he shuddered. He should have killed his father as soon as he returned home. But he did not. Rue would not have borne it. He closed his eyes, waiting for day to dawn once more.

Chapter Two

L ike a bubble rising from the bottom of a pond, Fenn came awake; he did not open his eyes, but lay still, allowing gentle sunlight to bath him in warmth. He was in the faire glade where the cold winds of autumn could not reach him. Grayson had told them the fairies abandoned the glade long ago, but Fenn remembered lying awake the night before—they came out of hiding and sang to him; and he understood their song. Sadie and Grayson would never believe him.

They were to have awakened at midnight to begin their journey across the boundary of the Ruud, escaping the king's guard into the hill country. Yet they had overslept; he could hear Sadie snoring not far away.

The night curse, yes, that was what woke him and his mother's charm was hot against his chest. He could hear her, a soft airy voice; in his vision, she grasped the robe of a wissende with her slender hand and said, "Keep him safe." He'd become accustomed to that image in his head.

But there had been more this time. "Tell him who he is." And those words startled him into pulling away from slumber. Was that truly a part of his vision, he wondered, or had he invented it himself, wishing she'd once said such a thing so he could confront the wissenry and demand to be told everything?

Darnit, the huntsman Rogget's brown bear, rustled his nose into someone's back pack. Jerky again?

"Darnit," Fenn said aloud, pulling his mother's charm from under his tunic to let his skin cool a bit. "Cut it out." But still he did not open his eyes until he heard the whisper of an unfamiliar voice.

"Gold."

Bolting upright, raising a hand to shield his eyes from the sun, Fenn startled to see a man standing over him, leering, his face pinched in a scowl. Three others dug through their supplies, tossing them about as if they were trash.

"Where did you get that?" The intruder reached out and lifted the charm from Fenn's chest.

"That's mine."

Grabbing Fenn's tunic, the grimy-haired folk lifted him in the air, giving him a shake.

"I said where did you get that?"

"It's mine, I tell you."

The man dropped Fenn and shoved him to the ground. Reaching out, he pulled Fenn's hemp rope from around his neck with a yank. Fenn tried to grab at it, but the thief batted him away as if he were a bug.

"That's mine," Fenn said. "Give it back. Grayson, Sadie!" He saw them startle awake.

"Now, now, let's not get excited," one of the others said.

"Tie them," the thief said.

The other men grabbed Sadie and Grayson.

"Give that back," Fenn demanded, but the folk sneered at him and pulled the hemp rope over his own head.

"You thieving little brat."

"Me? It's mine!"

Fenn jumped up and rushed at him, grabbing wildly for the rope, but the man seized him and held him and Fenn felt the cold blade of a knife scrape his neck. As Fenn's hands wrapped around the folk's thick arms, in a futile attempt to push him off, his first thought was of Darnit and Rogget. *Where were they?* Had the thieves killed them? Anger consumed him—then rage, hatred, and a lust for his gold charm. At first he directed it toward the sneering man holding him, pulling him to where Sadie and Grayson sat being tied up by the others. Then he felt as if he *were* the thief, as if he'd sunk down into the other man's clothes and *become* him—wanting the gold, wanting to kill Fenn, being held back by a confused feeling of remorse and hope buried deep within. As the folk pushed him to the ground beside Sadie, Fenn came back to himself, weak and trembling.

They huddled together, their hands tied behind their backs, watching as the thieves rifled through their supplies. Again, Fenn wondered where Rogget had gone.

"Look here, Clutch." One of the men, smaller and hunched, his face covered in dirt, limped toward him. "A pouch."

"Let me have it, Muck," the man who wore Fenn's charm growled, and the other tossed it at him. He opened it and smiled at the kids. "Coin." Closing the drawstring, he held the pouch up and shook it. "Thankee very much."

"Yo, Clutch." Muck returned to rooting in Sadie's knapsack. "What're they doing out here in the divide wood all 'lone, eh? It don't seem right."

"What do we care? Just get their valuables and let's head out. If we don't catch Grindelwell before his debtors do, we'll have to give him up for good."

"Aye, what's he worth anyway? What do we want with the likes o' him?"

"Eh, now. He's my brother." Stout and bald, this man tossed Grayson's belongings from his bag onto the ground.

"You don't see me begging special favors for *my* brother," Muck said.

"You ain't got one."

"Shut up, all o' you," Clutch yelled.

Grayson sucked in a deep breath and screamed, "Elrundt! I call on the spirit of Elrundt! Help us!"

Fenn winced and turned from him. "Do you have to yell?"

Clutch threw his head back and roared with laughter. He walked to where they sat, bound together on the ground, and leaned down to put his face very close to Grayson's.

"Elrundt's not going to help you today, boy."

"Are you sure?" one of Clutch's men said, turning in circles looking up at the sky. "Are you sure he ain't got a spirit helper?"

"It's only a legend, Gog. It isn't real."

"Wait a min'. I just thought o' something."

Clutch rolled his eyes. "What did I tell you about spouting off every stupid idea that pops into your noggin?"

"No, wait, Clutcher." He pulled a stationer's poster from his sack. "I got this here in Aaronland this morning as we passed through. They was posted all over the place."

Clutch shrugged. "So." He took the poster and glanced at it before handing it back to the other folk.

"So, it says here..."

"Oh, everybody stop stealing now." One of the others chuckled. "Goggle's planning on reading to us. Tell us a story now, Gog."

"Let him read it," Clutch said.

"It says these three kids be enemies of the king. The one in Michelruud, anyway."

"Three kids?"

"A girl, name of Sadie Pratt, daughter to the Path stationer; pale brown of hair and eye, with freckles."

"Freckles?" Sadie said. Grayson leaned into her with his shoulder to give her a nudge, frowning.

"A boy, Grayson Steppe, of the inn; dark in features—tall, scrawny."

Sadie giggled and once again, Grayson shoved at her.

"And a Fenn Foster of the wissenry—small, pale, but dark of hair and eye—who'll be havin' a mark on his right shoulder."

Clutch stared in amazement at the three of them crouched together at his feet. He stepped in front of Fenn and pulled at his tunic.

"That there's a mark right there." Muck said.

"You got him on the first try, Clutch!" Goggle said.

"Enemies of the king, eh?" Clutch said. "How much can we get for 'em?"

"It don't say how much. But it does say reward."

"A reward from the king?" Muck said.

"Aw, Clutch, no king's gonna give the likes of us no reward," the bald man said.

"The king of Michelruud will." Clutch nodded. "I think Grindelwell will have to be given up to his debtors, after all. Let's get these enemies to the king, eh? Goggle, you go on reading all you want. Don't nobody make fun of you anymore."

The crack of a tree branch echoed in the glade and Darnit burst into camp roaring and charging at the thieves. The folk scattered, shouting, running off in a panic. Darnit continued the chase into the wood as Rogget showed up with a few dead rabbits hanging by their back feet from a rope.

"Get up, get up." Rogget's thick fingers deftly worked the ties at their wrists, freeing them. "We need to move; they're likely to come back for you once they realize Darnit's got no bite nor sense of direction."

Chapter Three

The carriages stopped on the forest path to Michelruud and Leah looked up from her journal. She'd been remembering her trip so far with a heaviness that she attributed to homesickness. She was not enjoying herself in the Ruud as much as she'd expected.

Prenalin was kinder as the days wore on; he too must be longing for Ruhm and his family. Kirche was his usual hot and cold—one hour regaling her with stories of his childhood in the prestigious King's Chosen school back home, laughing at his own derogatory opinions on the folk of the Ruud, winking at her when he caught her staring at him—and the next moment sullen, brooding, quiet, and glaring.

Perhaps, she reasoned, Lord Kirche also missed home. Even the well-traveled must still wish for their own beds on occasion. That morning, Leah wished for any bed. They'd had the porters Gretchen and Zelda pack up their belongings for the short trip to Michelruud the night before and for some reason, probably known only to Rett himself, awoke before dawn to begin the trip without so much as a by your leave to King Arnot or his queen.

Only Cook was there to wave her a farewell after she'd shoved a napkin full of breakfast tarts at her. Leah was grateful for both the tarts and the goodbye. She realized now, as the carriage horses danced in their harnesses, how much she'd written in her journal of her mother: her meals, her baked goods, her face, hands, and smile. But she most fondly remembered their long sessions in front of the looking glass as her mother brushed out Leah's long brown hair while singing ancient songs of Mutterede, long since forgotten by the followers of Rett.

"Why have we stopped?" She asked when Prenalin peered into her carriage, took her journal from her and set it on the opposite bench with a smile. He offered her his hand to help her to the ground outside. A fresh rush of autumn filled her nose and she breathed deeply. All about her, forest golds, reds, and yellows mingled with deep evergreens and brought a smile to her lips.

"Did I not tell you?" Prenalin said, watching her. "We are to go on a hunt before we go to Michelruud. We have quite an adventure planned."

"Oh."

"Are you not up for adventure?"

They followed Lord Kirche and his guards Alphonse and Redd, while Kipling remained at the carriage with the porters.

"My apologies, Prenalin. I'm afraid I'm too tired to appreciate it." She smiled at him.

"As soon as we make stop, we'll start a fire and heat up some kaff bitters. We hunt at mid-morning."

She nodded, tightened up the ribbon holding her hair behind her back, and followed along into the woods silently. There was a cold moistness in the air; the hair at the nape of her neck stuck to her skin. Heady aromas of pine and jasmine floated all around her and the damp ground was cold through her shoes and stockings to her feet. Leah couldn't keep the smile from her lips. Truly the Ruud and the eastern continent had beauty that rivaled the marble city of Ruhm. She so wished she could tell Prenalin, even Kirche, how much she felt at home in the forests of the Ruud, even on the streets of their villages among their folk. How often she'd thought she could stay here, if only her mother and father would join her. But she knew such comments bordered on blasphemy.

Ruhm was to be first in her heart, and certainly her loyalty. Ruhm was supreme on Kell. The most glorious city, the most noble Hass, the wisest High Preist, Kirche. All these things she'd been taught and knew deep in her soul.

But never at the Hass school did they tell her of the greens and golds of the east—they'd noshed Ruud apples, with pleasure, but were often told it was the trip across the sea to the Great West that turned them sweet.

Leah smiled to herself. Such silly stories only a child could believe. But believe them, they all did. Now she had to admit, the rich soil beneath her feet, the temperate weather, the freshness of the air, the clean, cold water in the streams—these were surely the necessary ingredients for the juiciest apples on Kell.

And never at the Hass school did they show pictures of the beauty of the landscape in the east. In Ruhm, once you left the city, you gazed upon a rocky, brown horizon to the far off mountains in the north—crags of rock that beckoned only outlaws and escaped beast folk. The Ruud, quite to the contrary was covered in succulent, colorful, fecund life.

Leah, smiling, took a deep breath and walked into Prenalin's back.

"Oh." She gasped and fell backward onto her bottom on the cold pine-covered ground.

Prenalin was there in an instant to help her to her feet. He chuckled but placed a finger to his lips. Leah realized they'd met up with a small group of folk. Prenalin stepped behind her to guide her forward, but they remained behind Kirche and were not introduced.

"This way." The slithering weasel waved a hand to lead them.

Leah walked on in stunned silence. They were now accompanied by the vile folk Lord Kirche had met with secretly in the woods a few nights before. There, he'd mentioned a hunt—a hunt for brownies. She shook off her nagging suspicion. She must have misheard him. For what purpose would one kill a brownie? Lord Kirche couldn't intend to eat one—the very idea was absurd.

"What do we hunt, Prenalin?"

He shrugged. "The usual, I would imagine. They have large pheasant in these woods, and boar. We will take gifts to Michelruud, no doubt."

Leah followed on, trying to remain behind Prenalin, hoping not to be noticed by the weasel. She feared her expression would make him suspicious, though she was certain he never saw her hiding in the woods listening in on his conversation with Kirche.

They found a small glade and Alphonse and Redd dug a fire pit and set up tender. Once the fire was ablaze and they had mugs of bitters, she relaxed on the blanket Prenalin gave her, resting her back against a stump.

"Michelruud is always the key," Kirche was saying to the weasel. "The others tolerate us very well. But King Evan was forever difficult."

"You will find his son no less so, I'm afraid."

"Were they close?"

"Far from it. And that may be to your disadvantage. The newly crowned King Welk will have things done his own way. He is not familiar with the Hass and its dealings with the Ruud."

"Perhaps I can work that to my advantage," Kirche said. "And now he has a little beast of a boy to deal with. Hass can help him with that problem."

"It would be best to rid us all of the little brat as soon as possible. The folk are beginning to speak out, to stand up to the guard and the king, out of their fear of the boy."

"If they truly believe he is prophesied, that will work well for us."

196

"I suppose, my Lord. You know best."

The vile man reached up to smooth the hair on the sides of his head, and tugged at his collar. Leah sucked in a tiny breath. His hands and neck were covered with tiny scars. She'd seen the like before. With a twitch, the weasel glared across the fire at her and she flinched.

"Your new aide is rather interested."

Kirche laughed. "You prefer your aides to pretend to be occupied, no doubt." He cast a glance at the two guardsmen who had accompanied their guest, now distant, standing alert and uninterested.

"Well, I certainly expect that they do not stare."

Leah lowered her gaze to the dark brew in her mug.

"Leah Hallowsing," Kirche said and she looked up again. "This is Sorgood. He is one of us."

"Is he?"

Kirche laughed again and Sorgood sneered.

"Insolence."

"My apoligies, Sorgood," Leah said. "I was surprised that is all. I thought you a folk of the Ruud. I meant no disrespect."

"He is indeed of the Ruud. We have some loyalists here, even in the east. Ruhm is their fatherland, after all. And Hass their mother church."

"Yes, sir. Of course. Do they teach abqut the Hass in the east?"

Leah glanced at Prenalin, sensing his disapproval at her outspoken nature, but his eyes were on his own mug of bitters.

"They do not," Sorgood said. "They have no schools in the Ruud and prefer to leave their folk in ignorance. Such is the legacy of the great wissendes of Ruhm."

"Then, if I may be so bold, sir, how did you learn of Hass?"

Sorgood chuckled and rolled his eyes. "From the annual visits of course."

"You will see when we arrive in Michelruud," Kirche said. "We have a small following there among some of the older children."

"Why only in Michelruud?"

"We concentrate our attention there. We—how shall I say it—recruit some of their young folk."

"But, again, why only Michelruud?"

Lord Kirche smiled at her. And though she was sure he was just as condescending as his friend Sorgood, it warmed her heart and her cheeks blushed.

"Because Michelruud is the key. Michelruud has always been the dominant kingdom of the Ruud and one day, soon, she will make a play to reunite all the kingdoms into one, as they were in the beginning.

Michelruud is where the power concentrates. We do not want to train the youth of Aaronland and Damon Wall only to have them fight between themselves when the time comes. No, Michelruud will take the entire Ruud, and our recruits there will be ready."

"I see."

Both men smiled at her as if she were a child and went on in conversation between them. Leah turned again to Prenalin. He sipped his bitters and looked about him, avoiding her gaze. The kaff took root in her blood and she was energized. Leah stood and brushed imaginary soil from her skirt.

"Yes." Kirche also stood. "Let us be on the hunt. Alphonse and Redd will remain here with our things. We need only our firearms and bows."

"Surely, I am to remain behind as well," Leah said.

"Oh, no, no," Kirche said. "You must join us. I insist."

"I have no practice with the firearm, Lord."

"But you do with a bow, no doubt. I hear the archery classes at the Hass school are superb."

"Yes, of course."

Reluctantly, Leah took the bow and quiver she was offered. As they walked on, away from the warmth of the fire, she tested her string and examined her bow.

"And what will you be hunting today, Leah?" Prenalin smiled at her.

"I've bagged my share of squirrel and hundrat. But I do not think the king of Michelruud would be much impressed by them."

"Agreed. It's boars and elchen for a king's table."

"We won't find elchen in these woods, will we?"

"Quiet down," Sorgood said, glaring at the two of them. "From here out, we are silent. Even in our footsteps."

"I confess," Prenalin whispered in her ear, his right arm pulling at her right shoulder, drawing her close so that she could feel his breath on her neck. "I myself am not a hunter."

He let her go and moved a few paces in front of her, but looked back at her with a smile. They trod quietly as they could, with Sorgood and Kirche occasionally turning back to them with annoyed expressions or fingers to their lips. Sorgood led the way through the dense wood that grew darker as they walked; moistness now hung heavy in the air as fog just at their torsos and rising up past their heads. They could see through the mist only as if through a ratty worn bed sheet and thus snuck ever so slowly through the forest.

On occasion, Sorgood would stop, raise a hand, lower himself to the ground to peer beneath the fog, then stand, and motion for them to continue. While Leah felt out of place with the hunting party, the feel, the smell, the deep green of her surroundings lulled her into a fantasy dream in which she was on a great exploration in a foreign land, searching for the lost treasure of Ruhm.

Once again, Sorgood's arm popped up; they halted and waited. Sorgood knelt and peered through the wood under the fog. He stood and motioned for them to move on.

"Perhaps," Prenalin whispered again in her ear, "we should make our way on our hands and knees to better see whatever it is we look for."

Leah slapped her hand against her mouth and turned from the group, trying to hold in her laughter. Bent over and forcing herself to think upsetting thoughts of brownies fleeing their bows for their lives, she sucked in several deep breaths through her fingers. When she turned, Kirche and Sorgood were glaring at her. She could do nothing more than slug Prenalin in the shoulder, still smiling.

Sorgood held up his hand, turned and knelt. He stood again and beckoned them move forward. The fog eased as they hiked, lifted higher and higher as they crept behind Sorgood and Kirche. Leah's nose tickled at a familiar smell.

She turned to Prenalin; her face broke into a smile. Kettering's roses. The forest there was abloom. She could not see them, but she smelled the heady perfume, just as she did while passing Kettering's cart in the town square back home. Roses, like the ones that lined the gardens at the grand Hall of Hass. Prenalin turned to her, and smiled in response to hers, but she said nothing, not wanting another scolding form Sorgood.

Their steps slowed, the fog now lifted, and the forest opened into a clearing. Beyond, at the base of an enormous pine, a brownie rooted in the dirt. He dug a tiny hole only to replace the dirt, patted the ground with both hands, sniffed about, dug, refilled, and patted again, then bounced against the earth as if tamping it. Leah's heart sank. Without thinking, she shook her head and grimaced. So it was true.

Kirche raised his firearm and aimed, squinting into the sight. A shot shattered the woods, echoing in waves into the distance. Birds shrieked and flitted all around, fighting for the sky. Other beasts, unseen, darted away from them through the trees and shrubs. And the brownie, writhing on the mossy ground, began to scream.

Leah's gut churned and pushed against her throat as Kirche moved forward toward the poor creature and raised his firearm once more.

Chapter Four

The early morning mist tingled at his face as Lucas hiked through the woods of Timber on his way to Michelruud Castle. He'd dug his wissende's cloak out of his pack and wrapped himself in it, now pulling the hood over his head for extra warmth. Quarn and the eis assassin followed him—sometimes behind, sometimes to the left or right. Their scents mingled with the pine and honeysuckle. Lucas reached for the grip of Father Treacher's firearm at his hip, reassured.

In his last encounter with Quarn, Father had taken an arrow meant for him. His chest swelled with indignation at the thought that Father might have lost his life. But he was merely shot through the arm; Father Britt assured him Treacher would heal fully in a month or two.

"I am grateful for Father Treacher's bravery and sacrifice," he told Britt. "And I am glad I don't have to avenge his death."

"Avenge him?" Britt had sputtered. "We do not advocate such actions. They lead only to more death and strife."

"And a clear conscience."

"A clear conscience, my boy? Live long enough, and you will realize there is no such thing."

Lucas chuckled to himself. Perhaps Fenn Foster was right after all. The wissendes say much...and yet very little. A twig broke nearby and he stopped his trek. The hair on the back of his neck, and on his arms, stood erect. Slowly, he turned to find the frail Quarn and the taller eis hunter standing four yards distant among the trees.

"Come into the clearing," he told them and watched, every nerve in his body aquiver, as they made their way forward to greet him.

"And so you would still have me murdered, Quarn."

"You belittle our ways by remaining in that disgusting form."

"And yet you stand before me the same."

Quarn moved forward, his lips curled into a scowl. "You know not of what you speak, young felid. Once you are turned, you will see that this form is weak. It is vile. And only used when necessary."

Lucas' gaze was focused behind Quarn on the eis readying his bow.

"Has he paid you?" he asked him, his right hand finding Father Treacher's firearm.

The eis looked puzzled.

"He won't pay you," Lucas said. He pulled the gun from its holster and pointed it at the eis.

"That won't do enough harm to stop me from killing you." The eis chuckled. "Even should your aim be true, I would have your throat slit

200

before I succumb."

"Then I will shoot Quarn." Lucas aimed the gun at his uncle. "As I said, he won't pay you."

"You would murder your uncle?" Quarn said.

"You would have me murdered. What's the difference?"

"Life itself is the difference, you fool."

"Exactly," Lucas said. "I choose to live my life as folk. You have no right to deny me that."

Lucas sensed motion behind him; Quarn and the eis hunter stepped back several paces and the eis lowered his weapon. Quarn, threatened, shuddered into his feline form. Lucas turned to see Red Lichen and three other centaurs standing behind him.

"What have we here?" Lichen said, his front hoofs pound-ing the earth.

Quarn shook and trembled, his enormous head rocked back and forth in agitation, until he reformed as a felid folk.

"You have no right to interfere," he growled.

"You speak of rights?" Lucas said. "He means to have me murdered by this eis."

The eis stepped back another pace, shouldered his bow and raised his hands as if in surrender. Being trampled by powerful centaurs was not in his plans.

Lichen gazed upon the scene for a moment before speaking again.

"Do you wish an overthrow of Dag Voorspeld?" he asked Quarn. "Or do you attempt this for Lucas' sake only?"

"His name is not Lucas. His name is Frieden; he is my nephew and my responsibility."

"Your responsibility was severed when he was given up to the folk. Your actions now will be brought to the attention of the lord."

A low, guttural growl rolled from Quarn and he slunk back into his cat form, turned and padded away. The eis assassin bowed low.

"My apologies for offending you, Red Lichen."

"Stay away from Lucas."

"Of course." The eis smirked and turned to follow Quarn.

Lucas let himself breathe again and turned to Lichen and the others.

"What were you going to do?" Lichen said. "Shoot Quarn?"

Lucas tilted his head and smiled. "I had few choices."

"You need a guard. The eis will not defer from this challenge simply because we defended you this time. He would find pleasure in killing you. And he knows we are confined to the forest."

"And yet I find you here, out of the forest, in the Timber woods."

"The brownies and fairies alerted us. Being followed by an eis hunter, they said. I am surprised to find they were telling the truth."

"Well, you're most likely right about the eis continuing in this adventure. But why does he not snipe at me from a distance? Why does he show himself first?"

"It is not sporting to kill a folk by stealth. A guard will prevent him from approaching you."

"I intend to find myself a guard of sorts."

"See that you do. We will escort you to the edge of the wood. Stay in the open until you are with others."

Lucas felt like a lost lamb with his escort; but he couldn't deny the wisdom of it.

Chapter Five

They gathered their discarded sacks and returned to them all that the thieves had no use for—their second pair of clothes and Sadie's book of maps which they hadn't even opened. All their food was gone, Sadie's money and Fenn's charm—in the hands of thieves.

"Hurry." Rogget herded them out of the faire glade.

"What about Darnit?" Fenn said.

"He'll find us, come on."

Sadie stopped to spin around in a circle, getting her last look then turned to follow them.

"Grayson," she whispered. "What was all that about Elrundt? Huh?" And she giggled.

"What's so funny?"

"Nothing. I just didn't know you were the superstitious type."

"I don't believe in Elrundt, okay? I'd have been calling on him plenty of times before this if I did."

"Then why *did* you call him?"

"I was calling Rogget, you dope."

"Then why did you say Elrundt?"

"And let those thugs know we had someone else with us? Sometimes you think too much like a girl, Sadie."

"Well...well, I am a girl. And what does being a girl have to do with it? Honestly, Grayson, sometimes—"

"Hush," Rogget said in a loud whisper.

As they headed east toward the hill country, Fenn remembered the anger and hatred he'd felt when he grabbed Clutch; and when, for a moment he felt like he *was* Clutch, and filled with the pain of loss and fear. Clutch wanted the gold charm desperately; was it from hunger or just greed? And when Fenn felt he'd become himself again and lost the feelings of Clutch, it was still there, a deep connection with the gold charm and a strong desire for it. When Clutch had tossed him to the ground he felt something draw him thin as if he were far from the thing he needed most: the charm.

Strange as it was to feel he had become Clutch, he was more confused that their feelings had been so similar. Had he that much in common with a filthy criminal? He wished he could talk to Father Treacher about it. He would explain what had happened. Maybe it had something to do with being trained as a wissende. But Father Treacher, he remembered, while teaching him a great deal, had failed to explain the most important things to him. He'd probably say something nonsensical about skills and not worrying. Why were they trying to keep him in the dark?

Suddenly, he remembered the fairies in the trees and their song of the early morning, and he stopped walking; but Rogget continued ahead of him.

"We're going the wrong way." They all stopped and turned to look at him.

"The border's that way," Rogget said pointing behind him. "Through the divide wood."

"We've lost all our supplies. We have no food left."

Grayson and Sadie nodded.

"We need to go north, through Aaronland. We'll get supplies and head to the north border instead."

"But that will take us into the wasteland."

"Not exactly," Grayson said. "Let me see your maps." He'd pulled Sadie's pack from her back before she could agree and rifled through it for her book of maps.

"Why don't you just keep them," Sadie said, "if you're going to want to look at them every five minutes."

"Look here." Grayson pointed at the map of the northern outskirts of the Ruud. "If we cross the border north of the Waverly wissenry, we'll be at the northwestern edge of the hill country."

Fenn studied the map. The rapid river they'd crossed again and again in the last two weeks wove between the wasteland and the hill country just north of the Ruud, before disappearing off the map. There was a bridge several miles out. That was where he would cross into the wasteland.

"From there," Grayson said, "we can make our way farther in and to the east, if you want, before turning north toward the cold lands."

"I think the farther we can get from the Ruud the better," Sadie said.

Rogget shook his head. "It's dangerous to try for Aaronland. The guard's on the lookout for you now; all of the guard—even King Arnot's."

"What choice do we have? We need food and supplies," Fenn said.

"Really, Rogget." Sadie put her hands on her hips and frowned at him. "They even took our blankets."

"But," Rogget stammered. "You'll have to cross the plains of Aaron. Wide open."

"Maybe we'll be less conspicuous out in the open. They'd be expecting us to hide," Grayson said.

"And there won't be thieves out in the open either." Sadie's eyes pleaded with Rogget to see reason.

"You'll be finding worse in the hill country, so you best be prepared."

"We'll need weapons then," Fenn said. "Do you have any money?"

Rogget nodded. "I do."

After a pause and a careful study of the map, Rogget shrugged. "All right then. We pass through Town Village for supplies and make our way across the border to the north."

And so they plodded on in silence, only their footsteps on the forest floor thudding against the cold morning air. Fenn struggled again with his feelings of being Clutch, until the quiet boomed heavy in his ears. Why were they all so silent? Rogget, he could understand. As guide, he carried the safety of them all on his shoulders. Grayson seemed to have a new determination about him for their quest, while Sadie acted as if adventure was more than she'd bargained for.

"Freckles," she mumbled. "I bet it was that Jeopard Link who printed up the flyer. He knows how I feel about freckles."

"You have freckles on your nose, Sadie," Grayson said. "You can't deny it."

"But he didn't have to put it on a flyer."

"What's wrong with freckles?" Fenn smiled at her. "I think they're cute."

"You do?" Sadie said.

"Sure, they dabble across your nose and on top of your cheeks like... like a little patch of wild flowers."

Grayson let out a chortle and Sadie frowned at him.

"Maybe my freckles aren't so bad." She smiled.

Grayson turned to Fenn with a glare and they trod on without speaking for some time. When the silence was too much for Fenn and he felt the need to speak, Rogget put out a hand to stop their hike.

Muttering, cursing, and occasional whomps, echoed through the wood, as if someone were trying to chop a tree with his boot. Motioning them forward, Rogget peered around a thick pine. Fenn approached the other side of the tree and looked into a small clearing where a folk was spinning about thwacking trunks, stammering, and whining.

Chapter Six

Leah turned and darted from the scene, through the woods, back into the fog, branches and shrubs tearing at her face and arms, pulling at her hair. She heard the second shot and the brownie's piercing cries fell silent. A knotty vine reached up and tripped her ankles, sending her sprawling on the needle-covered earth. Scrambling to her knees, she crawled to a large rotwood trunk, nearly three times as wide as she was, and leaned against it. Pulling her knees to her chest, she buried her face there to quiet her wailing. Now the smell of Kettering's red roses smothered and nauseated her. Her stomach lurched and she turned to lie across the ground, but nothing came of it. Still, she lay there, her cheek cold on the earth of Kell, settling her breath and her mind.

When footsteps startled her, she sat up and found Prenalin settling himself against the tree beside her. His face was drawn and concerned, but he did not look at her. Prenalin was quite the opposite of Kirche, she thought, taking the opportunity of a long look. His was a rugged and timeworn appearance, while Kirche's skin was soft, almost delicate. And Prenalin's dark eyes could not pierce her thoughts as Kirche's pale gaze did; instead, they only brought confusion and mystery when he frowned at her.

"We must go back," he said.

She shook her head stubbornly, even as she knew she must do as she was told.

"He did not bring you along to upset you. I assure you."

Now Leah stared ahead of her and slightly nodded. Of course Kirche did not do such a thing. But what could he have been thinking?

"He thought I would enjoy the spectacle," she said.

"Yes."

Here she put her face in her hands and began to weep again. "But the poor creature. It is not to be eaten; why would he kill it?"

She wiped at her eyes and turned again to Prenalin, but he still would not look at her and gave no response.

"Tell me," she said. "He does not mean to eat it?"

He sighed and shook his head. "No, of course not. It is a trophy."

"A living, sentient being."

Now he turned to her, anger ablaze in his eyes. "You blaspheme."

Leah shuddered and returned his glare for a second or two, before breathing in an erratic gasp of air to calm her tears. "Of course, you are right. Forgive me."

"Leah, Leah," he said. "It is all he's been raised to believe. They are not equals. They have no spirit that lives on. And they do not worship Rett. They are therefore expendable."

"Of course."

"You cannot pretend to me to believe it. You are not alone. But you must keep your thoughts to yourself. They are zoo animals, nothing more."

A heavy silence hung between them while they looked at each other. It was the first time Leah felt understood in his presence and a light smile touched her lips even through her disgust at the hunt.

"How old are you, Pren?" she said, without thinking.

He smiled. "Twenty-seven."

"I always thought you much older. You behave much older than your years."

"As do you, Leah."

She stood, brushing the dirt and pine from her clothes and he rose as well.

"Understand," he said. Kirche's voice sounded their names several yards distant. "He meant to impress you."

"Impress me? Why would he want to do that?"

"For the same reason any young folk would want to impress a charming girl."

Prenalin had lost his smile, though what he said was certainly a joke.

"Come," he reached for her hand. "They are near."

They rounded the large rotwood and found their way toward Kirche's voice. He and Sorgood emerged from the wood, beaming, Sorgood's bloody sword still in his hand.

Kirche held up a burlap sack soaked in blood. "I have my trophy," he said. "Shall we try for another?"

Leah was startled first by Kirche's face, lit with joy and animation as she'd never seen it before, and then by the bag which she surmised contained the head of the poor brownie.

"Oh, no, Lord Kirche," Sorgood said. "We've certainly been spotted by the felidae already. We've lost the surprise for the rest of the trip, I'm afraid. There will be a next time. When their sense of security returns."

Undeterred in his triumph, Kirche shrugged. "Leah, you won't mind having my prize on your carriage. I'm sure there's no room on mine."

Leah belched and vomited her breakfast tarts at Kirche's feet.

Chapter Seven

Forbes Billings," Rogget moved from behind the tree. "Forbes Billings," he said louder.

The folk stopped his whirling and cursing and turned to Rogget with red, tear-stained cheeks.

"Rogget." The slender man fell to his knees, covering his face with his hands.

Startled, Rogget turned back to the trees at the children, fear and confusion on his face. Fenn led the others into the clearing and they all stood and stared at the dejected folk.

"What is it?" Grayson asked and moved to put a hand on the man's shoulder.

"I've lost my writ," he cried and sat back onto the ground. He threw up his hands and then let them drop aimlessly. "I've lost my writ."

Grayson looked at Fenn, but Fenn could only grimace. Rogget knew him, so the folk couldn't be completely insane; but he was clearly beside himself. When Grayson sat beside the man, Fenn turned, alarmed, to Rogget, but Rogget simply stared, agog.

"Who is he?" Fenn asked.

"It's Forbes Billings."

"I guessed that much."

"I grew up with him, in Timber. But I haven't seen him in nigh on ten years."

"What happened to your writ?" Grayson asked the man. "Go on, sit down," he told the others.

They dutifully dropped to the ground, Rogget hitting unceremoniously and all his huntsman's gear falling away from him. Forming a semicircle in front of the whimpering man, they waited to understand.

"You remember, Rogget. You remember my writ. Given to me by the prince himself."

"What's a writ?" Sadie said.

"It's a decree issued by the king, or his master of the guard," Grayson said.

"Like a law?"

"Or an order. Yes."

"I think my da has printed some of those."

"I remember the writ," Rogget said. "You've kept it all these years?"

"O' course."

"But Forbes, you can't expect Welk to settle on it. You don't think he actually meant it, do you?"

"O' course I do. He's king now, ain't he? And it decreed, 'Upon ascending to the throne.'"

"But Forbes, he was drunk."

"King Welk was drunk?" Sadie turned to Grayson, astonished.

"Aye, he was," Forbes said. The flow of tears stopped and was dutifully wiped from his face. "He came into our camp, carousing and drunken, with his circle of noble folk. They wanted cards and dice and some of our'n stew and loaves. We obliged, o' course. We hadn't much choice. And I won the writ fair and square in dice. You remember Rogget. I got sixes."

"I remember." Rogget was subdued and Fenn scanned his face for clues as to what it was all about.

Forbes burst into tears once more and fell full-bodied onto the forest floor. "And now it's gone. It's gone."

"What happened?" Grayson asked him again, standing to pull the man back to sitting.

Forbes choked on his tears for several seconds, wiped his face with his sleeve and managed to whine out something of the story.

"Soon as I heard he'd been crowned, I dug up the entire yard looking for it."

"You buried it?" Rogget said.

"Indeed. Such an important doc'ment. I couldn't let it get lost." Here he cried again for a moment before continuing. "I dug ever'where until I finally remembered where I'd hid it. Down in the basement in a jar. I thought, Lil, you'll ne'er forgive me for what I done to your garden, and all the time it was in the basement."

Sadie turned to Fenn wide-eyed and grinning.

"I went all about Woodside, boasting on my writ. Then I walked all the way to Town Village in Aaronland to see my brother. We went all over town, all the pubs and inns showin' off my writ. They all toasted me and wished me luck."

"What does the writ say?" Sadie asked.

"But after dark, when we stumbled out of The Crown, we was beset by thieves. They rifled through all my pockets. All they took was the writ."

"That's a might suspicious," Rogget said.

208

"Aye." Forbes fell into tears once more.

"Well, what did it say?" Grayson said.

Forbes only shook his head and cried.

"Forbes was married young," Rogget said. "His wife was with their first child when she was banished to the wasteland for shooting a guard."

"She shot a guard?" Fenn said.

"Only in the foot. She mistook him for an intruder. But no matter. He happened to be one of King Arnot's third cousin's second in-law or some such nonsense. And her firearm was illegal. They hauled her off to the wasteland without much of a trial nor two thinks on it."

"Oh, my Lil," Forbes wailed.

"And the writ freed her?" Grayson said.

"Aye, it done more than that," Rogget said. "The prince was drunker than a brownie on honey mead. He promised to pardon all the wastelanders once he became king."

"What?" Fenn said.

"That's right. Now Forbes, you know as well as I do that there weren't no possibility the king would honor that writ."

"It was signed by him," he said. "And the nobles with him. It's the law. He has to honor it."

Rogget sighed and shook his head sadly. "We all knew what had happened to him. They say he was run off to wed an eisen against the king's wishes. Welk was betrothed to Panter of Damon Wall, but he wanted none of it. Rumor had it, King Evan set the guard after them, had them all killed."

"Killed," Sadie's voice echoed.

"It was that bloody Sorgood." Forbes sniffled. "He was the only one willing to lead the party, so they say. Relished in it, if you ask me. And now he's Master of the Guard. Such wicked injustice."

"When was all of this?" Grayson said.

"Oh, before you were born, likely."

"It were nigh onto twelve years ago," Forbes said. "Twelve years of waiting for my Lil to be freed."

"Forbes, you can't seriously think King Welk would have honored it. He was grief-stricken drunk."

"It's the law," he cried.

"Rogget's right," Grayson said. "Don't fret over losing it. You have to realize the king would never acknowledge it."

"If anything," Rogget said, "you'd be banished yourself and never heard from again and your property gone to your King Ricker. And who would care for your children then?"

"That's probably true," Grayson said.

Forbes looked to Sadie and Fenn. Fenn turned to Sadie and nodded. Together they nodded their agreement at Forbes.

"Ah, maybe you're right." He sucked in a few ragged breaths. "But I thought I'd finally have my Lil home. I thought..."

"*Don't* think on it," Rogget said.

"Did you get a good look at the thieves?" Fenn said.

"Oh, sure. I seen the like of them before. They got that leader Clutch, the vilest folk in the hill country. They come through Woodside often, and no matter how much we give 'em, they always got to take more. I recognized 'em all right."

"What are you doing in the woods alone?" Sadie asked him.

Forbes threw up his hands and slapped them down on his pants. "I don't know. I left Aaronland after them, without my sack, without supplies. I can't go to Banished now and face Lil. She'll have heard about Welk being crowned. She'll be expecting to be set free. So I thought I'd get on home. And then I decided I'd be better off just sitting here in the woods until death found me."

"Don't be stupid," Rogget said. "You're going home."

"How can I go back to Woodside and face them all?"

"It's easy," Grayson said. "You tell them you were robbed. Regale them with a story. They'll forget it soon enough."

"Oh, sure they will. I'll be the fool who failed to get his loved ones out of the wasteland. That's who I'll be. I can't go back there."

"Where will you go?" Sadie said.

"I can't face Lil. I can't face home. I don't know what to do."

"Come on," Rogget said to them. "Let's set up camp and get him some food. Maybe we can figure this out."

Chapter Eight

As he emerged from the orchard hiking toward Michelruud Castle to the north, Lucas saw in the distance that the folk had convened at the gathering stage. He walked past the guards' barracks on his left; all was strangely quiet there. He came to the jail, but several of the townsfolk were standing in front of the guard, their arms folded across their chests, so he passed and moved along toward the gathering. The crowd was shouting and raising fists in the air.

Lucas made his way around the outskirts of folk, hoping he wouldn't be recognized too soon. Dunham, privy to King Welk sat in the listening chair while Karner Hardy, owner of the general store in Path, and Lancet Wolf, the leather worker, stood on stage before the throng.

"Their parents should be forced to tell," Hardy shouted. "Dragged out of the jail house and put into the stocks or shown to the noose. They must know where their children have gone with the evil bairn—as surely as they are parents."

The crowd shouted its approval.

"We must give time for King Welk to weigh the evidence and his options," Wolf said.

A folk in the crowd shouted out, "King Evan would have had this done long before now."

"Evan sent your children to Steingefan. Let them rot in that drafty old prison on the merest chance they might have the mark of prophecy," Wolf said.

"Aye, and it was because he had that great idea that we found the evil one," Hardy shouted. "The bairn led the escape. Why, Evan couldn't have planned it better."

"And walloped your own boy on the head, Wolf," someone in the mass of folk shouted. "Would you not have your retribution?"

"Please, I beg of you all," Wolf said. "The High Priest of Hass is due at any time. We must prepare—"

"The Hass could help us find the evil one," Hardy said and the crowd roared its approval.

"The Hass?" Wolf said. "The very folk who treat us so vilely? They lash our children in the streets for playing, send us to the stocks for the slightest affront. Think of those they've killed. The stationer and the innkeeper make regular visits to the burial grounds and you would ask favor from the folk who put their children under tombstones?"

"We would only ask that they capture the bairn," someone mumbled.

"But you would risk the lives of Sadie and Grayson," Wolf said. "And you would dare ally yourselves with the Hass when instead you should spit before them as they trod our villages."

"They deserve the respect of their station."

"It is not respect you show them, but fear."

"They have soldiers and firearms to outnumber ours by far. They can help us find the boy and kill him."

"Kill him?" Wolf stared at the crowd, stunned. "Folk, listen to yourselves. We don't have all the facts. We don't know the truth. And already you are prepared to ally yourselves with your enemy and murder a child."

"If our enemy will help us in this, why not ally with them?" Hardy said. "Dunham, what says the king?"

Dunham stood and raised his hands to quiet the crowd. "I will take all of your concerns to his Highness. In the meantime, the stationer and innkeeper are to be left alone in the jailhouse. I assure you King Welk takes the threat of the bairn very seriously."

"Then why does he let the parents of his accomplices sit in jail? Why does he not publicly interrogate them?"

Dunham again raised his hands and shook his head. "I will relay your message." He took the steps off the stage, the crowd mumbling against him.

Lucas made his way back to the jailhouse. He was pleased to see the angry folk were dispersing, apparently realizing there would be no public accusations this day. He stepped up to the guards and threw off his hood, shocked to see his friends. They too were surprised to see him.

"Edgar," he said. "I heard you were injured."

"Aye." Young footman Wolf showed off the now healing bruise on the side of his head. "The evil bairn hit me with a rock during the Steingefan escape."

"He did not hit you with a rock," Tildon Weeks, the other guard, said. "It were one of the other kids. Why do you keep saying—"

"What difference does it make?" Edgar said. And turning to Lucas, continued. "Your Father Treacher being run off to the port, they asked Ma'am Hardy to tend to me, and she told me I ought to be laid off active duty for just a while. So, here I am."

"This ain't *in*active duty," Tildon said. "It's very active."

"Aye." Edgar smirked. "'Tis very active standing at the jailhouse all day making sure no one goes in to bother the prisoners."

"Who do you have in there?"

"The usuals," Tildon said. "The pirate, the madman, and the witch."

"And the stationer," Edgar said. "You're forgetting the most valuable ones."

"Oh, right. The stationer and his wife, and the innkeeper. They got the best stalls, but still sleeping on straw. It ain't right, if you ask me."

"Oh it ain't right, is it? You didn't get hit in the face with a rock, did you? All in the aid of the evil little bairn, did you? No, you didn't."

"That don't make it right none, to lock up the stationer or Ma'am Stationer, of all folk."

"They should tell us all what they know, they should."

"They don't know nothing." Tildon turned to Lucas. "They don't know nothing. No sense keeping them locked away."

"Think what the townsfolk would do to them if they were freed, Til,"

Lucas said.

Tildon stared at him for several seconds before his face lit up and his mouth fell open. "Oh, aye, that's it. That's what they're in the jailhouse for."

"What are you going on about?" Edgar poked Tildon's shoulder.

"Protection."

"They protect the likes of the folk that brought me this?" He pointed to his face.

"Ah, Wolf," Lucas said. "It's all healed now. And it wasn't the stationer's fault."

Wolf shook his head. "They can stay locked up until the gray is gone around my eye at least."

"Might I see them, do you think?"

Tildon laughed. "Are you out of your mind, there, Lucas? Nobody is allowed in. By the king's orders."

"But, I'm one of the wissenry orphans. And without Father Treacher about, I'm practically next in line."

"Your lesser wissendes over there to the wissenry already tried that one with the madman."

"The madman?"

"Aye, their regular visit to tend him and calm him and feed him. Same with the witch though she don't want none of it."

"And you didn't let them in?"

"No one goes in. Didn't you hear me? No one."

"Who's feeding the prisoners then?"

"We are, o' course," Edgar said.

"I just want to make sure the stationer and innkeeper are all right."

"They're all right," Tildon said. "There. You made sure."

"Come on, Til. You won't even let *me* in?"

"Are you saying there, Lucas, that I do not take my position in the king's guard seriously?"

Lucas sighed. "No. I'm not saying that. Of course your duties are important."

"Indeed they are. So don't even think about trying to visit with them prisoners. I'm going to be on especial lookout now that I know you want to. I know how sneaky you think you are."

"He is sneaky, Tildon," Edgar said. "He don't just *think* it."

They both stared at Lucas with their eyes closed up into slits of suspicion and nodded slightly. He would have to figure out another way.

Chapter Nine

Leah's mind was numb and her body tingled when she moved to take the steps up to the porch of the inn at Path. The day was done and darkness had fallen. She'd spent the carriage ride forcing herself to think of anything but the brownie's head, bleeding in the sack on the floor near her feet. To be out of the carriage and away from it only brought it back to her thoughts and her stomach turned.

Prenalin held the door to the inn open for Kirche and his guard, the porters, and finally Leah. They stood in the lobby, looking on at the few folk left in the dining area beyond the staircase. A fiddle screeched out a rustic ditty somewhere in the distance and glasses clinked together. Prenalin leaned toward her and whispered, "They have a pub here in Path."

A pub? Leah began to regain her composure and her eyes widened. She'd heard Kirche speak of pubs on the second day of their trip east, aboard the *Treasure of the Seas*. Prenalin explained their purpose and that she would pass several while in Cold Sea Port. It was quite a feat for her to manage to look through the open doors of those they passed without Prenalin or Kirche discovering her curiosity. Pubs and public drunkenness were forbidden in Ruhm.

Kirche led the party up the staircase to the second floor and Leah, tired and weary, wanted only to find her bed and her journal. High-pitched giggling met her ears and she glanced up to see a little girl with red, bouncy curls bounding down the stairs. The child lost her footing and fell into Kirche's leg. Kirche raised an armed and smacked the child off him as if she were a wasp, sending her tumbling down the stairs.

Leah reached out for the girl, but she fell past in blur of ruffles and socks, landing in the lobby with a dull thud. Instinc-tively, Leah stepped down toward her, and several folk shouted, but Prenalin's hand held tight to her arm. She turned to him, and beyond him, saw Kirche continue up the steps without looking back.

"She will be tended to," Prenalin said sharply, pulling Leah to move along upward.

The child lay still at the bottom of the stairs and Leah forced herself to turn away once more and go to her room. Once inside, she heard the little girl begin to scream. Leah stumbled to a chair at a desk and sat staring into the darkness until a woman knocked and opened the door.

"My apologies, mistress," the woman said and lit the lanterns. "I was delayed."

A porter followed with Leah's bags; he set them with a thud on the floor under the window and hurried out. When the room was lit and the walls flickering with shadow and light, Leah realized there was a looking glass on a stand in the corner. She smiled at the memory of her mother brushing her hair back home in Ruhm.

As the woman pulled back the covers from the bed and fluffed the pillows, Leah turned and watched her. Her dress fell loose over her wiry frame and gray hair dangled about her face, escaped from the severe bun on the nape of her neck.

"Would you like the bed warmed, miss?" the woman said without looking at Leah.

"It's not nearly cold enough for that," Leah said. "But thank you for the offer."

"Yes'm. Can I bring you anything before you turn in for the night? Unpack your bags?"

Leah shook her head. "Is the little girl all right?"

The woman looked hard at her with a frown. "I'm sorry to appear rushed ma'am. I will do for you anything you wish."

"I understand. You need to get back to her. But please...is she going to be all right?"

For several seconds the old woman glared at Leah. Then she said, "Looks to be a broken arm. And she was out dead cold for a few moments. The wissende is gone, lesser wissendes are not well versed, and so she's off to Ma'am Hardy, but—" She stopped with a nod and a quick breath and turned to the door. "My apologies, ma'am. To have bothered you."

Leah wanted to stop her. To learn more. But she felt as if her mind and body were a step behind and the woman was gone before she could raise a hand. Weary, she dug open her bag to find her night clothes. She hid behind the dressing screen and changed. Stepping out, she went to stand before the glass and untied her hair. She ran her fingers through her long locks, pulling them out, away from her head. Then she spun, and caught glimpses of herself with her hair twirling about her in the mirror. She stood admiring its length for some time before taking out her brush from her bag and giving her tresses a long, thorough grooming.

That chore gladly completed, pulling her journal and a lead writer from her knapsack, Leah fell across the bed and lay there with the book open, willing herself to write.

But words would not come to her. Homesick. Confused. Angry. Disappointed. Leah could not bring herself to write the reality that she had been wrong about Kirche. No. Not wrong about him. Wrong about herself. How stupid could she be?

"Oh, Madam Always," she whispered. "You would not be proud of me now."

Chapter Ten

At midnight, Lucas moved silently in the darkness, past the sleeping Tildon Weeks and Edgar Wolf, dutiful soldiers in the king's guard. He lifted the latch and entered the stone jailhouse of Michelruud. The innkeeper's snoring echoed throughout the building and he followed it to its origin, down a long, cold hallway, peering into each barred cell as he passed. The pirate, smelling of whiskey, slept between bouts of unconscious cursing; the madman of Michelruud, frail and harmless, and a relative to the king so not to be sent off to the wasteland, tossed about as if frustrated by fleas; and Ma'am Eer, the sorceress, imprisoned again for setting fire to someone's summer crop was a solid lump of motionless slumber. The wastelanders had once more refused to allow Eer entry and as there was never any evidence against her, she spent much time in the jailhouse.

All slept as he strode past without sound. The innkeeper snored in a cell at the end of the hallway, and across from him, in another cell, lay the stationer and his wife.

"Stationer," Lucas whispered.

Ma'am Stationer sat up. "Who is that?"

"Lucas of the Path wissenry. Wake the stationer."

In the dark, Lucas watched her shake her husband awake.

"Pratt. Pratt, wake up."

The stationer's head popped up, turning this way and that.

"What is it?"

"Lucas, of the wissenry. Come to the bars; we must speak."

He sat up, rubbed his face, and crawled forward to the cold, steel bars of his cell.

"It is too dark; I cannot trust it is you."

"Do you not recognize my voice?"

"It's him," Ma'am Stationer said. "I'm sure it's him."

"But you told me the guard took him with the others." Pratt turned back to his wife.

"They did. 'Tis true."

"Aye, the guard took him," Pratt peered through the bars. "So, how might he find himself here?"

"They let him go, husband. I tell you, it's Lucas."

216

"We have no time for bickering," Lucas said.

"What do you want, then?" Pratt said. "Do you have Sadie and Grayson?"

"The children are in the care of Rogget, a wissenry guide. They are safe as can be expected."

"Does the king believe this bairn nonsense?" Ma'am Stationer whispered.

"He is confused. He does not have access to the histories, as you do."

Pratt's mouth fell agape for a brief second before he spoke. "How do you know about the histories?"

"Never mind that. Understand that war is approaching. Forces from the west and the north are rising. We cannot fight them both."

"What does this have to do with me?" Pratt said, disheart-ened. "I am jailed as a traitor to the king."

"Yet you remain the stationer of Michelruud. Welk is not so arrogant as his father was. He will find he requires your support. I feel you must trust him."

Stationer Pratt's eyes lowered to the ground. "There are things I should not know," he said. "Things I should not possess."

"I am aware," Lucas said.

"If I trust the king, I give myself up to the law for punish-ment."

"Perhaps. But you may save the Ruud in so doing."

The stationer's brow creased and he shook his head. "How?"

"Trust me in this. Knowledge is necessary at all times, but especially when one is faced with enemies he does not understand. You have knowledge the king needs."

Pratt nodded. "I see. But I have not heard of any threat, from the west or the north. I only hear the ranting and rumors about a bairn."

"That is the concern," Lucas said. "Our folk are disturbed and afraid. Our enemies will use this to their advantage. You know of whom I speak, Stationer. You know the threat the Great West poses."

"But how do *you* know this?"

"I cannot say. Remain skeptical if you like. But remember what I have said, when you are brought before the king."

"It is so highly unlikely that I should be brought before the king, that if that one small miracle occurs, I will consider you a great sage and follow your advice."

Lucas smiled. "I am no sage," he said. "I just know where to look for information."

Chapter Eleven

They'd spent the late afternoon the day before comforting Forbes Billings. Once Darnit rejoined them, Rogget took a brief hunt while they scoured for wild roots and berries. After they ate what they could, Rogget left Darnit as guard while he went off to scout the location of the thieves.

Fenn's sleep was troubled without dreams and visions. And when he woke, Rogget had bitters warmed over the fire and told him to drink.

"You look like a harpie's ghost."

"Thanks." Fenn was weary and his body felt as if it moved through mud. Something ached inside him for his charm—not thought, not feeling, but the emptiness of longing. The morning was cold and damp and did nothing to raise his spirits. When Forbes woke, he offered a weak smile.

"They've made their way into the port at Cold Sea," Rogget said. "Your writ is long gone."

"All right." Forbes' shoulders sank as all his hope seemed to leave him. "I'll go on home. I'll pack up the children from their grans and we'll have to go meet up with Lil. She has to know the truth." He shook his head. "I am one dumb folk."

"Don't be so hard on yourself," Grayson said wiping the tired from his face. "You were just hopeful that's all. Nothing wrong with that."

Forbes shrugged.

"I didn't realize," Sadie said, "that you could go and visit the folk in the wasteland."

"Oh, sure," Forbes said. "They rely on family, and the wissenry, to bring them supplies and food. It's a harsh life."

"Why don't their families stay with them?" Grayson said.

"Some have been known to. But they leave behind their property and the king takes possession."

"Aye," Rogget said. "If you want your children to have it, you have to stay in the Ruud and keep claim to it."

"Where are you four headed?" Forbes asked.

"Aaronland," Rogget said.

"Well, then, I'll go with you. I'll get my belongings from my brother and then head home to collect the children. No sense trying to make it all the way through the divide wood with nothing to eat and no knife."

As they hiked through the woods, Fenn lagged behind with Sadie and Grayson while Rogget and Forbes talked of their days of childhood in Timber.

"Are you sure that writ's no good?" Fenn asked Grayson.

"No. But no sense making Forbes feel awful about it."

"I think the king could be forced to acknowledge it," Sadie said. "If I learned anything from my da, it's the importance of the law."

Fenn nodded absentmindedly. The thief had his charms and hemp rope. And he had Forbes Billings' writ. In a way, he thought, Clutch had stolen both their dreams.

Chapter Twelve

Leah was groggy when she opened the door to the old woman again. She nearly shoved Leah aside and hurried to pull open the heavy curtains at the window; morning light streamed in across the floor. Next she busied herself making up the bed.

"Good morning," Leah murmured and went to the window to look out over the small town square.

"Morn. Bitters or tea? In room or down to the dining area?"

"I'll meet my party downstairs."

The woman nodded. "Will that be all, then?"

"How is the little girl this morning?"

"She'll be fine."

"What is her name?"

The woman stared at her, frowning. "Matilda Steppe. Daughter of the innkeeper."

"How old is she?"

"Eight."

"Are you the mistress of the inn?"

"No, miss."

Leah paused, wishing the woman would say more. But she stood stiff and imposing as if awaiting orders.

"And what is your name?"

"Dowling."

"Dowling?"

"Yes, miss."

Leah frowned and let out a short sigh. There would be no friend in Dowling, apparently. She turned to the window once more.

"This village isn't like the others I've seen of the Ruud. It's so small."

"It ain't small." Dowling joined her in looking out at the town square. "This village evolved more than it was built. It were once no more than the path from the original castle, now Steingefan, to the river."

"Path," Leah said and nodded. "So, this isn't all of it?"

"No, miss. Path is spread out into the woods and over through the orchards to the new castle. These here are the main square buildings. But you'll find the wissenry over into the woods and the smithy and chandlery, too. No, there's much more to Path than meets the eye."

"Thank you." Leah curtseyed.

Dowling's eyes closed up and her chin lifted. "Hmph," she said and left the room.

Downstairs, Leah found Kirche in high spirits at a small corner table finishing up his kaff. She picked at a biscuit and ate a bit of sausage until Prenalin arrived and sat with them.

"Today we investigate the woods to the north," Prenalin told her. "And then we meet with the king at his table."

She tried to smile but found herself dazed and saddened. Kirche and Prenalin chatted until Kipling, Alphonse, and Redd, Kirche's bodyguards, arrived to lead them. They left the inn through the back door, Leah absent-mindedly following Redd down the steps. When she looked up to find her way, she was staring into the eyes of the brownie Kirche had murdered the day before. She shrieked and fell backward onto the wood stairs.

Prenalin forced Alphonse and Redd away from her and pulled her up by the arms.

"What was that about?" Kirche said, his smooth purr of a voice now more sinister than mysterious to Leah.

"I'm sorry," she managed. "The brownie. I didn't..."

"Oh, yes," he said, smiling at her. "Drying out a bit before the preserving cloths can be placed."

The brownie's small head was mounted on a stick stuck into the ground outside the back door to the inn, his face frozen in a grimace, his eyes wide open; dried blood ran the length of the post to the dirt.

"Do you think it would be better to move it away from the building?" Prenalin said.

"And have some wild animal take it? Or worse, let the felidae claim it? No, no. Dowling said it would be fine here."

"Dowling?" Leah said.

"Yes. She runs the inn. Rumor tells us our innkeeper has found himself in jail. Dowling is his mother-in-law, I believe. Dour isn't she?"

Leah nodded and let Prenalin take her arm as they made their way into the woods. Gretchen and Zelda had come along to carry their baskets for a mid-morning snack and their formal cloaks for the later visit with King Welk. Xavier, the youngest porter, was charged with carrying the small chest in which Kirche's formal head wear, his tall mitre, was nestled. They traveled a series of paths for hours, Gretchen chatting along about this and that and nonsense, with Kirche and Alphonse occasionally veering off to investigate a hole or a cavern. Leah imagined they must be searching for the elusive kell stone and let herself chuckle.

She supposed her suspicions had been right all along. Kirche had no idea where the stone was and no plan for finding it. He seemed to quite enjoy the adventure of his visit to the Ruud, however, and that was no doubt the true point of the trip.

"Are you all right today?" Prenalin asked.

She nodded with a slight smile.

They stopped for a picnic at the edge of the woods looking out over a brief plain and the ruins of a castle.

"Steingefan," Prenalin said as he sat on one of the blankets with her. "A prison now, but once a castle. Beyond that is a path through a field of lilac clover that leads to the wastelands, where they banish their folk."

"Lilac clover. An entire field of it?"

"Yes, I hear tell it spans miles eastward. It helps to keep the banished from returning home. You've heard of it?"

"There is a patch southwest of Ruhm, beyond Madam Sponhide's mine. We were allowed to study there in school—capture fairy bees for..." the thought made her stomach lurch just a bit.

Prenalin nodded knowingly. "Yes, you see? This is how we are raised. They are not sentient beings, but zoo animals."

"The fairy bees are only somewhat sentient. And not fairies at all, in truth," she said. "Not really bees either."

He raised his brows and smiled.

"They are the gemein," she told him. "Angry little creatures. Powerful bite that often scars badly."

Prenalin took a bite of an apple. "So you did not mind so much harming them?"

"I didn't dissect mine."

"No?"

She shook her head. "Madam Always allowed me to defer that assignment."

He smiled at her and wiped apple juice from his chin. Leah turned to gaze at their party, the bodyguards and porters lounged and snacked while Kirche had Alphonse plodding with him about the edges of the wood examining flora.

"Do you remember on the boat over, you told me that Kirche could barely stand these visits?"

He tilted his head and his brow furrowed. "Did I say that?"

"Yes. You told me how base and crude the folk were here, and I asked you if Kirche felt the same."

"And you think I spoke a lie?" A slight smile lit up his face.

"I think Lord Kirche enjoys the visits here, yes."

Prenalin laughed—a loud, stout chortle that surprised her and made the others turn to watch them.

"Nonetheless, Leah Hallowsing," he said, grinning. "The standard answer will always be that the Ruud is a dreadful place and our Lord Kirche cannot wait to wipe its mud from his boots."

Leah couldn't help but giggle and shake her head. She felt the others' eyes on them both but she didn't care. Kirche was too busy walking this way and that, peering into the woods and pointing at birds to notice *her*.

"Pren, is this a test?"

He balked. "What?"

"Am I being tested?"

"Why would you ask such a thing?"

"Because I feel as if I am being tried. And found lacking."

He turned from her and watched the rest of the group eating and chatting. "Not a test. No," he said.

Leah could almost hear the rest of his answer hovering somewhere in his head, not daring to be spoken. When they'd finished their rest, they packed up and headed toward Michelruud castle.

Chapter Thirteen

King Welk gnawed on roast pig and spiced, stewed apples in the great hall. The noble folk, all kin to the founder of the Ruud, Michelruud himself, lounged about the heavy wood tables and benches lining the walls enjoying food, drink, music, and dancing. Welk sat at a table in front of his bed-chamber doors, next to the stairs to the upper floors. He watched the empty throne dais across the room and the young couples resting easily across its steps.

As a child, Welk would sit at his father's feet during meal times watching in amazement as servers, who knelt on either side of the king, held his food tray steady above his lap while he ate. Two others stood at his sides holding his golden chalices ever ready to let them go when the king grabbed at them for a guzzle. Welk shook off his disgust as the chamberlain approached his table.

"Tom Britt, from the wissenry at Cold Sea, Sire," he announced.

Welk waved a hand for the lad to approach and speak. The boy pulled a scroll from under his robes, unrolled it, and read.

"The wissenry of the Ruud wishes to make it known to King Welk of Michelruud that it is sorely grieved to have caused his Highness unpleasantness in the scandal involving the evil bairn of prophecy. None of our wissendes were aware of the origins of said bairn, nor understood the meaning of the mark he bore. He has thus been banished into the hill country, never more to take refuge in the wissenry. Let this be the end of our involvement. By your leave, Father Britt, Head of Affairs, Wissenry of the Ruud, Cold Sea Wissenry."

The lad bowed. "Return message, Sire?"

Welk shook his head and waved him away. The boy handed the scroll to the chamberlain, bowed and left.

"Is Sorgood still about?"

"Yes, Sire, still readying for another journey to the port."

"Summon him."

While he waited, Welk finished his meal and drank his wine, his stomach churning with fury. When Sorgood approached with several of his elite guard, he did not hide his anger.

"Why have you not left for the port?"

Sorgood bowed too slowly. "I have already sent a detach-ment, Sire. I meet with them shortly."

"Give him the scroll." Welk waved a hand to the chamberlain. He watched Sorgood as he read the declaration from the wissenry.

"But, what does this mean?" he stammered. "Did they have the boy and let him go?"

"It doesn't say...does it?"

"Does this mean he is traveling through the Ruud toward the hill country?"

"Or is this a ruse to keep us away from the port?" Welk added.

"I will call up two hundred men, Sire, and we will accost the wissenry at Cold Sea. They cannot be allowed this treachery."

Welk fumed, not looking at Sorgood, thinking about what that would mean. He could not move against the wissenry without losing the heart of the folk. They were with him, thus far; their fear of the evil bairn and the destruction of the Ruud kept them loyal to Welk. But they were devoted to their wissendes, who counseled them, represented them in the courts, gave them aid and comfort. No, he dare not take the wissenry by force.

It was likely the boy was being hidden under Father Britt's care all this time, even as the guard searched the port more than a week ago. But what else could he do? It was enough, for now, to be seen trying to find the bairn of prophecy. Welk turned to Sorgood, repulsed. Soon enough, he would have to take real action against the boy. This was no time to question his nerve.

He shook his head. "No. We will leave the wissenry alone... for now. You will strengthen your patrols on the borderlands. Build your perimeter. Go to Aaronland first and demand from Arnot all available guards. See to it they cover the border in the divide wood. Then go to Damon Wall and do the same and only after you have secured the northern and eastern boundaries, go to Cold Sea and see what you can learn of ships transporting children away from the Ruud."

Sorgood bowed. "You suspect he remains here still?"

"I do. They are children. They will be loath to leave their homes. And they travel slowly."

"We will find him, Sire."

"Do you have any in your ranks who are familiar with the boy and can recognize him at a distance?"

"Aye, Sire." Sorgood's face lit up. "A volunteer has come to aid us." He reached out his hand and beckoned a young folk forward and Welk sucked in a small breath in astonishment.

"Lucas Foster of the wissenry, Sire." The boy bowed stiffly, as if he was forced into the obeisance.

Welk stared at him, so much like his old friend Belfen his heart leapt. Frieden. Young Frieden would now enlist in finding the bairn of prophecy.

"Lucas was raised with the boy at the Path wissenry." Sogood smiled broadly.

"Of course," Welk managed to say. "Yes. Very good. Thank you for your help."

The boy nodded and rejoined the other guards. Sorgood turned to leave just as Welk's chamberlain approached flustered, and said, "Sire, the High Priest of Hass has entered the castle grounds."

Welk thought he saw Sorgood flinch before he turned to make his way across the lobby.

"Is it autumn already?" Welk said, watching Frieden, small and frail among the guardsmen. "Allow them entry."

The group, cloaked in soft shades of red, except for the priest, in purple, crossed the room making a great show of their patience and grace. Welk sneered. The priest still wore the same funny hat he remembered as a young lad sitting at his father's side. This priest was much younger than those he recalled visiting his father. The hat seemed larger, too, than Welk remembered.

They approached his table and stood before him. Each of them wore a chain and hanging from it was a large circular charm carved of white marble, etched and painted with a picture of a tree lit in flames.

Looking about haughtily, the priest moved forward but did not bow. The representatives of the Hass of Emorah never bowed before the king. Welk remembered questioning this practice when he was very young. But his father waved him away and learned to send him off on some errand or other whenever the Hass arrived.

"Allow me to express my sadness at the passing of your father, King Evan," the young priest said.

Welk nodded. His eye caught sight of a young girl in the group, her eyes roaming about the hall.

"I look forward to many years of service to you, my lord." The priest smiled. "It is customary," his voice rolled smoothly in the air, filled with disdain and charm, "for the king of Michelruud to stand before the high priest of Hass."

"Is it?" Welk sat back in his jeweled dinner chair and eyed the high priest curiously. He glanced at the girl, her attention suddenly on the conversation, and offered her a smile. Her glance flew to the floor and her cheeks flashed a blush.

"Yes," the priest said.

"My father stood before the Hass?"

"He did."

Welk shrugged. "I find that odd."

"Nonetheless," the man purred with expectation.

"I will not stand before you," Welk said. "But I will invite you to sit."

He raised his hand and called for chairs.

"It is customary for the priest of Hass to sit in the king's chair."

At that Welk laughed aloud and a silence fell over the great hall as folk turned to watch the meeting.

"My father gave you his chair did he? Did he also give you his throne?"

The priest smiled viciously at Welk, but Welk was not intimidated.

"Sit, or don't sit." He motioned to the low wood chair placed before him at the table. "But either way, tell me who you are and what you want."

For a brief second, the priest looked concerned, but his face quickly regained its snobbish glower.

"You are not familiar with the Hass of Emorah?"

"Of course I am."

"I am Kirche, High Priest. I have come to see the King of Michelruud as is customary, every year before winter."

"Aren't you all called Kirche?" Welk said.

The priest barely nodded. "It is customary for the king to receive us in his chambers."

"And why might that be?"

"It is no concern of mine."

"Then what is your concern?"

"Tribute."

"Tribute?"

"Yes." Kirche sighed and appeared angry. "The kings of the Ruud, Michelruud in particular, pay tribute in the form of monetary compensation and statements of fealty, to the Hass of Emorah."

"I believe you are mistaken." Welk frowned. "The kings of the Ruud pay tribute to the Kingdom of Ruhm."

"The Hass of Emorah *is* the Kingdom of Ruhm."

"Again," Welk said, smiling. "You are mistaken."

The young priest stepped closer to Welk and sneered. "I will not tolerate this insolence, young king."

Welk leaned forward with a clever smile and picked up his fork, just as a servant set a plate with a slice of berry pie on it before him.

"Apparently, you will," he said. "I am king in Michelruud. You are my honored guest, a representative of the Kingdom of Ruhm. That is where we are. You may sit, or you may stand, but you do not have my chair, nor my throne."

The priest fumed and glared at Welk as he ate. The young girl's eyes widened and she gawked at him. He chuckled and ate a second bite of pie. After several seconds, the priest took the chair and accepted a plate of food. Chairs were brought for his aide on the left, and the young girl on the right; the others in their party were sat at the far end of the table.

"I am Prenalin, Secretary to the High Priest of Hass," the aide said. "And this is Leah Hallowsing, Aide to the High Priest." They both bowed and sat before Welk.

Welk then turned his attention to Kirche who glared at him, his eyebrows raised.

"You needn't be insulted," Welk said. "I believe you were only given my father's chair near the end, because the king was too weak to sit in it himself."

"Are you accusing the Hass of taking advantage of the sick king?"

"Isn't that your *job*?"

The young priest leered at Welk for a moment, then smiled slightly and nodded. "Perhaps we will get along, after all."

They ate for a few moments in silence. Welk watched as Leah picked, uninterested, at the fowl and potatoes. Her hair was gathered at the nape of her neck and fell down the back of the chair nearly to the floor. Her features were delicate, and while her eyes were filled with curiosity at everything they came upon, Welk could see a strength of will behind them. Hers was very different from the dull, practiced gaze of the priest.

"I have often, as a lad and young prince," he said, raising his mug. "Wondered what tribute does the Kingdom of Ruhm need from our little realm?"

Kirche shrugged. "None, naturally. A token gesture is all that is expected. Your father sent pretty gold chains from the ore mines dug in the northern hill country."

"Very well."

"One day, if you're daring enough, we'd like to see a relic or two from the ice realm. Your father once promised us a rhinobear pelt. Alas, he fell ill shortly after, and was ill every year after that."

"I might visit the ice realm one day for adventure. I'll pick something up for you. Or is that...for the king of Ruhm?"

"Yes, yes of course." Kirche smiled devilishly. "For the king."

Both Leah and Prenalin looked to Kirche when he spoke and nodded in agreement often.

"Who is king of Ruhm these days?"

"Roren."

"I am told the king has always been a child, these past five generations."

Kirche nodded and his aides followed suit.

"Do many children in Ruhm die so young?"

Kirche shrugged but said nothing, while Leah looked squarely at Welk as if she'd never heard such a question.

"Is that an odd thing to ask?"

She seemed to realize she'd been looking at the king, shook her head and looked back to her plate.

"They do not die while king," Kirche said.

"If they do not die, how are they removed from the throne when they reach adulthood?"

Kirche frowned and stared at Welk. "These are questions regarding law and order in Ruhm and are not your business."

"Ah." Welk stuck another fork full of pie into his mouth and chewed with a smile. "But I'm wanting to know. Is it beheading? Banishment?"

Kirche shrugged. "Our kings are granted the privilege of tranquility at the end of their reign. It is a great honor. And none of your concern."

"Well, we'll find something appropriate to send the current boy king, anyway, shall we?"

"You are having troubles with a boy of your own, are you not? An evil little bairn running amok in the Ruud? Your folk are worked up into a frenzy over some ancient prophecy."

Welk nodded and eyed Kirche who seemed to have lost the edge of his sarcasm. They both ate in silence for a moment.

"You could use this situation to your advantage," Kirche said.

"And yours?"

"Perhaps."

"Explain."

"If you kill the boy, you can create a devotion surrounding him. You can make his memory whatever you wish and use it to calm the folk, to direct them."

Welk looked at him skeptically. "If I *kill* him?"

He could almost feel the energy bottling up in both Prenalin and Leah as their bodies tensed and they stared hard at their plates.

"You would not do it yourself, of course," Kirche said smoothly, ignorant of the turmoil he caused his aides. "The folk themselves will ask that it be done."

Welk creased his brow. "They will ask that he be killed, and then accept a devotion surrounding his memory?"

"Yes, it can be done. It was done in the southern lands long ago. Do you not know the story of Rett?"

"Ah." Welk nodded. "But I am of the wissenry line, you recall, and my ancestors did not subscribe to superstition and dogma."

"True, true. But you would be wise to consider them useful. Your position now, as king, cannot rest on truth and realism alone. Folk want to be led and they want to be comforted."

"Comfort is the duty of the wissenry."

"Hah. The wissenry of the Ruud is a mere shadow of its former days in Ruhm." Kirche nearly spat with this statement and Welk flinched, surprised at his passion.

"Perhaps we didn't battle the superstition of the Hass, here in the Ruud," he said, expecting to see Kirche fume.

Instead, a calm apathy fell over his face and Kirche waved his hand. "Enough of our bickering. I assure you, if you have the child killed, and convince the folk it was by their wishes the deed was done, you can then plant seeds of devotion in the land. A great superstition will arise from his death. The folk will worship him."

"And then?"

"And then you appoint a high priest to tell them *how* to worship."

228

Welk eyed Kirche carefully. He saw Leah, out of the corner of his eye, pull the cloth napkin from her lap and hold it to her lips.

It was all very familiar, what Kirche was saying. He'd been told the story of Rett when he was a child. His nurse implored him never to repeat it, though he'd asked for it over and over again.

"All right, dear prince," she would say, tucking him into his bed each night. "But remember, you must not share the story."

"But why?"

"It is forbidden."

It was long after Nanta had died that Welk had the epiphany: if it was forbidden, how had his Nanta known it? And why would any story such as that, a silly tale of superstition, be forbidden? Now, twenty years later, here sat the high priest of Hass alluding to the same story as if it were true.

Very odd things were happening of late. The Hass calling for the murder of a child; a child of prophecy with the mark of the faire. Welk frowned as he sat at table listening to the young priest of Hass regale him with stories of the greatness of the kingdom of Ruhm. But he paid little heed. His father told him many a time the Hass was all bluster and exaggeration. "Believe half of what they say, but suspect them double."

"You will find our ways very useful, should you require them," Kirche was saying; and Welk was sure now that he was desperate, deep in some part of him, for Welk to agree to his plans for the young bairn.

"I'll consider your words," he said.

"Good, good. And now, what news of the stone?"

"Stone?"

Kirche tilted his head and raised his brows. "Surely your father told you."

"I know nothing about a stone."

Kirche scowled, even while his secretary and aide relaxed and finished their meals. "The Hass has been assured that the entire realm has been searched for our stone."

"*Your* stone?"

"It belonged to Ruhm and was stolen by your ancestor. We will have it back."

"Who stole it?"

"Michelruud, who founded your kingdom, but he gave it back, eventually."

Welk laughed softly. "Then what's the problem?"

"One of our wissendes secreted it away and returned it to you."

"How would that then be our concern?"

"Your king received property stolen from us." The priest fumed.

"And you are certain of this?"

Kirche turned to Prenalin. "You have the declaration?"

Prenalin reached under his robes and pulled an envelope from his vest. Opening it, he withdrew a yellowed piece of parchment, unfolded it, and handed it to Kirche.

"When I was in the Ruud last, your father asked to see the proof. And here it is. Wissende Ferdwick Elson, in his own hand, tells of taking the stone from our most sacred museum of artifacts and sailing with it to Michelruud, returning it to its rightful place."

"Well, then," Welk said. "I imagine you will find it there, wherever that rightful place is."

Kirche glared at him. "Do you take us for fools? We know the beast do not have the stone."

"I see." Welk peered at him. "My apologies to the great representative of Hass." He smiled cleverly. "I know nothing of this stone, but I assure you I will look into the matter."

Kirche shrugged. "I am told the stone was a matter of great importance to the folk of the Ruud in the early days. How can you know nothing of it? Is your education system so poor?" He made a face as if he smelled a skunk.

Welk smiled broadly at him. "Indeed, we live rustic lives of farming and brewing. History is for scholars and priests." He turned to Leah. "Our deepest apologies for the debasement you must endure here."

To his surprise and delight, the young woman smiled and nodded; Welk knew that she was in on his joke.

"Do you require lodgings? I do not recall the high priest ever residing in the castle."

"We do not," Kirche said. "We have always stayed at the inn in Path. We still have more touring to do. We sail for home in a few weeks' time."

"Must be a tedious job having to leave the splendor of Ruhm and suffer the hardships of camping in the Ruud. Do you require a guard? I hear tell of a bear loose in our midst."

"Absolutely not. We are heavily armed."

Welk shrugged. "Very well then. Enjoy the hospitality of our folk. We will see you again next year. Chamberlain," he called. "Do we have a tribute to the king of Ruhm?"

He nodded. "Aye, Sire. It was prepared a month ago by your father's steward."

"Then it is goodbye," Welk said. He remained in his seat, smiling at Kirche, knowing that Kirche was waiting for him to stand. But he would not stand in the presence of this high priest of Hass.

230

After a long pause, Kirche rose and his attendants gathered around him. "I do not think you understand the nature of the relationship between the Hass and the Ruud, young king."

"I believe I understand what it has been, young priest," Welk said. "It is you who do not understand what it is now."

Kirche's jaw set hard and he glared at Welk. "There are ill omens in the air. I am thinking we will see each other again before the year is up."

Welk nodded. "Very well."

As the priest and his folk made their slow walk across the lobby toward the castle door, Leah turned back to give Welk another smile.

Welk looked to Chamberlain. "I could swear his hat is bigger than that of the last."

"They are taller hats every year, Sire." Chamberlain smiled and Welk laughed aloud, his voice ringing through the great lobby behind the Hass of Emorah.

"Dunham," he said, and Dunham appeared at his side. "Prepare lodgings here in the castle for the parents of our fugitives. I will tell you when the time is right to move them from the jail."

Chapter Fourteen

They returned to the inn after their meeting with King Welk and Leah went upstairs to put away her cloak. She was to meet Kirche and Prenalin downstairs for a late afternoon trek into the woods once again, for what purpose they didn't bother to tell her. She should lie down and rest, but her thoughts would not let her alone.

She dared not write in her journal her feelings of late—of Kirche's odd split in personality from a heartless killer to a prideful child; of her feelings of pleasure in being in the Ruud; of her homesickness for her mother even while she didn't want to return to Ruhm. But more and more, the gnawing realization in her mind that her father did indeed know the location of the kell stone wore her down.

After a quick brushing out and retying of her hair, she left her room and plodded down the stairs into the lobby. There was a foyer to the left of the front door and a large window let in light upon a set of chairs and a table. Leah went there, intending to sit in the sun in hopes the warmth would chase away the ache in her forehead, but instead, she found, on a dais, a stand holding a large, open book, covered in a thick layer of dust.

Using the bottom hem of her over tunic, she wiped the dust away. Closing the book, she read the title: *The History of the Ruud*. After looking back to see if anyone were watching, Leah lifted the tome and brought it to a chair by the window. She opened it on her lap and began reading.

In the year 1043, the great wissende Michelruud traveled to the eastern continents with his family, many wissendes, and others of Ruhm looking for adventure, where they settled into the three realms of the Ruud.

Leah skimmed the pages looking for any mention of their reasons for fleeing Ruhm, or of stealing the kell stone, or sending it back with Dakenruud, but none of that was mentioned. In this history, Ruhm was gracious enough to help rid the Ruud of its beast problem and all now lived in peace.

Pages and pages of genealogy followed and after that, stories of the various kings and queens of the Ruud and their children. Leah closed the book and a poof of dust billowed into her face. She sneezed, got up, and replaced the heavy tome onto its lonely dais; she now understood why no one ever looked at—she'd never seen such a boring history book.

Heavy footsteps thudded down the stairs and Leah saw Prenalin turn into the lobby. She followed and watched as he crossed through the dining area and entered the pub at the back of the kitchen. As she entered behind him, she heard Dowling in the dining room.

"That's no place for a young miss your age," she said.

Leah turned to her, curtseyed, but chose to ignore her warning. Prenalin had taken a seat with his back to her at a table by a window. An ink bottle sat in front of him and he dipped a quill into it and scribbled something. Several folk sat on stools at a long bar and they turned to watch her as she walked through the pub.

"I'm sorry to disturb you," she said as she approached.

Prenalin hurried to pull a blotting sheet into his journal and closed the book, setting down his quill. He smiled up at her.

"Forgive me," she said. "I didn't realize you were journaling."

"It's all right."

"I thought you were working sums for Kirche's inspections."

"No, no. Truly. Sit down. Join me."

She sat opposite him and the barman approached with a bottle and a small glass. He poured an amber liquid for Prenalin and asked, "Would the miss like something from the bar?"

"Tea for the young lady," Prenalin said.

Leah watched as Prenalin put the small glass to his lips and tipped it up, emptying its contents in one sip.

"Don't look surprised." He smiled. "Spirits are quite allowed in moderation—for the inner circle."

"Of course." She hated to behave like a child in front of him. She certainly knew that folk in Ruhm often took spirits. But it was highly regulated and public intoxication severely punished. Few folk bothered with it, so far as she knew. And she'd never actually seen anyone drink them before.

The barman brought tea in a dainty cup and once again, Leah was astonished. Tea in Ruhm was a treasure; the Ruud was seeming more and more like home all the time.

"I wanted to ask you about our meeting with King Welk," she said. "I'm confused about so many things."

"Of course you are. This trip was planned long before you were chosen for your present position. Once we return to Ruhm your duties and schedule will become more...defined. Now you must feel tossed about and unsure of what to make of much."

She smiled. "I feel very much like that at present, yes. But tell me. What was Kirche saying to King Welk about Rett? He made it sound as if Rett was killed on purpose—to be made into a devotion for the folk."

"Did he?" Prenalin shifted in his chair. "I don't think he meant to say that. Only that it worked out that way. The folk did call for his death, when they thought Rett had betrayed them. They only found out later the truth of what he'd done to save them from the manipulative power of the beasts. It's in the *Book of Rett*. You've read it, surely."

"Yes, of course. But what of the southern lands?"

He accepted another glass of amber from the barman and held it, but did not drink. "What do you mean?"

"Kirche said Rett was killed in the southern lands. But it says, in the *Book of Rett* that he was taken to the outer boundary of Ruhm, to Galdred."

He drank, but this time only took a small sip and set the glass back to the table.

"Are you certain you recall the conversation accurately? I can't imagine Kirche would make such a mistake. But then, the tales we've told the folk of the Ruud are vast and varied. It's possible he was simply keeping up a pretense."

"Do we have reason to keep the truth of Rett from the folk of the Ruud?"

At this, Prenalin sat up and leaned against the back of his booth, turning his gaze to the window. "These questions are unbecoming, Leah."

She sipped her tea. "My apologies. But..."

Prenalin chuckled. "Yes, all right. Just one more."

Smiling, she said, "What of the document about the wissende Ferdwick Elson taking the stone from Ruhm and bringing it to the east?"

"What of it?"

Leah shook her head. "Kirche himself told me that Michelruud, who led his folk here, gave the stone to an emissary who brought it home, and was instructed to hide it. No one is sure where. While Kirche believes the stone to be here in the east, we can't be certain. Can we?"

"Well, a little white lie to force the hand of the King of Michelruud does no harm, does it?"

"But why not name the emissary? Why make up the name of Ferdwick Elson?"

Prenalin eyed her, his head atilt. "Why do you say the name is a lie?"

Leah realized then that she'd made a mistake. How could she know that Elson was not the emissary? Kirche had certainly not told her it was Dakenruud who took the stone from his brother Michelruud and hid it somewhere.

"Perhaps..." Her mind raced wildly for some excuse. "I merely expected it was a lie because the document was."

"Of course," he said. But Leah was sure she hadn't fooled him.

It occurred to her that she ought to tell Prenalin that she knew that the emissary was Dakenruud. What harm could it do? But then, he might ask her where she learned the name. And she'd certainly not learned it from school. There were books in the school library, of course, that told small bits about the legend of the stone and the power it gave the beasts whenever they were near it. But she only learned of their quest for the kell stone from Prenalin when she accepted her position as Aide to the High Priest of Hass.

"We're off on our annual trip to the Ruud," he'd said so many weeks ago it felt like years. "We will visit, make notes, observe, and of course, look for the elusive kell stone."

She'd only made a questioning face and he'd continued. "Ah, yes. You'll learn all about that soon enough. Suffice it to say, we've been looking for it for years and haven't come close. But it's there. It must be there."

And that was the extent of her knowledge until her father told her about it being stolen from the beasts and hidden for centuries. Michelruud, brother of her ancestor, Dakenruud, had stolen it back and intended to hand it over to the beasts on the eastern continent. Instead, he'd given it to Daken in exchange for Ruhm's help in ridding the eastern lands of the beasts.

But she couldn't tell Prenalin what she knew. He might suspect that her father knows more than he should. She must find out for herself, first. Only if she could find the location of the kell stone could she explain to them her connection to it. Once Kirche held the stone in his hands, her short term of deception would surely be forgiven.

Chapter Fifteen

Lucas sat on the ground with the riders of the king's guard on the Michelruud side of South Bridge. He leaned against a tree, munching an apple. Across the river lay Aaronland. The guards were suspicious of the delay. Sorgood had run them all over Michelruud and into the port at Cold Sea and now had them pausing when they should be moving into Arnot's kingdom in search of the bairn. Every minute they waited meant further distance between them and the boy.

"Something ain't right, I tell ya," Brinkley whispered for the third time.

"It don't matter," Phil replied again.

"Don't you think something's not right?" Brinkley turned to Lucas and Lucas nodded.

"Look, we stopped 'cause we got to eat, don't we?" Phil said.

"You don't stop to eat when there's an evil bairn running loose in the Ruud."

"Yeah, well, you don't keep changing your mind about where to go, either."

"Sure you do. You got to go where you think the enemy is, don't you? But you don't stop and have a picnic by the river."

Phil shrugged. "You think too much. Just follow orders."

Lucas pondered the situation. The guard had left Michelruud Castle after Sorgood met with King Welk and made straight for South Bridge. That in itself was not surprising, as the news was that their new destination was Aaronland Castle for King Arnot's troops. But they'd stopped at the bridge and settled down for lunch. And while Phil was correct in that they had to eat—they were riders of the king's guard and could very well have eaten apples and hard tack while trotting across Aaronland.

"You really planning to turn the kid in?" Brinkley asked Lucas.

"You've asked me that twice already."

Phil and Brinkley looked at him keenly.

"Why wouldn't I turn him in? Wouldn't you?"

"Well, sure. He's the evil bairn and all. But you *knew* him."

"He came to the Path wissenry before you left for the guard. Don't you know him, too?"

They shook their heads and their eyes widened. "Oh, no. We don't know him. Never heard of him."

Lucas smiled. "Chickens. Squawking chickens."

"Not chickens. We're riders in the guard," Phil said. "What are you? A wissende?"

"You implying the wissendes are weak, Phil?" Brinkley said.

"They ain't soldiers."

"It's true, Brink," Lucas said. "There's no offense. Wissendes are thinking folk, not great warriors such as yourselves." He couldn't help giving them a wink.

Brinkley nodded. "So, you really planning on turning him over?"

"Wouldn't you?"

"Course we would," Phil said. "He's dangerous. Even if he don't seem so. I mean, look what he done already with the prison kids."

Brinkley chuckled. "That weren't nothing. We could have done that ourselves."

"But we wouldn't have, would we? It's against the law. Against the king."

Lucas watched Sorgood about twenty yards north; he tossed a knapsack over one shoulder, patted his horse on the back and trudged through the makeshift camp, disappearing into the woods.

"Well, then," he told his friends, not remembering the gist of their conversation. "There you have it."

He stood, stretched a moment to look unconcerned, and excused himself to make a trip into the forest.

Phil muttered behind him. "I don't think he ever did answer your question, Brink."

"Don't be running off now," Brinkley called after him.

Lucas turned back and smiled. "You know I wouldn't get you into trouble."

Brinkley laughed. "You're legend for trouble."

"I'll be back soon, don't worry." And neither Brinkley nor Phil followed.

Lucas made his way silently through the shady wood, winding around wide trees and over roots, sliding furtively through dense shrubs, until he heard horses and Sorgood's voice.

"Yes, Lord Kirche," the master of the guard said. "I am certain we can find him."

Hiding behind a thick pine, Lucas knelt to the ground, and slowly peered around it. There in the wood stood Sorgood, short and bent, looking up as if subordinate to a tall, blond folk—Lord Kirche, the High Priest of Hass. Lucas remembered passing him as he left King Welk's table earlier in the day. With the priest was another folk, darker of hair and eyes, and a girl with a long braid down her back.

"Carry on, then," the priest of Hass said. "You must find the boy and appeal to the folk for his death; but be careful that you do not request it directly. The folk will demand it, if the options are presented to them in the right manner."

"I understand," Sorgood wheezed and though he couldn't see it, Lucas could almost hear the man's slick smile at his lips.

"Welk is not quite as you said," the priest continued. "He is defiant, not at all timid. But he allows circumstances to take him where they lead. He is not a true ruler. He does not shape the world to suit himself, as a king ought to do."

"Aye."

"You should have little trouble using him."

As he was about to turn away, the young girl caught sight of Lucas' face in the woods; her eyes flew open but she stood mute. Standing, expecting her to alert them to his presence at once, Lucas stepped back and made his way quickly and silently back to the guard to pack up his sack to leave. Sorgood approached from the woods several minutes later and gave no hint that the girl had said anything about Lucas' spying.

"We move into Aaronland this evening to camp," the master announced. "Tomorrow we will enter Town Village to enlist the Aaronland guard in setting up a perimeter on the north border. Change out of your uniforms. We will dismount at the outskirts and walk through the village separately, without arousing interest. I will take Welk's orders to the first castle gate on the east side. If you see anything of the boy, contact me immediately."

The soldiers dug out their civvies and began to change as Sorgood approached Lucas, his dark face set hard in a frown. Lucas swallowed heavily, ready with his excuse for listening in on the vile man's private conversation in the woods.

"You'll stick with your guard," Sorgood told him. "And if you see the boy, you will alert them."

"Of course, sir. I serve the king." He bowed with a smirk.

"You ain't gonna turn him in," Brinkley said after Sorgood returned to his horse.

Lucas smiled and waited for them to get dressed.

Chapter Sixteen

They'd spent the day before hiking through the divide wood, with Rogget setting off on brief hunts to increase his load of rabbit and squirrel to share with Forbes for his long trek back home, and to trade for goods in Town Village.

"You've never been good with the bow, Forbes," Rogget chided him. "Admit it."

"It's true; I'm a farmer through and through."

They camped at the edge of the wood overlooking the plains of Aaron and woke to cross in the morning light. Dew wet their shoes and the ankles of their trousers as a soft breeze worked to dry the grasses. As they neared the village, Aaronland castle stood tall and imposing in the distance. At the southern outskirts of Town Village, Rogget sent Darnit off to the north.

"How will he find us again?" Sadie asked, watching him lumber off.

"Oh, he'll sniff me out one way or t'other."

They made their way into the village and familiar sounds of the waking town hit their ears. They waved hellos several times to folk off to market with their push carts, or tending to their cottage chores, feeding chickens and ducks, or beating rugs, hung from low tree limbs, with brooms. Rogget told them to act natural, but Fenn felt nothing like it as he pressed a worried smile to his lips. Once they arrived in the bustling town square in front of the castle, they bid their goodbyes to Forbes.

"Everything will work out all right," Fenn told him.

Rogget glared at him.

"It will," Fenn said. "I promise."

Once Forbes disappeared into the crowd, Rogget said, "You ain't got no right to promise such a thing."

"I don't have to mean about the writ."

"But you know that's what he thought you meant."

Fenn shrugged. "Maybe."

In his heart, he did believe it would all work out. There had to be a way to persuade the king to honor his promise to Forbes.

A short distance away, on a small wood stage by the well, a young man called out, "Hear ye! Hear ye! Proclamation from His Highness, King Welk of Michelruud."

Fenn stared at him in a panic and along with Grayson and Sadie inched closer to Rogget, but he continued walking, pushing them away.

"You don't see anyone else gawking, do you?" he said gruffly. "Keep walking, like it's none of your business."

238

And it was true; the villagers went on with their morning tasks, paying little heed to the town crier. As they passed through the center of town they heard him shout, "Three children, alone. The evil bairn, Fenn Foster of the wissenry at Path with a distinctive mark on his right shoulder."

Rogget put his arm around Fenn. "See there," he said. "They're looking for three runaway children. But you're with me, aren't you? You just tell anyone who asks that you're my kids."

Fenn raised his eyebrows at Grayson. They didn't look at all like siblings; nothing matched, neither hair, nor eyes, nor noses. And none of them looked like a child of Rogget's.

"Adopted," Rogget added.

The huntsman handed money to each of them, instructing them which shops to visit. Sadie was to get fresh and dried fruits from the market. Grayson was sent for flint sticks and candles. And Rogget would trade his rabbits for more wool blankets. Fenn was sent off to the butcher's with five coins for jerky.

"You wait for us out back of the butcher's," Rogget told him. "We'll meet up there and take the wood paths to Waverly wissenry before we try to cross the boundary."

Fenn walked through town keeping his gaze on the ground, but he felt that someone was following him. He wanted to look around, to see if there was a guard watching him, but feared that would give him away. When he reached the butcher shop north of town, he suddenly felt free, as if whoever was watching him had given up and left. He shook his head at his own silliness and entered the shop. At the counter, the butcher was chopping meat for the cure when he looked up and smiled at Fenn.

"I'd like five packets of jerky please." Fenn laid his coins on the counter.

"Well, son," the butcher said. "You either like your jerky quite a bit or you're heading out on a long journey."

Fenn flinched, but the butcher went about the business of wrapping the jerky without another comment. From the corner of his eye, Fenn saw someone approaching and turned. An old man hobbled close, looking at him with a peculiar, pinched face. He came to a stop in front of Fenn and put a long, bony finger out almost touching his nose.

"I know you," the old man said.

"I don't think so."

The butcher behind the counter handed him his packets and said, "Are you not from Town Village?"

Fenn shook his head and stuffed the jerky into his sack. "I live out in the divide wood with my da." The butcher peered at him suspiciously.

Fenn moved backward to leave but the old man grabbed his arm.

"I have something of yours," he said.

"No, you're thinking of someone else."

"Ah, leave him be, pa," the butcher said. Chuckling, he went back to his meat chopping.

"It belonged to your mother," the wrinkled man said.

"How do you know my mother?"

The old man tilted his gray-haired head at Fenn. "Come this way," he said and walked to the rear of the shop around the corner of the counter.

The butcher watched, still smiling, as Fenn followed the old man to the back of the store and into the butcher room. Fenn shuddered at the sight of beheaded, skinned, sheep carcasses hanging from large silver hooks along one wall. The crooked, limping old man kept on, waving him through the room and out the back door.

"Where are we going?"

A grizzled smile lit up the man's face; he pointed to a small hut just beyond the yard and hobbled toward it. Struggling to lift his feet up the few stone steps to the door, he pulled it open and disappeared inside. Fenn stood at the bottom step for a second or two, shrugged, and followed him. It took several moments for his eyes to adjust to the dim light of the one-room house. It was crowded with a desk and a bed and along every wall was a collection of oddities. Ticking, moving timepieces; chain mail; wheels of varying sizes connected by rods; metronomes, clicking off time; a firearm that looked like new. And in the corner, hanging from a nail was the most amazing thing of all: a wissenry robe.

The old man was rummaging in papers strewn all over his small wooden desk. He stopped, stood straight, turned and looked at Fenn. "What did I come in here for?"

"You had something for me. Something of my mother's. But I don't think you knew my mother."

"Oh, yes, yes. It was long ago."

Fenn didn't believe him, of course. He was an ancient folk, the oldest man Fenn had ever seen, and obviously, not completely in charge of his mind.

"Where did you get the wissenry robe?"

"Eh? Oh, oh, that. Yes, that's it, you see. I was a wissende many years ago. It was then I met your mother."

"I didn't know you could stop being a wissende...once you were one."

The old man tilted his head at him again and said, "Eh? No? None ever told me I wasn't one anymore...so maybe I still am."

"Then why don't you live at a wissenry?"

"I was banished, you know?"

Fenn shook his head. "No, I didn't know."

"Oh, yes. Banished." And as he talked, he continued to file through the papers on his desk that were covered from top to bottom in very small, but neat and squarish, writing. "I joined the wissenry after my dear wife Iselda died. I had the three boys, of course, and I know it was all selfishness to leave them to my brother. But I had to get far from the memories. And the wissenry took me. Ah, I was so very distraught. I didn't act quite right, for the wissenry, that is. And I was banished."

For a folk who must have been one-hundred years old, as old as the trees, he could say a lot in one breath.

"Well, then," Fenn said. "You aren't a wissende, anymore."

"Oh, no son. A banished wissende is still a wissende. I was sent to the hill country to tend to the rejected. And to the wasteland, to care for the poor castaways."

The hair on the back of Fenn's neck prickled. "You were in the wasteland?"

"Yes, yes. And then I left and came home. So, I'm not really banished anymore, except I don't know if the wissenry knows that. I suppose I'm something of a rogue wissende." He let out an airy laugh. "If you will." He put the papers down suddenly and said, "That's it. That's what I have for you. I couldn't remember. Merry me, but my mind isn't what it used to be."

The huddled figure stood in front of Fenn but gave him nothing.

"Well, what is it?"

"Ah, yes." He held up a finger. "Information."

"Information?"

"Yes. I have a name for you. Clara. In the wasteland, in one of the middle villages, on the outskirts, in a small cottage by a creek."

"Which village?" Fenn asked, curious, but still believing the man must be addlebrained and wrong.

The old man waved his hand. "I don't rightly recollect the name. And I have to tell you...I'm not sure...but I think...maybe ...I have given this information to others." He put his finger to his lips and stood there thinking, his eyes closed up and his wrinkled face squinched and focused.

"Is Clara my mother?"

"Oh, no, no," he whispered. "That name cannot be said here."

"Do you know her name?"

The old man waved both his hands in front of him.

"How do you know who I am?"

"You look like your parents."

"Who are my parents?"

The elderly folk looked at him sadly and shook his head. "I can't recall..." And he went back to the papers on his desk.

Fenn insides fell with disappointment. He should have known. The man was crazy, poor fool.

"They took my great grandsons," the old man said without turning back to Fenn. "Here, at the butcher shop, weeks ago. They took them because they thought one of them might be you. They thought maybe I took you and raised you. But I didn't. I gave you to the wissenry."

Fenn sucked in a small breath and stood still, a tingling spreading over his body.

"They told me you let them go. You freed them from Steingefan. I know who you are."

Fenn could see that parts of him were lucid and parts were lost. He knew, somehow, that if he reached out and touched him, he could sort through and find the lost things. He could know what this old wissende knew but couldn't remember. He stepped toward him and held out his hand, reaching for his shoulder.

With a bang, the door behind him flew open, hitting the wall. Arms grabbed Fenn from behind and dragged him out of the tiny cottage. He saw the old man's face lit with horror before the door swung back again and Fenn was dragged down the stone steps into the butchery yard.

Chapter Seventeen

Leah was surprised when Prenalin told her she had the entire day free. "Walk about Path," he suggested. "Visit the local shops or the orchards. We are allowed to take apples—as many as we wish."

She thanked him and left the inn, knowing exactly where she would like to spend her time—but first, she had a chore to see to. Most of her travels in the Ruud were by carriage, but once, she'd been asked to ride a horse, when Arnot insisted on taking their party along a trail to view the blooming fall flowers in a field west of Aaronland Castle. And Leah had watched, envious, the queen and her ladies straddle their mares easily, wearing pants. She'd not had much practice riding horses in Ruhm, going everywhere on foot or by carriage, and she struggled to keep herself properly covered sidesaddle while never finding a comfortable position in her dress and over tunic.

The tailor's shop was west of town nestled in a woodsy spot, shaded and cozy. Tailor Small welcomed her, though he was clearly nervous to serve her, and let his daughter measure Leah for riding pants. They would be delivered to the inn by day's end.

When she found herself once more in the small village square, she was exhilarated, and frightened, not knowing if she would be able to bring herself to wear pants in front of Prenalin and Kirche.

Two buildings south of the inn was the stationer's office, where Leah was certain to find comfort. The streets of Path were not crowded, but there were folk here and there who nodded and cast their gazes to the ground at her feet as she passed. Several folk gathered on the porch in front of the general store and eyed her suspiciously; she smiled and waved, but they did not respond.

In Path, the stationer lived on the second floor, just as her family did over her father's shop in Ruhm. The Path building had a wide porch with steps all around and on each side of the house were trellises in which it appeared Madam Stationer had attempted climbing roses with little success.

Leah walked up the steps to the front door and pushed it open. The air inside was stifling of books, papers, and ink and all sound was muted, soaked up by the tomes lining the walls.

Leah breathed in the memories of home.

"Hello?" she said, but no one answered.

A ticking clock paced the seconds somewhere nearby, but all else was silent. She walked through the first two rooms, letting her hand slide along shelves and spines and stacks of books.

"Hello," she said again.

There was a door, ajar, at the far end of the second room. She knocked on it lightly and it glided open. Stepping into a tiny office, tears filled her eyes as she thought of her father. How she missed him.

She sat at the desk and looked about at the disarray. Piles of paper sat precariously on the edges among books, inkwells, and a bin of pencils. The room was so much like her father's she smiled, but a tear trickled down her check. Leaning over, she put her elbows on the desk and wiped at her face, knocking several pencils to the floor.

She sat up and pushed herself back, bending down, search-ing for them. One had rolled far under, toward the wall, so she got onto her knees on the floor and reached for it. She had to laugh as she found more books and papers beneath the desk. Was it a rule that stationers must be untidy?

Grabbing at the writer, she noticed the title on the spine of a large tome. She pulled it from under the desk and sat on the floor with it. *The Book of Katze*. It was leather bound and looked very much like the *History of the Ruud* she'd seen at the inn. But it was much thicker and heavier.

On the first, yellowed, parchment page, in large calligraphy was the introduction: A Telling of the Kell Stone by The Modest Katze, Humble Servant to Our Sire, King of Michelruud. Leah turned the page and began to read.

Within these pages is the proper and unadulterated history of our Ruud, which begins, as all history must, with the beast. It is true that I, Modest Katze, have led a life of debauchery, drunkenness, and revelry. For that I was banished from the wissenry. But I was not the first and will not be the last. One must admit that at least a modest sum of eccentricity is necessary for a full life. I did my best. Perhaps I overly indulged. It will be for the future to decide. But despite this illustrious reputation, I adamantly swear that I have set down the story of the beast of the northern lands as the tale was given me by the beasts themselves. And the history of the Ruud is just as it was written by the sage wissendes of the days of old.

As all stories of the beast must begin with the kell stone, that is where I shall start...

Leah read until the light in the tiny office had shifted and a door opened and closed. She looked up and around the room, remembering where she was, the heavy book now open deep into the first half on her lap. Before she could gather her wits about her, the door hit the wall and a young man wearing round glasses, with a blond mustache at his upper lip, stood staring down at her, shock in his eyes.

"Who are you? What are you doing?"

"My apologies." She struggled to get to her feet with the heavy book in her hands. "My sincerest...I'm so sorry."

"What are you doing with that book? Why are you in here?"

Leah managed to get to standing and put the book, still open, on the desk. She curtseyed. "I'm dreadfully sorry. I wandered in, only looking for a feeling of home." A giggle escaped her and she slapped her hand to her mouth.

The young man glared at her and she feared he would shout some more, but instead, he stood aside and motioned for her to leave the office as if she were an unruly child. She stepped quickly past him into the next room. He closed the door with something of a slam and locked it with a key.

As Leah followed him into the front room, he said, "I'll be sacked for sure if anyone finds out I left that door open. No one's allowed in the stationer's private office. No one. Not you and not me. I'm in big trouble."

"I won't tell anyone. Honest, I won't."

He calmed down a bit, but wrung his hands on his apron. "I should have been here to greet you. It's my fault, really. What did you say your name was?"

"I'm Leah of Ruhm."

"Ruhm? You're not with the Hass?"

"Yes. I'm the aide to Lord Kirche, High Priest. I'm on the annual tour."

The young man's eyes widened and he stammered. "I see. My apologies. I could hardly have refused, had you come in and asked to search the premises. I didn't know, that's all."

"It's quite all right. My fault completely."

Leah curtseyed several times finding her way backwards to the front door. Giggling, she hurried outside, down the steps and back toward the inn.

Chapter Eighteen

Flung from the arms that dragged him from the hut behind the butcher's, Fenn turned to find a young guard standing before him with his firearm raised to Fenn's chest. Beside him stood Sorgood, the king's master of the guard, hunched and grinning like a rat with a slice of cheese. Fenn had seen Sorgood before, riding through Path, and then in the village square on the morning they'd rounded the children up to take them to Steingefan. He was much uglier up close, with black, greasy hair hanging to his shoulders. And beside Sorgood—

"Lucas?" Fenn said without thinking.

"This is him, then?" Sorgood sneered.

The young guard said, "It's him. It's him."

And Lucas nodded. "Yes."

Motioning to Lucas, the master of the guard said, "Tie him."

As Lucas moved forward, the door to the hut behind Fenn burst open and a shot rang out. Before he knew what had happened, Fenn saw the young guard's aim move from his chest to a point behind him and Fenn raised his arms as if to push the guard away and—whoosh! The guard, Sorgood, and Lucas all fell backward to the ground.

Fenn turned to see the old man standing behind him with a smoking firearm in his hands.

"Run," the old wissende said.

Fenn did as he was told and ran past the three on the ground, now stirring to get up, and toward the butcher shop where he saw Rogget, Grayson, and Sadie, their faces alert with fear.

"What was it? We heard a shot."

Rogget called out, "To the woods, quickly."

They darted into the forest behind the butcher's shop and ran north. Breathless, they stopped after a mile and began to walk.

"What happened?" Rogget asked.

"One of them must have spotted me in the village and gone for the other two when they saw me go into the butcher's." Fenn remembered the feeling he'd had of being watched. He would never again doubt his own senses.

"But what happened?" Grayson said. "They were on the ground. Did you shoot them?"

Fenn shook his head. "The old man did. He took me into his hut and told me about my mother. And then he shot at the guard."

"Mighty good shot to knock 'em all to the ground." Rogget said.

Fenn only nodded. What *had* happened? They fell to the ground after the shot—after he tried to push them away. But he was four or five feet from them. And even if he had physically tried to push them down, he wouldn't have been able to do it. He was a scrawny kid and there were three of them.

And Lucas. With the guard; helping them find him and identify him. Were those the skills Father Treacher had in mind when he told him not to worry about Lucas? Treachery? Betrayal?

"Well, I'd say we need to try to run again," Rogget said. "The guard will be alerted soon enough. We'll need to bypass the wissenry and head straight for the border."

"No," Fenn said. "We need more food. We'll just have to be quick about it."

"But it's a two-hour walk. They'll be alerted."

"They'll be expecting us to go straight for the border. They'd never suspect we'd turn west for Waverly."

Chapter Nineteen

Waverly wissenry was a large, square, two-story building, with a kitchen in the back, like all wissenry buildings. It was set on a large parcel of cleared land in the middle of the forest with easy paths leading out to the villages. Mother Carroll stared at them aghast for too long as they stood at the back door in the late afternoon sunlight.

246

"What's this?"

"As you see—" Rogget began.

"But why haven't you left? You should have been into the hill country."

At least they didn't have to explain themselves—they simply shrugged and offered her downcast, guilt-ridden faces and she hurried them into the kitchen and filled their knapsacks with biscuits and pieces of roasted fowl, and fresh fruits and vegetables to go along with those Sadie had purchased.

The kitchen was much like the kitchens of all the wissenry buildings—always a pot of stew over the fire. A desk or two in the corners. Oil lanterns hung over the center table. No one else was there and Mother Carroll wasn't at all concerned about keeping her voice down.

"Britt warned me you weren't the sort to go off and do as you're told. Fenn Foster, as I live and breathe, you'll never make wissende proper this way. A wissende is, above all, dutiful. Don't make that face—it's true. How can you come to be trusted if you don't first practice trust."

Fenn had no answer for that. He should tell her, he reasoned, that trust was meant for weeks ago, before he learned about secrets. He should tell her that Father Treacher and Father Britt couldn't be trusted—how was he to learn to trust from them?

"These are troubling times, Mother," Rogget said. "The boy hasn't even begun his training."

"Aye and it doesn't look like he will."

At that, Sadie grimaced and Grayson looked grief stricken.

"Oh, none of that children. Think of it as a grand adventure. You're off to explore—something few children of Path ever even dream of doing. Well, all right, they dream. But dream is all. You are living it."

"Thank you, Mother," Grayson said taking his now heavy sack and slipping it onto his back.

Mother sighed and put her hands to her hips. "You will take care, now, won't you?" she asked Rogget.

"Aye, Mother. I will let no harm come to my charges."

"And Fenn, when you—if you return to us. You will be oh so much wiser than you are today."

They were hurried out the back door and shooed from the porch. "Go on," Mother said. "And do as you're told, for once."

They jogged across the yard and disappeared into the north woods.

"Well, we can't be seen now," Sadie said. "We'd be caught for sure."

"Why do you say that?" Grayson said.

"Because my pack is so heavy, I'd never outrun a guard."

"Drop the pack then, silly."

"And give up all these supplies?"

"You won't need the supplies if you're caught."

Sadie rolled her eyes and shook her head. "Sometimes, Grayson, you don't make a lick of sense."

"*I* don't make sense?"

"Hush now," Rogget scolded. "Sadie's right. We want to keep our supplies, so we'll be quiet and move as quickly as we can."

Grayson turned an annoyed face to Fenn who could only smile.

They'd hiked east through the north wood for over an hour when Grayson said, "We must have crossed the border by now."

"The border is the end of the wood," Rogget said. "We step out of the wood and into the hills; that's your border."

They trudged on, silent, for another two hours. Fenn was once again troubled by the quiet. Sadie was angry and sad. But certainly she missed her parents and worried about them. Grayson too, though he just seemed sad. He wondered at himself and how he could go on betraying them by withholding secrets, even knowing that it hurt their friendship. But he couldn't seem to tell them the truth. And he still needed to have a private talk with Grayson about the history and the Hass of Emorah; but they never had a moment alone. Every time he tried to bring it up, Grayson insisted he didn't want Sadie to hear them discuss it.

The forest ended abruptly. They stood in a row looking out over a wide, grassy, shallow valley dotted here and there with shrubs and the occasional patch of trees.

"This isn't what I expected at all." Fenn stared at the darkening landscape.

A rising and falling horizon of hills beyond the valley beckoned them, lifted higher and higher until there was only a skyline of worn peaks.

"Me either," Grayson said. "I was thinking it would look like a lot of really big, green, haystacks...of a sort. If you know what I mean. And we'd be hiking up and down...or better, making a path around and through the valleys."

"Me too," Fenn said. "But it's just..."

"Slopey?" Sadie said.

"Aye, it slopes. Beyond are the hills. You can't see 'em now, but when we get closer, you'll find the sort you describe. Gnomes made 'em—all sizes. And look there." He pointed northeast where the setting sun lit up rocky mountain peaks in the far distance. "Beyond those mountains is the ice realm."

"How long will it take to get there?" Grayson asked.

"Oh, I'm thinking a few weeks walking."

"Weeks?"

"Probably more. It ain't so much the distance," Rogget said. "It's only maybe fifty miles through the hills. That'll take a few days for us. But then you've got maybe another hundred through the mountains. Much slower going, I'd think."

"Sadie has a rough map of the hill country," Grayson said. "And I'll see what she's got on the ice realm. We can make a good estimate in the morning."

"How will we find enough food?" Sadie said.

"How will we keep from getting caught?" Fenn asked.

Rogget began trekking down the slope into the valley and they stood watching him until he turned back to wait for them.

"What's your hurry?" He laughed at himself.

Fenn looked to Sadie and Grayson as they stared out into the darkening country in front of them.

"One more step," Grayson said, "and we're out of the Ruud."

"You hadn't been out of Path before a couple of weeks ago," Fenn said. "It's no different now."

Grayson looked at him, his eyes open wide. "No difference? The Ruud is home, just as Path is home."

"He's right," Sadie said. "This is the first real step toward adventure."

"Adventure," Grayson murmured. "I could do with a lot less of it."

"But look." Fenn walked out in front of them. "It's no different. See, I'm in the hill country. And now," he walked back. "I'm back in the Ruud. There's no real difference. There's no line. The Ruud is part of the eastern continent. And that is part of Kell. It's all the same. The border is all in your heads."

"And our hearts." Sadie smiled and moved past Fenn to where Rogget stood waiting for them.

"Sometimes Sadie can be very smart," Grayson said.

"Only sometimes, waiter boy?"

"She's a lot smarter than you give her credit for," Fenn told him.

"Waiter boy thinks anyone who doesn't read two books every week is downright dumb."

"I never said that."

Rogget rocked back onto his heels and fell forward a few times. "Any time you three are ready to move along..."

"You're awfully eager to leave home," Sadie said to Fenn.

"I wouldn't say I was eager. But the sooner we figure out how to get out of this mess, the sooner we can get back home and back to normal."

"You still think we can fix this?" Grayson said. "We're on the run, abandoned to the hills. We're refugees now. Nothing more."

"The guard isn't coming after us out here, are they?" Sadie said.

"Exactly," Fenn said. "We're banishing ourselves. We don't have to run anymore."

"And how is that better?"

"Living out here is better than running and hiding all the time. And without being chased, we can figure out a plan to get back home."

"Now, I wouldn't assume that," Rogget said. "It's true the guard is spread mighty thin. Most were headed toward the port at first because the prison children said you were headed south; then they turned and started fortifying the borders—until Welk got a message from the wissenry saying you were banished."

"I've been banished?"

"You just said you were," Sadie said.

"It's not the same if you do it yourself."

Rogget chuckled. "Not to worry. Your banishment is a ruse. And a clever one at that, I'd say. They've got the guard turned around so's they don't know what they're doing. First it's to the port, then to the perimeters. Then to the port again. And now they've caught you in Town Village at Aaronland. I don't know how they can rally quickly. And they don't know if you've left east of the castle, or north at Waverly."

"If the wissenry says they've banished him, they'd never expect us to have gone by Waverly to see Mother Carroll," Grayson said. "They don't know where we are at all."

"So, you agree with me. We're out of trouble," Fenn said.

"For now, we can get ourselves well into the hills. And Welk has little choice at this point but to accept you've escaped and spend time bulking up his perimeter to make sure you don't come back."

"That's a relief," Sadie said. "I guess."

"But that doesn't mean there won't be guard sent out into the hills after us. And that's going to be a problem."

"Why, exactly? Is it easier to find folk in the hill country?"

"In a manner of speaking. There's loads of gangs out here. Gangs like we ran into in the divide wood. They'd be only too happy to turn us over for a reward. We got to keep ourselves private and be careful who we trust. Don't start thinking we're out of danger."

Fenn turned to Grayson and nodded toward the hills. Grayson took in a long breath and let it out slowly before adjusting his knapsack on his back and trudging across the border and into adventure. Fenn smiled, following. They could fix this, he thought. They could fix everything. Just as they'd saved the children of Path from Steingefan, they could make folk understand that there was no prophecy and Fenn was not an evil bairn. And if he could find out who his parents were and have King Welk honor Forbes Billings' writ at the same time, more the better.

They walked on through the valley, up slopes, and down again, sometimes along brown dirt trails, other times in ankle deep grasses, until they'd climbed high above the timberline behind them, and down once more into a deep vale. The farther into the hill country they trekked, the more Fenn thought about Father Treacher and his wild grey hair and never seeing him again, never hearing him squeak with anger at Lucas again. Lucas. Fenn's heart sank. All that worrying he'd done about him being eaten by felidae only to find him a rat. Skills. Some skills—traitoring, and lying, and stabbing folk in the back. Now he didn't mind if he never got to go home again...so much.

"Well, I'm glad we're relatively safe," Fenn began, after they'd hiked in silence for some time. "Because I'm planning to head to the wasteland."

"You're what?" Rogget said, as they stopped to gape at him.

Fenn turned back to them. "I saw Sadie's map. Just into the hills there's a stone bridge crossing the river into the wasteland. And beyond it are several villages. I'm going to look for information about my parents."

Grayson's face gathered together into a glare and he opened his mouth to speak, but Rogget stepped forward.

"Do you ever plan to do what you're told?" Rogget asked.

"I can't answer that, really." Fenn smiled. "I might one day, though."

They stared at him in silence for some time, silhouetted against the deep red of the sinking sun behind them.

"You all can go to the ice realm without me, if you want," he said.

"But we made a pact; we stick together," Grayson said.

"What would be the point, anyway?" Sadie said.

"She's right. I think we're stuck going where you go, pact or not."

"So the pact stands," Rogget said.

"Of course it still stands. Pacts are forever," Sadie said.

They walked on, turning slightly north and set up camp against a slope out of the wind and slept on the soft grasses. Fenn bolted awake in the early morning light—he'd had no dreams, no visions. He reached for his hemp rope and charm, but there was no unusual heat on his neck. He was sickened at the thought of his charm against the skin of Clutch, the thief.

Chapter Twenty

The next morning, Leah was to travel with Kirche, Prenalin, and the bodyguards to visit Timber. They woke early, before dawn, for the long carriage ride south. Leah put on her riding pants, tucking one of her nightshirts into the waistband under her tunic. But she couldn't bare it. She liked the feel of the pants, but the look in the mirror was eerie and unfamiliar. She would have to wear the pants under the dress. At least she could hike it up and ride astraddle that way.

Timber was a bustling village without much of a town square. All the buildings and houses were huddled together in chaotic bunches on a plain nestled up against a northern wood.

"To the south," Prenalin told her, "is the beast forest. The villagers are wary of being carried away and eaten."

Leah smiled. "Certainly not."

"It's what we are told."

Leah remembered her chats with Wanda Kay at the Snapping Turtle Inn at Cold Sea. Wanda treated the relationship between the folk and the beast more as a rambunctious rivalry than a vicious battle. Though she did say the folk feared a war with the beast.

After their duties were settled in Timber, they took to horses provided by the villagers. When Leah waved away the side-saddled mare and asked to ride astride, her cheeks burned flush and she caught sight of Kirche's smirk. Neither he nor Prenalin said a word as she hiked up her skirt a bit and straddled the horse, exposing her new pants. She smiled, but Prenalin frowned and turned away.

They rode across the plain to the edges of the beast forest. Kirche told her it was necessary to patrol the area on his visits to be sure the beast were not flouting the laws that kept the most dangerous of them deep within the forest and away from the folk. And while he assured them all of their safety, he insisted they carry their bows for protection and he and the bodyguards had scabbards for their firearms draped over their horses' backs.

"What keeps them in the forest?" Leah asked.

"They were defeated once," Kirche told her. "And they know should they harm a folk here in the Ruud, all the soldiers of Ruhm will not think twice in slaughtering the lot of them."

They rode casually along the southwestern border of the wood and Leah watched as Kirche smiled up at the enormous pines. He was enjoying his tour immensely, she knew. But his smile soon disappeared and his right hand shot up in the air. They halted and Leah peered around

Alphonse and Prenalin to see what was the matter.

Rooting around the trunks of the pines along the edge of the forest was a bevy of brownies. Tiny brown creatures wearing pale tunics, they were on their knees digging and sniffing, and moving to dig some more.

Kirche turned back to the party with a finger at his lips. He pulled his firearm from its scabbard and slipped off his mount. Prenalin motioned for Leah to dismount as well and she fell to the ground with a thud. But the noise didn't deter Kirche. He prowled steadily closer and closer to the brownies and raised his firearm. Leah put her hands to her ears and closed her eyes tight just as the shot rang out.

When she opened her eyes, the horses were scurrying, Kirche and the bodyguards were running forward toward the brownies, popping off arrows, and another loud shot echoed through the air.

"Come," Prenalin said, and he took her hand to lead her forward, but she balked.

"We should not be separated." He forced her to jog to where Kirche and the others stood still attacking the brownies as they scurried away and into the trees.

Just as she reached Kipling and Alphonse, a thunderous clatter echoed from within the forest, and through the trees stomped a herd of centaurs. At their feet were enormous wolves and black cats. The ground shook and Alphonse fell in front of her, trampled by an enraged centaur.

"Run, Leah," Prenalin called above the shouts and screams. "Get to a horse."

Tripping, she fell to the ground, rolled several times to avoid a centaur's pounding, then clamored to her feet and ran blindly north. She saw no horses and seeking cover, ran into the trees to her left. Stumbling over roots and shrubs, she ran until her own terrified panting was deafening.

As the forest grew danker and darker, Leah slowed her pace and looked around her. Everywhere, she heard scampering, hooting, squawking. She was being watched and followed. She turned several times, changing direction, but she couldn't tell east from west. A terrified choking sound left her throat and she began to sob and shake. She was lost in the beast forest and, despite Wanda Kay's reassuring words, feared for her life.

When she saw shimmers of light twinkling ahead, Leah made her way toward a glen where streams of yellow sunlight sparkled with dust specks, warming the ground. She stood at the edge, alert to the sounds of creatures all around her. And then she saw it. At the opposite end of the clearing, encircled by a halo of light. Leah shuddered.

"It can't be," she whispered. "It can't be."

Unconsciously, she reached for her necklace and charm, but she wasn't wearing them. The marble amulet, much smaller than the one Kirche wore, etched with the flaming tree of Hass, was only worn for ceremony. But she knew the tree. She could trace its lines in her sleep, and recall the flames licking at its limbs. And there it stood before her in the beast forest. Its wide branches reaching out for her, alight in blazing red and fiery orange leaves glistening in the sun.

It was not possible. According the *Book of Rett*, when the folk of Ruhm learned of his betrayal, his love for the beast, they bound Rett's hands and feet and dragged him behind horses northeast to the flaming tree on the rocky, dry border between Ruhm and Galdred. They wrapped him in chains, hoisted him into the tree, and fastened him to a lower branch. Then they dug a circle pit around the base of the tree and lit it with fire.

When Rett's echoing screams ceased, the tree burned and fell quickly to ash, and the folk knew they had made a terrible mistake. And at that moment, every flaming tree on Kell fell in an instant into a pile of burnt embers. That is why there are no flaming trees left. Anywhere.

Of course it was just a story. Leah had known, deep within her, all along. But standing there in the beast forest looking at the tree, her heart fell. What she had always known was now at the fore; it could no longer be ignored. The *Book of Rett* was a lie.

She made her way, stunned, to the tree, staring up at its enormous limbs. Reaching out, she put a hand to its rough, flaked trunk. Was it called the flaming tree because of its scarlet leaves, she wondered. Or because they'd burnt Rett to death in one? She knew that one day she would have to find the answer—all of the answers.

A twig snapped and she turned, startled.

"H-hello?" she said.

A gray rock sailed across the glen, cutting into the sun's rays, and pelted her on the forehead just above her right eye. Leah fell to the ground against the flaming tree, dazed. She reached up to touch the spot and felt warm sticky blood oozing out of a gash in her skin. Another rock hit her on the arm. And another on the chest. More pummeled her face.

"Stop," she cried out.

"Murderer! Murderer!"

Brownies came out of the trees on the other side of the clearing screeching at her, throwing sharp pellets and branches. Leah curled herself into a ball and screamed.

"I know where the kell stone is!"

It did no good; the brownies moved closer continuing their attack. She raised a hand away from her face as if to block the stones and the

254

ground shook as centaurs entered the glen.

Chapter Twenty-one

It was sudden, Sire. There was no time to gather the rest of the guard."
Sorgood bent low before the king in his chambers by the hearth. Welk
sat in his comfortable chair staring at the round bald spot on the top of
Sorgood's head. A few of the guard, and young Frieden, stood behind
him. Welk was relieved that his shock upon seeing the son of Belfen was
wearing off. No doubt he would be seeing more of the lad now that he
was nearly grown. He was glad to be comfortable in his presence; it gave
him a melancholy hope for the future.

The guards' faces were bowed, but Frieden watched Sorgood with
disgust.

"You found him at the butcher's hut?"

"Yes, Sire. I dragged him out but the butcher followed me with a rifle
and fired at us."

"It wasn't the butcher," Footman Weeks said. "Begging your
pardons." He bowed curtly. "It was old Father Wold. I fired back...or
tried to."

"Poor shot."

"But it was old Father Wold. I couldn't..."

"Are you a footman in the king's guard or a wissende in training?"
Sorgood shouted.

"Enough," Welk raised his hand.

"That's when this oaf knocked us all down." Sorgood pointed at
young Frieden.

"I was protecting the master of the guard, Sire," he said.

Welk nodded and tried hard not to smile. He could not tell where
Frieden's loyalty was—but it was certainly not with Sorgood. And it was
now clear that all the digging, and march-ing, and packing and unpacking,
setting up tents and false perimeters—none of the guard's training had
prepared them to do anything more than ride about on horses chatting
with the guards of Damon Wall and Aaronland. How was he to fight off
the eis or Ruhm with these folk?

And what of the bairn? He'd now met with the butcher Wold—the
old wissende from the wasteland who told Sorgood weeks ago about the
boy's birth and his mark. How did the boy know to go there? He must
know more about his origins than the wissenry admits.

"And you let him out of your grasp," Welk mused.

"If I hadn't been knocked down, Sire."

"You'd have been shot," Welk said. "You were unprepared, Sorgood. I am, I have to say, beginning to doubt your worth."

Sorgood bowed lower. "I am sorry to disappoint, Sire."

"Why did you have so few guards in town?"

"There are not enough soldiers to patrol the towns as well as the borders, Sire."

"And no need now, I'm sure. He would have made for the hills by now, certainly."

"Yes, Sire," Sorgood mumbled. "We had yet to put the border in place north of Aaronland."

"As we should have done in the beginning. The boy has outwitted you," Welk sneered.

"He travels with an adult male, Sire. A woodsman."

"No, the boy is the intelligence that betters you, Sorgood. The sooner you realize that, the sooner you will learn to overcome your weakness."

"Yes, Sire."

"I believe I told you the boy would remain in the Ruud some time before slipping off. You would have done well to patrol the villages. But you chose to ignore my advice."

"Oh, no, Sire. I did not act quickly enough, it is true. But I heeded your words. Indeed, I did."

Welk shrugged. "I trust that at least *now* you will build your perimeter, Sorgood. Now that the boy has escaped us."

Sorgood hesitated before bouncing in a groveling nod. Welk dismissed him and his guards, watching Frieden's back as he left. How tall he stood, despite his frail folk form.

Once alone, Welk relaxed into his chair to ponder the situation as it was. Perhaps it was best that the search for the boy would now end in the hills, and not in the Ruud among the folk. They could be appeased and their lives return to nearly normal. But Welk knew he could not let the boy run amok in the outer lands for long. The folk of the Ruud will be complaining that one day the bairn of prophecy will return to destroy all. No. He must capture Fenn Foster and imprison him, as soon as can be.

The Hass of Emorah would like to see the bairn turned into a local devotion. But what trouble might that bring? And how might the Hass use such a situation to their advantage? And to kill a boy? The folk may be in a frenzy of fear, but to call for the death of a child...not likely.

"Dunham," he called and waited knowing the man was always just outside the door, perched, waiting to be summoned. As expected, a light knock sounded, the door opened.

256

"Sire."

"Where are the prisoners?"

"Hidden in the bower, Sire."

The bower? Welk looked at Dunham in surprise. The bower had been closed off many years ago after his mother's death.

"I am sorry Sire, if opening the room has offended."

"No, no." He waved his hand in the air. "It is good the room can be used for something."

He caught Dunham's slight smile as he turned toward the large double doors at the far end of the king's chambers.

"Come see what I have done," Dunham said, asking Welk to follow him.

Welk resided now on the first floor, in his father's old rooms. The bower, the queen's suite of rooms, would now await his wife, should he choose to marry. The thought hadn't occurred to him before.

"You see I have sent in the ladies to dust and air out the linens," Dunham said as they walked through the lobby and into the queen's bedchambers. "The prisoners are there," he motioned to a set of doors. "In the closet, where they would not be seen."

"It is a large closet, I presume."

"Indeed, Sire. The queen enjoyed a large closet."

Dunham held Welk in something of a hopeful gaze and Welk couldn't help feeling kindly toward him. He was more a father to him than his own father had been. But the queen's chambers did nothing to elicit in him a desire for marriage. He had little memory of his own mother and none whatsoever of these rooms heavy with tapestry and brocade.

"Very well, bring them to me in my chamber room."

The three folk of Path shuffled into Welk's chamber, wide-eyed and gawking, and bowing again and again as they approached him at his large, comfortable chair. The innkeeper, Steppe, a thick and intimidating figure, sported a shock of deep auburn hair, a face full of freckles, and pale green eyes. The Pratts were round and healthy, both with their pudgy fingers clasped at their bellies.

Welk's room, though once his father's, was simple. The bed had been cleared of its crimson velvet covers and the dark rugs exchanged for lighter, colorful throws. The wall above the fireplace was now freed of the ominous, dull-eyed stares of the eleshag and elk heads—those given to the guards at Steingefan for their cardroom. His father's jeweled throne was taken out and put into the hall and Welk's aged, soft chair from his old quarters brought in. Welk hoped the ease of his chamber would be comforting to the folk.

But once before him, they fell to their knees and cast their faces to the rug on the cold stone floor. Welk first fell forward to lift them to their feet, afraid they'd fallen ill, but remembered himself and sat back again.

"Dunham," he said. "Chairs, please."

Dunham looked surprised and hustled about the room dragging chairs over and doing his best to get the folk off the floor and into them.

"Please," Welk said. "Please sit."

They balanced on the edges of their seats, looking down still.

"Stationer to the King," Welk said and the stationer nodded. "This behavior is unlike you, is it not?"

"I am a prisoner of the king now, Sire. Begging only not to be hanged."

"Hanged? Please, I implore you all. We have much to speak of that concerns the Ruud. Can you please see me as an ordinary folk for a time?"

Ma'am Stationer nearly spit with surprise and looked up at Dunham who shrugged.

"We are not Ruhm," Welk said. "Have we not enjoyed a less formal hierarchy here in the Ruud?"

"Yes, yes." Innkeeper Steppe examined his hands in his lap. "And yet the folk of Path, Sire, as we were in the jail, would scream at us through the windows, telling us we would be hanged or tortured."

Welk shook his head. "My apologies for leaving you in the jailhouse for so long."

They all nodded their bowed heads.

"How can I speak with you if you will not look at me?"

The stationer finally raised his head and looked directly into Welk's eyes. "Sire, please tell us the fate of our children."

At that, Ma'am Stationer dared to glance up at his face briefly and the innkeeper nodded and wiped his eyes.

"Last news I have has them safe and off into the hill country with a woodsman."

"Rogget, the wayonder?" the innkeeper said.

"I am not sure who he is. But they are safe. I was hoping they would come to you at the jailhouse and we could capture them and be done with this mess. But they are led by Fenn Foster and he is clever."

"Aye." Ma'am Stationer smiled a bit. "He is a clever boy. He would not want any harm to come to them."

"We have no intention of harming your children," Welk said.

"I fear they are loyal to their friend, Sire," the stationer said. "But I do not think they understand the situation."

"Stationer," Welk said, leaning forward and looking at him closely. "I do not think I understand the situation. I was hoping you all could help me sort it out."

Ma'am Stationer looked directly at him now in surprise.

"It is true. I am confused. Certainly we must capture the boy and punish him for his escapade at the prison."

Ma'am Stationer's mouth hardened and her eyes shut into an angry glare.

Welk said, "All the children would have been returned home soon enough. We were desperate at the time to find this bairn foretold. The folk are concerned."

"Concerned, yes," she said. "But not so much as to see our children in Steingefan."

"Perhaps it was a hasty decision. But as I am at a disadvan-tage for information, I must stand by it. You see, I have here a history of the Ruud."

Welk put his hand atop the large book sitting on the table next to his chair.

"But I suspect this book is not the true history."

The stationer blinked rapidly.

The innkeeper spoke up. "We have the same book at the inn. It's available to all."

"Yes, but it isn't correct. You see, there is an error in it. I suspect this history of the Ruud is not accurate. Stationer, what can you tell me about it?"

"I..." The stationer looked to the ground and then back to Welk.

Welk felt for him, sensed his awe, and regretted it. While he'd spoken to a few folk from time to time as prince of the Ruud, and seen his father speak to them occasionally while sitting atop his horse on a tour, he knew that to sit in the presence of the king of Michelruud, especially in his private chambers, was, for the ordinary townsfolk, a miracle to be sure. Welk had long been disgusted with the hierarchy.

The stationer however, cowed as he was, held his own, as if pondering his options on what to say to him. And he finally spoke.

"It is my understanding Sire, that your sixth great grand-father, Roarn of Michelruud, commissioned the rewriting of the history."

The innkeeper looked at the stationer and seemed to chuckle. "What would he do that for?"

"The original history began with the Kingdom of Ruhm," he said. "It told of King Michelruud and his journey here, to establish the Ruud."

"This history begins there, as well," Welk said.

"No, Sire. It's not the same. The new history begins with Michelruud landing with his family and followers in the new land. It speaks of great adventure, freedom, bravado and the like. The original history begins much earlier and tells the story of why he left Ruhm."

Welk nodded. "I see. Why is the story of the prophecy different?"

"There is much that is different, Sire. The new history was commissioned after the Great Beast Revolt of 1070. The prophecy was supposedly made when the beast were defeated and driven off the lands surrounding the old castle. Many things that occurred shortly after were to be kept hidden...but..."

"But what?" Welk said.

"There was a wissende who was banished for a time for carousing. He apparently secreted away a copy of the original history and spent many years with the beast. He grew wise and determined to tell the truth. He added much to the history, about the beast folk, and published copies for all the wissendes under a pseudonym."

"A pseudo-what?" the innkeeper interrupted with another chuckle.

"A false name. He called his history, *The Book of Katze*. He knew to publish copies of the true history was worthy of punishment. But what he wrote about the beast could get him hanged."

"And why would that be?" Welk said. The innkeeper's head bobbed up and down in agreement. "Why was the history rewritten? Why was it forbidden? And why don't I know about it?"

"That, I believe, was the hope of Roarn, and all of the kings of the day. They wanted to erase the old history and hide what they'd done."

"What had they done?"

The stationer began wringing his hands together in his lap and his wife reached over and placed her hand over his.

"You are not supposed to have this information," Welk said.

The stationer shook his head. "No, Sire."

"How is it that you have it?"

"I do not know for certain how it came to be in the possession of the stationer, Sire, but my office has a copy of this *Book of Katze*." He began to talk quickly now, nervously twitching in his chair. "I have tried to cleverly ask about it at the wissenry, but of course, by law, we cannot speak of such things. So, I do not know if I possess one of the wissende's copies, or another. But my grandmother told me, she had it that a stationer to the king of Ruhm left it at our office in her grandfather's day, though she doubted the story greatly, Sire."

Welk smiled. "Does it not seem odd to you that the kings of the Ruud would not have this history? But the wissenry and the stationer do?"

"Oh, indeed, Sire. Indeed. But we who have dared look inside the book, Sire, we know that it was forbidden and the punishment is death. We dared not bring it to anyone, not even a king."

"Death?" Welk smiled broadly. "What could be in such a book to bring death on any who read it."

"I fear it is not so much what is in the book, Sire, as what is in the hearts of folk."

Welk tilted his head at the stationer and peered curiously at him. "I do not take your meaning."

"The book only tells the truth."

"If you are led home under guard, can you secure the copy for me?"

"Yes, Sire, yes."

"Very well. Dunham," he called, and Dunham appeared from behind a curtain looking curious and excited. "You will gather a small guard to escort the stationer to his office in Path. Before you go, find the lady of the upper rooms and have her prepare quarters for our guests. They will reside here secretly."

"Can we not return home, Sire?" Ma'am Stationer whispered and bowed her head.

"Aye, your lordship," the innkeeper mumbled. "I fear the state of my inn."

"I will send an emissary to the inn immediately to relate news back to you," Welk said. "Cook often travels there for your beef pies when she is too lazy to make her own. She would be an excellent spy, would she not, Dunham?"

"Must we hide?" Ma'am Stationer said and curtseyed.

"Indeed. The folk are caught up, I'm afraid. We'll let them think you are still held in the jailhouse for a time. And I'm sure you'll find the rooms here more comfortable."

"Thank you, Sire," Ma'am Stationer said. "I didn't mean to shun your kind hospitality. I think I'd rather like to live in the castle for a spell, even hidden away."

"I think you will like it. And you will have all the news of your children as soon as I have."

"Oh, thank you," she said.

Chapter Twenty-two

I know where the kell stone is," Leah cried out once more. But rocks and sticks struck her body and face again and again until she curled as tightly as she could into a ball, covering her head with her arms, waiting to be stoned to death.

"That's enough," one of the centaurs roared and pounded the ground near her head with his hooves; the attack ceased. The brownies nearly shrieked with each heavy, irate breath they let out and Leah lay still, huddled against the flaming tree of Rett, bruised and bleeding on her head and arms. Her body trembled violently. She was sure she would die. The centaur kicked at her.

"Get up."

"She is one of them," one of the brownies shouted. "Kill her!"

"Get up," the centaur roared and Leah forced herself to move.

First she lifted her head and squinted up at the silhouette of a centaur blocking out the bright rays of sun. Shading her eyes with a hand, she struggled to sit up.

"I know where the kell stone is." She was hoarse and her voice trembled as she spoke.

"Liar," the centaur said.

More centaurs and several wolves surrounded her. A deep growling hum rattled her through to her bones.

"What is this?"

The centaurs moved aside for one of their own to approach Leah.

"Red Lichen, she is one of them," a brownie said. "You must let us have our vengeance."

"She mentioned the kell stone," another centaur said.

Red Lichen looked down at Leah and she gave a slight nod.

"What do you know of the kell stone?" he asked.

"I am descended of Dakenruud." Blood trickled down her upper lip and she took hold of her tunic, wiping it away, wincing at the pain.

"What is that to us?"

"I know you know of Dakenruud. I read about it in *The Book of Katze.*"

"She lies," a brownie said, glaring at her.

Red Lichen shifted his hooves on the grass. "If the Hass knows where the stone is, why are they still here looking for it?"

"They don't know. I haven't told them."

"We should kill her," a brownie shouted.

"Wait," Red Lichen said. "We will take her to Dag Voorspeld for his counsel. If he decides that she is lying, you may have her."

"And if she is not lying," a brownie said, "we will torture her until she gives up the location of the stone. And *then* kill her."

Chapter Twenty-three

A cool, damp mist hovered among the slopes and valleys of the hill country. Back home in the Ruud, Fenn would be listening now to sparrows, cardinals, and chittenbirds chattering and peeping. Here in the hills, the stillness of the late morning was broken only by the occasional crow cawing far in the distance.

Rogget had a fire going and was warming kaff in a pot over the flames.

"Would you like some bitters?" he asked. "It's strong."

Fenn shook his head and packed his new blanket into his sack. Groggy with sleep, they sat around the fire while Grayson looked at Sadie's map of the hill country.

"It looks like the bridge is just before the larger hills begin. So if we keep heading northeast, we ought to find it."

"What makes you think you'll find out anything about your parents?" Sadie asked him.

"I was born in the wasteland, according to Father Britt."

"Just like the bairn of prophecy," Grayson said. He glared at Fenn, but his face softened quickly.

"I'm not the bairn," Fenn said. "There's no such thing as prophecy. The future isn't written yet; how could anyone predict it?"

"But you have the mark. And now we find out you were born in the wasteland. Even you must think there's something strange in all that."

"It's just coincidence. And anyway, Dag Anfang didn't say born in the wasteland; he said cast into it. There's a difference. And he didn't say anything about a mark. See? You're looking for reasons to think the prophecy is true and I'm the one. But I'm not."

They frowned at each other for several seconds until Rogget coughed.

"It was years ago," Sadie said, and Fenn was grateful for the interruption. "How's anybody going to remember anything about it now?"

"But, before you were saying that it ought to be easy to find my parents."

"That was when I thought you were born in the Ruud."

"She's right," Grayson said. "Finding your parents in the wasteland would be harder than in the Ruud. I doubt they keep track of births there."

"Well..." He hesitated. "The old man behind the butcher's told me my mother's nurse was named Clara and I could find her in a village in the wasteland."

They all raised their brows at him.

"How could he have possibly known that? He doesn't even know you. Nobody knows you, Fenn. You're an orphan."

Fenn shook his head. "I know it sounds strange, but I believe him. He had a wissende's robe in his hut. I think he did know me."

Grayson nodded. "If he was a wissende, I guess it's possible he knew you as a child."

"And..." He hesitated again and took in a large breath. He'd have to get it all out at once and act like he wasn't crazy for saying it. "And-the-fairies-told-me-to-go-and-find-the-truth-about-my-mother-in-the-wasteland-so-I-can-prove-there-is-no-prophecy."

"What?" Rogget said. "Huh? The fairies did what, you say?"

Grayson leered at him. "You heard fairies again?"

"I did. In the glade. Saw them, too."

"And they told you to go to the wasteland?"

"They did. Yes."

"Maybe you imagined it," Sadie said.

"I didn't imagine it any more than I imagined them in the beast forest making fun of Grayson's big feet."

Grayson laughed. "Well," he said. "He does have the faire mark. So..."

Sadie shrugged. "I suppose."

Fenn could tell they didn't believe him. Nobody, Grayson had told him, could understand fairy talk. Nobody. He wanted to tell them that his hemp rope and charm burned his skin, that he had visions of his past that were real, and that he thought he became the thief when he touched him, and he was sure he knocked Lucas and the guards over without touching them at all. Then maybe they would see that there was something odd happening and understanding fairies was the least of it. Then again, maybe that would convince them that he was crazy.

"Doesn't matter, either way," Sadie said. "If Fenn wants to go to the wasteland, we go to the wasteland."

"I thought you liked an adventure," Grayson said.

Sadie smirked. "You're right. Like Mother Carroll told us. It's a grand adventure. I'm just tired."

They were silent for a long time, enjoying the warmth of the fire in the chilly morning, waiting for the sun to dispel the mist and warm the air. Rogget put out the flame and drenched it with his leftover bitters and they all got up to leave.

"We'll get your parents out of jail," Fenn said. "We'll save them. We'll figure this out and end it, somehow. I promise."

Sadie tried to smile; she nodded bravely.

"I'm sorry," Fenn said.

"Don't keep apologizing," Grayson said. "It gets annoying. There's nothing we can do about it now and it wasn't your fault, anyway."

"He's right," Rogget said. "Let's just work from where we're at and not concern ourselves with how we got here."

Fenn looked at them all, standing there staring at him with half-smiles on their faces.

"All right then," Rogget said. "Let's get moving."

"Didn't you ever have folk at the inn come in from the hill country?" Fenn asked.

"If they did, they didn't brag on it. We got a lot from the port, heading out to the hills, so they said. And we got them from all over the Ruud. But I didn't ever hear any tell of being here."

"Then you'll have stories of your own to tell when you get back," Fenn said.

"If I ever get back."

"Haven't you ever been to the hills, Rogget?"

"I stick to the Ruud. But there are plenty who come and go. Most of the encampments will be nearby, close enough to sneak in and out of the Ruud."

"They get them mostly in Aaronland and Damonwall," Sadie said, and they all looked at her in surprise. "My da told me. He travels through the Ruud a lot. Folk from the hills don't come through Michelruud, mostly because it borders Steingefan and the wasteland."

"And why are the wasteland villages so far north?" Fenn asked. "Wouldn't they want to be nearer to the Ruud?"

"Well, now, they're banished out there. They're not allowed to be too near the Ruud." Rogget said.

"Aren't the folk in the hills banished?"

"Not exactly. But they would be, if anyone got the chance to banish 'em." He laughed. "In the hill country, the land is green and pleasant, so I was told, and so I see is true. The criminals and loners took control here. The banished stick to the wasteland and out of their way."

"Aren't the banished criminals?"

"Not always. Sometimes they're just folks who found themselves in a bad place and maybe made a mistake. Some of 'em, I hear tell, aren't quite right and leave the Ruud on their own."

"Yeah, that's what we hear," Grayson said.

"So, keep your ears and eyes wide open," Rogget said.

"How does a folk close his ears?" Sadie laughed.

"I think it's a metaphor," Grayson said.

"A metaphor," she murmured as if she liked the sound.

"What's it like in the wasteland?" Fenn asked.

"I hear tell the ground is rocky, bad for planting, bad for grazing. The folk there are very poor. Look there." Rogget pointed to an archway dug into the side of a slope and covered with rocks. "Gnomes. Watch for the holes; you don't want to fall in."

They laughed, but stepped carefully.

Sadie recited, "Stick a gnome, stick a gnome. Far from home you'll have to roam. Fall into the deepest hole. Never will you come back home." And she giggled, a sound that echoed off the slopes and hills and made Fenn feel lighter.

"I can't believe you remembered that," Grayson said. "I barely remember Bob Biddle."

Sadie began, "Kit kiddle, bob biddle."

Grayson joined in, "Tell us Brownie Tom's riddle."

Fenn and Rogget exchanged looks while Sadie and Grayson laughed together.

"Maybe there's something in the air," Rogget said.

Suddenly Grayson and Sadie stopped. Fenn followed their gaze to see two eleshags several yards in front of them stomping at the grass, wary of their presence. They were wide as small cabins and nearly as tall. Shaggy, brown coats of matted hair fell all over them and they shook it out, glaring at them impatiently.

"It's all right," Grayson whispered. "They're supposed to be very gentle."

When they all began to breathe regularly again, the eleshags went back to grazing. From around the hill three horses loped over to join them.

They heard a cry from the sky and looked up to see roster fiends and falcons circling in the east.

"Hunting for ground squirrels and hundrats, I imagine," Rogget said.

The autumn day wore on, the sun just barely warming their heads. They wandered the small valleys between the slopes keeping on a general northeastern path toward the bridge until they came to a row of curled, yellowed parchment signs on sticks stuck in the ground, about ten feet apart, leading around one of the large hills.

Rogget looked puzzled. "Now, I don't read well, mind you," he said. "But it looks to me like that says Scray Buts."

266

"It does," Grayson said. "What could it mean?'"

"It's an encampment perimeter. That much I know. I hear tell they put out signs to warn you so you don't bother 'em. Usually a mean-looking picture of something. But...Scray Buts. I'm not sure what to make of that."

"Hey, oi!"

A barefoot man approached them from around the hill, rags draped over his shoulders, his britches ripped to shreds at the knees. His face was black with dirt and mud, and his hair matted against his head.

"Toggle off with you," he yelled. "Didn't you read the sign? Go on... off!"

"But..." Grayson pointed to one of the parchments.

"Get out," the man yelled and two others joined him from behind the hill. They wore dirty, hole-filled tunics, their eyes were dull, and they had rags tied around their heads.

"We did read the sign," Grayson said.

"What are you still doing here, then?" The man picked up a rock.

"All right, all right." Rogget ushered the kids away. "We're leaving."

"What was that all about?" Sadie asked.

"Like I said. They're camped there, probably in the little valley between the slopes. Don't want us around."

"Well, they need a better sign," Grayson said.

"Let's get away from them and stop for some lunch," Fenn said. "I'm tired."

After lunch they hiked another two hours and came across another row of posted signs. These were sturdier, the parchment nailed to thin wood boards, and each had a picture of a bloodied gnome with Gnome Eaters written on the top and bottom in red.

"That's more like what I expected." Rogget smiled.

Sadie looked at him, disgusted. "They eat gnomes?"

"Well, now, for some, a gnome is not much different from a ground squirrel."

"Rogget," Sadie cried. "That's horrible."

"But you nab them," Fenn said.

"Just because we pick on them and carry them around as a lark doesn't mean we'd eat one."

"Do folk eat brownies?" Grayson asked.

"Grayson!"

"I'm only asking."

"I don't rightly know," Rogget said. "I've never heard of it. But the brownies are forest creatures. You won't find them out here."

"But they can talk," Sadie said. "How can you eat something that talks?"

"Just because you don't understand what ground squirrels are saying when they bark doesn't mean they aren't talking," Fenn said.

"It's not the same thing at all."

Grayson laughed. "She's right. The gnomes are beast folk—sentient. There's a difference."

"We'll see. Maybe we'll meet one," Rogget said.

"Well there you go," Sadie said. "You never talk about *meeting* a squirrel, do you? Anyway, I've met plenty of gnomes in the Ruud. They don't like being picked up. And they tell you about it."

"A ground squirrel will tell you about it, too," Grayson said. "And you'd understand his language perfectly well, then."

"I don't think squawking is language, Grayson. Honestly, you think you're so smart."

"Hey there," a strange voice bounced off the slopes and they looked up to see a gruff and dirty man standing next to one of the signs.

"What's all the noise?"

"Sorry," Rogget said. "We'll be moving on."

"Best be. You're all too fat to eat. What kind of spits you think we got over here? Battering ram spits? They don't' make 'em that big. So go on; off with you."

"We're not that fat," Sadie protested.

Rogget put a hand over her mouth. "No, no, you're right. Much too fat for the spits. We'll be moving on now."

But the man walked toward them, his eyes squinting and his head atilt.

"Is that Roggester? Roggester Reynold?"

Rogget peered closely at the man and Fenn saw his face brighten. "Wiley Arbus, is that you?"

"Tis! And you, what in the Ruud are you doing traipsing about the hills...and with children."

"They're my charges." Rogget beamed with pride. "Fenn Foster, Sadie Pratt, Grayson Steppe, this here's Wiley Arbus. We was stationed in the guard together years ago."

"You were in the guard?" Fenn said.

"His name is Roggester?" Grayson said.

"How do you do?" Sadie bent into a slight curtsey, holding out her hand.

Wiley gave her hand a gentle bobble. He took Grayson's with an enthusiastic pump and Fenn's with a jerky shake.

268

"Good to meet you as well, kidlings. Come along to camp; we won't eat you, really. I'll get a replacement guard so's I can hear all the news of the Ruud."

He led them around the slopes into a deep valley and Fenn was surprised to find a settlement with tents, even a few wood buildings, lines of rope hung with clothes drying in the dim morning sunlight, fire pits, pots and pans hanging at a mess tent, and dozens of grimy men lying about, smoking pipes, and playing cards.

"Hey, oi, Tanner. Go to the post. I found an old mate."

Tanner sneered. "It ain't my time yet."

"I says it's your time, now get."

Very slowly, Tanner rose and made his way out of the camp, huffing and grumbling as he went.

"Come on, sit here by my fire pit. This here's my tent."

They sat while Wiley built up a small fire and hung a pot on a spit over it. "I got a big treat for you kids. Some sweet honey brew. I wouldn't normally share, but I ain't seen a child in nigh on five years."

"You been out five years now?" Rogget said.

"I have. Left right after you. The guard just weren't no fun without you."

"You were in the guard?" Fenn said again, looking at Sadie and Grayson in amazement.

"He was," Wiley said.

Another man joined them around the fire saying, "Roggester Reynold, I never thought..."

"This here's Bruck Lerned, kids," Wiley said. "Aw, what d'you look all scared for? We ain't criminals. Well...well, yeah we are. But we ain't going to harm you none."

"No, they won't do us any harm," Rogget said.

"What sorts of criminals are you?" Grayson asked in awe.

Wiley shrugged but Bruck said, "Thieves mostly. We try to steal seeds and farm and such. But we ain't much for it. So we tend to steal food from town."

"We don't steal it from town," Wiley said. "In Aaronland, they got a mound near the border where they leave things for us. Kind folk. We have to steal from the Brutes and the Wretched. The Brutes mostly, cause they's the stupidest folk you'd ever meet. We try to keep away from the Wretched; ain't none meaner in these parts."

"Brutes!" Grayson said. "Scary Brutes! Is that what their sign's supposed to say?"

Wiley nodded. "Aye, it is." And they all laughed.

Wiley's honey tea was delicious and Fenn drank his fill, apologizing for taking so much. But Wiley seemed pleased to see them enjoy it. Grayson opened the map and showed them the stone bridge they were looking for.

"Passing Bridge. Over to the wasters. Just up north a bit. You're close now. But what do you want in the wasteland?"

"We're explorers," Fenn blurted out.

"Explorers, now?"

"That's right," Rogget told him.

"And Rogget here's your guide...your protection, I'm supposing?"

They all nodded.

"Well, that's a fine story. As fine a story as I've heard tell in these parts." He laughed. "Tell me the news, then."

They listened to Wiley and Rogget talk of the guard and the new King Welk of Michelruud and Rogget told him about Steingefan and the children of Path."

"Aye, we heard of that. The rumor of the evil bairn's been all over the hills for years. Came right out of the wasteland, he did."

"That's all the guard's about these days," Rogget said frowning. "Chasing after children, looking for this bairn."

"Well, they'd lost the adventure well before we left." Wiley said.

After their conversation began to lull, Sadie asked, "Do you eat gnomes, then?"

"Ard, no," Bruck said. "We call ourselves that to make 'em leave us alone."

"Are they bothersome?" Grayson asked.

The two men laughed. "We settled our camp here over a gnome city," Wiley said. "They didn't care much for us. They'd come out their little holes at night and tie our laces together, or pour honey in our pipes. Devilish little critters."

"So we changed our name to Gnome Eaters and that about did it."

"Just that?" Sadie said.

"Well, there was the unfortunate accident with the little gnome in the fire."

Sadie gasped.

"It was purely accident, I swear. But when he went off screaming like that, telling 'em all we was trying to roast him. Well, I guess they figured we were serious and they packed off right quickly."

"Well, Roggester," Bruck said. "I always thought you'd go back to the guard after your troubles were settled."

Rogget shot a glance at Fenn and shook his head. "Nope, nope."

"It weren't your fault. You know that by now, I figure."

"I don't rightly want to talk about it; and no I don't figure that. It was my fault. I didn't have to do it and I done it."

"You did have to do it," Wiley said. "It was a direct order from your superior. You kill the dang thing or you get hanged or something."

"I told you I don't want to talk about it. But I could have run right then. I don't think they'd a shot me in the back. Heck, they only had one firearm at the time and I was the one holding it."

"No, you did what you had to do."

"I said I don't want to talk about it."

"Fine then. But I can't believe you've been carrying it around for five years still thinking it was your fault."

"It *was* my fault. I don't care who told me to do it. It was wrong. And you know, sometimes I think he only told me to do it 'cause he knew it was wrong."

"Aye, I'll grant that," Bruck said. "I heard other stories about what they made guards do. But with most they start out when they're little ones, like these fine children here. And by the time they're old, like you was, they'll shoot a centaur with no more'n a blink of the eye."

"I told you I don't want to talk about it."

"You shot a centaur?" Sadie mumbled.

Rogget got up and took off his sack, bow, and quiver. "I'll be off for a stroll round about your lodgings, now, if you don't mind." He stomped heavily across the camp.

Wiley nodded and called out, "Rogget here's my friend. Give him leave." Several men looked up, a few waved and they went about their business of lounging and cards.

"Did Rogget kill a centaur?" Grayson asked.

Wiley nodded. "He was ordered to. He hesitated long time, hoping the darn beast would leave. But it didn't. Just dared 'em to shoot."

"But why?"

"The centaur was out of the forest, on the king's land, and we had orders to kill any beast we found without a pass. Lieutenant gave the firearm to Rogget, as he was new and all."

"So, he didn't join as a kid, like most?" Grayson said.

"No, he signed on older. His family needed the money and Rogget weren't no good at tailoring."

"Rogget's dad is Tailor Small?" Sadie said.

"In Timber," Wiley said.

"Oh, I don't know the tailor there."

Wiley nodded. "I joined up with him. Thought it'd be fun. And you make some good gold for your family. But neither of us took to it. And Rogget left after the centaur. Said he was going into the forest of the beast lord to ask forgiveness, but I don't think he ever went."

"And now he probably thinks it's too late for apologies." Fenn said remembering Rogget's refusal to enter the forest.

"True, true," Wiley said. "And he figures the beast folk have some sort of recip...recip ...uh, equal? What's the word, Bruck?"

"Give and take? Tit for tat?"

"The reciprocal law," Grayson said.

"What's that?" Sadie asked.

"It means Rogget thinks he'll have to give his life for the one he took."

"That won't bring the centaur back, will it? And anyway, it does sound like it wasn't entirely his fault."

"It's going to get a might cold here soon," Wiley said. "You kids have some warmer clothes with you...I hope."

They shook their heads.

"I don't think we thought we'd be running—"

"Exploring," Fenn interrupted Sadie. "We didn't expect to be exploring this long."

Wiley smiled and nodded. "Well, you head back through after you explore the wasteland and maybe we'll have found something for you. You know, something just lying around."

"Maybe you could find stuff lying around at my house," Grayson said. "I wouldn't feel so guilty about wearing it."

Wiley winked at him. "That's a possibility. But if not, you might can barter some stuff in the encampments on your adventures. I don't think they'll have anything in your sizes, though."

"Where you planning to explore after the wasteland?" Bruck said. "I don't think the hill country is someplace kids ought to be wandering about."

"We were headed to the ice realm," Fenn said. "They say it's beautiful."

"Aye, and filled with eis and angels. Beautiful and dangerous."

"No," Wiley said. "No. You can't be heading out to the ice realm. There's war coming up that way."

"War?"

"Aye, I'll be telling Rogget about it. Keep you out of trouble."

"Why war?" Grayson said.

"Ard, it's a mess. And the angels aren't helping matters any. They're the ones you got to look out for. I don't think you'd even make it to the ice realm without them taking you."

272

"Taking us?" Sadie said.

"Aye," Bruck said. "They come swoopin' in, a dozen or so, and they carry you off. They drop you in the ice mountains and leave you there."

"Dangerous and just plain mean," Wiley said.

"Then you got to walk all the way back, half-starved and weak—"

"If you make it back at all."

"True. Too true. Some of us didn't make it back. And up there in the ice, there's no burying the dead. The gargantuan crows and eagles will feast on your frozen, rotting body."

"Gargantuan crows," Sadie whispered.

"Well, technically," Grayson said. "If you're frozen..."

"Then," Wiley said, "a day or so after the poor souls are taken up by the angels, the eis come round with their poison arrows and demand that we take our kind elsewheres."

"And we always tells 'em, we stay here in the hills; we ain't none of your concern."

"But your kind are up there in our mountains, they say. And we say, 'your friends the angels took 'em up there.' But they don't believe us. They killed lots of us until we got the shields."

"What shields?" Grayson said.

"I'll show you one." Wiley stood and disappeared into his tent, emerging with a large silver plate of glistening metal. "They're heavy. But they're the only thing we've found to withstand the eis arrows. They shoot so much faster and stronger than folk."

"Ard, Wiley, they're eis; their arrows are imbued with the beast magic."

"Maybe so."

"Do our guards have those shields?" Grayson asked.

"No, no. They're stolen. Well, the Wretched stole 'em. Off ships that pass through Ice Port over there cross the Plains of Glisch."

"So you stole them from the Wretched?" Fenn said.

"No, they traded 'em."

"But aren't you enemies?"

"Enemies be a harsh and variable word round these parts." Bruck said.

"We're a brotherhood," Wiley said.

"Aye. A brotherhood of enemies."

"We'd run 'em off without a thought, mind you. But when it comes to fighting off the angels and eis, we're all of one mind."

"Not of one mind, Wiley," Bruck said. "There's those what want to fight and those what want to make a peace with the angels. There's no defeating them, some say. They got a knife even more powerful than the eis arrows." Bruck lashed the air with his hand as if slashing Fenn with his angel knife. "You stay away from them."

"Well, who wouldn't stay away from a knife?" Fenn said.

"Aye, but a knife with angel magic. One deep wound from it and you die a slow, slow death. Years! It can take years. Wasting away."

"Yes." Wiley stole a brief annoyed glance at Bruck. "What with the war coming from up to the north and the Wretched around here, I'd say you'd best be back in the Ruud."

"Where do the Wretched hide out?" Grayson asked.

"All over the hills. Land pirates. Steal anything they can find from anybody. No souls."

Bruck picked up a stick and poked the fire, fuming. "One o' these days we're gonna have to do something about 'em."

Wiley nodded. "One 'o these days. None of the gangs out here care for 'em much. If we could get together we could run 'em off. But nobody'll help us."

"Well, I don't see how we would know them...to avoid them," Grayson said.

"True," Wiley said. "By the time you knew who they were, it'd be too late. But they don't head north so much this time o' year. They do most of their foraging into Damon Wall and at the port."

"Is one of them named Clutch?" Fenn asked.

"You've met them already?" Bruck said.

"They robbed us in the faire glade on their way to the port."

"I'm surprised they didn't kill you, even though you are kids. Stay away from 'em if you can."

"We thought they might kill us. But Rogget and Darnit showed up."

"Darnit?"

"Rogget's bear."

"Rogget's got a bear, does he?"

"Sure, hasn't he always had a bear?"

"No, I don't rightly recollect a bear. Can't say as it's odd, though. He seems the type to be traipsing about the Ruud with a bear. Where'd he get it, anyway?"

Fenn shrugged. "Don't know."

"Is it an invisible bear, then?" Bruck looked all around.

"No, he sent it off without us when we went to town for new supplies. It should show up sooner or later. I hope."

"I don't know. Seems to me a bear might cause a disturbance out this way. Folk are more likely to shoot straight off."

274

"Are there a lot of firearms out here?"

"More so than in the Ruud."

"But aren't they hard to come by?" Grayson asked.

Bruck nodded and smiled. "They are."

"Do the Wretched steal firearms, too?"

"Indeed they do. They traded a whole lot of 'em to the Breathless to fight off raids from the Brutes."

"The Breathless?" Fenn said.

"Philosophers," Wiley said. "Never shut up."

"Can't understand a word out their mouths," Bruck said.

"But the Breathless turned right round and traded 'em to us and the Brutes as a sign of peace."

"We think that was their goal," Bruck said. "Like I told you—can't understand anything they say."

Wiley spit into the fire and the men chuckled to themselves for a few moments.

"Do you hear much about any of the orphans of the wasteland?" Fenn said.

Wiley shook his head. "There are some, I hear. But I don't know about 'em. Why?"

Fenn shrugged. "No reason."

"Mostly I think they aren't so orphaned as you might think," Bruck said.

"What do you mean?"

"A mother don't want her little one brought up in the wasteland, nor the hills. So she sends her wee one off with a traveling wissende or she sneaks it over to Waverly wissenry."

Fenn perked up at that.

From behind the tent they heard a roar and a scream.

"That'll be your bear, I guess," Bruck said and stoked the fire with a stick. "Don't shoot it!" he called out to no one in particular. "It's Rogget's darn bear!"

Chapter Twenty-four

The stationer sat in the second chair by the fire in Welk's chambers, a chair meant for a friend, an equal. But in the early days of the Ruud, the stationer to the King *was* nearly equal—a trusted confidante. He flipped through the gold-lined book on his lap; it looked nearly identical to the history of the Ruud Welk owned, but this one was larger and its early pages delicate with age.

"Here it is, Sire—the part that I have read. The Beast Uprising of 1070 has occurred and many of the beast were driven into the forest. But the beast lord returned to old Michelruud Castle, Steingefan now."

"I know as much as that, at least, good stationer."

"My apologies, Sire."

"Continue..."

"The beast lord returned with the felidae and created chaos and havoc outside the gate. It was as if he called up a storm overhead and his voice thundered until finally King Michelruud appeared outside to hear him speak. Do you care to read it? Or shall I?"

"You may read it," Welk said.

"Dag Anfang thundered, 'Michelruud, thief of lands, butcher of beast, heartless intruder, dead you are. Dead you will be. A new bairn, born of a king, cast into the wastelands, will rise against you, and destroy all that you hold dear. The kell stone he will wield and all folk will harken to his command. The dragon flies above him! All laid waste below!' But Michelruud only smiled and turned his back on the felidae, leaving the king's guard to escort them to the edge of the Ruud and into the ancient forest, never to be heard from again."

Welk sat in silence for a moment pondering what he'd heard and then said, "Well, then, there certainly was a prophecy. Of that much we can be sure."

"Perhaps, Sire. However, there is one small item after this entry. I never paid much attention before. But now it seems a bit relevant."

"What is it?"

"Here, in a report given by one of the king's guard. He states that he overheard Dag Anfang say to another felid, 'these folk don't cower and whimper as the others do.'"

"Others?"

"Yes. It is a puzzle, Sire. Though, we know that other folk from the Great West and parts beyond often landed north of Cold Sea Port, at Ice Port, before Damonruud built the harbor piers."

"And you think they are the others Anfang spoke of?"

The stationer shook his head. "I could not say, Sire. But it appears he thought he could frighten Michelruud."

"So, you think it was not a prophecy?"

"As a descendent of wissendes, Sire, no. I do not."

"I cannot believe that this is what Roarn and the other kings wished to hide from the folk."

"No, Sire. It was much more than that and it's all here in this book.

Originally, Michelruud speaks of wishing to create a world in which the threat of Emorah was unheard of. He wished to erase the fears of the Hass from the hearts of the folk. They were not to be spoken of."

"But it wasn't he who changed the history."

"No, he did not go that far. Damonruud, his son, had to deal with Emorah for trade at the port. And according to the history, he and the other kings accepted help from them to drive the beast folk out of the Ruud. They led raids and brutally tortured and murdered many of the beast, in the name of the Ruud."

"Ah," Welk said, nodding. "That is something they would wish to hide."

"Indeed Sire. We pay tribute to the Hass of Emorah annually for the deed, but none in the Ruud are aware of the savagery that was leveled against the beast. Even now, after some two hundred years, the main folk of the Ruud have no memory of their ancestors' past in the Kingdom of Ruhm. They believe that Ruhm helped Michelruud out of the west and we pay tribute only because they are our forefathers."

"Do folk forget so quickly, stationer?"

"That is what I meant, Sire, about the hearts of men. They will easily forget what they do not wish to remember. And they will do evil all too quickly in error."

Welk nodded and sighed. "Why did not the Hass of Emorah regain control of the Ruud when they were asked for help?"

"I cannot say, Sire. I confess, I have not read all the history. I haven't much time for doing secret things. Maybe the answer can be found within it. Especially in the history of the beasts that Katze put at the beginning."

"And you never read that?"

"I never found myself much interested before now."

"You are certainly not alone in that."

"I will leave the book with you, that you may read it all." The stationer stood and bowed, prepared to leave but stopped at the door. "One more thing, Sire, of grave import. When I went to retrieve the book from my office, it was not where it was supposed to be. And it was lying open."

"Someone has read it? Your apprentice, perhaps."

Stationer Pratt shook his head. "Jeopard has already read the book— and he didn't know of its last hiding place. Not only that, he is an honest young man and would never stoop to snooping."

Welk nodded. "So, others know what I will soon know. Can that be a bad thing?"

The stationer gave him a helpless shrug and left his quarters. Dunham approached and occupied the empty chair.

"What do you make of it all, Sire?"

"I believe the Hass of Emorah had something to do with the rewriting of the history. Folk who do not know the mistakes of the past are fated to the same errors again and again."

"Yes, Sire. Wisdom."

"I think they are looking for what they see as another beginning—here in the Ruud."

"Sire?"

"I will read the history first. But if my Nanta knew anything, I think she knew how this whole sordid mess began."

Dunham put a question on his face, but rose to prepare the king's plate.

"Will you dine in the hall, Sire?"

Welk nodded. Yes. The noise and gaiety of the great hall would help him think.

Chapter Twenty-five

Rogget returned to the fire when he heard Darnit had arrived and Fenn thought he had become his old self again.

"The thieves that stole my charm," Fenn said. "They're called the Wretched."

"That so?" Rogget said.

"And they have Forbes' writ."

"Aye, I reckon they do."

"What's this?" Wiley said.

"Forbes' writ. You remember."

"He still has that?"

"Not anymore," Fenn said. "The Wretched stole it from him outside a pub in Aaronland."

"Why would he take it to a pub where it could get stolen? Not that it's really worth anything."

"According to him," Grayson said. "That's all they took."

"That's a might suspicious."

"Exactly what I told him," Rogget said. "But like you say, it's worthless."

"Well, you never can tell with the Wretched. They'll steal anything. And they didn't know it was worthless, now did they?"

"I guess not. But why would they want it?"

278

"Maybe they'll take it to Welk," Sadie said.

"Hah," Bruck laughed and spit bitters into the fire. "I don't think a king of the Ruud is going to take a meeting with the likes of the Wretched."

They spent the rest of the day and night with the Gnome Eaters, sleeping by the fire as the gang sang and played cards into the night. The next day, they woke early, were treated to a hot breakfast and began saying their goodbyes.

"You were going to tell Rogget about the war," Fenn reminded Wiley, anxious to hear the news himself.

"Aye, the war."

"War?" Rogget's eyes lit up in alarm.

"It's the encampments in the northeast," Wiley said. "They're spreading out all over the hills and the eis of the realm don't want 'em any closer. They've sent messengers over to the kings of the Ruud telling 'em to get rid of the folk, but the kings think it's none of their concern."

"Are all these folk from the Ruud?" Fenn asked.

Wiley pointed at him with surprise. "Bright boy, there. No. No, most of the folk up farther north come from the Great West, from the Kingdom of Ruhm."

"Then it isn't the business of the Ruud," Rogget said.

"Tell that to the eis. Anyway, it's heating up near to boiling up that way. We hear rumors of civil unrest in the realm as well."

"In the ice realm? Aren't they peaceful among themselves?" Grayson said.

"Aye, that's what you hear in the stories, ain't it?" Wiley winked. "But they're just as cunning and crafty as folk, as it turns out. I hear tell of the maiden being ousted and planning a revolt to regain her throne."

"Then maybe they'll forget the settlers for a while."

"Rogget, I'm surprised at you. If anything, it only riles them against the settlers more. They got to put the blame on somebody, after all. Anyway, we told the kids last night they'd be better off in the Ruud."

Rogget shook his head. "I'm thinking...not so much. But thanks for the warning."

"Take care on your exploring expedition," Wiley told them with another wink.

They made their way north to Passing Bridge, a wide stone arc over the rapids of the river. The day was cool and the sky clear blue; light breezes whipped at their faces. The water rushed loudly below them as they crossed into the wasteland. Just on the other side of the river the land was changed. Mostly flat with sparse clumps of trees, the ground was rocky and much harder to trek. By noon, they'd headed northwest, upward across a long rise to look down into a shallow valley covered in a blanket of pale purple.

"It's beautiful," Sadie said.

"And dangerous," Grayson said.

"But they're just flowers."

"Grayson's right," Rogget said. "That there's a field of lilac clover—thirty yards wide. I plumb forgot about it." He scanned the horizon. "Blooms its sweetest in spring and autumn. We're smack dab in autumn. And it goes on for miles."

"But there's a wasteland village in the distance." Fenn pointed. "Let's cross."

"We'll have to head north or south to find a way around it," Grayson said.

"What are you talking about?" Sadie said.

"Bees."

"Ard no," Rogget said. "It ain't the bees you got to worry about. Fat, lazy things'll just hover out of your way. It's the fairy bees."

"That's what I meant," Grayson said.

"Fairy bees?" Fenn looked out across the peaceful, beckoning field of violet.

"They're not technically fairies," Grayson said.

"But they're sentient," Rogget said.

"The encyclopedia on the beast of the eastern realm says they're semi-sentient. They're self-aware; but prone to viciousness. They don't appear capable of, or even interested in, learning other languages and they can't be reasoned with."

"And they're dangerous?" Sadie said.

"Very," Grayson said.

"I guess reading my da's books does come in handy."

"You should try it sometime."

Fenn slugged him in the arm and gave him a stern look when Grayson turned to him.

"Sorry," Grayson said. "I guess I'm just out of sorts lately."

"Yeah, well, we all are, waiter boy. So, what do we do?"

Rogget looked at Fenn. "We could hike for miles trying to find a way around. The main entrance into the wasteland villages is north of Steingefan. There's a path through the clover there."

"All the way back to the Ruud?"

"Aye."

Grayson sat on the ground with Sadie's map of the hills and wasteland. "That must be what this hazy marking is. It's the clover. Sure enough," he said, putting his finger on the map. "Right there it says so. The patch runs from just west of Steingefan all the way up to a plain nearer to the ice realm."

"And no other way over or around?" Rogget said.

"There are bridges. The first looks to be about five miles north."

"Five miles?" Sadie said.

"It's not all that wide," Fenn said. "We should try to cross here."

Darnit shook his head slowly back and forth, arcing it down and up like a swing, and let out a deep growl.

"I'll set Darnit off again." Rogget slapped the bear on the backside. Darnit lumbered off northward. "He can meet up with us later."

"How does he understand you?" Sadie said.

Rogget shrugged. "I think he can smell the village. He don't like folk much. Can't say as I blame him. It's not like I trained him or anything. And I reckon he smells me out after a while. I like to think he wants my company. But I reckon it's the jerky."

"Would the fairy bees sting him, too?"

"Nah, they're not likely to sting an animal. They're just vicious. If you upset them, they'll sting you for spite. And they take great pleasure in it. But an animal? Nah. They know the animal didn't mean any harm."

"Well, what if we don't mean any harm?"

"They're fairy bees," Grayson said. "They think all folk mean them harm. We have to hike to the bridge."

"I've heard tell of folks crossing without harm," Rogget said. "But it's a risk is all."

They stood on the rise for some time, watching the field of clover and the village beyond. There was no indication of danger—all was peaceful and quiet.

"Well, what's it going to be?" Rogget eyed Fenn.

"I think we should try to cross."

"That's a really bad idea," Grayson said.

"We can't go back toward the Ruud. Do we really want to walk another five miles up and back for a bridge? Let's just be careful and cross here."

Rogget stared at Fenn longer than usual, making him restless. "Okay then," he said finally. "Let's be quick about it."

They walked downward toward the village and into the clover. Careful at first, stepping around as many plants as possible. Fenn's feet sunk deep between them, flowers grazing his boots at his ankles.

"I don't see any bees," Sadie said.

"Shh," Grayson warned. "Just keep moving quickly and don't talk."

As they trod, fat bees, rose from the ground around them, hovering, landing, buzzing.

"Which ones are fairy bees?" Sadie asked.

"They looked like wasps in the picture I saw."

"Wasps? Ouch!" Sadie slapped at her arm. "I got stung."

She turned this way and that, her arms flinging about her body and swiping at her hair. "They're all over me." She screamed and started to run.

Fenn watched as dozens of tiny bees swirled around her face and hands.

"Sadie, stop!" Grayson yelled. He ran forward and dove for her, tackling her to the ground. She screamed again batting furiously in the air. Rogget roared forward, grabbed Sadie up into his arms and ran through the clover heaving and wheezing.

Fenn ran ahead of him, slapping at the bees crying out, "Hurry, hurry."

Sadie screamed again. Grayson tumbled forward out of the field rolling to the ground knocking Fenn over. Rogget plodded out behind them and fell, dropping Sadie out of his grasp.

"Are they coming after us?" Fenn stood and gathered up his knapsack.

They looked back at the field; it was calm again.

"Sadie," Grayson said. "Are you okay?"

Rogget pulled at the neck of her tunic. She moaned and her head rolled to the side. Large, round red spots erupted all over her neck and face. Rogget looked up toward the village.

"We've got to get her to help fast."

He scooped Sadie up in his arms, gave Fenn a stern look, and headed off toward the village.

"I'm sorry," Fenn said.

"I'm not mad at you," Rogget said. Fenn heard him mumble under his breath, "Only myself to blame."

"Did you get stung?" Grayson asked.

"No. You?"

Grayson nodded. "Just twice. What do you suppose they have against Sadie?"

Chapter Twenty-six

Facing the beast lord in his den—a sunlit glade amid the dense, dark forest—her hands bound tightly behind her back, Leah wobbled and weaved, forcing herself to maintain balance. Her right eye was swollen, though she could still open it a sliver to see, and her body ached. Her damp hair was draped over her face and tickled her skin, but she could not shake it away.

Beasts of all sorts prowled about her as if she were prey—pacing wolves glaring at her with yellow eyes; brownies hissing; a fat, frowning troll snorting at her; large black cats padding in circles at the outer edges of the den, their loud purring echoing all about. Tinkling water drew Leah's attention to an enormous boulder with water running down its front and pouring into a basin of rock below.

She'd been marched through the forest by brownies, wolves, and centaurs—the brownies demanding she be killed without delay. When night fell, her hands were bound behind her around a small pine and she was allowed to sleep for a short time, though the fitful squirming on the root-covered forest floor could hardly have rested her. She woke once in the cold dampness of midnight and was glad for the extra protection of her new riding pants; at that thought, she let out a laugh, which only angered her captors. She'd lost the ribbon for her hair at some point in the attack and sat on her locks—with each shift of her sore, aching body, she felt ripping and tearing.

As they marched her to the den of the beast lord the next morning, she understood how she'd come to be in her present circumstance. The brownies were only too happy to make her aware of her crimes. News that Kirche had murdered a brownie in Aaronland had spread quickly through the beast communities. The brownie's head, drying out on a stick behind the inn in Path, was an added insult.

When they were stupid enough to attack the group of brownies just at the edge of the forest, the centaurs, wolverines, and felidae were already on guard. And there Leah was, enemy to the brownies, running into the forbidden forest of her own volition, and the brownies demanded their right to vengeance.

Once in the lair, the coolness of the day fell in a mist, and introductions of a sort were made to Dag Voorspeld, one of the huge black cats, who nodded his large head and growled something like words that she couldn't understand. He lounged atop a gray boulder overlooking the crowd of beasts, and stared at Leah as if bored.

"Ho-an uchen hin," he grumbled.

Leah watched as the cat trembled, as if shaking off the morning chill, but instead of settling down again, he shimmered and broke into a million tiny shards of shiny black glass, and twirled around in whirlwinds of bits and pieces until coming back to himself as a folk, wrapped in an ebony velvet cloak.

"You claim to know of the kell stone," he said, and every word vibrated across the glade and through her body.

She nodded.

"You will explain," Voorspeld commanded.

Leah fought to stay awake, wishing desperately to wipe the dried blood from her face. Her forehead throbbed and her wrists chafed against the ropes binding them; she could feel warm blood oozing onto her palms.

"My name is Leah Hallowsing." A sharp, slicing burn spread out on her upper lip as she spoke. "I am daughter of Edwin, Stationer to the King of Ruhm. I am kin to Dakenruud who took the kell stone from Michelruud and was commissioned to hide it somewhere on Kell."

She paused and wavered, fearing she would fall. She needed water desperately.

"And how does being kin to Daken save you?" the felid said.

Leah shuddered, realizing that her fate was Voorspeld's to decide. And what if he turned her over to the brownies?

"Before he was taken and killed by the Hass," she continued, trembling, "Daken gave his brother Abueruud a journal in which he told of his adventures across Kell. And in which he related where he hid the stone."

Snickers rippled through the group of brownies and centaurs pawed at the ground.

"She lies," one of the wolves growled.

"I must return to Ruhm and find the journal."

"You don't know where it is?" Voorspeld said.

"You see. She lies to save her life. Do not be fooled."

"Woolrich," Red Lichen said. "Do not insult the lord."

The brownie slunk back into the crowd and another stepped forward.

"She is not the one who killed our Zeelif."

"Do not listen to this one," Woolrich said. "He continues to use name given him by folk; he is traitor to his kin."

"Kwitcher is not traitor," the brownie said. "Like name. Keep it. That is all."

"Stop this bickering." Red Lichen stomped the ground for silence.

Dag Voorspeld gazed at Leah and she begged him with her eyes to

284

believe her, even as she knew she was lying. The journal was only legend. She would have no idea where to find it. And even if she did, there was no certainty that it contained any information about the kell stone. But she surprised herself by how little she cared; she wanted to live. She wanted to get out of the forest alive and go home. And she would tell any lie that might make that happen.

"What would you do with the stone if you found it?" Voorspeld asked.

Trying to sound truthful, she said, "I would consult with my father for advice, of course. But I am sure that he would agree with me that the stone should be returned to the beasts."

"You are a member of the Hass," Red Lichen said. "Why should we believe you?"

"It's true." She lifted her chin in defiance. "I came here as one of them. But I have seen Kirche's careless, even murderous, behavior toward the folk of the Ruud, both beast and mortal. I do not leave as one of them."

Voorspeld purred loudly for some time while Leah tried to stay focused on his green eyes. Somehow, she must convince him that she wanted only to help them. She could hear her father's voice in her head from long ago, after she'd been caught lying at the Hass school.

"A lie will always reveal itself in your eyes," he'd said. "It's there, an imprint on your heart, and your eyes betray you."

"Drop your beloved into the pool," the folk cat said.

Chapter Twenty-seven

As they approached the outer huts of the wasteland village, they found a sign posted on a stump. It read: Banished. They walked quietly along the main road lined with huts—some crafted of clumps of sod, others of branches, and a few of hewn logs. Fenn saw that each had a small fire pit dug just outside its entrance. Thin, sallow folk crouched outside their homes, or gathered in circles on the ground on mats, or in the dirt. Most paid them no attention, despite Sadie, pale and motionless, draped across Rogget's arms.

Banished was rocky and dry, warmed by a constant sun—no trees dotted the landscape, only huts. As they neared the center of the little make-shift town, folk turned to frown at them.

"Newcomers," someone said. But they did not approach to greet them.

As they stood at the well, a short, wrinkled woman with a long mane of gray hair dancing about her shoulders walked defiantly toward them.

"What is wrong with the child?" She reached out to pull the hair from Sadie's face and Sadie flinched. "It's the fairy bees."

"Aye. Have you anything for it?" Rogget said.

"Bring her to my hut, quickly."

They followed the old woman into a dark, suffocating room built of logs with mud, now dried, slathered between them. In the center, the woman pulled at a stick and a flap opened in the roof and sunlight streamed in, brightening up the little space. There were beds along the walls, no more than rags laid neatly on the ground.

"Put her there." She pointed and Rogget fell gently to his knees and laid Sadie on one of the beds. She moaned.

"Welcome to Banished." The woman dug through a chest, pulling out bowls and containers of herbs. "I'm Pinta. Never mind the others. They're leery of strangers. They'll warm up. But you aren't banished, are you?"

Grayson shook his head. "We're adventurers."

Sadie chuckled and coughed.

"She hasn't lost her mind," Pinta said. "So there is hope."

"Lost her mind?" Fenn said.

"The stings. They'll drive you mad from pain. Once that happens, death isn't far behind."

"Death?" Grayson said.

"Oh, don't worry, son." Pinta ground herbs, oil, and water in a stone mortar. "It's only the very weak, or the allergic, who succumb. I'm sure the girl will be well in no time. Now, sit. This will take a while."

They watched as Pinta sopped up her muddy mixture with bits of muslin and covered Sadie's red patches with it, pressing them gently onto the swollen sores. Smiling up at Rogget, she said, "Adventurers, now. Fancy that. You should know how to cross the clover properly."

An elderly man, bent over at the waist, supporting himself on a stick, shuffled into Pinta's hut. He pointed at Grayson and said, "Did you come from Ousted? Did you bring any writs or decrees from the board?"

"They're not banished, Havert. And from the looks of this one, they came straight over through the clover without any foreknowledge." Pinta looked at Rogget. "But...you didn't happen to go through Ousted, did you?"

"No ma'am," Rogget said.

"Where is that?" Fenn said.

"Ousted's the little patch just north of Steingefan. Where there's the

286

path through the lilac clover I told you about," Rogget said.

"It's the first place you go when you're banished from the Ruud," Pinta said.

"There's a board there where the kings have their decrees posted," Havert said.

"Yes, yes." Pinta rolled her eyes. "We haven't had a traveler through in months. But we rarely get a writ freeing anyone, anyway."

"It's good to have hope," Havert said. "At least."

"Ard," Pinta said. "Hope is nothing more than the disap-pointment that follows. Hollow. And unnecessary."

This reminded Fenn of Forbes. "Is there a Lil Billings living here?"

"Ah, Lil and her writ. Talk about hope." Pinta laughed. She finished pressing her bits of poultice onto Sadie's spots and ladled water out of a barrel. Rogget helped Sadie to sit up and she drank a few sips before smiling weakly and lying back down.

"Lil Billings lives over in a little plot yonder south a bit. She's got too many of us believing her husband's got a writ to set us all free. Any day now, she tells us."

"Do you read? Either of you?" Havert said.

Grayson nodded.

"Are you feeling better, Sadie?" Fenn asked when she rolled over onto her side to listen to their conversation.

"A little."

"She could use some meat." Pinta looked at Rogget. "But that's a rare treat around here."

"Aye," he said. "Meat. If you're of a mind to stay with these kind folk for a time," he said to Fenn, "I'll take the evening and try some hunting."

"They're fine. No harm will come to them in our little village. You'll have to travel far into the hills yonder for anything much."

"I'll bring us all back some juicy rabbit." Rogget adjusted his sack and patted the sheath at his hip. "Sadie will be back to strength in no time."

"Yes, go hunting. But you boys, come out and read for us," Havert said.

Fenn and Grayson followed Rogget out of the hut with Havert and bade him a good hunt.

"What is it you want us to read?" Grayson asked.

"This way, this way." The old man hobbled slowly across the dirt road through the town to another hut. "We keep them in my house, in a box."

"What do you keep?" Fenn said.

"Writs. The last we got we haven't read yet."

"No one here can read?" Grayson said.

"No, not a one. Well, there's a woman over to the river in the mountains, but it's a long trek to see her."

They entered Havert's tiny hut, made of logs without any material packed between; sunlight streamed in lines across the floor.

He pointed to a wooden chest. "There she is. Filled with writs." He lifted the lid and pulled several decrees from kings written on fine parchment. "These we got more than a month ago and we've had no one visit yet who could read them."

Grayson took the papers and looked at them with a frown. "From the stationers in the realms of the Ruud." He looked up to Havert. "Most of these are notices of property being seized."

Harvert frowned and nodded. "Aye. We get a lot of that. If you're not there to fight for it, they take it from you. You don't have to read those. No sense spreading bad news."

"But this one is for a Kindred Aldrick. It's a pass."

"A what?" Fenn said.

"He's allowed to go home for a short time."

"Oh, wonderful, wonderful." Havert clapped his hands together. "You see? We sometimes get good news. Let's go, let's go." He danced out of the hut and back into the dusty little village square. The boys followed, Grayson still holding the writ.

"Kindred, where's Kindred? He's got a pass."

Pinta came out of her hut. "Quiet down, Havert. The girl is resting. What's this all about?"

"Kindred has a pass."

"Is that so?"

"You called me?" A scrawny, bearded man hobbled toward them.

"Yes, Kindred. A writ for you. A pass. Read it to him, read it!" Havert slapped Grayson on the shoulder and shoved him gently toward Kindred.

Grayson nodded, nervous, and read, "Proclamation from Evan, King of Michelruud, attested by Ricker, King of Damon Wall. Kindred Aldrick, thief and liar, banished to the wasteland from his home in Damon Wall for a term of forty years, is hereby granted pass to return to the aid of his ailing parents."

The man shuffled his feet to and fro and cleared his throat with a rough cough.

"Aye," Kindred said. "Thank ye." He turned to leave.

"Don't you want it?" Fenn asked him.

"Nah," he said. "My daughter Lisha came here nigh on a month ago on her way north to join her sister. She told me my parents had passed into the ether."

"But, it's a pass," Fenn said. "Can't you use it to go home."

"It only says I'm granted a pass to see to my folks. They're gone. If I'd use it to get back home now—well, I'm not going to chance that."

"He's right," Grayson said. "It's not a pardon."

Aldrick nodded and left.

"But—" Fenn started after him and Pinta put a hand on his arm.

"There's nothing you can do to help us, boy. Come sit with your friend a while."

Sadie slept on the floor, her body occasionally jerking as if she were being stung again. Grayson and Fenn sat with Pinta as she cleaned out her bowls and mortar and packed away her goods.

"What did you do to be banished, Ma'am Pinta," Fenn asked quietly.

Grayson glared at him.

"If you don't mind my asking, I mean."

"Oh, no. Mine's a funny story. You'll enjoy it." She chuckled and shook her head as if lost in memory for a time.

"My family had all gone. My two sons were lost at sea—hadn't heard from them in nigh onto fifteen years. Their pa drowned when he fell from a fishing boat many, many years ago. And my daughter, poor darling, succumbed to the gasping fever shortly after she was born. So, I had no one and I thought to myself one day—I thought I'd come out to the wastelands with Father Britt and see to the sick in Banished. Father Britt introduced me to Father Wold, he was a banished wissende. He and I tended to the folk here."

"So you aren't banished?"

"No, it's not so boring a story as that. No, you see. We were plagued by a bit of the gasping fever and there were a few women who had babes. I knew I needed more orange root and spirim, and the only place I knew to find it growing free was in Timber at the outskirts of the western wood. So, I went to get some. But it had already been foraged. So I asked the apothecary in Timber if he could spare some. I had no money, so he chased me off. I managed to get some from the kind apothecary in Path on my way back. I came home, treated the sick and thought no more of it. Until some time later, a traveler from Ousted brought a writ declaring me banished."

She paused and Fenn said, "But why?"

Sighing, Pinta shrugged. She reached behind the chest of herbs and remedies and pulled a bag onto her lap. From inside, she found a yellowed, folded writ from the king.

"I'm told it says here, for willfully and recklessly spreading the gasping fever to the family of the apothecary in Timber, resulting in the death of his young son."

She handed the writ to Grayson and he nodded as he read it. "But, did you have the fever?"

"I never got sick."

"Father Treacher could have defended you at a court, at the meeting place," Fenn said.

Pinta laughed. "Maybe so. But as I'd already been banished, I couldn't go back home to try. And no court would have been allowed after the fact, anyway. They accused me and held that I was absent and so found me guilty without representation and no need of court."

"Can they do that?" Fenn said.

"Apparently."

Chapter Twenty-eight

Leah had been given a few sips of water and a biscuit, her hands unbound, and was now being escorted out of the forest. Only the brownie Kwitcher had been allowed to accompany the centaur Red Lichen, as the others could not stop arguing for her death. Her throat remained parched and her stomach growled occasionally, tightening itself into empty knots; her knees wobbled and threatened to give out several times. She struggled to make it out of the forest, fearing if she fell, her captors would leave her where she lay—and at the mercy of the brownies. She had never realized before how vicious brownies could be.

Red Lichen halted in front of her and held up his hand to have her stop. Kwitcher walked into the back of her knees.

"Apologies," he said.

"Shh." Red Lichen put a finger to his lips.

Ahead, Leah heard the crunching of needles on the forest floor and the brushing of shrub branches. A young, frail folk emerged from the wood. It was the boy she'd caught spying on Lord Kirche's meeting with Sorgood in the woods just outside Aaronland some days ago. His face, upon seeing her, told Leah she must look dreadful.

"Lucas," Red Lichen said. "You tramp through the woods like a boar. Have you no sense of stealth?"

"This is my forest, is it not?" he said, his concerned eyes still on Leah. "I have nothing to fear here."

They all stood silent for a moment staring at one another.

"What's this?" Lucas pointed at Leah.

"We are escorting her from the forest. It's a long story."

"I've heard some of it," he said. "I will join you. I am Lucas of the wissenry at Path."

"Leah." Her parched voice was barely a whisper.

"You are with the Hass."

Leah nodded. As they hiked through the wood toward the border at Timber where Kirche had attacked the brownies, Lucas told them that he'd heard there was trouble in the forest.

"The brownies are tightly knit," he said to Leah. "Among their various communities—except, of course, there is animosity between the displaced and woodland."

"Dirty, backward sorts," Kwitcher grumbled.

Leah nodded, not really understanding or caring what Lucas was saying.

"A few in Aaronland told me I was needed—that one of the Hass had been captured and their representatives were calling for her death."

"Dag Voorspeld has granted her reprieve," Red Lichen said.

"On what condition?"

"She claims to know of the kell stone."

"Is this true?" he asked her.

Leah nodded. Lucas looked at her carefully as they walked and she felt as if he knew she had lied. She was unsure why the beast lord had not known it. In his lair, Voorspeld had commanded that her hands be unbound. She was led to the boulder and stood staring at it, trembling with fear. She could hear Voorspeld purring, even in his folk form—an echoing, resonating hum—as he approached her.

"Drop your beloved into the pool," he'd said.

Leah shook her head and tears formed in her eyes. "I don't know what you mean."

"What is it that you cherish?"

She thought about it for a few seconds. "My mother. My father."

"What is your beloved?"

He was insistent, angry, and yet, a weariness tinged his words. Even in folk form, his smooth voice shuddered through her chest. It reminded her of Kirche's soothing speech and yet, she found herself trusting in Voorspeld—his was real and not rehearsed.

What did she cherish? Leah's chin fell to her chest and she closed her eyes; her cheeks burned hot with shame. "My hair," she said.

"Drop your beloved into the pool."

She slid her trembling hands along her head, gathering her locks at the nape of her neck and pulled them over her left shoulder. Kneeling on the ground, she let her hair fall into the water in the basin. While she knelt there, shadows emerged and mingled with the water falling over the face of the rock and Voorspeld stared down at her, then at the shadows, and back, as if reading her thoughts.

"She promised Voorspeld she would return with the stone," Red Lichen said.

"There is more," Kwitcher said. "She is to return the head of Zeelif to his tribe."

"And how will you do that?" Lucas asked her.

"They are to wait in the woods behind the inn tonight." She coughed.

Lucas pulled a canteen from under his tunic, popped out the cork and handed it to her.

"Drink," he said.

"Much obliged." She tried not to appear greedy as she swallowed several times. "Thank you."

"You may keep it, while we walk," he told her. "You are in more need of it than I."

Leah wished she could stop herself from finishing off Lucas' water, but was unable. She wanted to ask him who he was and what link he had with the beasts and their forest—she suspected he was one of the felidae, like she'd read about in the *Book of Katze*—but as captive, she felt it better to keep quiet. If she could only make it out of the forest and away from them, she would finally feel that her life was no longer in danger.

"The Hass has often had deadly run-ins with our kind," Lucas told her as they hiked. "They've killed felidae, centaurs, wolves. But never the little ones. We heard that your Kirche has been seen trying to hunt the brownies in years past, but he was unsuccessful. They aren't difficult to sneak up on, as they become engrossed in their digging for morels."

"We do concentrate," Kwitcher said.

"His efficiency at the hunt as apparently increased," Red Lichen said.

"He had help," Leah said. "From a folk called Sorgood. It was Sorgood who led him to the brownie."

Lucas nodded as if he knew of Sorgood already. "Here we are."

They pushed through the trees to the edge of the beast forest to look upon the plain of Timber. Leah found herself confronted by two folk on horseback surrounded by a dozen archers.

"There she is," Prenalin called out and the archers raised their bows.

"Frieden?" The king of Michelruud, sitting atop a horse beside Prenalin, gazed in shock at their party.

As the archers drew back their bows, Leah stepped in front of the group and put her arms wide.

"Please don't hurt them," she said. "They have escorted me out of the forest."

Prenalin dismounted his steed and ran toward her as Lucas, Red Lichen, and Kwitcher fled back into the forest. She fell as he met her and he lifted her into his arms, carrying her to his horse.

"Are you all right?" he said, clearly shaken.

"What have they done to you?" King Welk said when she found her seat on Prenalin's horse.

"Nothing more than I deserved." Tears fell down her cheeks, stinging her wounds. "It was revenge for the murder of one of their brownies. They did not hurt me without reason."

"You give them too much credit." Prenalin gazed up at her. "They should be punished."

"No, please. It would only lead to more fighting and more death."

King Welk nodded at Prenalin. "And what of the guard who was trampled? Does Kirche have plans to retaliate?"

"He has not confided any to me."

"Well, then, I am happy to have helped you, if only by lending you my horse. Let the girl ride back to the inn with you. I'll send someone for the horse later."

"Thank you, kindly, your Highness."

Prenalin climbed onto the horse behind her and spurred it toward Path at a lope.

"Are you sure you're all right?"

"I'm bruised."

"And bloodied."

"It probably looks much worse than it feels."

"Let us hope so."

"Will Alphonse be all right? Was he badly hurt?"

"Alphonse died of his wounds this morning. Kirche has already sent his body off to the port to be shipped home."

"I'm sorry." Leah thought back to the brief attack, and watching Alphonse trampled under the hooves of the centaur. She could not say if it had been purposeful or malicious. But it seemed at the time that the beasts intended only to protect the brownies. Though their response to her in the forest brought her many doubts.

"Will the soldiers of Ruhm come to the Ruud and kill all the beasts?" she asked.

"What on earth for?"

"But Kirche said, if they dared to harm a folk..."

Prenalin chuckled. "You put too much stock in Kirche's declarations.

But he will remember what has taken place here, and use it when he will."

"You engaged the king of Michelruud in my rescue?"

"Indeed. Though he was against it when we first approached him. He believed that you were likely lost forever, led over the falls to the mermaids or worse."

"But you persuaded him?"

"I did." His voice behind her sounded grave with concern. Leah breathed finally—a deep sigh of relief.

"And Lord Kirche, he stayed behind at the inn?"

"A rescue was much too dangerous for the Lord. But he was certainly for it. It was his idea, actually. At least...he didn't need to be convinced."

Once they reached the inn at Path, the others rejoiced in her return. Gretchen babbled continuously as she put an arm around Leah and led her to a chair in the front room where the thick *History of the Ruud* sat on its dusty perch. Zelda produced a ribbon and handed it to Leah, knowing she could not touch her hair.

"Prenalin, go and ask for Leah's room once again," Kirche said and then smiled down at Leah as she worked her hair smooth and tied it. "You look like death has tortured you. I hope you aren't permanently disfigured. We thought you gone forever, I'm afraid—knowing the murderous nature of the beast. We emptied your room and Zelda took possession of all your things. We'll have them back to you immediately."

"Yes, of course," Zelda bowed. "I'll run gather them now."

"Thank you," she said. "For coming for me."

Kirche laughed. "Prenalin would hear of nothing else. Insisted you still lived as if he was connected to you by telepathy. I told him we had no army with which to fight and he was bold enough to suggest asking the king, of all things. But it worked after all, didn't it?"

"I'm so sorry to hear about Alphonse."

"Ah, well." Kirche pulled his mouth into a deep frown. "Such are the dangers of the hunt."

Prenalin returned with her room assignment. "We weren't needed after all," he told Kirche. "She was emerging from the wood when we approached."

"See then?" Kirche said. "Much ado for nothing, as I said. But no matter. Our main business has done and we are off for adventures now. So, you didn't cause us any great delay."

"For that I am grateful, Lord Kirche." Leah smiled as best she could.

Chapter Twenty-nine

Welk returned to the castle at Michelruud and was forced to regale his cousins with the story of his brave rescue of the fair damsel in distress. He embellished as much as he dared, to make the story more interesting than it had turned out to be, but only a little. He was anxious to get back to his chambers and finish his reading of the history.

When he finally closed the heavy tome and lifted it with a heave back onto the table by the fire, he rubbed his eyes and let his hands remain against his face for some time. Finally, he pulled them away and blinked into the flames. The warmth of his chambers had left him; he was cold. He ground his teeth together unconsciously, seething with anger at his ancestors. Fools!

How could wissendes of science and logic have been so overcome with fear and suspicion that they would act with such vile against the beast? He could accept the behavior of the Hass for stealing the stone in the first place and casting the beast folk into confusion and despair. The Hass, after all, were always leading with their fears and insecurities and forever, it seems, hated the beast.

How Welk had applauded the story of the great wissende Michelruud, discovering the kell stone in the mines of Galdred in the west, risking his own life and those of his followers to steal it, escaping the Hass and sailing off to return the stone to the beast Rad. How his chest had filled with pride in reading that part—only to deflate into shame.

Thousands of years of cooperation among the various beast folk, cast away—their traditions thrown asunder and all because of mortal folk. It was no wonder to Welk, now, why the beast despised them so. His disgust at Michelruud, so easily persuaded by a crown and a castle, was strongest in his heart. The folk quest for power was only won by demeaning and dismantling that of the beast.

Anfang's words now made sense to Welk. He longed for a redeemer, to find the stone and return the Rad to power for the beast. But it was clear that the folk of the Ruud were justified in their fears. If the history was correct, once the kell stone is returned to the beast Rad, the folk are likely to be overcome and their lands retaken, cast off the continent with nowhere to go but back to their motherland and the Hass of Emorah.

Welk remembered Kirche and his desperation for the stone. Kirche and the Hass would not want the beast returned to power, even here in the east. No, the Hass want the stone to remain with the folk. And now it was clear why Ruhm had let the Ruud survive on its own for so many hundreds of years. They wanted, above all, to keep the beast inferior.

Welk sighed. He must find Fenn Foster of the wissenry. The mark! How could he have been so wrong about it? Why did Rue-Anna not tell him what it meant? They were too busy with forbidden love and defying their parents' kingdoms to bother themselves with matters of history. But now he understood. He alone, it seemed, knew who Fenn Foster truly was.

He needed advice. Welk needed to find the only person left in the world whom he could trust. And that task would not be an easy one. Luckily, the emissaries of the usurper queen of the ice realm had given him a reason to take control of the hill country without raising suspicion.

Chapter Thirty

Leah allowed Gretchen to help her up the stairs while Kirche and Prenalin remained in the dining area. Dowling was called to assist her in a bath in the bathing chamber. Leah knew the instant she saw Dowling's face that she must, indeed, look of death. The crotchety old woman nearly cried.

"Is it all that terrible?"

"Oh, miss," Dowling said. "Let's clean you up."

The bath chamber was on the second floor with a flume to the outside in which the used bath water was poured. But each bucket of fresh water had to be pumped from the well behind the inn, warmed over the fire, and carried up the stairs. While the tub was being filled, Dowling sat her in a chair, left and returned with a tray full of towels, soaps, and ointments.

"First, we must clean your wounds. Try not to flinch too much."

Dowling soaked a cloth in warm soapy water and gently dabbed at Leah's face. She winced at the stinging. The wound on her forehead thudded a dull ache through her head.

"We'll put the ointments on after your bath."

Leah stripped to her under slip and with Dowling's help, climbed into the tub of warm water. Her aching body tingled and relaxed.

"Miss, I'm afraid your hair will need washing. There is blood. I know I am not allowed to touch it."

"It's all right; I'll do it."

It took much of Leah's strength to lift her arms to scrub her scalp. She ducked under the water for a quick rinse, then stood and let Dowling climb on a stool to pour buckets of clean, warm water over her. She pulled the water out of her hair, wrung out her under slip, and climbed gingerly out of the tub.

Once in her room, she noticed immediately that Dowling had covered the looking glass with a bed sheet.

"No sense having a look until you heal up a bit, miss."

Behind the dressing screen, she pulled off her wet slip and put on her night shirt. Every muscle in her body demanded she stay still as she let Dowling help her into the soft bed.

"I'll be back shortly to dress your wounds."

After Dowling left, Leah turned to look at the mirror in the corner. How bad could it be? She crawled out of the bed and carried a candle to the looking glass. Lifting the sheet, Leah gasped at her reflection. Eerie shadows cast by the candle highlighted her swollen right cheek and brow. A red gash on her right forehead ran ragged to her hairline; both cheeks were lined with cuts and her right upper lip was fat and grotesque. She let the sheet drop and made her way back to the comfort of the pillow and blankets.

Dowling returned with another tray and set it on the table by the bed. On it was a teacup, on a saucer, with a string hanging over the rim, and a small brown packet of paper.

Seeing the packet, Leah said, "I do not wish to be anesthe-tized."

"No worry, miss, this is only willow bark, for the tea. It will help ease your pain."

She watched as Dowling pulled open the packet and poured pale, ground willow bark into the tea and stirred. Holding the teacup out to her, the woman said, "Drink it, you'll see."

Leah sipped the warm tea and grimaced. Dowling laughed.

"Ah, well, it's an acquired taste."

After forcing her into several more sips of tea, Dowling had her rest her head on the fluffed up pillows while she dabbed ointments on her forehead, cheeks, and upper lip. She gently pressed gauzy fabric over each wound and told Leah to finish the tea before she came back with her dinner.

"You must eat, miss," Dowling said when she returned with food. "And then you must sleep."

After eating, Leah requested more candles and promised she would sleep.

"The dark," she lied, lying coming easier and easier. "I'll sleep better with some light."

But instead, she sat at her desk, despite her aches, writing in her journal, waiting until the wee hours when she must fulfil her promise to Voorspeld and the brownies. Certainly, it was the only promise she could keep.

How would she ever find Dakenruud's journal? And even if it did reveal the location of the kell stone, how could she possibly get to it? It was most likely hidden deep in the kell somewhere, perhaps in the Ruud, but no doubt in a spot inaccessible to adventure seekers, much less a young girl of Ruhm. Even if she could get to it, she would certainly be found out by someone—Lord Kirche, probably, as he was looking for it as well.

No. Leah had told a terrible lie and she knew she'd have to get back home and hide forever from the beasts of the eastern continent. One thing she couldn't fathom, however, was why Voorspeld had believed her.

She shook her head at the thought and nearly dozed off writing mid-sentence. She darted awake when the picture of the flaming tree of Rett came back to her; she could still feel its rough trunk at her back as she lay huddled against it, believing she would die there at its base. Suddenly she realized all was quiet in the inn. She extinguished the desk candle, stood, wrapped her robe and tied it tightly at the waist, slid her feet into her slippers, and snuck downstairs.

The inn was dark as pitch. She was lucky to know that at the foot of the stairs there would be a clear path to the left, straight to the back door. She'd seen the latch lifted before and found it easily, sliding it up slowly and quietly. Pushing open the door, she let the latch drop so that it would hold the door open for her.

Leah was glad for the moonlight as she left the steps for the ground, grabbed at the stick that held Zeelif's now dried, dismembered head, and carried it into the woods behind the inn, forcing herself not to look at it. She was met by four brownies, glaring at her, tapping their tiny feet on the ground.

"Took long enough," one said.

The others hissed, "Murderer."

The largest of them took Zeelif's head and cradled it in his arms, then turned to her and spat. "Get back to the safety of your inn, mortal, before we stone you to death right here."

"Murderer," they called after her as she stumbled back to the door and ran into Dowling, knocking them both to the ground.

Chapter Thirty-one

Fenn woke once, in darkness, grasping for his lost charm, and realized he was in Pinta's hut in Banished; he let himself drift into sleep again. Rousing himself in the dim morning light, he heard Sadie and Grayson outside the hut talking in low voices. He pushed aside the fabric covering the doorway to join them.

They sat at Pinta's fire pit eating apples and hard biscuits. Sadie's marks were barely pink now and no longer swollen. Pinta was cooking in a pot over the fire and the smell of warm bread and gravy wafted to his nose.

Taking a seat next to Grayson, he said, "All better?"

"Oh, she'll be fine. Weak for a while," Pinta said. "She's lucky. She told me that she smacked a fairy bee and started dancing around. It's no wonder she was stung so many times."

"Pinta says that the fairy bees aren't really vicious," Grayson said.

"But you read about them," Sadie said.

"All I know is what it says in the encyclopedia."

"So," Sadie scooted herself around to face Grayson. "You're telling me that not everything in the encyclopedia is true?"

"Not vicious at all," Pinta interrupted. "Just frightened. Any time you cross the clover, except at night, you'll get stung once or twice. It's a warning is all. Learn to be calm, like an eis, and they'll let you cross."

"Like an eis?" Fenn said.

"Aye, the eis are very calm folk."

"What good are books if you can't trust them?" Sadie said.

"Just because you hear one little thing in the encyclopedia might be wrong, you're ready to toss all the books in the trash?" Grayson said.

"I didn't say that. I'm just learning to be skeptical is all."

"Nothing wrong with that," Fenn said.

"Take a plate." Pinta handed Fenn a few cracked pieces of ceramic. "And a slice of bread. We've got gravy for sopping."

"Where do you all find food?" Fenn asked, taking the bread from Pinta.

"We have little plots. Some of us are strong enough to hunt and share our take. But only once in a great while. We get rabbit, squirrel, and sometimes a boar. We have vegetables and some corn and wheat. We make our own flour."

Fenn raised his eyebrows at her.

"It's true. We don't starve. But we have to cooperate. And of course, we get folk from home on visit sometimes and they bring what they can—and folk travel through willing to trade."

"What do you have to trade?" Sadie asked and Grayson nudged her with a stern look. "What? I'm just asking."

"It's rude."

"Aw, that's all right," Pinta said. "We have our small crops, of course, and we make things. Jonesy has actually managed some fine mud pottery and every so often we get emissaries from the royals out to trade for 'em."

Fenn glanced quickly at the others, hoping they caught that as well. They would not be able to stay here long if any of the Ruud folk might happen along.

"It's a hard life, 'tis true," she said. "But we do what we can."

Fenn thought of Forbes Billings and his writ. If only it were real, all these folk could be freed. What could have been the harm in at least trying?

"What about Lil Billings and the writ?" he asked.

Pinta laughed and shook her head. "Waiting Lil, we call her. She thinks one day we'll all be going home—free as roster fiends in the sky."

"So, you don't believe there is a writ?"

"Writ, schmidt. No king would ever honor such a flimsy thing, if she had one. Don't worry about Waiting Lil. She'll come to terms soon enough. But if that husband o' hers dares to come back stirring us all up again, there'll be some sparring, no doubt."

"I was born in the wasteland," Fenn said, without thinking.

"Were you now?"

He nodded. "I was hoping I could find my nurse. Her name was Clara."

Pinta closed up her eyes and twisted her lips in thought. "There was a Clara out in Chosen, I think. Yes. She was a nurse. Worked with Father Wold for a time."

"That would be her." He jolted with excitement. "I need to get to Chosen."

"Leaving already?" Pinta said. "You should stay. It's dangerous for children wandering about the wasteland."

Fenn nodded politely. "I'm sorry, but I have a lot of exploring to do."

"Sadie at least should stay and rest."

"I'll stay behind," Sadie said. "I feel better, but I don't think I can walk very far yet. You and Grayson go off to Chosen."

"We can't leave you here alone," Grayson said.

"Maybe Rogget will stay with Sadie."

"Ard, what's that?" Rogget came around from behind Pinta's tent carrying three dead rabbits and two squirrels from his rope. "You want me to do what?"

Pinta smiled. "Come on over and join us."

"I've got some bitters if you've got water and a pot." Rogget smiled setting aside his game, shrugging off his pack and rubbing his hands together over the small flame.

"Bitters, now! I haven't had the bitters in forever, not since that fancy man in purple rode through about this time last year."

Rogget prepared a pot to boil their bitters and gratefully took a biscuit.

"Sadie needs to stay and rest while Grayson and I find Chosen," Fenn said. "You can stay with her."

"Hold on, there. I can't let you two go off alone in the wasteland."

"We can protect Sadie," Pinta said. "You boys go off and find Chosen. I can tell you where it is. It won't take but a half day to hike over."

Sadie looked stricken. "I'm not sure I want to stay here by myself."

Grayson sighed. "I'll stay with Sadie, then."

Pinta clapped her hands together. "It will be wonderful to have children about for a while."

"I'll try to teach you some reading," Grayson said to Pinta. "I'll try to teach everyone. To read their names, at least."

"And the words on a pardon," Fenn said.

He nodded. "Exactly."

"You can't teach folk to read in just a few days," Sadie said.

Grayson looked at the ground. "Maybe I should stay longer, then. Maybe I'm needed here."

"I didn't mean that," Sadie said. "I don't want you to stay here alone. And I don't want to stay. I want to go with Fenn to the ice realm."

They each looked quickly at Fenn, then Rogget, then Pinta. All their eyes were round except hers. She looked at them curiously.

"The ice realm? What sort of adventure are you on, anyway?"

"It's a dangerous one, Ma'am," Rogget said. "But very important."

She nodded. "I suppose that's why you're traveling about with three reading children. It must be a great mission for the kings."

"Aye," Rogget said. "But it's a very secret one as well. The children aren't so practiced at keeping secrets as at their other skills. We'd be pleased if you wouldn't spread the word to none of the guard."

She raised her head and looked down her nose at the three of them and then smiled and nodded at Rogget. "Aye, I'll be keeping my mouth shut. Of that you can be certain."

"But what about the situation here?" Grayson's voice held a hint of desperation. "We can't just leave this the way it is."

"Help me to write a proposal to the kings," Pinta said. "We can ask for a reader and a writer to visit on occasion."

"Would the kings offer help to you?" Grayson asked.

She shrugged.

"King Welk might be of a mind to be kind," Rogget said. "Being new and all."

"King Welk?" Pinta said.

"Aye, Evan the Fearsome is dead. His son Welk has the throne."

"Evan dead?" Pinta said. "I thought I heard long peeling of bells some time ago, come right over the wind, ever so faint. That must be why Lil Billings has been smiling so much more of late."

"Ah, about that writ," Rogget said. "Don't let her be getting your hopes up. I have it on good gossip that the writ's been—"

"Rogget," Sadie said.

"Oh, aye. It's all for Forbes Billings to explain."

"Any news of Elrundt?" Pinta broke in as if she hadn't been listening to them. "Now that his father's passed into the ether?"

"Elrundt?" Fenn said.

"Aye, Welk's younger brother, disappeared many a year ago after a row with his father. Any news?"

Rogget shook his head with a sly smile. "None ma'am. No news to be told there."

Fenn caught Rogget's brief glance and crinkled his brow. What was this about? Maybe Ma'am Stationer was right after all and there was a Prince Elrundt. But what would Rogget know about it? So many curiosities and questions to keep track of these days; he couldn't keep them all in his head.

"Yes, as you were saying," Pinta said. "Now would be the time for Forbes Billings to show up and get us all afluster again. I told the children I'd do him harm if he did."

"Ard, no worries there, ma'am. We put him to rights," Rogget said.

"You know him?"

"Long time friend."

"Maybe we'll meet Waiting Lil on our way to Chosen," Fenn said, hoping to end the talking and move on. He felt as if Clara was calling him to hurry.

"No, no," Pinta said. "It's the other direction."

Rogget left his rabbits and squirrels with Pinta for Sadie and to share with the village and in exchange, she'd given them dried apple slices and flat bread for their journey. They headed northeast just as Pinta had told them and hiked the flat rocky plains of the wasteland until, well after noon, they came upon a tiny village nestled up against a wood.

A few huts were neighbored by brick and wood buildings. Smoke poofed out of chimneys. A well sat in the center of the hut circle and folk went about their business, staring at them.

"New?" A man approached them, carrying a small wood pail.

"We're looking for Clara," Fenn said.

The man tilted his head at them then turned and spit into the bucket. "Seems quite a few folk are looking for Clara these days."

"Who else?" Rogget said.

"Soldiers."

"What would soldiers be wanting with an old lady?"

The old man smiled slyly. "It was the stories," he said. "Of the bairn. She lives out by the creek in the woods."

They hiked through the tiny village and over a slight ridge into the brief wood. They could hear the creek tinkling its way around them when they came to a clearing where a little cabin sat on the edge of the water. Fenn's heart pounded and he began to tremble.

"Well, come on," Rogget said. "We didn't come all this way to stand and gawk."

For a few moments, he couldn't move and stood trying to concentrate on the breeze rushing through the pines overhead. Finally, he managed to breathe, and walked to the door and knocked.

A woman, wearing an apron, and holding a damp towel, opened the door. She smiled at them and nodded.

"Clara?" Fenn said, his voice cracking.

She shook her head and motioned for them to enter the hut.

"I'll stay outside, if you don't mind," Rogget said.

"Are you sure?"

He nodded.

Fenn entered the dark hut and stood for a second letting his eyes adjust. The lady who answered the door took his arm and led him over to a bed in the corner. Lying there, propped up on two pillows, was a tiny, frail, old woman. She lay with her eyes closed and her mouth open and Fenn thought at first she was dead and took a step backward. But the lady patted the old woman on the arm and sat Fenn down beside her on a tall stool.

Clara opened her eyes and looked at Fenn. She closed her mouth and swallowed.

"Well, what is it? What do you want?" she said. Her voice was dry and scratchy.

"I..." Fenn couldn't remember what he'd come for at first and stared at her. Finally, he said, "I'm looking for my mother."

"Eh? What's that? Are you speaking?"

Fenn raised his voice. "I'm looking for my mother."

"Well, it ain't me." Clara closed her eyes again.

"But you knew my mother," he said. "You were my nurse."

She opened her eyes and looking up to the ceiling, shook her head. "I was only nurse to one child," she said. "It was long ago after my man and child died here in the wasteland. Father Wold came to me with a young woman." She stopped talking and peered at the ceiling for a long moment. "She was dressed all in white, like an angel," she said. "I was to tend to her. But she faded away so quickly after her bairn came into the world."

"Was that my mother?"

Clara turned her head to him, but instead of looking at his face, looked at his chest. "Do you have the charm?"

"Yes," he said, excited. "I have the charm." He reached for his neck and grappled for it until he realized it was gone. "But it was stolen," he said.

Clara turned away. "The child I nursed would have his charm."

"I did have it. It had a dragonfly on it. And the letters A, o, and E on the back. Can you tell me about it? Would you tell me who my mother was?"

She wouldn't look at him. "I can't tell you anything until I can feel the charm."

Fenn felt tears burning at his eyes and forced them away.

"Fine then," he said. "I'll go get it back and I'll bring it to you."

Clara closed her eyes, a frown at her lips. "You do that."

"But," he stammered. "But you don't know how hard it was just to get here. My friend even got stung all over by fairy bees—"

"Fairy bees? If you are the bairn I nursed, you'd have no trouble with fairy bees."

"Fine, fine," he said. "I'll go all the way back to the hill country and steal it back from the gang of thieves who took it from me."

"I'll be here. I'm not going anywhere."

Fenn sat staring at her, his mind searching for a better way. How could he get his charm back from Clutch? It was impossible. Suddenly, he thought, if he touched her, like he touched Clutch, maybe he would become her and know what she knew. He reached out his hand and put it gently on her arm. It was bony and thin and cold under her night shirt and he pulled his hand away. She did know something, but he felt as if he'd have to squeeze her to find out and she was too frail; he felt he'd break her if he tried.

He came out of the dark hut, squinting into the afternoon light, to find Rogget in the back yard tossing stones into the creek.

"Well?" he said.

"I have to find my charm," Fenn said sadly. "She won't tell me anything until she sees it."

Rogget nodded and paused for a moment before mumbling, "So, I'm thinking you're getting ready to take me into more trouble."

Fenn nodded and Rogget let out a chuckle.

Chapter Thirty-two

Lucas sat at a table in a dark corner of Dylan's Tavern at Cold Sea Port, keeping his hood pulled well over the top of his face. The bar was crowded as patrons drank and yelled and sloshed ale over the tops of their pitchers. Frantic waiters fought through the maze of folk with trays held high above their heads, serving those at table in the bustling lamplit pub.

"They've chased him out of the Ruud, at least," one gruff, unshaven folk called out.

"They should have caught him and hanged him," another countered. "What good is the king's guard if they can't get their hands on a child?"

"He ain't just any child; he's the bairn. Folk say he's got beast blood in him. He's dangerous."

"Aye, they shouldn't have let him escape in the first place."

The crowd roared approval.

"We should build up our own posse and head out to the hill country and drag him back for a hanging," one man said, standing up to raise his pitcher and staggering back against his stool. He was applauded.

"Hey, you! Wissende," someone called out. "You kept him safe all these years."

Lucas looked up and saw Father Britt's terrified face as he battled through the crowd. He rose quickly and made his way across the room, took Britt by the sleeve and pulled him back toward the door.

"That is not a good spot to meet this night," Lucas said.

"The panic has made its way clear to the port. I never expected..."

"Did you not?"

"No."

Lucas glanced at him as they made their way through the streets and to the wharf. There was a quiet alehouse there, more private, with booths and curtains. Madam Henry welcomed them in and showed them to a back booth and left to get them some refreshment.

"Father Britt, why does the wissenry appear unable to come to terms with reality? Is that not the purpose of the organiza-tion?"

"Reality has, for some time, been something to be avoided."

"By the folk, perhaps, but not the wissenry."

"What would you have us do?"

"Quell the fear. Speak some reason to the folk. Tell them there is no prophecy. The future is not something that can be foretold. End this madness."

Britt wrung his hands and looked up gratefully to Madam Henry when she appeared with pitchers of ale. How old he looked, how tired and red of face. The wissendes had, over two hundred years, degenerated from men of knowledge, to men of philosophy and comfort.

"We are not equipped to deal with this. We are not the wissenry of yore. We are the wissenry of the Ruud."

Lucas took his pitcher and drank long sips and put it down again.

"I did not know you drank ale," Britt said to him.

"I thought it was about time."

"You are hardly of age."

"I am older than you think," Lucas said, surprised that they had not figured that out by then. Did they not realize that felidae mature sooner than folk? Did they not have books on studies of the beast locked away in their old cabinets below ground? What did these wissendes spend their time on these days?

Britt smiled and shook his head. "You can't be more than fourteen."

Lucas waved a hand to quiet the old man. "Take the news. I must return to the guard. The folk all over the Ruud call for Fenn's death. He traipses about the wasteland with Rogget."

"The wasteland? But he was to—"

"He knows very well what he was told to do but he does not trust the wissenry any longer. He trusts only himself and I can't say I blame him."

"We had to keep these secrets."

"That is a lie."

"He is only a boy."

"He is more than just a boy, Britt. Or did the wissenry not know?"

Britt stared blankly at him.

"It's true then. The wissenry does not know who Fenn is."

"I only know that he has a mark that says he's part beast."

"That is not what the mark means."

306

Britt grimaced. "Then I know nothing."

"You must know something more. Tell me."

"Well, I hardly think I ought to be sharing our knowledge with—"

"Tell me what you know."

Britt looked at him now, with a hint of fear behind his eyes. "Only that the rumors spoke of a child with a mark. We assumed it was Fenn they feared. We kept him hidden as long as we could and planned to send him far away to the south lands as soon as he was of age to travel."

Lucas sipped his ale. "All right. Listen to me. Spread the word through the wissenry. Go to your cellars and get your books and read. Read them all. If they're under lock and key, they must be read."

"You want us to read?"

"Yes. Read. If you do not understand why we are in this mess, you will be of little help when it explodes."

"You think there will be an explosion?"

"I think so, yes."

"Of what sort?"

"Of the war sort, Father. You must decide on which side you will fight. And you must be available to the folk for information. That is your role. That is the duty of the wissenry. Why have you forgotten?"

"Why do you speak this way, young Lucas? You act as if you know much more than your few years of training would grant you."

Lucas smiled at Father Britt. "That's because I stole Father Treacher's cabinet keys and read all of his books. Now, tell me about my parents."

Britt sputtered. "What?"

"That is the reason I have summoned you. Tell me what you know. Why does King Welk know my felid name?"

Britt nodded and drank more ale. "Yes, he knows you. He was a good friend to your father. Belfen wanted peace with the mortal folk and he and your mother wanted to live the old ways."

"But what happened to my parents and what does Welk have to do with it? Quarn said that my father saved Welk's life."

"Welk was to marry his eisen, Rue. His father and her mother were against it. King Evan was not a folk to be trifled with—he'd already lost one son to the eis, and he would not lose Welk, his only heir, as well. But truth be told, his man Sorgood was all too eager to teach the eis a lesson. Evan sent Sorgood and some of the guard to stop the nuptials—to separate Welk and Rue. But they went too far. They killed everyone— everyone except Welk and Elrundt."

"My parents were there?"

"Indeed. Your father was to stand up with Welk and his brother."

"Murdered on Evan's orders?"

"It is unclear what he ordered. But that was the result. I came upon the massacre the same day. Welk held you in his arms. He...he fought against allowing Quarn to take you. The beast lord was there and he gave his consent to have you raised in the old ways as your parents wanted."

"Did my father give his life for Welk's?"

"Welk tells the story that Quarn and Yew, your other uncle, fled the scene leaving your father and mother to die."

Lucas stared at Father Britt, his jaw set so tight he felt pain and slackened.

"Thank you, Father, for being truthful."

"Have you seen Fenn, then?"

"Yes. And he saw me, I'm afraid. Fenn may end this journey believing he can trust no one."

Lucas stood, tossed a few doars on the table, and left Father Britt in the small alehouse at the wharf to make his way back to Sorgood and the guard.

Chapter Thirty-three

Fenn and Rogget returned to Banished after dark to find Sadie and Grayson sitting at the fire pit in the middle of the village, surrounded by the pale, gaunt folk on mats—the fire blazing, lighting up their faces with a yellow glow.

"They've taught us all our names," Pinta said. "And the word pardon. It's a start, but we sure could use them here all the time. Still, I guess I wouldn't wish such a thing on a free young."

"But, you can leave, can't you?" Fenn asked. "There are lots of places you could go besides the Ruud."

Pinta frowned. "Perhaps. But then they'd never know if they could go home. Here, there's always hope."

"But you don't like hope," Grayson said.

"No. I've never found much to appreciate in it. But they seem to require it." She looked at Havert with a smile.

Fenn turned to Rogget and whispered, "What about Forbes writ? Maybe there's a chance."

"Don't be settin' these folks' hopes on it, Fenn. I warn you. It's a fool's desire. Aren't no king who'd honor such a promise, made in a drunken fury."

Fenn frowned. "You're right, I guess." But he felt a tugging in his heart. There ought to be a way to make a king honor his word.

Rogget preferred to sleep outside on a small patch of smooth grass just behind Pinta's hut, and they decided to join him, curled up on Pinta's rag mats lying in the dark talking long into the night. Fenn told them his plan.

"I have to get my charm back."

"From the Wretched?" Sadie said.

"I've been thinking on it," Rogget said. "The Gnome Eaters know how to find them. We could try to sneak into their camp, but we couldn't let 'em see us. It's not likely at all we'll even get into their camp. And even if we could, how could you find such a small thing. And that's assuming they haven't melted it down already. I don't think you should get your hopes up much."

Fenn shuddered at the thought of the dragonfly melting into a small pool of gold. He fell into a deep sleep and woke in the morning feeling refreshed, but lost and alone. No visions haunted him. He remembered the slender hand, and the wissende's robe. But he'd forgotten his mother's voice in his dreams. He'd spent so much time before wishing the images would stop tormenting him, but now, without them, he felt empty and incomplete. A constant tugging tore at his insides and he felt the urge always to wrap his arms about his middle and weep.

"So you are to leave us now?" Pinta said as they bid their goodbyes.

"We'll be back soon," Sadie said.

"You're sure that the fairy bees won't hurt us if we stay calm?" Fenn asked her.

"I'm sure. But here." She handed Sadie a leather pouch. "It's more poultice, already soaking and ready if you need it."

"Thank you."

Fenn could hear fear in Sadie's voice, and as they left the village behind, she asked what he knew she would.

"Are you sure we have to go through the lilac clover?"

"I need my charm. You can stay in Banished until we come back."

"No," Grayson said. "We stick together, remember?"

"We'd be together again after I get my charm."

"Grayson's right," Rogget said. "There's still a guard out after us. We got to stay together."

"But can't we go around the clover?"

"Sadie, the bridge up north is miles out of the way." Fenn said. "And Pinta told us the bees are just scared. They don't really mean any harm."

"Tell that to my scars."

"They didn't leave scars," Grayson said. "Don't be so vain."

"I'm not being vain. It hurt. It hurt a lot. And Pinta said if they bite deep enough, they *will* leave scars."

"Well, if you hadn't flapped around like a madman, they wouldn't have stung you at all."

"I didn't know. Did you know?"

"Cut it out," Fenn said. "Anyway, even Clara told me that we should be able to calm the bees."

When they approached the stretch of clover, a sweet, heady aroma floated in the air and this time, they could see the bees hovering inches above the flowers.

"You should go back," Fenn said. "You don't have to come with me."

Sadie sucked in a loud breath. "No. We stick together. I'll stay calm."

They walked on, slowly, stepping gingerly, doing their best not to upset the bees.

"Calm, calm, calm," Sadie chanted. "I'm staying calm."

"Ouch," Grayson yelped.

"Don't slap at them," Rogget said.

"I'm not. Ouch."

"How can you not slap at it if it stings you?" Sadie said. "Calm. Calm."

"Just don't, that's all."

"Ow," Sadie stopped. "Ow. It stung me." She held up her arm and looked at the bee. About an inch long, it had a furry, golden abdomen that it wiggled back and forth teasingly, threatening another poke.

"No," Sadie scolded.

Its antennae were long and curled at the ends into spirals. The bee grabbed one in its front legs and pulled at it, letting it pop back into place before spreading its wings and flying off.

"See?" Fenn said.

"Why don't they sting you?"

"Maybe they sense that I'm a nice folk."

"Very funny. Ouch." Grayson slapped at the back of his neck. "Ouch, make them stop."

"You're egging them on, Grayson."

Sadie screamed and danced around.

"Calm down," Rogget swatted at the air. "Ouch. Darn bees."

"Stop it, you have to stay calm," Fenn shouted, as they dodged bees and slapped at themselves.

Fenn knew he had to do something. He sucked in a long deep breath and closed his eyes, letting serenity fall over him. He imagined his body as

310

a soft yellow light; it filled his chest and his head and shot out from his outstretched hands. Joy spilled out from him and he smiled. When he finally opened his eyes, Grayson, Sadie, and Rogget were standing, staring at him, still ankle deep in the lilac clover.

"What are you doing?" Sadie asked, a smirk on her face. "Why were you walking like a grub zombie?"

"How do you know what a grub zombie walks like?" Grayson said.

"I've seen plenty of kids pretend."

"He was communing with the fairy bees."

"Ard, he's calming them down," Rogget said. "Do it some more."

"That's right," Fenn said. "They stopped stinging you didn't they? You should try some communing yourselves."

Fenn kept his hands held out in front of him, trying to recapture the feeling of light emitting from his fingertips as he plodded across the clover patch.

"Well," Sadie said. "They did stop stinging us. That much is true."

"I am *not* communing," Grayson said. "You can't make me."

They exited the other side of the clover with only a few stings for Rogget, Sadie, and Grayson.

"I guess that wasn't too awful," Sadie said. "I'm going to want that poultice later. And I don't look forward to doing it again on the way back."

"Fenn will just have to commune the bees from the start." Rogget smiled.

They crossed the bridge into the hill country where Darnit roared and charged them, nearly knocking Rogget to the ground for jerky. The hike through the hills was a pleasant one and Fenn felt almost at home. Now all he needed was his mother's charm. It pulled at him from somewhere near.

At the outskirts of the Gnome Eater's camp, Rogget called out, "Oi, there." A young guard came around a hill and waved them over.

"Back so soon, Mr. Rogget?"

"Aye, and looking for trouble."

Wiley was glad to see them and they all relaxed around his fire pit while he and Rogget drank warm bitters and they all noshed on a batch of carrot root that Bruck had just dug up.

"We'll be looking for those Wretcheds you told us about," Rogget said.

Wiley looked around at them all in disbelief, shaking his head.

"I need to get my charm back."

"Consider it gone, lad," Wiley said. "Even if they did still have the thing, you'd never be able to get it back from 'em."

"I have to try."

Wiley sighed. "It just don't seem right. I'd like to help you. But if I tell you where they are, and you should get killed, it'd be my fault."

"I'll take responsibility," Rogget said. "They're in my charge."

"Aye, you're always taking on the responsibility, even when it ain't rightly yours."

"If you don't tell us where they are, we'll just wander all over and run into them by accident. But if we know where to find them, we can sneak up on them."

Wiley nodded. "All right. I'm seeing your persuasion there." He paused. "They have a main encampment some twenty miles from here, in Arrow Valley, nestled up close to the big hills. They're surrounded by wood on three sides and they post their guards well hidden in the trees. You can't come up at 'em from the north and through the valley or they'll see you right off across the brief plain."

They were silent for a moment before Wiley went on. "There's one way, I think. If you come straight at 'em from the Ruud, 'stead of from the north or south, they don't watch as much. They're not expecting regular folk. They watch for us and hungry banished from the north; and the Breathless, and the Hunters, and sailors come from the south. But the west. No, they don't usually get anyone that way."

Rogget nodded and looked at Fenn. "Sadie and Grayson will stay here, with you," he said. "I'll go in and get your charm."

Fenn shook his head. "No. You'll never find it alone."

"I have to say," Wiley said. "The kids are smaller and lighter. If we draw the Wretched away from camp, the children could sneak in and have a look."

Rogget looked to the ground. "Aye. You're not thinking of a battle, are you?"

"No, no. More like a chase. If we go at it right, they'll chase us all the way to Cold Sea Port." Wiley smiled and chuckled.

"They'll leave a few guard behind," Rogget said. "I'll handle them while the kids find the charm." He looked back to Fenn. "You're sure this is important?"

Fenn nodded. "Very important." And for a moment he didn't feel as if he were lying. He needed the visions, for one thing. Maybe they could help him. And the fairies seemed to think if he found out who his parents were he could stop the bairn of prophecy nonsense. So, it seemed true that finding his charm was very important. But what if someone got hurt or killed? He pushed that thought away, and tried to bury it deep inside him.

That evening, the plan was set. Under cover of darkness the next night, they'd approach the Wretched from the west. The Gnome Eaters would shoot fire arrows into their encampment where they were expected to be playing cards, drinking, and carousing. The Gnome Eaters would attack until all the Wretched were joined in and then run south toward the Plains of Glisch and Cold Sea. Rogget and Darnit would tend to the guard left behind while Sadie, Grayson, and Fenn found the charm.

It could actually work, Fenn thought as they crouched behind trees in the wood outside the Wretched encampment the next night. They were staring at a sign posted at the edge of the wood—a wooden plank, stuck in the ground, painted with a red skeleton, black wavy lines rising from it, to denote a rotten, stinky corpse. Very scary, Fenn thought; very much what he'd expect from Clutch and his dirty friends. And just beyond the sign, the land sloped downward into Arrow Valley. They could see the pale glow of firelight in the dark and hear voices of men yelling and laughing. They waited.

Suddenly there was a shout of pain and anger; Fenn imagined one of the fiery arrows must have hit its target. Then screaming rang out, high-pitched and frantic. The Gnome Eaters had attacked. Fenn looked, wide-eyed and afraid, to Rogget but Rogget put a finger to his lips. Darnit sniffed and rocked his head left to right until Rogget turned to the bear with a hard stare.

Grayson and Sadie looked on, edgy and excited, but the battle raged, noisily. Finally the sounds drifted off to the south as the Gnome Eaters led the Wretched out of their camp. Rogget gave the signal and they got up and made their way quickly into the valley.

Right away, Rogget and Darnit charged into the center of the village where Rogget jumped on a guard. Fenn, Sadie, and Grayson split up and began their search. Fenn was to look for a sign of Clutch's tent. He knew it right away. It was the largest, as Wiley had said it would be, and the only one with a chair and its own fire pit out front. Stuck on a stick outside the tent entrance was a sign that read: go away. Fenn darted for it and went into the tent. He stood there in the dark before remembering the lantern. Wiley told him there would be one and had given him a pack of flint sticks. He lit the candle and replaced the glass lid, returning the lantern to its hook. Rifling through the chest in the corner, he found jewels of all sorts, but not his charm. He tore apart the bed, but nothing. He looked all over but found only other folks' lost valuables.

Outside the tent, he came across Sadie and Grayson. "Anything?" he asked. They shook their heads and they all moved on to other tents and searched some more.

Too soon, they heard voices and Rogget whistled the signal for retreat. Fenn panicked. They couldn't return yet; he hadn't found it. But Sadie grabbed at his tunic and pulled him to come along. Reluctantly, he followed. They began to run as the voices drew nearer. As Fenn passed Clutch's tent again, he caught sight of a glint of gold and turned to look. There, hanging from the arm of the wooden chair out front was his hemp braid and his gold charm, with the stone charm the children of Path had given him dangling beside it. He pulled from Sadie and ran over to grab it.

"Come on," Sadie whispered. "Come on."

"I got it," he said, smiling broadly. As he turned to flee, he tripped over a duffle and landed on the edge of Clutch's wooden chair. As he struggled to work his foot out of the duffle's straps, he saw Forbes Billings' writ in the bag. Not believing his luck, Fenn grabbed it and kicked the duffle off.

"Hurry," Grayson called.

They ran toward the wood.

"Stop!" someone shouted from behind them.

Fenn turned to see Clutch and some of the Wretched running into the encampment. They were seen. "Get 'em," Clutch yelled.

They darted into the wood and saw Rogget turning into the trees behind them with Darnit at his side. A gunshot rang out; Darnit let out a painful roar.

Chapter Thirty-four

Leah had spent the last two days resting at the inn, sometimes in her room and often downstairs in the front lobby watching the town square through the large window. This evening she curled up on her bed and gently touched her face. Her wounds were healing, soon there would be little or no sign of the attack; but her soul was forever scarred.

Opening her journal, she wrote, as writing was the only thing that brought her relief from her anguish. There was no one here in the Ruud in whom she could confide. She'd begun her journey wanting nothing more than a coveted post within the inner circle of Hass. Neither Prenalin, nor Kirche seemed unhappy with her; she had no reason to think she could not still become historian if she worked at it. But she was no longer sure she wanted it. Kirche as always, from the time Leah was a young teenager pining after him from afar, was a beacon of all that was kind and beautiful. But up close, his goodness was turning out to be questionable—on the improper side of questionable, truth be told. His practiced smoothness was more facade than real; and his disregard for the beasts cruel, more than ignorant. Whenever she was in his presence of late, she struggled not to look upon him as if he were a murderer.

And now that she had seen the flaming tree of Rett in the beast forest, and knew the *Book of Rett* to be incorrect, at least on that point, she imagined Kirche and the devotion taught to her by the Hass of Emorah to be parallel—both well-crafted, partly good, but also false and cruel.

It was long past time for sleep when she heard a light rap on the door.

"Are you awake, miss?" Dowling whispered.

"Yes, I'm awake."

Dowling pushed open the door and peered in. "I saw the candle light under the door and hoped you were awake. May we come in?"

The door opened wider and young Matilda Steppe wandered into the room looking around, her dark red curls bouncing about her shoulders. Her left arm was in a sling and she wore her nightgown. When she caught sight of Leah sitting up against the pillows on her bed, her eyes opened wide.

"Did you fall down the stairs, too?"

Leah chuckled. "No, I fell on some rocks."

"The child couldn't sleep," Dowling said. "I thought you two might like to meet."

She made the introductions and Leah said, "It's a pleasure. Would you like to sit on the bed."

"Careful," Dowling warned as Matilda climbed onto the bed and bounced.

"Does Dowling make you drink the willow bark tea?" Matilda said.

"Yes, she does."

"She says we'll get used to it." The child rolled her eyes, opened her mouth wide and stuck her finger in, pretending to gag. "It tastes terrible."

"How is your arm feeling?"

"It's sore sometimes. But I'll be fine."

Leah looked to Dowling who sat at the writing desk and smiled.

"Dowling says you're very brave," Matilda said.

"Really? I don't think so."

"But you are. She said you were in the beast forest, so you must be."

"Well that's true enough, I guess."

"Was it scary?"

"Yes. But only because I didn't know what to expect. And because I didn't know the beasts and they didn't know me."

"But you're all friends now?"

Leah nodded. "All friends."

"Do you read? Would you read me a story? My brother is the best reader, but he's gone away."

"I'd be happy to."

Matilda bounced, excited, and reluctantly, Dowling left to find a book.

"What's this? Your diary?"

Matilda pulled Leah's journal from underneath her and held it open.

"Yes. Do you have one?"

"I did. My da wanted me to learn to write. So I wrote some things. But then my brothers found it and read my secrets."

"Oh, that's very rude," Leah said and her body shook slightly with the realization.

"It's too much trouble to write all the time, anyway."

"It takes practice."

Dowling returned with *Ginger Brown Bunny* and Leah read the story of Ginger Brown and her adventures in the wood, with Matilda resting next to her on the bed. Soon Matilda's eyes were closed and her breathing steady and Leah closed the book and smiled up at Dowling.

"Thank you."

"My pleasure, miss."

"You didn't like me very much when I first arrived," Leah said.

Dowling looked surprised.

"You didn't hide it well at all, Dowling."

She laughed. "Perhaps not. But you were of the Hass."

"Was? Am I not now?"

Dowling thought for a moment, her brow creased, biting her lower lip.

"When you first returned from your ordeal in the forest, I suspected. You took punishment for what your Lord Kirche did, but you never said anything about it. We all knew what had happened."

"What could I have said?"

She shrugged. "I'm not sure. Maybe nothing. But you took the incident with such grace, I was instantly softened. And then, that night, when you returned the brownie's head to his kin. Then I knew..."

"What?"

"That you aren't really one of them."

After Dowling carried Matilda back to her room, Leah opened her journal and flipped through the pages, tears forming in her eyes. She was a liar. Either she would never find the kell stone and so had lied to Dag Voorspeld and Lucas. Or, she would, and would thus lie to Lord Kirche and Prenalin. Either path she chose, she thought, right now she was lying to them all. She could not be trusted. And it hadn't occurred to her until moments ago, that perhaps, she couldn't trust others, either.

Unwillingly, Leah gathered the pages she'd written since returning from the beast forest—in which she'd confided to her journal her lies, her suspicions, sighting the flaming tree, and her feelings about Lord Kirche—and ripped them out. She carried them to the fireplace and tossed them into the embers watching them burn.

Lord Kirche must never know about the kell stone—until Leah herself did.

Chapter Thirty-five

Run!" Rogget yelled. "Don't stop." They sprinted without thinking about direction until they were out of the wood. Then they darted up the slopes and down, heading north toward the Gnome Eaters' encamp-ment. Finally, Rogget slowed, and they slowed with him.

"I don't think they're following anymore," he said, gasping. "You kids sure can run." He bent over and put his hands to his knees. "Darnit," he said and stumbled over to the bear who limped forward toward him. "Ah, Darnit. He's been shot."

Sadie gasped. "Is he all right?" She approached Darnit and, for the first time, dared to touch him. Darnit nuzzled her arm with his nose.

"I think it just grazed his back side," Rogget said. "I need to get him into some light."

They hiked on as fast as they could get Darnit to move and finally made their way into the Gnome Eaters' camp.

"It's you." Tanner guided them around the hill. "The others aren't back yet."

"They'll be here soon," Rogget said. "It went well, but I'm afraid we were seen. We'll have to leave right away."

"No worries," Tanner said. "It ain't like we never squawked at 'em and run before. They won't be back over any time soon."

"Is that what you do, then?" Sadie asked. "You fight back and forth."

Tanner nodded. "But usually we gots some reason for it." He smiled. "I like thinking of them darn Wretched ponderin' and ponderin' over what mischief they done to cause us to attack like that."

"I think they'll figure it out," Fenn said. "They're not stupid. They'll know you helped us."

Tanner smiled. "All the better."

"Just a grazing." Rogget relaxed after examining Darnit by the fire. He rubbed the bear behind the ears. "You'll be fine soon enough. But no more scuffles, you hear? Next time, you stay home."

"Won't he follow you?" Grayson asked. "He seems to."

Rogget nodded. "I reckon it'll be hard to keep him out o' things."

"Can you send him home?" Sadie said. "Back to the Ruud?"

"I don't think that's home for Darnit."

"Where'd you get him, anyway?"

"Out to the port. I won him in a game of cards. I think he came over on a boat from the Great West. I hear tell they got a lot of bears over that way."

"Well," Fenn said. "Let's just try to stay out of the way of the Wretched."

"You don't have to tell me twice," Grayson said. "They could have hit any one of us with that shot."

"I think you're right," Rogget said. "Be thankful for their poor marksmanship."

Wiley and the Gnome Eaters returned, whooping and triumphant.

"That was great fun," Wiley said. He saw Rogget patting Darnit nervously. "I see blood. Is the bear all right?"

"He was grazed."

"We heard the shot," Bruck approached. "I'm glad to see they didn't get one of the children."

"Is everyone else all right?" Sadie asked.

Wiley smiled. "Sure we are. We got pelted with some rocks, but they weren't prepared for much more. We need to start making plans for a dummy camp for when they come back at us."

Sadie shook her head. "I think they think they're playing a game."

"They don't have much else to do out here," Grayson said.

She rolled her eyes. "Maybe they could play cards together instead of trying to kill each other."

"Oh, we tried that." Wiley settled himself by his fire. "We ended up killing each other anyway. Might just as well skip the cards, eh?"

Fenn packed up his knapsack, preparing for their trek to the wasteland again.

"We're leaving already?" Grayson said.

"We have to move. The Wretched saw us and might come after us to get the charm back."

"How valuable could it be?" Wiley asked.

"It's very valuable to me," Fenn said. "And I don't want to risk losing it again."

"There's more reason to get moving," Rogget said, looking at Sadie and Grayson.

Fenn remembered Clutch's idea to ransom them to King Welk and he nodded in agreement.

"But it's dinner time," Sadie said. "It'll be dark soon."

"Darker is better." Rogget began packing up his gear.

"You and Darnit can stay," Fenn said. "Darnit needs to recover."

"He's fine now."

But Fenn was thinking more of Rogget recovering from the scare.

Rogget said, "The farther we get from the Wretched, the better I'll feel about it."

That much was true. They needed to get Darnit far from there quickly.

"Can I set you up with any provisions?" Wiley asked and he gave them some extra fruit and jerky. "Stop back and see us if you come back through."

"Aren't you all moving?" Grayson asked Wiley.

"Ah, maybe. But maybe they're expecting us to move and we'll fool them by staying."

The four traveled much of night through the hills and crossed the lilac clover without incident.

"They're asleep," Fenn whispered in the darkness.

"Well, step carefully," Grayson said. "I've seen Sadie when she wakes up. I don't want any grouchy fairy bees stinging me."

Once in Banished, they slept through to noon inside Pinta's hut while she tried to keep the villagers quiet for the adventurers' rest. Fenn tossed and turned fitfully; visions of his mother, his father, the old wissende's robe, and all their voices echoed in his head without ceasing. It was a nightmarish jumble of dreams that made no sense, but reached out for him and would not let him loose. He woke feverish and groggy, the hemp rope damp around his neck.

That afternoon, they were off to Chosen with the charm. When Fenn approached Clara's cabin for the second time, he was overwhelmed with fear that she was dead. But the same old woman opened the door to him, smiled, and waved him into the dimly lit hut and to Clara's bedside where she still lay, gaunt and shriveled.

"Miss Clara," he said. "It's me, Fenn. I brought the charm."

She opened her eyes and turned her head toward him. "Where is it?" She held out her hand; he took the rope from his neck and laid the gold charm in her palm. She looked up to the ceiling and felt the charm with her fingers, turning it over and over in her hands. Fenn suddenly realized that she was blind.

She held the charm out to him. "That's it," she said as he took it from her. "That's the charm."

Fenn's heart pounded in his chest. "What was her name?"

Clara shook her head, still staring at the ceiling. "She never said her name; she rarely spoke. But I called her Eseld. She was the most beautiful woman I'd ever seen. She was eisen."

"Eisen? Are you sure?"

"She didn't have to tell me. I'd never seen a folk look like that."

"What happened to her? Why was she here?"

Clara's face came together as if she were in pain. "It was so long ago and so frightening and the Father—he would not tell me much. I'm not sure."

"Please tell me all you know."

"He told me there had been an attack on an encampment in the wastelands. North, where sometimes the eis hunt. All were dead, but her." She smiled. "What do you look like?"

He grimaced. He didn't look at himself much. He couldn't remember the last time he'd seen a looking glass. "I have dark hair."

"And your eyes?"

"Dark also."

"You must have your father's features then. Your mother was pale, with hair like gold. Her eyes were blue as sapphires. Her face round and soft."

"I think mine's more pointy than round," Fenn said, beginning to doubt that this eisen was really his mother.

Clara nodded.

"Was my father killed in the attack?"

She shrugged slightly. "Father Wold didn't say. And I didn't ask. It was really none of my business. But she mourned as if he were dead, lost forever. So I reckon he was. She was in much pain. Her face and hair shone like the rising sun in the east. But her body was burned and mangled. She'd been felled by arrows. It took all of her strength to carry you those last days."

"Is she dead?" He knew the answer. But he hoped so badly he was wrong that he couldn't breathe.

Clara nodded, and swallowed hard. "She died just a few days after you were born. She was so frail and light, like air. It was too much for her. She tried to hang on for you. She did."

Fenn looked down and they were both silent for a long moment.

"You are the bairn of prophecy. Sent to us to destroy the monarchy and let the banished return to the Ruud." Her face glowed with adoration.

Fenn shook his head, but did not respond.

"I'm glad you haven't been captured," she said.

"Why do you think I'm the bairn?"

She frowned and closed her eyes. Her forehead creased as she thought hard. "I don't recollect. It was something the Father said. You were...to be neither prince of the Ruud, nor of the eis, but..."

"That doesn't mean anything."

"But cast out into the wastelands."

"What?"

"Cast into the wasteland. Orphaned. And you have the funny mark on your arm." She opened her eyes and turned her face toward him. Fenn trembled. She seemed to be looking directly at him.

"How long have you been blind?"

"It started several years ago," she said. "I see shadow."

He nodded and put his hand on her arm. He felt devotion and love travel through him like a wave of warm water and suddenly, he could see her. His mother. Lying before him, pale and drifting out of life. Her golden hair spread across the white pillow cover. She turned her face to him and opened her eyes, stunning him. He was sinking into the blue depths until Clara's nurse pulled him away.

Fenn left Clara's hut and was surrounded by Grayson, Sadie, and Rogget.

"Well?" Sadie said.

Fenn shrugged and began to hike back to Chosen.

"Come on, what did she say?" Grayson said. "You're not going to keep it secret are you?"

"She told me my mother was one of the eis."

Sadie gasped. "An eisen?"

"And my charm has RoE on it. It could be her name began with an R, like Rose. Rose of the Eis."

"Would not," Sadie said. "If it was for Rose of the Eis it'd be RotE."

"Not necessarily," Grayson said. "You don't have to have a letter for a little word like 'the.'"

"Oh, but you have one for a little word like 'of.'"

Fenn nodded. "She's right. It might all be a big mistake."

Suddenly, Rogget, who'd been silent for some time, coughed. "No," he muttered. "No I'm thinking this Clara is, or rather was, your nurse and she's telling the truth."

"I did get the sense she was being truthful."

"So, maybe she's insane," Sadie said. "Insane folk think they're being truthful so it might seem to us that they're telling the truth, but for the fact that, you know, they're crazy..."

Fenn smiled. But no, it was deeper than that. When he touched Clara, he felt deeply that she was telling him the reality of his mother, at least as far as Clara remembered it. But supposing Sadie was right. If a person was out of his mind and believed he was possessed by a doppelganger, for instance, if Fenn touched him, would he see that as the truth, even if it wasn't? What if it was all in his mind? What if he was insane and just thought he could be other folk and see into other folks' minds? That was the most likely explanation, after all. Unless... unless the eis could do it.

Once in the middle of Chosen, they paused.

"So, where to?" Rogget looked at Fenn.

"Well, I guess it's off to the ice realm then. Father Britt wanted me to go there to see the maiden. Maybe, if my mother was one of the eis, that's a good idea."

"Maybe that's why he wanted you to go there."

"I wouldn't be surprised," Fenn said. "He kept a lot of secrets from me. They all did. And I'm willing to bet there are more secrets they never told me."

Rogget coughed again. "All right then, this way." And he led them out of the village, across a broad, rocky plain, and then east along the lilac clover field.

"How about we take our time getting there?" Grayson said.

"Why?" Sadie said. "Are you scared, waiter boy?"

"Well, sure, there's the eis and the feeorin, and angels to be scared of and Wiley told us there was war going on and you should be scared, too. But it's not that; I'm just tired. I feel like I've been walking my whole life. I miss home. I miss doing nothing, you know? Oh, I had plenty of work. But I didn't have to go far to do it. And then when I didn't have work, I could sit at the lake up north for hours, or hang around town. I miss that."

"Or read in my da's shop." Sadie laughed. "I'm used to traveling more; but I'm tired, too."

"We can take it slow," Fenn said. "I'm in no hurry. Unless the guard decides to come after us. But, you all don't really have to come. You could stay in Banished. They could use you to read."

"Are you trying to get rid of us?" Sadie said.

"No."

"Then why do we have to keep saying it?" Grayson said. "We stick together. We made a pact."

"How binding are pacts, anyway?" Sadie said.

"What do you mean? It's a pact. Your honor and reputation are at stake."

"So nobody's going to jail if we break it?"

"Of course not."

"Why would you think that?" Fenn said. "You were the one to suggest the pact anyway."

She laughed. "I did. We stick together, through danger and calm, in peril and peace."

"And we're a team now," Grayson said. "No secrets among us."

"All right then." Fenn knew there were still secrets he hadn't shared. "Pact it is."

Chapter Thirty-six

In the days that followed, Leah found Dowling's mood much improved. She sang while making up the beds and working in the dining room and she smiled much more often, even around Kirche. She'd told Kirche that hundrats had made off with the brownie's head because he'd left it out too long.

"You told me I couldn't bring it into the inn," he'd protested. "So the fault is yours."

"I didn't prevent you from burying it, or storing it in the smoke-house."

This outraged Kirche and he ranted for some time in the lobby that it would have been absurd to bury it and have it overcome by worms or to have it smoked. But in the end there was nothing he could do to recover his trophy.

Once Leah was strong enough, and willing to cover much of her face with a scarf loaned to her by Dowling, she accompanied Kirche, Prenalin, Kipling, and Redd to tour the old prison Steingefan where they heard stories of the bairn who rescued the children of Path.

"It's a sad story that a king couldn't keep hold of a few children," Kirche purred as he grimaced, disgusted by the damp and barren rooms of the old castle.

The next day, they were off to train recruits from Path and Timber. It had been done once already on the day Leah had to herself, but this time she was invited along to see the young men's marching and shooting abilities. There were thirteen boys, small and large, various ages, barefoot and dirty.

"They're not much to look at," Kirche said as Leah stepped out of the carriage onto the field just outside the wood between Path and

Timber. "But they're eager to learn."

The boys marched and turned, and played at running and shooting, using sticks carved into the shape of long arms. Kirche enamored them with stories of the military in Ruhm and any time they wished to join, they could travel to the port and ask for passage on any ship of the Hass.

"How many have joined?" Leah asked Prenalin, as Kirche handed out hard candies to all the boys.

He smiled. "Over the years, a fair few have left home for the military. They had little to keep them here. And are you feeling much better?"

"I am."

"You'll have had quite a bit to write about in your journal," Kirche said, after dismissing his charges.

Leah eyed Kirche, but chided herself for her suspicions. Kirche had often mentioned her journal, and she'd never thought much of it before. Knowing what she'd written in recent days, and what she'd torn out and thrown away, on the off chance the book might come into possession of the wrong sort, had made her paranoid.

"I'd rather focus on positive thoughts," she said.

"But your time in the forest," he persisted, as they walked to the carriage. "You should perhaps write it all down in detail. It might later have some meaning."

"For finding the kell stone, you mean."

"Yes, of course. Did you see or hear anything that might lead you to some information about its location?"

Leah couldn't imagine what she might have found fighting for her life in the forest.

"Did any of the beast who harmed you say anything about the stone?"

"Why would they?"

Kirche looked at her as if she were speaking a foreign language. "Because you are a foreign folk, of course. Wouldn't they question you about it? Did they not ask you if you knew where it was?"

"My apologies, Lord Kirche. I don't understand why they would ask me that."

"Folk stole their stone. Wouldn't they question any they come across?"

"The stone was stolen generations ago. It would be highly unlikely that a folk such as I would know anything of its whereabouts."

Kirche smirked and climbed into the carriage. "Seems one would not want to leave any stone unturned." And at his own wit, he laughed loud and raucously, shaking the cart as Leah followed Prenalin to her seat.

Leah did her best to laugh with him. "No, I'm afraid there was no mention of the stone while I was there. They were more concerned about punishing me." She amazed herself at how easily she lied and continued to do so. She didn't flinch at all this time. Clearly, lies came more natural the more a folk told them.

"Punishment, yes. What cruel creatures, to punish you for something I did. Is that the sort of justice system they live by?"

"I couldn't say."

"Well, never mind that. It's over and done with now. Journal it. You may never know what ideas it might spark."

"If I may be so bold, Lord, what are we doing...to find the stone, I mean?"

Prenalin turned his face to the carriage window as the driver beckoned the horses and Leah thought he must wish she would not bother Kirche with her questions.

"We haven't done anything, yet. Not really. Certainly, we take a look when we come across some new cavern or hole we haven't seen before. And on this trip we will take a tour out to the caverns in the north. But in the past we have done little. The folk of the Ruud were charged with finding the stone for us."

Leah nodded. "I see."

"But this new bairn." Kirche beamed with a wide smile. "That's a boon, is it not? If we catch him, we can use him to our advantage in taking the Ruud. And if we do not succeed in that, we need only wait for him to find the stone for us."

"Do you suppose that is his goal, at present?" Prenalin said.

"Of course. That is what the prophecy told, did it not?"

"Do we know the words of the prophecy?"

Kirche let his head rattle back and forth on his neck and rolled his eyes. "We know what the folk tell us it said. Isn't that enough? The boy is meant to find the stone."

Leah shook her head. "Lord, begging your pardon. But I have found no folk here who know what the kell stone is."

Prenalin turned to her. "It's true," he said. "They don't know of it."

Kirche laughed. "The folk of the Ruud know nothing. Haven't I told you they are ignorant? Why, they don't even read. No, no. I understand we first heard the story from an angel eisen in Ruhm. We tried to find her after the story was revealed, but we were unsuccessful. Of all the creatures on Kell to be wary of, the angel eis are the most cunning and vile."

"An angel eis in Ruhm? But I thought they were—"

"Banished. Murdered. Yes. But angel eis have many powers and this one has apparently managed to live among us."

Leah shook her head.

"You are not convinced," Kirche said.

"Forgive me. But, how did you hear the angel eisen's story?"

"One of our community spies overheard her telling the story to charm folk at a fire gathering. The gathering itself was illegal and that is why he was there—to take names. After he reported, we searched for the eisen and found no trace of the woman."

"Of course. And the spy told the truth. Naturally."

"Naturally," Kirche said, failing to note the skepticism in Leah's voice.

But then, she thought, why would the spy lie? They are trained only to make note of blasphemies and incidents against the moral law. Where might a spy of Ruhm come up with such an idea if it were not true? But an angel eisen in the city? Why would she *be* there? What sort of life could an angel eis have living among the folk of Ruhm?

"Lord Kirche," she said. "Could this angel eisen, then, be a spy as well—for the ice realm, perhaps?"

Kirche's brows rose and his head fell back slightly before he let out another loud laugh. "For what purpose would the angels or the eis spy on the folk of Ruhm?"

The carriage slowed to a stop at the inn at Timber where they would have their dinner and Kirche continued his chuckling as he disembarked.

"It is a thought," Prenalin whispered to her as he scooted past her to leave the carriage.

He handed Leah down the steps to the ground and as they followed Kirche into the inn, Prenalin said quietly, "Kirche and the inner circle of Hass are of the mind that no other folk come near to Ruhm in power, among other things."

"Perhaps the eisen isn't a spy," Leah said. "But such arrogance for Ruhm doesn't bode well if she is ever faced with a real threat."

Prenalin smiled down at her and spoke unusually loudly. "Don't fear, Leah. Our circle is proud, yes, for our love of Ruhm. But is pride misplaced when its focus is valid? Ruhm is the greatest and most powerful city on Kell. Of that, you can be certain."

Leah turned to see Kirche watching them with a self-assured smile.

Chapter Thirty-seven

Darnit came bounding toward them two miles north of Banished and Rogget knelt to give him a rub about the ears.

"Ach. I've been so worried for you, darn bear. I wish you'd just take off.

He's such a mind of his own." Rogget turned to the kids, smiling.

"I think you'd be lost without him," Sadie said.

"Maybe. But I don't like these parts, with the criminals and the firearms. I'm thinking the ice realm, even with a war, will be safer for a bear."

Grayson shook his head. "It's rumored that even the criminals won't venture all the way into the ice realm, so I'm not sure safer is what we'll be."

"Oh, they're harsh there, on the criminal folk," Rogget said. "But I didn't ever hear tell of any of the faire eis being unkind to strangers... leastwise until they discovered their intent."

"Intent?"

"Well, sure. You know, there's some go off to the ice realm looking for gold and silver. Or the eisen women. I hear tell they're downright hard to resist...eh?" He looked at them and turned red in the face. "Uh, never mind that."

They made camp in the early evening at the foot of a row of large hills just north of the bridge over the lilac clover field. On the horizon to the northeast, Fenn could see the snow capped peaks of the ice realm.

"We'll have to make our way valley to valley, dale to dale, until we reach the mountains. Then we have to find Kingdom Pass," Rogget said. "That'll take us right into the realm... eventually."

"We'll need warmer clothes," Sadie said.

Rogget slapped his forehead. "Ach, I forgot. We were to pass by the Gnome Eaters again."

"But they wouldn't have had time to get us clothes," Fenn said. "They went with us to fight the Wretched and now they have to defend themselves."

"You'd be surprised, I think," Rogget said. "Wiley sent a few out right away to sneak into the Ruud for extra blankets and such."

Fenn frowned. He didn't want to delay the trip any longer than necessary. But they had forgotten about the clothes. He shrugged. What else could they do?

"All right then," he grumbled. "We'll have to head back."

"No, no. That won't be necessary," Rogget said. "There'll be more encampments up this way. We can barter for supplies and warmer clothing from them."

"We don't have much to trade."

"I think stories and news of the Ruud will do," Rogget smiled.

"How will we find water in the frozen realm?" Grayson said.

"We could melt chunks of ice in our mugs over the fire," Sadie said.

They all turned to look at her and smiled.

"What?" she said. "Can't we?"

"That's exactly what we'll do," Rogget said.

Fenn turned to Grayson and saw his cheeks redden, suddenly realizing a newfound respect for Sadie.

They hiked to the edge of a small copse of trees and after collecting enough firewood, Rogget set to work digging out a fire pit amid a circle of large rocks, while Grayson and Sadie disappeared into the wood to find branches for making a lean-to. Fenn sat on a boulder watching Rogget.

"It'll be all right to have a fire at this distance, I think," Rogget said. "Might be a risk to keep it aflame through the night."

"You think they'll come looking for us?"

Rogget nodded. "The plan was, o' course, for the Gnome Eaters to throw them off. But they saw you. And likely Clutch won't want to let you get away with taking back your charm. It would make him look bad, I expect. I don't think the guard will be this far out yet, though."

Fenn nodded. Rogget had finished the pit and piled sticks into the middle of the hole and took out his flint. Darnit roared from the woods and Rogget dropped the flint and jumped up.

"Darnit," he called and the bear peered out from the trees. "Don't scare me like that." He turned back to the kindling and knelt, but his hands shook as he tried to light the flint. "Darn bear. If he don't stay hidden it won't be my fault if he ends up shot again."

He lit three flints but they all burnt out before the kindling caught the flame. Rogget fumed. "Darn bear." He shook his head, rose, and walked the few feet to the trees and talked to Darnit. "You have to stay hidden, there, I tell you."

Fenn found this behavior puzzling. Darnit was hidden, like he'd been told. Except for the one outburst of a roar, he seemed rather content at curling up against a tree on the cold ground. Rogget must have been very worried still. Fenn tried to curl up in his tunic for warmth but the impatience of waiting for the fire made him shake off the cold. He stood up, walked to the fire pit, squatted down beside it and pushed his arms out toward the kindling and flint sticks lying burnt atop it. A feeling of power rushed through his chest and a small flame caught the sticks and began to billow. He quickly added more kindling and waved his hand over it. Rogget turned from Darnit in the trees and came back to watch him build up the fire.

"Your last flint must have worked, after all," Fenn told him with a smile.

Rogget muttered, "About time," and added a log to the pile.

Grayson and Sadie returned, pulling a pile of branches and logs behind them on a blanket. They set them up and tied them with Rogget's rope, building a nice lean-to under which they could sleep.

"There'll only be room for two." Sadie looked at Fenn, worried. "But we'll take turns."

"It's all right," Fenn said. "You two built it. You should sleep in it."

"Maybe tomorrow we can find more wood and build another one. Unless we decide to move on."

"We should keep moving for a few days until we're sure the Wretched aren't following us," Rogget said.

Grayson looked dejected, but he nodded.

They ate and talked and sat around the fire, until Rogget told them to go to bed. "I'll put out the fire in an hour or so, so bundle up in your blankets."

Fenn curled up against a boulder away from the wind, facing the fire, his knapsack at his feet, and tried to sleep. He had his charm back and reached to his neck to hold it. It was warm and his blood pulsed in his finger tips as he touched it.

Lucas was standing in the cellar of the Path wissenry with the woolen blanket pulled back, exposing the tunnel, its door slung wide open. "Go on," he said. "Get in." A wicked smile formed on his face and Fenn stepped back away from him. "No."

"Aw, come on, look, there's nothing in there to fear."

Fenn peered into the dark hole and saw a faint glow; it grew brighter and brighter until out of the tunnel floated the burning tree of the Hass of Emorah and Lucas laughed and laughed.

And then his mother's voice surrounded him. "Don't be afraid," she said. "It's only a dream."

Suddenly he was startled awake by a yell and the sound of a gunshot.

"No, Darnit, run!" Rogget screamed.

Fenn scrambled to his feet, only to find them caught in the straps of his knapsack, bringing him tumbling to his knees. He was grabbed from behind and wrapped in rope before he realized what was happening. Sadie screamed; another gunshot rang out and he heard Rogget's muffled shouting.

"Little thief," Clutch seethed in his ear and dragged him to a horse. He lifted him effortlessly onto its back, and then climbed on behind him.

"Let's go!" he called out and the horse shot off into the darkness.

With the wind rushing in his ears, Fenn thought he heard a crowd of men screeching a war cry. He looked back and saw only shadowy figures in the dim light of the cloud-covered moon.

Chapter Thirty-eight

Welk paced in front of the hearth with Dunham nervously twitching and clicking his tongue a few steps away, mirroring his movements. "Must you make all that noise?" Welk scolded.

Dunham made a shallow bow. "Your forgiveness, Sire."

Welk rolled his eyes and continued his pacing. It seemed hours since he'd received the crudely written note from the wide-eyed young guard. The boy had been on patrol, he'd said, at the border of the wasteland when he was approached in the early morning darkness by a gang of thieves. He looked as if he'd seen the devil. And where was Sorgood? How long ago had he been summoned?

All was working surprisingly in Welk's favor, with little or no effort on his part. He'd spent all the day before perfecting his plan to enter the hill country to gain support for something of an attack on the ice realm. It would allow him to meet with Clutch, to gain the loyalty of the folk of the hills, thus planting himself above the other kingdoms of the Ruud, and to begin the task of aiding the maiden and her loyal eis in their civil dispute. It was all so neatly packaged he was giddy with excitement to get started. Then he received the note. Clutch was, it seemed, right outside the Ruud. The days it would normally take to track him down were reduced to nothing. Now he only needed to get Sorgood out of the way.

Finally he heard the creak and boom of the old door to the lobby and Sorgood approached with his entourage, striding toward him with a look of power on his face that did not disappear until he reached Welk at the hearth.

Sorgood made a low bow and his guard followed suit. "You summoned, Sire?" he said.

Welk was sure he detected a faint hint of exasperation in Sorgood's voice, as if he fidgeted between showing loyalty to his king and dominance to his guard. But their faces remained stony and their eyes distant. If he was reading them correctly, the guard detested Sorgood as much as any other folk in the Ruud did.

Frieden, pale and blond, stood just beyond Sorgood, refusing to humble himself by hunching as the master of the guard tended to do. Welk forced himself not to look at the young felid folk. After meeting up with the boy outside the beast forest in Timber, he'd absentmindedly called his name out of surprise. The boy had eyed him suspiciously and took the first opportunity to dart away into the forest. But of course the wissenry hadn't told him of his connection to Welk. For all he knew, they hadn't bothered to tell the boy his real name.

Welk gave the chamberlain the note from the thieves and it was handed to Sorgood.

"This," he said, "came from the wasteland early this morning. Tell me what you make of it."

Sorgood took the paper to the wall, closer to the fire, and held it up in front of his face, studying it. Frieden followed and looked over Sorgood's shoulder. A slight, proud smile found its way to Welk's lips.

"Was it written by a child, Sire?"

"Read all of it." Welk watched Sorgood carefully.

"Ah." he walked back to Welk, with Frieden following like a curious kitten. Sorgood handed the note to the chamberlain. "The Wretched. I'm surprised to find they have a writer in the group."

Welk nodded. It would be Goggle, if he still lived. He remembered Goggle fondly. Clutch's favorite, and like a puppy—very hard not to like.

"Well," Welk raised his voice. "What do you make of it?"

"It's a trap, Sire," Sorgood said. "They mean to rob you."

Welk paused, looking over Sorgood's face. "Yes," he said and nodded. "I thought as much. Why did it take you so long to arrive?"

"I was on my way to Cold Sea Port, Sire. To interrogate some pirates regarding our quarry."

"Very well, Sorgood. Continue with your plans. I won't expect to see you again for some time."

"Yes, Sire."

Sorgood hesitated, his brows creased just a bit as if he fought with doubt, before bowing low again. His guard also bowed to the king and then followed the little man out.

"We should reinstate the backward bowing out rule, Dunham."

"Sire?"

"It would prolong his agony in trying to hide his smirk from me."

Dunham smiled and looked toward the door after Sorgood. He chuckled. "I'm glad to hear the king is not taken in by his obeisance, Sire."

"Ah, so you've decided Sorgood is against the king?"

"Oh, no, Sire. I wouldn't go that far. But I think..." He paused.

"You may speak freely Dunham. I need at least one person to always speak freely to me."

"Well, Sire. I think Sorgood is mostly for himself, rather than against the king."

"But he is also for Emorah, is he not?"

Dunham nodded. "That would be my thinking, Sire."

"And you, Dunham. Be truthful with me. I will not punish one way of thinking or the other. Where do you stand with Emorah?"

"Sire, I would willingly take the punishment if my way of thinking offended you. I stand against Emorah. But I stand with you. If you tell me that Emorah also stands for the king, I will stand with it."

Welk tilted his head and let a small smile come to his lips.

"You would stand with it out of loyalty?"

Dunham smiled. "I would stand with it, Sire. But that does not mean I would believe in its teachings. You recall the list I was to make, of possible enemies of your father?"

Welk nodded.

"It would appear, after my spy's reports, that Sorgood tops the list."

Welk's brow rose. "What is the report?"

"That he follows the representatives of Hass, or that they follow him. And spies report many a time that Sorgood was alone with your father, King Evan."

"You are a good and faithful servant, Dunham. I thank you for your candor."

"Aye, Sire. Always your servant." He bowed low.

Welk watched Dunham's shoulders as he bowed and wondered if it were true or not. Could he trust Dunham? How to tell? He was suddenly struck with loss. If only his father had not died young. If only his father had not betrayed him. All those he trusted were lost to him. Rue the fair, taken so young in life. His father, her betrayer, the cause of her death. They were both gone to the ether leaving him without counsel. Clutch, the only other he could confide in, well...he could at least find him on occasion. But he would do well to have someone handy, like Dunham.

"Sire?" Dunham looked concerned.

Welk shook his head, waved his hand as if to bat away the emotion.

"We need a guard, Dunham. Twenty men. Can you find them?"

Dunham nodded.

"Alert me when Sorgood has passed the boundary of Timber. We will ride out then."

Welk handed the poorly written note to Dunham and listened to his deep, fatherly voice as he read aloud.

"We have that boy. Come to get him. In the waste land. We'll let him go or else. We want ten big doars and ten gold rings." He paused and looked to Welk. "Ten gold rings, Sire?"

Welk chuckled. "Goggle doesn't know how to spell many words, I'm afraid. You'd better bring a lot of doars and gold. If Clutch told him to write bigger numbers and he didn't, he'll drag him behind a horse."

"You know these folk, Sire?"

332

Welk nodded. "I do." He raised his eyebrows at Dunham's surprise. "Do you not remember more than ten years ago, when we were both younger men. I ran away to live the life of a vagabond?"

"Ah, yes Sire." Dunham smiled.

"I met up with the Wretched for a time."

"And they didn't kill you, Sire? You, a prince of the Ruud?"

"Clutch had his reasons. Besides, I believe I'd renounced the throne at the time."

"I do recall." He began the tsk-tskinng with his tongue again. "Sad times, Sire."

Welk frowned. "And not so sad. At least then there was adventure. And hope for another chance at happiness."

Dunham nodded. Welk reached out and patted him soundly on the shoulder. "Let us not dwell on the past, then, good man." And he did feel the weight of it finally begin to slide. He could not yet completely trust Dunham, but he could see now that there was something bigger than himself. Something more important than Rue-Anna and their love. It was just as his father had tried to tell him, after all. The Ruud was the thing. The Ruud was his heart. He could trust the Ruud.

Chapter Thirty-nine

Fenn woke to the smell of campfire and bitters and to the snorting of horses in the misty cold morning. He sat up and winced; his body ached from head to foot. The wild horse ride the night before, the rocky spot on which he was forced to sleep, and his hands tied behind his back, all served to give him pain.

Clutch, Goggle, and Crud, another of the Wretched, sat by the fire watching him. Beyond them, to the north, Fenn could see the towers of Steingefan rising in the hazy distance over the tall grass. He was back home; most of him feared being so near to the place he knew he must flee, but some small part of him was joyous and he gulped deep breaths of Ruud air, sniffed out the morning aromas, and listened for the sparrow song.

"Here." Clutch held out a mug of bitters.

"I don't drink bitters," Fenn said. "Even if I could take the cup."

Clutch put the mug down at the edge of the fire and came up behind Fenn, untying his hands.

"You won't get far if you try to run. You might as well have your hands to drink."

Clutch offered him the mug and Fenn saw his hemp rope and gold charm dangling from the dirty man's neck as he took it from him. Instead of the stone the children of Path had carved for him, his mother's charm clinked up against a shard of amber rock.

"Where's the stone?" Fenn asked.

"Drink."

Fenn lifted the mug reluctantly and sniffed it. It smelled earthy, but he'd tasted it before and the name bitters didn't describe it well enough. He took a sip and grimaced.

"There was a stone charm on my rope. What did you do with it?"

"Ah," Clutch said. "Tossed it off somewhere."

Fenn's jaw set and he glared at Clutch. "Why are we here?"

"Border of Michelruud. Waiting on the king." Goggle smiled like he had a secret he couldn't wait to share. "I sent him a note about you."

"What if he doesn't come?"

Clutch smiled, then broke out in laughter. More horses approached from behind him and the straggling, tired Wretched joined them.

"Where are the rest?" Clutch said.

"Left behind," one said. "We was ambushed again, by the Gnome Eaters. They had the Scary Brutes with 'em and some others from round about."

Clutch growled and looked at Fenn. "This is your fault. We were all just fine, getting along, until you showed up."

"You didn't get along," Fenn said.

"We got along in our way."

Fenn chuckled. "If you want to call it that."

Clutch glared at him. "We'll be well rid of you soon enough."

Fenn realized they'd stolen his sack when he saw them digging jerky from it; at least they shared it with him and offered him a hard biscuit. He was forced to drink the bitters to moisten it. But his spirits woke shortly after and he felt alert, clear-headed, and energetic.

They heard horses and all turned to the south to see them approach.

"It's him, get up."

They moved forward, one of the men pushing Fenn along, to stand beyond the fire. It was the King of Michelruud, with ten horses behind him. Clutch smiled broadly as the horses slowed and formed a row some twenty yards away, in front of his men.

"Welk," Clutch called out gleefully. "I knew you couldn't resist an adventure. I got something you want."

Fenn looked over at the king, curious. He'd only seen the King of Michelruud, Evan at the time, in passing in Path or along the roads to the port. He'd certainly never been in conversation with a king before, and he was sure that Clutch was supposed to speak to him with more respect. He should say Sire and Highness and bow and all that. But maybe criminals didn't follow the rules of conduct the way regular folk did. Still, he would have thought a king would be angry at the insult of being called by name. But King Welk actually smiled and sat forward on his horse. With a light tap of his feet, the horse moved toward them.

Clutch and Goggle moved forward as well and met him halfway.

Fenn could hear some of their words. Money, ransom, evil bairn. And they laughed. The King of Michelruud was laughing with Clutch the crook. Fenn was stunned and looked around at the others who didn't seem to notice.

Clutch turned back to the group, whistled and waved his hand. One of the men tossed Fenn his knapsack, grabbed him by the scruff of his neck, and pushed him forward toward Clutch and the king. As he approached, Fenn kept his eyes on Welk of Michelruud. He didn't look half as mean as Clutch, though they both were dark of hair and eyes. King Welk peered curiously back at him.

"So," he said looking down at him from his horse, "you're the one causing all the trouble."

He didn't seem angry. "Yes, Sire," Fenn responded politely and the king laughed.

Welk looked him over, shaking his head. "We haven't decided what to do with you yet, but you're certainly worth a bounty." He raised his arm and signaled to his men and one of them approached with a large bag. Welk took it from him and held it out to Clutch. As Clutch stepped forward to take the bag, Fenn caught sight of something in the grasses to their right. Something prowled there, low to the ground, inching its way toward them.

"Hand over the boy first," Welk said with a sly smile at Clutch.

"I'll hand him over, but he's not to get on a horse until you toss the gold."

"Ah, Clutch, you don't trust me?"

Clutch laughed. "About as much as you trust me."

They both smiled, angering Fenn. Clutch grabbed at his knapsack and dragged him over to Welk who summoned one of his men to dismount and stand beside Fenn.

"Oh, and he had something of yours," Clutch said.

But just as Welk tossed the bag of ransom across to Clutch, one of his men screamed, "Felid!"

Fenn was startled and something or someone pushed him to the ground; horses reared and whinnied, men ran screaming this way and that. A shot rang out, whoops and hollers, almost gleeful, sailed through the air, and then Fenn heard the unmistakable growl of a bear.

He looked up in the panic and saw Clutch looking down at him with fierce rage on his face. Fenn reached up, grabbed his hemp rope from Clutch's neck and broke it off.

"You little—"

Clutch had Fenn by the throat, but suddenly the thief was pulled to the ground and dragged away.

Chapter Forty

In the chaos, Welk's horse reared up and tossed him into the grass. Pounding hooves and frantic whinnies echoed around him and the horses disappeared quickly, chased toward the Ruud, he assumed. He raised himself up to peer at the scene; felidae rounded up his and Clutch's men, pouncing on them and dragging them back toward the spot where they'd attacked. But Fenn Foster was left alone and running northward, flinging his knapsack onto his back. Welk crawled quickly, keeping as low as possible away from where the men were being captured and as soon as he felt his distance was enough, he stood and darted forward after the boy.

"Fenn, run!"

The other children sat on horses fifty yards away and Welk picked up his speed, but the boy was fast.

"Hurry," the innkeeper's son called. "Someone's coming."

But just as he'd reached his friends, the boy paused and bent forward to catch his breath and Welk sprinted to close in on him.

"Stop!"

Welk was almost at Fenn when he looked to one of the horses to see young Sadie Pratt, the stationer's daughter, had a firearm.

"Sadie, no," Fenn said. "It's the king."

"Get on the horse, Fenn," she demanded. The girl took a determined aim at Welk. The innkeeper's son sat with his mouth open and his eyes wide.

Welk turned to Fenn, who seemed confused. He looked at Welk, and then back to his friend. His eyes searched the meadow behind Welk for others but they still fought the felidae, and what looked like the Gnome Eaters, a hundred yards back.

"No one is coming to help you," Welk said. He must keep the boy on the ground long enough for his guard to arrive. But it sounded as if no reinforcement would come.

"I'm not the evil bairn. I'm not going to destroy the Ruud." The boy was desperate.

This was not the declaration Welk expected.

"The folk of the Ruud believe otherwise," he said.

"You can convince them. Tell them I mean no harm."

"It would change nothing."

"Fenn." Miss Pratt still aimed her firearm at Welk. "Get on the horse."

"If you were an adult," Welk said. "I'd have your head."

"Adults, you kill," the innkeeper's son responded, apparently his shock subsided. "Children are abandoned to Steingefan."

Welk smirked. Clever boy.

"You go on back to the battle," the girl said to him. "I don't want to shoot the king."

"No, I don't imagine your father would be pleased at the news."

"Does he get news in prison?"

Sarcasm. He never expected such from the daughter of the king's stationer. "Your father is a guest in the castle at Michelruud. He will be sorely disappointed to hear of your behavior."

"I don't believe you."

Welk shrugged and looked again at Fenn Foster of the wissenry. "I will hunt you across the eastern realm until you are captured. There is nowhere for you to run. Nowhere to hide."

"There is no prophecy," the boy said, clearly angry. "I'm not the new bairn."

"The folk believe in a prophecy; they will not be dissuaded. But if you are not the bairn, why do the beast folk fight for you now?"

"Maybe the beast folk don't like kings who pick on little kids."

"You are more than a child. You have the mark."

"The mark has nothing to do with it," the innkeeper's son said.

"You know of this mark?" Welk asked him.

"He reads." The Pratt girl smirked and raised her firearm again to her cheek.

"Why are we talking about this?" Fenn said. "I'm not going to destroy the Ruud. I don't know what the mark is, but is has nothing to do with prophecy because there's no such thing."

"You are a fine representative of the wissenry," Welk said. "All logic and no heart. The faire eis are gearing up for battle. Those marked are needed now more than ever. You may be the bairn, if one exists, but you are certainly the hope of the beast. Either way you pose a danger to the

Ruud."

"What are you talking about?"

Welk realized then for certain—Fenn Foster did not know who he was.

"Fenn, just get on the horse and let's get out of here," the innkeeper's boy said.

"Why do you hesitate to run?" Welk said. "What is it that you want?"

The boy paused as if thinking and Welk eyed him carefully. Finally, he seemed to have an answer ready.

"I want you to leave me alone," the boy said.

Welk sighed with anger, rolling his eyes. "Is that all?"

"No. I want the folk of the wasteland freed. I have a writ you signed to Forbes Billings twelve years ago. You swore that upon ascending to the throne you would pardon all those banished to the wastelands."

Welk sputtered and laughed, even as he felt the blood drain from his face. "You want...what?"

"I want you to honor your writ to Forbes Billings."

Welk creased his brow and peered at the boy. Perhaps Kirche was right. This was a boy who could be turned into a devotion for the folk most assuredly. How odd he was.

"I need a guarantee that you will leave the Ruud forever and I will not see you again unless I seek you out."

"I swear it."

"Then give me the writ."

Fenn dropped his backpack from his shoulders and pulled it open. He foraged through it until he found the paper and drew it carefully from the sack.

"I have it here, you see."

Welk held out his hand. "Bring it to me."

"No. You see that I have it. It stays with me. It's my guarantee that you will honor your promise and free them all."

Welk rolled his eyes and turned briefly to the still scuffling guard fifty yards behind him. "And then what of future criminals?"

"No more banishment."

Welk shook his head helplessly. He remembered the writ. The night he signed it was still clear in his mind despite his fill of drink. He'd wanted to sign it, thinking it would rile his father. But Forbes Billings didn't bring the writ to the king, as he'd hoped. The folk was smarter than that and Welk realized he was biding his time until Evan died. He should have known the writ would show up sooner or later.

"Very well," he said. "You will disappear. And I will proclaim the banished pardoned and end the punishment. But if you go against your word..." Welk stiffened his lips, forming his words carefully. "If you do not leave. I will have little choice but to have the folk of the wasteland executed even as they arrive home to meet their families."

"You wouldn't," Fenn whispered.

"Are you willing to test me?"

"Now will you get on the horse?" the innkeeper's boy pleaded and the young lad climbed on behind him. The Pratt girl lowered her firearm, looked off to the distance where felidae encircled Welk's men and Clutch's thieves, and then looked back at him with concern.

"Begging your greatest pardon, Sire," she said. "I'm just a stupid kid. I didn't mean any harm. But Fenn here's not like you say. He's not going to hurt anybody."

"You've staked your life on that, lass."

Welk clenched his fists in fury. Horseless, no sword, without arms at all. A gun aimed at him! He only wished he'd invited Sorgood along so he could have him whipped for the humility of it all. And worse, it was now clear that Fenn Foster of the wissenry had no knowledge of his own part in what was to come.

Chapter Forty-one

I am not the bairn," Fenn told the king sternly, trying one last time to reason with him before Sadie and Grayson forced the horses away. "There was never a prophecy. I don't want to destroy the Ruud. It's my home."

"Just because you feel that way now means little," King Welk said.

"I will leave as I promised. I was planning to leave anyway, to explore for the wissenry."

"There are more dangers outside the Ruud than in. If you come with me now, you may live your life in safety under guard."

"As a prisoner?" Grayson shook his head. "Come on, let's leave."

"What about my friends?"

"Never mind, Fenn," Sadie said. "He's stalling, waiting for help. We need to leave now."

"Would you let them and their parents go if I went with you?"

"Yes, of course. It's you we want."

"No, Fenn," Grayson said.

"I cannot guarantee your life or your safety if you run," the king said.

"But you just bargained with him to leave," Grayson said. "You promised to stop hunting him."

"That was not part of the agreement."

Horses galloped toward them. A herald called out, "The king!" Suddenly, Fenn heard small grouchy voices hissing at him.

"Run, you fool. Run."

Fenn looked around and saw several felidae crouching in the grass. One huddled there, in his folk form.

"We could not hold them forever. Run."

Before Fenn could decide what to do, Grayson kicked his horse and they turned and left the king of Michelruud standing alone in the meadow.

"Do you know where you're going?" Fenn asked Grayson over his shoulder.

"We're to meet Rogget in Banished."

"Did I see Gnome Eaters back there?"

"We have a story to tell you, for sure," Grayson said, but they were silent as the horses were driven hard, back toward the wasteland village.

At the first stop, to rest the horses at a stream, Fenn retrieved his hemp rope from the bottom of his knapsack. Holding it up, he laid the charm and shard of amber rock against the palm of his hand. The rock pulsated against his skin, much like his charm sometimes did, but the beats were harder, traveling deeper, up his arm and to his chest, beckoning Fenn to place it there. His first impulse was to close his hand around it and squeeze, but when he did so, both the charm and the shard dug into his skin and he was forced to relax his grip. Tying the rope around his neck, he sat for a moment watching the horses drink. Once the throbbing ceased and the charm and amber shard were at home against his skin, he begged Sadie and Grayson to tell him what they knew.

"Rogget would love to tell you all about it," Sadie said.

"I can't wait that long. What happened back at camp last night?"

"You know just as well as we do. The Wretched came and got you. And the Gnome Eaters showed up and there was fighting like mad for hours."

"It wasn't hours." Grayson rolled his eyes with a smile. "But it did seem to go on for a time. First we were held by some of the Wretched."

"And then the Gnome Eaters came and bashed 'em and then they took us."

"And then some of the Wretched grabbed us back."

"It was crazy."

"But you escaped."

"Eventually the Gnome Eaters ran the Wretched off. A bunch of us followed along as scouts were sent out to find you; but we all figured where they were taking you."

"Where is Rogget, then? I heard Darnit roaring back at the attack."

"Rogget stayed behind," Grayson said. "He's hurt. But it's not bad. He's being tended by Pinta."

"Yeah, he's probably in a fit right now. We weren't supposed to leave."

"It's a good thing we did, though." He looked at Sadie with a big grin. "We rescued Fenn."

"Yeah, we did."

They looked very pleased with themselves.

"But Sadie, you can never go home now," Fenn said. "You threatened the king. And where did you get a gun?"

"Don't you dare tell another soul," she said. "It belongs to Pinta."

They were right about Rogget. He was beside himself, lying on a rag mat in Pinta's hut, yelling one second and wincing with pain the next.

"But it's all right now," Pinta soothed him. "Look, the children are fine and well and they've brought Fenn back to us. And your bear, Darnit, is over across the way waiting for you."

"We've got to move," Rogget said. "We've got to get away before they come for him."

"The Wretched won't be coming too quickly, Rogget," Fenn said. "If they come at all. Their horses are tired. And anyway, we can stay here for as long as we want. I promised the king I'd never go back home. He won't come after me now."

"You talked to the king?" Rogget sat up amazed.

Fenn nodded.

"And you promised to stay out of the Ruud?"

Fenn nodded again.

"And you think he believes you?"

Fenn shrugged. "Why wouldn't he believe me? Besides, I had something to bargain with."

"Bargain?"

Fenn pulled out Forbes' writ and smiled.

"Where'd you get that?"

"I stole it back from Clutch when I found my charm. King Welk says he'll honor it; he'll pardon them all. And, no more banishment."

"Ah, pash," Pinta said, shaking her head. "You're not going on about the writ now too, are you?"

"But King Welk promised."

"And you believed him? He's a king, boy. He doesn't have to honor his word to the likes of us."

Rogget shook his head. "I don't like it. Not one bit. Pinta's right. It's a ruse, I tell you. I think we need to move and soon."

"But Rogget," Sadie said. "You can't move yet."

"I can. You got those horses don't you?"

"They're not ours," Grayson said. "The Wretched will come after them soon enough."

"But we can take them as far as the borderlands north and then set them off."

"Rogget's right, Fenn. I get the feeling we need to go far away," Grayson said.

"If you really think it's necessary," Fenn said. "But I don't want Rogget moving before he's ready."

"I'm ready," Rogget said.

Pinta nervously packed his things and Rogget climbed atop one of the horses while Sadie, Grayson, and Fenn climbed atop the other.

They sat around the fire a hundred miles out from Banished, long past the lilac clover range, wrapped in blankets, sheltered from the wind against huge white boulders. The sound of the great rushing river was dampened by its icy covering. Snow-capped mountains of the ice realm towered over them from the north as Grayson began to speak.

"Here is all I know," he said.

Fenn had cajoled him each day, every chance he had, during their trip north. He must tell what he knows of the history of the Ruud. If they were ever to figure out the mess they were in, they had to know everything they could. He was adamant at first that he would not share his information. It was forbidden; it was against the law. And any talk of the Hass of Emorah would only upset Sadie.

"Take a look around," Fenn had told him. "We're not in the Ruud anymore. We're outcast. There are no laws here and no Hass. Not to mention the fact that our lives may depend on what's in your head."

Finally, after days of persuading, he'd agreed and now sat bundled in a woolen, hooded overcoat bartered from a nomadic tribe just south, and covered in a blanket, in front of the fire. Rogget sat, as wide-eyed and curious as Sadie, waiting for him to begin the story that Fenn said he'd tell.

"A true story," he'd said, "that few other folk know."

"It was hundreds of years ago. Michelruud, the first king, was once a great wissende in the Kingdom of Ruhm."

"A wissende?" Sadie said. "Michelruud was a wissende?"

"A great wissende," Grayson said. "And the Kingdom of Ruhm is a great kingdom. The Ruud is nothing compared with it."

"How would you know?"

"Just let him tell us, Sadie," Fenn said, impatient.

"It's described in the history of the Ruud. The real history of the Ruud."

"What do you mean, the real history?"

"That's what Fenn wants me to tell you. There are two histories. One is the big book that sits out in the front room at the inn."

"And we have a copy at the stationer's," Sadie said.

"Yes," Grayson said. "Anyone can read it, if they can read. But that's not the real history."

"How do you know?"

"Because it said so in *The Book of Katze*. Katze said his was the original history."

"Let him finish the story," Rogget barked. Sadie flinched and hunkered deeper under her blanket.

"Michelruud was a great wissende. The wissenry in the Kingdom of Ruhm was not exactly like the wissenry here. They were scientists and learned folk. They studied the world. They didn't counsel folk and help them. That was the job of the Hass. Only, according to the history, they weren't always called the Hass. First they were the House of the Spirit. They studied philosophy."

"What's philosophy?" Sadie murmured.

"If the wissenry studied *how* things were, the Hass tried to say *why* they were."

Sadie shook her head.

"I don't really understand either," Fenn said.

"For instance, according to the history, there was a terrible plague in the Great West. The wissenry figured out that the disease was carried by tiny insects that fly around sucking the blood of eleshags and then laying eggs in folks' cured meat."

"That's gross."

"But the Hass would say that the plague was brought by Rett to punish the folk for misbehaving."

"Who is Rett?"

Grayson sighed. "This is going to be hard."

"Well, go on, just talk then. We'll listen."

"The Hass of Emorah tells folk how to behave and how to live. Rett is their devotion, the spirit being they follow. He used to live thousands of years ago, but the folk became angry with him when he told them that they should live in peace with the beasts. For that, they had him put to death. But later, realizing that they'd done wrong, they declared him a son of Mutterede and now they worship him. They say that Rett's spirit returned from the dead to create the Hass of Emorah, his representatives on Kell. Their job is to tell the folk how they are supposed to live and why Rett allows things happen. The wissenry was about facts and studies and things and they just told folk the truth."

"Okay. So what happened? Why did Michelruud leave?"

"The Hass of Emorah kept the folk in fear all the time over all sorts of things. But when the wissenry insisted that the beast folk and main folk are related, like brothers, the Hass didn't like it."

"Is that true?" Fenn said. "Are beast folk and main folk the same?"

"Related."

"I can see why the Hass wouldn't like to hear that," Rogget said. "Seeing as how they hate the beast."

"The Hass claimed that main folk were better than beast folk," Grayson said. "But the beast folk have greater power than the folk. The Hass said it was because they'd made a bargain with Mutterede's sister Horatia. They said the beasts were evil and wanted only to destroy the mortal folk."

"But I thought there were no beast folk in the west?" Sadie said.

"There were in the beginning. But as time went on, the folk pushed them off their lands. According to the book, there weren't many beast folk left after a few hundred years and the Hass made up stories about them raiding folk villages and causing all sorts of mayhem. And when the wissenry insisted that the beast were just like folk and not to be feared—that they were sentient, like folk—the Hass started saying that the wissenry was evil—in league with the beast folk and trying to destroy the Kingdom of Ruhm."

"So, Michelruud left?"

Grayson nodded. "He foresaw a great purge—a great killing. He believed their lives were in danger. But not all of the wissendes left."

"So, he wasn't a prince or anything?" Sadie asked, disap-pointed.

Grayson shook his head. "Just a wissende."

"So, that's why you were afraid when you saw the Hass in Cold Sea Port," Fenn said.

"No, not really," Grayson said. "This is only history. It was all long ago."

"We're afraid of the Hass because they're mean." Sadie stared intently into the fire and slowly shook her head.

"Did they do something to you?" Fenn asked her.

"My brother."

"I didn't know you had a brother."

"I'm sorry, Sadie," Grayson said. "I was hoping you wouldn't have to remember."

She wiped tears from her face and smiled weakly. "It's not something you ever forget, Grayson. You know that."

He nodded. "You're right. But it stays in the back of your mind, and deep in your heart. No need to bring it to the fore if you aren't ready."

"What are you talking about?" Fenn looked back and forth between them.

"My mother," Grayson said. "And Sadie's older brother."

"What happened?"

"Don't let's talk it out now," Rogget said. "If you're not up to it."

"I don't mind," Grayson said. "But I don't know how Sadie feels about it."

"You go ahead."

Grayson stared at Sadie for a few silent moments before nodding.

"My ma was fading away," he said. "She'd just given birth to my little sister Matilda. My grandmother said she would bleed to death without a dose of some special wissende medicine. My da tried to leave the inn to get some, but the Hass wouldn't let him pass. They'd been in the square, whipping children and one of their horses trampled Sadie's brother. There were folk outside the doors to the inn, front and back, enraged, calling out the Hass. Folk were screaming."

Grayson was suddenly far away, in his own memory and his eyes were wet with tears. Fenn wanted to make him stop, but didn't know if it was better to end it, or better to let him continue. Finally, Grayson spoke again.

"When Father Treacher arrived, he tended to Odom, but he died quickly. He couldn't get into the inn to see my ma until the next day when the crowd had calmed down and the Hass managed to leave. It was too late."

They were all silent for some time. The fire crackled and spit and a light wind washed them with smoke and then lifted it off them. Darnit whined and buried his nose under a paw.

"I'm sorry," Fenn said.

"Odom was seven years old," Sadie said. "I really don't remember much about it. Just that there was shouting and running and horses and my mother was screaming. And then they told me he was dead."

"We were both only about four years old at the time," Grayson said.

"Haven't you ever seen the Hass in Path?" Sadie said.

Fenn shook his head. "Never."

"The wissenry knows, like the rest of us, when they're due," Rogget said. "They keep their young fosters inside for the duration."

"Why do they come every year?" Fenn said.

"Tribute."

"Aye," Rogget said. "The Hass helped dispel the beast long ago and ever since they've demanded tribute."

"But what about the stone?" Grayson said. "Maybe they're looking to get it back."

"You mean the kell stone?" Fenn said. "From the prophecy?"

Grayson nodded. "The stone was a symbol of unity and power for the beast and the Hass stole it and hid it from them shortly after they came to the west. According to the history, Michelruud stole it back and returned it here. But later, he had to give it back to the Hass."

"Why?" Sadie said.

"You knew about the kell stone all along?" Fenn said.

Grayson nodded.

"We had a pact," Sadie said. "No more secrets, remember?"

Grayson looked to the fire and sighed. "It's forbidden to know these things. I couldn't tell anyone."

"How is it forbidden?" Sadie said. "And how would you even know that? I've never even heard of any of it."

"It says so on the very first page of the original history in *The Book of Katze*," Grayson said. "Roarn commissioned a rewriting of the history. The original history was destroyed and banned. Anyone caught with a copy would be put to death. You think I'm going to go around talking about it?"

"Now, come on," Rogget said. "We can't always know what's important to say and when. Grayson didn't mean us any harm by keeping quiet about this."

Grayson shrugged.

"It doesn't really make any sense," Fenn said.

"I didn't really read all of that part, about the stone, anyway," Grayson said. "It didn't seem important at the time. I thought it was legend."

Fenn rubbed his palms against his eyes and then stared into the fire. "I'm too tired to try to understand any of it."

"It's grown-up stuff," Sadie said. "We shouldn't have to understand it."

Grayson looked at her, tired and defeated.

"I'm just saying," Sadie said. "We shouldn't have to. That doesn't mean we don't have to."

"I feel out of place, too," he said.

"I didn't say I felt out of place."

"But you are. We all are. We don't belong here."

"But here we are." Fenn sighed. "I need to sleep. I think if I could sleep, I could figure some of it out."

"I won't argue with sleep," Grayson said.

"It's too early," Sadie complained. Her mouth fell open in a gaping yawn.

"As we go," Rogget said. "T'will get colder and colder. But we ought to find villages and encampments along the way where we'll get food and warmth, in exchange for this news of the Ruud."

"You mean you want to tell the history? We can't do that?"

Rogget shook his head. "It may be the only thing we have worth anything."

They nodded and bundled up for a spell of rest. But sleeping in the face of a journey into the ice realm would be hard fought, Fenn realized. And he lay watching the clouds in the darkening sky, listening to the crackling fire for hours.

When horses approached, they all darted up, and Rogget struggled to douse the embers left in the fire pit.

Chapter Forty-two

Leah sat in the front room of the inn in Path watching the small village square and the occasional passer-by. Soon they would be leaving for a rustic journey north to the caverns of the eastern continent, and into the hill country. A group of folk had arrived from Ruhm—spelunkers—to join them in what she assumed would be an adventure hunting the kell stone. Yet, she couldn't find any enthusiasm for the trip. She held her journal on her lap and looked at it. She could write as if speaking to her mother, but she found it difficult to stay away from topics that should not be broached. At some point, she realized she was not alone and flinched. Looking up, she saw Prenalin take a seat on a bench next to the window opposite her.

"You have not been yourself, of late," he said. "You are changed since..."

"Since the forest?"

He shook his head. "Before. Since the hunt."

She nodded. "Yes."

"It was not my idea that you would be taken on as aide so shortly before this trip. I felt it wasn't a proper introduction to the position."

She couldn't help chuckling. "No, I would say not."

"Kirche insisted. As soon as you graduated from the Hass school, he said, you were to be hired on."

Leah tilted her head and peered at him.

"What is it?" he said.

"I thought *you* chose me."

"No. You were Kirche's choice."

Her brow furrowed. She distinctly remembered the day in Aaronland, when Kirche had asked her to go up to his room and bring him the ledger and notes from his desk. And there, slightly hidden under a short stack of books, was a note he was writing to his brother back home in Ruhm. He'd said that Prenalin had selected her. He wondered why Prenalin would choose such a pretty girl for his aide.

"Is something wrong?"

"Nothing," she shook her head. More lies. Would they never end?

"I don't mean to speak out of turn, Leah." He leaned forward, putting his elbows on his thighs. "But I would like to offer you some advice."

"I am always happy to take advice from you, Pren."

"You know that I understand your feelings, with respect to the beasts."

She nodded.

"But I told you that you must not speak them. And I can see now that you are struggling with upsetting notions. Doubts have a way of eating away at us."

"You would simply have me not speak them."

"No, more than that. It's not enough to merely not say what is on our minds. We must examine our doubts, our fears, and any thoughts that do not ally with the Hass. And then we must accept that there will always be problems with our thinking. The goal is, and ought to be, to learn not to trust our own doubts and insecurities and instead learn to trust only the Hass."

Leah stared out the window for a time pondering what he'd said. She thought of the flaming tree in the beast forest and considered telling him about it. Would he believe her? Somehow she knew that he would find a way to disregard her find. It was only the Hass for Prenalin. Only the Hass had the answers, and to question Emorah was to question truth.

"But, what if our doubts regard matters of morality?" she said.

He shook his head when she turned to him, hopeful.

"The Hass is the arbiter of morality. It is well enough to think we have it right. But we must allow that the Hass controls the truth. The Hass determines what is good."

"I think I understand," she said. "If my view differs from that of the Hass, my view is wrong."

"Exactly. No matter how much you may feel otherwise."

Prenalin left her there at the window, more confused than before. There had been a short time during which she thought he could be made an ally in her fears. He seemed to think like she did, but was wise enough not to speak his mind where Kirche could hear him. But now she realized she would not be able to share her real feelings with him.

Rubbing her hands together atop her journal in her lap, Leah struggled to come to terms with her lies. She was guilty—she was in debt to so many—the beast lord, Lucas, Pren, and Kirche. How could she think herself moral when she had lied, and continued to lie, to so many folk?

She should tell all, at least to Prenalin and Kirche. She should tell them, at least, what she knew of the kell stone and that she was kin to Dakenruud. What difference would it make, really? And she should tell them how she escaped the beast forest—what she'd promised to the beast lord. But would Kirche send her home to look for the stone? Perhaps he would. She could have a new position within the Hass—she could be the one to find the kell stone. That was it. That was the answer. She must find the kell stone. It was the only way for her to atone—to save her dignity. She would not be a liar if she did so...well, not so much.

Kirche and Prenalin came into the lobby with the porters, Gretchen and Zelda. Xavier, the youngest porter had now been promoted to bodyguard to replace Alphonse and stood small and timid next to Kipling and Redd.

"Shall we make an evening tour of Path, before our trip north tomorrow?" Kirche beamed with excitement; he was already robed in purple and held his mitre under his arm. "Your face is healing quite nicely. You might not need your scarf after today."

"Lord Kirche." Leah stood, cupping her journal at her chest.

"Of course," Kirche said. "You may put away your journal first. Have you done much writing? Have you pieced together any information about the kell stone? Do you know where it might be?"

She froze, stunned, her mouth open, a slight shock on her face. Why would he ask that? Did he know about her lies? How could he? Out of the corner of her eye she saw Prenalin turn his face away from her.

"I..." She paused, her heart pounding in her chest. Even as she knew deep within her soul it was wrong to lie and to keep secrets, that very same conscience told Leah she must not trust in Kirche. Even that thought caused her pain and she winced.

"Are you ill?" Kirche said.

"Forgive me, Lord Kirche. I must tell you something. Something of great importance."

Prenalin turned to look at her, his face drawn and pale.

Chapter Forty-three

You're going to have to stop disappearing," Phil told Lucas as they hiked with the king's guard north through the woods toward the hill country. "We're supposed to be guarding you."

"I was with Sorgood, on an errand."

"Aye, you were with the master of the guard at that time. But where did you disappear to before that?"

"I'm not a member of the guard. I'm a citizen volunteer. I come and go as I please."

"Oh, yeah?" Brinkley said. "Then how come we were told to guard you?"

"You were just supposed to watch me and make sure I don't get into any trouble. You know, get hold of a firearm or something."

Tildon Weeks and Edgar Wolf had rejoined the guard and were happy to have Lucas' company for their tour of duty. They were assigned a perimeter guard north of the Waverly wissenry in Aaronland as Sorgood said that was the most likely reentry point for Fenn Foster and his traitorous abettors. But Lucas wondered how long it would be before they were ordered into the hill country to hunt the kids down and return them by force to Michelruud. He knew the folk would never let King Welk rest until they were certain that the evil bairn was under lock and key...or worse.

Lucas sat at the campfire while the guards marched their perimeter. Movement in a nearby shrub caught his eye.

"Psst there," a small brownie called to him. "I have news."

The brownie waved Lucas over. Knowing the creature would never want to be seen out in the open by the others, he left his cup of bitters by the fire and followed him into the wood.

"You asked that you be brought news of the Hass girl."

"And you are?"

"Pardons." The brownie bowed slightly. "I am Eerf today."

Lucas knelt on the ground and shook the small folk's hand.

"The girl did as she promised and returned the head of Zeelif, who will now be Zeelif forever." He frowned.

"It is a fine name for a memorial."

"We keep watch on Kirche. But there is little we can do should he decide to harm another. Many of the larger beast have come out of the forest to patrol. It is not good."

"No, it is not. But perhaps it is time to take this chance."

The brownie bowed again and trod off into the woods leaving Lucas to concentrate on Quarn, whose scent he'd caught as soon as he'd left the fire. He turned and watched as Quarn emerged from the wood and took his folk form to speak.

"Why do you continue to harass me? Even now that Dag Voorspeld knows of your treachery."

"Voorspeld's opinion doesn't change who you are. As your uncle—"

"Yes, yes, I know. You think being my uncle gives you the right to supercede my parents' wishes. It does not."

"I am your closest kin."

"You are no longer my kin. You have lost your honor with the felidae."

Quarn's face scowled in fury. Without a word, he fell into his felid form and leapt at Lucas knocking him to the ground.

"Och wen mudeh en," he growled.

"You will be outcast." Lucas struggled to keep the cat's drooling jaw from getting to his throat.

Suddenly Quarn roared and Lucas saw an arrow bouncing at his shoulder. The cat leapt off him; Lucas sat up to see the eis assassin pulling another arrow from his quiver.

"You attack my prey," the eis said to Quarn and raised his bow to aim.

"No!" Lucas dove in front of Quarn and the assassin lowered his bow.

"You would protect him?"

"I would protect anyone from senseless murder."

Quarn limped into the woods and Lucas heard his padded feet break into a slow run. He turned to the eis again, who smirked at him. But just as the assassin moved to take aim once more, this time at Lucas, Footman Wolf's voice echoed around them.

"Wissende warrior? Where have you gone to now?" He laughed at his own joke.

"I told you he was always running off," Phil said.

The eis lowered his bow and returned his arrow to the quiver.

"Another day perhaps," he said.

"I would know your name."

"Of course. It is well you should know the name of the eis who will kill you. I am called Na-Atten-tu."

"Why do you take such pleasure in the kill, Atten? You would risk the tenuous peace between our folk."

He laughed. "Perhaps that is the reason."

The guardsmen's footsteps tramped through the wood and Atten smiled at Lucas.

"One day soon, you will be my prize."

He turned and fled into the woods just as Edgar and Phil came upon Lucas.

Chapter Forty-four

Welk paced the library in his heavy robe and slippers. The castle was quiet this evening, no one stirred, not even Dunham. But Welk couldn't stop his thoughts enough to let him read or sleep. He could still see himself turning, stomping in a fury back to his men, Fenn Foster riding off to the east behind him. He'd fumed and shouted orders at his guard like a madman. Where were the horses? Where were their firearms? Why had they done nothing to stop the felidae?

It was only Clutch who could calm him. He'd called to him from where his men gathered up the remains of their dignity and supplies.

"It is done," he'd said. "There is nothing to be gained by rage. The boy is away once more."

Welk sucked in a heavy breath. "He is a sly one, isn't he?"

Clutch nodded and his men began to call to him to leave. They none of them liked being too near a king who could punish them. And so they had parted company.

He'd done as he'd promised Forbes Billings years ago. Welk had sent out the commands to Arnot and Ricker. They would allow the banished to return home and replace all property they could. From that point on, banishment was no longer a punishment to be used against a folk of the Ruud. And if the other kings refused, it would mean war. War, he'd said. The stationer sat at his writing desk frozen.

"War, Sire? You mean me to use that very word?"

Yes, he'd meant it. No more talking. No more pandering, trying to reason, and arguing over who controlled which borders and whose folk took whose sheep. The Ruud could not function as three kingdoms.

And as yet, he'd heard no grumbling against his commands from either Aaronland or Damon Wall. He would soon have the kingdoms of the Ruud united as one.

352

"We must call a meeting of all the representatives in the hills and the Ruud," he'd told Clutch before his men could drag him away. "Will you spread the word?"

"I will. What will be the purpose?"

"We will decide our rights to the hill country, and approach the eis with our demands."

Clutch had balked, but he smiled. "It was good to see you again."

"And you."

Welk turned back to his men, but Clutch had called out once more. "The girl," he'd said. "What will you do about her threat?"

"Nothing."

"But she aimed a gun at the king."

He laughed. And he could still hear himself say it. Where had it come from? And wasn't it true?

"I am no more a king than you are."

Chapter Forty-five

In the dim light of early evening, the kids scrambled behind the boulders and listened as horses approached. Rogget put an arm across the rock as if to hold them back from jumping out and betraying their position. The horses came into their tiny encampment and Fenn couldn't help but peer out at the intruders.

"Oi there'n," Wiley Arbus called out. "T'is that you, Rogget and company?"

Almost laughing in relief, they came out of hiding but the fierce roar of a large brown bear had them frozen.

"Oh, come now, Petunia," Wiley said. He dismounted and walked up to the bear, giving her a hesitant pat on the shoulder.

"That's not Darnit," Grayson mumbled.

"Indeed, no," Bruck said. "That there's Petunia. As fine a bear scout as we ever met."

Wiley laughed. "We wouldn't have rightly known what she was, if we hadn't met with your bear Darnit. Oh, look, she finally smelt him out."

Darnit had let out a grumble and Petunia lumbered toward him. Rogget and the others shook themselves out of their stunned silence and watched as Darnit and Petunia sniffed, nudged shoulders, and got to know each other.

"I think you got a story for me," Rogget said and built up the fire again to warm their guests. Wiley and Bruck Lerned sat with them around the pit rubbing their hands together over the flames.

"Like to thought we'd never find you, at first. And then, what you knows? A bear. And she seemed eager to make her way northeast," Wiley said.

"Aye," Bruck said. "She's got the smell o' Rogget's bear, I told him."

"That weren't your idea. It was mine."

"Nonsense. I said it first."

"And what coincidence. We needed to find you."

"But...another bear?" Sadie said.

Bruck slapped at his leg and fell slightly backward, laughing. "It were the Wretched again. Grindelwell was run off with a few doars he stole off Clutch—to the port. Everybody reckoned he would try to find a boat off to the south as he owed every other folk, and then some, more money than he could count."

"Aye, but instead, he took Clutch's doars and gambled himself into a fine fortune. Paid off his debtors and brought back Petunia. He thought she was all willing to be his partner in crime, but when he stopped walking, she didn't."

"Nope," Bruck said. "She kept right on, through every camp in the hills rooting out jerky, apples, and berries."

"It were Grindelwell what gave us the news."

"News?" Rogget said.

"Aye, we bring big news," Wiley said. "And we thought, what better way to find you than to follow a girlie bear obviously in search of a boy to run off with."

They all turned to watch Darnit and Petunia push their way into the shrubbery and disappear into the night.

"We may never see him back again," Rogget said.

"Amazing news," Bruck said.

"Right." Rogget turned back to the fire. "Let's have it."

"King Welk sent word through the Ruud that he is honoring a writ he signed some twelve years ago."

Rogget gasped. "You don't say?"

"It's true," Bruck said. "Forbes Billings' writ will be honored."

"All the banished are pardoned."

"And what's more, all their property what can be returned to them, will be."

"And how did he get Arnot and Ricker to agree to that?" Rogget said.

"He plain as out ordered them to accept it, as we heard tell it from Grindelwell."

"And Clutch confirmed it."

"You've spoken to him?" Fenn was suddenly nervous.

"Indeed. All the hills are in truce over the news. You never saw so much amity among fighting folk. Here tell a big meetin' is in the works."

"Did you tell them you were coming to find us?" Grayson said.

"Oh, no son," Bruck said. "But I don't think you need to worry yourselves about them."

"Not for another week or so, anyway," Wiley said. "There's going to be much to do about the hills with these changes."

"Aye," Bruck said. "Some of the hill folk are banished. They might up and head home to take on what you call normal lives."

Wiley laughed loud and Bruck joined him.

"Well, that is good news," Sadie said.

Rogget eyed Fenn warily. Fenn knew what he was thinking. Just because King Welk had honored the writ didn't mean he would stop hunting Fenn. As much as Fenn wanted to believe Welk's promise to leave him alone, he trusted Rogget's judgement more.

He, Grayson, and Sadie sat at the fire listening to the three folk talk of freedom and their days of youth until long into the wee hours of the morning when Fenn found himself nodding off to sleep, his hemp rope and charm pulsating warmth across his chest. The amber shard of crystal that Clutch had added to the rope was warmer than his charm and he often thought it throbbed and filled him with a sense of strength. But Father Treacher had once told him about the odd sensations of growing up and he surmised it wasn't the stone at all, but that he was becoming, finally, an adult.

Fenn was awakened by Lucas' screams in his head. And in that place between sleep and awake, he could see him, running forward toward him, screaming, "No!" Lucas reached out to him, to stop his floating away. But Fenn realized, gradually, that he was not floating away. He was being carried.

"Fenn!" Rogget called after him. "Fenn! No!"

Fenn woke, but couldn't move. He was cradled in the arms of a luminous being, shining so bright in the darkness he had to blink. He felt no arms holding him up; it was if he lay on a pillow of air. He tried to feel concerned about this situation, but he was almost giddy as he said to himself, "Kidnapped again." Still he thought he ought to be frightened, or angry. Instead, he was warm; he felt as if all was set to right again. No worries. He was going home.

As he was carried away into the cold darkness of the night sky, he heard Wiley Arbus' terrified scream.

"Angel!"

BOOK THREE

Mark of the Faire

Chapter One

1268 Autumn

Aliara woke, struggling to breathe, coughing... moving, crawling, before she knew where she was. The tent. The tent had collapsed. The child in her womb rolled and kicked. Her legs were on fire; she sat up to beat at them with her hands. Catching sight of an opening, she crawled over Rue-Anna and forced her head out, attempting a gulp of fresh air; the night was ablaze around her. Shouting echoed nearby. Horse hooves pounded the ground. She grabbed at her sister and tried to wake her, screaming her name again and again, but it was no use. She must find their men folk for help.

When Aliara stood outside the tent, she realized there would be no help. Their camp was burning, soldiers rode through smashing and cutting everything—the fine plates and cups for the wedding feast; casks of wine; her sister's wedding gown. Belfen lay motionless several yards away and a young, dark-haired guard stood over his body; he turned to her with a sly grin. When he raised his bow, she fled into the darkness away from camp.

She fell before she felt the sting of the arrow in her left thigh, crashing onto her stomach. Gasping, she caught her breath, stood and ran again. She was an esien, of the realm, kin to the maiden. She could outrun this scrawny folk any other time of life, but heavy with child, her chances were slim.

Another pang caught her in the right shoulder—she screamed but she did not fall. He was getting closer. She had to keep on. She must find a way. Then she remembered the clover and a surge of energy found her as another arrow pierced her hip. This time she fell but gave little time to suffering, darting up again, limping forward toward the patch. She could smell the clover, blooming in the warm night. Not as strong as it would be in later months, but the gemein would be there still.

Finally she felt the clover under her bare feet, struggled through, and fell to her knees. An arrow thumped into the ground just ahead of her. She lay down, exhausted, onto her side.

"Help me," she whispered. "Please."

She could see him, standing just outside the patch, and she thought she saw his smile in the dim light of the moon. The gemein rose around her as she raised her hand. The guard lifted a firearm and pointed it at her.

"Help me," she said.

Aliara watched as a cloud of bees buzzed from the clover and surrounded the folk; he dropped his weapon and shrieked, swatting at his face. He ran, his screams tore at the night all around her as she let herself lie back in the damp flowers and drift out of consciousness.

1280 Autumn

Leah Hallowsing cowered in the darkness, sobbing once again. She couldn't be sure how long she'd been lost, but it seemed weeks. She had little food left, and feared she could not fight off the cave rats again. They followed her as she crawled along the cavern floor, feeling her way, sure she'd plunge off a cliff to her death if she dared to walk; they scurried around her, occasionally nipping and pulling at her skirt. Several times now, one landed on her pack and, screaming, she battled him off. The time would come when it would be more than one. At some point, they'd have her pack and she'd have to consign herself to starving alone in the caves of the east, far from home.

She could crawl no more, she decided; she must rest. Every time she tried to sleep her mind brought her images she couldn't force away. Her father in his closet office, sitting across from her, the shadow of candle flame dancing on his face. "You are kin to the apostates," he kept saying. "What do you think of that?"

And Kirche, smirking. Watching her. She couldn't stop remembering the day she'd nearly told him about her father, about the journal of Dakenruud, about the kell stone.

"I must tell you," she heard herself say over and over again. "Something of great importance." Kirche had stared at her, almost as if he knew what she would say. And she stumbled. "I..." She could no longer remember why she'd thought to tell him the truth—could not recall what had stopped her. Was it the look on his face, the deadness in his eyes? "I'm frightened of the caves," she'd told him. It was a lie...then.

In her moments of hope, which were few of late, she'd see Prenalin —the horror in his eyes as he reached for her other hand, just as the one slipped from his grasp. She could still hear his screams. "Leah! Leah!"

"Oh, Pren," she whispered.

They'd gathered their gear in Path, and rode hard northeast with Kirche's spelunkers, Wivel and Pike. Wivel reminded Leah of the shepherds and cowmen she'd met on school field trips. Thick with strength and tanned, he had the sharp, dark features of a man who lived for physical exertion. And his wife, Pike, as lean and wiry as an acrobat, always a thin straight line of a smile on her lips. They were eager to tour the caverns of the eastern continent and Kirche was only glad to make a quick journey of it.

He'd heard tell of a meeting in the hills between King Welk and the land pirates and deserters of Ruhm who made the place their home. He wanted to get the spelunkers to work, enjoy a bit of cave hunting himself, and then move on, leaving them to search for his kell stone while he and his entourage traveled south to find out what they could of Welk's planned meeting with the eis.

The caverns of the eastern continent rose like a giant collection of sloping ant hills, rocky and brown, surrounded by forest. They'd lost track of the spelunkers within hours, but nobody worried; they were tasked with the find and would meet Kirche back in Ruhm.

"Keep to this path here," Wivel had told them. "It circles back around. Don't go off it or you could find yourselves lost."

And so she, Prenalin, and Kirche hiked in the dim light of the upper level near their campsite, up natural steps and down, in and out of pure rock, sometimes stopping to peer up at slits of sunlight highlighting enormous boulders resting uneasily against one another above their heads.

It happened so quickly, the slip, the tiny misstep that had Leah clinging to the rock, kicking her feet in search of some-thing beneath them to support her. Prenalin reached out and grabbed at her fingers just as she lost her grip. They stared at each other, frozen in time. All sound was muted but for her breath in her ears. Her hand pulled from his grasp like thick sap from a tree and though it seemed to take hours, she knew she only glimpsed his face and it was gone—she slid into the darkness, tumbled deep into the rock, tripping, falling, until the ground leveled beneath her. Prenalin's voice echoed far away, calling her name.

"Pren," she screamed.

He was no more than muffled noise and moving away, falling deeper into silence. She tried to climb out. For what seemed days she tried, until her fingertips and palms were bloodied and raw. She cried out; no one answered but herself.

At some point, she couldn't know how much time had passed, she feared they'd give up on her. It was then she began to move, determined to find a way out. And in her head, her own words did little to comfort her. "I'm frightened of caves."

Frightened. Leah pressed her hands against the sides of her head, forcing the sight of Prenalin's fear away. It wasn't true, she wanted to say. It was a lie. I'm not afraid. They must be searching for her, she promised herself. Prenalin wouldn't leave her to die in the dark.

Chapter Two

Dunham had assured Welk he had better sit on the throne. True, he'd thought as much himself; but now he felt silly, like he was playing at king. A heavy gold, jewel-encrusted crown sat atop his head, the purple velvet robe he wore pulled at his shoulders. He wanted to stand and readjust it, but that wouldn't be kingly. It wouldn't even be fitting for common folk. He winced, just as the representative of the ice realm began his approach followed by five others. They looked more comfortable in *their* refinements. And they glided across the stone floor effortlessly, with cold smiles on their faces.

"Luma, High Advisor to the Queen of the Eis," Chamberlain called out as Luma, pale as death, dressed in white robes, moved forward and bowed before him.

They were rather attached to formality, these eis. Prim, proper, always perfect in their dress and manner. Their smiles always barely there, as if their kindness wasn't meant to be taken too seriously. The eis were legendary for their strength, their resistance to wounds and an ability to heal. Even without the kell stone, while they could be killed, their skill with the bow and sword were formidable; their greatest weakness was in number.

In *The Book of Katze*, Welk had read as much as he'd time for about the history of the beast folk and their kell stone—a stone from which they drew not only strength and greater powers both physical and mental, but also those traits that exist, not in the *beasts* of the southern hemisphere of Kell, but in the *folk*. Katz surmised that the kell which influenced their evolution here in the north did not exist in the southern lands. Indeed, there are no eis, nor angels in the south, according to the explorers who managed to slip through Ruhm's grasp and travel to the Ruud to tell their stories. Nor any brownies, trolls, felidae, or other manner of creatures.

Similar creatures that exist in the south do not appear sentient—a condition the folk who left the south and settled in the Great West long ago wished to have revisited on the beast in the north.

Without their stone above ground in the north, the beast folk had not only grown weaker and fewer in number as the generations passed, but they fell away from their Rad—the beast governmental body. According to Katz, the kell stone forced the Rad, a council the angels and the eis wanted no part of. Only the beast lord, always a felid, could free them from it. Without the kell stone, the beast folk may one day be no more than legend.

"Rise, Luma," Welk said. "You may speak."

Welk smiled inwardly as he watched Luma compose his face for his memorized speech.

"Lara of Eidolon, Daughter of the Snow, Queen of the Eis, wishes to make known her dissatisfaction with the folk of the Ruud and their kings' refusal to remove their kin from her lands. Be warned that had not a most advantageous event occurred for your sake, Welk, King of Michelruud, this emissary would be a declaration of war. But fear not, you have one reprieve. Fenn of the Wasteland, child of prophecy, marked by the faire in infancy has been captured and is held for you now. If you will lead your kin out of our lands, you will have him."

Welk leaned forward, surprised. He expected a general plea, perhaps a threat, especially after the way the usurper queen's previous emissaries were summarily dismissed by his ailing father. But this? They have captured Fenn Foster and wish to ransom him?

"I must ponder this news," he said to Luma. "Please rest and join us in our mid-day meal." He held out his hand toward the set tables, the nobles all standing about watching, waiting, the wine stewards ready to pour. And as if on cue, fat chef came in from the kitchen leading a parade of tray-laden servers and the smell of roasted pig and duck wafted through the air. Surely, even eis could not resist a roasted pig.

Luma and his party bowed before the king. "I thank you for the invitation," he said, "but our queen is eager for your response."

"Very well," Welk said. He leaned back on the throne, put an elbow on the rest to his right and let his fingers scratch and play at his chin.

The boy is marked by the faire, he thought. And yet, the usurper queen would give him up. She does not fear his strength; but then why would she? The boy would have no interest in the eis; at least, not yet.

But this development would work out well for Welk. He was to leave for the hill country on the morrow. He would meet with the land pirates and representatives of those pilgrims from Ruhm and parts beyond, organize, make a stand for their rights to live on land the eis claimed, but of which they refused to take possession.

He chuckled and Luma, in his periphery, took in a deep, insulted breath. Yes, Welk thought, the usurper queen must want war. There could be no other explanation for her deigning to send emissaries to request anything, even the clearing of folk from her land. She and her angel consorts deemed the folk inferior, scum to be removed if possible, and if not, ignored. She wanted war. But without the kell stone, did the angels and the eis have enough power for it?

Welk sat upright and looked to Luma. She knows, he thought. She knows the prophecy. She expects Fenn Foster to find the stone—to wield it, destroy the Ruud, kill the kings. The *king*.

Here Welk laughed and Luma's left eye twitched. Could the usurper queen know of his efforts to unite the kingdoms of the Ruud under his throne? Thus making himself the one and only king—the only target of the prophecy? Nonsense. There is no real prophecy, he reminded himself.

"Tell your queen I will come for him," he said to the troubled Luma.

Perhaps she wants war. Or perhaps she wishes to take Welk as a better ransom. Could she be that ignorant of the tenuous relationships among Michelruud, Aaronland, and Damon Wall? Ricker and Arnot would let her have him—tell her to deal with the folk in the hill country herself, dirty her own, delicate eisen hands. No matter.

"And the folk?" Luma said, lifting his chin, no doubt wishing Welk was not above him on the throne so that he could look down his long, eis nose at him.

"Does the queen of the eis not understand that the winter folk are not from the Ruud? I'm sure she has been informed that these folk have no connection with us."

"They are folk. They are not eis nor angel. They are more your concern than hers."

"Very well. I will come for the lad and on my way I will see what I can do about your folk problem."

Luma waited for more. But there *was* no more. Welk waved a hand in dismissal and the eis and his entourage bowed again and backed away before turning to leave.

"Dunham, you will have to send for Sorgood," Welk said with a smile. "We must pull him from the port and let him know that he is to travel to the ice realm. He should be giddy."

Dunham raised an eyebrow.

"It will be the last I ask of him, before I discharge him from the guard."

Chapter Three

Her footsteps on the spiral stair woke Fenn in the dim light of the tower. The fires were no more than embers now and he saw only shadow as she scuttled across the floor; there was a rustling to her steps, as if she wore a gown and it brushed the floor as she passed. Groggy, he rubbed at his eyes and lifted his head, but she was not on her blanket by the fire on the other side of the room. He knew she must be hidden in one of the other alcoves; but, why?

The girl was there that first morning when Fenn woke to find himself in the top room of a tower, at the back of what he assumed was the ice palace. Though the room was large and round, eight thick stone walls jutted out from the exterior, forming cubbies, three with fireplaces, one with a heavy wooden door, and the other four with windows closed off by thin boards latched with rusty hooks. Only two fires were lit, those on opposite sides of the room—his, and the girl's. He'd nodded, that first day, but she ignored him and he'd gone on to explore on his own.

The locked door faced south and he could see from the window next to it, there was a landing outside it, and a wooden stair circling the tower to the room below. In the center of the room was a spiral stair. Pushing through a thin wooden door at the top, he found himself on a roof with a three-foot stone wall. Stacks of firewood blocked one portion and next to them were buckets, one for food, the other ice. There was a rack over his fire, where he could warm up the bits of meat and vegetables the angels left for them. He had a cup in which he could melt the ice for water.

The eisen was pale, as he'd heard they were, her hair the color of honey and her eyes the dark, angry blue of the wild burr petals that strangled out the white lilies Father Treacher tried to grow in his garden. She wore a hooded, full-length robe the color of straw, but at its bottom rim, a silky, gossamer gown slipped out occasionally and snagged on the stone floor. She said little and seemed to sneer at him when he struggled to chew the tough eleshag, or when he shivered at the icy wind whipping at him from the barely covered windows.

When she cried out in pain, Fenn sat upright, startled. She was still hidden in an alcove, away from her fire. She whimpered and cried again, though this time it was muffled, as if she were trying to hide her torment from him.

"Are you all right?" he said.

She sucked in a deep breath and Fenn scrambled to his feet.

"No," she said. "Don't come near me."

"What happened? Are you hurt?"

362

Here she let out a shrill scream and moaned.

Fenn took a few steps toward the shadows. "What can I do?"

"Nothing," she shouted. "Go away. Back to your fire."

He nodded and crept to the embers in his own cubby where he sat and wrapped his arms around his knees, wincing at her cries.

"Speak to me," she said, finally.

"What about?"

"Anything." Her voice was weak, trembling. "A story."

Fenn's mind went blank. "I don't know any stories."

"Your story then," she whimpered. "Who are you?"

"Fenn Foster, of the wissenry in Path. In the Ruud."

"And how do you come to find yourself imprisoned in the tower?"

He told her about being awakened by Father Treacher in the early morning, weeks ago, and sent away from the wissenry. He told her about Sadie and Grayson, and about Rogget and Darnit. He told her they went into the beast forest and met Dag Voorspeld, about Kwitcher the elf and the troll on the bridge. He told her how he, Sadie, and Grayson snuck all the kids out of Steingefan and how his mark was discovered and he was sent away from the Ruud, to the ice realm, to see the maiden. He told her of the Wretched and his charm and Forbes Billing's writ and Clara. And when he woke in the dawn of the next morning, he could not remember how much he had told, and how much he'd only dreamed.

When he sat up, he found logs had been added to his fire and there in his alcove were two eleshag pelts, a loaf of bread, and a bowl of apples and berries. Across the room he saw the girl in her cubby, curled up at her fire, sleeping.

Chapter Four

L ucas offered Brinkley his extra apple and it was gladly accepted. They sat on the ground while their horses wore their feed bags and waited for the break to be ended. There was much left to do in setting up camp. More tents needed to be staked, fire pits dug—the temperature here in the east, with the spires of the ice palace in the distance, were lower than any of Sorgood's men were accustomed to, they would need to dig them deep.

They were beyond the hills, through the winter woods, on a brief plain nestled at the opening of Kingdom Pass—a path through the towering foothills of the ice realm which jutted up through the ground as if they ached for the sky. They set up camp so close to the palace, they could be seen by the eis guards in their towers, no doubt.

"They got him there in the castle," Phil said to them. "Is that it?"

"That's the word," Brinkley said. "But this meeting here... this ain't nothing to do with the boy of prophecy."

"Too true. I heard the same," Phil said. He took Brinkley's apple from him and tore a large chunk into his mouth before handing it back.

Lucas smiled. He'd heard the rumors as well. Welk of Michelruud got the folk of the Ruud behind him by taking action to find Fenn. Then he'd ordered the freedom of all those outcast to the waste-lands and demanded King Ricker and King Arnot allow it. What choice did they have? The people were now more with Welk than before.

His idea to stand with the people in the hill country against the nonsensical complaints of the eis would secure him as leader of the Ruud, whether in name or not. But what did it mean for Fenn? That was Lucas' concern. Did Welk truly intend to retrieve the boy from the usurper queen? If not, Lucas would do it himself.

"Ho, there," Brinkley said, standing. "What's this?"

Lucas stood and turned, as all the camp did, to see the Hass of Emorah, their purple robes dancing as their horses dashed across the plain, riding in from the north.

"What are they doing out here?" Phil said. "Ain't it time they went back west?"

"Lucas, what do you know about it?" Brinkley nudged him, apple still in hand.

"Why would I know anything? Maybe they want to see how the meeting plays out. There are a lot of folk out here who escaped them, snuck out of Ruhm to live free."

"You think they'll make a try to haul 'em back?"

"Welk would never allow that," Phil said. "Would he?"

Lucas moved away from them, counting the horses—ten. Two laden only with supplies, seven sat with riders, and one, free of any encumbrance. He searched the group, as they neared, for Leah Hallowing and his heart sank when he realized she was not among them. But where could she be? When their horses rode into their burgeoning camp, Lucas was first to greet them, helping with their packs and supplies.

Their Lord Kirche was tired, but showed no sign of a problem. The other, his aide whose name Lucas did not know, was pale and drawn. One of the guards, a frail young man, wiped his nose and rubbed his red eyes as he dismounted and one of the porters, a woman, sobbed as soon as her feet touched ground.

"Enough," Kirche said. "You. Where is your Master of the Guard?"

Lucas bowed. "Scouting the woods nearby, sir. There."

When Kirche had stalked off in search of Sorgood, Lucas turned to the women, one wrapped around the other like mother and child.

"Can I be of any help?" he asked them. "Is someone wounded?"

"We'd like to set up our camp next to yours," the older man said.

"Yes, sir. We can spare some soldiers to help."

The man nodded and moved past him through the camp; the two guards followed, leading the horses, but the women remained, as if moving was too painful.

"Please," Lucas said to them. "What of Hallowsing?"

The younger woman sobbed again, burying her face in the older woman's bosom.

"There, there, Gretchen," the woman soothed. She looked to Lucas, her eyes brimming with tears. "We lost the dear thing in the caverns."

"Lost her?"

She winced. "Indeed. She slipped, fell into the darkness. We searched for an hour or so. But nothing. Not a sound."

"Only an hour?"

Gretchen raised her head and whispered, her voice throaty, "he wouldn't let us—"

"Hush, Gretchen," the old woman warned. "You'll not speak so. If you'll excuse us." She nodded and led the young girl to follow the others.

"That's a bad lot," Phil said coming to stand beside Lucas.

Lucas said nothing, but stood, looking to the north.

Chapter Five

Because there was nothing to do, Fenn spent much of his time wrapped in the eleshag pelts, standing on the roof overlooking the ice realm. To the south, below him, there was a small village in a little valley among the mountains, but beyond the snow-capped peaks he imagined only the sea. Behind him, east, and north, he saw only taller mountains of ice. But west he could see home. The ice palace was set at the eastern end of Kingdom Pass, the only route from the hill country into the realm. And beyond the pass was a brief plain, abutted by a wood, behind which sloping green hills rolled into the forests of the Ruud. His view of home was only interrupted by a taller tower rising up out of the west end of the palace, from which, he imagined, the angels and eis could watch the Ruud.

Sometimes when he gazed out toward home, it was a blur. Other times he could see as clearly as if through a powerful scope. He once was sure he saw Steingefan, but he struggled to keep it in view, as if his eyes had the power of great sight, but it was unused and weak.

The eisen still would not speak to him, even when he thanked her for the pelts and fruit. But he made sure he was first onto the roof every morning to bring in their food; and he always brought in enough extra firewood for her fire as well as his. It took her a few days to recover from her night of pain and once she seemed fully herself, Fenn woke one morning before dawn to find her gone.

He crept about the room, peering into the alcoves, but they were empty. He climbed the spiral stair to the roof but there was no one there. He could see sunlight, turning the darkness into gray just over the mountains in the east and a cold wind whipped at his cheeks. He grabbed a few logs and returned below, adding them to her fire and his. He sat, wrapping himself in a pelt, and waited.

He darted awake the next morning as the door in the roof was pulled open. When he saw an angel climbing down the stairs, he closed his eyes, feigning sleep, though his heart pounded with fear and he struggled to keep his hands from trembling. When he heard the rustling, as of a silken gown against the stone floor, he let his eyes open just enough to see between his lashes and watched as the girl darted into one of the alcoves.

Sitting up, he could see her in the warm glow of the firelight, and the streams of sunlight shining through the slits in the boards at the windows. She sat, huddled against the back wall, hidden behind enormous shimmering wings. They rose and shook and she screamed, gulped for air, one hand clawing at the wall in front of her; she sobbed. Fenn stood and walked toward her, but stopped when one of the wings fell away, leaving a raw, pulsating sore on her back. The wing on the floor shuddered and warped, curled and twisted into a black rotted root while the feathers fizzled into dust. The girl cried out as the other wing broke off and crumpled on the stone.

Struggling to calm her breathing, she glanced behind her, catching sight of him, then turned away. Fenn pulled the eleshag pelt from his shoulders, moved forward cautiously, and covered her with it.

"I built up your fire," he said. He pulled at her, lifting her, and led her into her own alcove where she fell weakly to the floor.

"The bag," she said, her voice hoarse and troubled. "More for you."

She was asleep before Fenn looked back to the cubby. There he found a muslin bag. Inside it were two loaves of bread, four red apples, handfuls of blackberries, and several tarts. He returned it all and set it by her fire before returning to his own.

366

Later in the day, she woke, and Fenn watched as she pulled open the bag and turned to him. Smiling, she stood, pulling the hooded robe over her gown. She brought him the bag and sat down with him in front of his fire. She ripped off a chunk of one of the loaves of bread and handed it to him.

"In the palace," she said, "we would have flavored spreads, cheese, and fruit jams."

He nodded. "In the Ruud, too."

She ate several bites, her gaze on the floor, before she said, "I imagine you would like an explanation."

"You're an angel."

She looked at him. "Angels do not shed their wings. I am angel eisen. My mother was an eisen. My father an angel. While that much is well known...the wings...there are few who know of that. My mother taught me to be cautious. And now, if I am caught with them, I will be chained."

"Why don't you fly away, then? Escape?"

"There are more important things."

"Could you help *me* escape?"

"I cannot carry you. I'm not angel enough for that. But I will help you escape, when the time is right."

"When would that be?"

"You were brought here by my aunt, the queen. She believes you draw the folk king, Welk."

"He promised he wouldn't come looking for me."

"And yet, he comes. He and thousands of folk have gathered in the hills before the realm. Soon they will take Kingdom Pass."

"Not for me."

"Partly for you. Partly for me."

"For you?"

She nodded.

"What would King Welk want you for? He has no say here in the realm."

"It's complicated."

"How complicated could it be?"

She chuckled and ripped off another hunk of bread for him. "The queen," she grimaced, "is seduced by the angel Noromir. If not for him, she would not even be queen. He has turned her against her kind. The eis have no qualms with the folk; it is only always the angels who wish to see them gone from the eastern continent. They would like to see the folk removed back to the southlands, no doubt.

"For years, Noromir has needled her to force the kings of the Ruud

367

to rid the hills of the folk, but her requests have been ignored. This has only succeeded in enraging him. And now, he has you, the great boy of prophecy."

"I am not."

"Of course not, but your folk are too stupid to know it."

"We're not stupid."

"They believe that mark on your arm means you're a prophecy come to pass."

Fenn unconsciously grabbed at his arm. "I'm told it's the mark of the faire, but I don't know what that means."

"It means you are chosen."

"Chosen for what?"

"It little matters now; it's not as if the angels will allow it. You've got folk blood in you. No folk has ever sat on the Rad before. It won't be only the angels who will forbid it. Your King Welk will march the pass and demand you be handed over to him, and Noromir has it in his head to fight him."

"King Welk wouldn't be so stupid as to walk right into the realm... would he?"

"Not ordinarily. I mean, it's not as stupid as it appears. Noromir will draw all his guard out to the pass to meet Welk and his army. Noromir is dumb enough to think Welk will request you be turned over to him in exchange for his promise to rid the hills of his folk. He does not understand that the folk will be ready to fight. It would never occur to him they'd be so bold as to think it, much less try."

"But they will fight? Can they win?"

"They needn't win. They only give time to my guard in captur-ing the queen."

"What?"

She nodded. "While Noromir is occupied, my guard will take the queen by force. We'll be marching her through the mountains to the sea before he has finished his pompous speech."

"Your guard?"

"Yes, of course. My aunt took my throne—another of Noromir's suggestions. But she never had all the guard beholden to her. It's too bad, of course, for she'll have to be brought back into the square and slit in half, once Noromir and the rest of his angels have been ejected."

"If you're part angel, maybe the other angels will fight for you."

"And if they do not, they will go the way of Noromir." She drew a finger across her neck and grinned.

"So, that's where you went at night...to your guards."

She nodded.

"When you get your throne back, you can keep the wings. I mean, it's painful, shedding them, isn't it?"

"My father told me, when I was very young, that the wings were a choice. When you choose them, they do not wish to be rejected. The angel in me, he said, will call to be awakened and it will fight to remain."

"I don't understand," he said. "They're just wings, aren't they?"

"Not at all. They are the essence of the angel. They come with more than the power of flight. See here?" She pulled the sleeve of her robe up to her shoulder and on her forearm, she bore the same mark Fenn had. "My father told me that I am chosen to represent those eis who struggle with the angel inside them. If I give in to the angel, I will not be eisen, nor angel eisen, but fully angel, and my mark will be taken from me."

Fenn was about to ask her to explain the mark—what did it mean to be chosen? But she pointed to his chest and said, "Your charm. It has the mark of the dragon."

Chapter Six

Leah dreamed there was light and the rats scurried from her, their pitter patter like a song in the silence of the cavern. A voice, soft, patient, said her name and she was lifted slightly, hair brushed from her face—she didn't care. Even when she realized it was no dream, as Lucas offered her water from a mug, she didn't care. He could touch her hair; it meant little to her, anymore. There seemed so many things of far greater importance than tiers and their sacred symbols.

"Are you awake?" he whispered.

She nodded. He lifted the lamp to see her face and she sipped more water, her hands trembling. The light was no more than a glass jar filled with lightning bugs, their abdomens glowing gold.

"How did you find me?" Her voice was rough and thick. She moved away from him to sit, leaning against cold, damp rock.

"I am felid. I smelled you out." He grinned and Leah chuckled.

He stood. "Come."

She took his hand, and his offer of a bug jar of her own, and together they walked the cave.

"How long have you been without food and water?"

She shook her head. "I don't know." She wished to tell him they'd entered the cavern for a tour with food, water, and honey mead; they'd planned to stop at a spot the spelunkers had told them about, where the rock opened and a stream splashed down into a pool. There they would stop for a rest, before finding their way above ground. But she was weary and it seemed too many words, so she merely offered him a smile.

"Why were you in the caverns?"

Leah adjusted her pack on her back. "Can you not imagine?"

"The kell stone," he said. "You will not find it here."

"Do you know where it is?"

"No. But you do."

"Do I?" Each time she saw him, he puzzled her. First, spying on Kirche in the woods. She thought he was fourteen at most; but the way he caught her eye and held her gaze, even for a second—he was no boy.

"You said as much to Dag Voorspeld."

She hesitated. "Yes." And in the beast forest, when he helped lead her to safety—still thin, a few inches shorter than she, but somehow older, speaking as one might imagine a man of many years and travels.

"But you don't know where it is, do you?"

"I only said what I had to, to be free. To live."

"I don't think Voorspeld would have allowed the brownies to kill you."

"He had me fooled, then." She smiled. "Did Kirche send you to find me?"

He would not look at her, held his jar up against the dark-ness and continued the trek.

"They left me," she said. "How did you know I was here?"

"Your party arrived at the meeting spot of winter folk southeast of here, against the foothills of the ice realm. The women told me you were lost, believed dead."

"How long did they search for me?"

"Leah," he said, as if to a child.

"Very well. Don't break my heart."

And now. Come into the caverns to find her. Why?

They walked for what seemed hours, sometimes downward, deeper into the cave, but Leah trusted Lucas. She marveled at that feeling, a feeling she didn't have for Kirche, even for Pren. Was it that he was felidae? Had he cast a spell? She didn't care. She would follow him.

"Here," he said, when she felt her legs could carry her no more. "A place to rest."

They sat and let their packs fall from their shoulders. Lucas took her jar of bugs, held both jars up and whispered, "Calm. You may calm. I thank you." The glow dimmed, faded, until it was no more. But there was still light. She turned to see cracks of pale green, glistening through the rocks on which they sat.

"What is it?" she asked him.

"Kell," he said. "We are deep within the earth here. And yet, this is the only spot we know of where the kell can be seen. The rest is much deeper."

"I thought it was a stone. A round, smooth rock, like polished crystal."

"Our stone was made from the kell. Would you like me to tell you one of the stories of how it came to be?"

"Are there more than one?"

He chuckled. "There are a few. No one knows the truth. But I will tell you my favorite."

Leah nodded. "All right."

"It is said the beast came out of the south with a small number of folk, long ago. So long ago it couldn't be written, for there was no language. When the passage was blocked and no more could find the north, time worked its magic and trans-formed the beast into sentient, powerful creatures, and the folk into the angels and the eis. And as beast and folk were at odds in the south, so they were still in the north.

"Generations ago, the angel Morimar returned from an expedition to the south with news of the folk. They were develop-ing a taste for explo-ration, she said, and domination. The sentients balked at the thought of such powerless creatures domi-nating the northern lands, but Morimar told them the folk had developed weapons that could fell a sentient from a distance. Their numbers were far greater than the sentients, and they had diseases that spread like plague and would leave thousands dead. Morimar insisted the sentients prepare for war."

"Your story does not visit well on my people," Leah said.

"There may be some bias in it," he admitted, "but it is the story, nonetheless."

"You are forgiven." She smiled and nodded, bidding him continue.

"The great felid sage Arngram, it is said, summoned all of his spirit and opened a passageway to Mutterede in Krone Mountain at the top of our world, and traveled deep into the kell to its source where he asked Mutterede for help. Mutterede told him to return to the surface and craft a scepter from an ebon tree with an open claw the size of the ancient screech raven, with a six-inch span, and bring back with him a represent-ative of each class of sentient.

"Arngram asked Mutter how he could persuade them to come with him, and she told him to tell them she would craft for them a weapon of such great power, they need never fear any enemy again. And so it was that Arngram was able to bring down into the kell, Morimar the angel,

Lendharf, the faire eis, Kitne, the centaur, Acksen, the wolverine, Orobon the Brownie, Asphor the fairy, and Anpart the duerger.

"All the sentients in the land gathered at the passageway to await the return of their kin, their representatives, with the great weapon. But only Arngram rose out of the passage with the kell stone, a perfect sphere of emerald kell, in the scepter claw on his staff. 'But where are Lendharf and Kitne?' the sentients asked. 'Where is Acksen?' The others, Arngram told them, had placed their hands on the stone and had given their lives so that all sentients would have great power and near immortality."

Here Lucas paused and dug into his pack for a canteen. He poured water for Leah, telling her she must drink, and she obeyed, gratefully. Then he produced an apple.

"Try to eat slowly," he cautioned and went on with the tale. "And so it was that Arngram passed the scepter to the felid Witherwoof and proclaimed him Lord of the Sentient, before vanishing into a wisp of mist.

"It is said that because Arngram brought the scepter to the felidae, the felidae will always be lords of the sentient and the immortals, and keepers of the kell stone. As soon as the stone was on the surface, all of the northern continent felt its power. Every asset they had was increased tenfold including, they would learn, their life spans.

"But it is told that the angel Morimar was skeptical and withheld her palm from the stone when she touched it and so the angels gained nothing, while the greed and jealousy in her fingertips was enhanced. And the angel Loda said, 'Where is the great weapon we were promised to defeat the folk?' To which Witherwoof replied, 'Our mutterede never promised such a thing. She has enhanced our assets so we may live in peace with the mortals.' Loda, believing the angels betrayed, then attacked Witherwoof, but Witherwoof caught the angel's wing in his powerful jaws and ripped it from his body. Loda limped away, vowing vengeance."

Leah winced.

"And so it was that the angels took to the northeast and plotted to capture the kell stone for themselves, thinking they would control the others with it. The eis followed, their hearts cold and their alliance resting with their kin. The others explored their new-found strengths and awaited the folk from the south. But they did not come. For many years, they waited, and their numbers grew; they lived in peace a thousand years."

"A thousand years?" Leah said. "Why did the folk not come?"

"We had lost the angels, and so had no news. We have theories. War. Plague, perhaps."

"But we did finally come."

"In small numbers at first, and so tolerated. As their number grew, the folk told their own stories, and one was that the beast had powers given them by the evil goddess Horatia, sister of Mutterede, banished to the ice kingdoms of the severe north. Deemed unnatural, we were looked upon with great suspicion and plots arose to find the stone and destroy it.

"Legend has it that Witherwoof sought to protect the stone and still allow its powers to be felt. He traveled deep into the northern forest and placed the scepter in a crevice in boulders by a stream and spent his days and nights guarding it. We are told that one day, the angel Serena came to him and brought him a meal of fawn and honey mead. She prostrated herself before him, showed him her stripped wing, a symbol of many of the angels' desire to accept their fault and to ask for acceptance back into the world of their beast brethren. Witherwoof accepted Serena's apologies, ate the meal, and fell into a deep sleep.

"Just as Serena went for the scepter, however, she was attacked by roster fiends, and because Loda had clipped her wing in hopes of fooling Witherwoof, she could not fly and was pecked to death."

"So much violence," Leah said.

"The makings of a great story." He smiled and pulled an apple of his own from his backpack.

"What happened, then? Did Witherwoof awaken?"

Lucas shook his head. "It was the sleep of death. We are told a young folk named Keirgen ran from home to avoid marriage to one of the elites of Rhum. He traveled into the great northern forest of the Great West hoping to find adventure and instead found our kell stone in the boulders by the stream. While they could not destroy it, the folk hid it deep within the earth where we could no longer connect with it. Our number dwindled and we were driven out of the west, to settle here, near to the angels and the eis who despise us. And so the folk not only have our lands, and our power, but also our stone."

"It is a sad story."

"Yes. But the felidae did recoup the scepter and fashioned a new stone face for it here in the east. We await the return of the kell stone." He turned to look at her, a faint emerald glow glisten-ing in his green eyes.

Leah was reminded of Dag Voorspeld and his steady gaze. There was that same question in Lucas' expression. They both wanted to trust her.

Chapter Seven

Welk sat in front of his tent. Some of the soldiers had dug out a long pit for fire and it now glowed and gave off warmth in front of him. Across from the flames sat a line of folk, representatives of the winter folk—refugees from the west—and gangs of land pirates in the hill country. Behind them mingled those not allied with any particular group, there to have their say. And beyond, miles distant, rising against the sky were the blue and white mountains of the ice realm.

"I am Welk of Michelruud," he said. "Welcome. Let us begin by introducing ourselves. There are some here who are not familiar to the others."

He motioned to the first folk seated on the left end, a well-dressed man who sat stiff and regal in his chair. He was the only folk who sat on a chair, except for Welk. The others had pulled over logs from the wood just west of the meeting place or sat on the cold ground.

The man stood, "I am Lech of the Freedom tribe. We reside at the base of the northeast mountain you call Risenpeak."

The next man stood and along down the line they stated their names. Flarneg of Brusia, in the Great West, representing a band of refugees from the Hass. Peter of Luscia, also of the Kingdom of Ruhm. A woman, Dania, fled the west with her college of women, now encamped too near the lower hills of the ice realm, two of her women already seduced and carried away by angels.

"I dare say." The next representative stood and grabbed hold of the lapels of his woolen long coat. "I am Sir Tain, of the tribe you call Breathless, though of course that is not our moniker in the Great West where we are philosophers of the highest order. We are well pleased to have been invited to this committee and, though we are thinkers as opposed to warriors, we will help in any manner we are able, perhaps strategy, if you will."

The next man rose and spoke. "I am Yriton of the lower east hills in the Kingdom of Ruhm. I would caution you not to give the floor to the Breathless philosophers or they will likely never cede it."

"I dare say, I finished my discourse and retook my seat."

"And for that we are all grateful."

"Hear, hear," Welk said. "We are all free to speak at this gathering. And I am sure we will all do well and allow our time to expire as it should." With a nod to the Breathless he turned to the other man.

"Do you have more to say?"

"We of Yriton offer Welk of Michelruud our promise to weigh his proposal with all due seriousness."

The next man rose. "Wiley of the Gnome Eaters. We land pirates are suspicious of any involvement of the Ruud in our parts." He sat again quickly.

A balding, dirty man stood and chewed on his lower lip for a second. "Scary Brutes," he said. "We's here to listen."

Clutch stood. "The Wretched have committed their support to Welk, King of Michelruud. We feel confident you will as well, when you have heard what he has to say."

"Eh." The balding man stood once more. "I did forget my name." And he sat again.

Wiley stood. "This here's Quince of the Scary Brutes."

"Right that." Quince chuckled. "I didn't mean I done forgot it. I done forgot to say it."

"Twice now," Wiley said and took his place on the ground again.

And lastly, a round man struggled to his feet from the ground and smiled at the group. "I represent the Wissenry of the Ruud." He lowered himself slowly and then fell with a thud back to the earth.

"Father Britt of the Wissenry at Cold Sea Port," Welk said. "Very well. Winter folk, those the eis wish to see removed from near their realm, I would like to know your feelings about the Great West, particularly the Hass of Emorah. Where do your loyalties lie?" He glanced to Sorgood, standing at a distance to his left with several of the guard, but the man didn't flinch. Welk was impressed.

"Certainly not with the Hass," Flarneg said.

"Certainly not, I dare say."

"We fled the Great West for the right to think and speak freely. The Hass no longer controls us."

"They're here now," Peter of Luscia said. "I saw them."

"They remain at their camp, Peter," Yriton said. "You needn't fear them."

"They can come listen for all I care," Dania said. "We are not afraid of the Hass."

"They are at the end of the annual tour," Welk said. "They should be on their way soon."

"Back where they came from; suits us," Lech of the Freedom tribe said. "When will you stop the tribute? How can we trust the Ruud when she's still connected to Ruhm?"

"But what does the Hass have to do with this meeting?" Flarneg asked.

"I will come to that," Welk said. "Others of the hills, you are mostly of the Ruud. May I assume you have no loyalty to the Hass?"

Wiley said, "We could not tell you who they are."

"Most of us are unfamiliar with the Hass," Clutch said. "But I can speak for them. If they knew, they would stand against them."

"But this Hass...they are not with the eis are they? What do they have to do with this?"

"This is where we stand," Welk said. "The eis have been content these generations to tolerate folk in the Ruud and beyond, but now claim we draw too near. They would wish folk to move away from the hill country and into the Ruud."

"But they do not defend their lands," Peter said. "They send emissaries to you, a king of the Ruud. To us, they send threats. Why do they not attempt to force us out?"

"Oh, you don't want that," Quince said. "They's gots great powers. They can kill you just by looking at you."

"If that's so, why don't they make us leave?"

"They cannot kill you with a look," Welk said. "Though they threaten war, I believe they are too few in number. They hide there in the ice and so know little of our alliances. They are not prepared for war that might involve Ruhm. They are not with-out advantages, however. Better sight, for one. They see us already from the tower against the great northern peak. They will surely see us at the base of Kingdom Pass, where we will camp before entering the realm."

They all turned to look behind them at the tops of the mountains beyond the hills and a ripple of fear agitated the group.

"They are a strong folk." Welk pulled at their attention. "Keen of hearing."

"Can they hear us now?" Wiley said.

Welk smiled. "Not as keen as that. They have superior bows and arrows. We have some good armor to repel them, though not enough to go around, as Ruhm refuses trade with us on the goods we lack. On their horses, the eis can be deadly. But if we can unseat them, we are the better soldiers. Better yet, if we can make it to the walls of the palace, their horses will be useless in the tight quarters of the outer village."

"But the angels," Clutch said.

"Yes, the have a few angels with them. Deadly creatures."

"Angels." Wiley shuddered. "They done carried off three wee ones and my man Rogget not a week ago."

Welk leaned forward. "All of them?"

"Aye. Left none but the bear."

"Why do they call on you?" Peter said with an apologetic nod to Wiley. "Why not one of the other kings of the Ruud? Why not one of us?"

"Even the eis recognize where the power of the Ruud lies," Clutch said.

"They have something I want," Welk said. "Their threat of war could be merely a ruse. Their hope is that I will force you off the land as a ransom. They believe I have some control over you."

"You must have told them you do not."

Welk looked for a moment at the speaker for the Gnome Eaters, fighting for the right words. "It has been explained to them several times that the winter folk are not folk of the Ruud. But to the eis, we are all the same. They see no difference."

"Is that why we are here, then?" Yriton of Luscia said. "You would attempt to force us off our lands?"

"I would not. I do not propose that you leave the eis lands. I propose we fight them together and let them know that if they cannot defend the outer hills, they have no claim to them."

"How are we to fare against them?"

"You will find them a worthy enemy," Welk said. "But we can show them we are willing to fight together to remain in the hill country."

"And why do you fight for us, Welk," Yriton said. "What do you want from us in return?"

"I want only good terms between our lands. We of the Ruud can offer you help in establishing law and order."

"And what if we don't want law and order?" Wiley of the Gnome Eaters said.

Many of the others grumbled and Welk raised a hand to quiet them.

"Maybe we do," Dania said. "Maybe we tire of the constant battling among the pirates and their threats against our lives and property."

"We leave you winter folk alone, mostly," Wiley said.

"Some of you do; but not all," Flarneg said. "Perhaps we need to form a government here."

"Oh, why yes," Sir Tain said. "That reflects beneficial to all so long as all our claims are secured."

"And what of our right to live free of government?" Wiley said.

"A government that allows the broadest freedoms for folk could suit you, could it not?" Welk said.

"A government may begin with the noblest of intentions, but it always ends up squelching rights and taking more power for those who serve it."

Strong words, Welk thought, for a man traipsing about the hills wearing stolen clothes. "I think we can manage a solution in which everyone may live peacefully."

"How is that?"

"Would you be satisfied if the winter folk carved out a piece of land and set up government? What harm would that cause you, except to forbid you from stealing from them without punishment?"

"Aye," Clutch spoke up. "The hills east of Damon Wall and the Plains of Glisch could be free of government, if Dania and her women's college are willing to move. Any who distrust government would still be free to live as we wish there. The settlements of winter folk and those of the wastelands could set up their governments in the hills north of Aaronland and the fertile lands north and east."

"But they'll be setting police forces against us, Clutch," Wiley protested.

"Why would we do that if you leave us alone?" Dania said.

"Well said." Welk smiled at Clutch. "Your victims have a right to organize against you."

"Aye," Clutch said with a smirk.

"So I propose we take a fight to the eis; we show them the winter folk will not move and folk do not fear them. What say you all?"

One by one, the folk stood and pledged their support to Welk, a king of the Ruud.

"And what of the Hass," Wiley said. "You were to come to that."

"If it were to come to war with the eis," Welk said, "Ruhm may offer aid, or we may find ourselves desperate to ask for it. I would, as King of the Ruud, forbid such association."

"Yes, yes," Dania said. "As much as we might need the help of a stronger power, it would only lead them to take control of the eastern continent, or at the very least, dominate us more completely than they do the Ruud now."

"But there are three kings of the Ruud," Clutch said.

"True," Welk said. "But it is not only that the people of the hills and the wastelands must unite with the Ruud against the eis; we must all together present a unified front to both the eis and Ruhm."

"And you propose we stand under your banner," Dania said.

Welk nodded. "I do."

"And what do the other kings of the Ruud think of that?" Yriton said.

"What do we care?" Clutch said.

"Where are they?" Flarneg said. "The eis deal with Welk."

"Too true," Clutch said. "And we are told Ruhm itself sees Michelruud as the dominant kingdom in the Ruud."

378

"I would tell you," Welk said, "to show you that my intentions are good and I mean to be only honest with you, that the other kings will arrive before we make for the ice realm. They would certainly have objections to this notion."

"It would be better to have a settlement on the issue before they arrive, I would think," Yriton said.

"What?" Sir Tain said. "No debate? Would we not wish to hear an offer from the others? Think mightily on the—"

"The way I see it," Yriton said, waving the representative of the Breathless away, "Welk brings us this proposal. He called on us and treats us as equals. Even the eis and Ruhm see Welk as King of the Ruud."

"I propose it, then," Dania said. "Though I can't say I am too taken with the idea of kings, I am happy to ally with Welk, King of the Ruud, where it benefits us both."

"Hear, hear," Flarneg called and the others joined him.

Welk turned to Clutch and offered the slightest smile.

Chapter Eight

Fenn grasped his charm. "It's a dragonfly," he said absent-mindedly.

"It is the symbol of forbidden love," the girl said, smiling. "You are quite young for such a thing, aren't you?" She laughed and it sounded like tinkling glass.

"What's your name?" he asked her.

"I am Brenna."

"Brenna." Fenn smiled.

"Daughter of the Snow, Queen of the Realm, Maiden Faire, if you please." She giggled.

"You're the maiden?"

"Alas, I am. It is a title I look forward to giving up. But I don't think I shall find a *forbidden* love. Too tragic."

"Father Britt told me to come to the ice realm, to see the maiden."

"For what purpose?"

"He said you might know my mother; if you hold my charm...you will know. He thought you could help me."

"Did he?"

Fenn nodded.

"This Father Britt—he is of the wissenry?"

"Yes."

"I have heard much of them."

Fenn pulled the hemp rope from his neck and handed it to her. She held the charm and the amber rock in her hand.

"Where did you get them?"

"The charm was my mother's. It was stolen from me for a while, and when I got it back, it had the red stone with it."

"I have seen the amber kell before; the angels have some. How long have you had it?"

"Not long. Why?"

"It's nothing." She let the stone drop from her palm and closed her hand around the gold charm. "Do you know the story of the dragonfly, then?"

"They have some in Aaronland, in a greenhouse."

"Yes," she said. "There was a prince of Aaronland, many generations ago, who lost his wife, as it was told. Grief stricken, he traveled to the ice realm; some say he wished to freeze to death. But instead he met an eisen who fell in love with him. Her name was Avrileis."

"Is this a kissing story?"

"I can leave out the kissing, if you like," she said. "Avrileis returned with the prince and lived for a time in Aaronland where she came to love the dragonflies he kept in his garden. But his father, the king, was unhappy with the match. Their children, he reasoned, would be folk eis, unnatural. They would be shunned and banished. And neither would their children be welcomed *here*. We do not tolerate split folk."

"Aren't you...split?"

"I am split of angel and eis. It is the folk part that is not tolerated. Do not look at me that way; I didn't start it."

Fenn smiled. "I suppose not."

"Avril could not bear the thought of causing pain to her prince; she would not ask him to live in the wastelands and she would not have her children treated as unnatural. So, she returned to the eis. The prince, vowing to love only Avrileis for the rest of his life, gave her a glass jar filled with dragonflies as a parting gift. Since that time, the dragonfly has been the symbol of the forbid-den love between eis and folk."

"Does that sort of thing happen a lot?"

"Much more often than you would think." She took his hand and placed his charm on his palm. "Tell me what visions the charm has given you."

He shook his head. "Only a few. I see a man, his back I mean. I see a woman's hand grasping a wissende's robe. Some-times I see her face. I hear her pleading for her child."

"It is as I suspected," Brenna said. "The charm is not your mother's."

Chapter Nine

How long was I lost?" Leah asked Lucas on the evening after their first ride toward the meeting place.

"About six days," he said. "I left to get you as soon as your party arrived at the encampment. It's a good three days' ride, though I made it in less time. I only had the one horse and didn't have to stop as often."

Leah stopped poking at the fire and looked at him. "Did you at least stop to sleep?"

He shrugged. "I will sleep tonight. I feel I owe you an apology; I could have gotten to you faster. Even as folk, felidae are fast. If I hadn't brought the horse..."

"Could you not have taken your felid form?"

"I have not entered that time of my life, no. The felidae once lived all their lives as folk, only to transform when their time was done. My parents wished that tradition for me."

"So you brought the horse because I would require one?"

"That, and it would have taken a week to get back on foot with you in tow." He grinned at her.

"I can run," she said, "but I'm no match for a felid."

They slept in an open field of grass sheltered against the cold autumn winds by blankets Lucas had brought along. Leah lay awake for hours after Lucas' soft breathing told her he slept, staring at the clear night sky full of pinpoints of light. There was a story told to her at the Hass school in Ruhm. The lights were the spirit eyes of the greatest followers of Rett, watching, always watching, ready to choose who among the living would be worthy of joining them in the afterlife. And what was it her father had told her?

"Eyes? Nonsense. Have you not peered into the night sky with the scope? Go out again this evening and watch the twinkling lanterns in the dark sky. Whisper a greeting. For somewhere, on one of those lights, a pretty little folk such as yourself is looking up, and wondering what your light might be."

"Hello," Leah whispered to the sky. She put a hand to her lips to stifle a homesick sob.

As the land passed under the horse the next morning, Leah found herself wishing Kirche, thinking her dead, had left for Ruhm. She didn't want to see him again, nor Prenalin. They would read her face, see there her doubts—more than that, her rejection of the Hass. It had been seeping in, somehow, since the meeting with her father in his little office before she left for the eastern continent. Those adoring eyes with which she'd looked upon Kirche every day had dimmed over time and now she knew there would be no love left in them. Perhaps Kirche wouldn't notice; he rarely noticed anyone but himself. But Prenalin would know. As soon as he caught sight of her, he would know they'd lost her.

"We will arrive tomorrow, I should think," Lucas told her by the fire their second night. "I believe the Hass is still in the Ruud, but if not, I will get you to a boat."

She nodded. "I thank you, again. For everything."

"It was no trouble."

"You jest. I would have died in the caverns if you had not come for me. I will never be able to repay you."

"What price your life, Leah? There is no payment due, but that you live."

"I do have something for you," she said. "A small token."

"I will accept no payment."

"It is but a story."

He smiled. "That I will take, gladly."

"When I was a little girl in Ruhm, my parents allowed me to attend the Hass school. I never knew why, really. All of my friends attended the common school. The Hass school only took those students who could pass a rigorous test of intelligence, as rigorous as one can be for small children." She looked across the fire with a grin. "But none of my friends even tried the test. I do not remem-ber asking to take it, or to attend the school, but my father has told me over the years that I begged to go."

"You sound doubtful."

"I am, but then, I am finding myself unsure of so many things of late. It spreads, this doubt, like a vine. Anyway, I went and was thoroughly, I think, indoctrinated with admiration for all things Hass, most especially our Lord Kirche."

"I can see where he would turn a girl's eyes."

Leah picked up a tiny pebble and tossed it at him over the fire. "I didn't mean that." But she couldn't force the smile from her face. "I studied diligently and behaved impressively, I must say. And I told my instructors I wished to be not just an historian of Ruhm, and work in the libraries and museum, but *the* Historian of Ruhm. I wanted to oversee the libraries and the museum. I thought being named Aide to the High Priest was the first step in that direction." Her voice faltered.

"And now?"

She shook her head. "Before I left to come here for the annual tour, my father sat me down in his office and told me a truth that has changed everything. I wonder now, if he knew it would—if he knew what I would find here in the east."

"Can you tell me?"

"Yes. And it is my gift to you." She gazed at him and was reassured that she was right to tell him. "I am kin to the great wissende, Michelruud, who left Ruhm generations ago with the kell stone."

Lucas sat straighter, his brow knit together and he looked as if he were going to speak, but he let her continue.

"I'm told Michelruud retrieved the stone from the mines of Galdred, where it had been hidden, and was planning to return it to the beast here in the east."

"Our grandfathers felt it returned to surface; they believed it would be found. But they were weakened by the generations without it."

"And of course, Michelruud did not return it to them. I didn't know why until I read the history book at the stationer's in Path."

"The big book on the front table?"

"No. I found another, in an office. I wasn't supposed to be in there, of course. I didn't mean to pry. I'd no idea what I was reading."

"*The Book of Katz?*"

She nodded.

"I confess to you, then," he said. "I have also read the history, though it is a forbidden book. And so, you know that upon arriving here, the folk, fearful of the beast, and of being so far from Ruhm, begged Michelruud to be their king—to protect them from my kin."

"Yes."

"And you know about the devices they constructed to capture and murder my kind?"

"But still they could not defeat you and needed help from Ruhm. In exchange for an army and weapons, Michelruud was to give the kell stone to his brother, Dakenruud, who had remained loyal to the Hass."

"This is why my folk have long believed it to be hidden once again in the west."

"Perhaps. My father told me Daken was commissioned to travel Kell and hide the stone; he was to tell no one where. When he returned home, he first went to his family and gave his brother Abueruud a journal of his travels. Two days later, he was taken by the Hass and never seen again."

"They couldn't let him disclose to his family where he'd hidden it."

"It's worse than that, I'm afraid. I heard it from Kirche that he was tortured. He would not tell even the Hass its place of hiding and he never did. They murdered him."

They were silent for a moment and Lucas lifted his face to the dark sky before looking at her. "The journal," he said. "You think he confessed it."

"I believe that was what my father was trying to tell me. I can feel it now, just as I did when I spoke with him, but didn't understand. He was trying to see how much he could reveal to me—how loyal I was to the Hass. In the end, he knew better than to reveal all."

"Do you know where the journal is?"

"I do not. But my father must know."

"When you told Voorspeld you would find it and return it to us, is that what you meant to do? Go to your father, find the journal?"

She shook her head. "Not at the time. I only wanted to get out of the forest alive."

"But he believed you wanted that."

"Yes, of course. I forgot. I'd already decided that if I could find the journal, and retrieve the stone for Kirche, my place as historian would be set. So, I suppose I did want to find the stone."

"What will you do now? It's a dangerous thing to be so close to the Hass and betray them."

"Perhaps my chances of finding the stone are better in my position. What if my father intended it all along? Maybe he knows where it is, but only a member of the inner circle can retrieve it."

"Would your father put you in such danger?"

She shrugged. "I confess, I cannot say. I thought I knew him— thought I knew myself—but I feel as lost and confused as I did deep within the earth in the darkness."

"You know what the kell stone means to me and to my folk. But I would not have you risk your life for it."

"Especially as you've gone through so much trouble to save it." She smiled.

"True enough," he said with a laugh. "The stone is ours to find."

"No," she said. "My folk stole it from you. It is our place to rectify the crime we committed."

"Then I will help you. I will follow you to Ruhm."

"Am I to allow you to risk *your* life?"

"You can't stop me, if you must know. And now I will give you a gift in return. No"—he held his hand up to stay her objection—"it is a trifle thing to folk, but I hope you will use it."

"You have already given me my life. Nothing you give now could compare."

"Nonetheless, I give you my name. I am called Frieden."

Leah blushed. "Frieden." Sighing, she shook her head and turned to the darkness surrounding them. "And once again, I am indebted to you."

When he laughed, she looked at him across the fire. "It is your plan to keep me thus; I see it now."

"I confess; I am enamored."

Laughing, Leah searched the ground at her feet for another pebble.

Chapter Ten

Dunham brought two covered plates of roasted pig, vege-tables, warmed bread, and gravy into Welk's large tent from the kitchen set up several yards away and set them on the small table where Welk sat across from Clutch.

"Thank you, Dunham," Clutch said with a nod.

"You are welcome, Sire." Dunham bowed and left them to eat alone.

"You won them over, Welk," Clutch said as he pulled apart his bread. "But you do not give them all the facts."

"They do not need all the facts. You know as well as I we ought to keep as much to ourselves as possible. But I will tell *you*, at least, this: I will aid the maiden against her aunt."

"You are sure she has not been killed?"

Welk chuckled. "The usurper dare not enrage her eis folk doing such a thing. The maiden lives in the palace under guard. My spies tell me Lara has been seduced by the angels and is overconfident in her power; but even so, it's unlikely she would harm her own kin."

"So it is only the usurper queen we fight."

"Perhaps. I believe the maiden, unlike Lara, is ready for peace and compromise. But it is Lara's relationship with the angels that is most troubling."

"They are the source of the problem?"

"They were always cruel, bitter creatures, even before folk came to the east, so I have come to understand."

"But what of this business with the boy? Do you not want the others aware of him? When the eis attempt to hand him over, will the winter folk not feel as if they've been used ill?"

"You may be right. Why don't you spread a little rumor that the boy is what the eis hold from me. Certainly they would not begrudge me possession of the child of prophecy; he's better off with us than with the immortals. The soldiers know of the boy already, of course. They may do the job for you."

"You are a sly one."

"I learned much from my father."

Clutch leaned back and laughed hard. "Indeed, more so than I. Should you ever have children, I hope you will not emulate him. It was because of him we found ourselves in the hill country together thieving and warring."

Welk smiled. "Those were the best times of my life."

"What?" Clutch laughed again. "You don't prefer the warm soft bed, the fire in every room, the lavish meals?"

Welk looked at the plate before him. "Ah, well, maybe so. But there is a pressure in being king that is not welcome."

"Come now," Clutch teased him. "If it is so stressful, why did you enlist the loyalty of the winter folk in gaining control of the entire Ruud?"

"I confess," Welk said, "it is a ruse."

Clutch's smile turned and he furrowed his brow. "What's this?"

"Do you remember what I said to you when we met at Steingefan last? On our parting."

"Remind me, for I've no idea what you're going on about."

"I told you I was no more a king than you are."

"I know you are the king; there is no doubt."

"That is not what I mean."

"No?"

"I cannot say why I said it to you. I wasn't thinking it. But after the words were out, it began to gnaw at me. A vision of a different way of living."

"You see visions, now?"

"Do you not?"

Clutch shook his head. "Visions are for kings and boys who were prophesied. Not tramps and pirates."

Welk shook his head. "You chose your lot."

"I did. And when I did so, I forsook visions. Tell me yours."

"For the Ruud. Do you not ever see it? One whole, unified realm. Stronger, healthier. No more bickering among cousins. All working toward a common goal."

Clutch chewed silently for a moment eyeing Welk with something of a smile. "No. I never had that vision. But, it was not mine to have, was it? I was not first born. I was not to be a king. I am only a pirate and a rogue."

Welk sighed. "By choice."

"And what were my options? No, this is the best life I could have chosen for myself."

"And now you are a legend."

"I am not that folk, anymore, and I will not embrace a good legend. A protector of travelers, of all things. I would try for something much more sordid. I want to be remembered for my evil ways." Clutch smiled broadly.

Welk laughed. "You aren't as vile as you like everyone to believe. No, I think you'll be stuck with being remembered as a good sort of folk." He sighed, saddened. "I did enjoy our time together here in the hills."

And for a long time they were both silent and distant.

Finally, Clutch spoke again. "But you said that was a ruse...a unified Ruud."

"The ruse is that I wish to be king."

"If not you, then it will be Ricker or Arnot."

Welk shook his head. "No one."

"No king? Why would they abide that?"

"I could see to it."

"But why?"

"Because we were not meant to be kings. We were once wissendes, not rulers."

Clutch stared at him, his fork raised almost to his mouth, a piece of meat dangling from a tine. When he dropped it onto his plate and fell backward with laughter, Welk couldn't help laughing with him.

"Well, I cannot stand against that," Clutch said, wiping his chin with a cloth. "I despise rulers, after all."

Welk's face fell as the words reminded him of his father, Evan, and the evil thing he'd done. He turned his gaze from Clutch and tried to force Rue-Anna's face from his mind; it only ever brought suffering. But she refused to yield, and he thought he felt a change, however slight.

"They would be happy for us now, I think," Clutch said.

Welk shook his head. "I do not wish to speak of them."

"It still pains you."

"Yes. Does it not you?"

Clutch shook his head. "I think, no. I found my peace with it. They were not like us. They were too perfect, too fair, too delicate for the likes of rogues, be they pirate or king. And the life I have chosen...I can freely live with her memory and never need consider marriage again."

Welk's jaw hardened. Clutch's meaning was clear. As King of the Ruud, Welk would have to marry and produce an heir. He would forget his beloved Rue and bind himself to another.

"Another reason to abolish the kingdom," Welk mused.

"I did mean to tell you something—"

Welk held up his hand. "I do not wish to speak more of our losses. Let us move on to another subject. I have a story to tell you."

"A story? Very well, regale me."

"Did you know that the history of the Ruud we spent so much time trying to avoid reading—"

"I believe I managed to avoid learning to read just to avoid it."

Welk chuckled. "Well, that history is false."

"False?"

"I have recently come into possession of the true history of the Ruud."

Clutch poured more wine into his goblet, sat back in his chair and said, "Ah, then, it was well and good that I did not bother with reading it. Tell me about it."

"It would seem much of what we know is not true. For instance, folk were not the first creatures on the world, not put here by Rett, the god of the Hass, or any other god."

"We never worshiped gods here, but we did assume we were first."

"According to the history, it was Michelruud who discovered the truth that the beast was first in the land and folk emerged from one of their ancestral lines. He learned this from sources he found in trades with a tinker, one of those who often brought treasures of books and discoveries to the wissendes. I haven't time to tell you all now; the important thing is, it was that truth and his refusal to recant it, that forced Michelruud from Ruhm. And believing the beast to have been wronged, he first intended to restore to them their kell stone, but once he tasted the same sort of power that drove him from Ruhm, instead he allowed the capture, torture, and murder of thousands of them."

"The kell stone is real?"

"Indeed. But not here in the east; at least we know Michelruud bartered it back to Ruhm in exchange for their help in forcing the beast into the forests and outskirts of our realm."

"Do we know what power the stone gives them?"

"It makes everything about them stronger, better, apparently. Gives them longer life; makes them more fertile. Their numbers have dwindled over the generations without the stone. I am certain *that* alone was enough to set them at our mercy."

"If the stone is returned to them, it could be the end of folk."

Welk mused for a moment and took a sip of wine. "Perhaps. But if that be so, we no doubt deserve it."

"And the boy with the mark? What is his part? Is there really a prophecy?"

"Of course not. But folk have a funny way of doing things they are convinced they will not do. I don't know why I fear it, but I do. I'm afraid he will find the kell stone and return it to the beast. I fear he is indeed on a prophetic mission, certainly not by design, but by choice, or by coincidence."

"He's just a boy."

"From the stories I am hearing, I am not the only folk who believes he will do this. The beast lord, Dag Voorspeld is it still? I hear he has set a spy to follow the boy. And the eis. Yes, I am certain they took him, not to ransom him, but to see if he is who they think he is."

"But if there is no true prophecy—"

"The future cannot be foretold."

"Why would the beast and the eis believe this?"

"He has the mark of the faire. A mark that until I read the true history, I thought only designated him as one of them."

"What more could it mean?"

"Did Aliara never tell you?"

Suddenly there was a roar from outside.

"Oh, yes," Clutch said. "I forgot. What shall we do with the bear?"

A gunshot, a yelp, and another roar ended their conversation.

Chapter Eleven

Brenna refused to tell Fenn more of the charm, pleading the need for rest.

"I will tell you the story of the charm when I have more strength," she said. "You must give me time."

He spent his days on the roof. With the warmth of his charm and the eleshag pelts Brenna had given him, he was able to spend longer hours there, watching the gathering of folk at the base of the pass. When he first spied them, he nearly waved, assuming they could see him as well as he saw them. But he realized, as he learned to focus his eyes closer and farther, they were too far away. This must be an eis gift, he decided. Clara was right. Despite what Brenna said, his mother must have been an eisen.

One day he was particularly tired and irritated. Brenna spent her time lying by her fire, sometimes it seemed she whispered poetry to herself, other times she stood at one of the windows and spoke quietly. But she refused to tell him the story of his charm. She hadn't disappeared again and he was glad. The pain she endured in shedding her wings was difficult for him to bear; he was unable to help and he hated the feeling.

He looked out toward the encampment of folk and cried out, "Sadie. Grayson. Where are you?"

"Fenn?" He heard Sadie call from below, as if from within the tower.

Then, "Fenn?" She was at a window, shouting out into the cold afternoon air.

"Sadie?"

He walked the perimeter of the roof, looking down, until he saw her.

"Fenn!" She laughed and called to Grayson and his head appeared.

Fenn let out a whoop of joy; how glad he was to see them. Sadie's brown hair hung down, dangling beneath her as she smiled up at him.

And Grayson, his dark hair and eyes, blacker it seemed against the backdrop of the ice, laughed and called out to him. "How long have you been up there?"

"I'm in the top room, just below the roof. Been here for at least a week. Maybe two. I've lost track."

"We've been here nearly the same," he said. "They took us first to the queen. She badgered us something awful."

"That's the truth," Sadie said. "Threatened to chain us in a dungeon if we didn't tell her everything we knew about you and the prophecy."

"What did you tell her?"

"Everything of course," Grayson said. "We were no match for her, I'm afraid."

Fenn laughed. "It's all right. There isn't much to tell. What of Rogget?"

"We don't know," Sadie said. "He and Wiley fought off the angels, but it did no good."

"It was the strangest thing, Fenn. I knew I should care, but I didn't."

"Same here. It's some sort of angel spell, I think."

Fenn realized Brenna was beside him. She leaned over the wall of the roof and said, "What's this?"

"My friends. The ones I told you about."

"Why were they brought here?"

"They said the queen questioned them."

"Who is that with you?" Sadie said.

"Brenna's a prisoner, too."

Fenn nearly told them Brenna was going to free them and only stopped himself just in time. They told him about their guards, who live in the tower and traveled to their room daily with food and water, but refused to speak to them or answer any questions.

"Do you think we'll be kept here forever?" Grayson called up to Fenn.

Brenna put a hand on his arm and he nodded to her, know-ing he had to be careful. "Not forever," he said. "Maybe just until the prophecy thing blows over."

"It's not so bad," Sadie said. "The fire is warm and the food is good."

"Why don't the guards bring us the food and water?" Fenn asked Brenna. "Why do angels leave it on the roof?"

"My aunt believes I am too powerful for her eis guards. You, however ...are a puzzle. Unless she knows you are split."

"Would that mean I'm powerful?"

"It would, indeed. But just as I did not know of my wings until my father taught me how to grow and shed them, you are likely not to know of your skills until they are required of you."

"What are you two going on about?" Sadie called out. "Let's think up a game to play, to pass the time."

"I know," Grayson said. "Choose and guess."

"Choose and guess it is," Fenn said. "Do you know how to play?" he asked Brenna. And for a long time, Fenn forgot he was trapped in a tower in the ice realm; he forgot King Welk would march the pass and demand the queen hand him over; he forgot that Brenna told him his charm was not his mother's.

Chapter Twelve

Leah struggled to decide if this was the reception she'd expected. For while she told herself as she and Lucas approached the encampment that Kirche, even Prenalin, had proven they cared little for her by spending so little time in search of her, and not sending anyone after her, she still found herself surprised at their easy acceptance of her appearance before them.

Kirche, after acknowledging her return with a nod, leered at Lucas, as if he'd rather the boy hadn't rescued his aide—as if he was not happy with his actions at all. Prenalin seethed with some emotion, but he controlled it well enough that Leah dared not assume it was relief or pleasure. Only Gretchen, Zelda, and Xavier let their happiness be known.

Leah allowed Gretchen to take her hand and lead her to a tent. She cast a glance at Lucas and he offered her a smile before he left. The tent was empty, only just erected. She was given a bed roll and a pillow and told to rest, but she could not. Instead, she asked for her things, worried they'd been left off somewhere on the trail from the caverns, or sent to Path to be packed in her trunks and shipped home to her parents. The latter was clearly the better outcome, but Leah wanted little more at the moment than to have her journal in her hands. She knew there was more in it that she should have removed, but she didn't expect to be lost from her party yet again and was too trusting that no one else would see it.

When her luggage case was brought to her, she rummaged through it, disappointed, then fearful. Her journal was gone. Just a fluke, she told herself, nothing to worry about. Gretchen probably took it for safekeeping, that was all. But when she found the girl at the kitchen tent and questioned her, she would only cower and shake her head.

"Leah."

She startled and turned to find Prenalin, his face still cons-trained.

"Kirche wishes to see you."

He turned abruptly and she followed, dread rising up in her throat. She hurriedly ran over her journal in her mind. What had she written? Certainly, she'd mentioned Daken; that much she'd have to own up to. But Daken's journal. Had she told that?

Kirche sat cross-legged on a large pillow in his spacious tent and motioned for her to sit opposite him, while Prenalin remained standing at the door flap. As soon as she put her hands in her lap to hear what Kirche had to say, he pulled her journal from behind him and she tensed noticeably.

"You are wanting this," he said, holding the book out for her.

She took it and felt her face grow hot; she could not look at him, nor Prenalin, only at the book in her hands.

"There are two things I must speak to you about," Kirche said.

She nodded, preparing to beg forgiveness for keeping this decidedly important information from him, knowing she must convince him she was still loyal to Hass.

"First, I imagine you have been left wondering why you were chosen as Aide to the High Priest. It is unusual for one with so little experience to have the position."

"Yes, my Lord," she whispered. No, she'd believed she was chosen because she'd shown herself to be worthy. She cringed at her own arrogance.

"It was because of your father, I'm afraid."

Here she looked at him. His blue eyes were cold and unreadable as usual. So leveled and simple he was. But was there turbulence beneath the bland facade?

"When I was named High Priest, I set out on a mission to unite Ruhm. She has lived with a schism since your ancestor, Michelruud the Betrayer, left us for the eastern continent. There have existed within our midst those still loyal to him, and to the ways of the wissendes he represented." He paused, as if expect-ing a reply of some kind, but Leah had nothing to say. "My thought was to bring these divisions together—to unite them through a common bond. We are as feuding families who only need two young lovers to force them to see reason, to see that we do better united, than torn." Again, he waited. Leah nodded, but could not fathom what he might wish her to say. "And so you were chosen to be my bride."

She sputtered, her eyes flying open as if they'd been closed tight and now hungered for sight—as if she'd slept and now was startled awake. "Your what?"

"Ancestor of the betrayer and the High Priest of Hass."

"I don't understand." She turned to Prenalin but he would not meet her eyes.

"It is so simple, you see," Kirche nearly purred. "You will speak for those who followed your father, those who still work against the Hass. As your father's heir, they will look to you for guidance. And you will lead them, with my help, to turn away from their treason, turn back to Hass. With your help and theirs, those who will not return to Hass will be found and purged."

"Purged?"

"Hass cannot lead the folk to paradise when there are demons in our midst."

"Demons?"

"They steal from us the hope of our folk. They spread deceit and turmoil, nothing more. Surely you agree that if we are to have peace, those who work against peace must be eliminated."

"But marry you?"

"As your father's heir, your willingness to embrace Hass, to extol its virtue, will convince them of its benefits."

"Lord Kirche, begging your pardon, but, even if my father has followers, why would they turn from him to listen to me?"

"Ah, well, that is the sad part. But we must get to it. I have already sent word that your father is to be arrested."

Leah gaped at him, forgetting herself. "On what charges?"

Kirche chuckled. "For possession of Dakenruud's journal. He won't tell us where it is, of course, but you will persuade him. Once you have the journal, your father will release a statement recanting both Michelruud's blasphemy and his own—"

"I am unaware of any such—"

"And he will name you his heir and ask his followers to honor you."

Leah giggled and shook her head. He was mad—lost his mind. She turned again to Prenalin, stared hard at him until his eyes met hers. He knew it, too; she could read it there on his face. The High Priest of Hass had gone to the wilds.

She looked back to Kirche. "My father has no followers. Daken's journal may be nothing more than legend. If my father cannot tell me where it is—"

"Then he will be hanged."

Her face froze, her breath caught in her throat. Still his face betrayed nothing, no kindness, no compassion, but neither hatred or cruelty.

"And if I do not marry you, will you hang me as well?"

Here he smiled, but it was not a pleasant sight. "You have no choice in that matter, I'm afraid. And now, to the second point, the boy Lucas. I care not why he left here to rescue you from the caverns. Whatever his motivations, they are no longer to be a consideration for you."

"I'm sure I don't know what you mean."

"You will not see or speak to him again."

"But why?"

"As my betrothed, it would be unseemly to encourage him in this matter."

Leah tried to shake herself out of her confusion, but nothing changed.

"Of course," Prenalin finally spoke and she turned to him, hopeful. But he only said, "The boy will be rewarded for returning Kirche's betrothed to him. If he had not acted, our plans would have taken much reworking."

Everything in her seemed to fall and she suddenly felt trapped— a mouse in a child's maze. If Prenalin would not help her, where would she turn? Perhaps, Lucas...

"You understand," Kirche said, "if you do not return to Ruhm as my wife, your father will be tortured in your presence. He will know his agony is your doing."

The tent spun around her and her nod felt out of balance. She stood, still holding fast to her journal, and forced a curtsy before staggering out, into the cold, sunlit day. There was a commotion at the other end of the encampment, south, and she made her way to the crowd, dazed, needing to find herself lost in the throng, somewhere away from Gretchen or Zelda. Even Xavier would try to pry from her what made her ill. And she could not speak it.

A trumpet sounded and the gathering of soldiers and winter folk all fell to a knee, leaving Leah standing, looking upon the sight of the king of Michelruud facing west. And approaching him, were Arnot and Ricker, uneasy, clearly anxious, their own soldiers standing back. Not desiring to be noticed, she knelt, but raised her eyes to watch as the other kings of the Ruud seemed to grow smaller and smaller as Welk spoke to them, until—Leah let out a gasp—they bowed before him.

The trumpet sounded once again and the crowd stood and roared its approval. Confused, Leah turned, only to find Kirche and Prenalin standing only yards distant, watching. Kirche had lost his calm demeanor; he turned briskly and stalked away.

Chapter Thirteen

When the sun found its way behind the peaks, it was too cold on the roof of the tower and Fenn had to say goodbye to Sadie and Grayson. He and Brenna built up their fires in their room and he sat huddled beneath warm pelts noshing an apple, the heat of the flames giving his cheeks a blush. When Brenna came to sit with him in his alcove, she reached out her hand and asked to hold the charm once again.

"Will you tell me its story now?" he asked.

She nodded.

"How do you know the charm didn't belong to my mother?"

"I'm not *certain*," she said. "But you clearly have the gift of touch; you are receiving visions from the charm. And yet, they are brief and without context. If this were your mother's charm, you would see more. Much more."

"What would I see?"

"You would see what I see."

He stared at her, confused, and waited for her to explain.

"This charm was carved by a folk," she said, rubbing her thumb across the grooves of the dragonfly on its front. "And given to an eisen. Their love was kept secret from their families for many months. They planned to marry, on the plain of Nergens, without consent. There is happiness and joy, laughter..." Brenna wrapped her hands around the charm and brought it to her chest; she shivered.

"What else?"

"Then there is darkness and glimpses of things not meant to be seen."

"I don't understand."

"There are none who can see anything of an object without connection to its owner. If you were the child of the woman who wore this charm, you would see her. With the kell stone, it was different, so I'm told. When the stone was with us, those of us with touch could glean much from any object we held, with no connection at all. Some say it was quite maddening and many are happy to be without the burden."

"But I do see stuff...I think."

"You may have a distant connection to the charm. Or perhaps your touch is in its infancy. I can't be sure that is not the case. And yet, I cannot fathom you would not be able to see what I see, if this did belong to your mother."

"What connection do you have to it?"

"Many years ago, we lost two of our eisen to murder. One was marked by the faire, heralded as the heir to the throne. Her name was Rue-Anna. She slipped out of the realm to meet and marry her lover, a young folk of the Ruud, we believe. This is her charm." She opened her palm to look at it. "He must have made it for her. It's crude; but I can feel that she cherished it."

"What happened to her?"

"I'm told the guards saw the flames of her encampment and felt the call of her spirit."

"Are you sure she couldn't have been my mother? My nurse, Clara, told me my mother had the charm with her when I was born."

Brenna shrugged. "Perhaps the party who raided Rue-Anna's camp were thieves."

"You're saying my mother was a thief?"

"I only know the charm is not your mother's and therefore not yours. If anyone has claim to it, it would be me."

"You?"

She nodded. "Rue-Anna was my sister. I was five years old when she was killed. I woke the morning of her death with the mark of the faire."

Fenn reached out and took his charm from her hand. "You could touch me. And you would know...if I was related to you."

"I have touched you. Just a moment ago, on the roof. But no, I cannot sense your kin; I see only the wissendes who raised you. I would know if Rue-Anna had a child. Or, if you had known her, I would be able to know it. But you were raised alone. I can't feel anything in you but what you know."

Tears pooled in his eyes and Fenn pulled at them with his fingertips then pressed the heels of his palm to his lids.

"Do not despair," she said.

He surprised himself with a laugh. "How can I not? This all seems so pointless. I don't know what everyone wants of me. The fairies told me to go to the wasteland and that did no good. Father Britt told me to come here, but you're no help either."

"What help are you seeking?"

"I want to know," he said. "I *need* to know who I am."

"Yes, exactly. You are split—part eis. That much I can say is certain. And the first thing a young eis must do to begin to live by the seven great principles, is know who he is."

Fenn shook his head, confused.

"We must find out who we are," she said.

"I've tried."

"No, Fenn. Who you are has nothing to do with who your parents were."

"It doesn't?"

"No. It doesn't have anything to do with where you were born, where you have lived, what skills or talents you possess, whether you are beast or folk. Who you are is right here." She poked him hard in the forehead.

"Ow."

"Who you are is determined by how much knowledge and experience you can fit into your head. Who you are is how much you know. It is the decisions you make, the actions you take, based on that knowledge. Who you are is what you think. An eis strives to work past what he believes, what he wishes to be true, to rely only on what he can know. That is who we are."

"That doesn't sound easy."

"It's not. But you must do it. Find out what you know to be true. Then you will know who you are and all decisions will come easy. Your path will be evident as if it's already been worn down by your feet. It will be lit up as a fairy parade at midnight. All will be clear and all will make sense."

"Do you know who you are?" he asked her.

"The greatest principle is one we eis strive for always."

"Oh, that's great," he said. "So what you're telling me is I have to do something that I will never do."

"Never perfect, perhaps. But trust me. You will come to know who you are."

"Where do I begin?"

"Begin with what you know."

"I only know what everyone else thinks I am."

"The child of prophecy, yes. The kell stone."

"I don't know what the kell stone is."

"Of course you do. *It is a place to start.*"

"You think I should look for it?"

She shrugged. "You sought the truth of the prophecy in the beast forest and found there was none. You sought your mother in the wastelands and found you were an eis. You sought the eisen maiden here in the realm and found that despite your mother being eisen, the charm is not yours. What is left for you to find?"

"I could find a place to hide and forget it all."

She laughed and it echoed on the stone walls around them. The fire lit the left side of her face and hid the right in shadow, as if there were two sides to her, one dark and one bright, one kind and one deceitful. But it was just a trick of the light.

"Where would you look for the kell stone," he asked her, "if you went in search of it?"

"I would sprout my wings and fly to Ruhm. The angels tell us it is there; they claim to feel it."

"Why haven't *they* found it?"

"Angels cannot go beneath the ground."

"How do you know it's underground?"

"If it were not, we would draw strength from it, even were it in the Great West."

"So, I should go to Ruhm."

She nodded, hopeful.

"What if I found it, and did what the prophecy said I would do? What if I killed King Welk and destroyed the Ruud?"

Brenna turned her face to the fire.

"That's what you want me to do, isn't it?"

"No," she whispered. "But there are few who would agree with me."

"Then why do you want me to find it?"

"I want it returned to my folk. I want us to live as we were meant to. But I would wish to live in peace with the folk of the Ruud. Think on it. The eis in you would have you seek the stone. You are the only one who can. For you are neither eis, nor angel, nor felidae. You are folk. Only you can get to the stone without being noticed and captured by the folk of Ruhm."

Fenn sighed and shook his head. "I'll think about it."

"Look to yourself, Fenn. Not to anyone else. Know yourself."

Chapter Fourteen

Leah found she was captive as soon as she returned to her tent, though it seemed Kirche was loath to part with Redd and Kipling too often and so it was Xavier who spent most of his time watching her.

"What do you make of it?" the boy asked when she emerged with her shawl. "The other kings of the Ruud, I mean. Have they abdicated?"

"That's unlikely, isn't it?"

He followed her through the encampment, winding around tents and well-tended fires, laundry lines, and make-shift kitchens. The sky was a powdery blue, dotted with puffy white clouds, and the sunlight shone timid, as if from hiding.

"Where are you off to?" he said, skipping to catch up to her.

"You don't have to come along." She breathed in the aromas of the camp—kaff, beans, roasting rabbit.

"But I do. I'm charged with keeping an eye on you."

"Is that so?"

"You're not allowed to leave the camp, nor see that young fellow what rescued you."

"Can I take a walk?"

"There's a bear somewhere about," he said. "I heard tell. Could we find it?"

Leah stopped, turned to him and smiled. "That's a plan, isn't it?"

Together they roamed through the camp, Xavier on the lookout for a bear, Leah simply trying to breathe. Every part of her told her to run, but to where? Home to Ruhm and her father? Could she save him? When they came to the northern edge of camp where there was a patch of woods to the northeast, set against the backdrop of the icy mountains of the eis, Xavier let out a whoop.

"Two bears," he cheered.

At the tree line was a camp of six tents, and there, just as Xavier said, were two bears rolling in a patch of grass.

"Can we ask to see them do you think?" Xavier said, his face lit with the smile of a child.

And so they walked several yards to the camp and were met by a group of what Leah could only describe as vagabonds. Grimy, every one. Three played at cards; two others napped; and one stood to greet them as they neared.

He introduced himself as Wiley of the Gnome Eaters.

"Do the bears eat gnomes?" Xavier asked.

"Not so far as I can tell," Wiley said. "What group are you with?"

"We are with the Hass," Leah told him.

Wiley's face hardened, but when Xavier beamed and said, "Can I touch one?" the man chuckled and led the boy to one of the bears as it sat up to greet them.

"Where did you come by bears?" Leah asked.

"Gambling. That there's Darnit. Our friend Rogget won him years ago. And this here is Petunia. One of the Wretched won her to the Port a little while ago and our man Tanner just took her off him yesterday."

"They ought to be together," Xavier said.

"Aye, I think that's why he won him so easy. She wouldn't stay with old Grindel, anyway."

Leah watched for several minutes, uncomfortable, while Xavier nuzzled the bear and scratched behind its ears.

"Why is it so friendly?" she asked Wiley.

He shrugged. "I can't be saying for sure he'd be friendly to everybody."

"We should go now, Xavier."

"Aw."

"It's all right," Wiley said. "Looks like Darnit's taken to you. Come back anytime you like. So long as me or one of the boys is here."

"Tomorrow then?"

Wiley nodded. "I'll be with the delegation to the ice palace day after tomorrow. After that, ask Tanner there if it'd be okay."

Xavier leaned down to hug Darnit.

"The kings of the Ruud," Leah said. "They've united?"

"Against the eis, yes."

"You think there will only be one Ruud, soon?" Xavier said.

"I imagine so. King Welk is the stronger of the three and he's got the people behind him. Ricker and Arnot gave over soldiers to him for confronting the eis and angels, and now they've gone off home."

"Would they give up their thrones so easily?" Leah said.

"Oh, I imagine there will be a fight. But I suspect Welk has more to bargain with than he lets on."

"What do you mean?"

"What? Ain't you heard? The eis have got the boy of prophecy —the one who's to destroy the Ruud. I saw him took up by an angel myself and carried off there. If Welk can get hold of him, all the Ruud will be behind him. It don't look too good for you folk."

"What have we got to do with it?" Xavier said.

"Ah, now, don't be pretending you don't know your Hass isn't wanting to come over here and start a fight of their own."

Xavier laughed. "If Ruhm wanted this little slap of land, she'd have it. It would take more than your little army of folk to run us off."

"Hush," Leah told him.

"But, it's true. If we wanted the Ruud we'd have had it a long time ago. We've got an army twice as big as anything you could come up with."

"And what have they been doing over there in Ruhm, eh? Patrolling for stray beast folk? Marching in parades? You think the winter folk who run off from the Hass and settle over here don't talk? You got a big bunch of pretty folk in costume, that's all. Out here in the hills, we been

400

fighting up close for years—real fighting, something your dressed up fancy boys haven't had to do."

"But we have firearms. Lots of them."

"And you don't think we do?"

"We know you don't."

"You think you know."

Xavier took a step closer to Wiley and Darnit let out a roar. The boy jumped and backed away.

"That's right," Wiley said. "We got bears, too."

Xavier was happy enough to leave after that, and Leah scolded him on their way through the camp.

"I'll tell Kirche what he said. We'll have them all searched."

"It would take an army just to do that."

"I'll tell him, even so."

"Your pride's been hurt, that's all."

The boy grumbled behind her and Leah pitied him. After all, she'd been in that frame of mind not too long ago, she realized —thinking Ruhm the best at everything.

"Leah?" A woman called to her. "Leah Hallowsing?"

She stopped in front of a large tent where several women stood wringing out wet clothing, hanging it on ropes tied to tall stakes sunk into the ground. An older woman came forward with a timid smile.

"Is that you?"

Finally, Leah recognized the face. "Madam Roths?"

Her smile widened. "I am called simply Dania, now." She glanced at Xavier. "What has brought you east?"

"She's the Aide to the High Priest of Hass," Xavier said.

"Are you now? And on the annual tour, no doubt."

"But what are you doing here?" Leah asked her.

"I represent the College of Women. One of the kings of the Ruud called us to meet regarding the eis."

"But what are you doing here in the east?"

"Hah," she laughed. "I suppose when we left, the Hass made up some story about our disappearance."

"You retired."

"That's as good an excuse as any. Did you know Byn Always is here, as well?"

"Madam Always?" Leah shook her head. "Here?"

"Well, not here at the meeting. She's back at our camp, some thirty miles south. There near the foot hills."

Leah turned to look. "So close."

"I imagine you would not be allowed to visit."

"No."

"Will your party be following when we confront the eis? Or waiting here in the hills for our return?"

She looked to Xavier, then shook her head. "I'm not sure why we haven't moved on as yet, but no. So far as I know, we will not join the march."

Madam Roths seemed to wish to say more. She took Leah's hands and frowned, squeezed them slightly and tried to smile.

"I wish you luck on your journey home," she said.

Chapter Fifteen

Welk woke from his dream with a start, the cold night air sending a chill through him. He sat up, reached for a log and tossed it onto the fire, stoked it, and sat for some time letting the warmth ease his mind. The camp was quiet now; even the card players and revelers nodded off. The crackle and spit of the fires echoed, and smoke whirled upward into darkness.

He heard it again. The voice, calling his name. In his dream it was Rue-Anna and he'd dared not answer, for even in sleep he knew she was dead and only a demon or a doppleganger would have called to him. He couldn't bear the heartache, even imaginary, of losing her again.

"Welk of Michelruud," the girl said.

Behind him, he found her standing between tents fifty yards north. An angel.

"I am still asleep," he mumbled. But he stood, wrapped himself in his cloak, and walked toward her. When he came near, she turned and made her way through the camp, out into the open field where the fires could not warm them and only the moonlight showed her face.

She could be Rue-Anna, he thought. Younger, taller, her hair a touch too much like honey, not enough like gold. Her eyes darker, like Rue-Anna's sapphires with a flare of anger to them. Another version of Rue, he thought, and realized he was not dreaming.

"I am Bren-Aian of Eidolon. Daughther of the Snow. Queen of the Eis."

Welk looked around them at the darkness. "Where is your entourage?"

"I come alone."

"I was not aware the queen of the eis was an angel."

"I am angel eisen."

"What does that mean?"

"My father was an angel."

Welk let his eyes gaze into hers for as long as she would stand it. He could see them both in her. Aliara's lips, always pursed in confidence. Rue's brow, curved with concern. But they were not angels. Of that much, he consoled himself, he could be sure. For no blur of mourning could erase wings such as those. Their shoulders rose to her ears. Thick with blinding white feathers, the tips of which danced with each breeze. When a strong wind whistled from the north, she lifted them, opened them slightly, and sent the wind off, shielding him.

"The queen has no plans to turn the boy over to you. She will attempt to take you. But her guard has dwindled low these past months, without her knowledge. She and Noromir have grown lazy. You will find a majority of the guard will turn against the others, once you make it clear you mean to fight."

He nodded. "Your emissaries told me as much."

"I wish to know when you march the pass."

"Day after tomorrow. We are hoping our delay makes her Highness restless."

The girl smiled. "Be assured you will make it to the first gate of the realm freely. Once a skirmish is raised, my allies will act swiftly. We will retake the realm."

"But this news is not why you came," he said. "You could have sent another of the eis on horseback."

"Yes," she said. "I would ask something of you."

He hesitated. "You may."

"I wish to touch you."

Welk flinched and drew back, unprepared for such a request. "Why?"

"You will know."

With that, Welk knew already; she needn't touch him at all. But he let her place her hand on his forearm. She closed her eyes and Welk fought to keep his open—to watch her lip tremble when she learned the truth of her suspicions. Why hadn't she known it was him? Did Rue never speak of him?

She lowered her head and her hand dropped to her side. "Thank you," she whispered.

"You are her kin," he said.

Her eyes seemed to sink to black there in the night when she looked at him. "I must know," she said. "Could she not have lived?"

Welk's jaw set hard and he fought to keep from grinding his teeth. "If she lived, she would be by my side."

"You're certain?"

"I watched the eis burn their bodies on the pyre."

She flinched when he spoke, as if his anger were thorns flung from his lips.

"You saw the bodies for yourself," she said, her chin raised, refusing to be cowed by his venom.

"I—" Welk realized the truth. "I did not."

He broke. He could feel the split in his heart. How could she do it to him? How could an eisen not be wary of his pain? It was unlike them—unlike Rue and Aliara, and so he thought all eisen—to purposefully cause harm. But there the eisen stood, forcing him to have hope where there could be none.

"Why?" he asked her.

She shook her head. "I cannot say."

"She is dead. They are both dead."

"Yes," she said.

"Then why do you question me?"

"It is when they died that is uncertain."

Chapter Sixteen

When he handed her the bow, Prenalin offered Leah a worried look, but she was still too angry to give him any solace. They followed Kirche, Kipling, and Redd into the woods west of the encampment and trudged on in silence for some time until she gave up and deigned to speak to him.

"He doesn't intend to find brownies here in this small wood, surely," she said.

Prenalin seemed to breathe finally, as if he hadn't had a decent intake since the day she'd returned from the caverns with Lucas—since Kirche made his vile threat of marriage.

"Merely rabbit." Pren tried to smile, but he only half managed. "I wish you to know," he whispered as the two of them fell farther behind Kirche, "it was not my doing that it happened as it did."

"The proposal you mean."

He nodded.

"But you knew he intended to marry me?"

"It was his plan all along. Yes."

They hiked the woods for two hours before Kirche let out a strangled growl and stomped off toward the camp. Not even a squirrel showed itself.

"How can one manage a decent hunt with all that racket?" Kirche said. "Do they carouse all day? What sort of army could they hope to make?"

When they exited the wood, Leah hesitated, watched their backs as they all left her there and disappeared among the tents. She flung her bow onto her shoulder and walked the edge of the wood to where Sorgood's guard were camped, hoping to see Lucas. He'd spied her twice since their return, both times nodding, smiling, not approaching, as if he understood she was under guard and warned against him. It wouldn't surprise her, as she found him much more intuitive than any folk of Ruhm. Perhaps it was the felid in him, she thought.

As she neared the last of the tents, she caught sight of him entering the wood twenty yards ahead and, thinking it best not to be seen following him, took to the woods there where she was. It was too bad she wasn't a felid herself, so she could smell him out, she thought with a smile. But better to search while hidden in the woods than get into trouble with Kirche.

As small as the wood east of the encampment was, it still had its dense, dark patches, and once caught within one, Leah couldn't help being reminded of the beast forest of the Ruud. Her heart quickened its pace and she caught her breath.

"Calm down," she whispered to the wind in the trees above her. But she began to fear, sure she was walking in circles. Perhaps the wood was not so small after all. When she felt a sob begin to rise in her throat, she startled at the sound of a strange voice.

"If you did not wish to die," the folk said, "why did you wander off from your fellows."

Leah shuddered, fearful now of being caught up in some-thing grisly. She moved forward slowly, let a hand reach for a thick pine to steady herself, and peered out from among the branches and shrubs.

"I do not seek you out," Lucas said and Leah's eyes widened. She could see the back of a folk, tall, thin but heavy with strength; he must tower over young Lucas. She strained to see the boy but could not.

"You must have sensed my presence."

"Hence my turning back to the camp."

Lucas was impatient, but fearful, she was sure; but the folk was cruelly playful, toying with him.

"No matter," the folk said.

Leah watched in horror as the folk raised a bow and she saw Lucas dart away; the folk rushed to follow. Without thinking, she pushed through the trees and shrubs after them. She caught sight of the tall folk as he glanced back at her. He smiled and continued after Lucas; she heard him chuckle, but Leah knew this could not be a game.

When she came upon him, stopped in a brief clearing, his bow raised, she pulled hers from her shoulder, nocked an arrow without thinking and let it fly. He jerked forward, stumbled, and turned toward her, frustration in his brow. He was set to shout at her, scold her like a child, but Leah nocked a second arrow and sent it into his throat before he had the chance—he fell. Once at him, she thrust her foot into his chest and glared, another arrow ready for his eye socket, her breath coming in raging gasps now.

"You are an eis," she said.

He nodded, shuddering.

"You will heal well enough, then."

His mouth opened and closed, but only blood flowed from it.

"I should kill you now."

"No," Lucas came through the trees, his hand held up to stay her. Leah didn't take her eyes from the eis at her feet. "Let him go."

"He was going to kill you."

"But he won't now. Not today."

Leah kicked at the eis and sucked in a deep breath, calming herself. "We should leave before he is healed."

Together they walked through the woods at a pace until they found their way into the encampment and Lucas faced her with a smile.

"How did you know he was an eis?"

"I studied them in school. I could have killed him, you know. An arrow in the brain will do it."

He shook his head and chuckled. "I had no idea you were so violent. And yet you shudder at my stories."

Leah finally let herself tremble from the fright and had to laugh at herself. "I am not violent," she said. "But I will do whatever is necessary to protect a friend."

"Now you have to say our debts are balanced."

"Would you care to tell me why an eis is intent upon killing you?"

"Would you tell me why you have been under guard since your return?"

They stood looking at each other, smiling, for several seconds until she laughed again. "I suppose neither of us is willing to burden the other."

His face softened and concern grew in his eyes. "Will you come with me to the ice palace? You don't have to tell me there is something wrong for me to help you. Come with me; your Lord Kirche needn't treat you this way. I will keep you safe from him."

Leah's heart lurched and settled back. How easy it would be to run from Kirche—run with Lucas. Even King Welk, no doubt, would protect her. And there lay the problem. She sighed. "I cannot ask our troubled truce be overthrown because of a dispute over me. For you know Kirche would blame the Ruud for my defection. He may say I was kidnapped, stolen, indoctrinated."

"Then tell me I am not to worry. You will be all right?"

"I will be," she said, though her voice quaked. "But will you?"

"I will. I promise the eis is no match for a felid." Here he offered a wily smile. "Will your party still be here when the delega-tion returns from the palace?"

"I think not. Kirche was not happy to see the other kings give up soldiers to Welk. He plans to return to the port on the morrow, though our ship is not due for a fortnight."

"Very well, then," he said. "I will see you at the port; I will find you there, before you sail."

"You still plan to follow me to Ruhm?"

He nodded.

"It is dangerous; much more so than an eis assassin, I'm afraid. If anything were to happen to you, I would feel...responsible."

"Then do not believe I go on your account. See me as concerned only with the kell stone. It's all I am after, I assure you." He smiled and put a hand on her arm. "I care not for you one whit."

She laughed and watched him take a path through the tents; he smiled at her, before disappearing from sight. When she turned to walk the edge of the wood back to her own camp, she found Redd and Kipling striding toward her. A pair of handcuffs rattled at Kipling's side.

"You leave him no choice," Prenalin said to her when she was deposited in her tent, chained to the center post.

Leah glared at him.

"He will release you, he says, once the boy is dealt with."

"What does that mean?"

"Don't concern yourself with the details."

"Tell me, Pren. What will he do? He can't harm him. Can he? It was my fault. Please tell Kirche not to blame Lucas. It was my doing, not his. Please tell him."

Prenalin lifted the flap of her tent to leave; he frowned at her. "I will tell him," he said, but he shook his head slightly before he was gone.

Chapter Seventeen

It is time," Brenna whispered. "The folk are gathering to confront the queen's guard."

Fenn nodded and winced. She was still weak from her last shedding, he knew. And when she returned the last time, she seemed changed—defeated somehow, saddened.

"How do we get out?" he asked her.

Brenna smiled and held up a long gold key. "Give me a lift," she said, beckoning him to the window in the cubby next to the door.

"Out the window?"

"There's a small ledge; trust me."

As Fenn cupped his hands for her slender foot and lifted her up, he thought of the children of Path, wondering if all tower walls might be clung to for daring escapes.

Her key tinkled in the lock and she pulled open the heavy door; a cold, thick wind rushed at Fenn's face.

"Did you have the key all the time?"

"For a while," she said.

"What about the guard?"

"We've done our best to keep those loyal to the queen out of our plans."

Outside there was a wood landing with a low rail, barely reaching his hip, and thin planks serving as steps circling the tower.

"Is it safe?" Fenn asked, shaking.

"There's no time for fear," Brenna said. "Hurry."

He followed her down the narrow stairs, around to the other side where there was another landing.

"These hardly seem like the sort of stairs a folk would find in the ice palace," Fenn said, his teeth chattering in the cold.

"This is a prison tower," she said, pulling open the door. "They're not designed to help you get down."

She pushed him into the dimly lit room where he saw Sadie and Grayson huddled in front of a fire. They jumped up, surprised, and Brenna held up a hand.

"Quiet," she said. "We do not know which guards are with us and which are not. Be wary."

"Oh, no," Sadie moaned as soon as they were out of the room and on the landing. "Isn't there a better way?"

"The only other way down is in the arms of an angel," Brenna said.

"Well, come on," Grayson said. "Let's get it done."

408

"To the next level," Brenna said. "There is another in your party there."

"Rogget?" Fenn said.

"A huntsman by the look of him."

They hugged the cold stone walls of the tower and stepped quickly, but gingerly, down the stairs. Fenn's legs trembled wildly. Finally, they wound round to the next door and found Rogget inside the room there. He grabbed them all into his arms and Fenn felt the man shudder with tears.

"You've all gone too thin," he muttered. Suddenly he tensed.

Fenn turned to find Brenna staring at them, her eyes wide in frustration.

"We must hurry."

"This is Brenna," Fenn said. "She was with me, on the top floor."

"We have no time for greetings. This way."

Together, they made their way down the stairs, around the tower, until they came to their fourth landing where Grayson begged for a rest. Fenn was glad to oblige. His legs wobbled as if he had no bones and his heart refused to calm. He decided, despite his rescue of the children of Path at Steingefan, he did not like heights.

"We come to the tenth floor," Brenna said. "You can go inside there and take the spiral stair in the center of the tower to the bottom."

When they neared the landing, the door swung open and three guards walked out, talking heatedly. As they headed up the steps, they looked upward and stopped abruptly at the sight of the three children, Rogget, and Brenna, staggered on the stair above them.

"What's this?" the taller of the eis said with a hint of amuse-ment. He glared at Brenna and tilted his head. "Is this an act of treason?"

"It is." She smiled. "Who is with me?"

The younger guards drew their swords. "I am not," one of them said.

The other shouted, "bring them into the ante chamber, we'll cuff them there."

But the taller guard drew his sword and faced them. "I stand with the true queen. We will help her in her quest."

"You will die," the other guard said.

Fenn watched in horror as the three guards began to fight—their swords glinting in the sunlight, clashes echoing off the tower walls.

"Quickly," Brenna said. "We must move past them."

"It's all right," he heard Rogget say from above him on the stairs. "Move carefully."

But as they stepped onto the landing and Fenn reached to grab

Sadie's arm, he was knocked over by one of the guards. Sadie fell over him and struggled to stand.

"Sadie," Grayson yelled, just as another guard's arm flew back and knocked her over the low railing.

Sadie's screams echoed all around, bouncing off the peaks. Fenn could see her hands grasping the low bar of the railing. Climbing to his knees, he was grabbed by one of the young soldiers.

"The ransom must not escape," he said. "You deal with these, let them loose if you have to."

The guard dragged Fenn toward the door, but Rogget grabbed the eis around the neck.

"Let him go."

The guard hung on tighter. Sadie screamed again and Fenn struggled to free himself. Brenna said something, in eis, and a sword fell to the ground at his feet. Finally, the guard's hold on him failed and Fenn stepped away from him as the folk slid sluggishly to the ground against the door. Fenn grabbed the heavy sword and called to Grayson.

"Do you need help?"

"I've got her," Grayson cried, kneeling on the landing and pulling Sadie up so she could grab the higher rung on the railing.

Fenn turned back to the door where Rogget was dragging the lifeless soldier out of the way. Brenna was backed into a corner, behind the tall eis who battled the younger guard. Fenn lifted the sword he'd claimed, closed his eyes, and stabbed toward the young guard.

"Ahh." With a terrible, shrieking gasp, the guard sank to the ground.

Fenn shuddered, opened his eyes and panicked. He dropped the bloodied sword to the floor of the landing and staggered, nauseated.

"Quickly," the older eis called.

Sadie climbed over the railing and Grayson grabbed her and pulled her toward the door. Fenn, shaking, took Brenna's hand and led her away from the corner.

"It's all right," Rogget was saying as they ran across the ante chamber floor and down the spiral stairs. "They aren't dead."

"Are you sure," Fenn said breathlessly, "I didn't kill him?"

"You got him in the side. He'll be fine."

But Fenn thought Rogget was only trying to make him feel better.

"Look here," Rogget said.

There against the wall were their knapsacks, their supplies strewn about the room. They gathered up their things as quickly as they could—blankets, tin mugs, Sadie's maps.

"What in Mutterede's name?" Rogget said.

Fenn stood and turned to the door; he gasped. Sadie and Grayson let Rogget step in front of them and he drew his knife to protect them.

"Step over here," Rogget told Fenn.

He shook his head. "It's all right, Rogget."

Brenna stood before them, her heavy white wings lifted and shuddered. "I have to leave you now," she said. "You must make your way to the front of the palace. Once out of the tower, the path winds through the gardens. It will take you to the eastern door. You will find it unlocked."

"Thank you," Fenn said. He reached his hand out to grasp hers, and she looked at it, hesitating, before taking it. In the brief moment they touched, she looked into his eyes and he thought he saw something familiar and warm there. But she released his hand before he was sure what had happened. They went to the door, stood on the landing, and watched as she let herself drop out of sight. Then she soared above them and flew into the sunlight.

"She was an angel?" Grayson said, his voice hollow.

"Angel eisen," Fenn said. "Split."

"All right then," Rogget said, sheathing his knife. "No time to dally."

They nearly fell the ten flights of spiral stairs toward the ground. Fenn struggled to keep tears from welling up in his eyes. He never thought he'd stab someone. He feared himself—wondered what other awful things he might be capable of. But he pushed that thought away; he must think only of getting to the bottom of the tower.

As they took the path through gardens and courtyards, the palace was abuzz with panic. Eis ran with them, passed them, crossed their path, but ignored them as they made their way, exhausted and panting, to the outer wall where the door stood, ten feet tall. Fenn put his hand on the latch, ready to pull it open.

"Listen to me," Rogget said, huffing and puffing, still not finding his breath. "You all run down the pass, you hear? They won't notice you."

"But what about you?" Sadie said.

"I'll run. I'm not saying I won't follow. But I'm bigger. I'll get noticed. If I should stop, you keep running."

"We will," Fenn promised, knowing it would never be that easy.

He pulled the door open and they found themselves in a mass of folk, on the opposite side of where they ought to be. To reach the pass, they'd have to make their way through a sea of white-robed eis who had filed out of the palace gates to meet the hundreds of soldiers of the Ruud, many on horseback, who had gathered at the walls of the palace.

Fenn followed Sadie and Grayson as best he could through the throng of white, but he knew at some point they'd be noticed, or fighting would break out. The thought of insanity ran through his head. But hadn't they done stupider things? Suddenly trumpets blared again and he heard the full throated, yet airy, voice of one of the eis.

Chapter Eighteen

Hundreds of eis had gathered before the first gate of the realm. Beyond it rose the towers and spires of the palace. All along the pass, Welk had expected an ambush, but Bren-Aian had fulfilled her promise; he detected not even a scout.

"This is not as the queen demanded," the tall, glowing eis who'd come forward bellowed.

Welk dismounted and let Sorgood's first lieutenant take his horse. He wrapped his arms across his chest and looked up slightly at the eis. Sorgood's men were gathered behind Welk, many on horseback, squeezed together in a long line from one end of the marbled wall to the other—a distance of some hundred yards. Many of the soldiers had dismounted on orders and attempted to flank the eis.

The eis guards stood like statues, their strong jaws set rigid, and their stares focused on something in the distance behind the folk. They were more disciplined than the guards of the Ruud, Welk knew; but he wondered if that discipline would make them vulnerable when faced with feverish young folk eager for battle.

"You agreed to sweep the land at our border of its refuse," the eis said. "Instead you bring it here."

"I never promised I would force folk from the hill country," Welk said. "I met with them and have heard their complaints."

"They must be removed from our lands," the eis roared. "It is the queen's command."

"Then the queen will have to move them off herself."

"If you wish to have the bairn, you must fulfill your part of the bargain."

"I made no bargain."

"Then the boy will remain with us."

"You do not have the boy," Welk said.

"He is this moment being shackled and brought out to a balcony where you may see him."

"You are mistaken."

The eis guard's eyes closed up a bit and he sneered. "Are all folk of the Ruud so ignorant? Or is it just your kings?"

Welk laughed. "We can debate which species of folk is the stupider another time, but I assure you, you no longer have the boy."

"How could you know?"

"Because he is there." Welk pointed to the boy in the crowd of angels and when the eis guard turned to see him, Welk grabbed him from behind and forced him to the ground. The sounds of confusion and pending chaos broke out all around him.

"You will send a message to the maiden," Welk said. "Seize the boy!" he called out to his guard. A shot rang out and the eis began a loud scream in unison as they moved forward toward the folk, their bows drawn. Too sudden, Welk thought, but it was done. If Bren-Aian was truthful, his folk would have little trouble getting the boy and leaving the eis to their own battle.

"Tell the maiden we are with her," he said to the guard. "She has but to call on us."

The eis, on his knees, struggled in Welk's grasp. "The maiden no longer has power here. It is the queen you must deal with. She will not ally with folk."

"Your false queen is too easily seduced by angels, my eis friend. And her throat is pricked by the point of sword as we speak."

He pointed to the balcony on the second floor and made sure the eis saw the young maiden standing there watching them.

Welk heard her voice, even from afar. "The throne is restored."

"No," the eis raged, pushing Welk off him and fumbling to his feet. He turned and drew his sword. "The eis will never ally with folk."

Welk smiled at him. "I have no time to fight with you. But I'm sure you'll find any number of soldiers willing."

Welk pushed through the throng after Fenn. The skirmish had billowed out from the gate, filling in the craggy grounds all the way toward the small pathway of the pass. Folk battled eis, eis battled eis and folk; it was a muddled, confused affair. He found Sorgood on the ground with his arm raised above his head as a shield.

"Get up," he said and dragged Sorgood up by his collar. "He's there, hurry."

He could see Fenn and the huntsman in the distance, struggling through the battling soldiers for the pass. He made his way forward, keeping his eyes on the boy.

Chapter Nineteen

Keep going," Fenn called to Sadie and Grayson. They'd stopped, panicked, amid the chaos. "Run!" he screamed.

They ran through the crowd, shoving their way around both folk and eis, none of whom appeared to care about their escape. Just as he let himself believe they'd made it out of the chaos, when he could see the road ahead leading away from the palace, that would take him through the pass and back into the hills, he heard a shout, and behind him, King Welk stood, his sword drawn, the tip red with blood.

The king grabbed him, first by his knapsack, yanking him to a stop, then by the back of his tunic. Fenn called out to Rogget but the huntsman was running with Sadie and Grayson, making for the pass.

"It's not safe," the king said to him. "Stay with the guard."

Fenn turned to look at him, confused, and caught sight of Lucas darting from the edges of the chaos, running toward him. Relief washed over him—Lucas was safe—but it was tinged with hurt and he realized then that he couldn't be sure if Lucas was coming to help him get away, or to help King Welk turn him over to Sorgood. He struggled against Welk's grasp, but Lucas was on them both within seconds, grabbing Welk from behind, surprising him, forcing him to let go of Fenn; the king's sword fell to the ground. Without thinking, Fenn picked it up. It felt strangely comfortable in his hand.

"Lucas?" he said.

"Run, Fenn. I cannot hold him long."

But Fenn stood there, his eyes wide, frantic.

"The boy should stay with the guard," Welk said, struggling free of Lucas' grasp.

Amid the shots and clanging of swords, the shouts and orders, one powerful bang rang out nearby, causing Fenn to jump. Everything went silent. Rogget caught hold of him as Fenn watched Lucas' face, his eyes wide, his mouth open as if he gasped for air. As Rogget pulled Fenn away, Lucas fell to his knees and Fenn's hearing returned.

"Lucas!" Fenn started forward, but Rogget lifted him off his feet. "Lucas!"

Lucas fell face down onto the ground; his back soaked in blood. Standing only a few yards behind him was Sorgood with a firearm, smiling, nodding. Fenn raged and pulled free of Rogget's grasp. Rushing toward Sorgood, he lifted Welk's heavy sword over his head. Sorgood, surprisingly, turned and ran, but Welk grabbed Fenn's arm. Struggling against the king, Fenn felt Rogget's huge arm wrap around his body once again, lifting him off the ground. He was pulled from Welk's grasp and dragged away. He watched a cluster of white-clad, glowing angels surround Welk.

"The King!" someone shouted.

Fenn saw the dagger, white and icy as the angels themselves, lifted high and brought down against the king's back. Welk caught Fenn's eye as he jerked with pain. A sadness washed over his face before he fell.

Rogget set Fenn on his feet and pushed him forward; he ran from the battle, down the road away from the ice realm, passing folk who'd followed to watch the scene.

"Lucas," he gasped as he ran behind Rogget. "They killed Lucas."

Chapter Twenty

1268 Autumn

Aliara was awakened by thumping footsteps in the clover; the geimen buzzed around her, telling her all was well. She opened her eyes to see an old, plump folk, in a brown robe, tied at his middle with a pale hemp rope. He stood just outside the clover patch, reached to the ground, and lifted the firearm her attacker had dropped. Her breathing quickened.

"All is well," the geimen sang. "All is well."

When he turned to her, he smiled and said, "You live," as if he hadn't expected it.

He tucked the firearm under his arm and walked into the field of clover to where she lay; he knelt at her side and cast his gaze along her body. She wondered how much blood there was to see.

"The geimen called to me," he said.

When she woke again, Aliara was in a hut built of tree branches, slits of sunlight danced between them spotted with specks of dust like fairies. Women, old as the wissende, haggard and gray, dressed her wounds. She was helped into a gown and the oldest of them offered a toothless grin.

"The finest we could find, my lady," she said.

Aliara opened her mouth to speak but no sound escaped; it was then she realized how quickly she was fading. The hag placed a hand on her engorged belly and nodded.

"The child lives; but you must fight."

She awoke and stared at the hut, at the collection of artifacts strewn about, hanging on the walls and from the ceiling. Utensils, ticking time-pieces, shoes without mates, bunches of dried flowers, and yellowed, peeling pages full of writing and drawings. The wissende entered and took a seat at her bedside; his eyes were rimmed red.

"I will take you to the midwife, but the journey is long. I have secured a wagon."

Aliara reached for him, her hand trembling violently until it found rest on his knee. Her brows knit together and she sucked in a ragged breath.

He seemed to understand and frowned, a sweet quiver at his lower lip. "There was a massacre," he said. "I find no evidence of survivors...other than you, my lady. I can send an emissary to—"

She closed her eyes and shook her head. Finally, she managed to speak. "No." The darkness invaded her once again as she told herself she must live.

1280 Autumn

Leah woke to a hand clasped over her mouth; she startled and struggled to sit, realizing she was cuffed and chained to the post in her tent.

"Quiet," Xavier said. "Kirche and his guard sleep."

Groggy, unsure of what was happening, Leah watched as Xavier carefully—so as not to let the keys jingle in his grasp—found the correct one and unlatched her cuffs. She rubbed the raw spots on her sore wrists. Her hands had not been unbound since the day Kipling found her speaking to Lucas.

"This way."

Xavier led Leah from the tent and they crept past the fire, now only embers, and the empty bedrolls of the porters, to the kitchen tent where Gretchen and Zelda stood, nervous and fumbling.

"This is for you," Zelda whispered, putting a pack on her shoulders. "Food, drink, clothing, blanket."

"But this is madness," she said. "Where can I go?"

"You must go to Ruhm," Gretchen said. "Warn your father."

"I can warn him when I arrive with Kirche."

Gretchen shook her head.

"Hurry," Xavier whispered. "Kipling is returned from the woods."

"He means to have your father hanged on Founding Day," Gretchen said.

"What?" Leah nearly called out loud. "But he said—"

"This is a man who threatens to torture your father if you do not obey him," Zelda said. "Can you believe anything he says?"

She stood staring at them in the dark, her mouth open, her stomach turning. Nodding, she felt the sting of her fingernails digging into her palms.

"Very well," she said. "Thank you." She hugged Gretchen, then Zelda, whose strong grip took her breath away, and then Xavier who she knew blushed heavily though she couldn't see it in the dark. "Mutterede's blessings be with you," she whispered and darted through the tents to the south.

Chapter Twenty-one

They hiked Kingdom Pass and in the night skirted around the guarded folk encampment and headed south toward the Plains of Glisch, camping at the base of a hill. Fenn wouldn't talk about the ice realm, or the battle, even when Rogget asked him. Lost and disoriented, he didn't think he could answer any questions if he tried.

He woke in the early morning sunlight, warmed by Rogget's fire, and wrapped his blanket around him. "It's gotten colder," he said quietly, taking a mug of hot bitters from Rogget.

"Sorry," Rogget said. "It's all I got for us until we can barter more food and drink."

Sadie nodded, took a mug and shivered.

"We'll head south to the coast," Rogget said. "It'll be a bit warmer there, especially if we can find a bit of forest."

"When can we go home?" Grayson asked, looking around at each of them. "I mean, any idea?"

They all seemed to look at Fenn for the answer. He needed to focus. He got up and walked to the top of the hill and peered across the slopes, to the plain beyond, reaching to the horizon. Then he turned back toward the mountains of the ice realm. The southeast tower rose high into the sky. He squinted, hoping he would see Brenna, standing in the tower, watching him. But she wasn't there.

He rejoined the others by the fire and sipped his bitters.

"Well?" Grayson said.

"Well, what?"

"What are we supposed to do now?"

"How should I know?"

Grayson sputtered. "How should you know? You're the whole reason we're in this mess. If you don't know, who will?"

"That's hardly fair," Sadie said. "It's not Fenn's fault."

"It is so. He had the mark all along. If he'd just told us, we might not be in this mess."

"Why? Would you have run to the village and handed him over to the guard?"

Grayson pouted and looked to the ground. "No."

"It wasn't Fenn's fault Father Treacher sent him through the tunnel. And it wasn't our fault we were sitting there when he came out. It just happened. And don't act like you haven't been having fun."

Grayson rolled his eyes. "Great fun! Traipsing all over the Ruud. Roster fiends. Angels and arrows flying through the air."

"Well, it wasn't Fenn's fault. You could be back in Banished, you know. Nobody made you come along."

"That's enough," Rogget said. "Bickering don't change any-thing."

They were silent for a moment while Fenn tried to think of what to say. Finally, he set his mug down by the fire pit and said, "Well, I don't know what to do now."

"No clue at all?" Grayson said.

"Did you see the queen, like we did? Did she tell you about your charm?"

Fenn shook his head. "That's a story to tell. It turns out the eisen you met wasn't the queen. It was Brenna all along. She is the maiden."

"But she's an angel," Sadie said.

"Angel eisen," Grayson corrected. "You showed her the charm then?"

Fenn nodded. "She wasn't much help." He couldn't bring himself to tell them that Brenna said the charm was not his mother's. He didn't understand it, still. He was deeply connected to it. Why would it not be his mother's? "She said I ought to go into the Great West."

"What for?" Rogget said.

Fenn shrugged. "Seems like nobody knows what I'm supposed to do and they don't want to deal with me, so they just tell me to go as far away from them as they can think of."

"Aw, come now," Rogget said.

"Father Treacher told me to go to Father Britt and he told me to go to the ice realm, and the maiden told me to go west. They're just trying to get rid of me."

"You really think so?" Sadie said.

Fenn nodded.

"We can't get a ship west," Rogget said. "We'd have to make our way back to the port and I don't think that's a good idea."

"Sorgood and a lot of the guard were at the battle," Grayson said. "Maybe there won't be many in the port."

"Father Britt said they don't have any control there," Fenn said.

Rogget shook his head. "I don't know."

"I thought there was another port," Sadie said, "east of Cold Sea, where the winter folk landed."

"Aye, but it isn't just the immigrants who use it. They're plenty of pirates and scalawags about."

"That's no different from Cold Sea," Grayson said.

"Well, if we can get into the Ruud and to the wissenry at Cold Sea," Sadie said, "Father Britt could find us a safe passage."

"You're all talking like we're going west," Fenn said.

"Do you have any other ideas?" Sadie said.

"Do we have to go anywhere?" Grayson said.

Fenn nodded. "Exactly. Why don't we just sit here?"

"Sit here?" Sadie said, raising her eyebrows. "For how long?"

"Forever. Let's just sit here and do nothing. I don't know what else to do. I should just go back and find King Welk and turn myself in already." Fenn felt a pang of regret at his words and put his face in his hands.

"What is it?" Grayson asked.

"I saw the king. Just after Sorgood shot Lucas, the angels attacked him. He was stabbed."

"Aye," Rogget said. "But I'm sure he lived."

"You can't know that."

They let Fenn sit in silence for a while, warming themselves at the fire, sipping their bitters.

"Well, we can't just sit here," Sadie said.

"Why not?" Fenn mumbled.

She growled and stood up. "We need more supplies. We lost too much when we were taken to the ice palace." She stomped a foot. "Stop acting like this. You're not the only one having trouble here, you know."

"Really?" Fenn looked up, his face streaked with tears. "Are you an evil bairn of prophecy? I didn't think so. Did you stab somebody yesterday? No? Did you see your brother killed yesterday? No, again."

"Lucas was your brother?" Sadie said.

"They're wissendes," Grayson said. "They call each other brothers."

"He was my brother; we grew up together."

"Okay, I'm sorry." Sadie looked around. "But we have to go somewhere."

"Aye," Rogget stood as well. "We'll see if we can't find a camp of winter folk who'll take us in for a while."

"How does that sound?" Sadie said to Fenn.

"Stop asking me, like I'm the leader."

"Fine." She rolled her eyes.

"Enough bickering," Rogget's voice boomed over the hills.

They were silent as they put out their fire and packed their sacks and made the long hike over the hills toward the Plains of Glisch.

"There," Fenn said later in the day, pointing southeast. "I see an encampment."

Across the plain, nestled up against the lower mountains on the far south side of the ice realm, he could see huts and tents and smoke from a fire.

"Where?" Grayson said.

"It's there."

"There's nothing there," Sadie said. "Just the blur of the mountains on the horizon."

"It's right there," he pointed.

"We can't see it," Rogget said. "Fenn's got the eyes of an eis—when he can control them."

Sadie and Grayson gaped at him, as if they didn't believe Rogget. But one look from the old huntsman and they accepted it. They hiked toward the encampment until dark, and made camp again.

The next afternoon they approached the little make-shift village and were hailed by a guard who limped hurriedly toward them with his hands raised.

"State your whereabouts," he said.

"We're standing right in front of you," Grayson said.

"Oh, aye. I mean, uh." He fumbled in his trouser pocket and pulled out a piece of thick parchment paper. "Uh," he mumbled to himself, "halt, where are you heading." And then he looked at them, "Where are you headed?"

"We came to see if you could spare some food and lodgings in exchange for another hunter," Rogget said. "I'm good with the bow and knife, though mine have been taken from me."

The guard looked back at his paper and scanned it. "Uh, state your business?" He looked at them anxiously.

"We're traveling," Sadie said. "Probably over to the west."

"The west, eh? Well, you're going the wrong way, aren't you?"

Sadie looked at Fenn, confused, and Fenn smiled.

"We're of the Ruud," Rogget said.

"Ah, our brothers of the Ruud. We were told much about your kind back home. Yes, yes, join us and tell us of this Ruud." He beckoned them to follow toward the encampment. "We hear you live amongst the beasts and have learned their magic."

"Really?" Grayson said. Then he turned to Fenn with a smile. "This

420

could be interesting."

The guard led them into the small encampment where women set about their chores. Several large pots were hung over fires and they stood with sticks, stirring clothes in the hot soapy water. Some pulled pieces of clothing out and set them through wringers, others took them and hung them on lines to dry in the cold air.

They all smiled at the visitors and said hellos.

"Found some travelers, eh, Wally?" a young woman said and winked at him.

"Where's Byn?" Wally asked.

She pointed behind her. "Cooking the rabbit."

Fenn could smell the stew and cider already. They approached a long house at the back of the encampment and entered. Three fire pits were lit down the middle of the rectangular hut and a woman sat at each, stirring. Around the fire pits were logs for sitting and along the sides of the house were tables for preparing meals and more logs.

Another woman stood over to the side at a long table with a short axe. She lifted it and brought it down quickly onto the thick wood table. Thwack!

"Madam Always," Wally called out and the woman with the axe turned the them. "Visitors from the Ruud." Wally's excite-ment beamed on his face.

"Come, come," the woman said and as they approached, she dipped her bloody hands into a pot of steaming water and wiped them on her apron.

"I'm Byn Always," she said. "Assistant to Dania Roths, head of the college."

"The college?" Sadie said.

"The Ruhm College of Women. Lena, would you be a dear and finish chopping the last bunny for the stew?"

Lena got up from the middle fire, smiled and bobbed her head. "Pleasure, madam." She seemed happy to take the axe and grab the skinned rabbit on the table. Thwack!

"This way." Byn ushered them over to the middle fire. "Sit, we'll get you something warm to drink. This pot's full of cider."

She ladled hot cider into mugs and handed them around and joined them on the logs.

"Yes," she said. "We come from the the Kingdom of Ruhm. Dania was head of the college for women there; but we were forced out. Women in Ruhm these days are not able to learn beyond level nine. Do you have any schools for women in the Ruud?"

Sadie shook her head. "We don't have schools at all."

Byn tilted her head and her brow furrowed. "But how have you continued the path of the wissenry?"

Grayson frowned. "We have not."

"We just found out our first king was a wissende," Sadie said. "Had no idea."

Byn sighed. "That is a shame, truth be told. But perhaps we now have a calling, if the king of the Ruud would permit us to teach. I will bring it up with Dania when she returns; she may have questions for you. But she has gone with your King Welk to confront the eis."

"We've just come from there," Rogget said. "There was a battle, I'm afraid."

"Was it a good little skirmish?" She smiled unexpectedly. "We had a rider just an hour ago tell us they'd marched to the palace. We expect some losses."

"Why did they go to the ice realm?" Sadie asked and Byn looked at her with a frown.

"To show strength. The eis have been pestering us, saying we're on their land. But we do not plan to leave. We want an end to the bickering and the king of the Ruud organized a bit of a confrontation. He said it would solidify us in the eyes of the ice realm and they would either fight us, or leave us alone. I prefer the latter. Leastwise, anyway, that's what Wally tells us. He took Dania overland to the meeting. Hard to say with Wally and all, though. Such as he is, the dear man."

"Why do you say, 'king of the Ruud,' like there's only one?" Fenn asked and looked around at them all. "Weren't the other kings involved?" His eyes fell on Rogget who was looking back at him as if he'd just discovered something.

"The skirmish with the eis unites the outlanders against the eis," Rogget said. "But it also unites them with Welk."

"Do you think he will try to unite the Ruud?" Grayson said.

Rogget nodded. "I'm not sure it's a bad idea, knowing of the Great West and all."

"What do you mean?" Sadie said.

"Welk isn't the first to try to make the Ruud into one king-dom and rule it for himself," Grayson said. "Alfred of Michelruud tried to do it ages ago. But he was betrayed by his wissende and killed by Prince John of Aaronland. And Alfred's wife, Osara, had John captured and beheaded as revenge. These thing rarely work out well."

"It might turn out better for Welk," Rogget said. "Think on it this way. If the ice realm and the winter folk recognize him as king, he's already got an advantage. They'll deal with him more and more and not with the others. And then, well, I hate to scare you all, but if Ruhm made a bid to overtake us—"

"You think they plan to do that?" Grayson said.

"We have no proof of it," Byn said. "Rumors, however." The woman's face went pale and her mouth fell open slightly. "If you'll excuse me." She bowed slightly and left them to the fire.

"I'll see what I can get for some hunting," Rogget said. "Then we can be on our way."

Fenn turned to watch Madam Always grab hold of a woman at the front of the tent. They embraced and he was sure they were both crying.

Chapter Twenty-two

Leah first bristled at the contact, being pulled into a tight hug; such intimacy between unrelated folk was quite forbidden in Ruhm. But she missed her mother so deeply, and remembering fondly Madam Always' clean soapy scent, she relaxed and let herself be comforted.

Madam Always led her through the camp to a small fire outside her private tent, where Leah gladly accepted a mug of warm kaff, though her hands trembled so much it was difficult to drink. She sat on a thick stump at the fire while her old teacher from the Hass school back in Ruhm, looking surprisingly at home camping in the wilds of the east, stoked it and added another log.

She'd run as much as she could, but was forced to walk much of the way, through the first night and another, guided only by hope and the general direction Madam Roths had pointed out. And though she was flooded with relief upon seeing Madam Always and finding herself safe in her encampment, she still feared Kirche would send someone after her.

"I didn't know where else to go," she whispered. "I'm glad I've found you, but I cannot stay here."

"You must tell me what has happened. What brought you to the eastern continent?" Madam Always sat next to her on a thick log.

Leah set her mug on the ground at her feet and wiped tears from her face. "I am aide to Kirche now."

"Of course, the annual tour. But what happened? Do speak of it quickly, my dear; you're frightening me. Are you ill? Was your party attacked?"

She shook her head and new tears filled her eyes. "We were camped with the others. Welk of Michelruud called a meeting with what they call the winter folk, those of you who live here in the hills."

"Madam Roths was there."

Nodding, Leah said, "That is how I knew to find you here. Some time after they marched, I was freed."

"Freed from whom?"

"Kirche."

Madam sat back, her head tilted and a question on her lips, but she held quiet and waited. Leah thought over the last several weeks, wondering where she should start her story. She shuddered and let out a sob.

"I'm so ashamed. So ashamed."

"What could you have to be ashamed of, my dear?" Her voice was so kind, gentle, it only made Leah weep all the more.

"I was so happy to be named Aid to the High Preist of Hass. I thought you would be proud of me."

"I am, indeed. Quite an honor."

Now there was a tone in Madam Always' voice that Leah didn't quite recognize. Certainly she wasn't lying, but something else.

"I truly believed I wanted it." She wiped the tears from her face, ashamed of them.

"Yes," Madam said, frowning. "You were always fond of Hass."

"I was enamored. But, oh, I'm so ashamed to say it."

"Leah Hallowsing, there is no shame in feelings, in truth, in owning up to our faults."

Leah flinched a bit. This was not the general practice in Ruhm. Blasphemous thoughts were to be kept to oneself, pushed deep and forgotten.

"You do not sound like a citizen of Ruhm," she said. "Not like my teacher."

Madam Always smiled and laid a hand atop Leah's. "But I'm not in Ruhm any longer, am I? Now, go on. What has you so troubled?"

"Oh, it's awful. I...I thought he liked me."

"Who?"

"Lord Kirche. I know, it's so stupid. I've behaved like a child."

"But you are still a child, my dear. Do not regret your inno-cence."

"Innocence, indeed! I was so wrong. Oh, Madam! Lord Kirche gave me a diary and told me to use it to parse my thoughts on...on..." Here Leah could not bring herself to tell Madam Always the truth about the kell stone. "And he stole it and read it. He read my most personal thoughts. Worse, he read what I wrote about my father. About something he told me, in confi-dence. Oh, how could I have been so stupid as to put down on paper such a secret? But I didn't know. I didn't realize what I was writing. And now Kirche has sent a message to Ruhm. My father will be arrested and he insists I—Madam it's too awful to say."

She waited, her hand giving Leah a patient pat.

"He wishes me to marry him."

Here Madam Always sat upright. "He what?"

"He believes a marriage between us will unite the Hass and its skeptics in Ruhm. He claims my father leads a contingent against Hass and once we are married...oh, I don't know. Madam, I am not meant for intrigue. I only know I was going to marry him because he told me Father would be tortured and hanged if I did not."

Madam Always was silent for several seconds before she whispered, "I'm so sorry, Leah."

"But the porters, Gretchen, Zelda...they say he will have Father hanged on Founding Day, before we return to Ruhm, whether I marry Kirche or not. They told me to run. And I did so." Leah broke into sobs. "I'm confused. I do not know if I have done the right thing."

Madam Always' body seemed to deflate, her face softened into deep concern and she shook her head.

"Never fear, Leah. Your father would not blame you."

"But it is my fault. I think I must get home. If I could get to him before Kirche's message..."

"Yes, of course you must try."

Leah stood suddenly. "I must go, then."

Madam Always pulled her to sitting again. "We will get you to a boat in time, I assure you. But the boat that could take Kirche's message does not arrive for days."

"How could you know?"

She smiled. "We have porters who barter with the captains; we send and receive news of Ruhm."

Leah sighed in relief. "Another boat, then."

"Leah, you can't get on just any boat and expect the captain to do your bidding."

"But he must."

Madam shook her head sadly. "I understand your pain, my dear."

"How could you?"

"Trust me. You have time. Try to relax a bit; we will get you home. But I have information that will help you to help your father."

"You do?"

"Indeed. Leah, you say your father told you some secrets. Did he tell you why he sent you to the Hass school?"

"What?" She waved a dismissive hand and sipped her kaff. "He said he wanted me to have a good education. And I wanted to go so badly."

"You were recruited, of course."

"Recruited?"

"Dania and your father needed a way to meet regularly with-out arousing suspicion. And so you were brought into the Hass school—against your parents' wishes. Your mother was staunchly against it. But your father realized it was the only way."

"The only way for what?"

"For Dania to have access to your father's library."

Leah shook her head in several tiny jerks and her eyes fluttered closed and opened. "What are you talking about?"

"There is a hidden cache of blasphemy at the stationer's. It was necessary to examine it, make copies of pertinent parts for distribution and—"

"Distribution of blasphemy?"

"Leah, you are young."

"Stop saying that. Stop calling me a child. I am the Aide to the High Preist of Hass."

"Are you now?"

"I mean..."

"You are a strong young woman. Strong enough to know the truth."

Madam Always hesitated and Leah watched the woman's eyes; they were kind, tender, sad. They were the same as her father's—burdened with knowledge that no one dared to learn. She nodded for her to continue.

"The Hass is a lie."

"A lie," Leah repeated.

"You thought Lord Kirche liked you? You were enamored of him? And now you see he is not as you thought he was. Good. Because Kirche represents all there is to the Hass. It's a pretty, vacuous lie."

"They are the keepers of the moral laws of Rett."

"Rett is a lie."

Leah's mouth fell open.

"It's true."

"I know," Leah said.

"Do you?"

She nodded and looked to the fire. "I saw the flaming tree of Rett, just like the one on which he was hanged and burned."

"Where?"

"There is a forest in the Ruud, where most of the beasts live. Deep within it, I saw the tree—I touched it; it was real. The story in *The Book of Rett* must be a lie. They did not all burn to ash."

"I would very much like to see that tree someday. Perhaps, when this has all come to fruition, you and I will travel there."

"Is everything a lie, then?"

"In *The Book of Rett*? No, of course not. There is just enough truth, just enough goodness, for the lies to pass, to be dismissed."

"Father knew this."

"Yes. And more proof is there, in the secret cache."

"And now Kirche knows about Daken's journal." She gasped and put a hand to her lips. "He was right about Father."

Madam nodded. "Your father will not tell them where it is; he will not give them the books that remain—for he and Dania have sent most away over the years. And he will not tell them where the kell stone is."

"You know about the stone? Of course you do."

"Yes."

"Does Father know where it is?"

"Dania told me your father has read the journal, yes. But she did not tell me what it said about the stone."

"Tell me everything you know."

Madam Always nodded and poured more kaff into their mugs. Leah first wanted to tell the woman to quiet down, whisper, but remembered they were not in Ruhm; there were no Hass spies here—no Hass to arrest them.

"Long ago," Madam Always began, "the wissendes were honored in Ruhm. They were discoverers, inventors, problem solvers. Our leadership looked to them for guidance. But the followers of Rett and his devotion were concerned over some of the changes in the land. Folk don't like change, in general, you know. And they have always been fearful of the beasts. Since we migrated from the south and encountered them, we've been trying to find ways to avoid them."

"There are few beasts in Ruhm."

"Now. But long ago, they were many. And the wissendes began to tell us their power was harmless to us as long as we lived in harmony with them."

"Why would anyone object to that?"

"Ah, because the beasts were stronger, smarter, faster. The folk wished to control them, as they had controlled the nonsentients on the southern continents, but they could not. So they clung to the ideas of Rett, as the newly emerging Hass extolled his virtues. The Hass told the folk the wissendes were liars. That their ideas about the folk being kin to the beast were vicious untruths."

"Kin to the beast?"

"The wissenry studied and learned and gathered evidence. The beast, they said, were not evil—not the product of Horatia any more than folk were the divine creation of Mutterede."

Leah's eyes widened.

"Yes, you see. Blasphemy. But it wasn't blasphemy so long ago. It was simply two competing world views: one of learning and discovery, and one of dominance and ignorance."

"But why would anyone choose ignorance?"

"To avoid change. To avoid fear."

"And so they banished the beasts and the wissendes."

"The beasts, yes. Once the kell stone was stolen from them, over time they were easier and easier to drive away. The wissendes were forced to recant their blasphemies and they continued for some time trying to work within the Hass to change things. But eventually, Michelruud sailed here to the east and the rest of us remained in darkness."

"But...Father, and Dania."

"Oh, yes. There remained always a small cadre of revolution-aries, determined to keep the truth safe. We have bided our time, secretly and smartly spreading our knowledge. The seeds of revolution are fomenting in Ruhm. Your father and Dania had a difference of opinion, I'm afraid. Dania fled before she was caught and I went with her. She tried to persuade your father to leave years ago, but he would not. He insisted on continuing there, goading the Hass into lighting the wick that will incite the revolution."

"What sort of wick?"

"Leah, sometimes it takes an act so vile, something so clearly wrong, to make the people finally wake up and take action."

"I don't understand."

Madam Always patted her hand again and smiled weakly. "I know."

Chapter Twenty-three

Where is Sorgood?"

Welk's voice was barely a rough whisper and when he coughed, sharp biting pain stabbed at his lungs. He'd allowed himself to be lifted onto a horse and led through the pass, but halted his party before they turned toward the encampments. Lucas' frail body, wrapped carefully in a blanket, lay draped over another horse, and when he was helped from his own, Welk took the reins and guided the steed northwest.

"Sorgood's run off, Sire," one of the young soldiers said.

"Footman Wolf, isn't it?"

428

"Yes, sir. Sire."

He tried to chuckle, but found his lungs had little enough in them for a sigh. "Here," he said, motioning to a spot on the grass where he dropped to his knees and let himself fall, lying with his face to the warm sun, the cold breezes of the ice realm wafting over him.

Clutch knelt beside him.

"I'm all right," Welk waved him away and forced himself to sit, grinding his jaw against the pain.

"Angel blade," one the folk said.

Welk nodded. He looked at those gathered with him. Clutch of the Wretched, several of Sorgood's men, a dozen soldiers wearing the colors of Arnot and Ricker. Good, he thought.

"Wolf," he said. The young guard stepped forward and knelt, bowing his head. "Who of Sorgood's men is loyal to me?"

The boy blustered. "Why, all of them, Sire."

"Who would choose me over Sorgood?"

Here the boy raised his face to Welk, his brow furrowed. He nodded slightly. "Not Lieutenant Drake, Sire. No. But Sergeant Cotton, yes."

"Very well. Wolf, you are to find Cotton. Tell him, with these soldiers here as your witness, that he is to arrest Sorgood for murder. Cotton is to take charge of the Michelruud guard." Welk forced a cough and winced in pain.

"Yes, Sire," Wolf said. "But sir, I saw that boy, the one with the mark. Will you set a party out to find him?"

"You will lead that party, Wolf, when the time comes."

The look on the young footman's face was nearly unbearable —pride and fear. Welk knew he must look pale as a linen sheet; he could feel the lack of blood in his own face. He struggled to regain some composure, to look alive and not of death.

"I'm taking young Lucas' body to the caverns just north. I'll need four men."

All but Footman Wolf stepped forward and Welk smiled. Suddenly, a jolt of energy surged through him and he pressed his shoulders back in a painful stretch. The wound would heal over and the pain subside, he knew, but the poison would work within him, over time, debilitating him. He'd heard tell of angel blades, stories spread by adventurers and hunters who dared travel into the ice for rare pelts and prizes.

He picked his four men and sent the rest on to the encamp-ment with a promise to meet his guard in Michelruud as soon as he could. "We have done well in the ice, my allies. Tell of it when you reach your peers. The usurper queen is unseated and we must now pledge to help the maiden; she will forge a peace between the eis and the folk of the Ruud."

The small gathering raised a meager cheer.

"Go then. I will be home again soon and we will plan for Ruhm, if she dares to come."

Another cheer and the folk hesitated, and slowly by twos and threes, drifted toward the camp.

Clutch reached a hand to help Welk to his feet. "Why the caverns?"

"There is a bit of exposed kell there. Belfen told me of the ceremony, when there were no folk here in the east, the felidae often carried their dead to the kell. I will do for Frieden what Belfen and Vreni would have done."

"And what of the boy?"

Welk shrugged. "The angels will try to get him back, I think; he makes a fine pawn. I will take a new approach as soon as I've dealt with Frieden. Don't look at me so, Clutch. I can't bear it."

The rugged folk's face was softened, sad. "How long?"

Welk shook his head. "I could live for years."

"Or?"

Welk put a hand on his shoulder. "What would you do if I died today?"

Clutch flinched and took a step back. "I do not wish to contem-plate it."

Welk chuckled, glad to be able to breathe freely once again, though there would always be pain now. "Perhaps you should begin to think on it."

Chapter Twenty-four

Leah went to Madam Always' tent before she was to meet the young folk and travel back to the Ruud with them. They all fled the ice realm, she was told, and were to get to Father Britt at Cold Sea. They seemed an odd assortment: a huntsman and three children. When she asked Madam Always whom they fled and why they'd been in the ice realm at all, Always smiled and said, "Your father and Dania would have differing opinions on that, as well." And she'd told Leah about the prophecy and King Welk chasing the boy all over the eastern continent. They both laughed over it and Leah confided in her that Kirche, too, was after the boy.

"He told King Welk that if he had the boy killed, he could turn his memory into a devotion and create something like the Hass out of it. Pren dismissed it; he said Kirche didn't mean to insinuate Rett was killed on purpose, just so a devotion to him could be used to give a moral law to the folk."

"Ah, and what do you make of that now?"

Leah had frowned and shook her head. "It seems a difficult thing to attempt. And I find myself wondering now, if Rett ever lived at all."

Madam Always smiled and held up a finger. "You are not alone in that suspicion. And you will find, I hope one day, your father's library holds the key to that question."

"But the boy," she'd said. "Welk couldn't seriously consider killing him?"

"So young to be so important," Madam Always said. "You must protect him. See that he gets back to the wissenry where he belongs."

"They sent him away."

"Indeed, and they'll likely do it again. Just help him get there and perhaps Britt can find you a boat."

Now, hesitating by the fire, hiding the kitchen knife behind her back, Leah gathered her wits and called for her former teacher.

"You must learn to call me Byn," the old woman said with a smile when she emerged from her tent.

"That, I think, is appropriate, considering what I am about to ask you to do for me."

"Why, what is it, dear? Why so grave?"

Leah showed her the knife.

"Who are you going to kill with that?"

"I should tell you of my meeting with an eis assassin recently."

"Oh?"

"I'm quite violent, as it turns out. But I mean no one harm. None but myself."

Madam Always crossed her arms at her chest. "Explain."

"I wish for you to cut off my hair."

The old woman gasped and put her hands to her mouth. "I could not."

"You must." She pulled her toward the fire and sat down on the stump in front of her. "I will return to Ruhm, but I cannot be in the upper tier. I will be an ordinary girl, and go unnoticed." She held up the knife. "Cut it all."

And as the woman sawed away at her hair, Leah drew in a ragged breath and wiped the tears from her face. As soon as the long mane fell, a heaviness lifted from her, more than the weight of the hair, more even than the weight of her station. She had a plan—a vision. She would save her father, take him far from Ruhm, but beyond that, she must continue her father's work. She must find his library, the journal...and the kell stone, if for no other reason than to keep it from the Hass.

She met the young folk and curtseyed, trying out the greeting she never would have offered to someone below her in Ruhm. The three children were about twelve in age, she was told. Rugged, as most of the eastern folk were. Fenn had sharp, dark features against a pale face, hardened by experience, she thought. Grayson was dark, but in a softer way. His eyes hinted at intelli-gence more than heroism. And Sadie...she lifted her chin upon meeting Leah and looked suspiciously at her. But she smiled when Leah ruffled her own mop of newly shorn, curly hair.

"What do you think?" Leah asked her. "I need a woman's opinion."

This brought a laugh out of the girl and Leah relaxed. Even the huntsman Rogget didn't frighten her. He called her *ma'am* and *miss* at every opportunity and nodded his head as if she were a noblewoman and he, her servant.

They were off, and after some hours hiking, Grayson pounded his feet against the cold ground, and kicked at the browned grass of the plain, grumpy and tired. Occasionally he mumbled something sour and Sadie turned to Leah with a smile.

"You've been traveling long with these male folk?" she asked the girl.

"It's not so bad."

"Sadie's hardly a girl, really," Grayson said.

Leah gasped. "What a rude thing to say about a girl."

"I didn't mean... I mean. Sorry Miss Hallowsing," Grayson said.

"Call me Leah, please. I do not wish to be miss or madam any longer."

They all agreed, but she knew they'd be back to it soon enough.

"I only meant Sadie's not like some of the other girls in Path. She's strong and brave and doesn't bat her eyelashes at the older boys."

Leah laughed. "I think you'd be surprised at how many girls are strong and brave and just don't think you need to know it, until they're ready to show you."

Grayson blushed.

She enjoyed her new company so much more than that of Kirche and his party, though she missed them, she had to admit to herself. Gretchen's babbling would fit with the young folk moving from topic to topic without a care. Zelda would be able to mother Sadie; goodness knows the girl could use it—all them could, even Rogget. Xavier, though only a boy, was always quick with a joke. Leah felt a pang tug at her heart. She missed even Kipling and Redd. And Alphonse. She thought back on the last time she'd seen him, in Timber, at the edge of the beast forest, just before he was trampled.

"Are you all right?" Sadie said, wrapping a hand around Leah's elbow.

"I miss my folk, I suppose."

"But you ran from them," Grayson said. He blushed again. "I'm sorry, Miss Hallowsing. I shouldn't tell tales."

"We heard it back at the camp. Is it true?" Sadie said.

"That I ran away? Yes. I'm afraid I'm in some trouble."

"So are we," Fenn told her.

"It's good that way," Sadie said. "We'll all understand one another."

"What sort of trouble are you in? I mean," Leah faltered. "Madam Always told me about the prophecy story. The king of Michelruud is after you. The angels, too."

"Do you suppose they still are?" Grayson said.

"Ard," Rogget said, "count on it."

"But why the angels?" Sadie said. "Fenn said Brenna was going to oust the usurper queen. She wouldn't send them after us."

"Brenna said they wanted the kell stone," Fenn said. "Maybe they think I can get it for them."

"I learned a lot about them angels while I was in the guard," Rogget said. "They're beautiful creatures and full of themselves over it. They spend a lot of time looking at their reflections. I know 'cause I saw one."

"You did?" Sadie said.

"Aye, I did. But don't tell anyone I said that. I was on a secret mission for King Evan and no one's supposed to know we went to them."

"What did you do? What was the mission?"

Rogget laughed. "I haven't the faintest clue. I was just a guard."

"I'm told angels are evil," Leah said. "But none too bright."

"But they seduced the queen," Fenn said, "or Brenna's aunt. Don't you need smarts to do that?"

"Well, that's their danger really," Rogget said. "They know how to charm you. They make you feel so good you do whatever they want you to do willingly."

"That's scary," Sadie said.

"Aye. We'll keep our eyes open. You especially Fenn."

Leah sighed and shifted her pack; it was heavy and growing heavier. The women's college sent them off with bedrolls and enough food and water for the journey straight across the Plains of Glisch, through Damon Wall to the port. The ground was flat at least; to her right she could see the hills sloping gently higher and higher toward the mountains. She expected to see horses riding toward them, and Kirche's mitre glistening against the muted autumn sun, and the thought had her always searching for a place to hide. The grass on the plain was knee-high in some spots and she wanted to crouch down in it and crawl her way to the Ruud; though there were small, brief bits of wood on the plain, she wouldn't feel safe until she was in the forest of Damon Wall.

On the second day, in the afternoon, they approached a small encampment of a half dozen tents surrounding a fire pit. A cheerful folk called out to them, "Salutations!" He waved his arm back and forth above his head.

"What's he saying?" Sadie said.

"It's like hello is all," Grayson said.

Gray smoke from the fire swirled toward the sky, and as they neared they smelled roasting meat, kaff, and cider. The folk who'd waved at them was short and round with black hair cropped closely except for long strands falling over his forehead. He smiled broadly when they met him just outside the circle of tents.

"Welcome unwonted viators." He took Rogget's hand and pumped it up and down. "You have no rantipoles along, I assume?"

Rogget sucked in a breath prepared to respond, but stared at the beaming folk with a curious look until he let his breath out without replying. Leah stifled a laugh.

"Did he say he didn't want us here?" Grayson whispered.

Leah shook her head. "I can't say for certain, but he doesn't act like it."

The folk rubbed his large belly, looked at the kids and shook his head. "Ah, well, we'll submit to providence then. Come, come. Join us. I am Walter, a bona fide philosopher. Here you will meet my brother Ned, a philosophaster. But don't speak of it. And we also have Sir John; you'll find him full to the brim with gasconade and I do say I often suspect him of being something of a footpad. So, you will be careful, won't you? But come, come."

Rogget gave Leah a worried look, and she shrugged and shook her head.

"Can't you translate what he's saying?" Fenn asked Grayson. He turned to Leah, "Grayson reads a lot."

"I see," she said with a smile.

Grayson shook his head. "There aren't many language books at the stationer's."

They followed the folk to the fire where two others sat on logs drinking out of tin mugs.

"Viators," he said to his fellows and they waved hellos.

"Salutations, I'm sure," the oldest man said, his hair gray and his face lined.

434

"This is Sir John," Walter told them. "And here, my brother Ned."

"Good afternoon," Sadie said with a slight curtsy.

Leah followed her lead while the boys, shuffling their feet, bowed slightly. Rogget merely grumbled.

"She's in fine fettle, I dare say," Sir John said looking Sadie over. "And you've brought us a hobbledehoy as well," he said turning to Fenn.

"I'm a what?" Fenn said.

Grayson nudged him sharply in the ribs and gave him a scornful look.

"Join us, join us," Walter said showing them to a few logs at the fire.

They all removed their packs. Sadie, Grayson, and Fenn sat on one log and Rogget labored to the ground beside it, while Leah took a short log next to him. Ned handed them mugs filled with steaming hot cider and Leah grasped hers with both her palms, warming them, and breathed in the wonderful smell. Rogget had kaff and the strong odor competed with the delicate fruity smell of her cider. She turned to see young Fenn with his nose in his mug. She smiled at him.

"I don't like the smell of bitters," he said. "It's mucking up my cider."

She laughed. "I quite agree, though I don't mind the smell of kaff."

"'Tis quite hiemal, this land, is it now?" Sir John said to Rogget.

"Aye," Rogget muttered.

"We're immigrants ourselves. We flee a kakistocracy, seeking eunomy. Have you much illth in the area?"

"Uh," Rogget looked to Leah and she raised her shoulders, wide-eyed, helpless to suggest a response. "Er..."

But no matter; Sir John went on talking. "We locomote from afar to seek out our brethren. They denominate themselves Breathless."

"Oh, no, Sir John," Walter broke in, "they write that they are designated Breathless by the querimonious ruddy folk hereabouts. We can't imagine why."

"Nonetheless our brethren have adopted the moniker. Have you heard of them? We will felicitate them on their success in this land, to be sure. It is said they have garnered much. We do not at all suspect them of improbity, I dare say. No, no, we do not."

"There is much improbity in our mother land," Ned said.

"Indeed, indeed." Sir John nodded. "Such ipsedixitism, such hypermimia, such farrago, and pseudodox all about."

"Stop, Sir John," Walter said. "You're infecting me with horripilation."

"Oh, don't be such a mythomane."

Walter turned to the kids and said, "From whence do you roam? Tell us of your interests."

They stared at him for a moment, until Grayson, as if in a daze, said,

"My da owns the inn."

Sir John gasped. "Do tell us all about it. You must, then, be quite expert in xenodocheionology. Why Ned here claims such knowledge, but he's all bluster and polylogy."

Ned snorted. "Least I don't brabble grandiloquence."

"Do you attempt to fustigate me, young Ned? I dare say your fetor and ozostomia do nothing to recommend you to our vulgus guests."

"Is that it, now?" Ned said. "You must resort to ad hominem attacks? Your logorrhea isn't enough?"

"I dare say!"

"Now, now," Walter said. "Let's not engage in ruction in front of our hebetudenous guests."

"Jackanapes," Ned said.

"Pygalgia," Sir John said.

Slowly, and with much grunting and gasping, Sir John and Ned stood, and began to swat at each other. Sadie gasped, but Grayson chuckled. Fenn looked at Rogget who just stared at the folk, confused. Leah put a hand to her mouth to keep from laughing aloud.

Walter tried to wedge himself between the two fighters, squeaking, "You're both grobians. Abdominous, amentiatic, anserine, blatherskites."

Finally, all three men stood apart and breathed heavily for a long moment.

"I dare say," Sir John said to Walter, "that was quite unneces-sary."

"You have become rather incondite of late, Sir John," Walter said, returning carefully to his log. He looked at his guests and said, "Just a velitation, my comrades. Nothing serious; do drink up." And he looked over to Sir John.

"Indeed," Sir John said.

"Uh..." Ned said.

Sir John spluttered, "My friend, you have lapsed into monepic utterings."

"I believe, I mean, I daresay, I see something of an ursiform in the distance."

Walter laughed. "Ursiform? Don't be duncical." To Rogget, he said, "You don't have bears about, do you?"

Just as Rogget turned, Sir John fell backward to the ground in trying to jump up, and screeched in a high-pitched voice from where he lay, "Bear!"

"Ah, I think we'll be going now," Rogget said, standing. "We've enjoyed your hospitality and the bitters."

Leah caught sight of a bear loping toward them from the north. She recalled the two bears at Wiley Arbus' camp and won-dered if one had escaped.

"But the bear," Walter said, beginning to sweat and ignoring John on the ground.

"It's only Darnit; he's nothing to worry about," Rogget said. "He won't come near your camp."

Walter wiped his forehead with his sleeve. "I daresay I was clamoring for additional engrossing conversation, especially as relates to the boy's expertise in xenodocheionology, but I'm afraid our trio is quite ursaphobic."

"Do they have bears where you come from?" Grayson asked.

Ned, who hadn't moved, but kept his wide gaze glued to Darnit, now pacing in the distance, said, "Indeed. Godless execution machines. They're soulless, I tell you. No souls!"

"Ah, yes. As I said. We thank you for your hospitality. But..."

"Yes, yes," Walter said. "I agree it would be for the best. Could you take the bear very, very far away?"

"Of course," Rogget said. He walked around the circle and held out a hand to Sir John, still lying on the ground. "Let me help you up."

Sir John whispered, "No, no. His visual acuity is motion sensitive. If I just lie here I'll be fine. Pretend you don't see me. Move along. Move along."

Leah, having lost control, laughed out loud and turned from the sight so as not to embarrass herself further. Rogget, too, let out a laugh and a loud roar escaped Darnit. Startled, Leah watched the bear, now standing, his back to the group. Looking beyond him, in the distance, against the mountains, she saw a glow.

"What is that?"

"Angels," Fenn said, standing and moving to her side.

Darnit lay on the ground and curled up as the angels flew over him toward the tents, their great white wings flapping easily in the air. There were three—glowing a pale subtle blue, wearing loose, stark white gowns shimmering in the sunlight, so long it looked as if they had no feet and could not walk on the ground. And they were singing.

"I'd forgotten how beautiful they are," Sadie said. Her face lit up and she smiled, walking toward them.

"No—" Fenn grabbed her arm—"Don't go near them."

Leah felt Fenn's other hand on her elbow.

"They won't hurt us," Rogget said.

"Are you crazy?" Fenn said.

But Rogget's face was also bright with a smile.

Fenn turned to Grayson. "You're not going to get all angel mushy are you?"

"No." He smiled. "But they do sing nicely, don't they? Let's have these folk offer them some bitters or something."

"You can't offer them bitters. They're here to catch us again, or worse, take us into the ice mountains and leave us there."

"Well, I daresay," Walter said, coming forward. "I do not believe I have ever witnessed such a luminous display. Angels, you say?"

"They're dangerous," Fenn said.

Leah watched them, her heart rising to rejoice, to sing their song. Their faces, pale and sharp, reminded her of the carved heads of the premiers of Ruhm on the Hall of Hass. Like gods. But sensing their deception, she winced against the desire to follow them. Though Sadie, Grayson, and Rogget, she realized, were falling quite in love with the creatures.

"They're evil," Leah said. "Get down."

"Oh, now that's harsh," Rogget said.

"But don't you remember what Wiley told us?" Fenn said. "Don't you remember when they took us and left us in the tower?"

"What is that refrain they're singing?" Sir John said, rolling this way and that on the ground trying to get up.

"Stop listening!" Fenn said.

Just as Sir John was on his knees ready to stand, the angels dove toward the campsite. Leah felt a smile tugging at the corners of her mouth and warmth floated up from her feet.

"Stop!" Fenn screamed.

She jerked awake and turned to him. "We should look away," she said.

Walter, Sir John, and Ned held out their arms and began twirling.

"Positively gleeful," Ned said.

"I daresay," said Sir John, "I've lost all fright of the bear."

The Breathless folk stopped spinning and walked toward one of the angels; Ned shouted up at him, "Shall we go with you? Will you take us away?"

Leah, unable to keep from looking at them, watched as a luminous young male floated down to the huntsman. Rogget merely stood before it, as if waiting to be carried off. The angel slipped its hands under his arms and picked the man off the ground as if he were weightless.

"Don't," Fenn said, grasping Rogget's leg as he floated away.

Rogget looked down at him and smiled. "Maybe if you use the fire," he said with a laugh, "you could scare them away."

Leah was awash with confusion—the desire to run, a yearning to leave with the angels, to fly, but more, wanting to protect the children. She grabbed for Fenn and dug her heels into the ground as she and the boy were pulled along with Rogget.

"Sir John," Leah called. "Take the children."

The three men paused, watching her hang on to Fenn by his waist while trying to keep Sadie and Grayson from the other two angels hovering over them. Then, as if she'd poked them with an iron from the fire, the men leapt forward, grabbed Sadie and Grayson, pushed them to the ground and fell atop them; there they remained huddled.

"Stop!" Fenn screamed.

He was lifted off the ground and Leah pulled hard, forcing the boy to let go of Rogget. Together they fell backward to the grass.

"No," Fenn cried, watching his friend being carried away.

The other two angels came for them, but Fenn dodged them, ran to the fire pit and threw his hands at the flames as if batting them away. Leah ran from the flying creatures, crouched low with the Breathless, and watched the boy swat at the fire, again and again, until he cried out in frustration. Finally, he swooped his hands deep, nearly to the burning logs, and with a great audible whoosh, flames flew in a torrent like a wave at the two angels hovering above their camp. Their soothing song erupted into screeches.

"Make it stop," Sadie called.

Fenn threw his hands at the fire again, swinging his arms in a circle, sending flames into the air. One angel twirled toward the sky, screaming, batting at his gown. Fenn attacked the fire again and again until finally, the last angel rose into the sky in a cloud of blue smoke. They both soared away, their angry cries ringing out across the plain.

Leah struggled to stand and made her way to the boy, now lying on the ground, gasping for air, trembling.

"Rogget," he said.

The Breathless folk stood and helped Sadie and Grayson to their feet where they watched Rogget, in the angel's arms, far in the distance.

"I daresay," Ned said, "the pennate beast is removing your compatriot to the sea."

Fenn stood, shakily, watching Darnit race toward Rogget and the angel. Seething with rage, he ran, too, reached his hand toward the sky and shouted, "Let him go!"

The angel stumbled in the air, dropping toward the ground.

"Now," Fenn ordered.

Rogget fell from the angel's grasp onto Darnit and they both tumbled to the ground. The three angels hovered in the distance while the huntsman and the bear hobbled back to the tents. Leah moved to stand next to Fenn and put a hand on his shoulder.

"Leave us alone," he said.

The angels shrieked, turned, and soared northeastward toward the mountains.

"The sooner we get you to Father Britt," Leah said, "the better for all of us."

Chapter Twenty-five

Fenn trudged forward, across the grassy field overlooking Cold Sea Port, toward the wissenry on the hill. He followed behind Sadie, pulled by Grayson who had tight hold on her hand. Her head was bowed and she stumbled often; Fenn reached out and lifted her back to her feet a few times without thinking.

"We'll sleep when we get there," Grayson told her again and again.

Darnit grumbled as he was set off into the woods behind the wissenry. Rogget yawned and nearly lost his balance. Leah Hallowsing had kept them going—the whole time—herding them like dazed sheep, telling them they mustn't stop, must keep walking, must get to safety.

"Come on," Grayson would say every few minutes and pull harder at Sadie. There was fear in his eyes—a fear Fenn didn't recognize. Not the fear of the beast forest, or the beast lord. Not the fear of the Wretched. Not of the battle in the ice realm or the angels.

It's me, he told himself. They're afraid of me.

Fenn remembered eating, but there lingered a nagging emptiness in his middle that made him want to vomit. His legs shook and his hands trembled as they walked up the steps to the back door and he knocked. The smell of roasted chicken wafted out a window to his nose and he reeled and almost lost balance completely. Sadie sank onto the first step and Grayson knocked again. Finally the door opened and Fenn was sure he fell asleep where he stood.

When he woke, Fenn found himself in the hidden rooms below the wissenry, in the same bed he'd slept in weeks before when they'd come to Father Britt for help. Sadie was in her bed, pale, but sleeping. Grayson sat at the table eating, slowly, as if he didn't enjoy it. Fenn sat up, put his feet to the floor and rubbed at his eyes.

"Where's Leah?"

Grayson shrugged and held out a biscuit. Fenn went to the table and accepted it; sitting, he sliced it in half and slathered butter on it, topped it with honey. He took a bite and closed his eyes. How long had it been since he'd had a fresh-baked biscuit? Sadie sat up, her brown hair twisted atop her head. She tried to smile but only half made it, before she yawned. Father Britt knocked at the door and smiled at them as he took a seat on Grayson's bed.

"Well, now," he said, slapping his knees with his hands, "tell me."

"We went out to the hill country," Grayson said. "Fenn told us he was to go to the ice realm, but he wanted to find out about his mother." He turned to Fenn and offered a bit of a smile. Fenn nodded to him, letting him know it was okay. Better *he* tell it. Father Britt was less likely to scold him. "So we went over to the wasteland. He found his mother's nurse, but she wasn't much help. Then Fenn was caught by the Wretched and they tried to give him over to King Welk."

Father Britt nodded. "I know all of that."

"You do?" Fenn said.

"Some I heard from Treacher—still wandering about in disguise teasing out the folk's whim with regard to you. The rest in the hill country where I traveled to join the league of folk organizing against the ice realm. There was much talk of your exploits there. While you are feared and hated here in the Ruud, you're all quite celebrated in the hills."

"You were with King Welk," Fenn whispered. "So, you know about Lucas."

Father nodded again and Fenn was relieved that at least that much of the story would not have to be told.

"What happened after you escaped the battle at the palace?"

"We first went to an encampment south," Grayson said. "We weren't sure what we should do, I think. We met up with Miss Hallowsing; she's going back to Ruhm. We all crossed the Plains of Glisch but were attacked by angels. Fenn cast fire at them. It was amazing."

"How did you do it?" Father Britt asked.

Fenn whispered, "Rogget told me to throw fire at them. So I just did it."

Father Britt smiled. Fenn balled his fists tight. There was nothing in the wissende's face hinting at sorrow for the loss of Lucas. Was this the demeanor expected of a wissende? It couldn't be, he thought. Father Treacher wouldn't be so callous; he'd let his emotions show—Father Treacher had a heart.

"We have reports," Britt said, "that the angels are furious. The usurper queen was taken prisoner. One of their own was on the side of the maiden and carried her aunt into the mountains; we are told she was left there to die."

"That's awful," Sadie said. She wrapped herself in a robe Tom had given her when they arrived, made her way to the small table against the wall and took a chair.

"It may not be true," Father Britt said. "And even so, it would be better than a public execution. But it is true enough that after the skirmish at the palace, there has been a great increase in the number of attacks on the people of the hill country. Many dozens have been carried off."

"So they weren't after me," Fenn said.

"It seems not."

"What about King Welk? I saw an angel stab him with a weird knife. Is he...is he alive?"

Father Britt sighed.

"The king is all right," Grayson said, as if saying it would make it so. "And he knows Fenn isn't the bairn of prophecy."

"Is it all over, Father?" Sadie said. "Can we go home?"

"I wish I could send you all away and not have to tell you what I know, but, alas, I cannot. My heart will not allow it."

"What is it?" Sadie said, worry on her face.

Britt slapped his hands on his knees once again and said, "Very well, I will out with it. We don't know where Welk has gone or if he lives; he's disappeared. Some of his guard approached Sorgood in Michelruud, attempting to take control, but Sorgood overcame them, had them hanged as traitors."

"What?" Grayson said.

"Aye, it is a gruesome business. There hasn't been a hanging in the Ruud for nigh on to two decades. I'm afraid there is more. Your parents were guests in Michelruud castle, we are told, but are now in the jailhouse. Sorgood has sent out a missive saying they, too, will be hanged, unless Fenn gives himself up."

Father Britt paused, as if waiting for them to speak, to ask questions, to sob. But they all sat very still. Fenn looked at Sadie and Grayson, but they wouldn't meet his gaze.

Finally Grayson nodded and said, "We won't let him have Fenn."

"Very well. Now that the wasteland has been emptied of those who wished to return home, we think it best you all make your way there. We can secret you back into the hills with Rogget."

"What about the kell stone?" Fenn asked him.

"The stone is not your problem."

"Isn't it? Father Treacher told me when he first sent me away...he said no matter what, I shouldn't go looking for it."

"Because of the prophecy," Grayson said.

"I don't think so," Fenn said. "Tell us the truth, Father."

"I'm not sure I know what the truth is."

"Try."

Britt sighed again and rubbed his hands through his short hair, leaving it sticking up wildly around his head. "A wise young folk told me recently that I could understand much if I took the time to read my own books. I've read more in these last weeks than I have in all my life, I'm willing to say. And I've learned much. But, alas, I've gained more questions in the process."

"You mean, you hadn't read all of the books before?" Fenn said, surprised.

Father shook his head. "Some. Bits and pieces. But not all. The wissen-ry is something of a brotherhood, you see. Our traditions and knowledge are passed along one to another; it's in the books, to be sure...as we are told. But it never seemed necessary to read it for ourselves."

"What did you learn?"

He gazed at the wall behind them as if he saw something far in the distance and wished to touch it. "I learned that folk are cruel and small." He turned to Fenn. "I learned that we have wronged our brothers. But knowing everything I know now, I still cannot say it would be wise to return the kell stone to the beast folk."

"Why not?" Sadie said.

"We are too entrenched here. Our lives are here. With the stone in their midst, the beast would rise once again—their power doubled, tripled."

"What power?" Fenn said.

"Strength, life span, intelligence. They would continue the path of evolution on which they were so speedily racing along. They would oust us."

"You don't know that for sure."

"Would we want to live here among such powerful creatures?"

"You mean...creatures we treated so badly?" Grayson said. "I read about it. I know. We tortured them, murdered them, forced them off their land."

"And where would you have read such a thing?"

"That's not important," Fenn said.

"No, it's okay," Grayson said. "I read some of *The Book of Katze.*"

Father Britt's eyes widened. "You what?"

"I did. And if we ever get out of this mess, I'm going to read the rest of it. Everybody should know the truth of what we did."

"And you think knowing that, the folk of the Ruud would allow the kell stone returned to the beasts?"

"They have no choice," Fenn said.

"Indeed, they do."

Fenn's jaw hardened and he fought to keep himself from grinding his teeth. "You know where the kell stone is, don't you?"

Britt sputtered. "I told you it was not your concern."

"How can it not be?"

"If I knew where it was, I certainly would not tell you. No. Your part in this story is done. You will take to the wasteland, or farther north. Stay out of Sorgood's way and let us deal with this mess."

"You know I can't do that."

Britt shook his head and closed his eyes. "Very well, hear this: we have found out where it might be"—he held up his hand to dissuade interruption—"but we do not know for certain. And we have learned there might be a way to destroy it."

"Destroy it?" Fenn said.

"The wissenry has decided this is the best course of action. We are searching now for a suitable candidate to travel to—to its place of hiding. We will secure it, and see to its demise. Surely you understand it would be unwise to give the beast folk enough power to bring us ruin."

Sadie and Grayson turned to Fenn. He hesitated, holding Britt's gaze, then nodded. "Give us a day or two here, to rest," Fenn said. "We'll go north and let the wissenry handle this."

Father Britt seemed to deflate; he let out a nervous chuckle. "Wise, my boy. You will indeed make a fine wissende one day. And you'll see— when this is all done and told, you three will be welcomed home and this sordid ordeal will be put behind us." He clapped his hands together and pulled them each into a jolly hug before leaving them to rest.

"Back to the wasteland?" Sadie said.

"Maybe," he said. "Let's think about it."

"Aren't you mad at him?" Grayson said. "They keep sending you away. Are they protecting *you*, or themselves?"

"I am angry, yes. But it won't do any good to express that to Britt."

Chapter Twenty-six

When the boy found her room, Leah was putting the last of her few things in the pack Madam Always had given her. An apple, two pieces of jerky, a locket of her own hair, bound in a length of blue ribbon. "For your mother," Madam had said.

"I saw you before," the boy said, standing in the doorway.

She sat at her small table and invited him to take the chair opposite. The hidden rooms in the wissenry were dark, chilly, but comfortable. She was grateful for Britt's hospitality, and sorry to have to sneak away, but the less he and Tom knew of her whereabouts the better for them, she reasoned.

"I think you'd only just arrived," Fenn said. "You were with the Hass. Grayson told me he recognized the flaming tree symbol one of you wore on a chain."

She nodded.

"You passed us on the street and looked back. Your hair was very long then."

"I don't recall," she said. "But my arrival here was rather exciting; much of it is a blur in my memory."

"Why did you cut it?"

She tilted her head at him; it seemed an odd question. "In Ruhm, only those of a higher station may wear their hair long."

"So, it's almost like a disguise."

"Yes." She smiled.

"Is the Hass after the kell stone?"

She chuckled. "That was rather abrupt, was it not?"

"No sense wandering down side roads. Father Britt doesn't want it returned to the beast folk."

"I would imagine not."

"He says the folk of the Ruud would agree."

"But you think differently?"

He turned to look around her room, hesitating. "I don't know what to think. Except, if I found the stone—if I gave it to King Arnot or King Ricker, or maybe...destroyed it—everybody would stop chasing me, stop thinking I'm going to do something awful with it. The kings of the Ruud would oust Sorgood from Michelruud and I could go back to the wissenry in Path. Sadie and Grayson could go home."

"But what of King Welk?"

He turned to look at her and his dark eyes reminded her of someone she couldn't place. She'd seen those eyes before, she was sure; but they were playful where his were filled with worry.

"You didn't know?"

She shook her head, fearful now of what he would say.

"He was stabbed by an angel; I saw it myself."

"Madam Always told me you fled the ice realm; she didn't say you were in the battle."

"I was," he said. "I saw Welk stabbed, just after Sorgood shot Lucas. They say—"

"Lucas? Shot?"

"Did you know him? He was my brother...at the wissenry in Path."

Leah could feel her face pale and she swallowed.

"He's dead," Fenn said. "And Welk has disappeared, probably dead, too. Sorgood took over Michelruud. You see, if I can get the stone, give it to King Arnot, say—"

"Or destroy it."

"Exactly. Sorgood would be ousted, if not by the other kings, then by the folk of Michelruud. They're only allowing all of this because of their fear of the prophecy and the stone; I'm sure of it."

"But if you destroy the stone, how would they know? Would they trust your word?"

Here he flinched, barely visible, and he suddenly looked less a child and more a...again, she couldn't quite place his eyes. He has cunning in him, she thought.

"That is a concern," he said. "Maybe I can bring it to them in pieces, or melted down, or..."

"How do you intend to find it?"

The boy got up from his chair and went to her doorway. Peering out, he looked this way and that, returned to the table and whispered, "I snuck into Father Britt's room this morning while he was at the port. He's been reading; he told me so, and all the most important books were lying open on his desk. It was easy enough to find the book with the location of the stone in it."

"What book?" Her heart sped at the thought that Daken's journal could be here in the Ruud.

"It was a book of wissenry interviews and biographies."

"I see." She let herself breathe with relief. "And what did you find out?"

He leaned back in his chair. "How do I know you aren't with the Hass any longer?"

Leah tried not to smile; patronizing the boy would be cruel, sure enough, but also inappropriate. After what she'd seen of him at the Breathless camp, the way he threw fire at the angels and commanded them, she knew he was at least split folk, if not an eis. How much should she tell him? And should she tell him about Lucas? Was Lucas' identity a secret? It must be; if the boy lived with him at the Path wissenry and yet, didn't know, then it was not her story to tell. It was a shame; she could see how sad-dened he was by the loss. Nonetheless, there was much she *could*

446

reveal.

After offering the boy a mug of cider, Leah told him of her travels with Kirche, of his cruelty to the brownies, to all the beast folk. And she told him, candidly, of Dakenruud's journal.

"That's as much as I found out," he said. "In Britt's book, several wissendes speak of a journal that can be found at the stationer's in Ruhm. The location of the kell stone is in there. Is that why you're going back?"

"No. I only ever wanted the stone to prove my loyalty to the Hass. My only concern now is my father. Kirche plans to have him killed."

"Because of the journal?"

She nodded. "I'm leaving now," she said. "Or I was until you came to see me."

He peered at her, as if he were trying to read her thoughts. He leaned forward, over the table and reached his hand across it, almost to her arm. "May I touch you?" he said.

A bit frightened, Leah nodded and he put his hand atop hers. His was warm and pulsed slightly. She looked up at him but his eyes were closed. After a few seconds he removed his hand and opened his eyes.

"What is it?" she said. "What did you do?"

He smiled timidly. "Apparently, I'm part eis; many of them have the power of touch."

"And what did you learn of me?"

"That you're honest, caring, frightened. Worried."

She sighed a ragged breath. "That I am."

"You have a boat?"

"No. But I know someone I could ask."

"Not someone from Ruhm?"

She shook her head. "A young woman at one of the inns in the port."

"Can I come with you?"

"You're determined to destroy it?"

He shrugged. "Not completely, no. But I'm going to find it."

"Very well, then. You'll have to hurry."

Fenn hid in the bathroom while Leah invited Sadie and Grayson to visit her room. She felt silly, showing them nothing. Her room was the same as theirs. Just as empty, just as ordinary. Nonetheless, she feigned excitement, telling them they could visit one another while they stayed there at the wissenry. When she imagined Fenn had enough time to pack up his things and sneak out of the hidden rooms, she yawned and said she must nap, shooing them out. Then she tied the top of her knapsack and snuck quietly up through the cellar, pilfering a few more apples on her way, into the main rooms, and out the front door, marveling at how easily she could engage in stealing, as well as lying.

She found Fenn waiting just down the hill and together they walked the long, steep path into the port and to the Snapping Turtle Inn.

Chapter Twenty-seven

It was dark when they went to board *Tansey's Sorrow*. They wouldn't sail until just before dawn, but Leah insisted they were safer on the boat than at the inn. Just as Fenn stepped on the gangplank, he felt a twinge of guilt at leaving the others behind. And just as that twinge welled up in his chest and threatened to become a sob, he heard Sadie's voice behind him.

"I can't believe you thought you could leave us behind."

"We had a pact," Grayson said, walking past him and onto the boat. "You know what a pact is, right?"

"What are you three doing here?"

"Leah sent Wanda for us," Rogget said. "Wanda said Captain Olgut promised there'd be plenty of room, if we're willing to work our passage."

Fenn hopped off the plank to the deck and caught Leah smiling at him. "But...Father Britt?"

"Wanda was clever," Grayson said. "She told him Leah had forgotten a message for us. Britt had us come up to the main floor—didn't want to give away the hidden rooms, I suppose."

"And she told him," Sadie said, "'Why Father, it's private,' so he had to leave us alone with her."

"Oh, he was listening from the hallway," Rogget said.

Sadie laughed. "He didn't hear a thing."

"Does he know you're gone?"

"Not yet," Grayson said. "We just snuck out a bit ago."

Sadie, Grayson, and Fenn had a small cubby in the hold, as Olgut said they would not be allowed with the sailors like Rogget was; there was plenty of room as he'd sold his lot at port. The captain was a tinker by trade, carrying whatever goods he thought profitable, and legal, from Ruhm to the Ruud. They were grateful to have a spot of their own after they met the crew—a rowdy bunch, but eager to be polite. Their chores were easy enough: laundry, helping out in the mess, swabbing decks, cleaning Olgut's cabin, and telling stories of the Ruud and Ruhm. Olgut gave Leah his own cabin, insisting he enjoyed sleeping out on deck.

The first night in their cubby, when Leah was on deck watch-ing the darkness, as she put it, and Rogget snored away down below, Grayson said, "What's the plan, then? Why Ruhm instead of north?"

448

"I want to find the kell stone," Fenn said. "I want this to be over."

"But Britt said—"

"I don't trust him, nor the wissenry."

"Why would he lie?"

"I'm not saying he lied. I looked at his books. It's true; they know a place to look for the stone and they had some ideas about how to destroy it. But I have to do it myself."

Sadie shook her head. "I understand we've done great things, Fenn," she said. "We rescued the children of Path from Steingefan and saw the beast lord. We fought the Wretched and...I even held a firearm on a king. But finding the kell stone and destroying it? Shouldn't we leave that to the adult folk?"

"But that's just it. It's the adult folk who started all this. Think of it. A wissende—not the sort in the Ruud, but a real wissende from the old days in Ruhm, when they were folk of logic and reason—he couldn't bring himself to give the stone to the beast folk. And now we should trust them?"

"But you're not planning to give it back, are you?"

"No, I didn't mean that. It's just...I won't be free of this unless I know for myself. I have to be the one to do it."

Grayson nodded. "But, folk have been looking for the kell stone for centuries; what makes you think we can find it?"

"I think they've only just started looking. The beast folk have looked longer, sure, but you said they've been weakened without it; they can't search for it without risking folk catching and killing them."

Grayson's frown cast a clownish shadow on his face in the lantern light, rocking slightly with the boat. "It looks as if you're doing what the prophecy said you'd do."

"I don't believe in prophecy. And anyway, I'm not going to destroy the Ruud. It's my home."

He watched them both carefully as they tried to avoid his gaze.

"Well," Grayson mumbled. "We made the pact. We stick together."

"You could have gone home," Fenn said. "Is the pact more important than your folks?"

"If we went to Path without you," Sadie said, "Sorgood wouldn't believe we didn't know where you were; we'd be put in jail, too. And my mother would be angry with me."

"It's true enough," Grayson said. "As much trouble as we've caused our folk, they'd want us safe, and as far from the Ruud as we can get."

Fenn's heart sank just a little and he felt as if he'd lost something. They'd come along, really, because they had nowhere else to go. "Well, I'm glad you came," he said, not sure he believed it himself.

Chapter Twenty-eight

W elk allowed Krup to carry Lucas' body into the caverns in the north, far beyond the Plain of Nergens —where he felt the spirit of Rue-Anna calling with each gust of wind—over the field of lilac clover, and through the northern forests. He would not allow Clutch to join them; the man had too much to do—the folk of the hill country had a lot to consider. And so Clutch sent along Krup, his stoutest man, in his stead. And it was Krup whom Welk had chosen to enter the caverns with him, for as he traveled farther from the Ruud, as his fears for Lucas grew, he felt less kinship with the soldiers of his guard and more for Clutch, and any folk he trusted.

Every time he was forced by the wound on his back, just at his left shoulder, to stop and rest, Welk watched Krup pull Lucas from over his shoulder, cradle the young felid in his arms, and lay him gently on the rocky floor before kneeling behind Welk and checking his bandages.

"Something about you surprises me," Welk found himself saying, his hollow voice echoing in the chamber.

Krup lit Welk's lantern and set it in front of him. "What's that, sir?"

"You suffer from a deplorable lack of curiosity."

"Do I?"

"Don't you?"

"Clutch tells me to go with the king of Michelruud, I go." The man wiped his face and stroked his beard, pulling at a knot. "The king of Michelruud tells me to carry a body into the caverns, I carry."

"And you care not why?"

"I think I know why."

"Tell me, then."

"Only for you to laugh at me when you find I've a fanciful imagination?"

"Would that bother you?"

"I s'pose not. Here's what I figure."

Welk leaned against the rock wall and winced.

"You know this boy; I'm not sure how, for he's a felid folk, no doubt in my mind. And you know it, too. So, you carry him away where none can see. So he can do his turning."

"Have you ever seen a turning?"

Here Krup let out a chortle and shook his head. "Mutterede, no. I ain't even sure it happens. You don't get any felid who live as folk, nowadays; they're turned right away."

"That much is true."

"I hear tell they slit their bellies before they can suckle once."

Welk shivered at the thought and nodded.

"Am I right, then?" Krup said.

"You are."

"But why are we in the cavern?"

"There is a rift in the rock, deep within, where the kell can be seen. Long ago, I'm told, the felidae held their turning ceremonies there, where they could sense the kell most strongly."

"If the kell is there," Krup said, "why do they need the stone?"

"You know of the stone?"

"I do. Us folk out in the hills, we meet up with gnomes and brownies, sometimes a felid or two. We gots some of us come up from the coast what consort with mermaids and centaurs. Stories go around. And since you chased that boy out of the Ruud, the stories start making sense. You see?"

"Yes."

"So, why do they need the stone if the kell is here?"

"That I cannot tell you, for I do not know."

"Perhaps the boy here will know."

Welk looked at Lucas' face, his jaw held shut with a sling tied atop his head, drained of color.

"You thinking what I'm thinking, sir?" Krup said. "What if it don't work? What if he don't turn?"

Shaking his head, Welk groaned and lifted himself to standing. Krup leapt up to steady him. "I would not wish to consider that."

They made their way deeper into the cavern, Welk led by Krup with his cargo slung over his shoulder, holding the lantern high to guide the way, as Welk gave him directions from the memories of his youth when he and Elrundt lost themselves in the caves during their father's hunting tours.

Four times he thought he'd lost his way, but each time found a mark on the wall, his, Elrundt's, or some other adventurer's scrawl.

"Here," he said. "Hand me the lantern."

When Krup did so, Welk lifted the lid and blew out the candle. He heard a slight gasp from the folk, then another when the pale green glow of kell lit the path.

"There," Welk said.

They made their way down a set of natural steps into the chamber of slit rocks, green rays of light bursting from them, and Welk pointed to a flat rock against a far wall. Krup laid Lucas on the slab as gently as a mother putting her child to nap.

"Now we wait," Welk said.

"But..." Krup turned to him, worry in his eyes. "What if he turns a cat and...?"

Welk took a seat on a flattened boulder across the room and eyed Lucas' still body warily. "I've no more idea than you what to expect. You may return to the surface if you like, but I fear you will become lost on the path."

Krup nodded and found himself a rock. "I'll take my chances with the king."

They waited an eternity, it seemed. Until Krup said, "You sure we ain't s'posed to say some ceremonial words? A song or something?"

"I don't believe it to be a magical occurrence. I assumed it was natural."

They were silent again and Welk found himself concentrating on the rhythmic throb of his shoulder, the pain rising and falling, until he was aware of his head lolling, his eyes closing, his breath deepening. He startled awake when Krup let out a shout.

There in front of them were four felidae, the purring echoing so loudly in Welk's ears he could feel it in his chest.

"Voorspeld?" he said.

The cats shimmered, seemed to break apart. In the light of the kell, each tiny piece reflected the sharpest green and Welk put a hand to his eyes until the brightness dulled and they stood before him in folk form, svelte, lithe, wrapped in fur cloaks. Perhaps it was magic after all, he reasoned.

"I am," the old folk said.

"How did you know?"

"I should like to tell you we felidae are of one mind and sense the turning through some sort of ethereal connection. But as you were a friend of Belfen, I will not toy with you. The gnomes of the hills told the brownies of the Ruud, who in turn, brought the news into the forest. Lucas was killed by a folk of the Ruud and King Welk carries him north. And here we find you."

"Is he all right?" Welk said. "Will he turn?"

Voorspeld nodded. "But you must go. Your friendship with his parents is not enough to allow you to witness so personal an event."

Welk stood, wincing in pain. "Krup." He motioned for the man to join him.

"Thank you," Voorspeld said.

Welk turned back to the felid. He started to speak, but paused, gathering his words carefully. "I would wish a peace between our folk."

"Then build it," the cat said.

Chapter Twenty-nine

I know it's maddening," Leah said.

The children looked like rabbits caught in traps as they stood on the docks in Port Wonder. There was movement everywhere but the sky, bustling and noise. And the smells of fish, seaweed, and sweat fought against those of the pier stalls—the scented candles, bouquets of flowers, the cakes and pies and fried foods for sale. After the sweet, natural calm of the Ruud and the eastern continent, Leah couldn't imagine how the children and Rogget would fare here in Ruhm.

"And this isn't even the largest landing. But you'll get used to it."

"I've never seen so many folk in my life," Grayson said.

Sadie put her hands to her ears. "Is it this loud everywhere?"

"I'm afraid so."

She led them down the pier to the main road and into the little dockside town of Wonder, southwest of Rhum, where she found Fargel's Inn. A warm meal would do well for all of them, and Leah silently thanked her mother for ensuring she had plenty of spending money of her own on her trip east.

"One ought never find oneself beholden to others, if one can help it," she'd said, slipping the doars into Leah's bag.

She sat them all down at a table away from the window and ordered plates of roasted pig, hot salad, sliced tomato, and bread.

Rogget cleared his throat and said, "Begging your pardon, Miss Hallowsing, but, what's the plan, here?"

She smiled and laid a hand on his arm. "Dear Rogget. Please don't use my name here."

"Aye, I'm sorry about that."

She gave him a gentle pat and turned to the kids. "We'll get to the stationer's, to my home. I'm hoping my father is still safe there, or at least secreted away by now. If we can get to him, I think he'll tell us where to find Daken's journal."

"And if he's already left?"

"We'll search every nook and cranny and see what we can come up with. As a last resort, we'll have to follow where my father has gone.

Their meal finished, Leah led the children along the streets of Ruhm. She wished they could take a hired carriage to the city, but that would draw too much attention. A young woman of her new station—apprentice, at best—should not have enough money to pay for one. It was risky enough paying for a full meal at the inn. And a girl accompanied by a huntsman and three children would raise many a brow and quite a bit of interest, as it was. So they walked, daring not to run as that again was simply inappropriate for a folk of her age. Up the hard dirt streets of Wonder, through Truthspoke Park, where she'd been once on an excursion with the Hass school. Into the Community of Good, where the streets were wide and lined with witherwood trees and flowering shrubs: roses, lilies, and the aptly named Kirche's Pearl, a delicate, pale little flower with a powerful, too-sweet, conflicting smell, a mix of rose and peach. Finally she found Humble Lane; it would take her to Premier Road, cobbled and busy, and to the stationer's, and home. She kept her head down, pleading with Mutterede that she would not be recognized, but the street was strangely empty.

Approaching the building, her spirits rose in relief. *Home.* The stationer's office took up the first floor and its door faced the street, while a stair in the back led up to the second and third floors, where she and her parents had lived all her life. Ready to mount the steps to the door, Leah stopped—she breathed in and struggled to let it out again. There were three slats of wood nailed to the door. It was as she'd feared—they'd arrested her father already.

"What is it?" Sadie whispered.

"Too late," she muttered, and hurried around to the back of the shop with the others following.

The Hass must keep up the appearance of justice, she thought—hold him in jail for a short time before executing him. Mother would know what to do; she would know how to end this madness. She raced around to the back of the building and up the stairs, and gasped at the sight of the door to her home, also boarded. Her heart pounded in her chest and her gaze darted about the backyard as she tried to make sense of it. Her mother, too?

"What's happened?" Rogget asked, heaving up the stairs behind her.

"I don't know," she said. "I can understand the stationer's... but this is where I live."

Rogget crossed the small porch and pulled at the wood slats covering the door. He had them off in a matter of seconds and pushed the door open. He stepped aside, and Leah, frightened, walked past him into the house.

It was dark and still.

"Mother?" She called timidly, knowing her mother wouldn't answer. She turned to Rogget and the three children standing in the dim kitchen, the silence of her home shrouding them. "Would they have arrested her, too?" They couldn't answer, of course. "This way."

She led them through the kitchen to the little doorway at the steps, and down the stairs into the stationer's shop. It still smelled of ink and paper and oil and Leah forced the tears out of her eyes. She must keep herself in check, if she was to be of any help to her parents at all. Down into the cellar, they followed, through the tiny hall and into the canning room. She dragged the rugs from the floor and pulled open the trapdoor.

"The vegetable house," she said. "It's the only place I know where a book might be hidden. You'll find lanterns and candles in the front room, but be careful of making too much noise. No one must know you're in here."

"Where are you going?" Fenn asked her.

"I've got to find out what happened to them." She saw the desperation on the children's faces, like lost pups. "I'll be back soon," she assured them as best she could.

"Not to worry," Rogget said. "If we don't meet up here, we'll all be back at Olgut's landing on the morrow to take the boat back east."

That seemed to knock the air back into their lungs and Fenn nodded. "Good luck," he told her.

Trying to keep the panic at bay, Leah left by the back door and hurried across the street into the Community of Hope. Her first thought was Wilkins, her father's first apprentice. He lived only a quarter mile away; but, could she trust him? As she walked, she wrapped her arms around her waist and tried to think back to the few times she'd spoken with him; he was stern, to say the least. Always proper, never off his mark. She shook her head. No, she couldn't imagine Wilkins would not question her presence back in Ruhm without Kirche, her hair shorn, and asking questions about her father.

Quickly, Leah turned down another street and made her way south. She passed three servants, carrying laundry baskets to the nearest washing house, and nodded without meeting their eyes. Down another street and to her left, her heart racing, she forced herself not to hesitate. She had no other choice—no one else to turn to. She walked the path to the tidy little house and knocked on the door.

When Marigold pulled the door open, Leah held her breath. The young girl's face went pale; she glanced quickly at the street before pulling Leah into the front room.

"I'm so sorry," Leah whispered. "I do not wish to put you in this position."

Mari drew her farther into the house, to a small sitting room where she nearly pushed her into a soft chair. The house was silent like a roar and Leah felt as if she'd entered a tomb. The walls were frayed, natural wood adorned only with a framed drawing of a sailing ship. A basket in the corner held balls of yarn, two pairs of knitting needles pierced one of gray wool. On the floor beside her chair was a pillow, indented, as if the family cat spent much time there. And across from her, Mari sat in a hard-backed wood chair next to a table with a candle-lit lantern. Nothing was untoward, but still Leah considered it too picturesque —as if Marigold had laid it all out perfectly to appear normal.

"What are you doing here?" the girl said.

She'd lost her usual, submissive behavior and Leah was reminded of how she'd long suspected Marigold only feigned respect. She no longer cared.

"I," Leah struggled to find the words, to explain. "Kirche is going to hang my father. I fled the east and came home to take him away. But the house and shop are boarded up. What happened? Do you know? Did they arrest my mother? I know it's madness—the idea that I could get them out of prison, but I have to find a way. Can you help me?" She put her face in her hands, exhausted from worry, realizing she'd come so far and still done nothing.

"Your mother sailed for the eastern continent two days ago," Marigold said. "She was difficult."

"What do you mean?"

"She didn't want to go. She believed it would be better if she shared your father's fate."

"Better?"

"Even those who are not allied with the wissenry would revolt at the thought of hanging her."

"The wissenry?"

Marigold drew her lids together and peered at Leah suspiciously. "Your father told me you knew nothing. But we'd hoped you were placed as a spy."

Leah blinked and leaned back in the chair, shaking her head, confused.

"Your father led an underground wissenry. They've been shipping the library of heresy out of Ruhm for years and secretly printing the truth about Hass, sending it out among the folk. After Kirche left, he was arrested. We believe it was Kirche's choice to remove himself from the act, so he could return and bring order, express his sorrow at what his stationer had done—the betrayal. If any evidence of your father's innocence could be presented, Kirche could absolve himself and lay the blame on his ministers."

"He planned to return with me as his wife," Leah said.

Marigold's eyes flew wide and her mouth fell open. Her gaze flitted about the room. "Yes." She nodded. "Even better. Is that why you fled?"

"No," Leah confessed. "I was prepared to marry him; he said he would torture and hang my father if I did not."

"And yet, here you are."

"Those who helped me escape said he planned to hang Father whether I wed him or not. On Founding Day."

"But Leah," Marigold whispered. The girl reached forward and put a hand on hers, surprising her. "It's too late."

"What do you mean?"

"He is on the gallows by now."

Chapter Thirty

Fenn couldn't say what irked him about their following him into the vegetable pantry, each with a lantern. He thought it was because he wanted to find Daken's journal on his own; he didn't want them touching it. But that seemed too silly an idea. Maybe, he reasoned, he wanted to be alone for a bit to think, to plan, away from their stares. Because they did stare. He found them watching him, wary, quite often and it was becoming frustrating, not because he blamed them for their distrust. No, it was precisely because he did *not* blame them. But he wouldn't add fuel to their belief, that he would become exactly what he claimed he would not, by telling them to let him find the book himself; so he let them follow.

They searched through all of the potato bins, looked on all of the shelves lined with canning goods, inside the cracker barrels, and stood staring into a murky barrel filled with pickles.

"Nope," Sadie said. "I'm not sticking my hand in there."

"It couldn't be in there," Grayson said. "It'd be ruined."

"We're going about this all wrong," Rogget said. "It can't be here."

"Why not?" Sadie said.

"It would stand out too much," Fenn said. "It's got to be in a library."

"But if the Hass knew about it, they'd look at every book the stationer owned."

"That's true enough," Rogget said. "But I'm saying we ought not be looking for the book itself here. We should look for a door."

"What sort of door?" Sadie said looking around, holding her lantern high above her head.

"A secret one," Fenn said. "Like the one in the cellar at the wissenry in Path. There." He pointed to the potato bins, and tried not to get his hopes up; it couldn't be that simple, could it? "Move them away from the wall."

When they pulled the bins from the wall, they found a small patch of hardwood against it, no more than two feet square. Fenn fell to his knees and pulled at it, but it didn't budge.

"I need something to wedge it away from the wall."

Rogget knelt beside him with his knife and dug at each side, twisting the wood until it popped off. Behind it was a gaping hole; it smelled of dirt and rotting grass, reminding Fenn of the tunnel Father Treacher had sent him into so many weeks before.

"I won't be fitting in there," Rogget said. "And I can't say I feel right about sending any of you in alone."

"It'll be all right," Fenn said. "If I get to where I can't hear you calling, I'll come back."

Rogget shook his head, but Fenn knew he wouldn't stop him. He set the lantern just inside the hole and, lying on the floor, pushed at it. He crawled after the lantern, pushing it farther and farther ahead of him, until he was fully surrounded by dank, damp kell, and slithering downward. The lantern dropped a few inches and fell to its side. Fenn grabbed it and pulled it back to standing before the candle went out. Inch by inch, the tunnel floor dropped and the ceiling lifted until he found himself in a rounded out hollow in the ground.

When he turned to look back, upward, he saw Rogget's head outlined in the lantern light behind him.

"I'm here," he said. "It's a room."

"I'm sending Grayson," Rogget said.

"And me," he heard Sadie protest.

Fenn could hear Grayson scooting through the tunnel as he looked around the room. Empty shelves stood against the walls, and three tables sat in the middle. A few pieces of parchment paper, some squares of wax paper, some ink wells, and pencils were strewn about.

When Sadie stood beside him, holding her lantern up, she marveled. "It looks like my dad's office, without the books."

"Exactly," Fenn said. "No books."

"But it was a hidden library."

They walked all around the room, shining light into the dark corners and cubbies, onto shelves and in bins. When he was sure there was nothing to be found, Fenn spied the corner of a book on the floor, tucked behind one of the shelves. He reached for it, daring not to hope, telling himself it was trash. As soon as his fingers touched the worn leather, he knew it was a journal. He pulled slightly on the shelf, forcing it to let go of the book, and held it up to his lantern.

"I found something," he said, carrying it to one of the tables.

Sadie and Grayson set their lanterns alongside his and they all three leaned over the table as he opened it. On the first page was a sketch of a tree, flames carved into its trunk.

"Herein lie all our reason, all our faith, all our sin," Fenn read aloud. He turned the page. "In the Year of Our Beloved Rett, 1045, I determine to set record of my journey to do his lord's bidding—a survey of the lands south and north."

"Is that it?" Grayson said.

Rogget called from the other end of the tunnel. "Did you find anything?"

Fenn continued to flip through the pages, looking for some sign of the kell stone, but it appeared to be a prayer manual more than anything, with drawings of the tree throughout.

"We won't know until we read it," Sadie said. "Let's take it upstairs."

Once through the tunnel and into the front room of stationer's where there was plenty of natural light, all but Rogget huddled over the book reading. Occasionally one of them would point out a passage and whisper.

"That's him," Fenn said. "His name is Daken; it must be the one."

So engrossed were they in reading that when the door in the back of the stationer's banged open, they jumped and the book flew across the table to the floor.

Chapter Thirty-one

Leah heard Marigold calling after her, telling her to wait, saying it was too late, no use, but she bolted from the house and darted through the streets, not caring if any-one saw her. She ran along Premier Road, past the shops and homes, seeing few other folk and finally realizing why—it was a hanging day. Once at the circle, at the base of Palace Mall, she staggered and paused, panting heavily for a solid breath, before forcing herself on, around the curves to the northern edge, where she raced along the street toward a large gathering of folk. Already they were shouting, but there was something different, something that frightened her more than the cheers that usually erupted on days such as these. Folk were not boisterous here, they were angry.

The crowd grew thicker, deeper, before she reached the Hall of Hass, where Kirche and Pren had their offices. When she could see the House of Premiers, she fought her way through, shoving folk aside. She raised her arms above her head, trying to make herself thinner, a wedge. It was unseemly, vulgar behavior but no one cared, no one noticed. They were tugging, pushing, fighting, yelling. Enraged. And then the smell of roses—sweet beauty—taking her back to the day she last saw Kettering with her flower cart on the mall—how joyous she'd been—and the day in the woods of the Ruud when Kirche murdered the brownie. The aroma filled the air around the mob, painting it bizarre.

Finally she could see the gallows. The rope. The hangman. And there he was—her father stood looking out at the folk, defiant, his chin high.

Leah screamed. But her cry was hidden in the shouts and protests of the folk around her.

"Father, no!"

She thought she heard a male folk calling her name but her father's lips did not move. She could see Kirche's Minister of Law standing at the front of the stage, reading from his scroll—no one could hear him. Suddenly, a folk was lifted onto the others' shoulders. Then another and another. They were carried toward the gallows stage on a wave but before they could climb onto it, the Hass guard marched up the steps and stood in front of her father, their firearms raised. Shots rang out and those folk fell into the crowd.

"No!" she screamed.

Undeterred, the folk surged and more shots pierced the noise. The hangman tried to put a hood over her father's head, but he shook it away. The brute looked to Kirche's minister, but the folk was cowering at the back of the stage. He shrugged and let the stationer's face remain visible.

Leah was near the foot of the stage now, looking up, scream-ing his name. If she could only get to him—climb onto the stage, take the noose off his neck, over his head, race with him down the steps behind, and into the crowd. Even as she saw it in her mind, she knew it was false, a dream, but even so, she struggled to the lip of the gallows.

"Please, no!"

Even over the panic and chaos of the folk, the shots that only urged them on, and her name, called again and again from behind her, Leah heard the thump as the floor broke away beneath her father. She thought she caught his eye, just as he dropped. She was only aware of screaming when someone grabbed her from behind and pulled her back through the throng.

Prenalin had her tucked against his right side, one arm around her shoulders, the other grasping her arm. His face was hard, but when he glanced at her, his eyes were filled with terror. They moved along the Palace Mall with a crowd of folk, shots echoing behind them, while others ran against them into the fray carrying firearms, swords, sticks.

Leah was numb and let herself be carried away. Pren took her to the circle, and onto Premier Road. When she saw Marigold standing at the stationer's, wringing her hands, she shook her head, as if to let her know it was over. It was done.

"This way," Marigold whispered. "Hurry."

Pren led her around to the back of the shop, to the back door, and into her parents' empty kitchen.

Chapter Thirty-two

Leah's head throbbed but she felt no pain. In her ears, a river seemed to rush along into some dark distance. When its flow eased, she was suddenly aware of Prenalin, sitting next to her, his arm still wrapped around her shoulders.

"I only made port early this morning," he was telling Marigold. "I knew she'd try to help him; but he refused to be released."

Across the table, in her kitchen, sat Rogget and the children, quiet, watching, concern and confusion in their eyes.

"I could have told you he would," Marigold said. "He said this was the plan all along."

"No," Leah wrenched herself out of Prenalin's grasp.

"It's true," Prenalin said. "Your father would not flee Ruhm. He wanted to stand for something."

Leah turned to Marigold sitting on her other side. "Why do you trust him? He is a spy."

"Yes," Prenalin said, "for the wissenry resistance."

She shook her head, unbelieving. "You allowed Kirche to murder my father."

"Leah," Marigold nearly hissed. "Prenalin has been working for the wissenry for seventeen years. Your father would hardly approve of you speaking to him in this manner."

"Did my father know?"

They both looked at her, but said nothing.

"Did he know Kirche's plan?" she asked Mari. "To marry me and force some bizarre peace between your revolutionaries and Ruhm?"

The girl shrugged. "I was not included in all of the plans."

"He did know," Prenalin said.

"I don't believe it." Leah scooted her chair away from the table, away from Prenalin, and stood to pace the floor.

"It wasn't to happen this way," he said. "Kirche planned to return engaged. He would call for a uniting of the old wissende class and the Hass, claim our differences resolved in the face of threats from the beast folk and the folk of the eastern continent. Edwin knew he would be called on to bless the union and he would refuse. Kirche believed your marriage to him, in the face of your father's death would be enough to keep the folk with Hass, turn them away from the resistance."

"Father would let me marry him?"

"No." Pren stood and took a step toward her but she backed away. "You were to flee with your mother before that could happen. As soon as I realized Kirche intended to marry you before returning to Ruhm, I knew I had to get you away from him. But...well, you managed it yourself."

"And still you let my father be hanged."

"I tried to get him out. But he would not leave. He believed if he ran, the cause would suffer; those who trusted in him, trusted he was telling them the truth about the Hass, would see him as nothing more than a coward. Don't you see? He had to die."

Leah surprised herself. Launching at him, she slapped him hard in the face, and turned to the others, planning to lead them out the door.

"Wait," Marigold grabbed her and pulled her back.

"Leave me alone," she raged. "Why should I trust either of you? How could you let me be deceived this way?"

"We couldn't trust you," Marigold said, "if you want to know the truth of it."

"And so you allowed me to go along with Kirche, knowing all the while he intended to murder my father?"

"You seemed to enjoy it well enough," Prenalin said.

Leah lurched toward him again but Marigold put herself between them.

"I'll not have any lovers' quarrels right now," she said.

"How dare you?" Leah scowled at her.

"I dare plenty. You think you're the only one who's lost something? You think the Hass haven't already killed my parents? Pren's father and brother? You kept yourself pent up at the school well enough, didn't you?"

"That's enough, Mari," Pren said. "That was the plan."

"And I know all about it," Leah said. "Madam Always told me. I was nothing but a pawn for all of you—someone to smooth the path for your machinations. And now you expect me to believe you would not have

462

forced me into a marriage to Kirche?"

"Are you certain you didn't want it?"

"I said there'd be none of that," Marigold scolded. "Come to the table. Your friends found the journal."

For a few seconds, Leah hesitated, eyeing them both. Marigold was sneering at her. Hadn't she always thought the girl was looking down on her in some way? And now she understood why. She was the snooty one as it turned out; Leah's cheeks flamed at the thought of it. All those years believing herself special, a student at the Hass school, and then appointed Aide to the High Preist. And all along her suspicions were correct, she was nothing at all as she pretended, while Marigold was the one true to her father.

Prenalin, unlike Mari, looked worried—as if he'd lost some-thing and didn't know where to look for it. Perhaps that is the face of a spy being found out, she wondered.

At the table, Fenn pushed the worn leather journal to her.

"It was downstairs, in a hidden room," he said.

"A cache," Prenalin said.

"We got the manuscripts out of the archives in Ruhm," Marigold said. "Some from the school, others from the offices of the Inner Circle. We stored them here."

"You saw them?" she asked Fenn.

"They are gone," Marigold said. "Shipped east, most of them. To Madam Dania. All that's left is this." She lifted the book and pushed it at Leah as if she were angry with it. "Your father wanted you to have it."

"Daken's journal," Leah said. "Shouldn't this have been one of the first books secreted away?"

"He insisted it be saved for you," Pren said.

Leah let out a laugh, even with the tears spilling down her cheeks. "He wanted me to run away."

"We've looked through it," Fenn said. "We can't find anything about the kell stone."

"You'll have time to read it, today," Marigold said. "Tomorrow is Founding Day. The Hass will have the people subdued well enough, but they'll be on alert during the festivities. We'll continue with our plan and make north with the king."

"The king?" Leah eyed the girl as if she were insane.

"Aye. We're taking the king east to keep him out of harm's way."

Leah shook her head. "You're going to kidnap the king? A child?"

"Not the new king," Prenalin said. "The old king."

"How many kings do you have?" Sadie said.

"You would take him from his privilege of tranquility?" Leah said.

"Mari, you must leave us and continue the plan," Prenalin said. "I'll see Leah and her friends back east."

"I'm not going back home," Fenn said. "I'm here to find the kell stone."

"You can't search for the stone here in Ruhm; it's dangerous."

"I don't care."

"If you think denying the king his right to tranquility is going to help the cause," Leah said, "you're mad."

"It's not tranquility," Prenalin said. "It's murder."

"Murder?" Leah nearly laughed.

"What?" Sadie said.

"Sit down," Marigold told Leah.

Leah stared at the girl for several seconds, wishing she didn't feel so small and confused, but sat at the table again, and only shuddered when Prenalin took his seat beside her.

Marigold looked to Rogget and the children. "These are matters for adults, I'm afraid. But you're caught up now. I can't see setting you loose in Ruhm on a quest for the kell stone. You'll likely be caught and hanged. I'm sure Leah wouldn't approve of that." Here she turned to Leah with a glare.

"I don't care what's going on in Ruhm," Fenn said.

"But you very well should."

"You'll have to tell them," Prenalin said.

"That much is true," Leah said. "I would very much appreciate it if you two would stop treating me like an imbecile. My father has just been hanged by the Hass, my mother has fled Ruhm. I deserve to be brought into the plan."

Marigold turned back to the children. "Let me explain. In Ruhm a new king is crowned on a Founding Day every fourteen years. He's only four years old when he gets the crown and he wears it only until he is eighteen."

"Why would you want a kid to be king?" Sadie asked.

"They're easier to control," Grayson said.

"That's right," Mari said. "The new king is chosen by the High Priest of Hass. Every fourteen years, the priest meets all of the children who will be aged four on Founding Day and chooses the king's heir. When the day arrives, there is a great parade. All the priests of Hass are in it. All the posts in Hass, all those who serve the king, and our soldiers and sailors too. The old king is at the end with his menagerie."

"A zoo?" Grayson said.

"That's right. A collection of beast folk caught in the mountains north."

"They're sentient beings," Grayson said.

"Unfortunately, in Ruhm, they are not treated that way. After the parade, all the people of Ruhm cheer the old king. As everyone else circles, and marches back to the palace, the old king remains behind with his menagerie. Once back at the Hall of Hass, the High Priest lifts the new king onto his own parade carriage, and together they make their way to the palace, where only a select few are allowed to attend the crowning."

"And what happens to the old king?" Sadie said. "And the menagerie? Are they all murdered?"

"The people of Ruhm are told the old king is granted the privilege of tranquility—that he ascends to the heavens to live eternally with Rett."

"And that is not true?" Leah said.

"Of course not."

Marigold glanced at Leah as if she were stupid, and Leah felt it. She wanted to protest, to tell Mari she'd doubted the tale herself, even as she recited phrases from *The Book of Rett* in school. She was not so dumb as she seemed, she wanted to say; but she dared not—unsure of herself.

"Some time ago," Mari was saying, "we learned that the old king is taken directly from the parade to the tomb of the kings—"

"We all knew that," Leah said. She turned to Sadie. "The old king worships at the tomb before he is taken—"

"He is not taken anywhere," Marigold said. "He's left there. Locked in the room with the bones of past kings. Left to starve to death."

"Easy, Mari," Prenalin said, nodding to the children.

Leah saw their eyes wide and their mouths open. "I hardly think," she murmured, "the Hass of Emorah, keepers of the morality of—" Leah stopped and turned to look at Prenalin. She shivered as the truth of it invaded her.

The kitchen was silent for several seconds. Mari seemed to be waiting, giving them all time to absorb the horror of it before she finally continued.

"It's all come to a point tomorrow. From what we can tell, Kirche was to be absent when your father was hanged so he can attempt to blame Edwin's death on infighting withing the wissende resistance movement. We assume he will attempt to link this with his preparations to overtake the Ruud."

"Overtake it?" Rogget blurted out.

"Indeed. He's been planning it for some time, hinting to the folk that the kings of the Ruud are aiding the resistence here. His ships are in port, ready to sail. We assume they will do so during the Founding Day celebrations."

"Can you stop them?" Grayson asked.

"Some of our folk are planning an attack. It will weaken the force, but not destroy it completely."

"And what of the king?" Leah said.

"I am to rescue him from the tomb and take him east. At some point, preferably once we've assumed control in Ruhm, we'll return him, put him before the folk. His presence will prove that the ascension is a lie. We will throw open the tomb. The folk will see the truth for themselves. Bones of past kings will convince them."

"I think," Prenalin said, his voice measured against Mari's passion, "you may find that folk without a sound education in logic and reasoning will hold tight to their faith, even in the face of irrefutable evidence."

Mari sighed. "Edwin was with me—"

"Edwin tolerated your enthusiasm."

"But," Sadie said, "there's an army going to the Ruud?"

"Yes, yes," Prenalin said. "This debate can wait." He offered Marigold a smile. "The Hass has long planned to retake the Ruud, and Kirche feels now is the best time. He hopes it will unite the folk, turn them from the resistance."

"We call it Kirche's folly," Marigold said.

"We call it home," Sadie said.

Leah leaned across the table, reaching her hand to Sadie's. "I do not think the wissendes would leave your folk under the rule of the Hass. If I knew my father, and I'm sure I did, he would not stop until all folk, beast and mortal, are free."

Chapter Thirty-three

Fenn thought if he didn't get to sit down in the next minute, he would keel over dead in the street. He was squeezed into the crowd like a fish in a barrel—he couldn't breathe, much less see anything of the festivities. There was a show, he was told. Sadie was perched atop Rogget's shoulders, her back pelted occasionally by a nut or a small rock, no doubt thrown by someone behind them who couldn't see past her. Grayson stood on his tiptoes for at least a half hour at a time watching, before bending down to yell something awful in Fenn's ear. Last time it was, "It's some kind of strange, hairy, folk-looking beast! It's playing a pop organ!" He'd laughed and crept back up on his toes to watch. Fenn could only look up at the sky at the fire displays, popping red and blue sparks, whistling and bursting over the noise of the crowd.

He grasped at his charm, clinking against the amber stone, under his tunic and closed his eyes. Where was she? Why had she deserted him? There had been, in the beginning, visions of a man as well. He once thought it must be his father. But now they were gone—his charm nothing more than a dead piece of gold. Brenna must have been right. It wasn't his mother's charm. It had no connection to him—only to the Ruud. The charm warmed him and sent him visions—only in the Ruud.

He was jostled from behind and tripped over his own feet, falling into Rogget. Rogget looked down at him and smiled, misunderstanding; he put a large arm around him and jostled him some more.

That morning, Marigold had given them money and sent them into the city, thronging with people. She, Prenalin, and Leah remained hidden and would meet them at the end of the parade route, when it turned back toward the palace. She told them to act as if they were enjoying themselves and so they wandered the booths of the market, eating all sorts of sweets and fruits and buying absurd trinkets—tiny kings made of sticks wearing crowns made of moss, and hand-carved wooden figures of various beasts, most of which they agreed had never existed and were stuff of legend. Fenn's favorite was a dragon, sculpted of hard clay, its wings pulled back as if it darted through the air. The woman who sold it to him—toothless and aged—claimed to have carved it from memory.

"Saw in on my early travels south, I did. Oh, but my days of traipsing about the kell are over. Told and done, they are."

Fenn only nodded politely. And now he found himself smothered while the others got to watch a show. Finally, the crowd began to disperse.

"What is it?" Fenn called out. "What's happening?"

Grayson lowered himself off his toes. "Speeches, I think. The old king and the new king are up on a stage. Can you see it?"

Fenn shook his head. The crowd quieted down somewhat, and Fenn thought he could hear a deep voice.

"He's got something like a trumpet," Grayson said. "And he's talking through it so we can hear him."

Fenn could hear little, but the crowd cheered occasionally. He heard war, and more war, and war again. And the crowd cheered. He heard about the east and evil. He heard about Rett and victory. And the crowd cheered. Grayson looked down slightly at him with a frown.

After a moment, though, he heard something else—some-thing constant, underneath the cheering. It was a grumbling—a discontent. The folk were restless, unhappy, but not quite willing as yet to show it.

The crowd thinned more and more as the sun set. Music played behind them even before the speeches were finished. Dancing broke out spontaneously all around. Torches and lanterns were lit. They wandered the streets together, weaving around pockets of dancers, folk selling torches, and folk calling at them to buy their sweet breads. Fenn's feet ached and his ears thundered. He was sure he'd never heard so much noise in all his life. He'd never seen so many folk in one place. And he'd never walked on such hard ground for so long. He did not like the Great West at all, he decided. And he especially did not like Ruhm.

They spent the evening walking the cobblestone street of the Palace Mall, back and forth, eyeing the new foods, avoiding the sellers hawking their goods. Back and forth, until Fenn was sure his feet would fall off. He trudged for what seemed like days. His eyelids grew puffy and heavy and he scowled at everyone he saw.

Finally a great bell somewhere in the distance began to toll and the people let out a loud cheer. They pushed toward the outer edge of the street to await the parade.

"This is it," Rogget said. "Miss Marigold said we should find a place at the end of the road."

Fenn wanted to scream—more walking—but he grudgingly followed Rogget and the others. They made their way slowly through the packed crowd to the foot of the mall where the road became a large circle, nearly the size of Path itself, Fenn thought, and three roads branched off it— one east, one southeast, and one southwest. More torches were lit along the edges of the circle. He looked for Leah, but there was little chance he could recognize a face in the huge throng of folk.

"She said all the folk will amass here," Rogget said. "I don't know where they'll all fit."

And they did not fit. An enormous mass of folk crowded around them, filling out all the streets jutting off the circle. They were jostled and pushed, but Rogget held fast, leaving them at the edge where Fenn could see the first of the parade as it marched toward them. Dancers, flag bearers, jugglers, and musicians, all filed past, around the circle and back up toward the city. Then the menagerie carts rolled by. Fenn gazed, awestruck, at cages filled with trolls, brownies, even an eis. A glass cart was filled with fairies. And then about a dozen rather round folk wearing tall hats and purple robes walked solemnly by. And lastly, on an open cart, standing and waving, the King of Ruhm. His cart stopped and a silence fell over the mob. Fenn watched expectantly for him to say something, goodbye and good luck perhaps. But instead, he merely held his hands over his face and bowed low while the parade continued back up Palace

Mall with the crowd of folk following.

Once the gathering was gone, their cheering and merrymaking now echoing in the distance, the torches and lanterns carried away, the young king sat in his cart in the darkness.

"They just left him here," Sadie said.

Leah was suddenly behind him, her hand on his shoulder. Marigold and Prenalin were there, guiding them all quickly out of the circle, down the southwestern road ahead of the king's cart.

"Hurry, now," Marigold whispered.

They broke into a jog and left the road when it curved into a wood. They barreled into the trees, still making their way south-west, until they were hidden from the road. Only the moonlight told Fenn that Prenalin and Leah were ahead of him, and Rogget's grunts told him he followed.

"Far enough," Marigold said. They stood in a circle, panting, all of them looking at Mari in the darkness, waiting for her to lead them. "We walk from here." She turned and they all followed her through the woods.

At one point, they hid themselves behind trees at the edge of the road and carefully slipped across it, one by one, unseen, into more woods, thick with shrubs and vines. When they found themselves at the edge of the wood once again, Fenn saw they were at an empty mining camp. A hill on the right boasted a gaping hole with torches on either side of it. Beyond, the hill reached upward, curved, and sloped down again. In front of him, a field of tents, dark and cold, no fires burning.

"They're all in the city," Marigold told them. "Their work is now done. No one watches the king being locked away but Madam Sponhide."

"Madam who?"

"She owns the land, and the mine. For many years, we thought it was her devotion to the Hass that led her to go along with this ugly ritual of murder. But we've since learned—"

Marigold stopped and held up her hand. The cart was approaching. Fenn peered through the trees and shrubs at the young king, still sitting in the front seat, his head in his hands.

"Welcome," a woman said on the other side of the cart.

Fenn struggled to see her, but the darkness hid her. She helped the king down from the cart and they disappeared into the mine. They all waited, silent, as if holding their breath, until the woman appeared again outside, no more than a shadow. He waited for her to leave, but instead, she walked toward the woods, straight at them. He felt every nerve twitch as he prepared to flee, but before he got the chance, Marigold stepped out from the bushes and greeted the dark figure.

"You can come out now," Mari called to them. She was still talking with the woman when Fenn approached.

The woman, he could see now, was tall, pale, and not fully folk. He was sure of it. She pulled a chain from around her neck and handed it to Marigold. Attached to it was a golden key that caught the moonlight. "They do not know I have this," she said. "I've left the torches burning. Follow them to the final door. You'll find him there."

The woman turned and glided away. Fenn looked to Marigold.

"Do we go get him, then?"

She shook her head. "Not yet. Let's let him stew a bit."

"You were going to say something about Madam Sponhide. About why she lets the Hass lock the kings away in her mine."

"Indeed," Marigold said. She walked a few paces toward the door of the cave and sat on the ground. The rest of the group followed. "It turns out, she's an angel eis. We don't know much about them and she won't say much. But she's been living here in Ruhm for many generations, apparently. She's managed to fool the Hass into thinking she's always the next generation of Sponhides to own the mine."

"She can manipulate simple folk," Rogget said. "I've heard tell of it with the split eisen."

"That wouldn't explain why she'd let the Hass murder folk in her mine," Sadie said.

"Sure it does," Grayson said. "After what the Hass has done to the beast folk..."

"That's hardly an excuse to aid in murder."

Marigold shrugged. "Seems enough of an excuse for her."

They sat and whispered among themselves for what seemed hours, until Fenn wanted desperately to lie down and sleep. Finally, Marigold stood and stretched, and led them down into the mine, following the path of torches to a dead end where an enormous iron door stood in front of them.

She slid the key in a huge metal lock hanging from the latch and turned it. She pulled the lock off and stood back letting Rogget pull the heavy door open. Rogget took a torch from the wall behind them and held it forward into the doorway and Fenn peered from behind Mari as the shuffling of feet brought the dethroned king to the door, the confusion on his face aglow.

"Rett?" The king said.

Chapter Thirty-four

You are Roren, are you not?" Marigold said to the young man with a smile.

"I am," he said.

He looked nothing like a king, Fenn thought. More like one of the children of the Ruud. Lanky, not quite grown into his bulk, as Father Treacher would say. He was fair and pale, like an eis, and had a look of innocence about him.

"Why are you here?" he asked, somewhat amused. "I was told only Rett would come for me."

"We've come to rescue you."

"I am to await Rett. He will take me to the hall of tranquility to live eternally with him."

"The only place you're going is on a shelf," Rogget said. He pushed his way past the king, into the room and lit the torches on the walls, illuminating rows and rows of shelves filled with bones.

Roren turned and watched as Rogget lifted a skull from its resting place. He walked to the first of the shelves and reached out to touch the velvet robes of one of the skeletons.

"Rett isn't coming?"

"Why would they need to lock you in a dark room to wait for him, anyway?" Fenn said.

The king shook his head and turned to Fenn. "Who are you? Why did you come?"

"I'm not Rett, if that's what you're thinking."

"And why rescue me?"

"Because it isn't right," Sadie said peeking into the room. "They're going to let you die in here."

The king seemed confused. "And so, you decided to free me?"

"Yes," Fenn said, wondering what was so difficult to understand.

Marigold held out her hand as if to guide him from the room. Prenalin and Leah walked out, followed by Sadie and Grayson.

"Wait," the king said. "I am to remain here and wait for Rett." Even while he said it, it seemed he was doubting it.

"It's all right," Marigold said to him, cooing. She took his arm and led him to the door. All the way through the cave, as Rogget doused the torches along the way in buckets of water below each one, Marigold explained to the king what she could about the Hass' manner of creating, and doing away with, its kings.

"And so I am now to be *your* puppet?" Roren said, his inno-cense

471

seeming to disappear.

Fenn could see humor dancing in Marigold's eyes by the light of the last of the torches when she smiled at him.

"We will not force you to do anything. But we would at least like to give you the chance to live."

"We're going to bring you with us to the eastern continent," Fenn said.

He stood there, his face aglow in the torchlight, confused. "I don't understand."

"It's really very simple," Grayson said. "They want a new king every fourteen years. So they have to get rid of the old one."

The young king nodded. It was a more succinct way of saying it than Mari had offered, but Fenn winced at its abruptness.

"They told you Rett would come for you and take you off to...what?" Grayson continued. "Paradise or something? And you believed it. But they lied to you. They were just trying to get you out of the way."

The king nodded again.

"Do you understand now?" Sadie said.

"Yes," he said. "I think I do."

"Well, come on then," Grayson said.

Surprisingly, to Fenn, the king followed Grayson out of the mine.

In the darkness of night, the small group walked the long way, westward and northward, around the grand city of Ruhm. Rogget, Leah, and Marigold periodically looked behind them, or stopped and let them all pass before continuing on, taking turns at the back of the group. The young king walked along with them in silence and refused to answer any of their questions. At first Fenn thought he was just being kingly, and not speaking to those of inferior rank, but he caught his face occasionally in the moonlight and thought he was dazed and probably not hearing them.

They slept on the ground against a small wood on a plain north of the city.

"Would you like to use my blanket?" Fenn asked him.

The king stared at him.

"We're going to get some sleep now," Fenn said.

The king only nodded and lay down on the ground, closing his eyes. Fenn shrugged.

In the morning, Fenn could see the marble buildings of the city far in the distance. He realized they'd walked most of the night and that only made him more groggy. Rogget dug a shallow fire pit and they all searched for kindling in the little wood. Northward, the landscape wasn't treeless, but their patches were few. Once Rogget got the kindling set, he stood over the pit and looked to Fenn.

"Go on then," he said. "Show them all what you can do."

Fenn cast a glance at the group, feeling small. "What if I can't?"

"I have every confidence you can."

Fenn squatted at the pit and held his hands over the kindling and fire sticks Rogget had tossed in. He sat still for several seconds, longer than was comfortable, and only when he thought he heard Marigold chuckle did he feel the fire burn through his fingers and catch the sticks. He wasn't sure how it had happened, why it had happened, or what it meant, but the gasps from all but Rogget told him it was unusual.

"He is beast folk?" Prenalin said.

"Split," Rogget said. "Born of an eisen and a folk, though we don't know who they were."

"But, how did you know?" Fenn said. "How does the wissenry know?"

Rogget shrugged. "Father Wold was there when you were born."

"And they thought it was okay to keep it from me?"

"It was for your protection. You know you wouldn't be trusted in the Ruud, nor in the beast forest."

"Don't bother with it now," Marigold said to him. She reached out and put a hand on his shoulder. "The world is changing. You'll see. The wissenry knows the truth—that beast and folk are the same. Soon, everyone will know and you'll be seen as no different from me."

Chapter Thirty-five

Leah was glad for a chance to rest and warm herself at the fire and Rogget's bitters were rustic, but welcome. They had a small breakfast of biscuits and roasted meats Marigold had packed for them. She was insistent they make their way quickly east to Lerringlass Port where she was to get Roren onto a boat. But she knew Fenn had other plans.

"If I may," she said, gathering the attention of the group. "I'd like to propose that we be open with one another. We're an odd lot, but I think our goals are, at the very least, similar. I am willing to share my secrets, if you are." She looked specifically at Fenn and he nodded.

Prenalin put a warning hand on her arm only once while she told them all about her father and Dakenruud and the kell stone. She did not shake him off, but put her hand over his. They were in deeply already, she reasoned. There could be no harm in revealing herself to the others, even to Roren. And so, in turn, Fenn told them of the wissenry and the prophecy, and his intention to find the kell stone and destroy it.

"You would do that to your own folk?" Marigold asked him.

The boy frowned. "The wissenry thinks it's best all around."

"And you think you know how to do it?" Prenalin said. "It was my understanding the Hass attempted it when they took it back from Michelruud, and failed."

"The wissenry in the Ruud has some ideas on how it could be done. I'm really just wanting to find it now. We can worry about destroying it later."

Leah nodded and glanced at Pren, wondering if he felt the same as she did. The boy was unsure, his opposing loyalties pulling at him. She took a look at Roren as she sipped her bitters. Odd that he seemed so ordinary now, when he was king just a few days ago. There was a pang of loss in her gut at the thought of her father; how wonderful it would have been had he fled, instead of allowing himself to be sacrificed. He could return to Ruhm with Roren as soon as the revolution started, triumphant, proven. Instead, he chose to leave Ruhm to its own devices. Leah cringed, realizing she was angry with him.

"Our man at Lerringlass will wait," Marigold said, "if you want us to stay together."

"I think that's best," Prenalin said.

"Was the location of the kell stone in Daken's journal, then?" Fenn asked her. "I couldn't make much of it.

"There were clues," she said, "but nothing definite."

"Marigold and I have read it also," Prenalin said. "We found nothing."

"When I read it," Leah said, "I kept hearing my father's voice as we sat together in his little office in the stationer's...just a day or so before I sailed east. I remember feeling as if he were playing a game, teasing me. But when I read Daken's journal, there were those same words, over and over again."

"And those were your clues?" Marigold said.

"Yes."

"Well," Prenalin said, "what were they?"

"First, both my father and Daken said he was to take the stone deep underground."

"That much is known to most," Marigold said. "It's believed that underground, it cannot aid the beast."

"But the repeated words—a good story. A story with a moral. It's all throughout the journal. My father said it referring to the story he was telling me—the story of Dakenruud. But Daken—he repeats it over and over as if in prayer; and he refers to the story of Rett."

"Yes," Marigold said. "He wrote poems about it, quoted *The Book of*

Rett, discussed it at length. But we only assumed he was devout."

"Father knew," Leah said. "He knew it was a clue."

"But a clue to what?" Rogget said.

Leah looked at their faces, hopeful, agitated. "I may be wrong..."

"Naturally," Roren said.

She smiled at him. "I believe the kell stone is buried beneath the site of Rett's sacrifice."

They were all silent for several seconds, until Prenalin said, "Why?"

"It was something else my father told me. He said I was born of the wissende class. I was, therefore, prone to logic and reason. The truth would nag at me, he said, until it forced its way out. And I know the story of Rett's sacrifice is a lie."

Roren sputtered and laughed. "What?"

"The wissendes," Marigold told the young king, "long ago learned that much of the story is untenable."

"But a lie? How could you know such a thing?"

"I saw the flaming tree," Leah said. "There is one in the beast forest on the eastern continent. I *saw* it."

"You were mistaken," Roren said.

She shook her head. "No. I was brought up revering it just as you were. I know the shape and texture of its leaves; I know the unique nature of its bark, through the study of our art and history, through my study of *The Book of Rett*. And I saw it, I tell you—the tree still exists."

"Still, what makes you think the kell stone is there?" Fenn asked.

"I believe that's the moral my father meant—not Rett's sacrifice for our purity, not our shame in burning him to fulfill it. No. He meant skepticism. I am to be always skeptical, always seeking the truth. That's what he was telling me."

"And there are the drawings," Marigold said.

Pren nodded in agreement.

"Yes," Leah said. She opened the journal and flipped through the pages, showing the pictures to them as she found them. "Always the flaming tree of Hass."

"But," Prenalin said, "we have been to the sacrificial site many times. There is nothing there—certainly no pathway beneath the ground."

"Ah," Roren said, "but there is a pathway, nonetheless."

They all turned to the young folk, astonished.

"There is a cell in the palace dungeons where the walls are covered with maps and drawings—graffiti. They call it the lunatic's room. I spent many hours there, tracing the lines on the maps, imagining I could travel our world."

"What would the king of Ruhm be doing in the dungeons?" Marigold said.

Roren smiled. "I often sought solitude; and the dungeons are ancient ruins now, uninhabited, except by the spirits of the dead. It was the one place my guards would not follow."

"And there were underground pathways on these maps?" Prenalin said.

Leah could almost feel Pren's doubt, and she shared it.

"Yes," Roren said. "There were drawings of the many mines in Ruhm, and some in the south I'd never heard of. Those who made the maps drew in the tunnels...from memory I liked to imagine. And in one small spot, I found a drawing of the place of Rett's sacrifice. Leading away from it, there is one long meander-ing line."

"Dakenruud," Marigold said.

"He was imprisoned in the palace," Prenalin said. "In the dungeons."

"How far is the underground entrance from the site?" Leah said.

"I could not say," Roren said. "It was only a drawing."

"How could we ever find it?" Fenn said.

"In the drawing it was marked by three fat toads."

"Rocks?" Grayson said.

"Don't all rocks look like toads?" Sadie said.

Roren turned to her with a smile. "I suppose we will have to see for ourselves."

"Are we prepared for an underground journey?" Prenalin said.

"Aye," Rogget said. "I've got two torches and a lantern from Sponhide's. Took the liberty. We've got enough food to get us to the north port, supposing this underground search don't take us too long."

"North port?" Marigold said.

"Aye. Begging your pardon Miss Marigold, but I wouldn't think your eastern port is safe, what with Ruhm's army preparing to sail."

"We can argue that later," Leah said. "What do you say, Fenn?"

"It's worth a try. But if we don't find it there, is there any other place to look?"

Leah shook her head. "The mines of Galdred, I suppose; but I doubt it's there. I feared it may be in the southern lands, but I cannot find that Daken went there at all."

"But there is much time missing," Marigold said, "after he traveled north of Ruhm, as if he wished not to tell what happened. He could have gone south to hide the stone and left it out of the journal on purpose."

"But if he did not mean for his brother to find the stone, why did he not reveal its location to the Hass?" Prenalin said.

"Let us not puzzle about it now," Leah said. "If we find nothing, then we can start again."

Breakfast done and the fire doused, the group headed out across the plain toward a small village. Smoke rose from the chim-neys of the small wood houses. Sheep and goats milled about in pens, kicking up dust, and several villagers tended plots of farmland.

"Good travel," a man called out to them. "Can I offer you any water, or a handful of carrots?"

Rogget accepted the man's generosity and thanked him with a promise to take a message to the next village. And so it went, from village to village, to encampment, to one lone woman living in a hut by a stream in a little wood. They were able to gather more food and a blanket for Roren. Roren made a trade for a knapsack, determined to carry his share of the load. As they neared the border of Ruhm, the land seemed to rise and rise until they were above the world and looking back, Leah paused to view the plain sloping downward gently to the city and the sea beyond. Eastward, she could see tiny white specks where the land ended and the blue ocean began—Ruhm's ships, readying for an attack on the Ruud.

When they came upon the site of Rett's sacrifice, just inside the province of Galdred, they stood quiet for a time. There was nothing there; Fenn looked disappointed.

"Not what you were expecting?" she teased him.

He shook his head.

Just east of the village of Sacrifice, the site was no more than a ring of stone markers around an empty piece of ground.

"It doesn't look as if anything remarkable happened here. How do you know it's the right spot?"

"If the sacrifice happened at all—"

Roren's gasp interrupted Marigold; he sputtered.

"If it happened at all," she said looking at the young king, "which we doubt, it was probably not here."

"The people of Sacrifice," Pren said, "claimed the site when they founded their village; they set up the markers and enjoyed the increase in travel from the pilgrims of Ruhm. At least, so far as our research can tell."

Roren stared at them all as if they'd gone insane. He shook his head and turned away. "North then," he said.

The landscape was still brown and dry, but suddenly, as if by magic, gray mountaintops, far in the distance, decorated the horizon. And their trek was now spotted by small bits of wood.

"They say this was all forest once," Leah told them.

"What became of the trees?" Sadie asked her.

"Taken down. Some used in the building of Ruhm. Some shipped off to the southern and eastern lands."

"I prefer the forests," Sadie said.

"I do, as well."

"There." Roren led the way toward a rocky hill in the distance. "Those are toads if ever I saw one."

Sadie shook her head. "Looks like a pile of rocks."

"Use your imagination," Roren said.

"Yes," Leah said. "And just think, underneath them is a secret passage."

"Aye," Rogget said. "The tunnel could be right under our feet."

Sadie stepped back and looked to the ground, lifting up one foot and then the other as if she might be stepping on someone. Leah laughed and took the girl's hand.

"You say it was one, long meander?" Rogget asked.

"On the drawing, yes."

"You're concerned," Leah said.

"Aye. The mine passages I am familiar with go on for miles, twists and turns, cliffs and drops, pathways to nowhere. Very dangerous."

Leah shuddered—well she knew. It only then occurred to her their plan was to go underground. When they came to the boulders, they walked around and around them, looking for an entrance, but there was nothing.

"Of course," Marigold said. "He wouldn't have left it open."

Rogget and Prenalin gripped the bottom edge of one of the rocks—the head of a toad—and lifted, but there was only dirt beneath it. In groups, they worked to lift the heads and feet of the toads, and Leah let out a yell.

"Here," she said, laughing, trying to regain her breath. "It's here. I can't believe it. It's true."

Beneath the larger of one of the toad's feet, lifted and rolled by her and Rogget, was a hole, wide enough for one small person to drop into. Smiling, Fenn looked to the dark crevice in the ground and then to Leah. She knew her excitement had vanished; she could see that her appearance frightened the boy. Still, she couldn't manage to stop herself from trembling as she felt the blood drain from her face.

Chapter Thirty-six

Are you all right?" Fenn asked Leah. She looked as if she were wound tight, ready to bolt.

Prenalin moved to stand beside her and she shivered. "You don't have to go," he said. "I'll stay here with you, above ground."

Relief seemed to wash over her.

"Aye," Rogget said. "We'll need someone to shout them out, help them find the opening again, in case there are many paths. Maybe someone just inside as well with the torch."

"Well, I'm going," Fenn said. He found the lantern among their bags.

Leah turned to him, frowning. "It's dangerous," she said. "Rogget should go; he's the one of us with the best tracking skills, I'd bet."

"I can't fit into that hole," Rogget said.

"I want to go," Sadie said.

"I'd rather you didn't," Leah said.

"But why not?"

"I was lost," she said, "for days, in the mines in the east. I would have died if it hadn't been for Fenn's friend, Lucas. If you were to go, I...well, my heart would break every moment you were gone."

"She's right," Rogget said. "We can't have you going just because you want an adventure."

"I'm going," Fenn said.

They stared at him for a moment. Leah nodded.

"Why is it all right for Fenn to go, and not me?" Sadie said.

"This is Fenn's challenge," Leah said, "not ours."

"But your father left the journal for you," Marigold said. "He wanted *you* to find the stone."

"I don't believe he did."

"But the journal—"

"My father wanted me to know the truth—about Rett, about Dakenruud, about the wissendes. I can't imagine he expected I would find the stone. No, I think he meant for the journal to be taken from Ruhm with the other texts...used against the Hass, if possible."

"You aren't going, then?"

"No. But only because I'm frightened. If I never go under-ground again, I'll be happy."

"I'm not sure any of us can fit through that hole but the children," Rogget said.

"I'd rather not," Grayson said.

"I don't care if I have to go alone," Fenn said.

"No," Leah said.

"She's right," Rogget said. "It's not a good idea."

"I'll go," Marigold said. "I think I can fit."

Rogget eyed the girl, sizing her up, admiration in his smile. "Take this, then," he said, giving her the knife and sheath he wore around his calf.

Mari wrapped it three times around her left wrist and let Rogget buckle it. "Perfect," she said.

"What do you think we're going to find down there?" Fenn asked.

"You never can tell," Marigold said.

"Take my bag," Roren said. "It's small and won't be in your way. You'll need something in which to carry the stone...if you find it."

Fenn slid a matchstick against one of the rock toads and lit the lantern. Rogget lowered a sturdy rope into the hole and wrapped the other end around one of the bigger rocks. "Hang on, in case there's a drop," he said. "And stick with the main path."

Fenn lowered himself into the ground, the lantern held above his head. It was a small space, but he was able to scoot himself downward until he felt the ground open against his back just as his feet hit the bottom. From there he crawled backward until the space was wide enough for him to stand. He watched as Marigold's feet came into view, her skirt twisted up in her legs.

When she stood and turned to him, she was smiling. "I'm going to be a right mess after this, aren't I?"

They walked along a large, main tunnel with smaller paths leading off into darkness.

"Those don't look big enough to have been made by miners," Marigold said.

"No. But how do you suppose this big tunnel was made?"

"I've no idea."

"Do you think it has anything to do with the story of Rett?"

"I don't see how."

"Don't you wonder how this Daken fellow found it?"

"I do now, yes. How far were we from the site?"

"A quarter mile at most."

A rustling echoed in the darkness around them.

"What was that?" Marigold said. She grabbed at the lantern and jerked Fenn's hand this way and that.

"It's probably just burrowing rats."

"Too big."

Fenn agreed with her, but didn't want to let her know that. It didn't matter; he wasn't going to let anything stop him. As soon as he'd stood in the tunnel and turned south toward the spot where Rett had supposedly been hanged and burned, he'd felt it. Something drew him along, promising him the answer to every question he had.

Scurrying and pattering of feet continued around them, just beyond the reach of the lantern's light.

"Do you have gnomes in the east?" Marigold said.

"Yes, lots."

"Are they...deadly?"

"Not at all. Mischievous, maybe. But it can't be gnomes; there aren't any mounds on the landscape."

"Perhaps some gnomes do not build mounds."

"I've never heard of such a thing; aren't the mounds created from the dirt they dig out?"

"Well, I've never heard of anything bigger than gnomes burrowing underground."

He looked behind him, to be sure Marigold wasn't frightened. She smiled at him pleasantly enough. When he turned toward their destination, he thought he saw light, but when he lifted the lantern it was gone.

"Take this," he said, giving the lantern to Marigold. "Put it behind your back."

When she did so, he was sure there was a faint green glow ahead.

"Go back twenty or so paces and hide it behind you again."

"And leave you here in the dark?"

"I'll be right here."

As she walked away, he saw it—a distinct green light.

"It's there," he said. "I see it. Come on."

He moved ahead, into the darkness, the light guiding him like a beacon. Marigold called to him to wait, but he kept on. A booming silence pulsed in his ears, louder and louder until Marigold's words were muffled and distant.

"Hurry," he said.

He hadn't realized he'd broken into a run until he could see it—a deep green sphere, giving off a brilliant light. The closer he got to it, the faster it seemed to pulse in his ears and in his chest. As soon as he was on it, he was certain it was part of him and the pulsing was his own heart beating. It sat atop a stone pillar in the middle of the path and Fenn reached out, put his hands on either side of it, and everything stopped—the pulsing gone, silenced, the light extinguished. Only Marigold's screams echoed in the tunnel behind him.

"Mari," he called.

Fenn grabbed the stone and turned toward the lantern, only to find it sitting alone on the path; he ran and grabbed it as he passed.

"Mari?"

He could hear her up ahead in the darkness—her screams had become guttural, angry, courageous, and when he finally came upon her, the lantern light dancing all around, she was battling shadows, a bloodied knife in her right hand.

Fenn darted forward, dropping the kell stone and the lantern to the floor of the tunnel. He grabbed at the shadows, flinging them off Marigold and against the walls where they hit and squealed, only to come at him again, growling, biting. Instinctively, he threw his hands at them and away, forcing them, as if with wind, against the walls, several at a time and Marigold with them. Finally, they scurried off into the darkness and Fenn turned to see the green glow of the stone bouncing along the tunnel—they'd taken it.

"Take the lantern," he said. "Get to the entrance."

"I'm not leaving you."

Fenn heard her running behind him and was grateful for the light of the lantern, aiding him in stepping over the uneven floor. He no longer needed to see the stone; he could feel it drawing him forward. When they caught up to the shadows, he dove into them, grasping for the stone and as soon as he'd got his hands on it, a wave of powerful wind exploded from it, forcing the creatures into the darkness once again.

He found Marigold sitting on the ground, her hands behind her, propping herself up.

"What was that?" she said.

Fenn struggled to catch his breath, looking to the stone in his hands. Its light, no longer cast outward, instead seeped into his hands and up his wrists.

"It was the kell stone," he said.

Chapter Thirty-seven

I think you were right," Fenn told Marigold, putting the stone in Roren's knapsack, as they made their way to the entrance where thin rays of sunlight beckoned. "They were gnomes. Changed into something different here underground."

"What's that, you say?" Rogget said as he grabbed Fenn's hand and pulled him from the hole after Mari.

As soon as Fenn was above ground, he was knocked to his knees as if someone had punched him. He watched as the others sank to the dirt around him, and he smiled. The pulse of the stone slowed and after a few seconds, Fenn felt as if he could breathe again and his ears popped open. Every noise—the chirp of a bird a mile west and Leah Hallowsing's gasp—was crisp, potent, and imbued with meaning somehow, as if the stone could portend which was most important, which would bring him more joy; it pulled those sounds closer to him, let them resonate within him.

"What happened?" Sadie said.

They all found their feet; Rogget pulled Fenn to standing.

"It's the stone," Rogget said. "You found it."

Fenn could see, as if for the first time. The largest towers of Ruhm in the distance, open windows, paintings on the walls inside. The mountains in the north, frozen, snow-capped—deer and hare loping in a clearing.

"Fenn," Rogget said, "what is it?"

"Nothing," he said.

"Do you have the kell stone?" Leah said. "Could it truly have been that simple?"

Fenn turned to Marigold; she was cut and bloodied. Her hair had escaped its binding and played wild about her head and shoulders. A jagged tear in her skirt cut from the middle to its hem. But she was smiling, her eyes dancing as if she'd had a great adventure.

"What's happened to you?" Leah said.

"Gnomes," she said. "Turned into vicious shadowy creatures. They attacked us."

"They were probably protecting the stone," Prenalin said.

"Indeed," Mari said. "When Fenn came to my aid with the beasts, they took it and ran. But he took it back and—" She looked to Fenn, her eyes wide, mouth open, without words.

"It was the kell stone," he said. "It just...knocked them all away."

"Not the stone," Rogget said. "It was you, yourself."

Fenn shook his head. He pulled Roren's pack from his shoulder and dug the stone out of it, holding it in one hand while they all stared at it.

"It's beautiful," Leah said.

"Perfectly," Marigold agreed.

"Don't you see, Fenn?" Rogget said. "You're part eis; having the stone above ground is enough to make you stronger. But you're *holding* it."

"What do you mean?" Sadie said.

"The beast folk get their power, their strength, from the stone," Grayson said.

"My guess is," Rogget said, "Fenn commands wind and fire. I've heard tell of many an eis who could do it; but it's strongest, they say, in the split folk."

"But he's already done that," Sadie said. "With the angels, remember? And you had him light the fire."

"That's so," Rogget said. "Imagine what he'll be able to do now."

"There's more," Leah said to Rogget. "With the angels. When they were taking you. He commanded the angel to drop you, and it did."

"Did I?"

She nodded at him. They were all watching him; their gazes vacillating from his face to the stone; they were afraid. But Fenn only cared about the kell in his hand. Energy emanated from it, traveled through him, through his chest, through his brain—he felt as if he were breaking apart, as if he might fade into nothing. No, not nothing—the stone itself.

Rogget stepped forward and put a hand on the kell stone. "Fenn," he said. "Fenn."

Finally, Fenn took his gaze from the sphere and looked to Rogget. "I think it be best to put the stone into your knapsack. For safekeeping, eh?"

Fenn nodded. He let Rogget take the stone and watched him, ready to pull the stone back, as he put it in Fenn's pack and handed the bag to him. And without thinking, without being truly certain, he blurted out, "I'm going to take it back to the Ruud and give it to the beast lord."

His words stunned Sadie and Grayson, he could tell. Leah, Prenalin, and Marigold considered them, and said nothing. Rogget nodded slightly; and Roren smiled.

"It does seem an awful thing to destroy," the young king said.

"But—" Sadie's face twisted with concern—"you'll give power back to the beast folk. They'll take the Ruud."

"They'll take back what was theirs," Grayson said.

"You can't mean that."

"I didn't say I agree with Fenn. But the kell stone was never ours. We stole it from them."

"Maybe for good reason."

Fenn turned to Leah. "What do you think?"

She opened her mouth to speak, shook her head, and closed it again.

"I believe," Prenalin said, "the wissenry originally intended to return the stone to the beast folk."

"Yes," Leah said. "My father would have us do what is right. The kell stone belongs to the beast folk. It always has."

"This is exactly what the prophecy foretold," Sadie said. "You're doing exactly what it said."

"I am not. I'm not wielding the stone and destroying the Ruud. I'm not going to kill a king."

"Returning the stone to the Ruud is what will destroy it."

"How do you know that?"

"Because that's what Dag Anfang said. That was his prophecy. And King Welk is likely already dead."

"But I didn't kill him."

"Didn't you?"

"Sadie," Grayson reached a hand to grasp her elbow and she shook him away.

"Would he have been in the ice realm if not for you?"

"We don't know that," Rogget said.

"I *knew* it," Sadie said. "I knew it all along. You are the bairn. You're fulfilling the prophecy."

"I am not."

"You are. Rogget, you can't let him do it. Even Father Britt wouldn't want him to. He told us it had to be destroyed."

Rogget looked to the ground and shook his head. "I don't know what the right thing is, Sadie. But I have to agree with Fenn. The stone does not belong to us. It belongs to the beast."

"Well, I'm not going to let you take it to the Ruud."

Sadie stepped toward him and grabbed for his knapsack. Before she could get her hands on it, she flew backward against Rogget and fell to the ground.

"I didn't do that," Fenn said. "I swear I didn't."

"Of course you did," Rogget said.

Sadie climbed to her feet and rushed at him. "I'm taking it," she growled.

"You are not." Fenn let her grab at his pack and pull it, but he wouldn't let her have it. He concentrated on not pushing her away, but as soon as he wrenched the strap from her grasp, she flew off her feet again landing hard on her backside.

"That's enough," Leah said, kneeling beside her. She looked up at Fenn, anger in her eyes.

"We're supposed to destroy it," Sadie yelled. "You promised us you would."

"I never promised."

"Why don't you let us have it," Grayson said. "It's best for everybody if it's destroyed."

"I thought you'd be on the beast folk's side," Fenn said.

"We won't destroy it; we'll take it to Father Britt. We'll let the wissenry decide."

"No one will be taking the stone from Fenn," Rogget said. "I'm not letting you do that."

"Nor I," Roren said in a smooth, calm voice.

There was a brief silence as Fenn watched a light breeze lift Sadie's hair.

"Then I'm leaving." Sadie rummaged around the site stuffing her belongings into her knapsack. "I'm going back to the Ruud to warn them about you. I can't believe I let you drag me all over two continents and you turn out to be the bairn of prophecy. I can't believe it."

"There is no bairn," Fenn said. "There wasn't even a prophecy."

"You knew all along you weren't going to destroy it. Didn't you?" She walked up to him, her face only a few inches from his, close enough to make Rogget step forward. "Didn't you?"

"Not at first," he said.

"Fenn Foster, you are a liar. You've done nothing but keep secrets from us—from the beginning—and we trusted you. Our parents are going to be hanged because of you."

"Now, Sadie," Rogget said.

Sadie stomped away from the group.

"She can't go by herself," Leah said.

"We need to stay together," Rogget said.

"You can't leave," Grayson said.

She turned back to glare at them. "I can and I will. There is no way I'm traveling to the Ruud with him and that stone, just be hanged as a traitor because of him."

"I'm going, too," Grayson said quietly and began packing his things.

"You don't have to go with her," Fenn said. "She'll be fine."

"I don't need looking after," Sadie said.

Grayson set a hard, angry face on Fenn. "I'm not going with her to take care of her. I'm going because I agree with her."

"Fine, then."

"It's not fine," Rogget said. "I can't let you two travel here in the west alone. You'll stay with us if I have to hogtie you and drag you along."

"I dare you," Grayson said walking toward Rogget. "Go on. I dare you."

"Sadie," Leah said, "listen to reason."

"Reason? I'm listening to what I should have been listening to all along—my gut. And my gut tells me this whole thing stinks. As soon as I saw the mark on his arm I should have turned him in."

"That's enough," Grayson said. "Let's just go."

"I can't let you go," Rogget protested.

"You don't have any choice."

"We'll go with them," Leah said. "It'll be all right." She gathered her knapsack and, as if waking from a sleep, Prenalin and Marigold did the same. "We'll get them home." She put a hand on Rogget's arm. "No harm will come to them."

Rogget frowned, but nodded. "Aye. The eastern port?"

"Lerringlass. You can follow at a distance if you like and find a boat as well."

"Not with the stone," he said. "We'll go on north and take an ice cutter."

"Roren," Marigold said, "come along."

"No," the young king said. "I will stay with Fenn."

"But, we were to take you east."

"I am no longer slave to the plots and fancies of others. I travel east with Rogget and Fenn. If I decide to return to Ruhm to aid you in your plans, I will let you know."

Leah, Prenalin, and Marigold stood looking at one another for several seconds until Marigold shrugged, helpless.

"My father would not have us force anyone," Leah said.

Mari nodded and they all said their goodbyes. As he, Fenn, and Roren watched them follow Sadie and Grayson, Rogget put his hands on his head and let out something of a sob.

"You cannot protect everyone," Roren said.

Rogget walked forward, toward Sadie and Grayson and the others, watching them trudge off across the plains toward Ruhm. Fenn's breathing quickened and his face burned hot. He paced back and forth as anger boiled inside him. He should have known. He should never have allowed himself to trust them. He should have been more careful from the beginning. Suddenly he walked to the fire and swung his arms wildly toward it and then up to sky.

"Watch it," Rogget yelled shoving Roren aside. "Don't be flinging fire at random. You've got to learn to control that."

"What difference does it make?" Fenn said. "There's nothing here to burn."

"There is your honor," Roren said.

"What's that supposed to mean?"

"To have power and use it recklessly is to live without honor."

Fenn sucked in a deep breath and struggled to let go of his anger. He nodded.

Chapter Thirty-eight

Seize them."
Rogget and Roren both put their hands out to stop Fenn when they realized they'd come upon a small encampment of beast folk—eis, trolls, and strange creatures that reminded Fenn of death itself.

They'd hiked north for two days—the stone's effect on Fenn had eased over that time. He found his sight and hearing had settled back to normal, with occasional bursts of intensity when he least expected them. This would be a part of him he would have to explore and learn, he realized. But he didn't fear it.

Rogget told him they were almost to the tiny port where they could take an ice-cutter ferry across the slushy sea to the eastern continent. They'd be north of the wasteland, he told them; they could make their way into the beast forest unseen, through the woods along the west coast of the Ruud.

Now they stood wary, as an eis, pale and blond, with eyes like a clear sky, approached them; behind him, two others readied their bows. The eis called out and two trolls lumbered forward.

Fenn startled and Rogget took a step forward.

"Hold," he whispered. "No need to let on who you are."

Relaxing, Fenn allowed the trolls to yank off their knapsacks and push them along to a stand of trees. The ghostly beast folk, a sort he'd never seen the like of before—tall and gangly, gray like the dead—joined the bulbous, ruddy trolls and helped lash them to the large pines.

"What is this about?" Rogget said. "We're folk of the Ruud, making our way back home. We mean no harm."

"Find it," the eis ordered and the trolls rummaged through their sacks until one of them roared in delight and held up the stone.

The eis looked at Fenn with relief. "If you had destroyed it, I would have killed you."

"How did you know?" Fenn said.

"I felt the stone when you were in the small valley of wither-wood some miles away," he said. "And I heard you discussing your quarrel over it as you approached."

"Then you know we weren't going to destroy it," Fenn said.

"It doesn't matter. I have it now and will keep it safe."

"Who are you?" Rogget asked.

The eis peered at him suspiciously. "I am Quiren of the eis. News is already spreading that the stone is with us again." He nodded at Fenn. "I thank you for your part."

"You have to give it back to the boy."

"I need do nothing of the sort."

"He's the fulfillment of the prophecy."

Stunned, Fenn looked at Rogget. "I am not."

Quiren frowned at Rogget. "Which prophecy?"

"I'm not part of any prophecy."

"You know very well which one."

"It's not true," Fenn protested.

Rogget gave him a stern look.

"The boy says it isn't true," Quiren said slyly.

"He's born of a king of the Ruud, orphaned to the waste-lands, and now here he is with the stone."

Fenn struggled to listen, but thoughts raced wildly in his head. What sort of game was Rogget playing? Quiren didn't say he planned to harm them; he only said he would have, if Fenn had destroyed the stone. Still, they *were* tied to trees. But what difference would it make if Quiren returned the stone to the east instead of him? Fenn shook his head and looked up at the eis.

"Is it true, boy?"

"I was born in the wasteland and I am an orphan. That's all I know."

"It's true," Rogget insisted. "Dag Voorspeld named him and gave me the task of helping him along."

Now Fenn was sure Rogget was lying.

"If that is true, then you know what the prophecy stated."

"I do," Rogget said.

Fenn looked quickly again at Rogget. Did he know it? Fenn tried hard to remember if he, Grayson, or Sadie had repeated it to him, but he was sure they hadn't.

"Then speak it," Quiren demanded.

"A new bairn. Born of a king, cast into the wasteland. Raised an orphan. He will rise up against you, King of Michelruud. Dead you are; dead you will be."

Fenn breathed a sigh of relief. He was sure that was correct. It was, at least, close enough. After all, how would Quiren know exactly what Anfang had said?

Quiren stared at them for a moment and turned to Roren. "And who is this?"

"I am Roren."

"We stole him," Rogget said, "from the Hass."

"Stole him?"

"He was their king. Revolution is brewing, resistance. The wissenry plans to—"

"Enough," Quiren said. He returned to the fire where the other beasts had gathered and together they spoke in whispers for some time. Fenn struggled to hear, but their words bounced about as if in a bubble, and he couldn't make them out. Somehow, he realized, eis must have the ability to keep their words from being heard by others; but he had no time, just then, for figuring that out. Finally Quiren returned and approached Fenn.

"And you say you plan to return the stone to the beast lord, Voorspeld?"

"Yes."

"But you do not claim to be the new bairn?"

Fenn shook his head. "I'm not the son of a king. I'm just another orphan from the wasteland. There's tons of them."

"Then why do you plan to return the stone?"

Fenn shrugged against the ropes that bound him and the stiff bark of the tree scratched against his back. "It belongs to the beasts."

"Then why don't you give it to me and let me take it to Voorspeld?"

"You know it has to be him," Rogget said.

Quiren stared silently at Rogget for a moment. He nodded slowly. "Very well; release them."

The strange beast folk came to them and untied them from the trees. Quiren led them to their encampment and they sat gratefully by the fire and accepted mugs of warm honey mead offered them.

"I will take you aboard the cutter and transport you to the east myself. I will ensure you do as you have promised. Will that be acceptable?"

"Aye," Rogget said. "That'll do."

The trolls were set to guard them while the eis walked away in their small group and the gray folk hovered at a distance.

"Rogget," Fenn whispered. "What are those strange creatures?"

"Anthropophagi."

"What?"

"Ann-throw-poff-uh-guy," he said. "Eaters of flesh."

"What does that mean?"

"Cannibals?" Roren said, looking startled.

Rogget nodded. "I have only seen them deep in the great mountains of the north. I didn't know they ventured this far out."

"What do you mean, cannibals?" Fenn said.

"They eat folk," Roren said, disgusted.

Fenn's eyes popped wide and he gawked at the creatures watching them. They were taller than Rogget, slender and willowy. Their gray skin almost glowed. But they stood quietly, hands clasped at their fronts or behind their backs, their faces placid. Still, his heart raced. The eis wouldn't let them be eaten, would they?

"They eat only dead flesh," Rogget said. "Long dead. Scavengers. Much too weak, or lazy, to kill you for food."

"That's helpful," Fenn muttered. But there were six cannibals and only three of them. "I hope they're not coming with us to the east."

Rogget shook his head. "I don't think they can stay long out of the

490

mountains. I've been told they melt in the higher tempera-tures."

Fenn decided he'd try to throw fire at them, if it came to it.

"When were you over here in the west?"

"Long time ago. When I first ran from the guard."

Finally the eis returned with baskets of breads, aged sharp cheeses, and fruit. They ate and Fenn filled himself so full he needed to lie down. He slept fitfully, jumping up and throwing off his blanket several times prepared to flee the cannibals in his dreams. But they remained standing about them in a circle, their hands clasped neatly, their white hair and dead skin lit dully in the moonlight.

The next morning they were awakened, fed, and led across the land all day until night fell again, where they camped and once more Fenn's sleep was tortured by anthropophagi and grub demons and Lucas rising from the dead only to be eaten up again by the cannibals. Exhausted, he hiked all the next morning to the edge of the western continent and a rocky wet shore, looking out across a blue sea dotted white with ice floes. The eis ship was anchored far off shore and they called out for a boat. It was not as large as Captain Olgut's and Fenn was glad. Even if the cannibals wanted to come, there would not be enough room.

The small rowboat was pulled up to the shore and Fenn waded into the frozen water to grasp it. He pulled himself over the rim and as soon as he landed in the boat, he felt a warmth that began in his chest and spread slowly out across his body. He reached to his neck and felt his mother's charm; it was hot against his skin. It knows, he thought. And then some-thing occurred to him. He pulled his sack off his back as a few of the eis remaining on shore pushed them off and two other eis rowed them toward the ship. He dug inside to the bottom and pulled the kell stone up into his hand, without removing it from the bag. It was warm. It glowed and shimmered. Home, Fenn thought. We're all going home.

One night, several days into their journey, Fenn couldn't sleep. He wrapped himself in a blanket and found Rogget on deck, in the frigid night air.

"Here," Rogget said, wrapping another blanket around Fenn's shoulders. "Can't you sleep?"

Fenn shook his head and his teeth chattered.

"We'll be home soon," Rogget said. "Like as I can tell from the eis maps, the continents aren't so far apart up here in the icy parts. But the trip's tougher on the boat."

"Rogget," Fenn said quietly. "When you told the eis about the prophecy, you were tricking them, weren't you?"

Rogget looked out into the darkness.

"You didn't really tell Dag Voorspeld you would help me fulfill the prophecy, did you?"

"Does it matter?"

Fenn didn't want to answer. He looked to the deck at his feet, kicked at the wood a bit with the tip of his long boot and shrugged.

"I suppose not," he said. But it did matter. "I just wondered, that's all. I mean, I wondered how you could have got into the beast forest when you said you couldn't go."

"Aye, I couldn't go in, not without the stone. It is my penance for killing the centaur. It was given me when I threw myself on his lord's mercy not days after it happened. I'm not allowed to enter the forest again until you and the stone are with me."

Fenn continued looking down. Tears stung at his eyelids. "So that's why you went west afterwards? You were trying to find out about the stone and all?"

"Aye."

"Okay, I was just wondering. Thanks." Fenn walked back toward the stairs to the sleeping deck below.

"Are you all right, Fenn?" Rogget said behind him.

He nodded, but didn't turn around. "I'm fine," he mumbled.

But he was not fine. He was alone and he realized it with a stabbing pain in his chest and a wave of nausea in his stomach. There was no one left. Father Treacher and Father Britt were useless fools. Lucas was dead. Sadie and Grayson had deserted him and their pact. And now Rogget betrayed him. He fumbled with his blankets on the straw bed and lay in the dark in the rocking ship as it plunged through the ice toward home. All he had now, he supposed, was the Ruud itself. But even that was gone. He could never go home and be a kid again, even if he was just a wissenry orphan.

Fenn sucked in a big breath and closed his eyes tight. Even though it was put on him, and he didn't choose it himself, he loved his life before the tunnel, before Sadie and Grayson and Rogget. He'd give anything to have it back. He let out a long breath. That wasn't true, he admitted. That wasn't really true.

Fenn tossed on his mat, just as the boat rocked him. In his sleep, the turning of his stomach sent waves of disjointed visions through his mind. The woman's hand was cut and bleeding. Lucas laughing. Father Britt's voice saying over and over, "you must escape north, you must escape north." Clutch of The Wretched smirking, Fenn's gold charm dangling from his dirty neck.

Fenn bolted upright, knocking his head on the curved wooden hull, breathing heavily. He darted from his mat and up the steps to the top deck, ran across the ship and fell forward against the the side, vomiting. Again and again he purged until he was gasping for breath and sobbing. Wiping his mouth on the sleeve of his tunic, he stared below him at the black waters, dotted with pale gray ice floes.

"You are unwell?"

Quiren leaned along the rail beside him, but Fenn didn't speak. He swatted the tears off his face with his hands, still trembling.

"We will arrive soon, young Fenn, and you will feel better. There is much to be done in the eastern realm. Much there I love and would fight for. Much for you to save."

They were both silent for some time until Quiren spoke again. "The hero's path is lonely, with no one to trust but himself."

Fenn finally turned to Quiren and smirked. "I'm no hero."

"Heros usually say such things."

Chapter Thirty-nine

1268 Autumn

Aliara grabbed for the midwife's hand and tried to scream, but still she could not make a sound. Her life had already left her, she knew, and her soul only remained to push her child into the world. The midwife and her folk had to help; they lifted her legs, pulled her knees to her sides. One sat behind her, propping her up.

"That's it, love," Clara cooed. "Try to push."

Panting, she did her best to pretend she felt something more than pain, but all that made her who she was, had fled. Elrundt, dead. Her sister Rue-Anna and her betrothed, murdered. Her home—for they were the only home she had after fleeing the ice—gone.

"I'm sorry," she managed to whisper to him when he was swaddled and put in her arms. If she hadn't been attacked by the guard, perhaps... she thought, she could have lived for him. But it was too late. "I'm sorry."

She woke to find she was nursing the infant and she felt a smile at her lips. A wetnurse had been sent for, Clara told her. In the meantime, the wissende, Father Wold, had arrived.

"He's here," Clara whispered. "Right here."

"Name?" the wissende said.

Aliara shook her head, knowing it was barely perceptible, but still it took all the energy she could muster. She dug deep, forcing herself to lift her eyelids, and turned to him.

"One of the ancient kings," she said, as a long breath escaped her. "One of Elurundt's..."

The wissende nodded and she let her eyes close again. She waited.

"I think," the wise old folk said after a moment, "there has not been a Fenn in the line, since the last one, oh, more than one hundred years ago. Way back to near the beginning. He was a son of Alfred, who was son of Roarn. Roarn being the son of Michelruud. Not *the* Michelruud, no, but Michelruud's son. Michelruud, our founder, had three sons."

And so the wissende spun the tale of the Ruud for her little Fenn. Aliara let her hand rest on his arm as he spoke, silently she asked him to take care of the orphan. With the last of her strength she bound the old man to him as best she could. And when the time came, Aliara could not tell if Fenn was being lifted from her arms, or if she was falling away from him. But the pain of the separation took her last breath.

1280 Autumn

It was not yet dawn when Leah heard the shout. She was used to the voices of the sailors, but this was different—fearful. The steps on deck above her cabin were not the soft, bare feet of the crew, but boots. They'd made port, she realized. And something was wrong.

Prenalin met her on the steps and gave her a warning look, before he bound her hands behind her back.

"This is necessary," he whispered, barely audible, before pushing her ahead of him upward and onto the main deck.

Kirche stood there, his feet apart, one hand on the hilt of his long sword, his cream colored cape glowing in the pale lights of the morning at Cold Sea Port. She heard another muffled cry and realized Sadie and Grayson were bundled up and gagged, being dragged down the gangplank into the city.

"Prenalin," Kirche said. "I can't tell you how relieved I am to see you've returned successful."

Leah's chest lifted with a ragged breath and she forced herself not to cry out. Was it true? Was he with Kirche all along? She cast her glance about the deck looking for Marigold, but the girl was nowhere to be seen.

"But...what's this?" Kirche walked forward, squinting in the dim morning light. He reached out and grabbed at her shorn locks, jerking her head toward him. "What have you done?"

"It was her attempt at disguise," Prenalin said.

Leah recognized the cold, impersonal tone of his voice and wondered how she could have been fooled by him. Was she fooled? Again she had to force herself not to let out a sob, instead, drawing a deep breath.

"It worked," Pren said. "Though she did witness the hanging."

Kirche's head tilted and his brow creased. He made a tsking sound with his lips pursed together. "I so wanted to shield you from that horror, my love. But I suppose it is in a daughter's nature to want to be at her father's side when he pays for his crimes. That is the story we shall tell." He motioned for them to follow.

Prenalin took her by the arm but she pulled away from him.

"I can walk on my own," she seethed.

"Concerned, of course," Kirche was purring, "and riddled with guilt over your father's abuses of his station, you ran dutifully to his side to witness his execution." He walked the gangway, his hand in the air, gesturing as he spoke. "And of course, you were unprepared for such an awful sight and out of shock, cut your hair. Yes, that's right." He held out his hand to help her step onto the pier. She refused him. "Such a sight would make a woman of Hass wish to rid herself of her past. To start over."

"Excellent, Lord Kirche," Prenalin said.

Finally a sob escaped her. Leah glanced behind her at the ship and caught a glimpse of a horrified Marigold before she was forced to follow Kirche into the bustling early morning of Cold Sea Port.

Chapter Forty

When Fenn, Rogget, and Roren followed Quiren off the ship at the rocky cliff shores of Imlich, gray clouds puffed up the sky like dirty cotton in a bowl. Fenn wrapped his arms around his waist against the cold. Imlich. He'd heard stories of this village from Father Treacher on occasion. Beasts of the Ruud were driven either into the ancient pine forest just southwest of Michelruud, or northwest, beyond the wasteland, into the lands of ice. There, they traveled back and forth along the base of snow-capped mountains, between the frozen sea and the ice realm. That was their only territory. Too far north, and they would interfere with the angels. Too far south and the folk of the wasteland and hill country would herd them off. Imlich—where folk dare not tread. Village of the beast, they called it.

Fenn had seen, in these last months, that there were beast folk living all over the land. Fairies still inhabited the faire glade in the Ruud. Gnomes buried themselves under the ground in the hill country.

Brownies occasioned the forests. Trolls roamed, though rarely, through Michelruud. But here, in Imlich, *he* was the rarity.

At the shore, Fenn looked up to the rocky ledge he must climb to reach the mainland and saw a large herd of rhinobears and eleshags lumbering across the path at the cliff's edge. And once they passed, a committee of gnomes, trolls, and what looked like elves the size of brownies appeared, frowning down at him. They wore rabbit fur coats and hats and most had pipes, smoke twirling about their heads in the cold morning.

"We were not expecting travelers today," a large, fat troll said.

"We did not expect to arrive today," Quiren said carelessly, and began the trek along a path upward through the rocks.

"We have enough of their kind already." The troll pointed a thick finger at Fenn and the others.

Quiren glanced back at Fenn briefly and continued his hike. "They only return home."

"They belong south, in the Ruud."

"And that is where they go."

"Hmph." The troll stomped a fat foot on the dirt. "That's what the others say."

Fenn was out of breath once he reached the summit. Across from the wide herd path, a village, spotted with huts and fires, filled the plain between two forests, south and north. The forests were populated mostly with pines, bright green against the dull gray sky; but other trees stood bare of leaves, like dead hands reaching for water from the clouds above.

"We need food and drink," Quiren told the committee.

"Take them to the holding place," the troll said. "They may eat with their own kind."

Quiren turned to Rogget as they headed in the direction the troll advised and said, "I have no idea what he's going on about. I've not seen folk this far north in all my years of travel for the eis."

But as they walked the outer edge of the village, along the tree line, they saw, beyond the easternmost point of the village, settled on a widened plain, an unorganized encampment of folk, cordoned off with thick heavy rope tied to stakes dug deep into the ground. Inside the large circle were tents, fires, and folk milling about.

"He's not welcome here." One folk stood and approached them, pointing at Quiren. "You folk come on over the ropes. No beasts allowed."

"He's not a beast," Fenn said. "He's an immortal."

"What's the difference?"

496

Quite a lot, actually, Fenn thought. *Grayson would give him an earful.* Fenn frowned at the thought. He hoped at least that Sadie and Grayson had made port by now; but anger still bubbled up within him when he let himself rest on the subject of his former friends.

"I will make camp in the village and find out what news explains this," Quiren said.

Fenn looked at Rogget and shrugged. The three of them stepped high over the ropes into the encampment.

"Where do you come from?" the old folk said. "Michelruud? Damon Wall?"

"Michelruud," Rogget said. "But we've been away to the west."

"Why would you be away from the Ruud?"

"It's a long story, and we're tired."

"Of course. Come to my tent. I am Hargodt of Aaronland."

"I'll be Rogget. This is my charge Fenn, and our friend, Roren."

They followed Hargodt around and between campsites to a large tent where a thin and haggard woman stoked a pot hanging on the spit over the fire and three children sat on the ground wrapped in blankets with wooden bowls in their hands.

"Agatha, my wife," Hargodt said with a wave of his hand. Agatha bounced up and down several times in greeting.

They all fell easily to the cold ground on one side of the fire and were grateful to receive large, round loaves of bread. Fenn showed Roren how to pull out the center and eat it, forming a bowl for soup. Agatha ladled soup for each of them with a slight smile and then handed them wooden spoons.

Over dinner Hargodt told them of the troubles in the Ruud.

"They came over in boats, I hear. Brought horses and firearms. Went into Michelruud and took over the castle first thing."

"No sign of King Welk?" Rogget asked.

"None for weeks, nigh on two months."

"And you left the Ruud?" Fenn said.

"Had to. They was slappin' bands around everyone's arms and tellin' 'em what to do and what to say...even what to think."

"What do you mean?"

"We was told the Ruud is dead and gone. Michelruud failed us. The Hass will free us. We got to smile all the time and be pleasant. We got to say thanks to Kett, or Bett, or some such folk, for nearly everything all day. And no arguin' even over money owed you. If you didn't obey, you got put in what they call stocks. Awful things."

"So the Hass has taken the Ruud," Rogget said.

Fenn could only think of Sadie and Grayson. And Miss Hallowsing. What must have happened when they sailed into port? Were they hidden? Were they all right?

A flurry of activity erupted eastward—people shouting. But it was a moment before Fenn could understand them.

"It's the king," someone said.

Rogget looked quickly at Fenn and Fenn's heart began to patter rapidly in his chest. Not King Welk, surely. But did it matter? Any of the kings of the Ruud would be after him.

"My boy here is not feeling well," Rogget said quickly to Hargodt. "Might he lie in the tent?"

"Of course," Hargodt nodded and his wife smiled and patted Fenn's shoulder as she led him into the tent. She busied herself punching down a mattress for him to lie on. Fenn huddled by the open flap and watched Rogget and Roren stand. A small crowd of folk gathered in front of Hargodt's tent chattering.

"Where have you been?" someone called out. "They've taken the Ruud."

"Good folk."

Fenn startled at the deep, scratchy whisper; in it he remem-bered the strong voice of King Welk.

"Give him some time to rest," another folk said. "He needs food and drink."

A member of the guard in a tattered, faded, red uniform pushed through the crowd toward Hargodt. Without a word, Hargodt waved him and the king to his fire pit where they lowered themselves, weary and worn, to the ground. Hargodt's wife silently pushed past Fenn with a blanket and left him alone in the tent to peer cautiously around the flap. He watched as Rogget and Roren sat to the left of the fire, giving him clear view of the king and his guardsman over the embers. Fenn pondered Welk's face, drawn into a exhausted frown. He took a mug of bitters from Hargodt, and shivered. Folk gathered around, squeezing in, jostling one another for a better spot to hear Welk speak.

"The king has been chased and accosted by the angels these last weeks," one of Welk's folk said.

Fenn suddenly recognized him as one of Clutch's men. He couldn't fathom how it happened that he would be with Welk.

"Our sire was near home when he received word that the Hass had taken over Michelruud," one of the guards said. "Nay, the entire Ruud. We were told to come here, that a gathering of refugees could be found and we are heartily glad to see Ruud folk once again."

"Can the king not speak?" A lanky, blond folk with a bushy beard peered at Welk, quivering in front of the fire.

"I can," Welk said. His voice was dry and quiet, "but I am severely injured."

A sigh floated around the crowd.

"Can I help, Sire?" A woman came forward, her hair tied tightly back from her face. She wore an apron and wiped her hands nervously on it. "I've tended many a soldier of the Ruud."

"Dear Madam," Welk said with a slight smile on his thin lips, "I am afraid it is angel magic that haunts my wound."

She gasped and whispers fluttered through the crowd. "Too true, that I am not versed in the evil arts of angels," she said. "But I will make you a place near our camp, just over there. We have a thick mattress stuffed with goose down. The softest in the Ruud. You can lie there and I'll feed you chicken soup."

Hargodt's wife stepped to the side, blocking Fenn's view. She put her hands on her hips, but she said nothing that Fenn could hear. By the time she'd moved out of the way, Fenn saw King Welk leaning against Clutch's man, hobbling across the encampment.

Fenn let out a deep breath and realized he'd been holding it for nearly two minutes. He breathed in and out for a time, calming his nervous hands.

"Now, now, dear," Hargodt soothed his wife. "It was for the best. We have three children, and travelers to care for. Liberna did you a favor by taking on the king."

When she returned to the tent, Agatha's cheeks glistened with tears. But she smiled at Fenn and patted his shoulder again.

"Thank you," Fenn said, "for taking us in, but we have to leave soon."

She nodded.

Fenn poked his head out of the tent. "Rogget, we have to get out of here."

Rogget smiled at Hargodt and then turned to Fenn. "Aye, we'll leave as soon as we can."

"But why?" Hargodt said. "There's nowhere to go."

Rogget smiled and nodded. "We'll see."

Fenn remained inside Hargodt's tent despite the old man's pleadings, and those of his three little girls, to come out and sit by the fire. King Welk was only two tents away, resting on a mat under a tarp strung to three trees. Fenn wished Rogget would join him inside the tent in hiding; but that would be suspicious. Rogget sat uncomfortably on the ground with his back to Welk and his guardsman all afternoon while Hargodt left and returned to his camp several times. Roren disappeared for long stretches at a time, exploring the camp.

Just as the sun was setting, the king rose from his mat and sat by Liberna's fire. Fenn watched his movement carefully from the door of the tent. Finally, darkness fell and only Welk's shadowy silhouette could be seen against the flames. When Roren returned, Fenn left the tent and grabbed his knapsack.

"Thank you for your hospitality," Rogget whispered to Hargodt and his wife.

Hargodt nodded weakly, the firelight below them casting strange shadows on his face.

The three of them walked behind Hargodt's tent and through the encampment eastward, crossed over the rope and picked up their pace as they headed across the small plain to the forest of pines. It occurred to Fenn that he should have left Rogget in the encampment and snuck off with Roren, or just on his own. It would serve Rogget right if he escaped him and returned the kell stone to the beast lord without him. He'd tell Dag Voorspeld that Rogget was a lying fink and not to be trusted. But Fenn's heart sank at the thought of it. He knew he'd never actually say such a thing. Suddenly, Fenn's eye caught movement ahead. Shadowy figures in the pale moonlight emerged from the trees up ahead and approached. Guards.

Chapter Forty-one

Halt," the guard up front said, pointing a firearm at them.
They were surrounded before they stopped walking. Rogget, as if sensing Fenn's fear, reached out to stay him, just as he'd done when they'd been accosted by Quiren's group of beasts. A warning.

"We're just travelin' through," Rogget said. "Wanderers, is all."

"Wandering where?" A familiar voice cut the night and Fenn turned, startled.

King Welk walked forward and peered at him in the darkness. "Fenn Foster," he said, drawing out the name as if he didn't know it so well. "We meet again. I trust the felidae will not divert our attention this time; nor will your friends ride up on horseback and whisk you away."

It occurred to Fenn, despite Rogget's hand on his arm, that he could simply push them all away; at least, he *thought* he could do it. Each time he'd managed this repelling, if that was what it was, he hadn't thought about it, hadn't done it on purpose. It came more from anger or fear. He lit the fire for Rogget without emotion, but could he do the same in shoving folk off? And should he? Rogget's grasp tightened and Fenn accepted his caution. He had to admit that King Welk should not know the truth about him; at least, not yet.

Welk motioned to his guard and they were all led back across the brief plain to an encampment separate from the refugees, about a quarter mile distant. A great tent was set up at one end with a fire pit burning orange and yellow. Two rows of smaller tents were pitched on each side of the king's tent. Another fire pit sat in the middle of these, to be shared by the guards.

Fenn was taken to one of the tents next to the king's, shoved inside and left there alone. A guard stood just outside the door and he heard the footsteps of others moving into position all around outside. Removing his knapsack, he felt inside for the kell stone, just to be sure it was safe. He sat quietly for a while, wondering what he should do next. Welk was right. Who would save him this time?

Roren's words returned to him and he frowned. He could force them all away and run; he was sure he could manage it. He could cast fire all about, burn the camp, and escape in the chaos. But should he? What was honor, really, anyway? It wasn't in running away, he was sure of that. A sense of calm come over him, a realization that he had choices. He could wait and see what might happen; he didn't have to use force against anyone...yet. And anyway, he doubted he could repel a bullet. More worrying, however...he knew that once he revealed himself, he would only convince folk that he *was* the bairn of prophecy; that would only make his situation worse.

Suddenly a guard peered into the tent and beckoned him. He followed and knew all the guards' eyes were on him as he was taken into the king's tent. Welk sat inside on a stuffed mat; lanterns hung all around casting shadows on the heavy fabric walls. Toward the back, silken sheets hung from ropes tied across the top of the tent and were pulled taut to hide the king's bed.

"Sit," Welk ordered and gestured to a mat nearby.

Fenn stepped gingerly through the tent and sat in front of the king. The charm against his neck warmed quickly, startling him. He had to force himself not to reach up and touch it—a gold charm of great worth was none of Welk's business.

"Are you hungry?"

Fenn shook his head.

"Thirsty?"

He shook again.

"No? What about honey mead?"

Fenn stared at Welk, his eyes felt wide open and he tried to close them up again and look normal.

"Honey mead," the king called out and suddenly Fenn realized a servant had been in the corner.

"Are you frightened?"

Fenn said nothing.

"You weren't frightened the last time we met."

"Yes I was," Fenn said, before he could stop himself.

The king smiled at him and his charm throbbed with heat.

"I'm glad I arrived ahead of my guardsmen and took brief respite in the refugee encampment. If I had not, I would not have heard that you were there in hiding."

Fenn's cheeks burned hot with betrayal. Who had given him away? Maybe he was recognized by one of the folk. Could it have been Roren? Or maybe it was Rogget. What if he wanted to take the stone back to the beast lord himself? No, no, Fenn told himself. He must stop all this nonsensical thinking; it only led to confusion.

The servant pushed through the tent flap carrying two mugs. He stood before Welk and sipped one mug before handing it to the king. He handed the second mug to Fenn.

"Richard." The king pointed to Fenn's mug.

Richard took it from Fenn and sipped it also, then handed it back.

Fenn stared at Welk and blinked several times. No matter what he did he could not get his eyes to soften, and his charm burned hotter, searing against his skin. Strangely, the amber stone that hung with it cooled, as if to counter the heat. His hands warmed quickly with the warm mug between them and he relaxed, if only a little.

"You never can tell," Welk said.

"Huh?" Fenn took his eyes off Welk and cast them down. That was a stupid thing to say to a king.

"Poison," Welk said. These days, Richard always tastes my drink and food. But I would not have anyone poison you, either."

"Why would anyone poison me?" Finally, Fenn's eyes felt normal again and he looked on the tired king. He brought his focus quickly to his mug, remembering too late that folk were not supposed to look into the eyes of the king. Why had Welk not scolded him before for staring? Fenn shuddered slightly and his hands shook.

"Look up, boy."

Fenn looked up, first by raising his head slightly, then his face, then his eyes to the king.

"That's better. Can you imagine going around talking to folk and having them not look at you?"

Fenn nodded."Why would anyone poison me?"

Welk smiled at him. "Don't you know?"

Fenn shook his head.

"You're the evil bairn, of course. Come to destroy the Ruud."

"I am not." His voice surprised himself. He sounded old, and tired, but resigned as well.

"Perhaps not."

"You think maybe I'm not?"

Welk nodded. "I think it's possible there has been a big misunderstanding."

Fenn sighed with some relief. Finally a grown-up who sounded like he knew things.

"But you do have the mark," Welk said.

"It doesn't mean anything."

"I think it does. I have seen its like before."

Fenn frowned at him. "What will you do with me?"

Welk peered at him and put his hand to his mouth and rubbed his chin. "I don't know."

"Can't you just let me go?" Fenn desperately wanted to tell the king about the stone. Maybe he would understand and let him return it to the beast. But his reason told him the king would not agree to it. It was too risky. Neither of them knew what the stone's effect on the beast might be.

The king shook his head and sighed. "It's not safe for you now. The Ruud is overtaken by the Hass. They would use you, I'm afraid, in a most despicable manner. In the hill country and the wasteland, the Wretched are arming and organizing. That is no place for a boy, either."

"What are they organizing for?"

"For battle. We will take back the Ruud. I think your place is here, in this northern land. When the battle is done, we will try to find a way for you to live in the Ruud. If the people will believe you are not a child of prophecy, nor plan to harm anyone. Do you want to go home?"

Fenn paused and said, "I don't know if it is my home."

"You lived in the Ruud all your life."

Fenn shrugged. "There's no one left there for me." His charm seemed to breathe hot air on his chest and he desperately wanted to pull it away from his skin. He thought of the amber stone, called for it to cool him...and it did.

"What of the wissendes who cared for you as a child? They would be much like parents, would they not?"

Fenn shook his head only slightly. "They kept sending me away. I think even they believe I'm the evil bairn."

"Your friends, then. The ones who so gallantly saved you from my grasp."

Welk was smiling at him now, teasing him. Fenn frowned deeper.

"They're not my friends, anymore."

The king nodded. "I see. What of the huntsman, Rogget?"

Fenn shook his head and let his eyes fall to his fingers wrapped tightly around his mug of mead. "He's only doing a favor for the beast lord in taking me back to the forest." He squared his shoulders and raised his head.

"Why do the beast folk want you?"

Fenn shrugged. "Maybe they believe Dag Anfang's prophecy."

Welk tilted his head and peered oddly at him for a second. "You know of Anfang?"

"I went into the beast forest, to the lord's lair; I heard Anfang speak the prophecy."

Welk smiled and rubbed his chin again. "You are an adven-turous sort, aren't you. Ah, well. The land of the Ruud is in your blood; it will beckon you back. I'm afraid for now you'll have to remain here under guard. But why don't we set you a mat here in my tent. It's warmer here, and there are books and trinkets to amuse you."

Fenn nodded in agreement; but he knew the king just wanted to keep an eye on him.

"What about Richard?" Fenn asked.

The king chuckled. "What about him?"

"I don't think he wants to get poisoned, either?"

"Then he'd better keep a sharp eye on the cook, hadn't he?" Welk laughed. "It's a nasty business, this kingship nonsense. I recommend highly against it."

Chapter Forty-two

There was such a flurry of activity that Fenn felt it, even tucked away inside the king's tent reading a book of fables about knights, ladies, and dragons. At one point, he heard someone shout something that sounded like "rebels" and he could stand it no more. He put the book down, cast off his blanket, and went to the door of the tent. He stood just inside with the flap raised and looked out at the folk gathered in the king's encampment.

"What's going on?" he asked the guard standing just outside the entrance.

"Meeting," he said. "The Wretched have arrived."

"Can I go?"

The guard, his hair gray and his face lined with age, smiled at him. "I am to bring you once the fire is full aflame and the stumps and logs are set."

Fenn waited, watching the commotion of folk until another guard approached and whistled at them.

"Let's go, then," the older folk said.

Fenn followed the guard through the crowd, thinking he should have brought his knapsack in case he saw an opportunity to flee. Gray clouds hovered low in the sky and a wind whipped at his overcoat, a gift from the king—one he said he'd bartered for among the refugees. They came to a large opening in the throng where logs and stumps had been placed in an imperfect circle with a fire pit in the middle. He was surprised to see Rogget with Hargodt and other folk from the refugee camp. He raised his hand briefly in greeting and Rogget smiled and winked, as if to reassure him all was well.

King Welk sat on a chair lined in rabbit fur; he was covered in a thick, worn quilt. Fenn was led to his left and sat on a folded blanket beside him. Despite the wool beneath him, he could feel the cold of the ground seeping into his body.

Welk raised his left hand and the crowd quieted.

"Let us hear from the Wretched of the hill country," he said. Though his voice was dry and laden with pain, it was deep and commanding, carried to all present.

When Clutch stood from his seat on the other side of the king, Fenn was startled, though he scolded himself for not expecting it. Somehow, the king and the thief were known to each other and shared a casual friendship—a fact Fenn had difficulty understanding, even more so now, after finding Welk kind and compassionate, nothing like the leader of The Wretched. Clutch sauntered toward the fire pit in the middle of the circle of folk—his face twisted in a sarcastic smile as he bowed ridiculously low. Fenn was certain he meant to mock Welk, but the king did nothing. And as Clutch bowed, Fenn caught sight of the stone charm, made for him by the children of Path, tied onto a hemp rope, dangling from the thief's dirty neck. Fenn caught Clutch's glance and frowned hard at him; he nearly forced the man off his feet, but remembered, once again, Roren's words. Honor. He must learn to use his skills with honor and respect. Still, he felt certain he could force the charm from Clutch's neck and into his own hand if he had the nerve. But he must not reveal himself.

"Word has spread quickly through the wasteland and the hill country," Clutch said. "We have heard from emissaries all about, willing to go to battle against the Hass to free the Ruud."

"And the eis?" Welk said.

A low hiss, like a sigh, rustled through the crowd.

"We don't need their kind to help us," someone called out.

"Rogget," the king called and Rogget stood with a nod.

Welk surprised Fenn, once again, with the friendly way he greeted the wayonder—as if they were equals.

"You have recently returned from the west. What can you tell us of their strength?"

Rogget fidgeted as he stood encircled by the crowd of folk, clearly unaccustomed to public speaking. "Aye. They've...well, they're...," he stammered. "I saw an army of ships, a dozen at least, ready to sail when we left a week or more ago."

"More ships?" someone in the crowd said.

"Aye. And their folk have got more firearms than we do. But I was told there was to be an uprising of the folk over there. They planned to burn as many ships at port as they could. I don't know if they managed it, though. So, I say we need all the help we can get."

"There's more," Clutch said, scanning the crowd. "The angels will fight with the Hass."

Confusion broke out for a moment while everyone talked and a few shouted to be heard over the grumbling. Finally, Welk held up his hand again.

"It's true," Clutch said. "The angels have agreed to help Hass take the Ruud in exchange for the ice realm. The eis are to be removed or killed. And all folk are to be contained within the boundaries of the Ruud. While that is their agreement, I think we can assume the folk will be slaughtered as soon as the angels get the chance."

There was less muttering this time and silence fell naturally after only a few seconds.

"It is agreed then" Welk said. "We need the eis as much as they need us. We will fight together to defeat the Hass. And if the beast will aid us, we will fight alongside them as well."

Welk allowed the crowd to mumble their complaints, but it was clear to Fenn they were fast resigning themselves to their situation.

"We need someone to return to the Ruud and spread the word of battle secretly. We have a network of spies set up already in Michelruud, and no doubt Damon Wall and Aaronland do as well. We will utilize these spies to our advantage. But we need someone to send messages between here and Michelruud. Who volunteers?"

"I'll go," Fenn said. Many folk squirmed and leaned to see him sitting on the ground beside the king, as if they only now noticed his presence.

Welk shook his head. "We will not send a boy to do a man's job," he said quietly. "No. We need an ordinary folk, used to traveling across the boundaries of the Ruud."

"I'll do it," Hargodt said, raising his hand. "I am a merchant and travel all the Ruud, trading tobacco and wheat."

"Very well," Welk said. "You will meet with us later to discuss the plan before you go."

Rogget stood again. "We need someone to travel to the beast forest and alert them, ask them for help."

Welk nodded. "And you volunteer?"

"Aye, but the boy will have to come with me."

Welk looked down at Fenn and then back to Rogget. "The boy must stay here under guard."

Rogget nodded, but said, "I am not allowed to enter the beast forest without him. And I'm likely the only folk willing to enter at all." He looked around at the faces in the crowd.

Welk shook his head. "Then we'll have to come up with another plan for the beast. The boy remains here."

Fenn found Hargodt's questioning eyes on him and returned his gaze.

"Who is the boy?" someone in the crowd said.

"Our meeting is ended," Welk said. "I ask that you disperse so that I may rest. The guard will keep you posted of our plans for battle."

Grudgingly, the folk muttered and meandered away, left with questions and a growing unease.

Two days later, while Fenn was alone in the king's tent looking through a book on planting seasons, he heard Hargodt talking to the guard outside.

"But I must accompany her," the old man was saying. "She cannot speak and only I can interpret for her."

"Why not the boy?" the guard said.

"A man understands his wife much better than her son."

As Fenn approached the tent flap, in walked Hargodt, his wife Agatha, beaming with a bright smile, and a thin boy about Fenn's size, with pale blond hair. Agatha carried a plate covered with a napkin. She bowed and rose several times, still smiling.

"Hello," Fenn said, happy for the company.

"Come, young Fenn," Hargodt said rather loudly. "Sit and enjoy Madam's sweet potato pie."

Hargodt nodded his head and winked.

"Thank you," Fenn said.

Agatha pulled the cover from her pie plate, but there was no pie. Fenn looked at the strange pile of blond hair on the plate and then to Hargodt, who put his finger to his lips. Hargodt pulled the hair off the plate and showed it to Fenn. It was sewn neatly onto a thin piece of cow hide. Hargodt plopped it on Fenn's head. Madam got a comb from her pocket and set about combing it. When she'd finished, she stepped back and clasped her hands to her chest.

"Oh, it is good," Hargodt said. "Madam is so happy you like it."

Fenn giggled a bit; he hadn't realized before that the Hargodts were insane. But as Hargodt took the blond boy by the shoulder and led him to the mat Fenn had been sleeping on, the whole plan began to put itself together in Fenn's head.

"Tired? Well of course you are," Hargodt called toward the front of the tent. "Yes, yes, you rest now. We'll bring more pie tomorrow."

Fenn stared at Hargodt, wide-eyed, and shook his head. This would never work. How stupid did he think the guards were? They'd never buy it. But Madam smiled at him and put her skinny arm around his shoulders and all three of them walked out of the tent and across the encampment as if they were heading back to the refugee camp.

"Are they following?" Fenn whispered.

"Don't look back. And don't worry. Benjamin will lie in your bed until the next check. We've been watching. They check on you only every two hours while the king is out of the tent. Once they make the next one, Ben will climb out the back as the sun sets. If a guard sees him outside the tent, he'll run. But you'll be far away by the time they figure out he's not you."

As they neared the refugee camp, Rogget and Roren joined them and they all smiled and nodded and pretended to take a walk about. Once they neared the trees of the forest, Hargodt and his wife turned and faced the camp.

"I see no one watching. Take care my friends. And good luck with your mission."

The three of them darted quickly into the trees and didn't stop running until they were three miles in.

Chapter Forty-three

Fenn decided it was better to be on his way to the beast lord and out of Welk's tent, even though he had to be in Rogget's charge again. And it wasn't as if Rogget had become mean or cruel. He was still Rogget. But Fenn couldn't help remembering his betrayal, every time he caught him looking at him with his worried face. Let him worry. He had lied, after all. He shouldn't be trusted again. Fenn refused to smile at Rogget and kept his glare firm and his mouth rigid, long after his jaw ached to be relaxed.

They walked for miles and miles in the forest seeing no one, folk or beast.

"This will lead into the deepest part of the western wood next to Steingefan." Rogget said after they'd all been silent for several hours.

Fenn shivered. "We've got to find shelter for the night. It's freezing."

"Aye."

They walked on for another hour and came to three huge boulders jutting from the ground among a dozen large rocks. There, Rogget dug a pit and lit a roaring fire without asking Fenn for help, and the three of them huddled around it, shivering. Finally, Fenn began to warm; he looked at Roren, who hadn't spoken in so long Fenn worried he could no longer do so. His cheeks were flushed pink and he stared into the flames, despair etched on his face.

"Are you all right?" Fenn whispered to him.

Roren stared at him for a moment before nodding.

"Can you talk, anymore?"

"Why do you ask?"

Fenn sighed with relief. "I don't know when the last time was you said anything."

Roren looked back into the flames. "There is nothing to say. I was king to my folk, servant of Rett; and yet, I had no power. I was discarded by them both so easily, and sent into a dungeon to starve to death. Rescued by strangers who cared for my life more than my own folk. And now I travel with you, a burden. I am adrift in this wood; adrift in the world."

"Sounds like there's a lot to say," Fenn said with a smile. But Roren didn't respond.

Rogget set up his spit over the fire and walked deep into the wood, without a word.

"A rift has formed between you and your guardian," Roren said.

Fenn only nodded.

"Despite his reasons for protecting you, it's clear he cares for you, much like a father for his son."

"Maybe." Fenn found a stick and poked at the fire with it.

"And you miss your friends."

Fenn tossed the stick into the flames, angry. "I don't miss them."

"No?"

He sighed. "I guess I do. I miss feeling like I had friends. But when I remember what they said, I think it was all a lie. I get so—" Fenn pushed at the fire with both hands and flames flew at the trees, licking the evergreen needles. He sat fuming for a moment before turning to look at Roren. "I keep thinking about what you said when they left, about how I had to act with honor."

"It is clear you are honorable; but you are young."

"It scares me. The way I knocked Sadie down without thinking at all—I didn't mean to do it. And when the guards took me to Welk, I did nothing. But, they had guns. I don't think I can repel a bullet."

"It is good to learn control."

"Is it? I mean...can I hurt someone if I'm not upset? It would seem...cold. Calculating. I don't think I want to be that way. It doesn't seem honorable."

Rogget returned with water in a leather pouch. They boiled potatoes, onions, and carrots given them by Agatha. They warmed honey mead in another pot and poured it into their mugs.

"What will you do," Fenn said to Roren, "now that you're free?"

"Free?" Roren shook his head and sipped his mead.

"You can stay with me."

"But where will *you* go?"

Fenn laughed. "I see what you mean. I suppose we'll have to be wayonders together, like Rogget."

"There's something I need to tell you, Fenn," Rogget said. "About this prophecy thing."

"You mean about how you made a deal with the beast lord to make sure I got the kell stone?"

"Aye. About that."

"What more is there to say? You lied to me."

"Not exactly."

"You let me think—wait, you let the wissenry think you were working for them to protect me. But—"

"I *was* protecting you."

"You were protecting yourself."

"I don't see the harm done," Roren said. "If he was also making sure you got the stone, he was still your guide and protector. What difference

510

does it make?"

"We made a pact," Fenn said. "We all four swore to not lie to one another anymore and to stick together. And I'm the only one who stuck to the pact. Sadie and Grayson ran off, and now Rogget turns out to be a traitor."

"That's a rather harsh description," Roren said.

"It's the truth."

"How so? What did he do to betray you? He did not tell you the whole truth. We are all guilty of that, at some time in our lives."

Fenn knew Roren was right, of course. He hadn't been honest with Sadie and Grayson about himself; not at first. And the truth was that he still hadn't told Sadie, Grayson, or Rogget everything. He hadn't told them about his visions. But that was different, he reasoned. His visions had nothing to do with them—they were personal. And Rogget working for Dag Voorspeld to bring Fenn to the beast forest had everything to do with Fenn.

"Why didn't you just tell me?" Fenn heard the disappointment in his own voice and struggled to not allow tears in his eyes.

Rogget shook his head, despondent. "How could I? You didn't believe you were the child of prophecy—for all I know you're not and this whole thing is nonsense. I was afraid it would scare you, thinking that Voorspeld was after you, on top of the kings of the Ruud. And then, you were determined to destroy the stone."

"What would you have done if he tried to destroy it?" Roren said.

"I would have let him—not that I think it can be done."

"You would?" Fenn said.

"Aye. I don't have to make peace with the beasts. I want forgiveness, but I can live without it. I was happy to help you and Sadie and Grayson—happy to protect you and guide you. There are so many secrets I've had to keep."

"There are more?"

Rogget nodded. "Aye. Father Britt would not allow me to tell you about your being a split folk and the powers you're likely to have."

"How did Father Britt know?"

"It was the mark, of course. It's the mark of split folk."

"No."

They all jumped as the darkness seemed to move. Quiren walked forward from behind one of the large boulders, smirking at them.

"It is not the mark of split folk."

"How did you find us?" Fenn said.

Quiren laughed.

"He's an eis," Rogget said. "He could probably hear our footsteps a thousand feet away."

"I mean you no harm." Quiren joined them on the ground around the fire. "Unless you do not fulfill your promise."

"We're taking the stone to the beast lord," Rogget said. "You have my word."

"Like that means anything," Fenn said.

"Hear now," Rogget said. "I'm sorry I didn't tell you the truth. I didn't do it to hurt you."

"Stop bickering," Roren said. "It no longer matters."

They were silent for a moment as Fenn fumed. Quiren watched him closely; he didn't trust Fenn. None of them really trusted one another and why should they? Fenn was unsure of Rogget's motives. Roren acted like he was lost and in shock, but there was something underneath his eyes that told Fenn he was smarter than he was pretending to be. Quiren had threatened to kill Fenn and now glared at him. And Fenn had to admit, he wasn't to be trusted, either. He'd lied about his mark as long as he could. And he'd kept his plans to himself, as well. Maybe if he'd talked to Sadie and Grayson about the stone earlier, instead of just telling them after he'd decided not to destroy it...maybe they'd still be there with him. Sadie would tell him what to do about Rogget. Sadie would still trust Rogget; Fenn was sure of that.

"What does the mark mean?" Fenn asked Quiren.

"Why would you believe what he tells you?" Roren said, still staring into the fire.

"I didn't say I would."

"You will believe. You will all believe—when the stone is set in its rightful place."

"Well, go on then," Rogget said.

The eis' smile deepened. He stood and pulled off his overcoat, then a long leather vest. He untied his tunic and pulled it down over his left shoulder. There was the mark of the faire on his arm, just like Fenn's.

Even Roren stared at Quiren now. "What is it?"

"The mark of the faire," Rogget said.

"Yes. And no," Quiren said, now pulling his overcoat back on and sitting again on the ground with them. "It's a fairy mark, given us at birth when they take our blood."

"They take our blood?" Fenn said. "Why?"

"For the stone. Those with the mark are bound to the stone and to the Rad—the council of the beast folk. We represent our kind there, when it is called. I am the consul for the eis."

512

Fenn let out a laugh and they all looked at him. "Who would I represent?"

"You are folk eis. You will represent those like you."

"But the folk have no consul," Rogget said. "Do they?"

"No," Quiren said. "The gathering was always for the immortals. There were never split folk represented before. But we have not had a Rad since the stone was stolen from us, many generations ago."

"What happens if a consul dies?" Roren said.

Quiren looked at Roren curiously, but Roren kept his eyes on the fire. "As the consul ages, a new bairn is selected of his kind."

"But what if he is killed suddenly?"

Quiren tilted his head and his brow furrowed. "Anoher would be selected."

"But they can be killed?"

"Why do you ask these questions?" Quiren said.

Roren shrugged and returned his attention to the fire. "I have lived my life in the west; we do not have such superstitious nonsense there."

"Ha," Fenn said with a laugh.

Roren looked at him, frowning.

"Sorry," Fenn said, trying to force the smile off his face. "But what about Rett?"

They all looked at Fenn while a cold wind whipped up and blew smoke suddenly into Rogget. He jumped up, coughing.

"Let's get some sleep, mind," he said. "We've still a long way to travel."

Chapter Forty-four

The next day they walked miles and miles through the wood until midday. They stopped to rest and have lunch and Rogget wandered off to find a rabbit or squirrel for the evening meal.

"Tell me, Fenn," Quiren said when they'd built up a fire. "What split skills do you have?"

"Split skills?" Roren said.

"He must have several odd things going on about him. They all do."

"How many folk eis have you come across?" Roren said.

"None. But the Hass is firm against them, even more so than against the beast. They say they possess unnatural talents. So, Fenn, what are your unnatural talents?"

They looked at him, smiling, waiting. Rogget reappeared carrying two dead rabbits by the feet.

"He can conjure fire, and toss it," Rogget said. "And he can read you when he touches you. He's got the eyesight of the eis. And when he was a small boy, he forced a playmate to eat a cricket with only his mind."

"How do you know about that?" Fenn said.

"I've been watching. And Father Treacher told me about the cricket."

"Darryl ate the cricket all by himself. I didn't have anything to do with it."

"Darryl said different, I guess. And don't you remember that was when you and Father came to live in Path? They had to move you around a couple of times because of that sort of behavior. It's a wonder you weren't branded the evil bairn when you were three."

After they ate a lunch of hard biscuits and jerky, Rogget was up and dousing the fire. "Let's pack up and move on. The animals were skittish. I'm thinking there might be some of the guard or the Hass roaming about. The sooner we get into the beast forest, the better, eh?"

They walked on until the sky darkened into a deeper shade of gray, and camped for the night in a thick wood where the wind was minimal. Rogget cooked the rabbits on wood spits over a small fire. Fenn wrapped his blanket around him and gathered pine needles into a pile to sit on, leaning against a tree not too far from the warmth of the flames.

And so they tramped for several days southward staying as far west as the forest would allow. At times, Fenn could smell the ocean and knew they bordered the sea. During the day, Quiren taught him and Roren sword and knife play, but each evening, they all grew more and more silent. Fenn was sure there was something wrong, but he didn't know what until one day, Rogget and Quiren returned from a brief hunt and had them pack up and begin moving again.

"Hurry," Rogget whispered. He pulled at Fenn's coat and together they darted through the trees.

They bolted, skirting thick trunks, jumping low shrubs, and batting at low-hung branches. Vines and leaves tore at Fenn's face and his feet caught roots and tangles of ferns. He got a glimpse of Roren, his face pale, scrambling to keep up; Quiren had disappeared into the trees westward. Cracks and thuds echoed around him, as if monstrous beasts plunged through the woods toward them from all directions. Turning back in search of Rogget, he felt something hard pitch against his legs and he was on the ground.

"Rogget," he screamed.

A shot rang out and Rogget roared. Soldiers of Hass, their heavy plum tunics emblazoned with a tree in flames, each one with a firearm, surrounded Fenn.

"Find the stone," one said as another pulled Fenn to standing.

He was bound at the wrists and feet, surrounded by guards, and marched through the woods alone.

Chapter Forty-five

Leah stood at the window of her upstairs room at the inn in Path, looking out on the center of the village. Soldiers of Hass paraded in the streets keeping watch on those citizens who had not escaped the Ruud before Kirche and his men took control. The villagers walked wide swaths around the soldiers, nodded politely as they tried to go about their routines. When she saw Dowling hurrying toward the inn, she backed away from the window and waited. She knew Dowling wouldn't come to her right away; that would arouse suspicion. So she paced and wrung her hands and worried.

When the knock at the door startled her, she hesitated so as not to appear eager. Finally, she opened the door and let the woman carry a tray into the room. The guard outside stood in the doorway and watched as Dowling set the tray on the table and left without a word. He watched as she picked at her food, ate a few bites, poured tea from the kettle into her cup, drizzled honey into it and stirred. He waited while she nibbled her bread, forced herself to eat as much stew as she could stomach. And finally, when she told him she was finished, he called for Dowling.

The woman entered and lifted the kettle from the tray.

"Why miss, you haven't had but one cup of tea. I'll leave the kettle for you and be back in an hour or so with something sweet to tempt you. You really must eat more."

Leah nodded and watched Dowling leave before closing the door behind her, offering her guard an angry stare as she did so. Once alone, she finished the tea in her cup and poured the remaining water out of the kettle into it, then flipped the kettle upside down. As quietly as she could, she unscrewed the bottom of the metal vessel until it popped off. A piece of writing paper flitted to the floor and Leah scooped it up.

Dowling's note was scribbled hastily: Children alive, Steingefan. Signs posted, rally tomorrow, bairn of prophecy to be hanged. Lord Kirche's secretary asks after you.

At that last, Leah folded the paper over and ripped it again and again, fuming. How dare he? When she thought back to the last time she saw Prenalin, his face like a stone, his eyes cold, not that he would look at her, she shuddered with rage. And still, always that doubt. She hated herself for it, but it gnawed at her, bit at her dreams, unsettled her stomach and pierced her head with pain. Whose side was Prenalin on?

Kirche and Prenalin took to Michelruud castle, so Dowling said in one of her notes, while Leah was imprisoned with the ranking soldiers at the inn. She felt so helpless. She knew she couldn't let them hang Fenn; but what could she do? She paced the floor the rest of the evening, leaving the sweet cakes Dowling brought her untouched, until darkness filled the room. Without lighting a candle, she took to the bed and lay there. Eventually, she decided she'd have to try to jump from her window, just before dawn. It was her only chance.

When she startled awake some time later, she realized someone was in the room. Before she could move to scream, a hand slapped over her mouth and Prenalin whispered, "Don't shout; you'll rouse the guard."

Leah struggled against him, trying to tell him she didn't care, let the guard come in. Slapping at his arm, she managed to sit up in the bed.

"Listen quickly," he said. "Kirche plans to hang the boy. I wanted to warn you...prepare you."

Gasping for breath against his hand, without thinking, she rotated her face slightly and sunk her teeth into whatever skin she could manage to fit between them.

"Aargh!" Prenalin jerked his hand from her.

She scurried out of the bed and shoved him. "Get out," she seethed.

"You think I planned this," he said. She couldn't tell if his shock was true or feigned. "You think I gave you up to Kirche, that it was my plan all along."

"Wasn't it?"

He stared down at her in the darkness. The moon outside the window lit the left side of his face; his jaw was set hard and cruel. She could hear his breath soften as he tried to force a calm.

"He intends to hide you here in the Ruud," he whispered, "until your hair has grown back to its appropriate length. He then believes he can return with you to Ruhm, victorious. He has yet to learn of the uprisings there. Ruhm's ships, what is left of them, are due to arrive soon and then he may become desperate."

"I won't be here that long."

"Don't attempt an escape, yet; it won't work."

"Why should I listen to you?"

"There will be a battle, soon. The soldiers will be called on; there will be chaos. Then you can make your move."

"And let Fenn be hanged?"

"What do you expect to do? The courtyard in front of the castle will be filled with soldiers of Hass. You'll be taken away, or killed, and that won't help the boy."

"You apparently won't help him."

"My concern is you," he said. His voice was softer now, his brows knit together.

Leah hesitated, uncertain. "You swear to me—"

"I do. I swear I am not with Hass."

She nodded, but made it curt, and wondered if she would ever believe him. "What of Marigold?"

"They thought she was the laundress on the boat. She's at the Snapping Turtle Inn in Cold Sea Port, still working with the resistance."

"Can you stop him?" she said. "Can you save the boy?"

He shook his head and backed away; she moved toward him, anyway.

"Promise me you'll try," she said. Without thinking, Leah reached out to put her hand on his cheek. She took another step, lifted herself up on her toes, and put her lips to his.

Chapter Forty-six

When they drew the heavy metal cell door open, Sadie rushed in and fell into her mother's waiting arms, sobbing. The door shut with a clang and Sadie jerked in surprise.

"There, now, girl. All's turned out well. You're here now in Ma's arms."

Sadie shook her head against her mother's scratchy wool coat. How like Ma to see the world so simply. Sadie was there, with her Ma, so all was right. But all was so desperately wrong.

They walked to the corner where Sadie hugged her father and all three sat huddled over a candle flame, the only warmth in the room.

"They told me you were here and I kept asking and asking to see you and they kept saying tomorrow, tomorrow. I thought they'd never let me. I thought they were lying and you weren't really here at all."

"Aye," her father said. "Same for us. They told us when you arrived but wouldn't bring you to us."

"Why are they so mean?"

"I'm sure they wanted to question you first. Did they?"

"Yes. And Grayson. Over and over again. They hurt him."

"What about you?"

"They just scared me, only slapped me once." Her mother gasped. "But Grayson has a blackened eye and a split lip. Ma, it's awful."

"What did you tell them?" her father asked. "What is it they're after?"

"The kell stone. I told them we went into the mines of Galdred and we got lost and we found our way out and waited and waited but Fenn and the others never came out. So we walked to Port Lerringlass and came home."

She looked at her parents carefully, back and forth.

"Is that all you told them?" her mother said.

She nodded. "I only said that much because they told me they had proof that Fenn had the kell stone."

"Is that what happened?"

She stared at them.

"Sadie Pratt." Her mother laughed, but it was a strangled, frightened sort of chuckle. "You don't think your ma and da are spies for the Hass?"

Sadie tried to smile and wiped the tears from her face. "Well, maybe."

"Oh, dear gnomes underground," her father muttered.

"Go on, girl—" her ma gave her a squeeze—"it's all right. You don't have to tell us anything you don't want to. But I want to hear about all your adventures. For a time we were getting word from one of the king's spies. We heard about your travels in the hill country and that you were at the battle of the eis, but escaped unharmed. And then you disappeared from the wissenry at Cold Sea and that got us worried. I'm just so glad you're back with us."

"The wissenry wanted us to go north, but we went west."

"We heard as much yesterday."

"How do folk know?"

"There's a network of spies all over," her father said, "as it turns out. I'm afraid a battle is looming and we must be prepared."

"That's what I'm confused about. I'm not sure whose side I've been on."

"Were you not on Fenn's side?"

Sadie lowered her voice to a whisper. "I came home with Grayson because, well, I fought with Fenn over the stone."

"Fought how?"

"I lied to the Hass. We didn't lose them in the mine; we didn't even go there. I only thought of it because Leah was telling us about it on the boat. It was where Michelruud found the stone a long time ago."

"They told us you'd left with a young woman; was that Leah?"

"Miss Hallowsing, yes. She's from Ruhm."

Her father gave her a stern look.

"It's a long story, Da, but I promise she wasn't a spy or anything. At least I don't think so."

"Well, go on then," he said. "Why did you fight about the kell stone?"

"Fenn found it, beneath some sort of shrine. The wissenry wanted it destroyed. But Fenn—"

"He didn't?" her father said.

Sadie shook her head. "He said he was going to give it to the beast lord. I was so angry; I called him a traitor." A tear rolled down her cheek and she wiped it away.

"It'll be all right, Sadie, dear. You'll see."

"How can you be so positive? Fenn's here by now, with the stone. If he gives it to the beast folk, who knows what will happen? And if the Hass gets it...what if they use it against us?"

"All we need to know is that we will fight to get the Hass out of the Ruud," her father said. "That's all that matters to us at this moment."

"And we're together now," her mother said with a smile.

"But I need to get back to Grayson and make sure he's all right."

"No doubt they've sent him off to his da."

Sadie sighed. "I hope so. But something's just not right, Ma."

"What do you mean?"

"I don't know. I just have this feeling Fenn is in danger. And I think Grayson and I are in big trouble."

Chapter Forty-seven

Metal cuffs were clamped to Fenn's wrists, and the cuffs were chained to the floor behind him in a barred cell in the eastern tower of Steingefan. The light and dark from an unseen window took turns until Fenn no longer counted the days. He was hungry and cold and alone. Forced to lie on his side and grapple food off a plate with his mouth and slurp water from a shallow bowl, he grew weaker and weaker. Visions haunted him. When he slept, he saw his mother's hand, pale and trembling, heard her voice softer and softer until she whispered. Awake, Rogget's painful cry in the woods stabbed at him; he imagined the huntsman's face, eyes staring at nothing, mouth open but no words escaping. Roren, the fear in his eyes, lost in the forest. Was he dead, as well?

When Fenn thought he would go mad from loneliness, soldiers of Hass opened his cell, forced a potato sack over his head and detached his cuffed hands from the bolt in the floor. He was taken through the prison, outside, and put on cart. He lay down to keep from being jostled too much in his blindness. After traveling for half an hour, the cart slowed and Fenn heard a voice in the distance. The cart stopped and the voice was loud and nearby. Fenn sensed many people, their bodies shuffling about, a low hum of voices.

The loud, weasely voice called out, "The beast folk vowed revenge on your Ruud, and it was within their grasp. But the Hass has saved you. We have found him."

Fenn was forced to climb five wooden steps, shoved forward, and the sack was pulled from his face.

"The bairn of the prophecy is here."

Fenn looked out on the crowd. He was standing on a wooden stage erected outside the courtyard of Michelruud castle, and before him mingled what looked to be most of the villages of Path, Timber, and Town. At least, he was certain he'd never seen so many people in one place in the Ruud before, except Cold Sea Port, perhaps.

Behind the throng of quiet, dull-looking folk, a copse of trees shielded the road to Steingefan. Just north, through the wood, was the spot he, Sadie, and Grayson met Rogget and waylaid the carriage to sneak into the stone prison and rescue the children of Path. Behind him lay the King's Orchard and beyond that, the western wood and his best chance for escape.

"And we can thank our young heroes for helping us capture him."

The weasel voice belonged to Sorgood, King Welk's master of the guard. Fenn's first thought was that Welk had lied to him and was working with the soldiers of Hass to hold him captive.

There was mild clapping among the crowd as footsteps clomped up the stairs behind the stage; Sadie and Grayson walked forward and stood next to Sorgood.

Traitors, Fenn thought. Rage swept through him and he fought to push them away, but nothing happened. He was drained and empty. Powerless.

"Without their help," Sorgood called, "we could not have found the bairn and saved your Ruud."

More lazy applause. Fenn looked to Sorgood; he, too, looked worn—unshaven, sweating, though it was cold enough for puffs of fog to exit his mouth when he spoke. Why did he keep saying 'your' Ruud? Wasn't it Sorgood's Ruud, too?

"They will tell you of their daring bravery," Sorgood said to the crowd.

Neither Sadie nor Grayson looked at Fenn as Sadie began to speak.

"We followed the new bairn across the Ruud and into the Great West until he found the kell stone in the mines of Galdred," she said. Her voice didn't carry nearly as far as Sorgood's.

"Yes," he said. "You say you followed him to the Great West and he found the stone. And you, innkeeper's son, how did you get the stone from the bairn?"

Sadie cast a nervous glance at Fenn and he saw despair and fear in her eyes.

Grayson said, "We waited until he was asleep and I stole it from his knapsack."

"That's not true," Fenn said.

From behind, someone grabbed both his arms behind him and squeezed them together, sending a shudder of pain through his body. A gruff angry voice whispered in his ear, "Keep quiet or I'll gag you."

Fenn glared at Sadie and Grayson, but they wouldn't look at him. There were more footsteps on the stairs and Fenn turned to see one of the Hass, in his purple robe; but this folk wore a tall, pointy hat on his head. He was blond and blue-eyed like the eis, frowning.

"It's true," Sorgood called out to the crowd. "We have the kell stone."

"Show us," someone yelled.

The Hass representative walked forward to stand on Fenn's other side and said, "Arrest that folk."

From the back of the crowd, a few folk pushed through toward the man who had dared to speak. Fenn suddenly realized the gathering was surrounded by Hass soldiers, dressed in purple tunics with the flaming tree emblem.

"Will you arrest us all?" someone else shouted. And suddenly the folk came alive as more Hass soldiers were drawn from their posts into the unruly mass.

"If you have the stone, show us."

"We demand to see proof."

"You can't arrest all of us."

"Very well." The Hass folk nodded to Sorgood.

Sorgood called for his guard and several soldiers in red approached the stage at Fenn's feet. The folk in the crowd hissed and booed. Fenn was suddenly struck with the urge to spit. How dare soldiers of the Ruud serve Sorgood and the Hass? Traitors. Not just to the king, but to their own folk. He leaned forward as if to move toward them, but his captor pulled harder at his arms.

One of the guard handed a velvet bag up to Sorgood and a hush fell over the gathering as Sorgood reached in and pulled out the smooth round stone.

"You see," Sorgood said. "The kell stone of legend is real. And we are now possessed of it."

Odd choice of words, Fenn thought.

"How do we know that's the one?" someone called from the back of the crowd.

Fenn looked wide-eyed at Sorgood, a smile erupting on his face. Sorgood seemed stuck for a moment, his brow furrowed and his head tilted and pushed back on his neck. He looked briefly to the folk standing beside Fenn and said, "Kirche?"

Kirche shrugged and said, "Arrest them."

Fenn smiled deeper.

"We can't arrest them all. We haven't enough room in Steingefan."

"Then answer them. I'm not used to such insolence. You folk of the Ruud need more authority. Ruffians."

Sorgood looked to his audience and said, "What other stone would be perfectly smooth and round? Do you think I conjured it out of air?"

"You could have made one," someone said.

"No one can make a stone like this."

"How do we know that?"

Fenn desperately bit his upper lip to keep from laughing. He never expected such skepticism from the folk of the Ruud. He took a look at Grayson, but his friend still shuddered in fear. They must have their parents, Fenn realized. Why else would they be so frightened? Maybe that's why they lied about stealing the stone from him.

"There is no other stone like the kell stone in this world," Kirche said.

"Then it must have some power," someone else called out. "Show us what it can do."

"We will use the power of the kell to control the beast and free you of fear. But first we must deal with the child of prophecy. How do you want him killed?"

Fenn's smile vanished as he cast his gaze over the crowd before him. His breath seized in his throat and his heart raced.

"You have the kell stone. Why harm the boy?"

"You have wanted him hanged," Sorgood said. "I have heard you call for his capture and death, myself. And now here he is. The Hass has found him for you and is willing that he should die as you wished."

"Aw, now, some of us, maybe. But I've never thought the boy ought to be killed."

"Maybe we were a bit hasty."

"Why kill him now? You've got the stone."

Sorgood looked past Fenn to Kirche. "You said they would cry out for his death."

"And you told me they wanted it."

"They did want it."

"Hear now," someone in the crowd called out. "What say we just

522

lock the boy up at Steingefan?"

"Or the wissenry. He could be under house arrest."

The crowd broke out into a mumbling discussion of possibilities.

Kirche held up his hand for silence. "I have tolerated enough insolence from this crowd. If you wish to escape spending the night at your stone prison, there will be no more outbursts. We will hang the boy, as the folk of the Ruud have demanded."

Fenn searched the now silent crowd, fearful—his breath a shallow panting. Could he save himself? With his hands bound and his body hollow and empty of strength, could he escape this? The folk who had hold of him led him toward Grayson and Sadie. A beam stuck out overhead—he hadn't noticed it before—and Fenn watched as a noosed rope was tossed over it.

"No," he heard Sadie say. "You can't do this."

"You will stand there," Sorgood said to them, "and watch."

Everything seemed to pause when the noose was dropped over Fenn's head. If the crowd was making any noise, he could not hear it. He was aware of shuffling, jostling, and voices perhaps, but couldn't tell from where they came. Sorgood held the kell stone high above his head; folk rushed toward the gallows, furious; soldiers of Hass fought to the middle of the crowd and grabbed at folk, trying to force them away.

Suddenly, Sorgood sank to his knees and Fenn watched as the kell stone fell from his hands and rolled off the edge of the stage to the ground below. Sorgood froze, suspended mid-fall, an arrow piercing his chest just below his heart. His mouth opened and closed but no sound escaped.

Chapter Forty-eight

Folk of the Ruud," someone shouted.

Fenn looked up, behind the crowd, as horses approached. King Welk sat astride his steed, a raised bow in his hands.

"It is time for you to fight," he said. "Choose freedom, or choose the Hass."

There was a brief, shocked lull before chaos erupted and Fenn stood paralyzed for a moment as the world seemed to have begun again. The noose still hung around his neck and he struggled to escape from the folk who held him. Sadie screamed; Grayson rushed forward and grabbed at the noose. His captor was down, an arrow in his chest. Folk pulled Sorgood, still gasping for air, from the stage and trampled his body.

Kirche had disappeared.

"We have to run," Sadie shouted over the din, lifting the noose from around Fenn's head.

"You run. Get your parents."

"Come with us," Grayson said.

"I have to get the stone. Uncuff my hands."

Grayson scrambled to the body of the dead soldier and dug into his tunic pockets, pulling out a set of keys. He grabbed at Fenn's wrists and fumbled with one key after another.

"We don't have time for this," Sadie said. "Get off the gallows."

"No," Fenn yelled. "Do it now." He could see the kell stone beneath the feet of fighting folk in the crowd, kicked this way and that.

Finally his hands were freed and without a glance at Sadie and Grayson, Fenn scrambled to the front of the stage and leapt off it. Folk were fighting Hass soldiers with short swords, knives, and hatchets. Fenn ducked and dove to the ground; several folk tripped and fell over him. He caught another sight of the stone and grabbed for it as it rolled forward under someone's feet; they kicked it back and he grabbed again but it slipped away.

Scrambling to his knees, an elbow smacked Fenn's cheek and he fell. Another folk stepped on him; he screamed and rolled over, curling up, covering his head. Kirche appeared in front of him, crawling along the ground, blood oozing from the right side of his mouth; he was grasping for the kell stone.

Fenn got to a his hands and knees and threw himself into Kirche, taking the stone from him. Kirche pulled it from Fenn's grip and thrust a blade toward him, a furious rage on his face. Fenn glared at him, wishing he could force him to do his bidding—force him to let go of the stone. Gradually, Kirche's face relaxed. His eyes clouded over and he dropped the stone. The man fell onto his face and Fenn looked up to find Ma'am Hardy, with her cast-iron frying pan, standing over him.

"Get a weapon or get out of here, Fenn," Ma'am Hardy scowled and disappeared into the melee.

Fenn clambered to his feet and ran, bumping into Grayson. They had no time for greetings and without thought, Fenn followed him. Grayson led him through the trees toward Path until he stopped and Fenn realized they'd come upon Ma'am Dowling, Grayson's grandmother.

"This way." The woman grabbed Grayson and led him to a small stand of trees in the middle of the brief wood surrounded by shrubs. She told them to hide and went back into the fray. After a moment, Ma'am Dowling returned with Sadie and then led them all through the woods surrounding Path until they came to the back of the inn where she took them downstairs into the basement next to the alehouse cellar.

"You must hide here," Ma'am Dowling said. "The Hass has taken over the inn."

"Where's Da? And my brothers? Where's Mattie?"

"Mattie's off to Aaronland; she's safe. And the others escaped north to join the king."

"And left you here?"

"I stayed of my own free will and I have good reason."

"Yes Ma'am."

"And that reason will be down to see you in a moment."

They were left alone in the basement, one small lamp at the steps leading to the back door cast a hesitant light on their faces. Fenn realized he still had the kell stone in his hands and he lifted it; as he did so, it let off a green glow that lit the room below the inn. Shelves lined with tools, kitchenware, linens, and soaps filled the back of the basement. A pantry of canned goods, and the laundry, hemmed them into the small space at the foot of the steps.

After surveying the room, Fenn found Sadie and Grayson staring at him as if they were waiting for him to speak. Instead, he merely met their gazes, defiant.

Finally, Sadie said, "You don't think we wanted that to happen."

And that was enough for the three of them to begin speaking at once.

"What did you *think* they would do to me, if you turned me in?"

"To Welk," Grayson said. "Not the Hass."

"You knew everyone was after me."

"But hanging?" Sadie said. "It's drastic, don't you think?"

"What else could you expect?"

"And anyway, we changed our minds before we got into port."

"But it was too late," Grayson said.

"Welk wasn't so bad, actually—" Fenn said.

"They took us to Steingefan!" Sadie said. "They tortured Grayson."

"—but he wouldn't let me leave; we had to escape."

"Not tortured, really," Grayson said. "More like bullied."

"We were on our way to the beast forest, when the Hass caught me and took me to Steingefan."

"And we only said those things on the gallows—" Sadie said.

"I still don't know what happened to Rogget, but I'm afraid he might be dead."

"—because they told us they'd kill our parents if we didn't."

"And the next thing I know, I'm going to be hanged and my two best friends are—"

"You were in Steingefan, too?" Grayson said.

"Rogget dead?" Sadie said.

"You didn't turn me in?"

"No, not exactly...but...Rogget?"

"We're your best friends?" Grayson said.

"Is that so surprising?" Fenn said.

"We *are* best friends," Sadie said, "and we always will be."

"What do you mean, 'not exactly?'"

"I told you before," Sadie said. "They questioned us. I know I shouldn't have said anything about the stone, but they tortured Grayson."

"They did not."

"You still have a black eye."

"That's from a fight. One of the Hass soldiers kept saying stuff and I punched him. He hit me back, that's all."

"You punched someone?" Fenn said.

"In the face." Grayson beamed.

"What was he saying?" Sadie said.

Grayson frowned. "I'd rather not say."

Fenn was sure he was blushing.

"Why do you think Rogget's dead?" Sadie said.

"He was shot...I think."

They were silent—Fenn watching them in the dim light of the kell stone, Sadie looking back and forth at both their faces, and Grayson refusing to meet her eyes. When the door opened and Leah Hallowsing came in, they all jumped. She rushed down the steps and took them into her arms, kissing each one on the top of his head.

"Oh, Fenn, you have no idea how glad I am you're safe. And the stone, you still have it."

"I was trying to take it to Dag Voorspeld; but I didn't make it."

Leah shook her head. "I'm afraid it will have to wait. The battles are begun—skirmishes in the villages now. Dowling says the Hass is rounding up the young; we fear they're going to ship them off to Ruhm."

"Why?" Sadie said.

"Ransom of a sort. It keeps the folk in line, knowing the Hass has their children. I've got to get you all north, where your King Welk is planning to draw the Hass...to Steingefan."

Grayson nodded. "My brothers and my da are there. They'll be fighting and I plan to join them."

"You're not quite old enough for soldiering," Leah said.

"Age doesn't matter so much right now, does it?"

526

"Of course it does. Your grandmother, your father...they wouldn't want you to fight. But you could help with the wounded, perhaps."

Grayson scowled.

"But what about the children of Path?" Sadie said. "We should take them with us."

"Dowling is spreading the word as she can—telling all the children to sneak out and head north."

"We should gather them up and *take* them."

"You three are being gathered up and taken."

Fenn thought Sadie would burst. She sucked in a breath and glared at Leah. "I don't want to be taken away while the others are left behind."

"They're not, Sadie. Trust me. Everyone is working to help them."

"Do you know anything about Rogget and Roren?" Fenn said.

"They've not been heard from, nor seen, not that Dowling's found out."

She left them again with the promise of returning. The three of them sat huddled in the basement listening to the muted sounds of their village under attack. Occasional shots from firearms prefaced screams and shouts. The smell of smoke and burning wood filtered in through the cracks around the doorjamb and Fenn trembled, worried the Hass would burn the inn above them.

When Fenn woke from a restless sleep, Ma'am Dowling and Leah were standing in the darkened basement near the steps, fretting. As soon as he touched the kell stone, it let off a glow and he saw immediately that Sadie and Grayson were gone.

"Where did they go?" Leah asked him.

"After what you told me earlier," Ma'am Dowling said, "I think it's clear where they've gone."

Ma'am Dowling retrieved an empty flour sack from a shelf and placed inside it a small blanket, some food, and a flask of water for Fenn. When he put the kell stone inside it, its glow ceased and the room was darkened once again. He looked at Leah hopefully in the dim light of the cellar. They left him—Grayson to fight with his brothers, Sadie to help the other children escape. They knew he would have wanted to go with them, so they snuck out and left him. He was surprised at his lack of anger toward them as he lifted his brows at Leah.

She shook her head. "I know you'll want to find Sadie, at least, but you've got to think of the kell stone. We've got to get it out from amid the Hass."

The door above them flung open with a bang and a large figure stood silhouetted against the dim moonlight.

Chapter Forty-nine

Sadie made her way in the dark through the pines and stood just at the edge of the woods listening for their voices. Some time after dark, while Fenn and Grayson slept soundly in the basement, she'd heard kid folk at the back door to the inn collecting food from Ma'am Dowling. She waited for her chance, snuck out, and followed them as they took the path behind the inn and around toward the wissenry. When Sadie came upon it, she stopped and gaped. The wissenry building was a burnt out hull; brown smoke still billowed from its center.

Behind her, Sadie heard footsteps on the crisp pine covered ground and she turned. Jeopard Link, her father's apprentice, stuck a finger to her lips and pressed hard.

"Don't make a sound," he whispered and took her hand, pulling her back into the woods.

They walked hastily until Sadie's breath was quick and her heart pumped. He took her south to the high crossing where dozens of the young men and women of Path sat huddled in the cold night. She recognized Taylor and Winfred right away, and Dora, the daughter of the smithy. They stared at her, their faces wide-eyed and alert. She remembered the last time she'd seen them—they were running through the orchard playing tag; it seemed so long ago.

"What are you doing here?" Jeopard asked her.

"Looking for you; I wanted to help the children make their way north, to Steingefan."

"We've already got the young ones out."

"Then what are you waiting for?"

"We're watching the Hass. There's a battalion stationed just outside Michelruud castle and as soon as they begin to move, we're going to alert Welk's guard."

"We should move on them ourselves," Eller said.

Sadie nodded at him. She barely knew Eller; his folks lived on the border between Michelruud and Aaronland and sold their vegetables at market every two weeks—the only time he came into the village.

"We should steal their weapons and use them against them," Dora said.

"That's not a bad idea." Sadie walked forward into the group. She sat on the ground among them and began to recognize more faces in the dark. Drew and Gettel who lived north in the woods by the pond; Cammie, one of Ma'am Hardy's daughters; the shoemaker's son, Kirk.

"We have our instructions," Jeopard said. "We're only supposed to watch."

"Are they drinking ale?" Sadie said.

Jeopard shook his head. "These soldiers of Hass don't imbibe like ours do. And anyway, the battle is on. No soldier would drink when they have to fight in the morning."

Sadie smiled. "You don't know much about soldiers, do you?"

"Do you think they're drinking?" Milford, a young worker in the king's orchard said.

"I told you they are not."

"The inn is still standing," Sadie said.

"Their higher ranking officers are there."

"All right then. We'll sneak into the ale cellar next to the basement and take casks to the soldiers at the castle. What time is it?"

"Ten, I think," Milford said.

Sadie smiled. "Let's do it."

"What for?" Jeopard said.

"To let them have some ale of course. It's such a cold night. I'm sure we can persuade them. And the ale cellar's always open at the inn. The lock broke last year and Mr. Steppe hasn't a put a new one on."

"How do you know?"

Sadie shrugged. "How do you not?" She waited and, slowly, several of the others stood with her.

"How will we get it there? It's a long walk."

"We need carts and horses."

"The Hass has horses and carts in our stable," Kor Wolf whispered. "No one's guarding them."

"It's settled then."

At the inn, Jeopard snuck a look through the windows and reported that the soldiers downstairs were sleeping; ale mugs littered the floor around them.

"So much for your special Hass soldiers," Sadie told him.

They climbed into the cellar, one by one, and carried out the smaller kegs of ale and jugs of cheap wines imported from the west. They loaded up four carts and led the horses quietly around the outskirts of the burned town, onto the path through the wood and approached Town Village. The hanging stage still stood and soldiers of Hass had built small fires all over the grounds outside the castle walls.

Sadie and three others led the horses toward the soldiers' camp while the rest stayed hidden in the woods.

"Ho there, what's this?" One of the soldiers stood to greet them.

"We were told to bring you refreshment from the inn in Path," Sadie said. "A gift from your superiors who are encamped there."

"We do not drink ale," another said.

"They're drinking ale at the inn. They said they missed the Founding Day celebration while preparing to sail. They're celebrating late."

The soldiers gathered around, murmuring.

"We were told to leave it here and return quickly with the carts. We have more chores to do for the others."

"Very well." The first soldier waved them away.

Sadie smiled when she turned toward the wood. She and her three companions met up with the others several yards along the path.

"Now what?" Jeopard said.

"We wait. If they aren't used to ale, they'll sleep soundly and we'll go in and load the carts with their weapons."

Jeopard shook his head. "Your parents won't be happy to know I helped you with this."

"Well, then, don't tell them."

"Sadie Pratt," he said, his eyes wide. "You've got to be the worst behaved kid in the Ruud. And I couldn't be more glad of it."

And so they waited and watched from the woods while the soldiers of Hass enjoyed the ale, singing songs and staggering about. They fell into their fires and screamed and laughed. They shot their firearms into the air; they danced and tripped over one another until finally they settled down and dozed off.

The young people of Path followed Sadie into the camp and pilfered firearms, bows, arrows, long swords, short swords, and knives where they could find them. They snuck them back into the woods on Michelwood path and loaded them into the carts. Sadie crept through the darkness toward the castle wall on which soldiers of Hass had leaned their firearms. She picked them up, one by one, five in all, and struggled to cradle them in her arms. As she stepped over soldiers on her way back, she tripped and fell and found herself lying over a pair of legs. A soldier sat up and smiled at her in the darkness.

"Rutherford, what are you doing here?" he said.

"I...uh." Sadie looked around at the firearms lying about, one in particular lay across the soldier's lap. Sadie said the first thing that came to her. "I was trying to get home."

"Oh, aye," the soldier said. "You were always one for home. What's this?" He lifted the gun from his lap.

"It's my firearm."

The soldier laughed. "Rutherford, I'm going to tell Ma."

"No, don't tell Ma. I promise I'll put it away."

"What's this?" he said, looking at the firearms strewn about him.

Sadie still lay over his legs, her elbows resting on the ground. The soldier tried to move to reach for another musket.

"I can't move. Rutherford, help me."

He grabbed at Sadie and she began to roll over his feet. He pulled at her, dragging her forward.

"Help me up," he said.

Sadie started to scream, but thought better of it. If she woke all the soldiers now, they'd be caught.

"Let me go," she seethed.

"Well, you don't have to be mad about it. I just, I can't...oh, all's well now. I can move my legs. See?"

Sadie stood and brushed herself off.

"Of course you can move your legs," she said.

But the soldier had already lain back to the ground. "Tell Ma I miss her," he mumbled and began to snore almost immediately. Sadie collected the guns. Her legs shook like jelly as she tiptoed through the sleeping men to the woods. Ma was right, she thought. Too much ale addles the brain.

Finally, one of the carts was heavily laden with weapons.

"Now for the hard part," Sadie said.

"What's that?" Milford looked at her sleepily.

"We have to get the cart through Path and out to the Steingefan road."

"They're so drunk, they wouldn't hear it if we drove a hundred horses through," Jeopard said.

Slowly, Sadie drove the horses along the edge of the wood, north, as the children walked alongside. She didn't feel secure until they were well into the trees. Soon, the wood would be behind them and Steingefan's towers would rise into the moonlit night.

"We've missed you in the village," Jeopard whispered to her in the dark. "But it looks as if your adventures have done you well. You've changed."

"Have not," Sadie shrugged, embarrassed.

"No," he said, "you have. You've found courage somewhere along the way."

"Maybe courage isn't found, so much as enjoyed."

Her father's apprentice drew his brows into a question; but he smiled.

Chapter Fifty

Leah gasped and stepped forward to shield Fenn as three figures stumbled down the stairs into the basement. When the larger folk tripped and grunted as he fell to his knees and his smaller mate barreled into him and landed on his backside at the bottom of the steps, she let out a chuckle. The third shadowy figure stood atop the steps, head tilted, hands on her hips.

"Knew it was a basement," Rogget said struggling to his feet, "and still didn't expect the stairs."

"We'll light candles," Leah said. "Marigold, take care on the steps."

"No time," Rogget said. "We come to fetch the young folk and get them north. Is that you, Fenn?"

Fenn stepped forward and hugged the large folk, then turned to Roren in the darkness, shaking his hand. "I'm glad you're all right. Rogget, I thought you'd been shot."

"He had been," Roren said.

"Aye, and Roren good enough to get me to the beast forest."

"They let you in?"

"Your young king there managed to persuade his lordship, yes."

"How'd you do that?"

"I'll let you know one day," Roren said. "But now we must—"

"But where are Sadie and Grayson?" Rogget said. "Ma'am Hardy said Dowling got you all from the skirmish."

"It's my fault," Leah told him. "I left them here alone and they've snuck away."

"But why?"

"Grayson wants to fight," Fenn told him. "I guess he didn't think Miss Hallowsing would let him. And Sadie's gone to gather up the other kids in Path, to take them north."

"Ard," Rogget rubbed his hands through his hair.

"Shall I find her?" Marigold said, making her way in the dark down the steps.

"Out of the question," Leah said. "She was my responsibility—"

"Let's just get Fenn north," Rogget said, "and then I'll come back for our firebrand, eh?"

Leah tried to dissuade him, but Rogget wouldn't allow it. Her stomach twisted itself into knots, as she vacillated between anger at the girl for putting herself in danger and guilt at not foreseeing it. She armed herself with her bow, even knocked an arrow, so deep was her fear at the girl's daring, and followed Rogget, now carrying a small firearm, and

Roren with his bow. Marigold and Fenn walked between them as they snuck out from the basement—while Dowling made certain any soldiers who might awaken didn't find them out—and into the woods.

They hiked the path north, away from the inn, behind other buildings along the main road of the village, as far north as they could before having to leave the woods.

"We've got to go west," Rogget said, "behind Michelruud castle and make our way through the woods to the western side of Steingefan. Your Kirche's soldiers are already gathering on the plain in—" Rogget went silent, holding up his hand. He motioned for them to split up and Leah let him take Fenn while she and Marigold headed back into the woods and huddled there.

When she heard the smooth, snide voice in the distance, as if he were laughing, she launched herself forward, pulling out of Mari's grasp, and made a wide arc around the area in which his voice had arisen.

Through the trees, in a clearing, she saw Fenn and Rogget standing together—Rogget behind the boy, his arms around him protectively—surrounded by soldiers of Hass. She watched as Kirche moved forward, his smooth chiseled face lit up by the lanterns his aids carried.

He chuckled snidely. "It seems we play at cat and mouse."

"The boy's of no use to you," Rogget said.

"Drop your weapon."

Leah's heart raced as she saw Kirche raise his firearm at Rogget. The huntsman dropped his own small weapon to the dirt and one of his soldiers moved to take it.

"Let him go, and get back to your battle for the Ruud, eh?" Rogget said. "Capturing him's not going to do you any good."

Kirche shook his head and smiled. "Oh, I've no intention of capturing the boy, again. That proved too risky. Clearly, if I want him dead, I'll have to do it myself."

Leah let out a light gasp at the sight of Prenalin across the clearing; he looked into her eyes but no sign of recognition flickered on his face. It was dark, she reasoned; perhaps he couldn't see her hidden in the bushes. But would he stand there and let Kirche kill Fenn? She darted back, and made her way swiftly, silently, around the group, coming up to the trees behind Kirche.

"I won't let you do it." Rogget pulled Fenn behind him.

Fenn struggled against the man, cried out a mangled, "No."

Before Leah could hide, she felt the force of his power—a wall of wind left her splayed on the ground. Quickly, she told herself. She must get to her feet. Grabbing at her bow, she managed to nock an arrow as she clambered to standing and turned to the scene.

All were on the ground but Fenn, his fists balled tightly at his sides, his eyes raging at Kirche, now on his knees, now standing. Kirche chuckled, impatient, and shook his head. Leah watched his back straighten, his pride hurt, she knew. He raised his musket.

"Repel this," he said.

Leah didn't think about it; it didn't even enter her mind to hesitate. She raised her bow and let the arrow fly and when it hit its target, and Kirche dropped his firearm but stood for a few seconds, she could hear only her own breath. She'd pulled another arrow from her quiver, nocked it, and sent it deep into Kirche's back before she let herself care.

When Kirche sank to the ground, she expected a scene akin to the one at the gallows after Welk felled Sorgood, but instead, the soldiers of Hass fled, every one of them, scampering into the trees. Prenalin raced forward as Leah nocked another arrow; she moved into the clearing and aimed at him, expecting him to rush to Kirche. Instead, he came at her, his hand raised.

"Here," he said. "Do you see?" At his side he held a firearm. "If you had not done it, I would have."

She couldn't lower her bow, however, and kept it trained on him. "I don't believe you."

"Leah, stop it," Marigold said coming off the path from behind Rogget.

"It's all right," Prenalin said. "But come, we must hasten north. You shocked the soldiers well enough, but do not think this puts an end to Ruhm's plans."

"They will look to you," Leah said.

"No," Prenalin shook his head. He pushed Rogget and Fenn forward. "Where is Roren?"

"I am here," the young man whispered, scrambling to his feet.

"The mere secretary?" Pren continued. "No, they will find one of Kirche's commanders. Nothing has changed, I tell you. Leah, come."

She nodded to him and the others, lowered her bow and walked a few paces to where Kirche lay, his right cheek in the dirt. Kneeling at his side, she put a hand on his back, now soaked with blood. He was still breathing; he moaned at her touch.

"Are you sorry?" Prenalin said, standing at her side.

She nodded. "For myself."

Kirche's eyes fluttered open and he looked up at her. She drew her hand away.

"Pren," Kirche groaned.

534

"Quickly," Prenalin said, his hand on her shoulder. "They'll return any moment."

"Pren, help me."

Suddenly, Leah shuddered and cried out. She stood and put a hand to her mouth, then realizing it was wet with his blood, cried out again. Prenalin hurried her from the scene.

"It's not an easy thing," he told her as they fled, "to take a man's life. But Kirche was only too willing to take Fenn's, as he did your father's. You did the right thing."

But for the wrong reasons, she wanted to tell him. For she knew, even as everything in her seemed to deaden as she took the shot, there was a hard core of hate deep within her, and a terrible release of joy when Kirche reeled toward the ground. This would not make her father proud, she knew.

Capter Fifty-one

Welk paced the open, dirt-covered ground that was once the old bailey behind the gate at Steingefan. They'd taken the dilapidated stone prison from the Hass soon after thwarting Kirche's plans for hanging young Fenn Foster. There, they'd gathered forces, sending out spies, and finally all was in place. The Hass would fight today, whether they wanted to or not. Word reached him the day before that all in the country north and east of Steingefan were poised and ready for the battle to commence. They awaited only word from Welk. As soon as he gave it, select members of the king's archers would leave the castle on horseback through the front gate and engage the Hass. Hass muskets would be no match for his archers, who could fire upon them from a safe distance.

A thousand folk stood just over the bridge, facing the Hass army, many clad in leather armor in hopes of withstanding musket fire. But while the Hass had more firearms than the king's guard, they still had only one for every ten of their folk. And their supply of gunpowder, and their slow reloading gave the Ruud folk all the advantage they needed to dash toward them and engage them hand to hand. Clutch would sound the alarm and the people of the hill country would come at the Hass from the east, while Hargodt and the northerners, joined by the able from the wasteland, would attack from the western side of the stone prison. The Hass had another few hundred men coming from Path this morning, as his scouts had informed him; and their ships had made port from which more folk would embark. The Ruud seemed already in the hands of

Ruhm; Welk wished only to live long enough to see this battle won and his folk safe.

The sky eastward glowed in a pale bronze light as the sun rose over the horizon miles away. It was time. Welk raised his hand to the lead rider of his mounted archers, and nodded. The gate was raised and they crossed the bridge over the moat and rode out, kicking up dust. Welk turned to the castle behind him. The gentler of the ladies and several of the elderly peered out of the windows. Welk shrugged; these noble folk women were not well suited to battle. But the folk women of the Ruud were willing to fight. And those who were too small for battle were ready to tend the wounded or care for the children and frail wherever they found them.

He looked about him at the folk who had managed to find refuge behind the walls of Steingefan after the initial battle the day before. Snuck in right under the noses of the Hass who were too busy singing and sipping the spiced bitters of the Ruud to see them making their way through the tall grasses all around and swimming the moat.

Suddenly he heard the shouts. It had begun. The archers on the stone roof of the prison fired arrays of arrows while the crowd of folk, carrying whatever weapons they could find, surged forward. Welk climbed the stone steps to the top of the barbican and looked out at the scene. Folk rushed forward from Steingefan, across a span of the plain, into a throng of Hass. Spats of musket fire resounded and black smoke billowed. The mounted archers remained on the outward edges and continued their attack, being reloaded by folk children running back and forth from their positions along the outer edge of the castle moat. Hundreds of folk ran in from both sides, hacking at the Hass. As he predicted, their few muskets were abandoned for the sword once the folk were upon them.

Welk spied Hass reinforcements coming from Michelruud Castle on foot. So soon, he thought. Something, he was certain, was amiss. But there was no time to consider what—the battle was engaged. It was time for him to make his way off the barbican and into the fray. He took a deep breath, winced slightly at the pain from his wound, and gazed once more to the Ruud, his beloved homeland. It was as he predicted after all—he would leave Michelruud without an heir. But this was not his worry any longer, not his Ruud. She belonged now to those who came after.

As he turned to start his climb toward his own end, he caught sight of angels in the distance, east; they hovered, focused on a folk running along the outer edge of the battle toward the prison. Welk sucked in a sudden breath. Fenn Foster. The angels swooped down at him, but the boy waved his arms at them and they were thrown back, as if he'd hit them hard.

Chapter Fifty-two

With the sounds of Kirche's men returning to the scene, perhaps suffering guilt for having left their posts, or more likely caught by a superior and herded back, Leah and the others fled north. Leah lost Rogget and Fenn first, then Roren. Soon enough, Marigold was into the woods ahead of her and vanished. Only Prenalin kept pace with her. She led him west, behind Michelruud castle, just as Rogget had planned, and they came out at the edge of the battle, where she caught sight of Sadie Pratt atop a horse-drawn wagon heading toward Steingefan followed by a group of young folk.

She called to the girl as she and Prenalin ran forward. The battle was on, and there sat Sadie, out in the open, daring herself to be shot.

"Miss Hallowsing," she shouted with a smile. "Climb aboard. But be careful, I think they're all loaded."

Leah peered into the back of the cart. "What have you done?"

Sadie beamed. "We stole them. And we got the soldiers drunk on ale. I don't think but half of them will make it to the battle today."

Leah found a seat next to her while Prenalin preferred to walk.

"Very well, then," she said. "I suppose the folk of the Ruud could use some extra firearms."

Sadie swatted at the horses and they broke into a trot, while Prenalin ran alongside the wagon with the young folk. With every sound of musket shot, she and Sadie ducked low on the seat as if that would save them. But the archers on horseback rode some fifty yards from them and Leah knew they must at least be mildly skilled at staying out of musket range. Still, every shot brought her head down, her shoulders hunched. She forced herself to sit upright again as Sadie courageously whipped wildly at the reins. Faster; they must ride faster.

Finally, Sadie turned toward the old stone prison and they raced across the plain where the tall grass, browned and brittle from the cold, folded easily under the horses' hooves. Before they pulled up to the side of the castle, folk were bridging the moat with thin wide planks of wood for them to cross.

"Firearms," Sadie shouted. "We have muskets and powder."

The cart was taken over by folk and driven toward the field of battle. Leah stood with Sadie and watched them race into the throng.

"I fear the others are already out there," she told the girl. "Marigold,

Rogget, Roren...perhaps even Fenn."

"My parents are out there, too," Sadie said.

"Are you sure? They could be in the castle."

Sadie shook her head. "We've never known a battle like this. At least, I've never heard stories of such. But the stories we do tell...no, all of our folk who can be, are out there in the smoke and clang, fighting for the Ruud."

Leah pulled her bow off her shoulder. "Well," she said to Prenalin, a tremor of a smile at her lips. "Shall we?"

Chapter Fifty-three

Fenn ripped holes in the sides of Dowling's flour sack and slung the bag, with the kell stone safe inside it, on his arm as best he could. He ran, with Rogget and Roren, through the forest and onto the plain, where they found themselves behind the Hass battle lines. They made their way eastward to where the folk of the hill country were advancing into the melee. They lost Roren there, who'd picked up a sword from an early wounded, or more likely a Hass deserter, and joined the folk, darting into the fight.

He and Rogget almost made it to the moat, when the angels, sensing the stone, he imagined, found them. Each time Fenn flung them away, nearly falling to the ground from the force of it himself, they came at him again. Rogget fired on them and for that, one of them grabbed him and carried him off toward the center of the battle; Fenn was now alone. With each thrust of energy from his hands he was weakened and the angels gave him no time to recover before they came at him again.

Still, he made progress, finding himself near the eastern side of the old stone castle, where the remains of the outer wall stood, broken and in disarray, just on the other side of the moat. Folk rushed this way and that inside the bailey, carrying swords, hatchets, and pitchforks. Some carried wounded soldiers and laid them down. Wounded already, he thought.

Urgency spurred him on and he stepped forward, looking into the murky waters of the moat. He struggled to breathe cleanly. Turning, he saw another angel swooping down at him. He threw his arms up at it, repelling it. The angel let out a shriek as it tumbled in the air. Fenn rushed forward, slid down the hill and fell into the water. He swam as best as he could, struggling to keep the flour sack secured on his arm, and turned again, flinging his hands upward, forcing the angel away once more; but the energy pushed his face under water. He struggled for the surface and found his way to the steep slope on the other side. A hand grasped at his and he looked up to see Grayson reaching for him; he pulled Fenn up and out of the water.

"This way." Grayson led Fenn into the crowded courtyard where he could hide.

Fenn looked up at his friend and smiled. "You're filthy."

"War is a dirty business, it seems."

"Your father and brothers, are they all right?"

"I can't say."

"I'm sorry."

Grayson put a hand on Fenn's shoulder. "This isn't your fault."

Fenn nodded.

"I've got to get back out there."

"I should go, too. I can hide the stone—"

"No, Fenn. You know you can't."

"But why?"

"The mark. You know what it means, don't you?"

"Do you?"

"Sadie's da told mine. You've got to stay here with the stone. When all of this is over, then you can do whatever it is you have to do. But now, stay safe."

Fenn watched as Grayson ran into the crowd of folk crossing the bridge, making their way out into the battle, and disappeared. A woman screamed and Fenn turned to see the angels, three of them, surging toward the folk as they scattered. He knew there was no safety, not truly. They would find him and they would hurt a lot of folk in doing so. Fenn knew it was crazy, but when he saw King Welk on the old barbican that stretched over the fractured prison gate, he ran through the folk to the stone steps and climbed, taking himself closer to the angels.

When Fenn pulled himself atop the barbican, Welk gasped.

"I'm sorry," Fenn said, panting and watching the skies. "They're after me."

The three angels caught sight of him and raced forward. Fenn threw his arms at them and they fell back, tumbling through the air, their faces filled with rage. But the force of his own repel left him flopping backwards. King Welk grabbed him by the shoulders, dragging him back, keeping him balanced.

"Get down from here," the king demanded. "I'll take care of them."

"They'll follow me," he said. "I can't let them near the folk."

Suddenly an angel swooped up from behind them and grabbed at Fenn's long coat. King Welk raised his sword and slashed at the angel's arm sending it shrieking away.

"Get down, I tell you."

Fenn ducked as another angel came at him. The king raised his sword, but too late, the angel knocked him down and off the edge of the barbican where he dangled, fighting to hold on.

"Look out," Welk yelled as he struggled back onto the stones, groaning with pain.

The angels dove at Fenn. The largest swatted at him with a short, icy blue blade. Fenn ducked again, this time falling flat to the stone, while the king lunged toward the angels. Fenn rolled over onto his back and threw his hands at them again, forcing them higher into the sky.

"How are you doing that?" King Welk asked.

"I don't know, but I'm tired. I don't think I can do it much longer."

Fenn lay on the stones looking up at Welk. The king's hair was wet with sweat—his dark eyes gazing down at Fenn with a mix of concern and anger. Fenn's charm throbbed heatedly against his skin in time with the king's heavy breathing—even the amber stone could do nothing to alleviate it.

"You need to get down," Welk said.

"I can't. They won't leave me alone. I have to do something."

Suddenly an angel swooped at Fenn and King Welk threw himself in the angel's path. Fenn watched, horrified, as the short blue blade pierced the king's back tearing through his tunic. The angel shrieked, triumphant, as Welk, limp as a rag doll, disappeared over the edge of the barbican. Fenn rolled and looked down—his charm and the amber stone, dangling out of his tunic, pulled hard against him, reaching out to the king as he landed with a splash into the murky moat below.

"No," Fenn screamed and searched the sky for the angels.

He scrambled to his feet, pulled the flour sack from his arm and reached for the kell stone. Anger rose through his legs, to his stomach, and into his throat. His breathing came so heavy spit flew from his mouth with each heave. The angels approached once more, this time smiling with anticipated victory.

Fenn glared at them and waited. *Let them come*. When they were mere feet from him, he thrust the stone above his head and held it there, repelling with all his might.

For several seconds, everything blazed a shocking white. There was no sound; the battle silent, the shrieking of the angels muted. He heard no horses, no firearms, no screams of the wounded. And then pulsating waves, like drumbeats, echoed from the stone—both outward, away, and at the same time, into his arms, to his chest, throughout his body, threatening to

540

crumble the barbican under his feet. Circles of white heat flew against the angels, hammering across the sky. The first wave hit the trees of Michelruud far in the distance and bent them toward the sea.

The angels had flown a hundred yards, thudding to the ground amid the battle, before the stone stopped emitting its thunderous power. Fenn screamed in rage—at what he wasn't sure—and tossed the stone hard at the bridge below him; he watched as it crumpled into the moat. The waters bubbled and fizzed and spewed and the ground began to quake. Fenn fell to the floor of the barbican as it shook violently.

He saw King Welk climbing weakly out of the moat below. The ground all around began to break up; in the distance, trees buckled and fell. Quickly Fenn scooted himself to the steps and climbed down. He let King Welk lean on him and they hobbled away from the barbican as it crumbled and fell. People ran from the castle as its walls caved.

"What's happening?" Fenn shouted over the din.

Everywhere people were running and screaming, except the wounded, who lay on the ground reaching out with bloody hands, calling for help.

"Get low," the king said, his voice filled with pain. "Get low."

King Welk pulled Fenn to the ground and they lay there while the earth shook all around. Fenn's mind raced frantically. Rogget. Sadie. Grayson. Where were they? Were they all right? His charm burnt against his chest but he couldn't move to pull it away. The amber stone sought to cool him, but failed. He fell onto his back and lay staring up at the blue, cloudless sky. What had he done?

Finally, there was silence and the ground only trembled like a purring cat. Fenn stood on shaky legs and looked out across the moat. The kell was in upheaval, cracks and crevices spread across the land like a spider's web. The moat had drained. Few trees stood in the distant Ruud.

The battlefield began to stir. The soldiers of Hass stood, found their weapons and the folk of the Ruud did the same. Horns sounded in the distance, from Michelruud.

"What is it?" King Welk asked him, struggling to sit up.

"Someone's coming."

Screams echoed from the battlefield, from both the Hass and the folk and in unison they all began to back away, toward the castle. Fenn walked forward and climbed some of the stones that remained of the barbican. Suddenly he caught site of a centaur, then a troll.

"It's the beast folk," Fenn said, turning back to the king. "The beast folk are here."

Fenn looked again as the folk of the Ruud took up their swords against the Hass once again. Now the Hass was caught between them and the beast.

"The eis," Welk said and Fenn looked eastward. A sea of pale green robes rushed forward battling both soldiers of Hass on the ground, and angels in the sky.

Chapter Fifty-four

The folk of the Ruud were divided on the question of Michelruud Castle, the only castle in the Ruud left untouched by the shattering of the kell stone, or the burning scorn of Hass. There were those who insisted it was simply a matter of superior construction; and some who charted out the force of the upheaval and claimed location mattered. But there were those who believed its ability to endure symbolized Michelruud's dominance and whispers of a united Ruud spread folk to folk and village to village.

Marigold oversaw the return of the soldiers of Hass, in the few ships left unburned, to Ruhm. They were humbled, both at their defeat and the kindness shown them by the folk of the Ruud. Kirche's death was taken as a sign of vulnerability, a sign of change.

Fenn was allowed to walk beside Welk's cot as he was carried home. Aware of the folks' stares, he kept his gaze on the ground, his jaw set firm and determined; he would not cry. When the king's hand lifted from where he lay and one of the guards nudged Fenn, he glanced at the dying folk and saw him smiling.

"Look," Welk told him. "See."

And so Fenn lifted his eyes to watch the line of folk from Path and villages beyond as he moved among them. There were none on bended knee, nor bent, as Welk had spread word that there would be no more of that in the Ruud. Tear-stained cheeks, rounded and plumped by smiles. Worn, tired, dirty from their work in rebuilding and putting their homes back to rights. When they were not gazing worriedly at the king, they eyed Fenn kindly, offering him nods of encouragement. All was well, he realized. Perhaps he hadn't destroyed the Ruud, though it was by all measurements quite ruined; instead, he seemed to have strengthened it.

While the dead were being buried, orders for lumber being sent north and south, requests sent to stone quarries in the west, and considerations made for some show of thanks to all the beast, Fenn waited in the lobby of the castle, told to remain there until summoned by the king. He could not sit still so he paced in front of one of the hearths, letting its warmth compete with the heat from his charm—pulsing with every beat of his heart.

"Well..."

Fenn heard Grayson's voice. He and Sadie, with the king's new master of the guard, walked toward him, smiling. Grayson's dark hair was stuck to his face with sweat and Sadie's tunic was riddled with stains of grass and dirt.

"...you managed to destroy the Ruud, after all."

Without thinking, he grabbed them both and they stood in a tight circle, laughing, crying, relieved.

"I didn't know it would happen; I didn't even know what I was doing."

"You don't have to know," he said. "It's a prophecy. It's not like you could help it."

"The Ruud isn't completely destroyed," Sadie said.

"Are you kidding?" Grayson laughed. "The ground's uplifted. The trees are down. And the Hass burned just about everything."

"You can't blame the fires on me," Fenn said.

The doors flew open and Clutch and two of his gang trudged in. Fenn stepped back and looked to the master of the guard.

"What are they doing here?"

Clutch nodded at him, but walked past, to the back of the room and into the king's chambers.

Fenn turned to Sadie and Grayson, shocked. "I knew they were acquainted, but—"

"The king has summoned you," Dunham said, standing at the back of the room. "Your friends may join you, if you wish."

Fenn nodded. "Will you come with me?"

Sadie took his hand and together they let Dunham, solemn and grave, lead them through the small sitting area, into the bedchamber, to the king's bed, where Welk lay, frail and gray. Clutch was kneeling at his side, one hand clasping the king's, their faces only inches apart; they whispered. Fenn struggled to hear their words, to make sense of them, but he could not. Confused, he reached to the charm at his neck, lifting it from his burning skin. Clutch looked at Fenn, and then nodded to Dunham, who put a hand on Fenn's back, giving him a gentle push.

"You will approach the king," Dunham said.

Fenn looked to Grayson for some support, but he and Sadie only stared at him, wide-eyed. He walked slowly to the bed and looked down at Welk with a slight bow. But the king, he realized, wasn't looking at him; instead, his gaze was locked on Fenn's chest and his charm.

"Where did you get that?" Welk whispered.

"It was my mother's."

Welk shook his head and winced in pain. "That's not possible."

"My mother was as eisen."

Welk looked at him carefully. "My brother," he said. "The charm, Dunham." Each word seared with pain and Clutch put a hand to Welk's chest as if to quiet his suffering.

The king's aide snapped his fingers and a guard, hidden in a darkened corner of the room, approached Fenn and held him, firmly, but gently, by the arms while Dunham took his rope from around his neck.

"It's mine," Fenn protested, squirming to free himself from the guard's grasp. "It was my mother's."

"It was not your mother's," Clutch said quietly.

"It was!"

Dunham handed the hemp rope, with the gold charm and the amber stone strung on it, to Welk who grasped it to his chest. "Rue-Anna," he whispered and closed his eyes.

Fenn struggled to free himself but a look of warning from Dunham calmed him. The room went silent and all eyes were on the king. His face was serene, a slight smile at his lips, a tear rolled out of the corner of his eye toward his ear. As the seconds passed, the smile faded and the king paled. Dunham moved in front of Clutch, reached for Welk's wrist and held it for a moment, then placed his ear at the king's mouth. He stood and nodded mournfully to the guard, who let go of Fenn.

"The king is dead," Dunham said, choking on a sob. "Long live the king."

"But," the guard mumbled, "who is king?"

With a ragged sigh, Dunham looked up at the small gathering. Three young women, dressed in silk, cousins of the king, if he remembered Father Treacher's lessons correctly, huddled tearfully in a corner. Their brothers, younger still, stood sullenly near the fireplace. King Arnot lounged on a divan, wounded in the leg, and Queen Felisha of Damon Wall, mourning her husband's death in battle sat stiffly in a soft chair. The new master of the guard and three of his men—no doubt they were close to Welk—stood aside, near the door. Servants, Dunham, and Clutch. An odd assortment.

Dunham moved away from Welk's bed and Clutch stepped forward, looking down at the king's body. No one spoke, no one dared cough or cry. Clutch pulled the hemp rope from Welk's grasp, pulled it apart with a snap, removed the amber stone and retied it. He unclasped the kings fingers, replaced the charm, folding his hand around it, then—startling the gathering of folk—Clutch bent and kissed Welk's cheek.

Dunham sank to his knees. "Elrundt, King of Michelruud. King of the Ruud."

Whispers and murmurs flew through the group as the folk sank to the floor. Only Fenn remained standing, staring at Clutch, the thief.

"I want my charm back," he said. He tried to sound brazen, but his voice cracked with anguish.

Clutch looked at him peculiarly—a mix of sadness and joy. He reached into a pocket on the side of his trousers and held his hand out to Fenn. In his palm lay the stone charm the children of Path had carved for him after he rescued them from Steingefan, along with the amber stone Fenn had taken from Clutch's tent.

Fenn moved forward a few steps and took them both. "But I want the other," he said. "I want my mother's charm."

Clutch waved his hand at the folk in the room. "Leave us," he said. They rose and moved to the door. Clutch looked at Sadie and Grayson. "You may remain," he said. The rest, all but Dunham, filed out of the bedchamber. When they were alone, Clutch put his hand on his brother's, still grasping the charm against his motionless chest.

"That is not your mother's charm," Clutch said. "It belonged to Rue-Anna. She was a daughter of the eis, as was her sister, your mother."

"I don't believe you. My nurse Clara said my mother had it."

Clutch nodded. "Aye. Rue gave it to her, on the eve of her wedding. A tradition of the eisen. One is wed free of jewels and charms. Aliara would have returned it to her after the ceremony. If she'd survived..."

Fenn shook his head, confused.

"Welk carved the charm for his betrothed, and braided for her that rope. But he never married Rue-Anna; she was taken from us before the day arrived. She never had a child. It was Aliara who married the prince. Aliara...had a child?" Clutch's voice drifted into a hollow silence.

Fenn looked carefully at Welk's graying face, at Dunham standing at the door, his head bowed, and then back to Clutch. There was confusion and doubt in the thief.

"May I touch you?" he said.

Clutch held out his palm, and Fenn put his hand atop it. He looked at Clutch, who smiled weakly, his eyes brimming with tears. At first, instead of visions or memories rushing at him, Fenn felt only trust, devotion, and that sadness and pain he'd known long ago when Clutch had first stolen his charm from him. Then came a rush of images—the woman, his mother; he was sure of it. Smiling, laughing. And Clutch.

"Tell me what you see," the thief said.

"My mother."

His smile deepened. "She was taken from me, before our child was born. Or so I thought."

Dunham cleared his throat. "Sire," he said, "we can call for the wissendes and find the truth."

"No need," Clutch said, pulling his hand from Fenn's.

"Who are you?" Fenn said.

"Have you not guessed? I am Elrundt, second son of Evan the Fearsome. And now—" he shrugged—"king of the Ruud."

"He's your father, Fenn," Sadie whispered from behind him.

"My father?"

"It would appear thus," Clutch said. "Come, my son. We have much to discuss."

Clutch wrapped his hand around Fenn's, engulfing it. Together, they left Welk's chambers, walked through the lobby and out the huge double doors into the courtyard where a thousand folk had gathered. A cheer rang out among them.

"Long live the King! Long live the King!"

"I must confess," Clutch told him, giving his hand a squeeze. "I've no mind to be a king."

Chapter Fifty-five

While Damon Castle and the wissenry building at Cold Sea Port had been burned, the port city itself was largely untouched by the kell stone, and Leah was grateful for Wanda's hospitality. She'd prepared a grand lunch and sectioned off a small corner of the dining room for their last meeting. Leah fluffed her hair, bringing out a laugh from Wanda, and determined to leave it uncovered even when she set foot in the palace at Ruhm. A rush of daring tingled in her chest at the thought and she blushed.

"You'll be sure to come visit again, won't you?" Wanda said as they walked downstairs to the lobby of the Snapping Turtle Inn.

"Indeed. I'll miss the Ruud while I'm away. I think Pren and I will embark on a project to restore the forests of the west."

"And invite the gnomes and trolls to explore, no doubt."

"No doubt." She laughed. "I've already got a brownie begging for a ride on our return trip."

"Watch him," Wanda said. "He'll take root in your house and do terrible mischief."

"Pren." Leah took his hands when she reached the bottom of the stairs and let him kiss her cheeks. "Are they arrived?"

"They are."

She slipped her hand through the crook of his arm and walked with him into the dining room where she was nearly knocked over by Sadie Pratt's hug. Leah tousled Grayson's hair and gave Rogget a kiss on his beard, for which he blushed and offered a deep thanks.

"What became of you at the battle, Mr. Reynold? I imagine you'll be telling heroic tales for a month or two."

"You've no idea," Rogget gruffed. "It was chaos, o'course. But chaos and me, we got an understanding."

"And what of Darnit?"

"He's out back, miss, waiting for a visit and a scratch behind the ears."

Leah laughed, but stopped suddenly when she saw Fenn standing with Marigold and Roren at the long table now set with plates and utensils. She moved away from the group and went to him, smiling.

"Your Highness," she teased and bowed low.

When she stood and looked to him, for a moment she feared she'd insulted him—he was prince of the Ruud, after all. Instead, he bowed as well, rose and said, "Lady Hallowsing of the Hass?"

"You've heard?"

They all laughed and sat, and let Wanda's waiters bring out trays of roasted fowl, potatoes, turnips, and greens. She told Sadie and Grayson that Prenalin was not yet discovered as a spy and would return to Ruhm, with her as Kirche's widow. Together, they would work toward change in the Hass.

"But the soldiers saw you in the woods," Rogget said. "You killed Kirche."

"It's not likely they'll remember her," Pren said. "They'll be easily convinced it was just another folk of the Ruud."

"But I thought you two would marry," Marigold said with a smile.

Leah blushed and hissed at her, "Hold your tongue, or I will take back my offer to make you Stationer to the King."

Marigold held up a potato stuck onto her fork. "Tell me you have plans to marry and I will keep quiet."

Prenalin coughed and Leah caught his face reddening.

"Very well," Leah said to the now silent table, "we have plans."

"More wine," Rogget called out and they all cheered.

"And tell me," she said. "Grayson and Sadie, what are *your* plans for the future?"

"Please don't talk as if we'll never see one another again," Sadie said.

"You're right, of course," Leah reassured her. "Still, humor me."

"I'm going to start a university," Grayson said.

"Is that so?"

"What a wonderful idea," Wanda said, bringing in another tray.

"I agree," Rogget said.

"Maybe you should start the wissenry all over again," Fenn said. "The way it used to be, all about facts and learning."

"That's what I was thinking," Grayson said. "But, open to anyone who wants to learn."

"And what about you, Sadie?"

She shrugged. "I'm too young to have to decide my future."

Laughter echoed all around.

"It's true," she protested. "But I have an idea I'll be exploring. Maybe I can lead tours all over Kell for Grayson's students."

"That's a great idea," Grayson said.

"And Rogget?" Leah said.

"Ard, miss. I'd like to be Fenn's guard."

"Done," Fenn said.

"Just like that?" Rogget said.

"Just like that."

"You'll make a great king," Sadie said.

"I don't plan on being one."

"No king?" Roren said.

"Ruhm had one in name only," Fenn said.

"Too true, and look what took the king's place—the Hass."

"I'm thinking of something different. Well, my da is, anyway."

"It's lovely to hear you say *da*," Sadie said.

"It's not lovely," Fenn said. "It's powerful." He grinned at her.

"You're saying King Elrundt hasn't a mind to be king?" Wanda said, taking her seat at the table.

"About time you let yourself eat," Leah needled her with a smile.

"That's right," Fenn said. "But please don't go talking about it, yet. He's got some weird idea folk ought to decide on who they want to be in charge. Committees or something."

"Why that's right interesting," Wanda said. "Word of it will not pass my lips afore your father speaks of it, I promise."

"I think Ruhm would want to know more about this," Marigold said. "We'll need someone here, an ambassador, to keep us abreast of the news."

"Aye," Rogget said. "And the Ruud should have one in Ruhm as well."

"It sounds as if we're making progress already," Pren said, smiling at Leah.

"I'm going to miss you all," Fenn said suddenly and the group quieted.

"You can come to Ruhm, anytime," Leah told him. "And you'll have Sadie and Grayson and Rogget, still."

"And me," Roren said.

"You're staying in the Ruud?" Fenn asked him.

"For a while, at least."

"But," Leah said, "what will you do?"

"He could be our new ambassador," Pren said.

Roren shrugged. "I think perhaps I will tell my secrets at a later time. This gathering is for remembering how we came to be together and how we have each changed one another's lives."

"No, no, hold on," Fenn said. "There's one secret that has to be told. Grayson."

Grayson looked up from his plate of food, still chewing. "I have no secrets," he said.

"Oh, yes you do. Tell us what the guard at Steingefan said to make you hit him."

"What's this?" Rogget said.

"I thought they'd tortured him," Sadie said. "But as it happened, he'd just got himself into a fight."

"Our Grayson?" Leah said. "Studious and smart...fighting?"

Grayson blushed and Leah winked at him. *Poor, sweet child.* But she still wanted to hear his secret.

"Go on," she begged. "Tell."

Grayson put his fork down and took a drink of cold tea from his glass. He wiped his mouth with a napkin and looked around the table at them all.

"Very well," he said. "I will not give you the details—"

"Aw, come on," Fenn said.

"If you'll be quiet, you'll understand."

"Yes, Fenn," Sadie said. "Let him talk."

"If you must know, one of the Hass guards said something unkind about our Sadie. He hinted she wasn't as brave as one might expect."

The table was silent. Mouths fell open, into smiles. Ripples of giggles broke out and were quickly shushed. Finally, they all turned to Sadie. She sat, her eyes wide as saucers, her gaze on her roasted fowl and potatoes, her cheeks flushed pink.

"And so you hit him," Fenn said.

"Thank you," Sadie whispered with a smile, "waiter boy."

Grayson laughed and Fenn stood, his chair groaning against the wood floor as he pushed it back. He raised his glass. "We must drink to Sadie's champion. Grayson, defender of her honor."

"Hear, hear!" They all sang out.

Leah couldn't help feel this may be the last time she would experience such warmth—at least for a very long time. She would sail with Pren and Mari in the morning. She'd only been able to send a message to her mother, in the care of Madam Always, across the hill country. She'd see her eventually, she knew; but the delay wore at her day and night. She and her mother must comfort each other in the face of her father's hanging, but it would have to wait. A kingdom must be reset, freedoms restored, a community of folk not used to thinking for themselves must be guided. Leah had no time at present to think of herself alone. She could feel the weight of the truth on her shoulders—its telling a matter of saving Ruhm—and knew her father must have felt it, too. She smiled at his memory, though her eyes were filled to the brim.

Chapter Fifty-six

When Rogget rustled him awake before the sun tipped at the edges of the horizon, it took Fenn several seconds to remember. He was still at the Snapping Turtle Inn in Cold Sea Port. Leah Hallowsing was sailing west to take Ruhm and rework her into a kingdom in which the beast and folk could learn to accept each other. The folk of the Ruud were rebuilding, already working with the beast folk to ensure villages were welcoming to them. His charm was gone—buried with King Welk on the plain of Nergens where he lost his betrothed. Clutch, the thief, was Fenn's father. He opened his eyes.

"Aye," Rogget said, smiling at him. "It were no dream."

Rogget helped him dress in the fine silk tunic and pants Wanda had pressed for him and as he wrapped the oiled leather belt around his waist, he heard a light rap on the door. Instinctively, he reached to his chest for the gold charm. In its place, on a hemp rope his father wove for him, hung the stone charm from the children of Path, and the amber kell— Clutch told him he'd have given it to him, anyway.

"Before we let him in," Rogget said, "I should prepare you."

"Who is it?"

"Name's Budden. Representative of the gnomes, so he says. He's got the kell stone."

"What?" Fenn cross the room in an instant and pulled the door open to find a squat, greenish brown folk, tall as Fenn's waist, with a broad, rugged smile on his rough, lined face and thin wisps of gray hair dancing about his head. He held the stone out to Fenn with something of a nod.

"But...?"

"Wen groeven hetuit," Budden said. "Means...sorry, I have not spoke folk in many an age."

Fenn took the stone and beckoned Budden into his room where the old gnome looked around and whistled.

"Fijne accom," he said. "Ard, I done again. Nice room."

"Where'd you get the kell stone?" Fenn said.

The stone glowed and its green color leaked into Fenn's fingers, traveled up to his wrists, just as it had done when he first found it.

Budden nodded. "Yes, see. It is yours. We dug it out. The gnomes."

"I thought I'd lost it. I thought the kell had taken it back."

"The beast lord summons you with the stone. The young king of Ruhm is to...how do you say? He must travel with us."

"Roren?"

"Aye."

"Wanda's already had a pack made up for me to carry," Rogget said. "Blankets, a lantern, food."

"Can Sadie and Grayson come?"

Budden whistled again. "Into the forest, I say yes. But not to Rad."

Fenn looked to Rogget and the huntsman shrugged.

They said their goodbyes to Leah, Prenalin, and Marigold, and set off that morning with Roren, who didn't seem surprised at the invitation. Sadie's ma was against the trip, but after some negotiation with Rogget, finally allowed it. Grayson's da was in Path helping with the restoration of the village and Grayson acted rather grown up about being on his own.

When they all reached the edge of the forest later that morning, Grayson turned to Rogget and said, "You start counting and you'll see. It'll only take one day to get in, see the beast lord, and come back out."

Rogget's brow creased and Sadie laughed so loud a flock of roster fiends squawked and lifted off the tops of the trees into the sky. Once in the forest, the daylight dimmed and only shimmered in dusty rays through the trees.

Rogget whispered, "The forest still brings a touch of fear out of me."

"Nothing to fear," Budden said. "We have the stone."

As they traveled, they were joined by many others. Talkative fairies followed, flitting above their heads. Brownies, both woodland and displaced, skipped along beside them. Wolves and felidae prowled on either side. When the centaurs plodded into view ahead of them on the path, Rogget stopped and gawked. The largest of them stepped forward and glared, his rusty orange coat and wild brown hair and beard glistening in the sun's rays.

"Huntsman," the centaur said. "It was you who shot me many years ago, on orders from your superior, I am told."

Rogget stammered but couldn't manage to form the sounds into anything resembling words.

"He thought he killed you," Fenn said.

"Aye," Rogget managed to blurt out, "and Dag Voorspeld let me think it."

"Such was your penance."

Rogget huffed and snorted along the path for some minutes after the meeting, but eventually calmed down. "I suppose I should be glad the creature lives."

"He's not a creature," Sadie said. "He's a folk."

"He is Red Lichen," Budden said. "Very wise. Most respected."

"It's going to take the folk of the Ruud a bit of getting used to," Rogget said, "this fraternizing with the beasts."

The trek was much like the last time Fenn had ventured to the lord's lair. They crossed the river, but no troll demanded payment on the bridge. They hiked until after lunchtime and stopped to eat, with little discussion, as if they all had worries none wished to share. When they finally approached the lair, in what seemed the darkest part of the forest, Kwitcher bounded into the group and grabbed Sadie's kneecap.

"Scared and Bitten," he said. "Pretty. You are now Grown Wise. So good to see you once again."

"What is your name now?" Grayson asked him.

"I remain Kwitcher. Catch much anger and trouble. But is new trend. All the best displaced brownies taking names."

"And what are you going to call me now?"

"You are also grown wise; I will call you Learned, today. Nearly Orphaned!" Kwitcher squealed and hugged Fenn's knee.

"Hello, Kwitcher."

"But you are no longer nearly orphaned, are you?"

"How did you know?"

Kwitcher breathed in deeply. "You smell of comfort and finding home. Come, come, friends of my friends. I will take you all to the lair."

"I am guiding the bearer of the stone," Budden said.

"Very well, then," Kwitcher said with a bow. "I follow Budden of the gnomes."

When they arrived outside the lair, Rogget nervously tousled Fenn's hair and punched him lightly on the shoulder. "Go on, then," he said. "Make us proud."

"How exactly do I do that?"

Rogget roared with laughter. "I haven't any idea. Maybe, it would be best if you simply be yourself. Ard, yes. That would make us proud."

"The stone," Budden said.

Fenn dug the stone from his knapsack and held it, watching its glow permeate the skin of his wrists.

"You and the young king," Budden said, "will follow me."

"Why Roren?" Fenn asked.

"That is a question only the lord can answer."

Fenn smiled at Sadie and Grayson. "I'll be out soon."

"Try to remember everything," Sadie said. "I want the whole story on the way home."

He nodded, turned, and carried the kell stone into the lair of the beast lord where he was enveloped in cool, damp air. Several beast folk sat in a semicircle on stone benches, looking at Fenn and Roren—a troll, a displaced brownie, and a woodland brownie. One of the wolves sat nearby. Red Lichen stood at the edge of the trees, his arms folded at his chest.

"Take your place," a purring voice said.

Fenn looked up to the beast lord's throne and stumbled back two steps. "Lucas?"

Chapter Fifty-seven

Lucas nodded and pulled the hood of his velvety black robe from his head.

"But, you're dead," Fenn said.

"I am."

Fenn shook his head, trying to find some sense in Lucas' words. "Then why are you sitting on the throne of the beast lord?"

Lucas chuckled, a throaty, cat-like sound. "I suppose because I am the beast lord. I am Dag Frieden. Day of Freedom."

"How'd that happen?"

"Being felidae helped. Did Father Treacher not tell you, at least after I was killed?"

"The wissendes never told me much of anything useful."

"I'm sorry for that. Felidae are conceived and born as folk. Long ago, we lived our first lives as folk. But when the folk invaded our lands, we shunned the form and turn our young to felidae shortly after birth; it is a grisly business. I am told my parents wished me to live as folk in honor of the ancients, and so when the choice was offered, I felt it already made."

"So, when you died, you didn't die all the way?"

"My form only changed to shiftling. And I have the mark, as you do."

Lucas bared his right shoulder and there, on his pale thin arm was the mark of the faire.

"The beast lord has the mark?"

"It is how we are chosen."

"Didn't the guards see it in Path, when you were taken to Steingefan?"

Lucas shook his head slowly. "Folk can be easily persuaded."

"By felidae," Red Lichen said.

"We have the gift of seduction," Lucas said, smiling, "but I could not have remained undiscovered long. Fearing I would be harmed, my brethren took me from the danger."

Fenn sighed with relief; events were starting to make sense. "So, Quiren told the truth."

"Truth?"

"About the Rad and the mark meaning I'm consul for split folk."

"You thought it meant you were the child of prophecy?"

Fenn nodded. "I didn't want to believe it; but what else could it mean?"

"None, neither immortal nor mortal, can foretell the future. The mark is shared by all who will enter here this day."

Fenn looked around at the beast folk until finally his gaze fell upon Roren. Every folk present, he realized, was concentrated on Roren.

"The woodland brownies demand an explanation for his presence," the little brownie said.

"So do we," the troll said. "What is *his* kind is doing here?"

"Show them," Lucas said to Roren with a nod.

Roren, looking perplexed and fearful, pulled off his overcoat and bared his shoulder. There, Fenn saw the same mark. Three long tapered lines tipped with dots.

"You never said anything," Fenn said.

"I was unsure of its meaning."

"But, Quiren told us."

Roren shook his head. "I was still uncertain of who to trust."

"Do not blame the folk," Lucas said. "We have never had a folk consul. They have no tradition to help them along."

"Nor split consul," the troll said. "Soon the Rad will be overrun with splits of all sorts."

"The kell stone decides."

Fenn looked at the stone, still in his hands.

"That is not an explanation," the brownie said.

The other beast folk nodded.

"If the fairies have decided the folk deserve a seat at the Rad," Lucas said, "we dare not shun them for no reason."

"We shun the harpy and the doppelganger consuls."

"I said for no reason. And the fairies tell us none of the harpies or doppelgangers have been marked."

"But these folk are not beast."

"That's not what the wissendes would say," Fenn said. "That's the whole reason we came to the Ruud in the first place. Michelruud, the first king, was a wissende in Ruhm. He discovered beast and folk are all...just folk. We're kin."

"The folk forced us off our land," the troll said. "If they be part of the Rad, trolls will not participate."

"It's true," Lucas said. "The folk have dealt wrongly with us. But we must put it behind us and move forward."

"We have the kell stone again," the wolf said, more of a growl than actual speech, though Fenn understood him well enough. "We can force their retreat, now. All the way back to the southern continents where they belong. Already we feel its power."

"You don't own the land," Fenn said. "Mountains and rivers, the plains, the forests. They belong to all the creatures of Kell."

"Put the stone in the basin," the troll shouted. "See if those two are cast out."

"Yes," Lucas said. "We will consult the Rad. Fenn, you wield the stone. You must deliver it to its rightful place."

Lucas pulled the staff from beside his throne and carried it to the stone basin, where the water dripped over the face of the rock into the pool below. Fenn joined him there and when Lucas lowered the claw end of the staff toward him, Fenn pushed the kell stone into the claw until it set with a pop.

Lucas lowered the staff into a small hole in the pool of water and pushed it down deep until the kell stone sat just above the water's surface. The huge boulder began to tremble and the water stopped running over its face. Fenn stepped back and watched as the trees surrounding them shuddered. Roster fiends shrieked. Lucas pulled him away from the basin and he watched, stunned, as Quiren, the eis, appeared, as if from nothing, before the rock.

Quiren nodded at Fenn and moved to the stone benches where he sat with the troll. A feeorin, larger than a fairy of the Ruud, but clearly, to Fenn, a fairy, appeared next. Her wings fluttered, she blinked several times, and flitted off to find a spot to perch with the brownies. A duergar raged through, shouting what Fenn thought could possibly be obscenities, flitting off to sit as far away from the feeorin as she could get.

Fenn gasped when Brenna stood before him and seemed to float across the lair to stand with him. She looked around briefly before turning to Fenn and taking his hands.

"It is good to see you again. I've been worried about you."

When an angel fell through the portal, stumbled, and stood, fluttering his wings, the gathering grew noticeably cold and several beasts shouted.

"The angels sided with the Hass," the troll cried out. "We must not allow them a representative at the Rad."

"He is Durahn," Brenna said and the others hushed, "my ally. Part of a new coven of angels, looking for peace."

A grumbling rippled through the gathering but Brenna glared at them each in turn until they quieted.

"Greetings, all," Lucas said. "The kell stone has been returned to us after many generations of absence. It would have passed into legend had it not been for the bravery of Fenn Foster, a folk eis of the Ruud."

"It is a shame on our history that a split had to restore the stone," the woodland brownie said, angry.

"It didn't need to be so," Brenna said. "Any of us could have retrieved it."

"Not so," the brownie said. "We are not all capable, and therefore not all culpable."

"The beast face certain death in the west," the troll said. "And you propose we could have simply traveled there and searched for it?"

"I contend we use the decorum of meeting and speak only when called upon," Red Lichen said.

"Don't be foolish, Lichen," Lucas teased with a smile. "It has always been speak as desired in the Rad."

"We do not run centaurian meetings in such chaos."

"Freedom is chaos," Quiren said.

"And chaos freedom?" the troll said. "I think not."

Lucas raised his hand and all were silent. "We may speak as we wish, but at least let us keep on topic."

And thus began the first council of the Rad in generations. Fenn sat with Roren and Brenna and he was keenly aware of the way they eyed each other, trying not to smile. He shook his head, but couldn't help smile himself.

When the meeting ended, hours later, and little had been decided, but much discussed and argued over, Lucas approached him outside the lair where he'd met Sadie, Grayson, and Rogget.

"What will you do now?" Lucas asked him.

"I have to get back to Path, to Clutch. I mean, Elrundt. I mean...my father."

Lucas nodded. "I will come with you and offer him my condolences on the loss of his brother. And after that?"

"My father—" the words were coming easier and easier to him— "wants to leave the folk to govern themselves and venture southward."

"And you will go with him?"

"He says he won't go if I don't want him to."

"And so you will go with him."

Fenn sighed. "I think I will."

"They say there are dragons on the southern continents," Grayson said. "*If* they exist," he added with a smile.

"And a different sort of kell in the south, I'm told," Rogget said. "Amber."

"I hope there aren't any prophecies about that one," Fenn said.

"So, it's all over then," Sadie said. "No more bairn of prophecy. No more running."

"But Fenn did destroy the Ruud," Grayson said, looking hopefully at Lucas.

Lucas shook his head. "There is no such thing as prophecy; the future cannot be foretold."

Roren left Brenna and joined them. "We have been invited to visit the ice realm," he said. "I do hope you all will join me."

"I will," Sadie said. "I'd like to see inside the palace, not a prison tower."

And so it was settled. Fenn, Rogget, Sadie, and Grayson let Lucas lead them along with Roren out of the forest on a path northward that would take them through Timber. As they hiked, surrounded always by some group of beast or another, Fenn couldn't help catching glimpses of Roren. Something nagged at him—a truth he dared not say aloud. How could Dag Frieden be wrong? How could the wissenry be wrong?

And yet, there it was. The young king of Ruhm, destined to die of starvation in the mines of the Great West, marked as a consul of the Rad by the fairies. As if they knew...as if it had all come to pass as it was meant to. And then there were the dragons! What was it the prophecy said? The dragon flies above him. All laid waste below.

"I think I will," he blurted out. "I'd like to see this southern kell for myself."

Books by this author

Fantasy by Dana Trantham
Children of Path: The Kell Stone Prophecy Book One
The Wretched: The Kell Stone Prophecy Book Two
Mark of the Faire: The Kell Stone Prophecy Book Three
The Kell Stone Prophecy: Complete Trilogy

Story Runners: Awakening

Women's, Literary, Romantic Comedy, and Young Adult
by Dianna Dann

Camelia
Always Magnolia
Bookish Meets Boy

Paranormal Humor by by D.D. Charles
Zombie Revolution

Children's fiction by Dana Trantham
Zombie Cats (middle grades)
Wayward Cat Finds a Home (children's chapter book)

www.waywardcatpublishing.com
Dianna Dann   Dana Trantham   D.D. Charles

* 9 7 8 1 9 3 8 9 9 9 2 6 0 *